LAVIE TIDHAR

The Bookman
Histories

THE BOOKMAN • CAMERA OBSCURA
THE GREAT GAME

ANGRY
ROBOT

ANGRY ROBOT
A member of the Osprey Group

Lace Market House,
54-56 High Pavement,
Nottingham,
NG1 1HW, UK

www.angryrobotbooks.com
Steamed

This omnibus first published by Angry Robot 2012
1

The Bookman copyright © Lavie Tidhar 2010
Camera Obscura copyright © Lavie Tidhar 2011
The Great Game copyright © Lavie Tidhar 2012

Lavie Tidhar asserts the moral right to be
identified as the author of this work.

A catalogue record for this book is available
from the British Library.

ISBN: 978 0 85766 298 9
eBook ISBN: 978 0 85766 300 9

Cover artist: John Coulhart.
Set in Meridien by THL Design.

Printed in the UK by CPI Group (UK) Ltd, Croydon, CR0 4YY

All rights reserved. No part of this publication may be reproduced,
stored in a retrieval system, or transmitted, in any form or by any
means, electronic, mechanical, photocopying, recording or
otherwise, without the prio...

This book is sold subject to
way of trade or otherwise,
otherwise circulated witho
any form of binding or cov
published and without a si
condition being imposed o

This novel is entirely a worl
incidents portrayed in it are
Any resemblance to actual
localities is entirely coincide

LANCASHIRE COUNTY
LIBRARY

3011812852965 2	
Askews & Holts	24-Feb-2014
AF FANTASY	£12.99
CPP 4/14	

Praise for Mr. LAVIE TIDHAR

This book should be returned to any branch of the
Lancashire County Library on or before the date

− 4 JUL 2014

− 4 AUG 2014

0 5 SEP 2014

0 1 JUN 2015
1 9 JAN 2017

CPP 4/14
June '18

CONDITION
NOTED
08.04.21
SR@HAC

Lancashire County Library
Bowran Street
Preston PR1 2UX

www.lancashire.gov.uk/libraries

LANCASHIRE COUNTY LIBRARY

3011812852965 2

By the same revered gentleman

Osama

The Tel Aviv Dossier (with Nir Yaniv)
Hebrewpunk (stories)
An Occupation of Angels (novella)
Cloud Permutations (novella)

A Dick & Jane Primer for Adults (editor)
The Apex Book of World SF (editor)

To Elizabeth – in love – always

Introduction
page 9

THE BOOKMAN
page 15

CAMERA OBSCURA
page 319

THE GREAT GAME
page 671

Introduction

The Bookman began to take shape years ago, hazy at first, a mere outline. I remember, for instance, unrealised plans for a novella that involved automatons and a detective on the Strand, cycling along on his bicycle to Simpson's, there to investigate the murder of a certain chess-playing machine...

It crystalized for me in the beginning of two thousand and six, however, with two unrelated things. One was the appearance in the Thames of a Northern Bottlenose whale, which drew me, like many Londoners, to watch for it on the South Bank; and the other was going to watch, in that fine old cinema in Richmond-upon-Thames, the movie *Munich*.

These are strange seeds for a novel, perhaps. There was a moment in the film where the assassins wire a telephone to explode; and it occurred to me, as I came out, that an assassin could do the same thing to an object as innocent as a book. It would be years before I found out a real Bookman existed, in Indonesia. Reality is *always* stranger than fiction.

Then, too, I had an image of the Thames as the river Styx, impossibly wide and dark; and of my hero having to traverse it to save his love from the lord of the underworld. There would be whales in my Thames, I knew. And so these images began to coalesce.

I had only recently finished my first novel, one destined never to see the light of day. I had then decided to write something purely for my own enjoinment. I have loved the stories that came to be called steampunk – those early works by Tim Powers and James Blaylock and others, which paid homage to my own childhood reading. The amazing adventures of Jules Verne and the fog-bound mysteries of Sherlock Holmes, the westerns of Karl May and the swashbuckling tales of the musketeers. And many more. I decided to write a book I'd enjoy and that, just possibly, a younger me would also have enjoyed. To begin with it was only going to be a novella, but when I told my friend Nicola Sinclair about it she told me I had to make it a novel. Little did we know there would be three books in the series, one day…

I had borrowed freely from those works I enjoyed – pirates from Powers, Babbage engines from Gibson and Sterling, a giant lizard for a queen straight out of Paul di Filippo's madcap *"Victoria"* – and the mythic resonance of those Greek stories I grew up on (in Edith Hamilton's wonderful *Mythology*). I had the whole of London for a canvas, the streets I walked on, the bookshops I went to, the old pubs I drank in – and I began to write at my little flat in Surbiton, on the outskirts of London, over 2006.

In 2007, I left London for the South Pacific island of Vanua Lava, somewhere off most maps, in the Republic of Vanuatu. I lived in a bamboo hut facing the volcano, with no electricity or clean water, and not much contact with the outside world. *The Bookman* remained on a hard drive, untouched.

In early 2008, I spent a couple of months in South Africa visiting my parents, on my way to Laos. My friend John Berlyne had read the book. In many ways my ideal reader, he shared my love of these Victorian fantasies on which *The Bookman* was founded. Moreover, he was in the process of setting up his own literary agency. John, I was gratified to know, had liked the book – but also (I was less gratified to know!) thought it required a lot of work.

A *lot* of work.

We had one of those long and excruciatingly uncomfortable Skype conversations, where an editor tells a writer just what they are doing wrong, and the writer squirms in his chair and mumbles defiance every now and then. And shakes his fist. And swears vengeance.

Then I went away and did everything John said… beginning with cutting out sixteen thousand words right in the middle of the book and replacing them with a single sentence.

While mumbling obscenities and shaking my fist in the air and swearing vengeance.

Naturally.

At last it was done. I finished the rewrites, then flew to Laos to join my wife. Time, as they say, passed. I began to work on a new novel, *Osama*, and in due course signed up with John as a client. John still liked *The Bookman*, and proposed to sell it. I graciously agreed to let him. And, a mere few months later, he did.

This was my first intimation that books you write might actually be published. Moreover, the gentlemen of Angry Robot Books asked not only for *The Bookman*, but for a further book or two. This caused something of a dilemma. While I have since seen several reviews commenting on how *The Bookman* is clearly the first in a series, it clearly is not. It is a self-contained book and was never meant to have sequels. Moreover, I get bored easily: I do not like to write the same thing again, and I have already written *The Bookman*. I was not going to write it a second time.

It occurred to me, however, that there were still plenty of stories left to tell in the world of *The Bookman*, and that I could tell them in any way I pleased.

I wrote *Camera Obscura* while living in Laos. *The Bookman* was a book about books. *Camera Obscura* is a book about movies. Years ago, in Zimbabwe, I watched the great blaxploitation classic *Cleopatra Jones and the Casino of Gold*, and it had stuck with me ever since. In Laos I watched any number of kung fu movies out of Hong Kong, learning about the genre of martial art stories called *wuxia*. I wanted my heroine to be Tamara Dobson, to be Pam Greer. And I wanted to tribute the wuxia tropes, the secret societies, the masters and assassins, the novitiates and the temples. I also wanted it to be noir, but at the same time I wanted to preserve the feel of the original book, the same sense of fun and literary referencing that runs like a hum in the background, there for whoever wants to pick it up.

Writing *Camera Obscura* was a lot of fun. It was a different book – a crime novel set mostly in Paris – and yet it was also a continuation of what appeared to me an obvious arc continuing from the first book, all leading back to the one choice Orphan had to make. When it was done I knew I messed up though. I had tried to take it in a darker direction – a sort of *Heart of Darkness* vibe throughout the whole second half. John and I had one of those awkward telephone conversations again. He told me it didn't work. I told him I knew. I went back and rewrote the entire second half of the book, around forty-five thousand words.

It was by far the right decision.

By this point *The Bookman* was actually about to come out. We'd just left Laos in early 2010; a single copy of the book chased us to Thailand, courtesy of Angry Robot. It would be another change of continents and a few months later that I could finally arrange for the rest of my copies to follow. I moved to Israel, settled for a time with the same old sluggish laptop that took five minutes just to boot up, and tried to write.

The Great Game was initially going to be *Night Music*. It's a fun book, but it never took hold – it was a prequel to *The Bookman*, following David Livingstone in Africa. We spent the summer of 2011 in Indonesia, where I got about a third of the way through it before stopping. I went to the UK for the launch of *Camera Obscura*. Came back to Israel. Began working on *The Great Game* again.

It's a spy novel. Some of it comes from the discarded *Night Music*. A couple of characters disappeared in *The Bookman* rewrites way back when but found their way back, particularly the villainous Fogg. *The Great Game* ties up the three books with what I thought was the obvious end for the arc began by Orphan's choice in *The Bookman* though, admittedly, this is not a series hung-up on particularly neat endings!

A lot of *The Great Game* was created by sitting for morning coffees with my friend Nir Yaniv by the seaside, in Jaffa. It was by far the most difficult book in the series, though none of them have been particularly easy. It couldn't just be done to fulfil a contract: it had to work. I hope it does.

By late 2011 we moved back to London. *The Bookman* had been well received. *Camera Obscura* was nominated for a couple of awards. Now here we are. An omnibus. All three books together at last, like slightly belligerent siblings.

I hope you enjoy them.

Lavie Tidhar
London
2012

I
THE BOOKMAN

PART I
Orpheus & Eurydice

I must frankly own, that if I had known, beforehand, that this book would have cost me the labour which it has, I should never have been courageous enough to commence it.
  – Isabella Beeton, *Mrs. Beeton's Book of Household Management*

ONE
Orphan

Under Waterloo Bridge Gilgamesh slept
wrapped in darkness and the weak light of stars
his breath feeble in the fog:

He dreamt of Ur, and of fish,
slow-roasting on an open fire,
and the scent of spring
  – L.T., "The Epic of Gilgamesh"

Orphan came down to see the old man by the Thames. The old man sat alone on the embankment under Waterloo Bridge, wrapped in a horse blanket, beside a small fire, a rod extending from his gloved hands into the dark waters of the river below. Orphan came stealthily, but the old man's blind eyes nevertheless followed his progress. Orphan sat down beside Gilgamesh on the hard stone floor and warmed his hands on the fire. In the distance, whale song rose around the setting sun.

For a while there was silence. Then, "Did you catch anything?" Orphan asked.

Gilgamesh sighed and shook his head. His long hair was matted into grey locks that made a dry rustling sound as they moved. "Change is unsparing," he said enigmatically.

Orphan echoed his sigh. "But did you catch anything?"

"If I had," Gilgamesh said reasonably, "it would have been roasting on the fire by now."

"I brought bread," Orphan said, and he reached into his bag and brought out, like a magician, a loaf of bread and a bottle of wine, both wrapped in newspaper, which he put down carefully on the ground beside them.

"Red?" Gilgamesh said.

Instead of an answer Orphan uncorked the wine, allowing its aroma to escape into the cold air above the Thames.

"Ahh..."

Gilgamesh's brown fingers broke a piece of the bread and shoved it into his mouth, and he followed it by taking a swig of wine from the open bottle. "Château des Rêves," he said appreciatively, "now where would a young lad like you find a bottle like that?"

"I stole it," Orphan said.

The old man turned his blind eyes on Orphan and slowly nodded. "Yes," he said, "but where did you steal it, young Orphan?"

Orphan shrugged, suddenly uncomfortable. "From Mr. Eliot's Wine Merchants on Gloucester Road. Why?"

"It's a long way to come, with a bottle of red wine," Gilgamesh said, as if reciting a half-forgotten poem. "As much as I appreciate the visit, I doubt you came all this way on a social call. So," the blind eyes held Orphan in their gaze, "what is it you want?"

Orphan smiled at that. "Tonight," he said, "is the night, I think."

"Indeed?" The eyes turned, the hands checked the anchored fishing-rod, returned to the bread. "Lucy?"

Orphan smiled. "Lucy," he said.

"You will ask her?"

"I will."

Gilgamesh smiled, but his face looked old and, for a moment, wistful. "But you are both so young..."

"I love her." It was said simply, with the honesty only the young possess. Gilgamesh rose, and surprised Orphan by hugging

him. The old man felt frail in Orphan's arms. "Let's drink. For
the two of you."

They drank, sharing the bottle, Orphan grinning inanely.

"Read me the paper," Gilgamesh said. They sat together, looking
at the Thames.

Obligingly, Orphan reached for the stained newspaper. He
scanned the small print, the ink already running, searching for
an item of news to interest Gilgamesh. "Here," he said at last.
He cleared his throat and read the title, which was: "TERRORIST
GANG STRIKES AGAIN!"

"Go on," Gilgamesh said, spraying him with crumbs of bread.

"'Last night,'" read Orphan, "' notorious terrorist organisation
known as the Persons from Porlock struck again at the very heart
of the capital. Their target this time was none other than the famed
playwright Oscar Wilde, who was engaged, by his own words, in
a work of composition of the highest order when he heard an insistent knock on the door, followed by shouts from outside. Rising
to see what the commotion was about – having, for reasons of his
own, dismissed all his servants for the night – Wilde was confronted by several men dressed as clowns who shouted fragmented
lines from Lear's *A Book of Nonsense* at him, enclosed him in a circle
and danced around him until his mind, so he himself says, had
been set awhirl with chaos. The Persons departed as suddenly as
they had come, evading the police force that was already on its
way to the scene. In his statement, a confused Wilde said the title
of his new play was to be called *The Importance of Being Something*,
but for the life of him he could no longer recall what that something was. "How long will this campaign of terror continue?"
Wilde asked, and called for the Prime Minister's resignation. "This
cannot go on," he said; "this is a violation of everything our country stands for." Prime Minister Moriarty's Office was not available
for comment.'"

He finished, and all was quiet save for Gilgamesh's chuckle.
"Was he really 'engaged in a work of composition of the highest
order'?" he said, "or was he entertaining the young Alfred

Douglas? I suspect the Persons from Porlock wasted their time on this one. But you wouldn't know anything about that, would you?" he said.

Orphan glanced away and was silent. Again, Gilgamesh chuckled. He took another long swig on the bottle and said, "What else is there?"

"Moriarty to launch Martian space-probe," Orphan said, "ceremony to take place tomorrow at dusk. The probe will carry an Edison record containing the songs of birds and whales, as well as a small volume of Elizabeth Barrett Browning's *Sonnets from the Portuguese*."

Gilgamesh nodded approvingly. "Lucy is going to be there," Orphan said. "She has been doing the whale recordings for the past two months, and she was selected to put the record and the book into the probe at the ceremony." He grinned, trying to picture it. The Queen might be there!

"Whales are worth listening to," Gilgamesh said mildly, though his eyes twinkled. "Pray, continue."

Orphan did so. "Fresh fly supply for the Queen was halted temporarily on Tuesday due to suspicion of a contaminated source – most of her public appearances have been cancelled for the next week. The Byron simulacrum gave a poetry recital at the Royal Society…" He turned the page over. "Oh, and rumours the Bookman is back in town."

Beside him, Gilgamesh had gone very still. "Says who?" he asked quietly.

"An unnamed source at the Metropolitan Police," Orphan said. "Why?"

Gilgamesh shook his head. "No one knows where the Bookman will strike. Not unless he chooses to make it known, for reasons of his own."

"I'm not sure I understand you," Orphan said patiently. "Why would he do that?"

"As a warning, perhaps," Gilgamesh said, "to his next victim."

"The Bookman's only a myth," Orphan said. Beside him, Gilgamesh slowly smiled.

"A myth," he said. "Oh, Orphan. This is the time of myths. They are woven into the present like silk strands from the past, like a wire mesh from the future, creating an interlacing pattern, a grand design, a repeating motif. Don't dismiss myth, boy. And never, ever, dismiss the Bookman." And he touched his fingers to his blind eyes, and covered his face with his hands. Orphan knew he would speak no more that night.

That was how Orphan left him, there on the water's edge: an old man, hunched into an unmoving figure, like a pensive statue. Orphan never again saw him in life.

Who was Orphan and how had he come to inhabit that great city, the Capital of the Everlasting Empire, the seat of the royal family, the ancestral home of Les Lézards? His father was a Vespuccian sailor, his mother an enigma: both were dead, and had been so for many years. His skin was copper-red, his eyes green like the sea. He had spent his early life on the docks, running errands between the feet of sailors, a minute employee of the East India Company. His knowledge of languages was haphazard if wide, his education colourful and colloquial, his circle of friends and acquaintances far-ranging, if odd.

He learned poetry in the gutter, and from the public readings given by the great men and women of the age; in pubs and dockyards, in halls of learning and in the streets at dawn – and once, from a sword-wielding girl from France, who appeared mysteriously on the deck of a ship Orphan was helping to load with cargo bound for China, and recounted to him, in glorious, beautiful verse, a vision of God (he had never forgotten her) – and he learned it from the books in the public library, until words spun in his head all day and all night, and he agonised at writing them down on paper, his hand bleeding as the pen scratched against the surface of the page.

Who was Orphan? A poet, certainly; a young man, that too. He had aspirations for greatness, and had once met, by chance, the ancient Wordsworth, as the great man was leaving a coffee house in Soho and the five-year-old Orphan was squatting in the street outside, talking to his friend, the beggar Lame Menachem. The great man had smiled at him then, and – perhaps mistaking him for a beggar himself – handed him a coin, a half-crown showing the profile of the mad old Lizard King, George III, which Orphan had kept ever since for good luck.

At present, Orphan was engaged, himself, in a "work of composition of the highest order": he was busy crafting a long poem, a cycle of poems in fact, about life in this great city. He was moderately proud of his efforts, though he felt the poem, somehow, lacked substance. But he was young, and could not worry himself too long; and, having seen his old friend Gilgamesh, the wanderer, and ascertained his (relative) well-being, he proceeded with a light heart to his primary destination of the evening, which was the newly rebuilt Rose Theatre in Southwark.

Orphan walked along the river; in the distance the constant song of whales rose and fell like the tides as the giant, mysterious beings rose from the dark waters for a breath of air. Occasionally he paused, and looked, with a poet's longing for the muse, at the cityscape sprawling before him on the other side of the river. Smoke rose from chimneys, low-lying and dense like industrial clouds, merging with the fog that wrapped itself about the buildings. In the distance, too, were the lights of the Babbage Tower, its arcane mechanisms pointed at the skies, its light a beacon and a warning to the mail airships that flew at night, like busy bumblebees delivering dew from flower to flower. Almost, he was tempted to stop, to scribble a hasty poem: but the cold of the air rising from the river compelled him onwards, and at his back Big Ben began to strike ten, hurrying him on. Already he was late for the performance.

Lucy wasn't there and must therefore have been inside; and so he bought a ticket outside the theatre and entered the courtyard, where people still milled about. So there was still time, he thought. He bought himself a mug of mulled wine and sipped at the hot, spicy drink gratefully before making his way inside the building, into the groundlings' floor.

In the spirit of authenticity, the Rose was lit not with gas but burning torches, and their jumping light made the shadows dance and turned the faces of people into fantastical beings, so that Orphan imagined he was sharing this space with a race of lizards and porcupines, ravens and frogs. The thought amused him, for it occurred to him to wonder how he himself appeared: was he a raven, or a frog?

He settled himself against the balustrade separating the groundlings from the lower seats and waited. There was a slim, dark-haired girl standing beside him, whose face kept coming in and out of shadow. In her hands she held a pen and a notebook, in which she was scribbling notes. She had a pale, delicately drawn face – seen in profile it was quite remarkable, or so Orphan always thought – and her ears were small and pointed at their tip, and drawn back against her head so that she appeared to him in the light of the moon coming from above like some creature of legend and myth, an elf, perhaps, or a Muse.

He leaned towards her. "One day I will write a play for you they would show here at the Rose," he said.

Her smile was like moonlight. She grinned and said, "Do you say that to all the girls?"

"I don't need to," Orphan said, and he swept her to him and kissed her, the notebook pressed between their bodies. "Not when I have you."

"Let go!" she laughed. "You have to stop reading those romance novels, Orphan."

"I don't–"

"Sure." She grinned up at him again, and kissed him. Two old ladies close by tutted. "Now shush. It's about to start."

Orphan relented. They leaned together against the balustrade, fingers entwined. Presently, a hush fell over the crowd, and a moment later the empty stage was no longer empty, and Henry Irving had come on.

At the sight of the great actor the crowd burst into spontaneous applause. Orphan took another sip from his drink. The torchlight shuddered, and a cold wind blew from the open roof of the theatre, sending a shiver down Orphan's spine. On stage,

Irving was saying, "…The bridegroom's doors are opened wide, and I am next of kin. The guests are met, the feast is set: may'st hear the merry din–" and the celebrated performance of the stage adaptation of *The Rime of the Ancient Mariner* began.

Orphan, though he had seen the performance before, was nevertheless spellbound anew. As Irving's booming voice filled the theatre the strange and grotesque story took life, and the stage filled with masked dancers, enacting the wedding ball into which the Ancient Mariner had come like an ill-begotten creature rising from the Thames. The story took shape around Orphan: how the young mariner, Amerigo Vespucci, took sail on his voyage of exploration under the auspices of the British court; how, on Caliban's Island, he discovered and shot the lizard-like inhabitant of that island, by that callous act bringing upon himself unwanted, unwholesome immortality and on his masters, the British, the full might of Les Lézards, the Lizard Kings, who now sat on Britannia's throne. It was an old, fanciful story, woven together of gossip and myth. Irving's adaptation, Orphan knew, had been wildly popular with the theatre-going public – particularly those of a young, mildly radical disposition – but was decried as dangerous nonsense by the palace, though Prime Minister Moriarty himself had so far kept silent on the issue. Either way, it was becoming evident that the play's stage-life would be kept short – which only added to the public's enthusiasm. Speculation in the press as to Irving's motivations in staging it was rife, but insubstantial.

When Vespucci began his return journey home, Lucy leaned forward, focused, as he knew she would. It was the portion that told of the coming of the whales: how they had accompanied the ill-fated ship all through the crossing of the Atlantic, and further, until they arrived at Greenwich and the city awoke, for the first time, to their song.

He edged towards her. Her hair was pulled back behind her ears, and her fingers were long, smudged with ink and with dirt under the nails as if she had been digging in Thames mud.

"How are the whales today?" he asked.

"Restless. I'm not sure why. Have you noticed the change in their song when you walked along the embankment?"

Leaning together against the balustrade, the crowd closing them in, it was like they had found themselves, momentarily, in a small, dark, comfortable alcove, a private space in which they were alone.

"You're the marine biologist," Orphan said. "I'm only a poet."

"Working with whales is like working with poets," Lucy said. She put away her pad and her pen. She had a small bag hanging over her shoulder. "They're unruly, obtuse, and self-important."

Orphan laughed. He took her hand in his. The skin of her palm always surprised him in its roughness; it was a hand used to hard work. Her eyes were dark and mesmerising, like lodestars, and small, almost invisible laughter-lines gathered like a fine web at the corners. "I love you," Orphan said.

She smiled, and he kissed her.

On stage, Henry Irving abandoned the role of narrator as the final act began to unfold. Now, with all the considerable verve and power he was capable of, he played Shakespeare, the poet and playwright who rose to prominence in the court of the Lizard King and became the first of the Poet-Prime Ministers.

Both Orphan and Lucy watched as the Ancient Mariner shuffled onto the stage to deliver the story of his life to Lord Shakespeare: Orphan, who had a natural interest in books, observed it closely. It was a heavy, leather-bound folio, the spine facing the audience, with the title *The Rime of the Ancient Mariner* etched in gilt onto it.

"I pass," cried the Ancient Mariner (a young actor, Beerbohm Tree, whom Orphan vaguely recognised), "like night, from land to land, I have strange power of speech," (here he took a deep breath, and continued), "that morning that his face I see, I know the man that must hear me: to him my tale I teach!" And he passed the heavy book to Shakespeare, who took it from him with a graceful nod, laid it on the table before him, and opened it–

There was the sound of an explosion, a deafening bang (and for Orphan, everything slowed, as)–

The book disintegrated in a cloud of dust–

Not dust, shrapnel (and Orphan, moving in jerky, dreamlike motions, grabbed hold of Lucy and let himself fall to the ground, his weight dragging her with him, his body first cushioning her fall and then covering her in a protective embrace)–

That tore into Shakespeare/Irving and cut his head away from his body and sent plumes of blood into the air.

The air filled with screams. The stage collapsed. It was, Orphan thought in his dazed, confused state on the floor of the theatre, holding on to the girl he loved, the definite end of the performance.

TWO
Lucy

And now we reach'd the orchard-plot;
And, as we climb'd the hill,
The sinking moon to Lucy's cot
Came near and nearer still.
  – William Wordsworth, "Lucy"

They walked together along the embankment. At their back the Rose was wreathed in flames. Orphan had a cut on his shoulder, bandaged with a strip of cloth. Lucy's heavy coat was covered in plaster and dust that wouldn't come off. Both were shaken.

A police automaton passed them by on its way to the scene of the explosion, a blue light flashing over its head. "Clear the area!" it shrieked at them. "Clear the area! Unsafe! Unsafe!"

"Yes," Lucy murmured, "I noticed. The big explosion was a definite clue."

They both laughed, and Orphan felt some of his tension ease. The automaton, borne fast on its hidden wheels, disappeared behind them.

"Who do you think was behind it?" Lucy said.

"You mean, who hired the Bookman?"

"Yes," Lucy said. "I guess that is what I mean."

The fog swirled about them, muting the glow of the fire from

29

behind. Without consciously realising it, they drew closer; Orphan felt Lucy's warmth even through the heavy coat and it made him feel better. It made him feel alive.

"I don't know," he said. "I expect we'll read about it in the papers tomorrow. Could have been anyone with a grudge against Irving. He didn't exactly make himself popular with the *Ancient Mariner* production."

"Like the Persons from Porlock?" She threaded her arm in his and smiled. "Tell me, Master Orphan, did you dress as a clown last night and quote limericks at Mr. Wilde?"

"I…" Orphan began to say, but Lucy reached to him and put her finger against his lips, sealing them. Orphan closed his eyes and let his senses flood him: Lucy's taste was a mixture of flavour and scent, of spice and river water.

"We all have our secrets," she said in a soft voice. She removed her finger, and Orphan opened his eyes, found himself standing face to face with her. She was his height, and her dark eyes looked directly into his, her mouth smiled, a crescent moon. She had white, uneven teeth, with slightly extended canines.

They kissed. Whether she kissed him first, or he kissed her, it was immaterial. It was a mutual coming together, the two opposing poles of a magnet meeting. Her lips were cold, then hot; her eyes consumed him. He thought without words, without poetry.

When they came away both were somewhat breathless, and Lucy was grinning.

"Come on!" she said. She took Orphan's hand and he followed her: she ran down the embankment and he ran with her, the cold air whipping their faces, and the fog parted in their passing. Orphan, flushed, still breathless from the kiss, felt a rare kind of happiness take hold of him; he threw his head back and laughed, and the clouds parted. For a moment he could see the moon, shining yellow, its face misshapen. Then the clouds closed again overhead and he ran on, following Lucy, running towards the growing whale song emanating from underneath Westminster Bridge.

Nearby, on the other side of the river, Big Ben began, majestically, to count the midnight strokes.

What does Orphan remember of that night? It is a cacophony of the senses, a bazaar through which he can amble, picking and discarding sensation like curios or used books. Here a stand of sounds, and he pauses and lifts again the noise of the explosion, compares it with the rising whale-song into which Lucy led him, as they approached the south side of Westminster Bridge and the pod welcomed them with a symphony that somehow wove inside itself the distant light of stars and the warning flashes of the mail-ships in the air, the dying fire down-river and the salty taste of a kiss. He pauses beside a canopy and sorts through touch, experiencing again the heat of an embrace, the wet, slippery feel against his hand of a whale rising silently from the Thames, a plume of water interacting with the moon to form a rainbow, making laughter rise inside him like bubbles.

They visited the pod that night, and the whales, who rose one by one to the surface, were dark, beautiful shapes like sleek submarines, acknowledging them.

"Come on!" Lucy had said, and he had followed, and knew that he would follow her anywhere, even beyond life itself.

In the light of the moon, under Westminster Bridge, he kissed her again. "Will you marry me?" he asked.

"I'll be with you everywhere," she said. Her eyes were veiled with shimmering stars. "We will never be apart."

"Where have you been?" Jack demanded as soon as Orphan walked in. "Were you at the Rose? Do you have any idea what's going on?" He surveyed Orphan through his dark glasses with a frown. "Have you been out *enjoying yourself*? I've been worried sick waiting for you!"

"I'm fine," Orphan said. "Couldn't be better," he added. His mouth kept trying to shape itself into a grin, which he was trying to suppress for Jack's benefit. "I was at the Rose, but I wasn't hurt. I was with Lucy."

"He was with Lucy!" Jack said. Orphan's grin fought one last time and was released; Jack, on seeing it, shook his head and muttered, "Well, that's all right then."

"We're getting married."

"Married!"

"Don't look so horrified."

"Delighted for you, my boy! Married!"

"Are you sure you're feeling all right, Jack?"

They sat down together in the back room of Payne's Booksellers. Orphan sprawled on his bed (which sat between AEGYPTIAN ARCHAEOLOGY and ELECKTRONICKA – GENERAL) while Jack took the single chair (beside the small, but choice, selection of technical tomes on the shelf marked STEAM ENGINES – THEORY AND PRACTICAL APPLICATIONS). Jack himself slept in the basement, which was large and filled with old books and which was always damp, embellished by the constant smell of mould and a strange, tangy breeze which had no obvious source.

"Married," Jack said. He seemed to mull the idea over in his head. "Nothing against marriage, me, but… Oh hell. Congratulations, boy! Let's drink."

"I thought you'd never offer."

Jack rose nimbly and reached for a thick bible on one of the shelves. He removed it, carrying it carefully, and laid it on the small side-table. Opened, it revealed a bottle of Old Bushmills. "Would this do? There are a couple of glasses in that *Illustrated Mother Goose* on the lower shelf next to your bed, if you could trouble yourself to fetching them."

Orphan sighed. Jack constantly worried him; he was afraid to ask what else was hidden in some of the books. More than words, he was sure.

Eventually, they clinked glasses. "To Lucy and yourself! To matrimony – may it make you forever happy and never come near to me!"

"I'll drink to that," Orphan said, and grinned, and he drank the toast. The whiskey, from the first distillery licensed by the Lizard Kings, slid down his throat with almost no resistance.

Heat rose from his feet to his face. "Put scales on your chest," Jack said, and laughed. "To Les Lézards!" Jack said. "We must drink to them too. May they end up on a spit above a fire as the food for drunken sailors."

"One day," Orphan said, "you'll go too far."

"Not far enough," Jack said.

"So the Bookman's back in town," Jack said, a little later, putting his hand on his chin (index finger resting against his cheek) in a faux-thoughtful gesture. "And poor old Irving's career is finally over." He sighed, theatrically. "Everyone's a critic."

"What have you heard?" Orphan said. Jack spread his hands in a shrug. Had he been French, it might have been called a Gallic shrug; as he weren't, it was a decidedly English one. "I heard the police closed off Southwark and are diligently hunting for clues, headed by the admirably efficient Inspector Adler. It must have been chaos there if they let you all go – there's a public appeal going out in the papers first thing in the morning for any witnesses to come forward."

"*Irene* Adler?" Orphan said, and Jack smiled unpleasantly and said, "The very same who is in charge of the Persons from Porlock investigation."

"Then they could do without my testimony," Orphan said. "What else does your abominable Tesla set say? And by the way," he added, "do we have some wine?"

Orphan coughed, said, "So what else did you hear?" Jack had an illegal Tesla set in the basement, modified to listen to police and government communications; he spent most of his time down there, scanning the airwaves. He was – he thought of himself as – a Radical. He was also the editor of the *Tempest*, an anti-Calibanic broadsheet published irregularly and distributed poorly. Lastly, he was proprietor of Payne's, having acquired the ramshackle bookshop (so the story went) one night four years ago at a game of cards.

"Well," Jack said, slowly swirling the drink in his hand, "rumour has it the Bookman's not left town. They're panicking,

Orphan. *They* are panicking. There's increased security at the Palace, but for all they know his next victim could be the Byron automaton, or Prime Minister Moriarty, or just some dumb fool who buys the wrong book at the wrong time." He looked up from his drink and his mouth twisted into a smile. "The Establishment is teetering, Orphan. And they are all going to end up against the wall, when the revolution comes."

Orphan looked at his friend, concerned. Usually, Jack was good company, but when he was like this – when his revolutionary sentiments got the better of him – he could be savage, almost frightening. Orphan didn't know what grievance his friend had against the Calibanic dynasty. He didn't need to. There were many other people like Jack, angry people, people who hated lizards, or poetry, or both. People, he thought, like the Bookman.

He finished his drink and, mirroring him, Jack did the same. "I'm going to sleep," Jack said. He stood up and laid the glass on the table with a little more force than was necessary. "Make sure you open the shop in the morning. And try to get some sleep. See you tomorrow, china. And congratulations."

When he was gone, Orphan blew out the two half-melted candles that perched precariously on two opposing shelves and stretched himself on the bed. Sleep claimed him at once, and his dreams were full of Lucy.

THREE
The Parliament of Payne

As with the commander of an army, or the leader of any enterprise,
so is it with the mistress of a house.
  – Isabella Beeton, *The Book of Household Management*

Orphan had first met Lucy one day at the bookshop. She came
through the door like – sunshine? Wind? Like spice? Orphan
wasn't that much of a poet – looking for a book about whales.
He fell in love the way trees do, which is to say, forever. It was
a love with roots that burrowed deep, entangled, grew together.
Like two trees they leaned into each other, sheltering each other
with their leaves, finding solace and strength in the wide en-
compassing forest that was the city, holding together in the
multitude of alien trees. Orphan loved her the way people do in
romantic novels, from the first page, beyond even The End.

When the door opened he hoped it was her, but it wasn't. The
door opened and closed, the bell rang, and footsteps – their
sound a dry shuffle – approached the counter behind which Orphan sat, bleary-eyed and untidy, a mug of coffee (the largest
that was available) and the morning paper resting by his side.

"Good morning, good morning!" a voice said chirpily. Orphan,
wincing, looked up from his reading. "Good morning to you too,
Mr. Marx. All's well?"

"All's well that ends well," Marx said, and sniggered. He ran his fingers through his large, overgrown beard, as if searching for a lost item within. "Jack about?"

Orphan mutely pointed towards the small door that led to the basement. Marx nodded thoughtfully but didn't move. "Have you, um, come across any of the volumes I ordered?"

"Let's see," Orphan said. He reached down to the shelves built into the counter. "We have–"

"Quietly, please," Marx said. He looked left and right and back again and said, apologetically, "The walls have ears."

"Quite," Orphan said. Though he usually liked Karl, the man's constant movement, like an ancient grandfather clock, between high paranoia and boisterous cheer, grated on his fragile nerves that morning. "Well," he whispered, "we managed to acquire M. Verne's narrative of his expedition to Caliban's Island, *L'Île mystérieuse*, that you asked for, and also the revolutionary poems of Baudelaire, *Les Fleurs du mal*. I think Jack is still looking for de Sade's *Histoire de Juliette* for you."

"Not for me!" Marx said quickly. "For a friend of mine." He straightened up. "Good work, my young friend. Can I trust you to..."

"I'll deliver them to the Red Lion myself," Orphan said.

Marx smiled. "How is your poetry coming along?" He didn't wait for a reply. "I think Jack is waiting for me. I'll, um, show myself in. And remember – mum's the word."

Orphan put his finger to his lips. Marx nodded, ran his fingers through his beard again, and disappeared through the small door that led down to the basement.

"For a friend of mine," Orphan said aloud, and laughed. Then he took a healthy swig of his coffee and bent back down to the newspaper which was, of course, full of last night's events at the Rose.

"IRVING FINALLY LOSES HEAD!" screamed the headline. "SHOW ENDS WITH A BANG!" The name of the writer, an R. Kipling, was familiar to him: they were of about the same age, and had come across one another several times in town, though they had not formed a friendship. Kipling was a staunch Caliban supporter, as was evident from his reporting of the explosion:

"Late last night (wrote Kipling), a bomb went off at the controversial production of *The Rime of the Ancient Mariner*, killing the show's star and artistic director, Mr. Henry Irving, and wounding several others. Police have closed off the area and investigation has been undertaken by Scotland Yard's new and formidable inspector, Irene Adler. Eyewitness testimony suggests Irving was killed by a booby-trapped copy of the book of the play that was delivered to him on stage by the young actor Beerbohm Tree, playing the Ancient Mariner to Irving's Shakespeare. The play raised much antipathy in official circles and was justly avoided by all law-abiding citizens and faithful servants of Les Lézards. It was, however, popular with a certain type of revolutionary rabble, and sadly tolerated under our Queen's benign rule and her commitment to our nation's principles of the freedom of speech."

Orphan sighed and rubbed his eyes; he needed a shave. He took another sip of (by now cooling) coffee and continued reading, though his mind wasn't in it: his head was awhirl with images of Lucy, and he kept returning to the night before, to the words they spoke to each other, to their kiss like a seal of the future… He sighed and scratched the beginning of a beard and decided he'd take the afternoon off to go see her. Let Jack do some work, for a change: he, Orphan, had better things to do on this day.

"Though there is official silence regarding the investigation (Kipling continued) this reporter has managed to make a startling discovery. It has come to my attention that, though Irving's co-star, the young Beerbohm, was apparently killed in the explosion alongside his master, a man corresponding exactly to Beerbohm's description was taken in for questioning earlier today! If Beerbohm is still alive, who was the man delivering the book on stage? If, indeed, it was a man at all…"

The doorbell rang again, and Orphan lifted his head at the new set of approaching footsteps. He knew who it would be before looking. At that time of day, in this shop, no casual browser was likely to come in. Only members of what Orphan, only half-jokingly, had come to call the Parliament of Payne.

"Greetings, young Orphan!" said a booming voice, and a hand reached out and plucked a well-worn penny from behind Orphan's ear. Orphan grinned up at John Maskelyne. "Hello, Nevil."

Maskelyne frowned and scratched his bushy moustache. "No one," he said, "dares use my second name, you lout." He threw the coin in the air, where it disappeared. "Jack in?"

Orphan mutely nodded towards the basement door.

"Good, good," Maskelyne said, but he seemed in no hurry to depart. He began wandering around the shop, pulling books at random from the shelves, humming to himself. "Have you heard about Beerbohm?" his disembodied voice called from the black hole of the COOKERY – BEETON TO GOODFELLOW section. "Rumour has it the police found him trussed up like a turkey with its feathers plucked out, but alive and safely tucked away at home, if a little dazed around the edges."

"I'm sure that it must be a mistake," Orphan called back. "I was at the Rose last night and I can assure you Beerbohm was as effectively made extinct as the dodo."

He tried to follow Maskelyne's route through the shop; now he could see the top of his head, peeking behind the BERBER COOKERY shelf; a moment later, his voice rose from the other end of the room, muttering the words of an exotic recipe as if trying to memorise it. Then Orphan blinked, and when his eyes re-opened, only a fraction of a second later, the magician stood before him once again, his eyes twinkling. "I hope I didn't give you a start."

Orphan, who luckily had laid the coffee back on the counter a moment earlier, waved his hand as if to say, think nothing of it. "He is still alive, young Orphan," Maskelyne said, and his countenance was no longer cheery, but deep in an abyss of dark thoughts. "And what's more, no doctor was called to treat the man at the Rose. Let me riddle you this, my friend. When is a man not a man?"

He opened his hand, showing it empty. He laid it, for a moment, on the surface of the counter, and when it was raised a small toy rested on the wood, a little man-like doll with a key at its back. "Come to the Egyptian Hall when you next have need of counsel," the magician said, almost, it seemed to Orphan, sadly, and then he turned away and was gone through the door to the basement.

But Orphan had no time to think further of the magician's words. No sooner had Maskelyne departed that the door chimed again, and in walked an elegant lady. Enter the third murderer, Orphan thought, and hurriedly came around the counter to hold the door. It was the woman for whom an entire section of a bookcase was dedicated, and he had always felt awed in her presence. "Mrs Beeton!"

"Hello, Orphan," said Isabella Beeton cordially. "You look positively radiant today. Could it be that the rays of marital bliss have finally chanced upon illuminating your countenance?"

Orphan grinned and shut the door carefully after her. "Can't get anything past you," he said, and Isabella Beeton smiled and patted his shoulder.

"I know the look," she said. "Also, Jack did happen to mention something of the sort in this morning's missive. Congratulations." She walked past, her long dress held up demurely lest it come in touch with the dusty floor. "I won't keep you, Orphan. You are no doubt eager to go in pursuit of your newly bound love." She tossed her hair over her shoulder and smiled at him; her hair was gold, still, though woven with fine white strands that resembled silk. "Our number is complete. Go, seek out Tom, and get that idle fellow to replace you. Your watch is done."

And, so saying, she too disappeared through the small door that led to Jack's basement, and was gone.

Orphan managed to locate Tom Thumb in his quarters near Charing Cross Station, and after rousing the small man from his slumber extracted from him a promise to take his place at the shop for the day.

"Bleedin' poets," Tom Thumb muttered as he exchanged his pyjamas for a crumpled suit. "Always bleating of love and flowers and sheep grazing in fields. The only sheep I like are ones resting on a spit."

"I owe you one," Orphan said, grinning, and Tom shook his head and buttoned his shirt and said, "I've heard that one before, laddie. Just show me the shekels."

"Soon as Jack pays me," Orphan promised, and before Tom could change his mind he was out of the door and walking down the Strand, whistling the latest tune from Gilbert and Sullivan's *Ruddigore*.

He crossed the river at Westminster, still whistling. Already, on the other side of the river, he could see the whales, and their song rose to meet him, weaving into his whistle like a chorus. He felt light and clear-headed, and he stepped jauntily on, descending the steps towards the figure that was standing on the water's edge.

"Orphan?"

He was suddenly shy. Lucy, turning, regarded him with a dazzling smile. Behind her, a whale rose to the surface and snorted, and a cloud of fine mist rose and fell in the air.

"I missed you," Orphan said, simply.

They stood and grinned at each other. The whale exhaled again, breathed, and disappeared inside the blue-green waters of the Thames.

"I hoped you'd come," Lucy said. Her eyes, he noticed, were large and bright, the colour of the water. Sun speckled her irises.

He said, "I'd follow you anywhere," and Lucy laughed, a surprised, delighted sound, and kissed him.

Later, he would remember that moment. Everything seemed to slow, the wheel of the sun burning through the whale's cloud of breath and breaking into a thousand little rainbows; a cool breeze blew but he was warm, his fingers intertwined with Lucy's, and her lips tasted hot, like cinnamon-spiced tea. He whispered, "I love you," and knew it was true.

He saw his face reflected in her eyes. She blinked. She was

crying. "I love you too," she said, and for a long moment, the world was entirely still.

Then they came apart, the cloud of mist dispersed, blown apart by the breeze, and the sun resumed its slow course across the sky. Lucy, pointing at a bucket that stood nearby, said, "Help me feed the whales?" and Orphan, in response, purposefully grabbed the still-writhing tentacles of a squid and threw it in an arc into the river.

A baby whale rose, exhaled loudly (the sound like a snort of laughter), and descended with its prey.

On the opposite bank of the river Big Ben began to chime, and the strikes sounded, momentarily, like the final syllables of a sonnet.

FOUR
Gilgamesh

And all the while his blind brown fingers
Traced a webbed message in the dirt
That said
Gilgamesh was here.
  – L.T., "The Epic of Gilgamesh"

When they parted it was dusk, and the first stars were rising, winking into existence like baleful eyes. Orphan felt buoyant: and he was going to see Lucy again that night, at Richmond-upon-Thames, for the Martian probe ceremony. He'd promised he'd be there as soon as he saw Gilgamesh again. The truth was, he was worried about his old friend. He was the closest thing to a family Orphan ever had. Gilgamesh lived rough, and the years had not been kind to him. "Seven-thirty!" Lucy said as she kissed him a last time. "And don't be late!"

He walked the short distance along the embankment to Waterloo Bridge. He thought he'd talk with Gilgamesh, but when he reached the arches there was no sign of his old friend there.

Orphan called for him; his voice came back in a dreary echo. He went closer to the edge of the water. There was the small ring of stones where Gilgamesh's fire had burned. Cold ash lay between the stones, dark and fine. "Gilgamesh?" he called again, but all was quiet; even the sounds of the whales had died down, so that Orphan felt himself in a vast silence that stretched all around him, across the waters and into the city itself. "Gilgamesh?"

Then he saw it. An arc of dark spots, leading from the fire towards the river. He bent down and touched them with his fingers, and they came back moist.

He looked around him wildly. What had happened? Resting against the wall he found Gilgamesh's blanket. It was stained, in great dark spots, with a smell that left a metallic taste in the back of his throat.

But not blood.

Oil? Or, he thought for a moment, ridiculously – ink?

The blanket was torn. No, he saw. Not torn. Cut, with a sharp implement, like a knife… or a scythe.

He rolled the old blanket open, panic mounting. What had happened to Gilgamesh? The blanket was empty, but soaked in some dark liquid. Wide gashes opened in the dirty cloth like gaping mouths.

Orphan knew he should call the police. But what would they do? They had better things to do than worry about an old beggar, with the explosion at the Rose and the Ripper loose in Whitechapel. He stood up, pulling away from the blanket. His hands were smudged.

Orphan felt ill, and panic settled in the pit of his stomach like a snake, coiling slowly awake and rising with a hiss. What had happened? What could he do?

The silence lay all around him. He could hear no birds and no traffic. The light had almost disappeared entirely, and the world was one hair's breadth away from true and total darkness.

Frightened, he nevertheless followed the arc of spilled ink from the dead fire to the water's edge. He bent down to the river and washed his hands in the cold, murky water.

It occurred to him that Gilgamesh's fishing-rod, too, was missing. He looked sideways and down, but could see nothing.

Then a curious sound made him turn. It came from the water, to his left, a clinking sound, like champagne glasses touching. Still crouching, he made his way carefully to the left, his fingers running against the side of the embankment. The stones were slimy and cold, unpleasant to the touch – then he found it. His fingers encountered something solid and round, and the sound stopped.

It was a tall round shape made of smooth glass, and it was tied with a fishing line, Orphan discovered, to a rusting hook that protruded underwater from the side of the embankment. His fingers growing numb with cold, he managed to untie it and finally lifted his find from the water. It was a bottle.

Raised voices came suddenly from the river path and Orphan, jolted, withdrew into the darkness of the arches. The final rays of the sun faded and now the streetlamps began to come alive all along the river, winking into existence one by one, casting a comforting yellow haze across the darkened world. His heart beating fast, Orphan waited in the safety of the shadows until the voices, sounding drunk, passed. Then, clutching the bottle in his hands, he hurried away from the bridge, away from the blood-like substance and the dark absence of his friend. For when he withdrew it from the water Orphan recognised two things about the bottle: that it was the one he had brought Gilgamesh only the night before, the stolen bottle of Chateau des Rêves, and that though it had been emptied of wine it was not yet empty: for the bottle was sealed tight, and a dry sheaf of paper rustled inside it, like a caged butterfly the colour of sorrow, waiting to be freed.

He took shelter on the other side of the river, in the welcoming, warm and well-lit halls of Charing Cross Station. He stood alone amidst the constant, hurried movement of people to and from the great waiting trains that stood like giant metal beasts of burden along the platforms, bellowing smoke and steam into the cool night air. His back against the wall, the smell of freshly baked pastries from a nearby stall wafting past him, Orphan broke the crude seal on the bottle and withdrew, with great care, the sheaf of paper that nestled inside.

Gilgamesh's jagged handwriting ran along the page in cramped and hurried lines that left no blank space. It was addressed – and here Orphan stopped, for he felt cold again despite the warmth of the station, and his fingers tingled as if still dipped in the cold water of the Thames – to him.

Alone amidst the masses of humanity at the great station of Charing Cross, his ears full of the short, sharp whistle-blows from the platforms and their accompanying clacking of wheels as trains accelerated away into the dark, and his stomach (despite all that he had found) rumbling quietly at the pervading smells of pastries baking and coffee brewing, he began reading Gilgamesh's letter to him:

My Dear Orphan –

As I write this a hot explosion lights up (I imagine) the skies above the Thames, and rather than worry I am exhilarated – for that ball of fire and heat is a signal, and it tells me of my impending doom. I shall try to post this to you, but already I grow anaesthetised and dull, for I do not believe I will have the time. He is coming back for me, me who had been forgotten for all those centuries. But the Bookman never forgets, and his creations are forever his –

You scoffed when I spoke of the Bookman. You called him nothing but a legend. But the Bookman is real, as real – more so – than I am. Who am I, Orphan? You and I played together in believing me Gilgamesh, the lone remnant of an ancient civilisation, a poet-warrior of a bygone age. We were humouring each other, I think – though the truth is not that far from the fiction, perhaps. In either case you, of all people, deserve to know–

Every creed has its myth of immortals. The sailors have their Flying Dutchman, the explorers their Vespucci, the Jews their Lamed-Vav. Poets, perhaps, have Gilgamesh–

I, too, have been immortal. Until the knife descends I shall be immortal still, but that, I fear, is soon to end. Who was I? I, too, was a poet, and of the worst kind – one with delusions of grandeur. When Vespucci went on his voyage of exploration I went with him, for there must always be someone to record great discoveries. I was with him on Caliban's Island, when he roused Les Lézards from their deep slumber in the deep metal chambers inside the great crater at the heart of that terrible island. Almost alone, I managed to escape, blinded by the terrible sights I had seen. I took to sea and for days I floated, half-crazed and dying. When at last he found me I had all but departed this earth—

He – fixed me? Healed me? But he did more than that – and he took the knowledge of the island from me, and then let me go. But he had not repaired my sight. Perhaps, already, he thought I had seen too much—

I had thought he had forgotten me, but the Bookman never forgets.

Now, I fear, he is coming back for me, and perhaps it would finally be an end. Perhaps I could rest, now, after all the cold long years. But I fear him, and know that he would not rest, not until what was started on that cursed island can be brought to an end. He is bound with the lizards, I believe, and vengeful. Perhaps he was theirs, once. Their stories are interlinked—

But why, you ask, I am telling you this? Perhaps because I suspect you, too, will have a role to play in this unfolding tragedy. Perhaps because I knew your father, who was a good man, and your mother, who you didn't know—

No. I have not the heart to tell their story. Not now. For me, as I sit here, alone, on the water's edge, waiting for him to come, no words remain, and language withers. Only a final warning will I deliver to you, my friend: beware the books, for they are his servants. Above all, beware the Bookman.

Yours, in affection—
Gilgamesh

Orphan, stunned, leaning against the wall as if seeking support in the solid stone, scanned the letter again, the words leaping up at him like dark waves against a shore. He felt pounded by them, and fearful. His vision blurred and he blinked, finding that tears, unbidden, unwanted, were the cause. He wiped them away, and a drop fell onto the page, near Gilgamesh's signature, and he noticed something he had missed.

In the small margin of the letter, Gilgamesh had scribbled a couple of lines in small, barely legible writing, almost as if hiding them there. He cleared his eyes again and tried to decipher the words. When meaning came, dread wrapped itself around his neck like an executioner's rope, for it said: "*I know now that he is near, and moving. His next target may be the Martian space probe you told me about. For your sake, and Lucy's – stay away from it. If I can I will tell you myself–*"

There was no more.

And time, for Orphan, stopped.

He was a point of profound silence in the midst of chaos and noise. That silence, holy and absolute, was his as he stood against the wall of the train station, the letter falling slowly from his hand to the floor, too heavy to be carried any more. Lucy. The thought threatened to consume him. Lucy, and her gift to the planet Mars: a small, innocent volume of verse. Elizabeth Barrett Browning's *Sonnets from the Portuguese*.

Somewhere in the distance a whistle blew, rose in the air, and combined with the clear, heavy notes that echoed from Big Ben. They tolled seven times, and their sound jarred against Orphan's own bell of silence, until at last, on the final stroke, it cracked.

Lucy, he thought. And, *my love*.

He had half an hour to save her.

FIVE
The Martian Probe

Once in about every fifteen years a startling visitant makes his appearance upon our midnight skies, a great red star that rises at sunset through the haze about the eastern horizon, and then, mounting higher with the deepening night, blazes forth against the dark background of space with a splendour that outshines Sirius and rivals the giant Jupiter himself. Startling for its size, the stranger looks the more fateful for being a fiery red. Small wonder that by many folk it is taken for a portent.

– Percival Lowell, *Mars*

Picture, for a moment, the great city from above. On one side of the river rise ancient stone buildings, their chimneys puffing out smoke into the night air. Interspersed between them are newer, taller edifices, magnificent constructions in metal and glass, returning the glare of gas and lights from their smooth surfaces. Here is the Strand, the wide avenue overflowing with ladies in their fineries and beggars with their bowls, with hansom cabs and baruch-landaus. The stench of abandoned rubbish mingles here with the latest perfumes. Here is Charing Cross Station, looking from above like a great diving helmet, its faceplate open to the world, its wide mouth spewing out metal slugs who chug merrily away across the wide bridge and over the river.

Here are the Houses of Parliament, cast in the strange, scaly material so beloved of the Queen and her line. They glow in the darkness, an eerie green that casts flickering shadows over the water. Here, too, is the palace, that magnificent, impenetrable dome, surrounded by the famous Royal Gardens with their many acres of marshes and ponds.

At a distance, instantly recognisable, is the Babbage Tower, rising into the dark skies like an ancient obelisk, strange devices marring its smooth surface like the marks of an alien alphabet. A light flickers constantly at its apex, warning away the airships that fly, day and night, above the city. Rise higher and you can see them, flying in a great dark cloud over the cityscape like an unkindness of ravens, like a siege of herons. Night and day the airships fly, the eyes and ears (so it is said) of the Lizard Kings, landing and taking off from the distant Great Western Aerodrome that lies beyond Chiswick and Hounslow.

Pull away, return to the great avenue of the Strand and to the train station that belches constant smoke and steam at its extremity. One train, one metal slug, departs from its gaping mouth and snakes away, departing this side of the river, going south and west. Past grimy industrial Clapham it runs, and onwards, through the genteel surroundings of Putney, where wealthy residents dine in well-lit riverside establishments, past the guarded, hushed mansions of Kew, until it arrives at last in that sea of greenery and country charm that is the Queen's summer abode, the calm and prosperous town of Richmond-upon-Thames.

A lone figure spews out of the metal slug. Orphan, running out of the station and onto the High Street, past rows of quaint, orderly shops dispensing gilt-tooled, Morocco-bound books, fresh flies (by Royal licence! screams the sign), fishing-rods and boat trips, delicate delicatessens and chemists and florists. Turning, he runs, breathing heavily up Hill Street, past the White Hart and the Spread Eagle and the Lizard and Crown, arriving, at last, out of breath, eyes stinging with sweat, at the open gates of the Royal Park.

Harsh lights illuminated the wide open space now crammed with people. There was an air of festivity to the event and the smells of roasting peanuts and mulled wine wafted in the air, coming from the many stands that littered the outskirts of the crowd. Many people wore large, round, commemorative red hats – for Mars – or lizard-green – for Her Majesty. Many waved flags.

Orphan pushed his way through the crowds, feeling desperation overcome him. Ahead of him he could see the outline of the majestic black airship that was to take the probe on the next, slow leg of its journey, over land and sea to Caliban's Island, where the launch would take place. Cursing, he pushed further, not heeding the resentful looks he received. Where was Lucy?

Above the noise of the crowd a familiar voice rose amplified: Prime Minister Moriarty, delivering the last lines of a speech. He still had time!

Glancing higher he saw the raised platform where Moriarty stood. It only took him an instant to recognise the assembled dignitaries: sitting beside the Prime Minister was the Prince Consort, a short, squat, lizardine being in full regalia, whose reptilian eyes scanned the crowd, his head moving from side to side. Occasionally a long, thin tongue whipped out as if tasting the air and disappeared back inside the elongated snout. Several seats down he thought he recognised Sir Harry Flashman, VC, the Queen's favourite, the celebrated soldier and hero of Jalalabad. On the Prime Minister's other side sat Inspector Adler, her face serious and alert. Surely, Orphan thought, such people could sense the danger before them!

But no. Onwards he pushed, hoping against hope, but Moriarty's voice faded, the speech completed (too soon!) and the crowd burst into applause. Orphan made a last, desperate dash forward, and found himself at last in the front row of the waiting audience.

Before him, the airship loomed. Below it, the probe rested, a small, metallic object, dwarfed by the ship, looking like an innocent ladybird turned upside down.

The belly of the probe was open, and before it, approaching it with small, careful steps, was Lucy.

She had almost reached the probe. In her hands was a book, resting on the Edison record she had so meticulously prepared. She bent down to place the objects in the hold of the probe...

"Lucy!"

The shout tore out of him like a jagged blade ripping loose, tearing at his insides. It rose in the open air and seemed to linger, its notes like motes of dust coming slowly to rest, trailing through the air...

She paused. Her back straightened and she turned, and looked at him. Their eyes met. She smiled; she was radiant; she was happy he came.

The book was still held in her hands.

"Get away from the probe! The book is–"

He began to run towards her. He saw her face, confused, her smile dissipating.

And the book exploded.

The sight was imprinted on Orphan's retinas. Lucy, incinerated in a split second. The airship burning, black silk billowing in flames. The probe hissing, its metal deforming. In that split second a burst of burning wind knocked Orphan back against the screams of the crowd. He landed on his back, winded, blinded, deaf.

Shame filled him like molten silver, and with it the pain, spreading slowly across his body.

I failed, he thought. She's dead. I failed her.

Incinerated. Black silk billowing in flames. The book, disintegrating, and with it...

Then the crawling pain reached his head and he screamed, and the darkness claimed him.

SIX

The Bookman Cometh

What fond and wayward thoughts will slide
Into a Lover's head!
"O mercy!" to myself I cried,
"If Lucy should be dead!"
 – William Wordsworth, "Lucy"

The darkness came and went. In moments of lucidity he could hear voices speaking in a murmur beside him, and his battered senses were assaulted by the wafting smell of boiled cabbage.

He shunned those moments of awakening, seeking only to return to the comforting darkness, where no dreams came and he was free of thought. But light came more and more frequently, accompanied by voices, cabbage, the feel of starched sheets against his cheek, until at last he was awake and could not escape.

He lay with his eyes closed, his back pressed against the mattress. Perhaps if he lay like this long enough he could escape again into dreamless sleep.

But no. The voices intruded, heedless of his despair. "He's coming around," said a firm, no-nonsense kind of voice, male and authoritative: a doctor, Orphan thought.

A feminine voice, less harsh but carrying with it an equal – even greater – seal of authority, said, "It's about time."

"I won't let you interrogate him," the first voice said, sounding angry. "He needs to be left in peace."

The reply, Orphan thought, sounded tired, but there was a note of iron in the voice. "What he *needs* and what he is going to get are two different things, *Doctor*." She sighed; she had the trace of a Vespuccian accent. "Look, I'm sure you appreciate the importance of this investigation. I don't need to tell you what kind of pressure I'm under to get results. Moriarty–"

"Moriarty isn't head of this hospital," the doctor said, but he sounded resigned, as if the battle was lost even before it started. "If you ask me, the whole Martian debacle was inevitable, and the idea of flight into space preposterous."

"So vain is man, and so blinded by his vanity…" said his opponent quietly; it sounded like a well-used quote.

Orphan opened his eyes.

Leaning into him, their faces at an odd angle, so for a moment they seemed to him conjoined, the opposing faces of Janus, perhaps, one shadow and one light, were the two speakers. One was a man in his forties, with tanned, healthy skin, a thick moustache and friendly eyes that nevertheless, just at this moment, did not seem particularly pleased to be observing Orphan. The other face Orphan dimly recognised, and wished he hadn't: Inspector Adler, the one woman he had hoped against odds to continue to avoid.

"I'm awake," he said.

"Good, good," the doctor said. A small cough. "Welcome to Guy's Hospital." He glanced sideways at Inspector Adler and pulled back a little. "You've had quite a severe shock. Now, I don't want to do this, but the Inspector over here needs to ask you some questions, and she's been waiting for over two days for you to come around. Do you think you could talk to her? You don't have to."

Orphan tried to laugh; it came out as a cough. "Oh, but I think I do," he said, and saw the doctor's small, helpless nod in reply. "I shall leave you then," the doctor said brusquely. "I will make sure there is a nurse immediately outside. If you need to terminate the interview at any point, just call for her."

"Thank you," Orphan said. "I will."

The doctor departed, and a moment later a nurse came in, a large woman in white, with a cheerful countenance. She helped Orphan sit up in his bed and propped two pillows under his head. "Don't you mind Dr W.," she said. "He's not had any sleep in two days, ever since that terrible accident in Richmond Park. He's a good man." She gave Irene Adler (who, throughout this, stood back without a word) an indecipherable look, said, "If you need anything, call. I'll be outside," and disappeared through the door.

Orphan was left alone in the room with Inspector Adler.

Now that she had him alone and to herself, the Inspector seemed in no hurry to begin the interview. She stood in silence and gazed at Orphan as if examining a small but fascinating exhibit. She looked, Orphan thought, like a person used to waiting; she looked like a copper.

Orphan was grateful for the silence. In his mind Lucy's image still burned, a flame that threatened to consume him. Gilgamesh's letter, his maddened flight to Richmond, his push through the crowds, Moriarty's speech, Lucy's dissipating smile...

Waves of black despair threatened to drown him.

"You heard the nurse," Irene Adler said. She approached Orphan's bed and stood looking down at him, her face thoughtful, a little – he thought – sad. "What happened in the park was a terrible accident." Her arms were folded on her chest. She had, Orphan thought, a beautiful voice. A singer's voice. He looked into her eyes and found unexpected sympathy.

"An accident," he said. The words were bitter in his mouth. They had the taste of preserved limes, needing to be spat out.

"Yes," Irene Adler said. She let the silence drag. Then, "You know, I have been interested in you for a while."

"Me?" His surprise was genuine. The Inspector smiled and shook her head at him, as if admonishing a wayward boy. "You are part of the Persons from Porlock, aren't you, Orphan? You and Tom Thumb and Wee Billy Conroy and 'Scalpel' Reece DuBois? Taking such delight in disrupting the work of eminent writers in the capital, dressed like clowns, quoting poor Ed Lear like the words of a mad Biblical prophet… and so sure of your invincibility, your invisibility, as if no one and nothing could touch you."

The Persons from Porlock! He looked up at her, suddenly confused. "You knew?"

"Of course I bloody knew," Irene Adler said. "As little as you clearly think of Scotland Yard, we are not fools… and certainly not clowns."

"I…" He faltered. "Have you come to arrest me?"

"Arrest you?" She seemed to contemplate the question. "For making a fool of yourself and sending up dear Oscar into the bargain? As tempting as that is, I think I'll decline."

Orphan's confusion deepened. "But what we did… the Queen…"

The Inspector shrugged. "Les Lézards may be overly fond of poetry," she said. "I, on the other hand, am not."

Orphan felt himself blinking stupidly. The Inspector's words were close to treason. Why, he wondered, was she telling him this? What did she want? He said, "I don't understand."

"No," Irene Adler said. "I don't suppose you do." She came closer to him then, and sat down on the edge of the bed, her face looking down directly into Orphan's. There were fine lines at the corners of her eyes, which were a deep, calm blue. "You're an enigma, Orphan," she said at last. "You show up at the Rose Theatre, and it ends up in flames. You show up a day later in Richmond Park – it ends up in flames. You belong to an organisation that terrorises writers and you live and work in the bookshop of a known seditionist. Why is it that trouble follows you around like a dog on a leash?" She leaned even closer towards him, and when she spoke, though her words were no more than a murmur, barely audible, they nevertheless hit Orphan like cold water evicted from a bucket and shook away the remnants of his dark sleep. "What is it about you that so draws the attention of the Bookman?"

Orphan wandered through the streets like a lost minotaur in a hostile, alien maze. Somewhere, unseen but deadly, was the

Bookman: Orphan felt his presence like a ghostly outline, a shapeless, formless thing, a disembodied entity that hid in the fog and watched him from the rooftops and the drains.

What is it about you, Irene Adler had said, *that so draws the attention of the Bookman?*

Her words kept running through his mind, a question lost in a maze of its own, seeking an answer he didn't know.

He had not answered her. Irene Adler, after examining him for a long, uncomfortable moment, said, "Do you miss her?"

A wave of anger took over Orphan. He could think of nothing to say, no suitable reply to that meaningless, cruel question. Looking at him, Irene Adler sighed. She said, "If it was in your power, would you bring her back?"

Their eyes locked. It seemed to Orphan that an invisible contest was taking place, a battle of wills between them, like a jousting tournament for a prize that was unknown.

He said, "She's dead."

The silence stretched between them, dark as an ocean under a moonless sky. Irene Adler stretched and walked away from him. She paced around the room, circling, coming closer, drawing back, as if trying to decide something unpleasant. She stopped by the window and looked out. When she spoke her face was turned away from Orphan. She said, "Death is the undiscovered country…"

She waited. The light from the window touched her face and pronounced the fineness of her features. She turned her head and looked at Orphan, eyes tired but still full of life, containing within them both a challenge and a question.

Orphan completed, as if compelled to answer, the Inspector's quote, the words torn out of him. "From whose bourn no traveller returns…" He sat up in the bed. "What do you want from me?" he whispered.

The Inspector, unexpectedly, smiled. "You still don't understand, do you?" she said. "Did your friend Gilgamesh not try to tell you?" She saw his startled expression and shook her head. "Oh, Orphan. Why is it that everyone you touch seems to die?

You are like Hamlet, Prince of Denmark, wandering the halls of your mind, not daring to act until all is lost. This is the time of myths, Orphan. They are the cables that run under the floors and power the world, the conduits of unseen currents, the steam that powers the great engines of the earth. Would you bring her back if you could?"

The question again, flung at him like a hook on a fishing line. Ready to reel him in.

And Orphan, caught, said, "Tell me how."

He walked away from Guy's Hospital through the maze of Southwark's streets. "Not here," Irene Adler had said. She had glanced about her, and Orphan, following the direction of her eyes, saw they were focused on an ancient-looking bible that rested by his bedside. "Here." She handed him a piece of paper. Orphan opened it, read an address and a time.

"Get well," Irene Adler said, and then she was gone, closing the door softly behind her.

It had taken Orphan two more days before the doctor released him. The waves of darkness came and went, grief washing over him, Lucy's burning image waking him in the night with screams that echoed only inside his head.

Yet overlaying the grief was Irene Adler's question. *Would you bring her back?* she had asked – and the question, with its implication, its insane promise, had consumed Orphan until he could think of little else.

He did examine the bible that rested by his bedside. It was an old volume, printed the previous century, rebound in contemporary cloth. Grubby and worn, it had the look of a bible that had rested, over the decades, in the hands of more than one dying patient. It was a King James bible, of the translation sanctioned, for his own mysterious reasons, by that greatest of all Lizard Kings, yet it was not published by the King's printer: it was an illegal publication. Orphan turned the book in his hands, intrigued. The publisher's name was given as Thomas Guy. Orphan seemed to remember, vaguely, that the founder of the hospital had indeed begun his career in the printing and selling of illegal bibles. That must be, therefore, one of them, he thought. But why had Irene Adler looked to it before falling quiet? What was it about the book (if that was indeed what had concerned her) to prevent her from speaking further? It was just a book.

Restless, alone with his dark thoughts in his room, Orphan began paging through Thomas Guy's bible. First he shook the book, edges down, but nothing had fallen from within its pages. Next he thumbed through the book, seeking to see where it would open: it should, he knew, come to the place that had been most used. And so it did, and the old bible opened in his lap onto the eighth chapter of the first book of Samuel. It was the part where the elders of Israel come to Samuel, an old man now, and ask him to make them a king. Orphan read Samuel's reply to the elders, and felt a strange apprehension reach out to wrap cold fingers around his chest, as if the ancient, anonymous writer of the text was addressing him, replying to an unanswered question.

And he said, This will be the manner of the King that shall reign over you: He will take your sons, and appoint them for himself, for his chariots, and to be his horsemen; and some shall run before his chariots.

And he will appoint him captains over thousands, and captains over fifties; and will set them to ear his ground, and to reap his harvest, and to make his instruments of war, and instruments of his chariots.

And he will take your daughters to be confectionaries, and to be cooks, and to be bakers.

And he will take your fields, and your vineyards, and your oliveyards, even the best of them, and give them to his servants.

And he will take the tenth of your seed, and of your vineyards, and give to his officers, and to his servants.

And he will take your menservants, and your maidservants, and your goodliest young men, and your asses, and put them to his work.

He will take the tenth of your sheep: and ye shall be his servants.

And ye shall be his servants. Something was crystallising in Orphan's head, the beginning of understanding; that in the maze of texts there was hidden a message, an interpretation of a past like a thread that aimed to lead him onwards, to traverse the filthy streets of history. Numbly, he wondered how King James, and all his get who came after, had allowed passages like this to be printed. And then, at the bottom left corner of the page, in a pencil mark so faint that he almost missed it, he saw the inscription that waited there, almost as if it had been waiting for him, just him, through all the patient years: *The Bookman Cometh.*

SEVEN
Body-Snatchers

The body-snatchers, they have come
And made a snatch at me.
It's very hard them kind of men
Won't let a body be.

You thought that I was buried deep
Quite decent like and chary;
But from her grave in Mary-bone
They've come and bon'd your Mary!

The arm that us'd to take your arm
Is took to Dr Vyse,
And both my legs are gone to walk
The Hospital at Guy's.
   – Thomas Hood, *Whims and Oddities*

Away from Guy's, through the narrow maze of Southwark streets. Dusk was falling, and on the other side of the river, through the fog, the great city lit up in thousands of moth-like flames, in hundreds and hundreds of lit butterflies, their wings beating against the stillness of dark, fighting the night with their simple existence. A week before, and Orphan would have stopped, taken out his small notepad and his pen, scribbled a few lines, composed a minor poem, recorded the motion of the light in dark air.

Not now.

Away from the hospital, away from the echoing corridors and the hushed expectant silence punctuated by dying screams. Away from the cold stone and the musty watching bibles in every room, and away from the food that churned the stomach, and the sharp stench of industrial cleaning fluids. He walked through the fog and felt the presence of the Bookman like a ghostly outline, a shapeless, formless thing, a disembodied entity that hid in the foul air and watched him from the rooftops and the drains.

The second night at Guy's, unable to sleep, uneasy with the presence of the pirate bible by his bedside, he stood from his bed. The floor was cold under his feet but he welcomed the sensation. He walked out of the room and shut the door behind him.

He walked through empty corridors and listened to the sick behind their doors. No one stopped him, no one challenged him to return to his bed. He was alone as a wraith, haunting the hospital as if he were already dead.

The cold wrapped itself around him, rising like the shoots of a flower from the ground and into his feet and up, entombing him. He passed through ill-lit wards and looked out of the windows and saw nothing but black night draped across the hospital.

His footsteps led him, by twists and turns, downwards, so that he passed floor after floor in this fashion, his bare feet padding silently in his journey through the endless corridors.

He pushed open a door marked MEDICAL SCHOOL, and descended a flight of stairs, and the air grew even colder, and was filled with a chemical tang that burned the back of his throat. I should wake, he thought. I should not be walking here. But he could not stop; he was trapped in a dream and could not rouse.

And yet, now that he was here he could go no further. The basement, he realised. A long corridor stretched before him. Electric lights hummed and flared and dimmed in naked bulbs suspended from the ceiling like grotesque blinking eyes. A row of doors stood shut like the flooded mouths of underwater caves. He heard voices, approaching, and turned back, and hid against the wall, his head turned to observe the happenings in the corridor he had just vacated.

There was the sound of something heavy being dragged against the floor, and the laboured breathing of two or more men. Orphan looked, and saw that there were indeed two men there, and that each was dragging behind him a sack. Both had clean-shaven faces of ordinary features, almost pleasant. They stopped before a door in the middle of the corridor and the one on the left knocked twice.

The door opened and a man came out. He looked from side to side furtively, and on his face was a nervous, almost frightened expression. Orphan recognised him – it was the doctor who had first examined him.

"What ho, Dr W.?" the man on the left said. "We got you a good one, on my word of honour." He looked at his companion and smiled. "Two good ones, and fresh."

"Shut up, fool," the doctor growled. He raised his hand and touched his moustache nervously, then motioned the two men. "Bring the Things in. Quickly." As the door opened Orphan saw there were other men in the room, though he could not see them clearly.

As the two men walked through the door they struggled with their sacks, and the one on the right momentarily came loose; and Orphan watched with horror as a slender, white leg protruded from its opening.

The doctor halted when he saw this.

"I did not ask you for a female, Bishop," he said. "I will not pay for a Thing I do not need."

"It is not a woman but a big small," the man – Bishop – said in a wounded tone. "Look." And he opened the sack fully as it lay on the threshold of the room.

The corpse that sprawled out was indeed not that of a woman. It was a boy, aged, Orphan thought, around fifteen or sixteen. His face were strangely peaceful, as if he were only asleep and would soon wake up and demand his tea, and his features were strong but delicate, a face that had once known comfortable living.

The doctor looked with distaste at the two men. "What did he die of, Bishop?" He turned to look at the other man, who was standing grinning with his sack held securely in his hand, "May?"

"I neither know nor care," Bishop said, and his companion, May, nodded and said, "It is quite indifferent what he died of, for here he is, stiff enough."

"Get in, damn it!" The voice that came from within the room had the tone of command in it, and the doctor and the two body-snatchers (for that, Orphan realised, was what they must be, two resurrection men plying their trade) hurried through the door, the doctor shutting it behind him in a hurry.

Orphan, for whom the whole gruesome scene still seemed no more than a part of his nightmare, padded around the corner into the corridor, and peered through the keyhole.

Inside, the argument was continuing.

"This subject is too fresh," the doctor said, and the two men laughed. "The fact is," Bishop said, "you are not in the habit of seeing fresh subjects and you don't know anything about it!"

The same commanding voice Orphan heard before now growled, "We need the Thing fresh, so stop arguing about it and get to work!"

But the doctor did not easily give up. "I don't think it was ever buried," he said. "Where had it come from?"

"You know nothing about raising bodies!" Bishop said. He seemed truly exasperated.

"Enough," the man who seemed to be in charge said, and all fell quiet. Orphan, peering through, could not make out his face: all he could discern was a remarkable bulk, coupled with power.

Orphan squirmed against the door, trying for a better angle.

For a moment, the whole room spread out before him: there were the two resurrection men, standing to one side with their gruesome merchandise; the doctor, hovering nervously beside what appeared to be a huge coffin; the fat man, sitting in an arm-chair, himself surveying the room; two more men, strangely similar in appearance, dressed in white medical smocks, standing next to a vast array of machinery pulsating with lights.

What was in the coffin? Vapours rose from it, icy white tendrils that turned the room into a still, cold space like the inside of a slaughterhouse. A mortuary, Orphan thought. The coffin was long, metallic, over six feet long. It must have held a tall person, he thought. But who?

He blinked, took a slow, quiet breath. Yes. He could discern a face, thin, with a hawkish nose and a square, prominent chin. The eyes were open and stared into nothing, as if the man was not quite dead but rather drugged to an extreme, until he had taken on the semblance of death.

The fat man stirred in his armchair. "Pay them and get rid of them," he said to the doctor. "You must try the procedure again."

Then he turned his head towards the door. He seemed to be looking directly at Orphan.

Orphan froze. Then the fat man shook his head, minutely, as if saying, "This is not for you," and he lifted a cane that rested by his side and made a motion with it, and one of the men moved against the door and blocked Orphan's view. Orphan ran from the door, but it remained unopened. No one was pursuing him.

Did the fat man know that he was there? He had warned him away. Hadn't he? Did he know him? He shuddered, suddenly feeling the cold. He felt entirely awake now. The body-snatchers will come out any minute, he thought. He did not want to be there. The cold overwhelmed him, made his teeth chatter. Everywhere he turned there was death.

He turned and ran away the way he had come, his feet noise-less on the stone floor.

Away from Guy's, away from its ghoulish dreams, its baroque mysteries. Away from the hospital with the falling of night, through the cobblestone streets and onto the south bank. The fog intensified around him, became a thick screen that blotted out the stars and erased the city as if it had never existed. Orphan hurried, shivering despite his coat. The lonely sound of his footsteps was muffled by the fog.

He walked past streetlamps that bled a wet yellow light, making his way by memory rather than sight. A chill wind rose from the Thames and pummelled him, and he drew the coat tighter around himself and turned away from the river bank, until at last he reached the great edifice of Waterloo Station, jutting out of the fog like a dark citadel. It seemed to him a living thing then, a grotesque, giant face that breathed loudly, the sound of its inhaling and exhaling composed of the steady rhythm of trains. He skirted the station, encountering few people. Those who were out in this foul weather hurried past him without glancing his way, and Orphan had the sudden feeling that he was invisible, a ghost wandering in an unreal world.

He stopped by one of the great stone arches. A lonely figure lay huddled on the floor, wrapped in grey blankets. Orphan crouched down, and the figure stirred. A mane of shaggy hair emerged and two large eyes, milky-white and unseeing, stared up at Orphan. "Spare some change?" the beggar said hopefully.

Orphan was startled. He had almost, for a moment, believed it was Gilgamesh, returned. "What is your name?" he asked, and he reached into his pocket for what money he had.

He dropped the meagre coins he found into the beggar's bowl. The man raised his face further; his blind eyes seemed to search Orphan's face, to study them. Then the unblinking eyes grew wider, and his pale face turned paler still, and his breath caught in his throat; and Orphan, worried for the man's health, grabbed him by the shoulder and said, "What ails you, my friend?"

The beggar moved away, as if the touch of Orphan's hand was more than he could bear. "Not so much noise, my lord!" he hissed. "Sweet prince, speak low: the King your father is disposed to sleep."

Was the man a failed Shakespearean actor? Orphan wondered. He said, gently, "My name is Orphan."

The beggar did a thing that startled Orphan. He laughed. It was a curious sound, hoarse and weak like a failing engine. Then he said, "Sweet prince, the untainted virtue of your years hath not yet dived into the world's deceit, nor more can you distinguish of a man than of his outward show."

He spoke, it seemed to Orphan, with great intensity, as if his words carried a meaning far beyond their stage-use. But, "I'm sorry," Orphan said, "I don't understand."

Sighing, he rose to leave. He was already late for his meeting with the Inspector.

The beggar bowed his head. Then he said, half-muttering before retreating back into his blankets, "Now cracks a noble heart. Good night sweet prince: and flights of angels sing thee to thy rest!"

"Thank you," Orphan said, "I think." And he walked onwards, as the beggar under his arch was swallowed in the fog.

He walked around the great edifice of the station; and it was not long before he reached another arch where, underneath, small glass windows glowed with an internal warmth, and a small door stood waiting like a welcoming embrace, and a small sign hanging above the door said, The Lizard's Head.

EIGHT
Lord Byron's Simulacrum

The beings of the mind are not of clay;
Essentially immortal, they create
And multiply in us a brighter ray.
  – Lord Byron, "Childe Harold's Pilgrimage"

He pushed the door open and went inside. Heat assailed him, a cloud of tobacco smoke engulfed him, and with them came the sizzle of frying sausages, and the smell of beer that had, over the years, seeped into the very foundations of the pub.

The pub was dark, smoky, and full of hazily seen figures. Orphan removed his coat and looked about him for Irene Adler. He saw a white hand beckoning to him from a booth in the corner, and went to join her, next to a small ship's-window that had fog climbing to it outside like ivy.

"Sit down," Irene Adler said.

She was sitting alone, a half-drunk glass of white wine before her. Her bright, alert eyes had dark rings around. "I'll get a drink," Orphan said.

He went to the bar, paid, and returned with a tall glass. As he sat down opposite the inspector a shadow fell across the table.

He had seen that face before. The black curly hair, the sharp nose, the smooth features: Lord Byron. A youthful Lord Byron, without the ravages of time. "Byron," Irene Adler said. "Please, sit down. Orphan, this is Lord Byron."

Byron sat next to the Inspector, opposite Orphan. He didn't speak. Orphan, captivated – he had seldom seen one of its kind before – studied him overtly.

It was disconcerting. The youthful features, the hair, even the eyes seemed that of a young man, but now, as he examined them, he thought: they are precise and unchanging, the way a doll's are. This was not Byron, the poet, the rebel, who was long time dead. It was a remarkable simulation of a man, yet a simulation all the same, and now that he could see that, could examine him in this way, in an almost intimate fashion, Orphan noticed the way the face moved mechanically from one expression to another, the too-sharp angles of the body, even, when Byron turned his head to look at Irene, the small, tell-tale metal tag that was embedded discreetly in his neck.

Byron turned his head back to Orphan and now Orphan could see that the eyes, too, were unreal: they were glassy, marble-like, devoid of feeling or even true sight. The Byron simulacrum sighed (and Orphan marvelled at the way his chest moved, the way the air travelled through its throat and nose) and said, "I am not human."

There was a silence. Orphan could think of nothing to say in reply.

At last, it was Irene who spoke. She looked across the table at Orphan and said, "Do you remember what happened at the Rose?"

Orphan, looking at her, thought of Lucy.

"Describe it to me."

He shook himself. His mind slipped back to what he had seen. Henry Irving, in his guise as Shakespeare. Beerbohm Tree stepping onto the stage as the Ancient Mariner holding in his hands a heavy, leather-bound folio. Irving opening the book.

The book exploding.

"What happened to Beerbohm?"

Orphan, lost, looked into Irene's eyes. He had not thought of the young actor. He tried to think back, but could conjure no clear image. "Did he not die in the explosion?"

Irene looked down into her wine glass. The Byron simulacrum sat quietly, like a machine that had been temporarily switched off. "What I tell you is a state secret," Irene said at last. "But I think we are beyond secrets now, Orphan." She raised her face, and he could see the deep weariness in her eyes, the moving shadows.

"Beerbohm Tree was found, dead, in an abandoned warehouse by the docks a few hours after the explosion at the Rose. He had been there since at least the previous day. He had not been at the Rose at all." She twisted the stem of the wine glass. "When we… when I found him, there was not much left of him. His hands were clasped about what was left of his chest. They held a blackened, broken object. It might have once been a book."

"The Bookman…" Orphan said. "But I saw him there," he objected. "I saw him at the theatre." Even to himself he sounded petulant. Then his eyes fell on Byron and he whispered, "It was a machine."

The Byron automaton stirred. "Was it?" he said. "What is a machine, Orphan? La Mettrie wrote that 'the human body is a machine which winds its own springs'. Can a machine act in a play? Can a machine play music? Can a machine love?"

"I… I don't know," Orphan said. He looked from Byron to Irene. "I don't understand." He wanted to shout. "What has this got to do with Lucy?"

"Following the explosion in Richmond Park," Irene Adler said, "a brief, powerful burst of concentrated energy was recorded, originating at the very moment the book exploded in Lucy's hands. We have recorded a similar transmission after the explosion at the Rose. These books with which the Bookman so cunningly kills – they are not mere books. They are devices."

Orphan swallowed. The beer stood forgotten on the table before him. He said, "Devices of what?"

"Perhaps," Irene said, so quietly she may have been speaking to herself, "they are recording devices."

"And they record... what?" He thought back to the Rose, to the counterfeit Beerbohm Tree, indistin-guishable from the real thing. As if the man had been copied in his entirety, as if he had been recreated, made anew, and left to perform his role as if nothing had happened... And he said, in a hushed voice, the thought cooling him down as if he were still outside, and it was snowing, "You think he takes people's souls."

Lucy, he suddenly thought. So that was what the Inspector had wanted him to understand. If she was not killed, but merely... what? Abducted? Translated? Taken by the lord of Hades, to reside forever in his dark and lonely court?

"Perhaps," Irene Adler said. There was such pain in her eyes that, for a moment, Orphan couldn't bear to look at them. She was, he thought, gazing inwards, looking deep within herself at a memory he could not see. She, too, he thought suddenly, the realisation striking him, had lost someone she loved to the Book-man. And he wondered who it was.

Across the table from him Byron stirred again. "La Mettrie," Byron said, "says that 'the soul is but an empty word, of which no one has any idea, and which an enlightened man should only use to signify the part in us that thinks. Given the least principle of motion, animated bodies will have all that is necessary for moving, feeling, thinking, repenting, or in a word for conducting themselves in the physical realm, and in the moral realm which depends upon it.'" He sighed and looked down at himself, and shook his head as if confused. "I will ask you again," he said. "What is a machine?"

But Orphan didn't answer. Could it be, he wondered – could Lucy, somehow, still be alive? Could she come back, the way Beerbohm Tree had come back, if only for a short while? He said, his voice choking, "How could I get her back?"

"Listen," Irene said. She inched her ear at Byron, prompting him to speak.

"I don't know who – what – the Bookman is," Byron said. "But I know this: there are more artificers on this earth than the bureaucrats of the Babbage company who made me. I am but a machine. I am human-made, and as imperfect as a human. But I listen." His eyes, those great and vacant marbles, were no longer empty, and he turned his head in a delicate movement, as if listening to something unheard. "I listen to the talk of machines, to the exchange of Tesla communications, to the constant hum of the aether. We simulacra are rare and far apart, so far. But we talk to each other, and to others who are not like us in form, but whose souls are. And the rumours persist."

He spoke with a great gravity, and a little sadness. And it seemed to Orphan that he knew why, for surely what he was learning was a secret to these beings, and not easily shared. Impulsively he said, "Thank you, my Lord," and saw the Byron simulacrum smile. "I am not Byron," he said. "I am made to look like him, to sound like him, to quote his words and pretend his moods. But I do not have his talent for poetry, nor his love of it…" He sighed again, and for a moment he was Byron, an older, wiser lord who carried a heavier burden on his slim shoulders.

After a moment, Orphan said, "What rumours do you hear?"

Byron raised his head and his fingers tapped a gentle rhythm on the tabletop. "That there are others, like us and not. That there are other, alien beings, not human nor mechanical, but something of both." He shook his head. "A storm is coming, Orphan. A great storm that travels over the sea and lashes the waves into submission, whose origin is one island and its destination another. We believe…"

He fell silent.

"Believe what?"

"It is of no importance."

"Please," Orphan said. The simulacrum smiled. "I do not know who, or what, the Bookman is," he said. "All I know is that he is bound, whether in love or in hate – and the two are often merely two aspects of the same emotion – with Les Lézard. And the story is told that – like love and hate, perhaps – the Bookman too has an opposite. Perhaps another aspect of himself. Who knows? Is he real? Is the Bookman?"

"He killed… he killed Lucy."

"Ah, empirical evidence," Byron said. "Yes. Again, I'm sorry."

"What do you believe?"

Byron laughed. It was a grating, harsh sound. "We believe in the Translation," he said.

"Translation of what?"

"The translation, perhaps, of us all. Goodbye, Orphan." He stood, then, pushing his chair back, his movements stiff and unnatural like those of a toy. "But what your part in this is, if any, I do not know."

He made to turn away from them. But Orphan stopped him, rising and putting his hand on the simulacrum's shoulder. "Please," he said. "Who can I turn to?"

Byron turned to him, and for a long moment they stood facing each other, unmoving, Orphan's hand resting on Byron's shoulder.

At last Byron turned away. Orphan's arm dropped to his side. The simulacrum began to make his way towards the door, his steps slow and heavy and mechanical.

Halfway he stopped, and turned back. Orphan watched him, the fine, pale, manufactured face looking back at him as if seeking an answer to a different question. Then it changed, as if a corner of a picture-puzzle had become suddenly clear to him, and he smiled and said, in a quiet voice that nevertheless carried across the room, "Ask the Turk."

NINE
At the Cock-Pit

A forum there is for debate,
A Fives Court for milling in fun, Sirs,
A Parliament House for the great,
With a cock-pit for cruelty's sport, Sirs.
  – John Ashton, *The Treats of London*

Orphan walked home across the bridge, deep in thought. When Byron left he had finished his drink and thanked Irene Adler. They barely spoke, each of them isolated in a separate pool of thought. He wanted again to ask her who she had lost, but thought better of it when he saw the expression in her eyes. Instead, he rose from the table and made his way outside, where an icy fog had settled over the city like a pale northern invader.

His footsteps barely echoed as he walked across the bridge. He could see no living thing, as if the city was deserted, and he was alone in it, the last living man left in a ghost town. Even the whales were silent. To save Lucy, he thought, I must find the Bookman. But where do I start? He missed her, with a terrible urgency that surprised him even as it hurt. They were bound together, he and her.

When he reached the Strand he thought he heard a soft smooth sound coming from above his head and, raising it, glimpsed for a moment the movement of a velvety darkness low in the skies. An unmarked black airship, he thought, and almost laughed to himself. It was a fanciful idea, one of Jack's. He continued past St Martin in the Fields, and thought he caught another glimpse of the blimp, passing high to his left. He walked up St Martin's Lane and turned left with relief into Cecil Court.

Payne's was a haven of light in a dark world. Stepping inside, he was nearly overwhelmed with the feeling of home. The familiar, conflicting smells of the books vied for his attention. The musty tang of old volumes, the polished smell of new leather bindings, the crisp clear scent of freshly printed books, all rose to greet him, like a horde of somewhat-dysfunctional relatives at a family event.

Lit candles were scattered haphazardly around the room, perched precariously on piles of books and on the long counter. They cast spheres of light interlinked by shadows that fluttered like painted eyelids. He made his way into the back room and found his bed unaltered and waiting for him, a worn, comfortable companion.

On the small table rested a sputtering candle and beside it were two glasses and Jack's bottle of Old Bushmills.

It's like I hadn't left, Orphan thought. It's as if the last few days never happened, as if I only just came back from meeting Lucy. He felt a sense of unreality steal over him, but the sense of loss he felt was real enough, and would not let him sink into comforting dreams. Instead he lay down on the bed. Behind closed eyelids the candle flickered, lulling him into sleep. He felt exhausted, still weak from his injuries, and cold.

"Orphan."

When he opened his eyes the candle had burned down to a stub. One of the glasses on the table was missing and the bottle had been moved. A shadow-cowled figure watched him from the doorway and for a moment he felt panic, ascribing to the unseen face the hideous countenance of a nightmare: he had fallen asleep, he realised, and he dreamed... he dreamed of the Bookman, a monstrous being made of the yellowing pages of thousands of books, with a face like bleached vellum and gilt-edged eyes, who stalked him through a maze of bookshelves where no light penetrated.

The figure in the doorway moved and it was only Jack, holding a glass half-full with amber liquid. His face was drawn and tired, with shadows around his eyes.

"Jack."

He sat up, feeling groggy. His foot hit a shelf and sent books flying to the floor. He shook his head, trying to dispel the cobwebs that stretched inside it, and with them the last images of his dream. Jack came forward and sat down in the chair opposite. He poured drink into the remaining glass and offered it to Orphan. "I'm sorry."

Orphan nodded and accepted the drink, and they sat in silence. Orphan contemplated the glass in his hands and could think of nothing to say. It was Jack, therefore, who finally broke the silence. "What will you do now?" he said, and he looked at Orphan with his head cocked to one side, a strangely sorrowful expression on his face.

But Orphan didn't know. He felt disorientated, unsure of the time, unsure even if it was still night, or whether day had crept over the city while he was sleeping. So he said, "What's the time?" and watched Jack nod, as if Orphan's question had confirmed something he had previously only suspected. "Four, four-thirty." He must have seen the confusion in Orphan's eyes. "In the morning." He stood up suddenly, depositing an empty glass on the table. "Come with me."

"What is it, Jack?"

His friend shook his head. "I want to show you something. Come."

With a groan, Orphan rose from the bed. He felt curiously light-headed, as if this was all but part of a bad dream, and he was still asleep. He left his untouched drink on the table besides Jack's glass and followed him out of the room.

The door banged behind them as they stepped outside the shop. Though the fog had abated the air was cold and damp, and a strong stench, as of an open sewer, filled the air. It had rained while Orphan slept, but it had done nothing to cleanse the city. Black velvety night pressed oppressively over Cecil Court, unhindered by the feeble gas lights that stood on St Martin's Lane.

He followed Jack without speaking. They crossed St Martin's and went through New Row, past shuttered shops and onto King Street. He could hear the sounds of a fight, screams and breaking glass followed by hoarse, wild laughter coming from the old Bucket of Blood pub on nearby Rose Street.

Jack led him on. The market square, lit by gaslight, was a place of shadows and squalor. Tired prostitutes, mainly women but with two or three bare-chested men amidst them, converged in small groups underneath the roofed market, negotiating with late revellers who seemed unsteady on their feet. A man cursed loudly and was pushed away; he walked off, still swearing loudly. On the corner of the Opera House a man stood behind a stall and a small fire, and the heavy smell of frying onions and sausage-meat filled the square like a march of invading soldiers.

Orphan liked Covent Garden during the day, when the fruit and vegetable market was open and continental restaurants filled the air with the scents of garlic and cooking spices. He avoided it at night, when it became, or so it seemed, the lodestone that exerted its powerful pull on every lecher and drunk in the Lizardine Empire. Even this late the barely discreet bawdy-houses on the side streets were no doubt operating, and the pubs and drinking establishments were still seeing out the late stragglers who refused to wave goodbye to the night and adjourn at last to their beds. He wondered what they were doing there at this hour, Jack and him, but his will seemed to have seeped out of him, and he merely followed in Jack's footsteps, not asking the question, content to merely walk on through the haze of the market.

They walked past a group of drunk students half-shouting and half-singing the words to the old favourite, "If I Had A Donkey Wot Wouldn't Go". Orphan smiled when he heard the closing words, followed by a last, spirited chorus:

> *Bill's donkey was ordered into Court,*
> *In which he caused a deal of sport,*
> *He cocked his ears, and opened his jaws,*
> *As if he wished to plead his cause.*
> *I proved I'd been uncommonly kind,*
> *The ass got a verdict – Bill got fined;*
> *For his worship and me was of one mind –*

And he said... (and here the chanting students raised their voices even higher, and shouted again the refrain) – *and he said!*

> *If I had a donkey wot wouldn't go,*
> *I never would wollop him, no, no, no!*
> *I'd give him some hay, and cry Gee! Whoa!*
> *And come up, Neddy! And come up, Neddy!*

And they disappeared in a burst of laughter around the corner. Jack marched on. Orphan followed.

It wasn't long before they arrived in Drury Lane. Jack stopped outside a deserted-looking building. A fading sign that looked like a remnant from another century entirely declared the place as the King's Arms Tavern. The windows were boarded up and the gas-lamp outside was broken, casting the area into gloom. Orphan found himself wondering if the sun would ever rise again. He blew on his hands to try to warm them. He could taste the faint tang of leaking gas in the air.

Jack went to a small door set into the side of the building. It was plain, made of rough, unvarnished wood. Jack knocked, a complicated beat.

They waited.

Presently they could hear steps, and the door opened.

"Wha' do you want?"

The woman filled the doorway. Fat rolled down her neck as she surveyed them with small hard eyes. The fat spread down to her arms and disappeared underneath the long fur coat that must have been made from the skins of an entire skulk of foxes.

She raised a languid hand on which heavy rings cut into fleshy fingers. "Jackie, issat you?"

Jack surprised Orphan by reaching out and taking the woman's hand in his. "Mother Jolley," he said, and almost, it seemed to Orphan, bent down to kiss the woman's – who did not look at all jolly, to him – hand. "You get prettier every time I see you."

"Spare me yer flattery, cur," but she looked momentarily pleased.

Then the small, suspicious eyes shifted to Orphan. "Who's your friend?" She reached out her hand, extending it before her like a crane, and grasped Orphan's face between her fingers, pulling hard at his cheeks. "He has doleful eyes like a dog what's been kicked by 'is mistress." And she cackled at her own words, until a bout of coughing took her over and she let go of Orphan's face, though he knew she had left her mark on his skin before doing so.

"A friend," Jack said, and a look was exchanged between him and Mother Jolley whose meaning became clear to Orphan only when Jack added, "a comrade."

The fat woman surveyed Orphan for a moment longer, as if dubious of his entitlement to such distinction. Finally, with a reluctant nod, she moved back and pulled the door open. "Follow me, gents."

Orphan, shooting Jack a glance that said, *what the hell is going on?*, followed him nevertheless, and the three of them, like an ill-matched family of nestling dolls, walked in single file into a narrow hallway, where the accumulated decades of tobacco smoke lay sedately in the still air.

They walked down a flight of stairs that opened onto a stone-walled antechamber, empty save for a large, stout oak door. Mother Jolley moved aside, allowing Orphan and Jack to crowd beside her. The door had no handle; Mother Jolley pressed a hidden lever on the wall and the door swung open, making no sound.

But noise erupted through the open door, as startling as a gale. The hoarse shouts of excited men and women mingled with the scream of animals, and a heavy, musky scent ebbed into the air of the antechamber, the mixture of human sweat and excitement – and of fear and animal faeces.

Jack walked through, and Orphan followed. Mother Jolley herded them in and the door closed behind her, shutting out the above-stairs world.

"Welcome to the cock pit," she said.

Orphan looked around. They were in a wide basement. Burning torches hung on the walls, giving the place the aura of a Middle Ages torture chamber. The ground was uneven and sloped down until it became a circular arena. It was surrounded by people – mostly men, but some women too – all shouting, waving fists, flashing money.

Inside the ring two large roosters fought in a cloud of blood and feathers. Orphan, sickened, followed Jack to the edge of the crowd. The roosters had small, thin blades attached where their spurs should have been. The blades flashed in the torchlight. The screaming of the fighting birds filled the air with menace.

Jack was circling the ring. Orphan followed him, and they finally came to a stop in a dark corner of the basement, where Jack leaned against the wooden supports that rose from ground to ceiling. He motioned to Orphan to do the same.

"Why," Orphan said, having to almost shout to be heard over the noise of the fight, "are we here?"

Jack nodded. "Now, that is the question," he agreed. "Why are any of us here? What is our purpose on this earth?"

He flashed Orphan a grin, which wasn't returned.

In the ring, a red-and-black rooster was crowned the winner. The lifeless corpse of its opponent was scooped off the ground. Orphan followed the man who lifted it – a short, stocky man wearing a bloodied butcher's apron – as he carried the dead bird to the opposite side of the basement from them. Coals glowed in a brazier, and on a wire mesh chicken pieces sizzled and smoked. The man in the apron laid the latest carcass on the surface of a table by the coals and began plucking feathers.

"I wasn't joking," Jack said. He turned to Orphan and looked hard into his face. "Why we are here – why we are here – that's a question I think you need to have answered for you."

The umpire, a tall moustachioed man with pale, blotchy skin that made his head look like a mushroom that had never seen the sun, announced the next bout, and two fresh roosters were kicked into the ring, where they immediately set on each other.

"Did you think to ask yourself," Jack said, speaking softly despite the noise of the crowd, forcing Orphan to bend closer to listen to him, "just why the Bookman wished to destroy the Martian probe in the park? Or did you think, as you seem to, that his one and only purpose was to hurt you? That he launched that public, spectacular attack just to hurt the girl you loved?"

The girl he still loved, Orphan thought. He resented Jack that moment. He straightened, avoiding Jack's eyes. The truth, he realised, was that he did think that, did not – could not – comprehend another reason, no sense in the act that took Lucy away. He turned his head from his friend, focusing on the crowd. Movement caught his attention. That head. It looked familiar. As if in response a man in the crowd turned and their eyes met, and though the man did not give any sign that he knew him, Orphan recognised him immediately: it was Karl Marx.

When Marx turned back to the fight Orphan noticed that the figure next to him, though it was dressed in a long coat and its head was cowled, was that of a woman; and he was not surprised when, a moment later, the cowled head turned towards him, revealing the face of Isabella Beeton.

So the Parliament of Payne was complete and present.

Mrs Beeton, too, did not acknowledge him; and a moment later she had turned back and was swallowed in the crowd as though she had never been.

"What are *they* doing here?"

"The same thing we are doing," Jack said beside him. "Watching."

"The cockfight?"

Jack drew further into the shadows. He lifted his hand, his finger pointing upwards. "Them."

Orphan looked up.

Though the ceiling was low, a small balcony was erected halfway above the floor, made of wooden boards and surrounded by a thin balustrade. Three figures stood there: and though one was a man, the other two were of aristocratic stock.

They were lizards.

TEN
The Woman in White

The paleness grew whiter on her face, and she turned it farther away from me.
"Don't speak of to-morrow," she said. "Let the music speak to us of to-night, in a happier language than ours."
  – Wilkie Collins, *The Woman in White*

In the ring, a wounded rooster and a dead one were taken away. Something that was not quite a hush settled over the crowd then: a kind of tense, anticipatory stillness.

The umpire reappeared. He looked tense himself, and kept casting quick, darting glances at the balcony.

"Ladies and gentlemen, doxies and rakes!" the umpire cried. "Get ready to be shocked, prepare to be amazed! The fight of the night is about to commence!" Again he looked up, saw the silent watchers on the balcony, hesitated. His Adam's apple bobbed up and down.

Leaning against the wall, in the shadows, Orphan, too, was watching the lizards. They were two tall, distinguished beings, dressed in simple (yet obviously expensive), sober suits, with gentlemen's hats perched on their scaly heads. They moved forward now, their claws resting on the balustrade. They watched the ring intensely. Their tongues hissed out every so often and tasted the air.

The man beside them was uncommonly fat. He stood apart from the lizards, his attention not on the ring but on its audience. His head moved, slowly and methodically, as he scanned the room. Suddenly, as if aware he was being watched, he turned his head sharply and met Orphan's eyes.

It was the man from the mortuary at Guy's.

The man nodded, once, then winked at Orphan. Orphan hurriedly turned his eyes back to the ring. He was discomfited by the fat man, and not just by the memory of their previous encounter. He could not tell what it was that had so unnerved him. He knows me, he thought. He was waiting for me. He reminded him of a spider that had lain in wait in the centre of a cobweb, the trap so light it could not be seen until it sprung. He looked to Jack for help, but his friend's eyes were on the ring, and there was a strange, hungry expression in them that made Orphan uneasy.

"All the way from the ancient empire of Egypt," the umpire was saying, "now under the protection of our own Everlasting Empire – from the deadly deserts of the Nile, the most hostile region known to man – and *lizard* –" and here he glanced again at the balcony, like an unruly child afraid of being punished for his misbehaviour – "it's… Goliath!"

Orphan watched, incredulous, as into the ring came, on all fours, stepping slowly and majestically across the pit – a most immense lizard.

It was not a royal lizard, a Les Lézard, but rather an animal, that walked on four legs and was dark brown, with yellow bands crossing its naked body like war-paint. It raised its head and hissed loudly at the audience, a long, forked tongue darting out like a weapon.

The umpire took a step back, swallowed, glanced again at the balcony and said, apparently determined to play his role through to the end, regardless of possible consequences – "And in the other corner, all the way from the savannahs of the Dark Continent, the reigning champion – it's the Red King!"

The lizard that entered the ring second was not red – it was more olive-brown, Orphan thought, and mostly without bands

– but it looked fierce, and as soon as it saw Goliath it raised its head and hissed, and the two lizards began circling each other, while the umpire exited the ring with a look of relief on his pale face.

The Red King inflated its neck. The other lizard backed away, then hissed. Its tail lashed against the floor, and metal flashed. A long, silver knife was attached to Goliath's tail. Orphan felt sick, and suddenly terrified by the obscenity of the scene. He looked up and saw the two lizards on the balcony standing immobile, and beside them the fat man, who was looking not at the ring but at him, Orphan.

Sweat dampened his palms. He looked around him, seeking a way out, but the one door was shut and Mother Jolley was leaning against it with a body as heavy and shapeless as a sack of grain. She is a barricade, he thought. She would not let me through.

The Red King rose on its hind legs. It stood tall, and the silent crowd fell back as if cowed – or as if faced with a superior, a royal lizard. The Red King's tongue darted out, tasting the air.

Goliath struck.

The giant lizard darted forward and its tail lashed at its standing opponent. The knife cut into flesh and the Red King fell down. Its jaws closed around Goliath's neck and its claws dug into Goliath's body. The two lizards rolled on the floor, biting and clawing at each other. The Red King's tail lashed at Goliath and inflicted a wound.

"Watch." It was barely a whisper. Beside Orphan, Jack's eyes were moving wildly, looking on the audience, on the fight, on the balcony with its royal watchers. Jack's pupils swam in his eyes like foul-weather moons.

Orphan looked at the crowd. They stood away from the ring, immobile and silent until they seemed like statues. He searched for Marx and found him standing to one end. They were all cowled, he realised. Something about the audience… and then he realised.

It was not merely human.

Slowly, he found them. Following Jack's gaze, his own instinct. The lizards standing in the crowd. The hint of a tail, the impression of an elongated snout. Les Lézards.

Caliban's get was at the King's Arms.

In the ring, the two fighting lizards disengaged and withdrew from each other, hissing. Deep cuts could be seen in both their bodies, and they left bloodied footprints on the floor.

Goliath inflated its throat. The Red King hissed and stood on its hind legs again. Goliath followed it, and the two lizards stood and faced each other. They were a grotesque parody, Orphan thought. Like two princes stripped of their finery of clothes and of their title, undressed of civilisation. They were two savages, fighting for the entertainment of their brothers and their former servants.

Is this what Jack wanted me to see? he wondered. How his hatred of the lizards could be justified, that they would allow such a thing to be, that they would glory in it? And yet, there were humans there too, allowed to watch this degradation, and to enjoy it. It was a dangerous game Jack was playing, he realised. Orphan had thought him a mere public-house revolutionary, safe amidst his intellectual friends, his harmless Tesla set and his illicit printing press, but it wasn't so. He was a different thing altogether, much more dangerous and unexpected than he had ever seemed to Orphan: he glanced now at his friend and realised he had never really known him.

Jack looked back at him, and smiled; and his smile seemed to say that he knew what Orphan was thinking, and that he was glad, for now Orphan could no longer hide behind mere words, or childish pranks such as the Persons from Porlock had perpetrated, that he would now have to choose a side. *Why we are here – that's a question I think you need to have answered for you*, he had said. Orphan turned his head away; he could not meet his friend's eyes.

In the ring the Red King lashed out and its tail hit Goliath's leg, the blade flashing, cutting deep, and the lizard collapsed with a sound of pain, and then the Red King was on top of it, biting at its opponent's throat, its claws falling like knives on the wounded Goliath. It ripped Goliath's body open, cutting and biting until, gradually, the other lizard's movements slowed down.

Goliath's body gradually wound down, the way an old clock comes to a halt and stops beating the hours until, by degrees, time and sound die. It shuddered at last under the Red King, and was still.

Pandemonium broke around the ring. New torches were lit around the room and in their light Orphan could see Marx, his face contorted in rage or ecstasy – it was hard to tell which – exchanging money with a man beside him, saw Isabella Beeton turning to talk to a tall, dignified lizard with a navy uniform visible under his black robe, saw the lizards up on the balcony turn away (the fat man had disappeared), saw Jack's taut smile floating in the air beside him: more than anything, he saw the dead and broken lizard lying on the floor of the ring like a discarded toy. For one crazy moment he wondered if it, too, had once had a lover who might now mourn it.

He turned away from Jack. The air felt heavy with smoke and blood and he could stand it no longer. Looking towards the door he saw that Mother Jolley had moved away and was circling amidst her clientele, who now spread throughout the room in small groups. He saw the umpire entering the ring, ready to announce the winner. He saw the man in the bloodied apron also approaching, and wondered if he would serve up Goliath's remains. It would be cannibalism, he thought. He turned away and ran for the door, knocking people out of his path. He crashed into the door, and it moved open for him, and he escaped through it and up the stairs, and outside.

The cold air revived him. He walked away from Drury Lane, down to the Strand. The fog weaved in and out of his sight like a ghostly quilt. The sky seemed lighter, and he thought the sun must be rising, slowly, ever so slowly over the cold capital of the world. He walked to the river and stopped, hemmed in between Somerset House and King's College. A piece of darkness seemed momentarily to move in the sky, and he glanced up at it nervously, thinking again of black airships. But he could discern nothing beyond that first, hazy sense of movement, and his eyes returned to the flowing water, his thoughts liquid and disordered in his mind.

Revolution, he thought. That was Jack's ambition, his dream, his purpose. To fight their overlords, to overthrow the Queen and her line. To replace it with... what? He thought of the wounded birds in the ring, their silver blades flashing in the torchlight. And it seemed to Orphan that it didn't matter: that whoever ruled the empire, lizard or human, would be a being who would stand and watch a fight like that, and coldly make odds on the winner. He thought of Lord Shakespeare, the first of the great Poet-Prime Ministers, the greatest of them all. "As flies to wanton boys are we to the gods," he whispered into the mist. "They kill us for their sport..."

A damp breeze rose and touched his skin, sending a shiver through his body. Perhaps the automatons, he thought. Perhaps they had their own political ambition, perhaps they too were gathering in secret, preparing for a revolution. The thought neither cheered nor oppressed him. It left him unmoved. He thought of the revolution that had taken place in France, the Quiet Revolution of which so little was known. The French had resisted the might of Les Lézards – and for the most part, the Queen seemed happy in return simply to ignore the new Republic across the Channel. A cold peace lasted between the two nations, though now that he thought of it, Orphan found himself wondering how long that would last for.

The French were difficult. The words of a Carroll ditty rose in his head, and he smiled. "They are the frogs, and we have lizards," he whispered into the wind, "we play the first, and they the second fiddle."

From within the fog he heard a sound like that of a slow-moving boat, waves brushing against a hard, rocking body. He strained but could see nothing, and his thoughts returned to their meandering track. In *L'Île mystérieuse*, which was banned under the Empire, the author, Jules Verne, claimed to have made a voyage to Caliban's Island, though Orphan suspected it was a mere fancy of the author, who was known for his tales of wild imagination. I'd like to visit France, he thought. Then a boat came sailing out of the mist, a single person sitting in the prow, and his breath slammed into his lungs and froze his thoughts into small hard diamonds.

The person in the boat was Lucy.

She was dressed in a fine white dress that seemed to form a part of the fog, and she sat in an unnatural calm as the boat sailed without anyone to steer it, coming close to the bank of the river, close enough for Orphan to almost reach a hand and touch her. Almost.

He tried to shout her name. It came as a hoarse whisper. She was in profile to him and unmoving, and her head did not turn to him. She was staring out into the fog, into the boat's invisible path and he thought, suddenly and with a dull dread spreading through his bones, She is a ghost.

The fog hid her like a dance of scarves. The boat, the flow of the river itself, seemed to slow. He shouted, "Lucy!" and thought – for just a moment – that her face was turning to look at him.

Then she was gone, and the boat was swallowed by the mist rising from the water and disappeared like the last lingering trace of a dream, leaving only emptiness in its wake.

ELEVEN
Mycroft

You are right in thinking that he is under the British government. You would also be right in a sense if you said that occasionally he is the British government.
 – Arthur Conan Doyle, *His Last Bow*

Orphan stumbled away from the Thames like a drunk, and his hand ached for paper and pen, for something to write with. It was all too much of a poem, he thought. The woman in white. It made him suddenly giggle. He was too tired, too worn-out. Hallucinating, perhaps. And perhaps, he thought, Inspector Adler was right, and the Bookman had the power of life, as well as death.

She hadn't looked at him. That was what mattered, what hurt him the most. She neither looked at him nor spoke. It was as if one of them had not existed, as if one were a ghost and the other real, and the two passed each other in two different worlds. He didn't know which one he was, the real or the ghost.

I need sleep, he thought. I need a cup of tea, a bath and a warm bed. Sleep, above all. Sleep.

But it was not to be. For, as he made his way away from the river, a piece of the black night detached itself from the sky and came floating, as silent as a dark balloon, directly above his head.

Orphan looked up.

It was a blimp.

It was entirely black, with no markings, no legend on its side, no identity code describing its existence or purpose. No beacons were lit on the vehicle: it drifted in perfect darkness, invisible and sinister, like a bat hunting in the night.

Orphan's first thought was: so I did not imagine it.

His second: so it's true!

He had been followed by one of the legendary, mythical black airships. What do they want? he thought, panic rising inside him like heated water in bottled glass. And then, government. For who else could command a ship that did not exist?

The blimp hovered above him. He could see its small gondola, as dark as the balloon, the envelope itself. Were there windows cut into the passenger car? If so, they too were darkened.

Then, full-blown panic settled in. Already unsettled by the vision of Lucy, he did not notice until too late when two indistinct, towering figures rushed him from either side and pinned him between them. He struggled, but the two men held him tight and a cloth was thrown over his head and blinded him. He lashed out, heard one of the men grunt in pain. Then a blow caught him on the back of the head and pain exploded inside him, and he fell loose in his captors' arms.

He was dimly aware of being carried. When he returned to himself he found that he was sitting down (the chair soft and comfortable against his aching body), and the air was warm. He heard the clinking of glasses and voices speak, too softly for him to make out what they were saying.

The cloth was removed from his head.

He blinked. His arms were free, and he touched the back of his head gingerly, but there was no blood, only a small swelling starting up that hurt, but not too badly.

He looked up.

In a wide, plush armchair, a round glass in his hand with an amber drink sloshing inside it, sat the fat man from the King's Arms. The fat man from the mortuary at Guy's. And Orphan thought: Oh, no.

"You," Orphan said. He felt foolish as soon as he said it.

The fat man nodded companionably. "Me," he agreed.

What did he look like? The considerable bulk was spread over the tall body of the man. His head was large, too, with a prominent forehead and dark receding hair that was once – but no longer – lush, and his nose was sharp and prominent, commanding respect. His eyes, deep-set, seemed to penetrate into Orphan's soul. He was a man who missed nothing, who knew everything. He almost, Orphan thought, looked like one of Babbage's analytical engines.

But he was human enough. His fingers were chubby though strong, and his breath condensed on the glass as he raised it to his mouth. Red appeared in his cheeks then, and as he closed his eyes and savoured the taste of the drink there was something sensual in his action. This was a man, and a man who took great delight in drink, and in food.

They sat like this, without speaking. The room they were in was dimly lit and plush, covered in mahogany and dark velvet, like a club-room. Beside their chairs were side-tables. Behind the fat man was a drinks cabinet. Two small lamps burned, electric, behind sombre shades.

The fat man clicked his fingers and a dark-suited butler glided over and handed Orphan a drink of his own. He tasted it, found it to be a whiskey much superior to the brand favoured by Jack. He turned his head, feeling the back of his head hurt as he did so. To his right was a window. He looked outside – and saw the city spread out below.

From high above, the Thames was a silver snake curled into an unknowable glyph. Lights winked in and out of existence as the city breathed below. The lights seemed to spell out a message, a hidden truth that he could decipher if only he tried, if only he concentrated hard enough. The Houses of Parliament were a face, craggy and huge, studded with jewels, whispering secrets that reached out to him and went past, still unknown. The blimp swerved slowly, giving him a view of the north-east side of the river and of the dome of St Paul's, looking like the bald head of a secretive monk. He took another sip of his drink and felt it burn away the pain in his head, and he turned away from the window and said, "Who are you?"

The fat man nodded in approval. "You go straight to the heart of the matter. That's good." But he seemed in no hurry to reply to the question. He sipped again from his drink (the butler had long since withdrawn from the room, as silent and efficient as an automaton) and gazed at Orphan with those clear, penetrating eyes. "Perhaps," he said, "the question of who I am is not as significant as you suggest. I am intrigued more, my young friend, by the much more interesting question of who you are."

Surely you already know, you miserable old bastard, Orphan thought. He was tired and his eyes hurt, and his mouth tasted like ash. All he wanted was a bed to sleep on, and silence.

"Well?"

"My name is Orphan."

The fat man seemed to consider it. "It isn't much of a name," he said at last.

"That's the name I was given."

The fat man leaned forward. "Ah, but by whom?" he said. "Orphan, after all, is not a name, as such. It is a moniker, a nickname, an alias – a designation. It is a description of what you are. So what was your name before you were–" he coughed a laugh – "Orphaned?"

"Who are you?" Orphan repeated. The fat man's question had hit him like a punch to the liver.

"My name is Mycroft," the fat man said levelly. "What's yours?"

"Orphan."

"No."

The silence between them felt charged, like the air before a storm.

Finally the fat man – Mycroft – stirred. "Very well," he said. And, "Interesting."

"What is?"

"You do not know your own name."

Orphan gently put down the glass he was holding. He was afraid he would otherwise throw it in Mycroft's face.

"Do you?" he said.

Mycroft shook his head. "No. And that, I find, is even more interesting, for you see, I know a great many things."

"You seem to know a great many people," Orphan said. "Vivisectionists, for instance?"

Mycroft sighed. "It is a queer fate that led you down to the basement at Guy's that night. If fate is what it was. Perhaps I owe you an explanation."

"You could start by telling me why you had me followed and then abducted on board this airship," Orphan said.

"You see," Mycroft said, as if he hadn't heard him, "I despise the resurrection men. The thought of grave robbers operating in this city, in this time – it is abhorrent. And yet..." He, too, put down his glass. "Were it not for my brother," he said, "I would have nothing to do with such scum as Bishop and May."

"Your brother," Orphan said, and suddenly the image of the man in the icy coffin rose in his mind, the long and prominent nose, and something about the eyes... He said, "What happened to him?"

Mycroft shrugged and his eyes filled, for a moment, with pain. "I don't know." His fist hit the side-table and made the empty glass jump. "I don't know! I who am the central-exchange, the clearing house for every decision and conclusion, for every branch and department and organ of government – I don't know."

"Is he dead?"

"Yes. No." There was frustration in the fat man's eyes. "He was found. In Switzerland. At the bottom off... the details do not matter. No doubt my secretive brother was on the trail of some conspiracy of crime. But what, or who, he was pursuing, I do not know."

"He was a policeman?"

"A consulting detective," Mycroft said.

Orphan nodded politely.

Then, as the thought occurred to him, he said, "But you suspect foul play."

Mycroft nodded. "Perceptive," he said. "Yes."

"Who?"

Mycroft laughed. It was a short, bitter sound. "Why should I tell you?" he said. But in his eyes Orphan could see that he had already decided that he would. He wondered why the man wished to confide in him – and the thought made him afraid. He did not want the man's secrets.

"Moriarty."

Surprise widened Orphan's eyes. "The Prime Minister?"

"A puppet," Mycroft said, "serving the Queen and her line like a simulacrum. While the job of governing, the thousand and one acts required every hour of every day to make the wheels of empire move in unison, is done by other, more capable hands."

Such as yourself? Orphan thought – but he didn't express it out loud. He said, "Why Moriarty?"

Mycroft shrugged. Weariness formed lines at the corners of his eyes. "Odd hints, careful suggestions. An incidental fragment of data suddenly startling in a field of information where it was not expected." He stopped speaking and his eyes stared into Orphan's. "The Martian probe."

Hot anger burst inside Orphan's skull. Mycroft raised a hand as if to ward him off. "I think my brother was investigating Moriarty's space programme. A programme so secret even I was kept unaware of it. I think he was – disposed of – to protect its true nature."

Orphan was about to speak, but Mycroft suddenly roared, silencing him. "I will not let him die!" When he raised his eyes they seemed to hold a silent plea. "The best doctors have examined him," he said, almost plaintively. "The specialists in matters of life itself: Jekyll, Narbondo, Mabuse, Moreau, West… he has been treated with serums, with gland extracts, with electricity, with a spectrum of rays and with devices too arcane and tortuous and numerous to mention. Yet he remains as he is… dead to the world." He looked up at Orphan and said, "You and I are not so unlike. Both of us, after all, are seeking solution for death."

"Enough!" Orphan said. "Who are you? What are you? What do you want?" He felt rising anger and with it something akin to panic. He didn't care for this man, or about his brother.

"Again," Mycroft said, and his expression changed, became almost jovial. "You ask good questions. I hear you are one of our more promising young poets? Exactitude and directness are good qualities for a poet."

Orphan began to rise from his chair. Mycroft merely shook his head. "Don't," he advised. He clicked his fingers and beside him, the silent butler materialised like condensation on a glass of dark beer.

Orphan looked out of the window. The ground was far below. He sat back down.

The butler departed.

He was playing a game with him, Orphan thought. But what sort of game? It was a strange exchange of questions and half-answers, of things implied but not said – what did the fat man want from him? He had referred to himself as someone in government – well, that was clear enough. But whose interest did he represent? And what did he want from him?

It was a strange interrogation, he thought. Almost as if it was he who needed to find out the answers from Mycroft, and not the other way around. Or perhaps, not find them as much as decipher them on his own. He said, "At the cockpit."

"Yes?"

"You weren't watching the fight."

"No."

"Were you there for me?"

"What do you think?"

"No."

Mycroft nodded. "Very good," he said.

"You work for the government, but you are not in government. You have the power to commandeer a black airship, and you consider yourself a clearing house for information. So you must be in Intelligence."

Mycroft inched his head. "That seems obvious," he said. "But do go on."

"Which means that you are a loyal servant of Les Lézards."

"I serve Britannia," Mycroft said, a little stiff.

Orphan nodded thoughtfully. "That's what puzzled me," he said. "There seem to be so many factions at play here that I am quite lost. You claim to serve the empire, but show reticence with regards to Les Lézards." He smiled; he felt his mouth turning in a grimace. "You were watching Jack."

"Jack…" Mycroft mused. He, too, smiled. His expression, too, was ugly. "Your friend, Jack. Yes. An interesting specimen. But of course, he was not alone, was he, Orphan? He and that European troublemaker, Marx, and that beautiful, determined woman, Isabella Beeton… Yes. I was watching them quite carefully. And I was watching you, too. Will you join them?"

The sudden question took Orphan by surprise. "Is that what concerns you?" he asked. "You think they represent a threat to the empire?"

Mycroft shrugged. "There are a hundred different factions and organisations and secret societies in this city at any given time, all conspiring the downfall of the lizards, or of the government, or even of my own department. Do they represent a threat? Possibly. Quite possibly."

He fell into a brooding silence. Orphan glanced again out of the window. They were passing over the palace now, and the great, greenish pyramid rose out of the capital's ancient ground like a tombstone catching the starlight. He watched the Royal Gardens for a long moment, the silvery pools of water over which the shadow of the blimp passed almost unnoticed. He said, "What do you want from me?"

Mycroft, too, looked out of the window. At last, turning his eyes back to Orphan, he said, "I want you to find the Bookman."

There was a silence.

Orphan sank deeper into his chair. I want to find him too, he wanted to say. But what makes you think that I will? The tiredness threatened to consume him. He said, "For what purpose," not quite forming it into a question. Intuition told him what the answer would be.

"Tell him," Mycroft said, and his voice was heavy and suddenly old, the voice of a man making a compromise against his will, against his very nature, "that I am willing to bargain with him. He is the enemy of Les Lézards. He will want to talk to me."

"Bargain for what?" Orphan whispered, but he knew the answer even before he heard it, and before the blimp turned, away from the palace, and back towards the river.

"For my brother's life," Mycroft said. "Tell him that, when you finally find your Lucy."

TWELVE
At the Nell Gwynne

Love in these Labyrinths his Slaves detains,
And mighty Hearts are held in slender Chains.
  – Alexander Pope, "The Rape of the Lock"

He had been left on the riverbank, at the same place from which
he was taken. The blimp touched down softly. The silent butler
escorted him out of the car and deposited him outside. There
was no sign of the other man who helped abduct him. It was
still dark. The blimp rose into the air and silently departed, gliding as soft as a whisper into the sky.

He could barely think. His feet felt heavy and unresponsive
underneath him. He made his slow, weary way up the Strand.
Soon he would have to open the shop. Did Jack expect him to
work today? Then he thought of Tom, and a small smile formed
on his tired face.

He walked past Simpson's and the Savoy Theatre. Stopping to
rest for a moment, he stood outside the newly relocated abode
of Stanley Gibbons and admired the display in the windows.
Though the streetlights still burned the sun was slowly climbing
out of the depths of night and natural light began to awaken the
capital's streets. How long have I been awake? Orphan thought.
His body ached for sleep.

Nevertheless, he was captivated by Gibbons' display: stamps of all shapes and sizes and colours collected in the window like a cloud of still butterflies. There was, for instance, a Penny Black, the first stamp ever issued, bearing the profile of the young Queen Victoria, her scaly face regal underneath the burden of the crown. There was a rare, triangular Cape of Good Hope stamp bearing the smiling head of Mpande, the third of the Zulu kings and the father, so the note in the window said, of Cetshwayo kaMpande, the current king of that far-off protectorate of the Everlasting Empire. For a moment, Orphan was a child again, pressing his nose against the window, where a whole, unknown, exciting world was compressed into small pieces of paper. There was a Kashmiri "Old Rectangular" from twenty years before, with a script he couldn't read; there was a celebratory stamp bearing the grinning face of Harry Flashman, the Hero of Jalalabad; there was a Vespuccian First Day Cover with three stamps bearing the proud heads of leaders of the Great Sioux Nation; there was even a series of French stamps depicting artists' wildly romantic impressions of what Caliban's Island might look like. He lingered over the display for a long moment, savouring each of these tiny mementos of a world he hadn't seen. It was also, he realised, a thorough display of the greatness of the empire, of its boundless reach. It was meant to excite – but also to humble.

He walked away from the closed shop at last, feeling a small regret, as if he had lost something but hadn't known what it was. His tired feet carried him onwards, across the wakening Strand. Just before the Adelphi Theatre he turned right, and into the dark confines of Bull Inn Court. The alleyway was always dark; tall grey-brick walls rose on either side of it, permanently obscuring the sun. It was a narrow path, almost a scratch on the face of the city, a thin line connecting the Strand with Maiden Lane above it. It was too narrow for gas lamps, a small, hidden way one could have passed a hundred times when walking along the busy Strand without noticing its existence.

On the left, its walls adjoining the Adelphi, was, of course, a pub.

There were always pubs, Orphan thought. Wherever you turned in the capital you would find one, and in the unlikeliest of places. They were the glue that held society together, a fixture of history and culture, as permanent and as pervasive as the gloomy weather.

This pub was a small, nondescript building that merged into its surroundings like a smear of coal-dust on the grey walls. Small, rectangular windows looked like dark glasses worn by a retreating professor. The pub used to be called the Bull's Head, but under the edict of its mischievous new owner the name was changed to the Nell Gwynne, and the sign above the door depicted the famous actress – who grew up in Covent Garden, performed in the Theatre Royal, and was whisperingly told to have been a mistress to Charles II, who people still called the Merry King – entwined with a smiling lizardine gentleman, neither of them dressed, her pale flesh startling against his bright scales. It was a typical sign for his friend to have had commissioned, Orphan thought; and, shaking his head, he reached for the low door and knocked.

He had to knock several more times, and more and more loudly, before the door finally opened, and a ruffled-haired Tom Thumb stood in the doorway, looking at first annoyed and then, as he spied Orphan, concerned.

"What happened to you?" the little man said, and he grabbed hold of Orphan's arm and pulled him into the dim interior, closing the door behind them with a practised kick. "Sit down, china. You look terrible."

He propped Orphan on a red velvety chair before the fireplace, where a comforting blaze was slowly consuming a large tree log. Orphan sat down gratefully and felt the exhaustion overcome him. The warmth from the fire threatened to send him to sleep, and his eyes slowly closed.

A giggle made him open his eyes again. On the other side of the small room (the inside of the Nell Gwynne, Orphan had decided on his first visit there, was about the size of a large wardrobe) a large bed covered most of the raised area which would have once held, perhaps, a couple of tables for the pub's customers. Two young women – each easily twice the height of his friend – were sitting up in the bed now, their nakedness covered half-heartedly by a blanket. Behind the long bar counter Tom was pouring a drink. "We was having a bit of a party before you showed up," he said. "Orphan, I'd like you to meet my dear friends Belinda and Ariel – girls, this is Orphan." He turned to Orphan and offered him a sheepish grin. "I was telling them about youse only last night."

"You poor thing!" the two girls said in unison and, rising from the bed – the blanket falling to reveal two perfect Rubenesque nudes – came over to Orphan and began fussing over him. "It's *so* sad," said one of them – he couldn't tell which was Belinda, and which was Ariel – and the other said, "You have been *so* brave!" She turned towards the bar and bellowed, "Tom Thumb, stop mucking about there and bring your friend something to drink! Look at the state of him!"

"I'm getting it!" Tom growled. "You can't rush the drink, you insufferable doxy!"

Orphan, who felt rather confused, looked on helplessly as the two girls set about plumping pillows for him, taking off his shoes, and then sat down on either side of him and looked at him with large, sorrowful eyes. "You look terrible," one of them said, touching a cool hand to his forehead. "You're so pale and weak." She nodded and her hand sleeked the hair off Orphan's brow. "It's a broken 'eart what does that to you. I know."

"Leave him be!" Tom Thumb bellowed as he approached from behind the counter, a large, round glass held in his hand. "Here, laddie, drink this."

Strangely, the drink in the glass looked like the skies in sunrise, red and yellow hues suffusing the liquid with an internal glow. Tom Thumb, as if reading Orphan's mind, said, "It's one of me own little inventions. I call it a Mezcal Sunrise. I first made it when I was travelling through Mexica. Did I ever tell you about my time with the Aztecs? Barnum took us all there in the good old days…" He stopped and sighed, lost in memories. "I wish you could see it, Orphan. It's a magnificent place, and the women!"

"Oi!" one of the girls – Orphan had decided, in his dazed state, that she must be Ariel, if only for the sake of convenience – said. "You said there was naught as good as Britannia's girls last night!"

"Oh, Ariel," Tom Thumb said (and Orphan was relieved to find he was right), "the world is full of mysteries and beauties too numerous to ever fully explore, but all are enthralling and captivating in equal measure!" He grinned, then said, "It was Barnum's favourite line, that was."

Orphan held the bulbous glass in his hands. It had two straws sticking out of it, and he took a careful sip. The drink was sweet and yet refreshing, and he felt for a moment as if he had indeed swallowed a little bit of sunshine. He smiled sleepily and said, "You are all too kind. Too kind." Then he closed his eyes and, without even realising, fell asleep.

In his sleep, he didn't see Tom extract the drink carefully from his hands and lay it on the counter of the bar, nor did he feel it when the two girls helped Tom carry him to the large bed and laid him there, as peaceful as a child. No dreams came to him, just a deep, deep blackness that soothed his aching, fevered mind, and calmed him, and a hush filled him until it overflowed.

When he woke the Nell Gwynne was quiet and empty. A small fire still burned in the fireplace, a new, slender log being consumed, and he sat still for a long moment in the unfamiliar bed, and watched the flames dance like sprites across the burning wood. Haltingly, he reached out for a pen and paper, finding some on the table by the bed (an old pub table, scarred with countless cigarette burns and the acidity of spilled drinks), and having done so, began writing a poem.

> *like air rushing into a bone-white vessel* (Orphan wrote)
> *silence fills you;*
> *it wraps in your hair and turns it mute*
>
> *and courses through your blood vessels*
> *breathing your inner skin, and sighs*
> *residing in the hollows of your throat*

it fills you to the rim and lashes of your eyes:
silence bursts out of you, a rupture of ears and touch –
I stopper you with my mouth and you sigh,

and turn over in your sleep.

He thought of Lucy, then, and of all the things he never got to say to her, and all the futures, all the possibilities that were now gone, like a road that once branched into hundreds of unexplored paths but now lay blocked and abandoned, all its promises gone. If I can, he thought, I will get her back: even if it means going to the Bookman himself.

He left the poem on the side of the bed. More mundane things made him shake his head, then rise. He made the short, dangerous trip to the bathroom, walking down the narrow stairs on unsteady feet (ducking just in time before his head could hit the low ceiling) until he reached the water-closet at the bottom. He returned to the bed then, and sat in silence, watching the flames, thinking of nothing in particular. He didn't know if it was night or day. Outside was the same twilight that always lingered in Bull Inn Court, and Tom kept no clocks. "Clocks are the enemies of time," his diminutive friend liked to say, "they are the gaolers of day and the turnkeys of night." Perhaps it was his friend's own attempt at poetry, or perhaps, Orphan thought, it was another Barnum saying – and he wished, then, that he had witnessed the spectacle of the P.T. Barnum Grand Travelling Museum, Menagerie, Caravan, and Circus that Tom always referred to, simply and with an utter conviction, as The Greatest Show on Earth.

Tom was a Vespuccian, born to English parents in the lands of the Mohegan tribe in Quinnehtukqut, which meant – so Tom had once told him – Long River Place, and which the immigrants had called Connecticut. Born small, he was discovered by Barnum and joined the circus at a young age. Fearless, charming, and wild, he left the circus when it came to the capital, for reasons he had never discussed, and settled in the dilapidated old pub, the size of which, he said, made him feel comfortable. He was a friend, a fellow member of the Persons from Porlock, and seemed happy to work at Payne's when Orphan couldn't, taking his payment not in money but in books.

Those books covered the walls of the Nell Gwynne. On crooked shelves and windowsills and, here and there, propping the short legs of a table or hiding behind a cushion or an empty pint glass, the books lay like sleeping domestic cats glorying in the dimness of the room and the heat of the fireplace. The small pub-cum-home was full of unexpected, small discoveries reflecting Tom's eclectic and erratic interests. Lying on the bar counter, for example, Orphan found a heavy, illustrated volume of *The Sedge Moths of Northern Vespuccia (Lepidoptera: Glyphipterigidae), With Woodcuts and Annotations By The Author,* while on a half-hidden shelf behind the door he found a vellum-bound copy of *The Floating Island, A Tragi-Comedy,* written by the students of Christ Church in Oxford, dating from 1655 and notorious for being an early and venomous treatment of Les Lézards' journey to Britannia, set to music by Henry Lawes but never performed. By the sink he could leaf through the latest catalogue of Smedley's Hydropathic Company, advertising their brand new electrocution water tanks (Heal Any Disease!), and near the fireplace, precariously balanced, was a pile of technical tomes that included Ripper's *Steam-Engine: Theory and Practice,* Babbage's *Some Thoughts on Simulacra,* Moriarty's *Treatise Upon the Binomial Theorem* and Lady Ada Lovelace's *Basic Programming Explained.* Behind the bar, leaning against a label-less bottle of creamy liqueur, was a copy of poet William Ashbless's *The Twelve Hours of the Night,* and by the bedside he discovered Tom's latest reading material, *The Chronic Argonauts,* a debut novel by a young writer unknown to Orphan, by the name of Herbert Wells.

It was a treasure trove and a scrapyard, a library that was also a maze, with little sense of purpose or direction, in which one could become easily lost. Orphan loved it.

He was just leafing through a well-thumbed copy of Flashman's *Dawns and Departures of a Soldier's Life* when he heard voices outside, raised in song, and recognised Tom's bellowing, cheerful voice as he sang, "In taking a walk on a cold winter day, by hill side and valley I careless did stray, till I came to a cottage all rustic and wild, and heard a voice cry, I'm a poor drunkard's child!"

Feminine voices joined in, shouting the refrain. "I'm a poor drunkard's child!"

The voices came closer, and Orphan smiled as he listened to the old drinking song. "In this lonely place I in misery cry, there is no one to look to me, no one comes nigh. I am hungry and cold, and distracted and wild – kind heaven look down on a poor drunkard's child!"

"Poor drunkard's child!" Orphan murmured, and just then the door opened, and Tom Thumb, accompanied by Ariel and Belinda, came through.

"My father was drunken and wasted his store, which left us in misery our lot to deplore, his glass soon run out, he died frantic and wild, and now I must wander a poor drunkard's child!"

Tom Thumb stopped his singing, slung a bag full of groceries on the bar counter, and said, "How are you feeling, china?"

"A lot better," Orphan admitted, and the two friends smiled at each other. Belinda and Ariel came over to Orphan, fruity perfume following them in a summery cloud, and they fussed over him rather as if he were a kitten or a puppy before they pulled him to his feet and made him dance with them, each holding one of his hands.

"My mother so good, in the cold grave lies low, she left me all friendless in want and in woe, broken-hearted, in death, she looked heavenward and smiled, but still I am left here, a poor drunkard's child!"

Orphan spun and spun, grinning, caught in the dance and the song, and the two girls laughed and held him, like nymphs risen from a secluded pool in an ancient forest.

"My clothing is scant, and all tattered and torn, kind friends, I have none. I am sad and forlorn! And far from this cottage so lonely and wild, I'll wander away, cried the poor drunkard's child!"

And they fell, still laughing, onto the wide bed.

Orphan sat up on the edge of the bed. "What time is it?"

Tom Thumb grinned and said, "It is twelve o' the clock, and all is well."

Orphan stood up. A sudden sense of urgency seized him. "Midnight?"

"You slept for a long time."

"You needed to!" Ariel said. "You was like Hamlet's ghost, coming in 'ere last night."

"I have something for you," Tom said. "From the shop."

"From Jack?"

Tom shook his head. "I didn't see him at all. Perhaps he was in the basement, but if so, he wasn't coming out."

He took out a folded sheaf of paper from his back pocket and handed it to Orphan, who opened it.

"From that infernal magician," Tom said. "That Maskelyne fellow. He asked about you, then made the note appear in the pages of the book I was reading. The ass."

Orphan smiled, knowing the magician's fondness for elaborate illusion, and read the short note.

> *Dear Orphan* (Maskelyne wrote),
> *I was dreadfully sorry to hear of recent events, and am only glad that you yourself are alive, and on the road to recovery.*
> *If you recall, the last time we spoke I offered you to come and see me at the Egyptian Hall if you ever had need of counsel.*
> *Let me once more extend this offer. If magic is an illusion, the act of smoke and mirrors, then nevertheless the mirrors we hide may reflect, sometimes, a deeper truth, one not so visible to the naked eye.*
> *Come, and come soon.*
> *Yours,*
> *J. Maskelyne*

"What does he want?" Tom asked.

Orphan shrugged. The words of the magician's simple sympathy had affected him, and for a moment he couldn't speak. Once again he was overwhelmed with that image of Lucy, smiling, the book held in her hands, and then the bright searing explosion that had ended her life, and changed his forever. And he thought, I must act. I must find the Bookman. He had almost forgotten, in this momentary haven; but now that ghostly, mist-like figure seemed to re-form around him, to press against the windows with its silence and to watch him as he stood there helpless. The words of his friend Gilgamesh returned to him. *This is the time of myth*, he had said, and Orphan thought, then I am the minotaur, and I am trapped in the Bookman's maze.

"He invited me to visit him at the Egyptian Hall," he said. "He was very kind."

"The Egyptian Hall?" Belinda said. She rose from the bed (where Ariel was now sitting cross-legged, an open tin box on her knees, and rolled a cigarette with Tom Thumb's cannabis, which he regularly bought at Captain Powers' Pipe Shop near Leicester Square), "Me and Ariel went there only last week. You must go see it! They have the most amazing machine there, an old, old automaton that plays chess and can beat any man or woman what tries to challenge it!"

More automatons. Was his life now bound into the aspirations of machines as well as human beings? He thought, I would send him a note and apologise for not being able to come. He would understand.

"Yes!" Ariel said, "And the funny thing is, it's made up to look like an old Turk!"

The words trickled, slow and with a stealthy smoothness, into Orphan's mind. "What did you say?"

His voice sounded to him like it emerged not from him at all but from some place far away. What had Byron said?

Ask the Turk. And he had not paid it much attention. Why?

"I said it looks like an old Turk," Ariel said, her fingers smooth-ing out a cone-shaped cigarette. She lit it with a match and a sweet, pungent smoke rose into the air. "With a turban and a drooping moustache and hands that move across the board like they was real." She inhaled deeply from the cigarette, shrugged, and said, "You should go see it. There's also a mechanical duck that eats food and then shits it out."

"French," Belinda added.

Orphan looked at the two of them, turning from one to the other. *Ask the Turk*, he thought. And here, then, was the Turk.

"Is it open now?" he found himself saying.

"It's always open," Tom said. "There's always a show on at the Egyptian Hall." He looked at Orphan for a long moment, as if trying to decipher something he could only half-see. He said, "Are you sure it's a good idea?"

Orphan said, "No."

Tom slowly nodded.

With a sense of inevitability stealing over him Orphan went to the door and put on his shoes and his coat. He turned to Tom, began to say, "Thank you," but Tom merely shook his head. "You're always welcome at Old Nelly's," he said. "Just be careful, OK, china?"

"I'll try," Orphan said. "But I seem to be doing a bad job of that, recently."

Tom shook his head. "It can't be that bad," he said, "if you're still around."

Orphan smiled in return.

"If you're going to the Hall," Tom said, "say hello to my old friend Theo. He works there as Jo Jo the Dog-Faced Boy."

"How will I recog... ah," Orphan said. And, "I'll do that."

Then he said goodbye to the two girls, who both hugged him and told him to come back soon and, if they weren't there, to ask for them at the Shakespeare's Head.

"I will," he promised. Then he opened the door and, stepping out into the cold dark night, left both warmth and the Nell Gwynne behind him.

THIRTEEN
A Night on the Town

"Oranges and Lemons," say the bells of St Clement's.
"Bull's eyes and targets," say the bells of St Margaret's.
"Brickbats and tiles," say the bells of St Giles'.
"Halfpence and farthings," say the bells of St Martin's.
"Pancakes and fritters," say the bells of St Peter's.
"Two sticks and an apple," say the bells of Whitechapel.
"Pokers and tongs," say the bells of St John's.
"Kettles and pans," say the bells of St Anne's.
"Old Father Baldpate," say the slow bells of Aldgate.
"You owe me ten shillings," say the bells of St Helen's.
"When will you pay me?" say the bells of Old Bailey.
"When I grow rich," say the bells of Shoreditch.
"Pray when will that be?" say the bells of Stepney.
"I do not know," says the great bell of Bow.
  – Traditional nursery rhyme

It was a surprisingly warm night, and the residents of the great capital, welcoming this unexpected change in the always-precarious weather, had abandoned their homes and taken en masse to the streets. Orphan walked up Charing Cross Road and listened to the cries of hawkers who, even at this late hour, were busy advertising their wares to the busy burghers of the city.

"Ripe strawberries!"

"Buy a fine table-basket!"

"Eels! Eels!"

"Buy a fine singing bird?"

"Old shoes for some brooms!"

"Fine writing ink!"

"Buy a rabbit, a rabbit!"

"Crabs, fat crabs!"

"Fair lemons and oranges!"

"Buy a new almanac!"

"White mice, see the white mice!"

"Knives or scissors to grind?"

"A brass pot or an iron pot to mend!"

"Pens and ink, pens and ink of the highest quality!"

"Bread, fresh bread!"

"Figs!"

"Sausages, good sausages!"

He stopped in his walk through Leicester Square and bought one of the sausages so advertised, covered in oil, dripping fried onions, held in a soggy bun. Everywhere there was the smell of cooking foods, and the lights in all the public houses were burning, and the cries of the drinking class sounded, merry and loud, from every open window but were drowned by the street merchants.

"Buy a pair of shoes!"

"Buy any garters?"

"Wigs! The best wigs in town!"

"Maps on display! See the wilds of Vespuccia, admire the steppes of Siberia, marvel at the secrets of Zululand!"

"Worcestershire salt!"

"Buy a fine brush?"

"Ripe chestnuts!"

"Buy a case for a hat?"

"Fine potatoes!"

"Hot eel pies!"

"A tormentor for your fleas!"

He stopped at the last one and watched the old man whose cry this was, trying to decipher what the tormentor was, but all he could see was a series of strange, pen-shaped devices that could serve no obvious purpose. He shrugged and walked on through the throng, towards Piccadilly.

"New-born eggs!"

"Spices! Spices from Zanzibar!"

"Hot curry powder!"

"Cannabis! Home-grown cannabis!"

"Puppy dogs!"

"Bananas! Bananas fresh off the ship!"

"Ladders! Sturdy ladders!"

"Marjoram and sage!"

"Do you want any matches?"

He passed a solitary woman standing on the corner of Haymarket who was singing in a high, clear, beautiful voice. It was a wordless song, a melody that, for a moment, reminded him of the songs of the whales, and he stopped on a whim and put a coin into the box that lay beside her on the pavement.

She did not stop her singing but she looked at him, and inched her head slightly in acknowledgment, and he was moved by the beauty of her face, and by the unexpected sadness that he found there, reflecting his own. He hurried away then, suddenly uncomfortable. He kept glancing at women in the crowd only to think he had discovered Lucy, but as he looked the women always turned out to be someone else, without the remotest resemblance to his love. Would she appear to him again? he wondered. Was she even now seeking him out, lost in undeath, a prisoner of the Bookman?

But she did not reappear.

"Hot spiced gingerbread, smoking hot!"

"Turnips and carrots!"

"New love songs, very cheap!"

"Primroses!"

"Jam! Blackberry jam!"

"Onions! Buy a rope of onions!"

"Music boxes for sale!"

"Edison records! Get the latest sounds for a peaceful sleep! The call of African birds and the sleep-song of the Nile!"

And here and there as he walked past the Circus the songs of merchants, as old as the city itself, rose to greet him as he passed, a hundred salutations assailing his ears.

> *Young gentlemen attend my cry,*
> *And bring forth all your knives;*
> *The barbers razors too I grind;*
> *Bring out your scissors, wives.*

And:

> *With mutton we nice turnips eat;*
> *Beef and carrots never cloy;*
> *Cabbage comes up with Summer meat,*
> *With winter nice Savoy.*

He was nearly there. The street was clogged with horse-drawn carriages and, in between them, though much aloof, were the curious steam-powered baruch-landaus that carried inside their shining metal bodies those rich enough to afford them. They were shaped a little like a conventional carriage, but with a large, round, black pipe sitting on their heads like a top hat, and they belched constant steam. The wheels were large and wide. In the back of the machine an enclosed black box contained the engine, and a stoker could be seen crouching in his own small space (similar to a theatre's whisper-box, Orphan thought) like a semi-naked demon caught in an eternal inferno. Past the engine was the passenger box, windows darkened to prevent the rabble from looking in on the distinguished riders, while in the front the driver sat in full majestic uniform and controlled the vehicle by means of a large metal stick.

The baruch-landau drivers had at their disposal an array of loud noises (to clear traffic) and flashing lights (for purpose of the same) and as they passed through Piccadilly they were cursed at by the common drivers of the public carriages, to which they replied with cool indifference and the application of louder and even less wholesome noise.

"Sand! Buy my nice white sand!"

"Young radishes!"

"Read the *Tempest*! Read the publication they don't want you to read! Find out the truth about–"

This one cut short as two uniformed bobbies came past (walking slowly) and the caller hastily disappeared up Glasshouse Street. It was Jack's publication; and Orphan shrugged and walked on. He was not interested in conspiracies.

"Door mats!"

"Quick periwinkles!"

"Song sheets! Get the latest Gilbert and Sullivan for half the price of the theatre!"

"Southernwood that's very good!"

"New Yorkshire muffins!"

And from a seller of brooms and combs came:

> All cleanly folk must like my ware,
> For wood is sweet and clean;
> Time was when platters served Lord Mayor
> And, as I've heard, a Queen.

And from a stall nearby:

> Let fame puff her trumpet, for muffin and crumpet,
> They cannot compare with my dainty hot rolls;
> When mornings are chilly, sweet Fanny, young Billy,
> Your hearts they will comfort, my gay little souls.

And then, almost without noticing, Orphan was there. He stood outside the imposing façade of the Egyptian Hall.

What did it look like?

Imagine a grand and ancient temple built for the long-vanished kings of a desert country, wide and rich beyond imaginings. To either side of it stood ordinary, red-and-grey bricked apartment buildings, as ordinary and staid as two elderly gentlemen who had stayed out too late. The Hall, though... Wide columns rose on either side of the entrance, each twice the height of a man, and above them, in lonely splendour, stood the goddess Isis and her husband, the god Osiris, magnificent and tall, while above and all around them the rest of this mock-temple sprawled, covered in unknowable hieroglyphs, a sturdy and faithful imitation of the temple in Tentyra.

Above them all stood, in giant letters, the single word: MUSEUM.

Carriages and baruch-landaus alike carried people to and from the busy entrance, and a steady trickle of visitors, both wealthy and less well-to-do, came and went through the large front doors of this temple of learning. Even lizards, Orphan saw – a party of five, all dressed in full regalia and attended by a host of human servants – came to this place of wonder, and paid the admission price.

He could still taste the mustard in his mouth from the sausage he had earlier devoured; it was not a bad taste, exactly, but it lingered unpleasantly. Like the Egyptian Hall, he thought. It looked, for all its mock-antiquated brashness, like a doll dressed up in once-fine rags.

At the door he showed the usher his letter from Maskelyne and was admitted in without questions.

The inside of the Egyptian Hall was a wide, cavernous space. It was an amalgamation of junk and of rarities, of curiosities and oddities: a mixture of the deeply strange and the everyday.

In the centre of the room stood a rounded enclosure and, inside it, all manner of animals were on display, identified with large signs that were hung around the enclosure: there was a giraffe from Zululand and an elephant from Jaunpur; a dancing bear from the forests of Transylvania and a zebra from the Swahili kingdoms; a peacock from Abyssinia and, in a cage all to itself, a sleepy tiger from Bengal. The animals looked lethargic to Orphan, almost as if they were drugged. The tiger opened one eye when Orphan passed him, looked at him for a short moment and then, as if that exercise was too much for it, closed it again. The bear declined to dance, and crouched on the ground like an elderly fisherman, while the peacock seemed reluctant to spread its plumage to the onlookers, who tried to encourage it by cheering at it and waving their hands in the air, to no avail.

Dotted around the room were the human curiosities. Here, in an alcove with a gas lamp burning on its wall, sat the human whale, a giant male dressed only in a loincloth, whose naked flesh rolled and rolled, like waves in a pool, each time he stirred. He had his own crowd of admirers, who came up to him by turns and poked him with their fingers, in order to better see the fat roll from the point of contact and spread outwards across the giant frame.

Here, sitting on long raised chairs like the legs of flamingos (there was one of those birds, too, in the animals' enclosure), were the Scarletti Twins, one smaller than a child and as fat as she was tall, the other towering over six feet up and as thin as a rope. "They look like a small fat mushroom under a tall and gangly tree, the poor dears!" Orphan heard an excited customer say to her husband, who nodded with obvious satisfaction at his wife's wit.

Here was the Skeleton Dude, a thin, ill-looking man in a tuxedo (hence the name, dude being a Vespuccian slang-term for urbanite), and beside him was the Translucent Man, whose pale skin allowed the observers to examine the circulation of his blood through his arteries and veins. Here, too, was the Fungus Man, whose body sprouted numerous additional appendages, spots and boils (which you could pop at your leisure for a modest sum).

Orphan walked in a daze through this gallery of unfortunates. Everywhere he looked in that wide, open space some man or woman stood or sat or – in one instance – floated (the Mermaid, a woman floating inside a large water-tank, whose lower body was made to look like the tail of a fish), some unfortunate soul was displaying an affliction for the amusement and elucidation of the paying public. On and on it went: in a side room he saw

a man with no legs and a man with no arms ride a bicycle together; in another, a bearded lady shared a rolled-up cigarette
and a cup of tea (apparently on her break) with a woman who
had three breasts (and drew an unwanted crowd of male admirers even as she sat there).

Where was Maskelyne?

As he passed a man with bricks on his head – the bricks were
being pounded into rubble by a second man with the use of a
great sledgehammer – a small figure bounded up to him and
grabbed him by the arm.

"Are you Orphan?" this startling person asked.

Recovering from his momentary surprised, Orphan nodded,
then said, "You must be Theo."

The man who had stopped him was short of stature, and
dressed in short, loose-fitting trousers and an open vest that exposed his hairy chest. His arms were equally hairy, as were his
legs. His face was dark and deeply grooved, covered in a straggly
beard all over that looked like wild-growing weeds. Deep, sorrowful eyes looked up at Orphan from that extraordinary face.

"You can call me Jo Jo," he said. Then he shook his head, twice,
as if shaking invisible water from it, and said, "Come with me."

"Where?" Orphan said. He felt a sudden, desperate desire to
leave the Hall. Its damp, dark interior, filled with the smells of
human sweat and the manure of its trapped animals and the re-
lentless gaze of the massed crowds, left him with a mixture of
feelings, a sanctimonious (if heart-felt) pity vying with a cerebral
excitement (for he, too, like the rest of the crowd, was thrilled
by the grotesques). I am no different to anyone here, he thought.
And – It's why this place is so successful.

"Come with me," Jo Jo the Dog-Faced Boy said again, and
tugged on Orphan's sleeve. "There is someone what wants to
meet you."

He walked off. Orphan, after a short hesitation, followed. I left
my will at the door, he thought. This place is like a prison; if it's
a museum, it is one that houses only human misery.

But it was not quite true. For, as he followed Jo Jo out of the central hall and through a long, narrow corridor, he began to notice an exhibition of curious devices lining their path. The corridor branched into small, alcove-like rooms, dimly lit like the rest of the Hall, and there were fewer and fewer people venturing this way; for here there were no animals and no human curiosities, but only machines.

In a room to the left of him he saw a mechanical menagerie, birds in the plumage of gold and silver leaves, who moved in slow jerks and called in rusted voices. They sat on the branches of a machine made to look like a tree, its chest cut open to display a series of cogs and wheels. Steam rose out of small vents in the branches, and the birds twittered and fluttered their wings each time there was a belch of steam, which came about every ten seconds.

In another room he saw several people gathered around a naked female torso that stood on top of a dais, as still as a statue, until, as to the beat of an unseen clock, she jerked her hands and turned in a circle, then subsided again into mechanical slumber.

"It's a very sad thing," Jo Jo commented while they walked. "These machines were once the apex of scientific achievement. Even five, ten years ago, I'm told, people flocked in their thousands to see them and marvel." He had the same wild-frontier accent as Tom, Orphan thought. "But now – look at them. Lost, lonely, discarded like used toys. If it wasn't for Mr. Maskelyne taking pity on them they would have soon found themselves on the rubbish heap – or worse."

That last was said with an ominous whisper. "Why?" Orphan said. "What would happen to them?"

They had left the corridor and entered another, then turned again, and again. It's a maze, he thought, as Jo Jo led him. Soon he could not remember which way they had come. Was it left-left-right, or was it left-right-left? The dark corridors were now empty of people, and the rooms they passed were unlit and smelled of dust and disuse.

"The Babbage Company, that's what would happen to them,"

Jo Jo said darkly. "Old Charlie Company's been trying to buy these automatons for years." He barked a laugh. "For their *archives*. For the benefit of the *scientific community*. Ha. They can't wait to cut these guys open and dissect them." He looked over his shoulder at Orphan. "'Cause they didn't build them, see? So they have to know."

"Know what?"

He was getting thoroughly disorientated by the walk. The corridors never seemed to end – he was beginning to suspect they were simply walking in circles.

Jo Jo stopped, turned, and tapped his own head with a hairy finger. "Know how they work. Know if they think. 'Cause if they do, china – then how can they do it without old Charlie's engines? We're here."

They stood in the middle of a corridor identical to all the ones before. Jo Jo ran his hand along the wall, pressed something invisible – and a section of the wall smoothly detached itself from the rest of the surrounding structure and swung open, revealing a small dark room hidden beyond.

Jo Jo motioned with his hand for Orphan to enter. He saw Orphan's bemused expression and his face softened, and those great soulful eyes blinked. "If you need me – bark." He laughed. "Don't worry, mate. You're expected."

Orphan looked into the dark room. Was it a trap? It was possible – but even then, was that not what he had wanted? Perhaps it was the Bookman inside there, ready to reveal himself at last. Or perhaps…

He took a deep breath. Tom said he could trust Jo Jo, and he, in his turn, trusted Tom.

So…

He stepped into the dark room, and the door swung shut behind him without a sound.

FOURTEEN
The Mechanical Turk

Let us not say that every machine or every animal perishes altogether or assumes another form after death, for we know absolutely nothing about the subject. On the other hand, to assert that an immortal machine is a chimera or a logical fiction, is to reason as absurdly as caterpillars would reason if, seeing the cast-off skins of their fellow caterpillars, they should bitterly deplore the fate of their species, which to them would seem to come to nothing.

– Julien Offray de La Mettrie, *L'Homme Machine*

The room was dark and warm. There was a dry, not unpleasant smell in the air, as of a cupboard that had been left closed for a long period of time, containing gently fading clothes and the dying scent of lavender. Orphan stood still and let his eyes adjust to the darkness. There was no movement, no sound in the room but for his own breathing.

He took a cautious step forward.

"Play with me," a voice said. It had a scratchy, echoey quality, as of an old Edison record.

Orphan, keeping silent, took another step forward.

Light, flickering and low, came into existence before him. It emanated from a series of small electrical bulbs set in a half-ring around a square wooden table with a chessboard laid in its middle. A figure was sitting on the other side of the chess table.

It was the Turk.

The machine looked remarkably like a man. Only the upper half of the body could be seen, and Orphan had the distinct, uncomfortable notion that that was all there was to the Turk; that, had he looked behind the table, there would be nothing there. The Turk's face was ivory-white, as unchanging as a statue's. A long, thin moustache emerged from its upper lip and curved down. On the Turk's head was a turban, and a heavy fur coat covered its body. The coat looked old; it was moth-eaten. The Turk's hands rested on the table. They were pale, the fingers long and slender. One of his hands held a long-stemmed pipe which disappeared into a side drawer as Orphan watched.

An empty chair waited on the side of the table opposite the Turk.

"Please," the voice said. "Sit down." There was a short, mechanical chuckle. "I have been waiting for you for some time."

The Turk's mouth did not move. The voice seemed to emerge from somewhere around his midriff.

"Please, sit."

He sat in the chair. It was high-backed and once grand, but now the paint was peeling and the cushions had been eaten away by insects. When he sat, he was at eye level with the Turk. The chess pieces were arranged on the board. He sat on the side of white.

"Play with me. Please."

Though the tone of the voice never varied there was something almost desperate, a lonely quality to the voice. Orphan surveyed the board. The pieces had once been lovingly crafted, he thought. But now they were chipped, the white king was missing half its crown, and the pawns looked battered and scarred like ageing mercenaries.

On a whim, he moved a white pawn two squares. "E2 to E4," he said.

The Turk gave another wheezing chuckle. "A good opening," he said. "It frees your queen, and your bishop, and gives you early domination of the centre. Very good."

The Turk's right hand moved jerkily across the board. "E7 to E5."
The two pawns faced each other across the board.

"Queen to F3," Orphan said. Somehow, the game was important. He said, "What do the automatons want?"

"Knight to C6," the Turk announced. The artificial eyes blinked at Orphan. "The right to exist. Freedom."

"But you are machines," Orphan said, and the Turk's head turned in a slow odd shake, left to right to left.

"So are you," it said.

"Bishop to C4," Orphan said. "Byron said something similar to me. But you are constructs. Created by human hands."

The Turk's response was a loud snort. Then, "Knight to F6."

The thought suddenly occurred to him and made him uncomfortable. How old was the Turk? The one simulacrum he had met, Lord Byron's, was manufactured by the Babbage Company. It was a recent construct, the product of an entire scientific age... He said, "Weren't you?"

"Play," the Turk said.

Orphan looked at the board. "Knight to E2."

"Bishop to C5," the Turk said, his pale slender hand moving almost languidly across the board. Then, "What do you know of Jacques de Vaucanson?"

"A2 to A3," Orphan said, moving his leftmost pawn. "Was he a poet?"

The Turk did laugh now, a full-throated, lasing sound full of scratches and distant echoes. "D7 to D6."

No piece had yet been taken.

"Who was he?" Orphan said.

"Play."

Orphan examined the board. The space between his king and rook was now empty. He said, "Castling," and moved the king and rook so that his king was now safe behind a row of pawns.

The Turk nodded its head. "Ah, *Rochieren*," he said. "Very good. Bishop to G4."

The black bishop now threatened the white queen. Orphan didn't pay it attention. He said, "Vaucanson?"

"Let me tell you a story," the Turk said. "Which is relevant, perhaps, to your quest." The machine's eyes looked at Orphan's. They were like a blind man's eyes, void of depth, white and unseeing. "You came here for help, no?"

"I'm looking for the Bookman," Orphan said. Now that the words left his mouth they seemed to hang in the air for a moment, unburdened by weight. The Bookman. I am coming, he wanted to say. And the image of Lucy rose in his mind, clear as if she were standing beside him, so vivid that he almost turned and reached for her.

The bulbs seemed to dim, their feeble light fading.

"The Bookman…" the Turk said. "That great invisible Machiavelli." Again, that chuckle. "Do you think I can help you find him?"

"Do you think I can win this game?" Orphan asked in return, coming back to himself. He motioned at the still chess pieces.

"It's unlikely," the Turk said. Then, "I take your meaning."

"So you can help me?"

"Let me tell you a story. But first, play."

"Queen to D3." Orphan moved his queen away from the bishop's threat.

"Knight to H5." The Turk's hand fluttered and settled on the table. The lights behind it grew and dimmed. "Back when France had kings," he said, "a secret project was initiated by Louis the Fourteenth, and carried out by the greatest automaton-maker the world had yet seen. Jacques de Vaucanson." The Turk sighed, as if remembering a painful past, and his hand fluttered away from the table, pointing at a gloomy corner of the room. "That is one of his early constructions," he said.

Lights winked into being above a small display table. Orphan looked, and saw a duck squatting on the table.

"Do have a look," the Turk said. "There are some seeds beside it."

Orphan rose. The duck, of course, was a mechanical duck, and though it might once have been lively it now looked like the rest of these forgotten mechanical curiosities, worn down by the passing of the years. The duck looked up at him, and its beak opened and closed weakly.

"Feed it."

There was, indeed, a small store of seeds beside the table. He took some in his hand and put his open palm before the duck's beak. The duck pecked at them without overdue enthusiasm. The seeds disappeared inside it.

"Watch," the Turk said. "It is marvellous."

Orphan watched. For a while, nothing seemed to be happening. Then, with a soft "poop" sound, the duck raised its behind and delicately deposited a small smear of excrement on the table.

"Bravo!" the Turk cried. "Do you know, Voltaire once said that, without Vaucanson's duck, there would be nothing to remind us of the glory that was France?" His head shook sadly, and he said, "Gone now, of course. They are all gone, and only I remain..."

Orphan, unable to decide if he was amused or disgusted, returned to his chair.

He reached for the board and found a piece. "Pawn to H3," Orphan said.

"Bishop takes E2," the Turk said, his hand moved, and Orphan's white knight was no longer on the board. "Do pay attention."

"Queen takes E2," Orphan said, removing in his turn the Turk's bishop. "You were saying?"

"Knight to F4," the Turk said, unperturbed. His knight was now threatening Orphan's queen. "So, what did you think of the duck?"

The lights above the duck's display dimmed and disappeared. "Interesting," Orphan said.

The Turk sighed. "Once it was the grandest attraction!" he said. "Even now... even now people come to see the duck. To marvel at its ingenuity."

"Queen to E1," Orphan said, rescuing the queen. He stared at the board for a long moment. "What was Vaucanson's project?"

"Knight to D4," the Turk said. The black knight stood now

between the white bishop and pawn. "Louis was sick. Already, in his time, France was in decline as the power of *les rosbifs'* unholy lizards grew. And so, as you may have already gathered for yourself, wherever there is opposition to Les Lézards, a certain shadowy presence makes itself known…"

"The Bookman," Orphan whispered. And he thought, always, it is the Bookman. Wherever he turned, the Bookman had been and gone, leaving only a ghostly outline in its wake.

"Perhaps that is so," the Turk said. "I have lived for many years, but even I do not understand the exact circumstances. The Bookman almost never deals directly. I only suspect his influence. Play."

"Bishop to B3."

"Knight takes H3," the Turk said, removing Orphan's pawn. "Check."

"Tell me what you have to tell me!" Orphan said. Anger made him raise his hand as if he intended to wipe clear the pieces off the table.

The Turk only stared at him, as mute as a doll.

"King to H2," Orphan said at last.

The Turk chuckled. "Good, good. You truly fascinate me, Orphan. You may only be a pawn, at the moment – but what you may yet turn into!"

"The project?"

"Of course." The hand moved again. "Queen to H4. You see, Louis, a dying man, was deeply, intensely interested in life. What, after all, was life? If man is a machine, could he not then build a machine to simulate life? To live life?"

"Vaucanson set out to build a simulacrum," Orphan said.

"Correct! Very good!"

Absent-mindedly, Orphan moved. "G2 to G3."

His pawn now threatened the Turk's queen.

"Pawns are such fascinating pieces, too…" the Turk said. "So small, almost insignificant, and yet – they can depose kings. Don't you find that interesting? Knight to F3."

And now the Turk was threatening Orphan's queen.

"Did he succeed?"

"Perhaps," the Turk said, "in another time... if the lizards had not appeared... if the Bookman had not existed... Perhaps in that time he had failed. A fanciful notion, but the longer I exist – the longer I live? – I think a lot about the might-have-beens, the what-ifs. About the little places in history where one tiny, minute change can lead to a new and unimaginable future. It's like chess. So many permutations, so many possibilities, probabilities, choices, cross-roads... I think a lot about the future, our future. And I see uncertainty." It stopped, then sighed, the same, repeating sound, each scratch and dim echo a repeat of the last one. There was something desperate and lonely in his voice when he spoke again. "Please, play."

"King to G2," Orphan said. His king moved, now threatening both the Turk's knights. He was in a purely defensive position. None of his pieces had managed to progress across the board. The Turk had brought the battle entirely to Orphan's side. "Damn."

"Knight takes E1," the Turk said, removing Orphan's queen with his long, deft fingers. "Check."

"Damn," Orphan said again. The Turk merely stared at him.

"Rook takes E1," Orphan said at last, removing the Turk's knight from the table.

"Queen to G4," the Turk said. Now there was only a pawn separating the Turk's queen and Orphan's king.

"D2 to D3," Orphan said, moving a pawn. "So Vaucanson succeeded."

"Bishop takes F2," the Turk said, taking Orphan's pawn. The bishop now stood next to the white king and threatened Orphan's rook.

"He built a simulacrum."

"You insist on reducing probabilities to certainties," the Turk murmured, making no sense to Orphan. "But fine, yes. Roughly speaking."

"Rook to H1," Orphan said.

"Queen takes G3," the Turk said, removing the pawn that

stood between him and the white king. "Check." He sighed again, and Orphan thought: it must be a recording. A hidden system of miniature discs, perhaps, each with its own sound, a word or a phrase or some non-verbal expression. He wondered whose voice it had originally been, and how old it was. "Who gave you your voice?" he said.

There was a silence. The Turk sat motionless, as if his energy had run out. And Orphan thought, You speak in a dead man's voice.

At last the Turk stirred, his head moving from side to side as if seeking an invisible presence. The lights flickered behind it. "Vaucanson worked for many years on the project," he said. He did not acknowledge Orphan's earlier question. "He was a student of Le Cat, you know –" Orphan didn't, but he remained quiet – "there was quite a lot of animosity between them, towards the end. Le Cat, too, was working on an artificial man." The Turk made a coughing sound, as of a man clearing his throat. When he spoke again his voice was different, deeper and less monotonous, as if someone else was now speaking through him – through it. "'You are working, so I am told, on your artificial man and you are right in doing so. You must not let Monsieur de Vaucanson accept the glory for ideas he may have borrowed from you. But he has applied himself only to mechanics, and has used all his shrewdness for that purpose – and he is not a man who is afraid to take extreme measures.'"

An image of the two men rose in Orphan's mind then, two scientists, each working in secrecy over the inert body of a man who was not a man, each suspicious of the other, careful, always careful not to reveal to the world the work that they were doing… he wondered why, if one was once a pupil of the other, they had fallen out.

"De Cideville wrote that to Le Cat," the Turk said. "Another of Voltaire's friends… But Le Cat's man came to nothing."

"And Vaucanson's? What happened to him?"

"Play," the Turk said.

Orphan, frustrated, glanced at the board. "King to F1," he said reluctantly. The white king made his temporary retreat.

"Bishop to D4." The Turk's head bobbed up and down. "Officially, in the books of history, Vaucanson never completed his project. His artificial man never existed. The project was abandoned, and Vaucanson himself died in 1782, an old and wealthy man."

"King to E2," Orphan said. He knew he was losing. Then: "The revolution. In France."

The Turk looked up. "Yes?"

"It took place in 1789."

"Yes?"

"Seven years after Vaucanson's death."

"Yes... Queen to G2. Check."

"Why the Bookman? You implied he led Vaucanson to build his simulacrum. Why?"

The Turk nodded. "What do you think?"

"To counter-balance the Everlasting Empire. To check the growing power of Les Lézards." He looked at the Turk. "What exactly did happen in the Quiet Revolution?"

"Perhaps," the Turk said enigmatically, "you will soon have occasion to find out for yourself. Play."

"King to D1," Orphan said, retreating further.

"Queen takes H1," the Turk said, removing Orphan's rook. "Check."

"Do you know where the Bookman is hiding?"

"Do you?"

"No. I..."

A horrible thought rose unbidden in his mind.

The Turk's head bobbed up and down. The lights flickered, on and off and on. "The Bookman wants you to find him," the Turk said. "He has kept his eyes on you for a long time now. Have you thought to ask yourself why?"

"Tell me," Orphan whispered. And then, "Tell me!"

"Play."

"King to D2."

"Queen to G2. Check."

"King to E1!"

"Knight to G1."

"Tell me."

"I sit here," the Turk said, "every hour of every day, alone in the darkness. I have a lot of time to think. To look at the strands of the past weave themselves into the knot of the present, and to imagine how the future might unfold from them. So many possibilities. Like a game of chess. And you, my little pawn, you are the catalyst, walking through the board one small step at a time, towards... what? What sort of endgame will you bring us all, Orphan?"

"I don't know. Tell me."

"Play."

"Knight to C3."

"Bishop takes C3. Do you know, I have played an identical game to this, once. He was a young soldier in the revolution... a short, angry, quite brilliant man, Bonaparte. In another history, another life, he may have been great. In this one, I think he was happier, growing grapes and pressing wine on his farm. Happiness must count for something, don't you think?"

"I don't want destiny," Orphan said. "I want..."

"Happiness? To get the girl and live happily ever after, raising fat babies, writing mediocre poetry? Perhaps in another life, Orphan. Play."

"I can't win, can I?" Orphan said.

"No."

"Pawn takes C3," Orphan said, removing the Turk's bishop. He felt as though something heavy and painful now rested on his chest, pressing against him until he couldn't breathe. "How many?" he asked. "How many sides does this game have?"

"Queen to E2," the Turk said, almost sadly. "Checkmate."

"How many sides?"

"Two," the Turk said. "There are only ever two."

"Les Lézards," Orphan said. Then, slowly, "And the Bookman."

"And we are all their pawns," the Turk said.

Then the lights behind the automaton dimmed for the last time, and died. Orphan was left in darkness.

"Wait," Orphan said.

There was merely silence.

"I don't believe that. Byron mentioned something... the Translation."

A lone bulb flickered into half-light above the Turk's head.

"The Binder story," the Turk said. "Yes... The probabilities are small."

"The Binder?"

"A being like the Bookman, if he exists at all," the Turk said. "It is a belief of – of my kind. A myth for a time of myths. The Translation... somewhere, they say, the Binder lives, and where the Bookman kills the Binder restores."

"What is the Translation?"

"Who knows? A device, perhaps. Or a way of thinking, a way of being... There is a story of a time when human and machine will be as one, life biological and life mechanical and all life animate and inanimate will be joined, will be made one. The Translation..." The dim bulb faded. Darkness settled, again and finally.

Orphan turned. Behind him, the door to the room had opened. Jo Jo stood in the corridor outside.

Orphan took a step towards him. Stopped. Turned back. The Turk was wrapped in the darkness. The Bookman, Orphan thought. And he took a deep breath, half-angry, half-surprised. For he knew then; he knew where the Bookman was hiding. He turned again, ready now. Jo Jo waited silently in the doorway.

FIFTEEN
Jack

Just the place for a Snark! I have said it twice:
That alone should encourage the crew.
Just the place for a Snark! I have said it thrice:
What I tell you three times is true.
  – Lewis Carroll, "The Hunting of the Snark"

"Orphan."

The girls were gone. Tom was on his own, dressed in silk pyjamas, reclining in a chair. He had a book in one hand, a rolled-up cigarette in the other.

Orphan glanced at the title. Moriarty's *The Dynamics of an Asteroid.* "I need to borrow your gun."

Tom stood up. "What happened?" he said carefully. "Orphan, are you well?"

Orphan giggled. He felt feverish, and yet, inside, there was an icy calm. "I'm very well," he said. "I need to borrow your gun."

"What happened at the Hall?"

"It was as Maskelyne said in his note," Orphan said. "Smoke and mirrors. Mirrors and smoke."

"You don't make no sense. Sit down. I will make you some tea." He turned to go to the bar area. "Did you meet Theo?"

"Jo Jo the Dog-Faced Boy," Orphan said. "I met him. Or, rather, he met me."

"Did you find what you were looking for?"

"Ask me later tonight." He looked at Tom and suddenly shouted, "I don't need tea!"

"What do you need?"

"Your gun."

"What," Tom said levelly, "for?"

Orphan giggled again, ignoring the concerned look Tom was giving him. "Hunting," he said. "I'm going hunting."

"It's a bit late to go a-hunting." Tom said. "Perhaps you should stay here tonight."

"Your gun," Orphan said, and now his voice was quiet and hard, with no trace of laughter left, and he stood tall against the door.

Tom, too, was quiet. He stood in his pyjamas and regarded Orphan without blinking.

"Please," Orphan said.

It was the please that perhaps did it; for when he said it, Orphan came as close as he had ever been to breaking. Perhaps Tom saw that. Maybe he had his own reasons. Either way, he went behind the bar without a comment, and returned a moment later with a giant revolver in his hands. Orphan took an involuntary step back.

Tom smiled. "My old Peacemaker," he said, holding the gun with obvious affection. He needed both his hands to hold it. Then he proffered the revolver to Orphan, holding it by the barrel, and Orphan took it cautiously, suddenly wondering if what he was doing was making any kind of sense at all.

"The Colt forty-five, single-action revolver," Tom said. "A six-shooter. So who are you planning to shoot?"

"No one," Orphan said. "Hopefully."

Tom nodded. "I should hope so too. Here." He went again behind the bar and returned with a belt and a handful of bullets. "You know how to use it?"

"I'll figure it out," Orphan said. Tom merely nodded, and helped him put on the gun belt. "Of course you will."

With expert hands he loaded five bullets, one after the other, into the chamber. "Cock it before you want to shoot. Always leave it on the empty chamber, or you'll end up shooting yourself. Have fun – try not to kill anyone."

"I will," Orphan said. The gun felt heavy on his hips, yet reassuring. I would need it, he thought. If only to make me bold enough to proceed.

"Here," Tom said. "You need a hat, too." He went to the right corner of the room, rooted in a small cupboard, and returned with a wide-brimmed hat that he put on Orphan's head. "Now you look proper, like."

Tom kept a full-length (at least, full-length for him) mirror close to the stairs. Orphan positioned himself far enough and examined himself in the mirror. He saw a tired face looking back at him, covered in stubble, a face shaded by the hat, a poet's hands clenching and unclenching into fists. He looked like a gunfighter, he thought. Like one of the men from Buffalo Bill's Wild West Show, which he had seen in Earl's Court once when they performed in the capital.

"You look like a kid," Tom said, not quite hiding his laugh. "If you were performing with Barnum and me, that's what you'd 'ave been billed as. The Kid." He laughed again, but Orphan didn't. The Kid, he thought. It resonated with him.

"The Kid," he said out loud. Tom stopped laughing and regarded him almost solemnly. "Take care of yourself, Orphan."

"I will," Orphan said. He turned away from the mirror and marched out of the Nell Gwynne.

"And bring back my gun!" Tom shouted after him. "It was a present from Colt himself!"

He leaned against the doorframe and watched Orphan disappear as he walked out of the alleyway.

"I wonder if I'll see you again," he murmured into the empty night, "Take care of yourself, Orphan. For all of us."

He walked along St Martin's Lane and thought of endgames. There are many players, he thought. But only two sides. And the objective of the game is to topple the king. But what if there was no king? What if a queen ruled the board? The objective, he thought, would be the same.

It was a cold night, the earlier warmth departing under the threat of a bank of clouds that sailed overhead, a fleet of warships announcing their dominion of the weather. The street was almost empty, the gas lamps casting weak light and strong shadows. They twisted and turned like barbarians in a dance. He thought, I want to come back to my old life. To return to the shop, sell books, write poetry. Talk to Gilgamesh by the bridge, watch the theatre, love Lucy and be loved... but it had already happened, and passed. And here I am.

He turned left into Cecil Court. Payne's stood in darkness. His footsteps made the only sound.

He stepped into the interior of the shop. Age-old books dozed in the darkness on countless shelves. They seemed to murmur sleepily to him when they sensed his presence. He thought again of the bible at Guy's, the book that lay in wait in every room, the one Irene Adler had glanced at, nervously it seemed to him, before falling silent.

The books have ears, he thought, and giggled.

The sound was muffled by the room, absorbed by all the paper. He thought, There is nothing sadder than an unused bookshop. Volumes of words, ideas and stories, blueprints and diagnostics, illustrations and notes scribbled in the margins – they did not exist unless there was someone there to hold them, to open their pages, to read them and make them come alive, however briefly.

Out of habit he went to his room. His bed lay undisturbed beneath the burden of the bookcase. The table was bare. His eyes were used to the darkness now, and he ignored the stub of a candle still sitting in its saucer. The dark was better, he thought. His days of sunshine and light were gone, the clock his body followed had been twisted and changed. He did not like night, yet now he lived inside it. I will live in it for just a little while longer, he thought. He left his room and returned to the main area of the shop. There.

He approached the door to the basement and put his palm against the wood. He pushed, and it opened.

Worn stone stairs led underground. The stairwell was dark. Orphan walked down the steps, placing each foot carefully before continuing to the next one.

At the bottom of the stairs was a second door. Faint light spilled through the narrow gap with the floor underneath it. A small sign on the door said, BIBLIOTHECA LIBRORUM IMAGINARIORUM.

He paused for a long moment, unsure of himself. He could hear nothing behind the door. He thought he could hear the Turk speaking, inside his head. You are a pawn, it said, laughing at him. Pawns can never go back. They can only move forward. To capture or be captured.

This isn't chess, he wanted to say, but the Turk had already faded away, had never been there to begin with.

He pressed the door handle down and pushed, and the door opened.

The basement was in reality a small, rather comfortable room. Bookshelves lined the walls here just as they did upstairs. An old sofa sat against the wall and doubled up, as far as Orphan knew, as Jack's bed, though he had never seen his friend sleep. Three tables sat at opposite corners, covered in books. Through that small room a doorless opening led onto a second, slightly larger room.

Inside the second room was Jack.

He was hunched over a small desk with a large headset nearly covering all of his head. Apart from the desk there were more bookshelves in the room, a small stove, and a rather large dresser.

"Jack," Orphan said.

There was no response. Jack was hunched over the desk, listening to sounds Orphan couldn't hear, scribbling furiously onto a notepad.

"Jack!"

He approached the sitting figure and tapped him on the shoulder.

For a few moments, nothing happened. Jack continued to scribble on his pad, seemingly unaware of Orphan's presence.

At last, however, he put down his pen, stretched his back, and removed the headset.

"Orphan, what happened?" He did not seem pleased at this intrusion into his personal space. "I've not seen you since last night. Are you all right?"

"No," Orphan said quietly.

"No?"

"No, I'm not all right."

Jack looked irritated. He rubbed his face with his hands, then said, "It's late."

"Or early," Orphan said. "Depends on how you look at it."

"What are you talking about? Look, did you want anything? Because I'm quite busy and if it can wait for tomorrow–"

"No, it can't," Orphan said, and suddenly the gun, the Colt Peacemaker, was in his hand, and pointing at Jack.

Jack stood up, his hands making a nervous, calming motion at Orphan. "What the hell are you doing? And where did you get that thing?"

"It's loaded," Orphan said. His voice shook, but only a little. "Don't make any sudden moves."

"I don't doubt it is," Jack said. "Look, what is this about, mate?" He glanced at the gun and then looked into Orphan's eyes. "Please put that thing away."

"Where is he?" Orphan said. The words constricted in his throat.

"Where is who?" Jack said, but there was a sudden look of horror on his face, brief yet powerful, and Orphan knew, with a helpless, sinking feeling, that he was right.

"Where is the Bookman?"

"Put down the gun, Orphan."

"Where is he?" Orphan said. The gun did not move. It pointed at Jack's chest. It made Orphan sick, to be threatening his friend. Yet he didn't remove it.

"Please," Jack said. There was something small and helpless in the simple word. He took a step forward, raised his arm as if to gesture, and his mouth opened, his lips parted in the beginning of speech...

And froze instead.

He made an ungainly statue. He was fixed in a position of frozen movement, the raised arm suspended in mid-air, the open lips just about to blow out air and with it their first word... His foot had not quite touched the ground, remained hovering just above the floor.

Orphan, uncertain, said, "Jack?"

There was no answer.

He put the gun away in his belt. It was not as if he would have ever used it. He approached his friend cautiously. Confusion made him hesitate. He touched Jack's arm. His flesh was hard. He put his hand before his friend's mouth, but could feel nothing, no breath blowing against his fingers.

"What the...?"

He stepped back. The room suddenly felt very small and crowded. The books stared at him from their shelves with sly expressions.

He stepped forward. Concern made him go back to his friend. He stood close to him, reached to check his pulse...

With a smooth, flowing motion Jack sprang into life. One moment he was still. The next, he was returned to life, and his foot came down with force on Orphan's, sending a hot flame of pain into Orphan's mind, bringing with it, sickeningly loud, the sound of delicate bones breaking.

Jack's arm came down, hard. His fingers bunched into a fist. The fist connected with Orphan's nose, and more pain flowered, and he was thrown back.

His back connected with a bookcase. His hat had fallen off. More pain, and then it was raining: volume after volume of antique books fell on him in ones and twos, a dribble that built into a flood. He lashed out, blinded, connected with nothing but air. The books continued to fall, hitting him on his head, his shoulders, his arms.

He blinked sweat from his eyes and tried to scramble away. From nowhere came Jack's foot, a kick that connected with a furious impact with his ribs, and he screamed.

"What are you *doing*?" he cried, but realisation, working its slow, inefficient way through his sluggish brain, had finally arrived, and for a moment he, too, froze.

He was backed into a corner of the room. Jack towered above him, unspeaking, his face impassive. His eyes stared down at Orphan but did not see him. For Jack, Orphan realised, was no longer there.

Jack kicked him again. The kick just missed his left kneecap and hit his shin. Pain shot through him, weaving a bright spider-web through his body. Stars exploded behind Orphan's eyes. Amongst them he thought, for a fleeting moment, that he could see a red, large star winking at him.

The starscape faded to black. When he opened his eyes again Jack was still there, his foot raised high. Ready to stomp down on Orphan. Ready to finish him.

With no conscious thought, like a spider with its own mind, his fingers reached down to his side and pulled out the old gun, fumbling at it, cocking the hammer. Jack's foot descended –

Orphan pulled the trigger.

SIXTEEN
At the Bibliotheca Librorum Imaginariorum

There thou mayst brain him,
Having first seized his books, or with a log
Batter his skull, or paunch him with a stake,
Or cut his wezand with thy knife. Remember
First to possess his books; for without them
He's but a sot, as I am, nor hath not
One spirit to command: they all do hate him
As rootedly as I. Burn but his books.

– William Shakespeare, *The Tempest*

The recoil threw him back. He felt his shoulder and arm slapped as by a giant stone hand. The sound of an explosion deafened him.

A book landed in his lap, and when he looked at it, blinking, realised for the first time that he was bleeding. The blood congealed on the leather cover, mixed with the dust that lay on the book like a thick layer of pollen.

A choked laugh escaped from his lips. The book in his lap was *Gray's Anatomy*.

I'm going to need that, he thought.

He raised his head. His fingers clutched the book.

Jack was crumpled against the wall on the other side of the room. There was a hole in his chest.

But there was no blood.

Orphan pulled himself up, his bloodied hands leaving palm-prints on the wall. The gun remained on the floor, beside the fallen book.

He took a deep breath and felt pain, like a jagged nail, cut across his ribs. His nose was blocked and hurting. One leg refused to carry him, and he leaned with his back against the wall, letting the leg dangle.

Jack remained unmoving on the other side. He, too, had hit a bookcase. He lay surrounded by silent, fallen books.

Slowly, carefully, one hand trailing against the wall and the contours of the room, Orphan made his way toward him.

There was a whistling sound in his ears. And, somehow, he could smell – there was a burning smell in the room, a mix of gunpowder and something else, as of scorched rubber...

He stood above Jack. His friend's face was lax, empty, as if its features had half-melted away, leaving behind a mask devoid of animation. His eyes were closed.

He forced himself to look below the face. His eyes moved down slowly, hesitating as they went. They felt, he thought, reluctant to obey his brain.

There was a hole in Jack's chest. And in the hole... blue fire.

A spark flew in the air and made Orphan stagger back. Sparks were coming out of the open hole in Jack's chest, one and then another one and another, until a small electric storm seemed to erupt out of that still body and jump into the air.

He is bleeding electricity, Orphan thought. And then, at last, he formulated to himself the thought that had insinuated itself into his mind when Jack attacked him.

Simulacrum.

He knelt beside Jack and took his hand in his. There was no pulse, but the skin felt warm and, now that he looked closer, lines of light were moving beneath the skin.

He peered into the hole in Jack's chest. Sparks were still flying, but they were diminishing. Inside... he could not comprehend it. Perhaps, he thought, he was expecting gears and cogs. But the inside of Jack's body resembled no machine he had ever seen. It was like a vast, strangely beautiful painting of incomprehensible, miniature elements, not human, not machine, but some sort of unknowable technology that was, perhaps, a little of both.

Jack, he thought, numb. Why? Who?

But he already knew the answer. He rose from his crouching position and looked around the room. Books lay everywhere, like wounded soldiers on a battlefield. The desk, the Tesla set. Nothing else. He began scanning the shelves, pressing his hand against the wall as he moved around the room. Searching.

"I know you're here," he said into the silence. "I know you can hear me."

The books, he thought. He needed a key. He began riffling through the ones still left on the shelves, picking each for the brief moment it took him to read the title, then tossing the book on the floor. Jack, he thought. That's where he would hide things. In books.

Jo March's *A Phantom Hand.* William Ashbless's *Accounts of London Scientists.* Hawthorne Abendsen's *The Grasshopper Lies Heavy. The Encyclopedia Donkaniara. The Book of Three.* Emmanuel Goldstein's *The Theory and Practice of Oligarchical Collectivism.* Captain Eustacio Binky's *Coffee Making as a Fine Art.* Ludvig Prinn's *De Vermis Mysteriis.* Gulliver Fairborn's *A Talent for Sacrifice.* Colonel Sebastian Moran's *Heavy Game of the Western Himalayas.* Gottfried Mulder's *Secret Mysteries of Asia, with Commentary on the Ghorl Nigral.* Cosmo Cowperthwait's *Sexual Dimorphism Among The Echinoderms, Focusing Particularly Upon the Asteroidea and Holothuroidea.* George Edward Challenger's *Some Observations Upon a Series of Kalmuk Skulls.*

What were those books? Orphan thought, exasperated. Most of these titles were completely unknown to him. He almost wanted to stop, to take his time, browse through the titles at leisure, leaf through the enigmatic books, study their contents. Instead, he pulled each book, opened it and shook it upside down, searching for something hidden inside. Some things did fall out – a pressed flower here, its startling blue preserved amidst the pages of Josephine M. Bettany's *Mystery at Heron Lake;*

a folded currency note there, bearing an unknown script, that fluttered to the ground from within Flashman's *Twixt Cossack and Cannon* – but nothing to give him a clue, a hint as to his next move. Yet as he continued ransacking the shelves he became more and more convinced that what he was doing was right, that the books were the twine that could lead him across the floor of the maze to the minotaur who waited at its centre.

Gossip Gone Wild by Dr Jubal Harshaw. *In My Father's House* by Princess Irulan. *Burlesdon on Ancient Theories and Modern Facts* by James Rassendyll, Lord Burlesdon. *The Truth of Alchemy* by Mr. Karswell. *Stud City* by Gordon Lachance. *Boxing the Compass* by Bobbi Anderson. *The Relationship of Extradigitalism to Genius*, by Zubarin. *Megapolisomancy* by Thibaut de Castries. *De Impossibilitate Prognoscendi* by Cezar Kouska. Eustace Clarence Scrubb's *Diary*. *Azathoth and Other Horrors* by Edward Pickman Derby.

More things fell from the books. A coin, so blackened that its face could no longer be discerned. A map of an island drawn in a child's hand. A butterfly, the wings black save for two emerald spots. A newspaper cutting from the *Daily Journal*, that read:

12 June 1730.

Seven Kings or Chiefs of the Chirakee Indians, bordering upon the area called Croatoan, are come over in the Fox Man of War, Capt. Arnold, in order to pay their duty to his Majesty, and assure him of their attachment to his person and Government, &c.

Aunt Susan's Compendium of Pleasant Knowledge. Broomstick or the Midnight Practice. R. Blastem's *Sea Gunner's Practice, with Description of Captain Shotgun's Murdering Piece. The Libellus Leibowitz.* Augustus Whiffle's *The Care of the Pig.* Dr Stephen Maturin's *Thoughts on the Prevention of Diseases most usual among Seamen.* Professor Radcliffe Emerson's *Development of the Egyptian Coffin from Predynastic Times to the End of the Twenty-sixth Dynasty, With Particular Reference to Its Reflection of Religious, Social, and Artistic Conventions. The Book of Bokonon.* Kilgore Trout's *Now It Can Be*

Told. James Bailey's *Life of William Ashbless*. Hugo Rune's *The Book of Ultimate Truths*. Harriet Vane's *The Sands of Crime*. Jean-Baptiste Colbert's *Grand System of Universal Monarchy*. Toby Shandy's *Apologetical Oration*. Coleridge's *The Rime of the Ancient Mari–*

There.

He was on his knees, a dull throbbing pain in his hurt leg. He saw the title, bottom shelf, Coleridge's name. But the book did not move.

And then he noticed the dust.

A layer of dust had settled over time on the tops of the books and lay there undisturbed. Yet on *The Rime of the Ancient Mariner* there was no dust.

And the book would not move, would not be pulled away from the shelf.

Orphan stared at it for a long moment. That long, strange poem of Coleridge... He traced the edges of the slim book with his fingers.

It did not feel like the rest. It was hard, metallic, not leather. He gave up on trying to pull it out and, instead, gave it a push with his thumb.

The book slid effortlessly away from him.

There was a soft *click*.

The bookcase moved. It hit Orphan, sending more pain through his body, and he scrambled away and fell on the floor, cushioned uncomfortably by books.

The bookcase moved, swinging, and behind it was an emptiness, a lack of a wall and beyond that was a darkness. Somewhere in the distance he could hear what sounded like waves, and taste a sharp, almost rancid smell.

He stood up, looked one last time towards Jack. Then he retrieved the gun from where it lay on the floor and tucked it into its holster. He lifted the wide-brimmed hat from the floor and put it carefully back on his head, at an angle.

He stared into the darkness for a long moment, but could discern nothing beyond the bookcase. Then he took a deep breath and stepped forward, and into the darkness.

SEVENTEEN
The Man Behind the Screen

The Lion thought it might be as well to frighten the Wizard, so he gave a large, loud roar, which was so fierce and dreadful that Toto jumped away from him in alarm and tipped over the screen that stood in a corner. As it fell with a crash they looked that way, and the next moment all of them were filled with wonder. For they saw, standing in just the spot the screen had hidden, a little old man, with a bald head and a wrinkled face, who seemed to be as much surprised as they were. The Tin Woodman, raising his axe, rushed toward the little man and cried out, "Who are you?"

– L. Frank Baum, *The Wonderful Wizard of Oz*

The ground sloped gradually beneath his feet. The earth felt moist, and his feet sank slightly into it with each step he took. The darkness was complete; he felt that he was set loose in the space between the stars, with no up or down, no weight...

There was the sound of waves. The air was warm, but a small breeze blew against his face. He had the sense of unseen things scuttling away from him in the darkness.

Where was he? he wondered. Somewhere underneath Charing Cross Road? He could not tell which direction he was taking. What was this place?

As he walked further he could discern a glow of light in the distance. Coming closer, the glow resolved and separated into strange orbs that cast a dim, greenish light over the surroundings.

He was standing in a cavern, and the orbs were hung on the walls. Before him was a black lake, and he was standing on its shore. There was sand at his feet.

He bent down and touched the water. It was cool to the touch, and he lifted some in his palm and drank from the lake. The water had almost no taste, yet it revived him.

He began to walk along the shore, his body casting two shadows onto the ground. A short way off, by the cavern's wall, he found an empty boat beached on the sand.

He knows I am coming, he thought. He is waiting. The thought did not upset him. The Bookman wants you to find him, the Turk had said. He has kept his eyes on you for a long time now...

"I know you are watching," he said aloud. There was no other sound but the lapping of the waves. "I'm coming."

He pushed the boat into the water and climbed inside. It was made of wood and smelled of disuse. Once in the water it began to move of its own accord.

He sat back. There was nothing else for him to do, and he was suddenly glad. He let his hand trail in the water of that dark lake. Perhaps it is the same boat Lucy had travelled on, he thought. Soon we could come back, together in it.

His hand touched something soft in the water. He looked overboard and nearly fell over: there was a body floating in the water, its eyes open and looking straight at him.

The body floated just below the surface of the water. It was that of a man, naked, not alive and yet not dead, either, and he recognised it: it was Henry Irving, the actor. He had last seen him blown up into pieces at the Rose.

He pulled away from the side of the boat, feeling sudden revulsion. As he looked now, he could see other bodies submerged in the water of the lake. The water was very clear, translucent. The lake, he realised, was very shallow. He sat back, unsettled. Henry Irving's body diminished behind him.

As the shore grew farther in the distance a shape loomed ahead, rising out of the lake. A small island, he thought. The boat, of its own, unknown will, headed towards it.

It was not a long journey. Soon, too soon, the boat ran aground on the island, and he stepped out. He felt better now, and the various pains in his body had disappeared. Touching his nose, he could not feel the break. Instead, he felt light and clear-headed. Something in the water, he thought.

His feet touched black sand. Before him the island was almost flat, a disc floating on the water. He scraped away at the sand and was not surprised to discover a greenish metal underneath. An artificial island. He took a step forward, then another. The ground rose, then, after only a few more steps, gently sloped downwards.

Above his head the globes of light slowly faded, leaving him in total darkness. He stood for a long moment, not moving, and waited.

Though he thought he was prepared, when the voice came it nevertheless startled him. "Mr. Orphan. What a delight to finally meet you." It was a deep, mellow voice.

A light came to life directly ahead of him. An old-fashioned, ornamental streetlamp planted in the sand. It illuminated a small square of chequered tiles, black and white like a chess set. In the centre of the square was a table. On the table stood a tea pot, a small milk jug, a jar of sugar and two delicate china cups. On a saucer he could discern what looked like ginger biscuits.

One chair was unoccupied. In the other sat a man.

He rose when Orphan approached. He was a tall, athletic-looking man. Black hair was only just beginning to recede across his forehead. He was dressed in a smart suit, like that of a well-to-do City worker. He was clean-shaven. He came towards Orphan with his hand outstretched, and shook his hand. His handshake was strong and confident. His eyes twinkled. Orphan felt completely lost.

"Please," the man said, gesturing at the table. "Sit down. Have some tea. I have been looking forward to talking with you." Not waiting for Orphan, he returned to his seat and began pouring tea into the cups. Orphan, not knowing what to do, and feeling a vague sense of unease – or perhaps, he thought, it was disappointment? He couldn't tell what he had been expecting, but it wasn't this – sat down opposite.

"Milk? Sugar?"

"Yes, please. Two sugars," Orphan said. His voice felt unreal to him. Maybe, he thought, maybe I never shot Jack. Perhaps I am still lying on the floor of the basement, concussed, and I am merely hallucinating this. I will be glad if it turns out I never shot him. It wasn't like me. He was my friend. Then he wondered, if that was true, what hospital he would go to. Would it be Guy's again? He didn't relish that idea.

"I am sure you have a lot of questions," the man said, handing him his tea.

Orphan smelled the tea. It smelled good, an Earl Grey, and when he tasted it warmth spread through his body. "One or two," he said cautiously. Something is wrong, he thought. But I don't know what it is.

The man nodded as if Orphan's reply confirmed some deep point of conversation. "You are wondering who I am." He smiled. His teeth were white and even. "I am, of course, the Bookman." He laughed and shook his head. "I am one of the Bookmen, rather," he said. "I am afraid you were rather misled to think of us as one person. One mysterious and quite nefarious person, no doubt." He sighed and took a sip from his tea. "I am afraid the reality is quite a bit more mundane. Would you like a biscuit?"

"No, thank you," Orphan said. His companion shrugged and helped himself to one, which he bit into with relish. "They're very good," he said.

"I have no doubt on that score," Orphan said. "You were saying?"

"Ah, straight to business. Quite. You see, Orphan, we are not some monstrous and alien entity – though we like people to think that – but rather, we are simple patriots. Men – and women – who have made it their goal to free our homeland from the shackles of oppression." He looked at Orphan with an earnest, searching gaze. "The oppression of Les Lézards."

"By killing innocent people?" Orphan said. He was coming back to himself, a little. "By killing Lucy?" Anger flared and he seized it with gratitude, trying to pull himself out of the spreading numbness.

The man shook his head. His face bore a sad, dignified countenance. "We had no choice," he said. "Though, in the event, we were wrong. Misled."

"Wrong?" Orphan said. "*Wrong?*"

"Yes," the man – the Bookman – agreed. "You see, our target was, of course, the Martian probe. Yet–"

"Why? Why the probe?" He pushed away his tea. "What harm can it possibly do?"

"Let me riddle you this, Orphan," the Bookman said. "Where do Les Lézards come from?"

"I was told they come from an island whose location is kept secret."

"Come, come," the Bookman said. "You've read Darwin. Surely you realise this idea of parallel evolution, of this other race evolving naturally away from humanity on a small island, surely this idea is preposterous?"

"I had not given it much thought," Orphan said.

There was something about the way the man talked, about the way he moved his head...

Suddenly, it reminded him of the Turk.

"The truth, Orphan." the man leaned forward, and his eyes looked deep into Orphan's with a gaze both trusting and wise. "A truth many men died to obtain proof of, I should tell you –" and here he lay his hand on the table, as if it were a bible and he a witness at a court of law – "the truth is this: the lizards *have no earthly origin.*"

Orphan looked into the Bookman's eyes. There was, he thought, a lack in them, an absence he could not quite describe. Something was missing in the man, some subtle part of a man that simply wasn't there. He said, "I see."

"Do you? Do you, Orphan? Do you comprehend the magnitude of this affront?" The man grasped him by the arm. "They are intruders, invaders, an occupying force from – from beyond. From beyond space. They want nothing else than to rule the whole world – and they are using us, humans, to do this – until the day when they no longer need us…"

"You sound like Jack," Orphan said distractedly. He turned his face away from the man. He couldn't see the lake from where he sat, it was as if he were sitting in an upturned bowl. Beyond the little square, beyond the streetlamp's light, there was nothing.

An absence within an absence, he thought. He said, "Jack was my friend."

"Yes, yes," the man said. "Do try to pay attention."

"You were going to explain to me about the probe," Orphan said. Was it really an absence? He looked harder. It seemed to him that there was something out there, on the edge of his vision, something vast and powerful moving in the darkness, watching him. "Then you can explain to me about the mistake you made. And then you can give me back Lucy."

"Look," the Bookman said, his face colouring in anger. "You don't seem to understand what is at stake here. I thought you would be sensible. Us humans need to stick together, to–"

But Orphan was no longer listening. He stood up, pushing back the chair, and stalked off beyond the streetlamp, into the outlining darkness.

"Hey, where are you going?" the Bookman shouted after him.

Orphan turned back. "You're another simulacrum, aren't you?" he said. Then he pulled out the Peacemaker and shot the Bookman in the chest.

EIGHTEEN
The Bookman

Facile credo, plures esse Naturas invisibiles quam visibiles in rerum universitate
 – Thomas Burnet

"Bravo," said a voice. It wasn't the man who had spoken. He was lying on the ground on his back, with a hole in his chest. Like Jack, he was bleeding sparks. Lines of light ran underneath his skin and gave him an unhealthy, eerie glow.

Orphan turned to the darkness and said, "Show yourself."

The voice sounded amused. "I'd be afraid you'd shoot me too," it said. "You've become awfully proficient with that gun awfully fast." There was a sigh, long and heavy like a wave. "So you have come at last."

Orphan squinted into the darkness. He felt unnerved. Something was moving there, a shape he could not quite make out, large and malevolent. He said, "Where is Lucy?"

"Nearby," the voice said, and Orphan felt his heart quicken; he took a deep breath, exhaling the air slowly to try to calm himself. He said, "Release her."

"So you have come at last," the voice said again, and again, there was the sense of deep amusement coming from it. "Descended to the Underworld to bargain with the lord of death.

But what, Orphan, do you have to bargain with?"

"Show yourself," Orphan said again. He felt suddenly like a small boy, lost, his voice weak and lonely in the immense dark. The Bookman was toying with him.

The Bookman laughed. Then he said, "I can give you Lucy back. Alive again. Better than alive. But for what price, my young poet? Do you think you can just wander in here like a lost figure of myth and demand your love back?"

Orphan looked into the darkness and saw only moving shadows. "What do you want from me?" he whispered into the dark.

"Ah. Good." A movement, and a disturbing sense of something like a giant insect, multi-legged and with too many eyes. "You are seeing reason."

"Why did you kill her?"

The voice returned to him from the other side of the square now, and he turned to it. I'm bound to him, he realised. For Lucy I will serve him.

"I began to tell you, when you killed Mr. Worth," the voice said, sounding surprisingly peevish. "You leave quite a trail in your wake."

An image of Jack lying on the floor came unbidden into Orphan's mind, and he felt his heart constrict. "Will you...?" he said. "Could you fix him? Jack?"

"I could," the Bookman said. Moving again. Circling around Orphan, like a hunter who had closed on his prey. "I might. Should I?"

"He was my friend," Orphan said. As the words left his mouth he thought again of Jack. He had taken him in, at Payne's. He had cared about him. And Orphan had shot him. Suddenly he felt disgusted with himself. And angry.

"I know," the Bookman said. "Ironic, isn't it? You see, I could bring him back if I chose, but how would Jack react?" The voice sighed, a gust of wind that stroked Orphan's cheek. "He never knew he was a simulacrum."

The Bookman laughed. In the distance the waves rolled

against the shore. On the table undrunk tea sat cooling. On the black-and-white squares a man lay dead.

Orphan felt tired, old. He sat back in his chair. So Jack really was his friend. "Please," he said. "Bring him back."

"First Lucy, now Jack?" the Bookman said. "What will you give me?"

But Orphan had played that game before. Ever since that night by the Thames he had played a riddle-game, his opponents changing but the questions remaining the same. A question for a question, he thought. You will tell me what you want from me when you decide it's time. I know you now. What is it that you want me to do? What is it that you want me to learn?

"Who was he?" he asked, pointing to the dead, suited man.

"Adam Worth," the Bookman said. "Quite an ingenious, ruthless criminal. I assimilated him some years ago, following his theft of the Duchess of Devonshire – ever seen that painting? quite marvellous – from Agnew & Sons. He already had an extremely successful network of criminals working under him – in fact, I believe your friend at Scotland Yard once called him the Caesar of crime."

"My friend?" He felt a sudden chill.

"Come, Orphan," the Bookman said. Moving again. Orphan felt too tired to try to follow him with his eyes. Yet he was aware of the movement. "Let us keep no secrets between us. Even now Inspector Adler is keeping watch over the entrance to Payne's. She's had you under surveillance ever since you left Guy's Hospital. Didn't you know that?" The Bookman laughed, and said, "Of course not. She is very good. She felt – quite rightly, of course – that you could lead her to me. Mistakenly, though, as it turns out – by the time she realises you will not come out and makes her move, she will be able to find nothing."

The chill he felt spread, numbing him. "What do you mean?"

The Bookman's answer did not give him cause for relief. "You'll find out."

"Why?" Orphan said. Real bewilderment made him belligerent. "Why kill Lucy? Why bring me here?" Then the words of the suited man – Adam Worth, he thought – came back to him, and he said, "The Martian probe."

"Yes," the Bookman said.

"It keeps coming back to that," Orphan said. "But why? Why destroy it?"

"Because it was not – is not – a probe," the Bookman said, and his voice was very close now, almost caressing, issuing behind Orphan's shoulder. Orphan sat very still, as if, by his stillness, he could fool the Bookman into moving away.

"It is a beacon," the Bookman said.

His voice was low and soft, whispering directly into Orphan's ear. Something scaly and inhuman touched his shoulder, and he almost jumped.

"A beacon," the Bookman said. "To be carried into space by the design and engineering of humans, but for a purpose of which they know nothing. Think of it, Orphan," that awful voice said, "think of a great cannon booming, a cloud of smoke, heat torching the ground below as the cannon fires, shooting its cargo into the atmosphere, and beyond. Into the coldness of space. To float alone amongst the stars – isn't that poetic?"

"Yes," Orphan whispered, paralysed by the Bookman's touch. What was he, he thought, desperately, helplessly – what strange, alien being had trapped him here, to speak to him of poetry?

"Poetry has its own irony," the Bookman said. "The probe would reach space, but it would not head to Mars, to explore its arid deserts and its false canals. Instead, it will spread out dishes like the opening petals of a flower. And it will begin to broadcast a poem out to the distant stars. In the language of the creatures you, in your ignorance, call Les Lézards. Do you know what message it will carry, Orphan? What poem will make its way into galactic space?"

He could feel the Bookman behind him, a shadowy presence made solid, made real and threatening beyond anything he had ever imagined. He whispered, "No," and heard his own voice come back to him, not recognisable as his own.

"It will be a song of surpassing beauty," the Bookman said. "And it will be a poem of summons. It will whisper of the beauty of this world, of Earth, of its blue oceans and green lands, of its abundance of life, its riches, its minerals and fuel and rare metals. A world ready for the taking. A world already half-subdued." Something like a lizard's tongue, yet different, hissed in the air beside his ear, tasting the words. "Come, it would say. Come, our brothers and sisters. We have been lost for a long time, but now we are found. Come to this world we have taken for ourselves, and we could rule it together."

The words took on a seductive tone, forcing tendrils into Orphan's mind, conjuring new, disturbing images inside his head. Whether it was his imagination alone, or some influence of the Bookman, he didn't know, but suddenly he was no longer sitting at the table but flying, disembodied, through a space strewn with stars, and below him was a globe, a blue world streaked with the white of clouds and the green of living things. It was beautiful – but then he turned, and he saw the small black body he had last seen, blown apart, in Richmond Park. The probe sailed through space, as small as a pebble, only seen by the occasional glint of light from its side. He turned again, facing away from the Earth, and his breath caught in a mixture of wonder and fear. For amongst the stars rose a fleet, thousands upon thousands of silver discs burning in the rays of the distant suns, coming closer and closer.

"Invasion," the Bookman whispered in his ear, jolting him back into awareness. His – hand? – tightened on Orphan's shoulder. "When the probe is released, it will sing its song out to the stars. And amongst the stars, Les Lézards' ancient kin will listen. And they will come, Orphan. They will come. And they will take this world for themselves."

"But it was destroyed," Orphan said. "You destroyed it!"

"I was misled," the Bookman said. His touch on Orphan's shoulder slackened. His voice took on an aspect of haunting sadness. "The probe in the park was a decoy. The real one is at this very minute making its way by airship to Caliban's Island, where the launch facility is all but complete. It has to be destroyed, Orphan. Do you see?" It seemed the Bookman was almost pleading with him. "This is not about a single human life, however regrettable. The fate of the world itself lies, as they say, in the balance."

He released Orphan. On a sudden instinct Orphan stood up and turned, looking for the Bookman.

He had already retreated back into the shadows. Yet Orphan caught a glimpse of him, as he moved away: he was not human and not lizard, but a giant, caterpillar-like creature, its scaly head adorned with eye-stalks that, even as they were disappearing in the darkness, for one small moment seemed to wink at him.

"Destroy the probe," the voice of the Bookman said, growing faint, "and I will return Lucy to you."

"Why me?" Orphan said. Pleaded.

"A pawn does not ask for its player's strategy," the Bookman said. "And I have been playing this particular game for more centuries than you can imagine. You must destroy the probe."

He felt himself sinking into the Bookman's web. A fly caught in a silk mesh from which there was no escape. Finally, he said, "How?"

"Will you do it?" the Bookman said. His voice echoed in Orphan's mind, over the black-and-white squares, the miniature board on which he played his game with Orphan.

And Orphan, a captured pawn, whispered at last –

"Yes."

PART II
The Odyssey

NINETEEN
Across the Channel

I travelled among unknown men,
In lands beyond the sea;
Nor, England! did I know till then
What love I bore to thee.
  – William Wordsworth, "Lucy"

It was some time later. The place was France.

Orphan arrived at Nantes train station in the early hours of the morning. He had crossed the Channel, travelled by train to Paris and from there took the night journey across France. He got to see little of the country. His only reading material along the way had been a newspaper: and the news was not reassuring. One item in particular concerned Orphan:

EXPLOSION ROCKS CHARING CROSS ROAD!
BY OUR SPECIAL CORRESPONDENT

In the early hours of yesterday morning a subterranean explosion rocked the foundations of Charing Cross Road and its environs. The explosion sent shockwaves throughout the nearby neighbourhoods, causing damage to property and health. Two people were mildly hurt when their baruch-landau fell into an opening in the ground, and several people were rushed into hospital with minor injuries. The explosion caused damage to roads and houses, and destroyed a bookshop, Payne's, in Cecil Court. Scotland Yard Inspector Irene Adler was on the spot immediately after the explosion, with a full team of constables and police automatons. She and her team were seen by this reporter to dig through the ruins of Payne's, where the proprietor and his assistant are feared to be missing amidst the rubble. Inspector Adler was not available for comment. The cause of the explosion is unknown, though experts suggest it was caused by a build-up of natural gas deep under the city—

He found himself worrying about the Inspector. And he worried about his journey, about where he should go, and wondered how he would accomplish the seemingly impossible goal the Bookman had set him. But most of all he missed Lucy, and he worried, worried until he could barely think or eat: for, just before his interview with the Bookman was at an end, he saw her again.

"I can give you back Lucy," the Bookman had said, and then—

She came to him out of the water of that dark lake. Her hair fell down to her shoulders. Her body was as he remembered it. She ran to him, appearing at the edge of the light and rushing forward, and she embraced him, and her lips on his were the taste of happiness. He kissed her, holding her close to him, the cold water of the lake soaking his shirt. "Oh, Orphan," she whispered, and she looked into his eyes and he could have remained that way forever.

"Touching," the Bookman said. And then, as quickly and mysteriously as she had come, Lucy was gone again, and Orphan, helpless, could do nothing. He, too, had to obey the Bookman's commands.

And the Bookman had given him papers, and money, and instructions. He was to go to France, to the city of Nantes which lies close to the Atlantic Ocean, and there he would be met. He wondered who it would be to welcome him.

In the event, the Bookman's agent waited for him at the station, and Orphan got a bit of a shock.

As the train came to rest against the platform Orphan glimpsed, through the window, two figures standing outside. One was a large, fat man holding a cane: the other was short and balding and even from a distance Orphan could see he had a scar down his left cheek that ended just below the eye. When he got off the train the two men approached him, and the short one made directly for Orphan's luggage. The fat man beamed at Orphan and threw his cane to his servant, took Orphan's outstretched hand in both of his, and shook it energetically. "Welcome to my home town," he said. "Welcome to Nantes."

"Thank you," Orphan said, "Mr–?"

The fat man looked taken aback. "Why, I thought my name is well known even in that lizards'-spawn hell of yours across the Channel," he said.

"I'm sorry, I don't–"

The fat man drew himself up. He snapped his fingers and his servant threw him his cane. The man caught it single-handedly and twirled it. "The name," he said stiffly, "is Verne. Jules Verne."

"Jules Verne? The author of *L'Île mystérieuse*?"

"Amongst many others," the writer said modestly. "Is this all the luggage you have?" He barked an order in French at his manservant, then turned to Orphan with a shrug. "This is my man, Robur," he said. Then he smirked. "I call him 'the conqueror'."

"How so?"

"Because of, shall we say, his prowess, with the ladies?"

Robur grinned at Orphan from behind the luggage.

They went in a coach and Robur did the driving. He drove the horses very fast. As they went through the narrow streets Orphan saw strange figures gathered and thought, for a moment, that he had seen royal lizards. In France?

"What," he said, and then wasn't sure what to say and merely pointed through the window. Verne turned to look.

"Punks de Lézard," he said.

They were an odd, mixed crowd, Orphan saw, watching them in horrified fascination: their hair was cut off entirely for both the males and the females, save for several who had a curious ridge or spine made of a narrow strip of hair in the middle of their scalp, that stood in tall spikes from their otherwise-bare heads. Their naked skulls were painted in a greenish-brown imitation of Les Lézards' skin, and were then patterned with bands of alternating colour. Their faces, too, were painted to resemble those of lizards, and their clothes were sparse and made to resemble scales. They walked around in small groups, and when one opened his mouth to speak, perhaps to shout at the passing coach, Orphan saw he had had his tongue cut so that it, too, resembled a lizard's.

"What are they?" he asked, overwhelmed.

"Lizard boys," Verne said, and snorted. And then, more quietly. "Children at play, but nasty, the way children sometimes turn. Ignore them."

But Orphan found them hard to ignore.

They sped away and soon the town, and the strange youths he saw, were gone behind them. At last they halted outside a large villa that stood in isolated grounds outside of the city. The house sat on the bank of a wide river – the Loire, Verne informed him; a large sailboat was moored outside.

"Welcome, welcome," Verne said, ushering Orphan through the large doors of the house into a cluttered living area. He clapped his hands twice and lights came on. Another clap and unseen heaters began to send tendrils of heat into the room.

"Amazing," Orphan said. The room, he saw, was a treasure trove of quaint mechanical constructions and odd automatons: a replica of Vaucanson's duck, for instance, sat in a cage beside one window, mechanically eating and disposing of its food at the two opposite ends of its body. Another, a replica of a young boy, sat writing, over and over again, a short message on a slate. Elsewhere there were calculating machines, toy soldiers that marched on the spot, the model of a blowfish growing and thinning, as constant as a clock, a miniature flute player, a Tesla set, an Edison player, a steam-powered, miniature ship moving in a large aquarium of water with metal fish swimming underneath it, and a mechanical giant squid that reached out tentacles for the ship, never quite seizing it; there were clocks and records, spy-glasses and microscopes, mirrors like something out of a carnival, each reflection different and contrary: and everywhere there was space it was occupied by books, lying haphazard over this museum of curiosities like sleepy attendants.

"The wife and kids are away for a while," Verne said. "Italy. They love it there. And it will keep them out of the way…" He sighed. "Bedrooms are upstairs, also shower, bath, et cetera. Kitchen through here. Robur!"

"Sir?" The small man appeared beside him.

"Fix our guest some food," Verne said.

Robur disappeared towards the kitchen.

"How did you get involved in all this," Orphan said to Verne. "Sir?"

"Oh, call me Jules," Verne said. His face became serious, almost stern. "I will tell you all," he said, "but all in good time. There will be plenty of time to talk – on the ship."

"You?" Orphan said. "You are coming with me to Caliban's Island?"

It seemed like madness.

The writer chuckled. "Who better?" he said, patting his stomach. "So I am not as young or as lithe as I used to be, but trust me, there is life and spirit in this old man yet! Robur!"

"Sir?"

He seemed to have simply materialised there.

"Fix our guest a drink."

"Sir."

"Drink, my young friend?"

"Please," Orphan said, a little dazed. "Some red wine would be lovely."

Verne smiled, Robur did his disappearing act, and in a moment Orphan was left holding a large goblet filled almost to the brim with a dark cabernet sauvignon. He gulped it down and felt wel-come warmth and a relaxing haze settle over his mind. He would do what he could to work against the Bookman, he thought. Were it not for Lucy. Then he stood up with a shout and nearly spilled his drink.

A massive lizard had entered the room.

It was, he saw a moment later, not a royal lizard, but a crea-ture very similar to those he last saw underneath the King's Arms in Drury Lane. It was six feet or more in length, with yel-low bands and spots forming broken crosses on its body and powerful tail. The lizard ambled into the room, paused, and its tongue tasted the air.

"This is Victoria," Verne said.

"Victoria."

"My pet. Isn't she beautiful?"

Orphan downed the rest of his wine.

TWENTY
The Nautilus

Now would I give a thousand furlongs of sea for an
acre of barren ground, long heath, brown furze, any
thing. The wills above be done! but I would fain
die a dry death.
  – William Shakespeare, *The Tempest*

Orphan woke up to dim light streaming in through the open
blinds. The black-velvet blinds; early-morning light; the cold
breeze coming in through an open window, making him shiver:
finally, Verne's full-moon face rising disembodied above him.

"Argh!" Orphan said, and shook himself awake. Above him,
Verne grinned. "Good morning, young Orphan," he said. "You
slept for a long time, and now it is time to set forth. It is time, Orphan." His smile melted away, leaving him looking solemn and
introspected. "It is time," he said again, then fell silent.

Orphan rose, stood up, began hunting for his clothes. A fresh
suit of clothing was lying neatly on a chair beside the bed. "Robur
is serving breakfast in the kitchen," Verne said. "Meet me there
in fifteen minutes. We sail with the tide."

He felt clear-headed that morning, and he stood in the centre of
the room for a long moment and stretched, and breathed in the
sea air and felt it whisper promises. To go on the sea: it conjured

images from books he had read in his youth, of treasures and battles and tropical storms. He thought, There is a book of poems in that. But he had not written a poem since that day at the Nell Gwynne, and his poetry had been bottled up, locked away together with Lucy: neither of them were as yet coming back from the dead.

He dressed and went downstairs. Verne was sitting alone at the kitchen table, a plate heaped with food before him. Robur was cooking eggs and bacon on the stove.

Verne indicated a vacant seat with the tip of his butter-smeared knife. "Sit down."

Robur served him a plate to accompany Verne's. Eggs, bacon, slices of toast, a strong sweet coffee, butter and jam: they were a powerful wake-up tonic. "English cooking," Robur said with a shake of his head, and disappeared into the adjoining room.

"Orphan," Verne said, "you are very much thrown into this without direction. You are a brave man; an honourable man. I respect that. As you know, I had attempted to go to Caliban's Island before. In that I was not successful. I was unable to land. Consequently, you must understand I know little more than you do. I do not know what expects us there. But I do know how to pilot a ship, which I have, as I have the men to operate it. I will give you all the help I can, and will tell you what little I know." He stood and reached out for Orphan, took his hand awkwardly in both of his. "I will do everything in my power to bring you there, and bring you back alive, too. If I can. Do you believe me?"

Orphan looked at the writer. For all that he was mixed up in these conspiracies of the Bookman, and for all of his effusive theatricality and his way of filling in its entirety the space around him, he found himself liking Verne. There was something almost innocent about the man, mixed with a childish, wicked glee at everything, as if life was one big game, a puzzle put out there for him to fathom one section at a time. "I do," he said, and meant it. Verne smiled. "Good."

They ate the rest of the meal in silence. When it was over, Verne stretched, sighed in satisfaction, and rose from his seat. Orphan, knowing the time had come, rose too. He felt jittery, but expectant too. The books he'd read kept flittering through his mind. Adventure on the high seas. He smiled to himself. Verne looked at him and replied with a smile of his own. For a moment they were two boys together, and the future was a bright game that would last all afternoon.

"Are you ready?"

"As ready as I'll ever be."

"Then let's go."

And so they did.

The clipper ship was magnificent. Three masts rose high above their heads, a white canopy of sails growing out of them like the first leaves of the season. The body was long and narrow, metal and wood intertwined, 18-pounder guns (as Orphan later learned) peeking out of portholes in the side of the ship. Sailors were already on board, and were busy with preparations.

"We're going in that?" Orphan said.

"She was built in Birmingham," Verne said, not a little proudly. "Served her time in the India trade. She's got some scars–" he pointed like a tour guide– "there, there, and there, where she was hit in a pirate attack a few years ago. But she's sturdy, and fast."

"It's huge. How many people have to be in on this?"

Verne smiled. "Only the captain. A funny old bird. The crew know nothing. As far as they are concerned they're taking cargo to King's Town – that's in Xaymaco, what you may see on some maps as Jamaica – and we're coming on board simply as additional cargo."

"I thought..." Orphan stopped. It hadn't really occurred to him just how he was meant to reach the island. "Maybe a steamer..."

"A steamer!" Verne said, and he pulled hard at his beard. "Those monstrosities pollute and destroy the ocean. They have no soul!"

"I thought you wrote stories about such vessels," Orphan said.

"Some things," Verne said, "are better left in books."

Orphan fell silent. They climbed on board, trying to get out of the way of the sailors. Robur hurried ahead with Verne's luggage. Orphan had a small pack, and was carrying it himself.

The wind blew at his hair, stirring it, and he realised it was growing long. He had shaved, earlier, standing before an enormous mirror with book cover paintings covering the walls, usually depicting some sort of futuristic vehicle or brooding menace. He had almost cut himself, but now on deck, leaning over the railings, the wind felt soft against his naked cheeks, and he raised his head high and breathed in the sea air. Adventure, he thought. Pirates and secret maps and treasure islands. He felt good, then, fresh and alive, and his determination returned like a full-blown wind. He would do this and return.

He followed Verne, who followed Robur, who followed a boy no more than sixteen who moved over the deck with the gait of someone who had spent his life on water. Orphan and Verne had neighbouring cabins on the middle deck, near the prow.

Orphan remained for only a few moments. Once he had settled his meagre belongings he left and returned to the deck and a comfortable position out of the way but with a good all-around view.

Sailors were hauling up cargo, whose nature Orphan couldn't discern (it came in large wooden boxes, and seemed heavy), while others were moving all about the ship, performing tasks of which he knew nothing. It reminded him, with a sudden intensity, of the docks in London, the ships coming and going, the bustling porters and sailors and merchants and officials and, in the distance, the song of the whales.

"Welcome," a deep voice said, close behind him, "to the *Nautilus.*"

Orphan turned. A dark-skinned man with sharp, austere features, wearing a stiffly ironed uniform, stood there.

"A beautiful ship," Orphan said.

"A good ship," the man said. "I wouldn't give her up easily."

Orphan knew without being told that the captain of the *Nautilus* was speaking.

"I am Captain Dakkar," the man said, nodding. "And you must be our passenger, sir."

"It's a pleasure to meet you, captain," Orphan said. Dakkar had a lean, intense feel about him – the feel of a hunter, Orphan thought. On an impulse, he said, "My name is Orphan," and saw the captain's eyes narrow in thought.

"Orphan, then," Captain Dakkar said. "Welcome on board. You have every possibility of enjoying your journey, as long as you stay out of the way of my crew." He smiled, though his eyes didn't.

Orphan nodded. "Of course."

"Then I shall speak with you and Mr. Verne later," Dakkar said. "Please join me at my table tonight." His eyes, bright and curious, examined Orphan for a long moment. What did he see, Orphan wondered? And more importantly, how much did he know?

"Later," Dakkar said, touched two fingers to his forehead in a brief salute, and turned away. Orphan abandoned the deck and returned to his cabin. He needed some answers, and Verne, it seemed, had them all.

When he knocked on Verne's door, however, there was no answer, and as he went into his own cabin the room moved about him and for a moment he lost his balance. Then, peering out of the porthole, he realised they were moving.

The *Nautilus* was leaving port and heading to the open sea.

What can be said of this, the last ever voyage of the clipper *Nautilus*? It was a ship of misfits and rogues, of men from every nationality, their tones ranging from a Swede's pale eyes through their Indian captain's earth-dark skin, to the Nubian darkness, like a polished obsidian rock, of the second mate's muscle-twined arms. Sailors spoke and sang and cursed and took orders in a confusing babble of tongues of which Hindi, English, French, Portuguese and Zulu were only the most common. It had seemed to Orphan, after a few days, that there were, in fact, more languages than people on board the ship.

It was, he had to admit, a magnificent ship, though it was, in other terms, also an old one: steam-power was muscling in on the clipper ships, taking over their routes, speeding along from continent to continent and market to market, making the old sail-ships slowly redundant. The *Nautilus*, having sailed the trade routes all over the Everlasting Kingdom's domain, and beyond, was now a ship-for-hire, commanded by the eccentric Dakkar (the son of an Indian rajah, according to Verne's whispered comment) and run by a rag-tag crew of ex-navy sailors, ex-buccaneers, even (so said Verne) ex-pirates. Where Dakkar had picked his crew Verne didn't know. "Here and there and everywhere," he had said, spreading his arms wide, "wherever there is unrest and injustice and wherever men run foul of the law."

"Whose law?" Orphan had said, and the writer shrugged expansively and said, "On this planet, at this time, there is only one law."

"So Dakkar is not…" Orphan hesitated. "Like you…"

"Of the Bookman's party?" Verne shook his head. "Not as such. He is his own man."

What could be said about the *Nautilus*? She had a long, slim body, narrow hips and billowing sails; her decks were sturdy and sure, her bow rounded, her quarter-deck and forecastle joined, by closing in the waist, to form one continuous upper deck. The *Nautilus* carried ten mounted 18-pounder guns on the upper deck, firing through ports in the low bulwarks of the waist. The middle deck, where Orphan and Verne's cabins were also situated, carried twenty 18-pounders. It was less a trade-ship than a warship, Orphan privately thought, and he wondered what Verne – or indeed Dakkar – had in mind for her, and for him. Would they sail direct to Caliban's Island with all guns blazing? Would they attempt a stealthy landing, with a small boat lowered off the side of the ship at night? Or… But there was no point in wondering.

It was time to get some answers.

TWENTY-ONE
Gilgamesh's Journal

In few, they hurried us aboard a bark,
Bore us some leagues to sea; where they prepared
A rotten carcass of a boat, not rigg'd,
Nor tackle, sail, nor mast; the very rats
Instinctively had quit it: there they hoist us,
To cry to the sea that roar'd to us, to sigh
To the winds whose pity, sighing back again,
Did us but loving wrong.
    – William Shakespeare, *The Tempest*

Answers, however, were slow in coming. When he confronted Verne in his cabin the writer spread his arms wide and said apologetically, "There is not much that I do know. What I found out – most of it – is in my book. Surely you've read it?"

"*L'Île mystérieuse*? Well…"

"No?" Verne looked childishly hurt. "Well, there is not much there to help us, I'm afraid," he said. "It is only an account of a journey, you understand. I was never able to actually reach the island, as I mentioned to you. Oh, I have attempted to describe it, from what little obscure records I managed to locate, from drunken sailors' tales, from people who have claimed to have been shipwrecked on the island… but there are too many mysterious islands, Orphan, too many wild tales and flights of wild fancy, to really give an accurate idea of what awaits you – us – there. Do you know, they say that on another island, some-where in the Carib Sea, there is a being just like the Bookman? A brother to him, a twin who plots his own mysterious plots? They call him the Binder." Verne snorted. Orphan kept very still. "The Binder. And what does he bind, I wonder?"

Orphan, thinking of Byron's words, of the Turk's, kept very still. Where the Bookman kills, the Binder restores. But restores what?

"Tell me what you know," Orphan said.

In place of an answer the writer spread a map onto the desk. "This," he said, pointing, "is the Gulf of Mexica. This is where the mass of land we call Vespuccia ends. And this mass of water is the Carib Sea. This is the island of Xaymaco; this is the island of Hayti, and this is the place Vespucci called Cuba. They are rough, yet prosperous places, populated by a mixture of Arawak, Carib, Aztec and Europeans. They are nominally under rule of Les Lézards, but only just." He stood up and began pacing up and down the cabin, his hands clasped behind his back. "Some-where in that sea, I am sure of it, is Caliban's Island." he stopped and looked at Orphan, frustration in his eyes. "There are stories that the island... that the island moves. That it is never in the same place. I am referring to sightings, reported by ships all over the Carib Sea and beyond it. Of course, most of these can be dis-counted, ignored, the ramblings of the drunk or easily impressionable. And yet..."

"You don't know where the island is?" Orphan said, surpris-ing himself by nearly shouting. Verne grinned a little sheepishly. "There are ways to find it," he said. He gestured to a sea-chest that stood, closed and locked, by the porthole. "Before we left I arranged for some – specialised – scientific equipment to be delivered."

"Delivered from?" Orphan said, but he already knew the answer.

"Our employer," Verne said. "Don't worry, getting there this time is going to be as easy as – how do you say? – falling off a log."

As he stood alone on the deck and watched the water parting before the ship, Orphan was less than comforted by Verne's assurance. Falling off a log, he decided, was most likely painful, and possibly fatal. Not something he was quite looking forward to.

He watched the sun dipping into the sea. He looked back at the wake of the ship and the foaming water. Back on the deck, two sailors were playing cards, and another was lying asleep in a hammock.

Dinner that night was served at the captain's cabin, a simple but delicious affair of grilled fresh fish, potatoes (one of Vespucci's – or rather the lizards' – most widely appreciated gifts brought to Europe), shiny and fragrant in oil and spices, served with a good French white wine supplied by Verne. The captain didn't drink, though he raised his glass in toast to, "The King of England, may he take his rightful place once more!" which Orphan found oddly discomforting.

Two cryptic things had happened during the meal. One was said, during an otherwise ordinary, civil conversation that ranged over many topics and remained cautiously general on each. In the middle of the dessert course (xocolatl, perhaps the greatest of the gifts brought back), Verne had turned to Dakkar and said, in the middle of a discussion about giant squid, "Did you bring her?"

Dakkar had dabbed his lips with a napkin and said, "Yes," in a soft, almost imperceptible voice. Verne then began to talk about the weather.

At the end of the meal the second occurred. Verne had commended the captain's cook, and Orphan enthusiastically joined him, and the pleased captain ordered the cook to be called. When he arrived Orphan was surprised to see a tall, slim youth – no more than seventeen in his appearance – who smiled at them shyly. Verne spoke passionately of the menu, offered to hire the chef away from Dakkar, to great hilarity, and was vividly and amusingly drunk.

The boy had long, fine hair and a smooth, almost featureless face that had never, it seemed, been shaved. Before he left, as they were wishing him well, his eyes locked with Orphan's, for just a moment, and the boy nodded. It was a nod of acknowledgment, of recognition. It was the briefest of movements. Then the boy turned and walked out of the cabin.

"A really most excellent cook," Verne said, sloshing the wine in his glass just a little. Dakkar acknowledged him with a smile. He then ordered his men to leave.

"Caliban's Island," he said then, speaking to Orphan, fixing his cold dark eyes on him. "I have often tried to find it. A place of great evil, for it is the place the lizards come from. The place where they crashed to Earth." His fist thumped the table. "They must be destroyed!"

"Really, old boy," Verne said, "you need to calm down about this. You're scaring the kid."

"India shall have its independence!" Dakkar said.

"No doubt," Verne said.

The conversation concluded soon after that. If he had learned something from it, Orphan thought, it was only that neither Dakkar nor Verne knew anything about the island. They didn't even know how to find it.

Yet Verne had instruments. A chest full of them in his cabin. He did not want to think of what they might be. They were the tools of the Bookman, just as Orphan was, a blunted tool made to strike at the Bookman's enemies.

Orphan climbed onto the deck and stood there, looking at the night. For a moment he thought he heard a whale's call in the distance. There were a lot of stars.

He swore again to himself that he would return. That he would save Lucy. And as for the Bookman…

Then he laughed, because he knew he was being absurd, and he joined a game of cards with three sailors and after an hour won a handful of coins, half of them unknown to him.

Days on the ship spent under bright clear skies… Flying fish pursued the *Nautilus*, silver fins flashing in the sunlight as they arced through the air. In the second week a pod of dolphins accompanied them from a distance. Occasionally, far away, he saw the disappearing hump of a giant whale.

He still had Tom Thumb's gun, and he practised shooting on the deck with some of the sailors. He played cards, and lost more than he'd won. Then, a week into the voyage, he returned to his cabin and found a book waiting for him on the bed.

He sat down and looked at it curiously. It was an old, weather-beaten notebook, bound in peeling leather. He lifted it in his hands, traced damage on the cover, opened it. Old, brittle paper. Foxed pages and water damage. Many of the pages were torn.

The handwriting inside jolted him.

Jagged and cramped, packed tight into the page. It was the handwriting of his friend.

It was Gilgamesh's.

He closed the book and held it for a long moment, his eyes staring into nothing, thinking of his dead friend. Where had this come from?

Then he noticed the note that must have fallen to the floor as he entered the cabin, and he picked it up and read it. *I have tried to rely on primary sources as much as possible*, it said. *I found this journal fifteen years ago, in a junk shop in Marseille. Perhaps you would find it interesting. How true its account is I cannot say.* The note was signed by Verne.

Orphan lifted up the journal and felt suddenly very far from home. He looked out of the porthole at the endless sea beyond, and thought back. Gilgamesh had been... a friend, and a part of his life. And now he was dead, and here was his journal, as old as a drowned ship.

He took a deep breath to calm himself, and blinked several times. Then he opened the journal – really, a small collection of leaves, incomplete and beguiling – and began to read.

A clear, calm day. The sea lies flat. We have left the
Aztecs last night with a mutual exchange of many gifts,
dancing and singing and drinking. I shall miss [unread-
able], her smooth dark skin and her smile in the

darkness... Everyone looks downcast today, despite the
weather – we are all suffering last night's excess. Our
course is leisurely, for now, and we plan to stop at one of
the islands before entering the Atlantic and further stock
up with provisions. A successful trip, and Amerigo is
happy and carefree, almost a new man after the trials of
the journey here.

...

An amazing land! I have never thought to see such wild
beauties as the forests of this new land, its strange animals
and unknown flora. My notebook is filling up fast with
lines of poetry, which I will attempt to structure into an
epic narrative poem upon our return. I lie in a hammock
on the deck and dream of glory, success following publication, a long life with many women, children and
grand-children, at last, rich and old and famous, burial in
Westminster Abbey... I smile even as I write this. But it is
good to daydream. Our journey is nearly at an end, and
has been successful beyond all expectations. We will be
welcomed like heroes. I wonder – have we opened up this
new world for good? Will the navy sail here now, to take
control of this wild continent and its wilder islands, to establish trade missions and new colonies for the glory of
Britannia? No doubt. Yet the people of these lands have
civilisations of their own, some quite powerful and old. I
do not take the Aztecs lightly, nor the others, the [unread-
able] who are fierce warriors. Tomorrow we shall stop at
Xaymaco, then home.

...

The island is like a mirage, a tropical paradise unlike anything I have seen in my travels. Several of the crew
disappeared today, seduced by this place, and I doubt
they will be back. Amerigo is furious, but there is little he
can do. Our priority now is to return and bring back the
fortune we have found. The cook brewed xocolatl today
– we have all become overly fond – nay, dependent! – on

it, and I can only imagine what the response will be like back home! We are all going to be rich beyond our wildest dreams.

...

Open sea again. The weather is turning, wind building up and slowing us down. There is a storm on the horizon, coming near. Something has been troubling me, something in Amerigo's behaviour...

...

I am filled with foreboding. The nature of the [unreadable] I have found out piecemeal, first from the Mexicas and later from the Arawak, although the stories are pervasive all around the Carib Sea. They concern an island which has no name, and they are told in whispers, though what they describe must have happened – if it happened at all – beyond any living man's memory. This is the way I heard the story for the first time, from a priest of Atlacamani, the goddess of storms. It tells of an epic journey – not unlike our own, perhaps – of a people called the Toltec, who lived in this part of the world and had built a flotilla of ships to go and explore the ocean, to find new lands and bring back their treasures. The fleet was not gone far (which I take to mean it was still in the Carib Sea or only recently outside it) when night – the priest was very specific on this, though I do wonder if it isn't some sort of an allegory – became day. Brightness washed the decks of the ships and the wind stood still, so that the ships found themselves stranded in mid-sea, and there was much panic. Not only light came from the skies, but heat, and as the sailors raised their heads to the heavens they saw a shooting star, growing in the skies as it plummeted down to earth. It grew so large and so bright that they had to shield their eyes against it. Many died that night. The star fell down and – by luck, or divine intervention – landed not in open water but on a small, remote island that was [unreadable[from the ships. The resultant explosion blinded many of the men, and many died later, in months and years to come, of blisters and growths and sickness. The ships did not attempt to approach the island. The flotilla turned and sailed back from that place, which is known to this day only as the Place of Sickness. This is what the priest told me, and it is an old tale, more of a ghost story to be told around the fire than any exact account of a long-gone event. Yet I wonder... and so, I fear, does Amerigo.

...

I should perhaps record the other stories, too, though I am wary of them. Little-told tales, heard as jokes or whispers from the Arawak. It seemed strange to me, indeed, that the ancient Toltec – or their inheritors the Mexica – never attempted to sail to the island, to examine it, perhaps to find traces of that fallen star. Yet the people of the islands were not so unified in fear, and I have heard tell of fisher folk and others who had, by accident or design, found themselves near this nameless island. Some have never returned. And some have come back sick, or dying, or insane, with tales no one would believe. Some even say the island moves, that it is rarely at the same place twice, and that it is haunted by a malevolent ghost. All nonsense, no doubt, yet Amerigo, who has heard the stories as much as I have, is enchanted by them. "It must have been a meteor," he said to me, "of an unusual size." His eyes became dreamy then and he said, "Would it not be a perfect ending to our voyage, [unreadable], that, after we have explored this world, we can perhaps explore the stones of another?"

I, too, was taken in by his enthusiasm, but only momentarily. Though the weather is now clear again and our speed stays at peak, Amerigo is suggesting a detour. He is determined to explore this island. I am fearful, but do not know why.

...

Before leaving Xaymaco, Amerigo has taken on board a
young Arawak man who claims to have seen the island.
We are goin [unreadable] direction, though there is not
yet a trace of it. The sailors are treating this as merely another excursion, and I wish I could share their lightness
of heart. Yet, though I am wary, I too am compelled to
this island: I too want to discover this possible visitor
from another world and learn of the truth in the old stories of the Mexica. The aura of mystery surrounds this
island, and it is more attractive and irresistible than anything we have yet discovered. Tomorrow...

...

We have found it! Even as I write the island lies before
us, wrapped in clouds, cloaked in dusk. It is beautiful,
though the eyes cannot penetrate far beyond the shore.
Everyone on board is quiet as the island exerts a not-in-
considerable influence over us. It is at the same time
inviting and brooding, peaceful – yet with an underlying,
almost sinister feeling. I must know what lies beyond the
clouds. I now regard those trifling lines of poetry I had
written as just that – trifling. My masterpiece will be this
island, its mysteries explored in verse so beautiful as to
make the ladies weep. The landing party, with Amerigo
and myself, will go at first light tomorrow. I–

It was the end of the writing. There had been more pages, before and after, but they had been removed at some time in the
past. Orphan held the journal close to his chest, almost hugging
it, and curled up on the narrow bed. He thought of all the people
he had lost, from the parents he never knew, to Gilgamesh, to
Lucy, and with each one the pain came harsher and more threatening, like tropical lightning. I can't bring back my parents, he
thought, and I can't bring back Gilgamesh. But Lucy... and he
thought of her laugh, and the way she had looked at him, and
he fell asleep at last, still clutching the ancient journal to his chest.

TWENTY-TWO
Pirates

Lastly, the crime of piracy, or robbery and depredation upon the high seas, is an offence against the universal law of society; a pirate being, according to Sir Edward Coke, hostis humani generis. *As therefore he has renounced all the benefits of society and government, and has reduced himself afresh to the same state of nature, by declaring war against all mankind, all mankind must declare war against him.*
   – William Blackstone, *Commentaries on the Laws of England*

It was a full two weeks later when the *Nautilus* entered the region of water known as the Carib Sea. A storm was building up on the horizon, where the setting sun cast blood-red and stained-yellow hues across a cloudscape of rain. Lightning flashed amidst the distant build-up, sizzling silver spears reaching from the heavens to the sea. The air felt hot and clammy, and the sailors had a tense, almost haunted look in their eyes.

The gunners manned their positions in full shift. The crew was silent, and the vessel had the feel of a ghost ship sailing other, ethereal seas. A single word caught Orphan's attention, pushing away all others, a whisper caught in the stillness of the charged air: *pirates!*

"What does it mean?" Orphan whispered to Verne.

The Frenchman looked tense. "This storm," he said. He looked like he would have said more, but at that moment a shout rose on the deck, and one of the guns discharged, the ball arcing over the water ahead, landing with an explosion of foam in the dark water below.

"Hold your fire!" came the shouted order of Captain Dakkar, cold and sharp like a sliver of ice. He stood at the prow, looking intently through his eyepiece at the horizon. Verne and Orphan had come and stood behind him. Orphan tried, but could see little in the distance. It was turning dark, the sea illuminated only by the flash of the incessant lightning.

"What is it?" Verne said, softly, to Dakkar, echoing Orphan. The captain folded his eyepiece and turned to him, tension etched into the lines on his face. "Perhaps nothing," he said.

At that moment thunder filled the air, close and unexpected, and seemed to go on forever. Rain burst out of the sky and fell on the *Nautilus*, making the deck slick and mirror-like. A wind rose and pummelled the ship.

The storm had arrived.

And with it, with a scream that rose from the lookout above and spread like water amongst the crew, were pirates.

Orphan, holding on to a rope to keep himself steady, peered out through raindrops and saw the pirate ship.

It was a dark shadow, moving across a deceptively calm sea towards them, almost gliding, its movement as smooth and uninterrupted as that of a heated knife. It sailed towards them, and its sails were black.

The pirate ship was a thing of darkness and dread. At the prow a giant, chalk-white head looked forward, severed at the neck, its nose a malevolent red. A giant, leering smile was painted on its face.

"The *Joker*!" called the lookout, and Dakkar had to shout at the crew to be quiet. They were frightened, Orphan thought. They recognised and dreaded the name.

He felt only a ball of excitement, taut and hard, forming in his stomach. Dread, exhilaration – he felt awake, alive, his senses growing to perceive minute details, each crack and line in the clown's wooden face that sailed towards them.

"Hold your fire!"

The men were tense.

"On my command – shoot!"

But the first shot came from the *Joker*.

Orphan saw the ball before he heard the discharge. The ball whistled as it flew towards them. It smashed into the side of the ship, and Dakkar, momentarily losing his balance, shouted hoarsely for the men to fire.

A volley of shots emerged from the 18-pounders and flew towards the enemy ship. Several hit, and a cheer rose, only to be silenced almost immediately.

The pirate ship was closing in fast.

It was close enough now for Orphan to see her name, tattooed to her side like a scar. The *Joker*. And the hideous clown face, the ship's mascot, grinned and leered at the *Nautilus* incessantly as if maddened.

"Fire!"

The guns fired, the *Joker* was hit, and continued to come. It was firing back, and the balls whispered overhead and sent exploding plumes of water high into the air when they missed, blood and wood where they hit.

"Fire!"

Then the *Joker* was close, close enough to reach out, almost to touch the dark figures that could now be seen on its deck, moving with silent determination.

The two ships touched, side to side.

The pirates swooped on the *Nautilus*. They sailed overboard with long thick hemp ropes and landed with cutlasses at the ready. They were an ugly, ferocious bunch, half-savage men with maps of scars over their naked torsos.

Lightning struck, and struck again, and again, and the sky was full of electric light, and illuminated the pirates' savage faces.

The lightning! Orphan thought. It was coming from the pirate ship. Everything was illuminated now, the air humming with electricity, and he could see its source, and his excitement (which had not yet abated) began at last turning into fear.

Rising from the top of the central mast of the *Joker*, a bright metallic ball shone like a moon as it was hit, over and over again, by lightning.

Then he had to turn his gaze, and draw his gun, because pirates were now swarming the deck. He shot, once, and a man fell down. Then he had to duck, and someone kicked him and connected with the side of his head, and he fell back.

The man was almost on him when Orphan shot him through the chest.

Then he pushed the fallen man off him and stood up. The deck was full of fighting men. Bodies littered the ground and their blood was washed away by the rain and the wind. The deck was red and shone in the light. It was sleek with blood.

He scanned through the faces as the lightning struck ferociously down. He could see no trace of Verne, or Robur. His eyes stopped on the sight of the young ship's cook, who seemed an island of calm in the midst of battle. He was fighting three men at once, and was unarmed, while they had swords, and one was reaching for a gun. The boy's leg shot out and took one pirate in the face, breaking his nose. He whirled round then, snatched the gun from the other pirate, shot the third in the same movement, then returned the gun in an arc that took in the remaining pirate's head and connected with it.

He looked up and saw Orphan. Again, there was that nod of recognition, as if they somehow knew each other. He made a movement with his hand that said, stay low. Then he returned to the fight.

Thunder shook the deck. Orphan ducked against a threatening cutlass, slipped, fell on his back, shot. If he had hit – or who – he didn't know. He remained down and realised no one was paying him much attention. Many other bodies already littered the deck.

Thunder boomed again, the sound seeming to emerge from everywhere at once, a shockwave of noise sweeping the deck, and the lightning struck again. It illuminated the deck of the *Joker* and, as Orphan raised his head, what he saw made him freeze as if he had been struck.

Standing majestically on the forward-deck of the *Joker* was a lizard.

It was a royal lizard, a Les Lézard, and for a long moment Orphan couldn't think, could not understand what he was seeing. Then lightning flashed again and he saw the figure in stark relief, and the sailors on the deck, seeing it too, seemed to lose heart in the fight, to be pushed back by the pirates as if the appearance of the lizard signalled the end of the fight, and of the *Nautilus* itself.

Feet passed closed to Orphan and someone kicked him in the ribs and made him shout. A grinning, leering face loomed above him, and with it a gun that was pointed at his heart. He tried to roll, then heard a shot go off.

When he opened his eyes he was still alive, and instead of the pirate the face he saw was that of the boy-cook. "Stay down!" he said, and then he himself crouched down beside Orphan, and pointed ahead. "Wyvern," he said, his voice soft and emotionless.

The lizard had stepped onto the *Nautilus'* deck. He was tall and dignified-looking. He was white, decorated in pale bands, and one of his eyes was missing. He wore a black eye-patch; his other eye was red, like dying fire. He wore loose, colourful clothes, with a cutlass and a gun on either side of the body, and his tongue darted and tasted the air. He seemed to smile...

He stepped forward and the battle surged away from him. Then Orphan noticed it. The lizard wore large metal gloves, and they were pointed forward now, towards the battle, and his digits were spread evenly, and shone silver.

"Stay down!" the boy-cook hissed.

"Who is that?" Orphan hissed back. The white lizard stepped slowly forward, arms raised, digits pointing.

"Captain Wyvern."

Lightning struck.

It struck the ball on the top of the mast but, this time, did not stop there. Down the lightning went, through wires that fell down the sails and reached the deck, and continued... overboard, over to the *Nautilus*, where they appeared again and rose into Captain Wyvern's hands.

Lightning flashed.

Bars of hissing, sizzling electricity shot out of Captain Wyvern's hands and hit the men fighting on the deck. Here, he pointed, and here, and here, and with each imperceptible movement lightning fell from the tips of his digits and hit one of the *Nautilus'* sailors.

Lightning flashed, again and again and again.

The men who were hit screamed, but only briefly.

The air on the deck filled with the smell of cooking meat.

Strangely, horrifyingly, even as he was gagging, Orphan's stomach made a growling noise, his body reacting to the smell the way it would to any cooking meat: with hunger. Then a wave hit the ship and the deck moved, and one of the corpses came rolling down and almost crashed into him and he screamed, and was sick all over himself.

The boiled face of the corpse looked at him with the glazed look of a mounted fish.

It was Robur.

Slowly, with the same serene expression on his face, the young cook stood up with his hands raised. He kicked Orphan, not hard. Orphan rose with his hands up and tried not to retch.

There was movement behind him. He half-turned, saw the face of a pirate, sunburnt skin livid with blood, broken teeth exposed in an animalistic grin, and something raised to strike…

He tried to escape but his movements were slow and sluggish, as if he was drowning in water, and then something connected with the back of his head and pain shot through him and brought with it darkness.

TWENTY-THREE
Mr. Spoons

I steer'd from sound to sound, as I sail'd, as I sail'd,
I steer'd from sound to sound, as I sail'd,
I steer'd from sound to sound and many ships I found
And most of them I burned, as I sail'd.
  – Captain Kidd

Orphan came to on the *Joker*'s deck. He was lying on his side, his head resting painfully against the hard boards. His hands were tied behind his back.

Rain was falling, and his clothes were soaked. The rain got into his eyes and ran down his face. He blinked, and the world came into sharp focus and he cried out involuntarily.

Ahead of him, the *Nautilus* burned.

It was growing smaller in the distance. The *Joker* must have turned around, he thought. He was lying by the stern. He watched, helpless, as the sails flamed and billowed in the wind of the storm. The flames licked the sides of the ship. The masts burned like beacons.

Orphan turned his head away. Beside him on the deck, he saw, were others, a half-dozen sailors from the *Nautilus* that he vaguely recognised. Like him, they were tied up. Like him, too, they were still alive.

He saw no sign of Verne or Dakkar. No sign of the cook, either, when he thought about it. He wondered what the pirates had in store for them. The rain worked its way into his clothes and wrapped cold hands around his belly. He shivered and looked back at the burning *Nautilus*.

The ship was falling into the sea. He wondered what had happened to Verne. Then he thought, Does it matter? He was alone again, and in trouble.

No change there, then.

The lightning, he noticed, had abated. The *Joker* was sailing away, growing faster, and the storm seemed to be receding, the dark clouds beginning to edge away from each other like a crowd of people at the scene of an accident. He tried to turn, moving his legs, and his hands scraped against the floor. He managed a half-turn. There was a dark pool where his head had been.

"Well, well," a rich, cultured voice said. "Look what the cat dragged in."

It was Captain Wyvern. The pirate stood facing the group of captured sailors, his single eye shining red. His tongue snaked out in a hiss of amusement. He stepped forward. He was no longer wearing the lightning gloves. Beside him stood a bulky, mean-looking pirate: his head was a smooth shaved dome, and a scar ran all the way down his bare chest, as if someone had once tried to cut him open and nearly succeeded. He wore hooped earrings in both ears and held a cutlass in his hand as if it were a toy. His eyes moved slowly over the sailors with a strange, serene smile that scared Orphan more than anything else about the situation.

"Eeny, meeny, miny, moe," Captain Wyvern said, almost singing, raising his pistol and pointing it at each bound sailor in turn, "catch a sailor by the toe." He continued to move the pistol from man to man. Orphan watched the horror on the sailors' faces, and felt fear clawing at his own. The bald pirate continued to smile.

"Please!" one of the sailors, a burly, red-headed man, said.

"If he squeals then let him go," Captain Wyvern said, more softly now, ignoring him. "Eeny, meeny, miny... moe."

The shot was a deafening thunder, a remnant of the storm. The ball from the pirate's pistol hit the sailor closest to Orphan, a short, badly wounded man whose head exploded with the impact, spraying Orphan with blood and brain.

Orphan screamed.

The bald pirate said something quietly to Captain Wyvern. The lizard nodded and seemed to smile. "Gentlemen!" he cried, lifting his hands as though wanting to embrace the bound sailors. "Welcome to the *Joker*!"

He nodded, as if making a note to himself of their response, and said, "This is Mr. Spoons."

The bald pirate took one step forward. Again, he scanned the row of captive sailors. Again, he wore that strange, detached smile.

"Mr. Spoons is my boatswain," Captain Wyvern said. "I will now leave you in Mr. Spoons' capable hands. He is here to ask you a very simple question, gentlemen. Sink or swim. Live or die. Turn pirate, or turn fish-bait. No," he said, raising his hand to silence one of the sailors, "don't answer me. It is Mr. Spoons that you answer to now. Mr. Spoons – they're yours." And he turned and marched away from them, leaving the men alone with the bald pirate.

"Thank you, captain," Mr. Spoons said. He had a surprisingly high, though rather pleasant, voice. "You," he said, and pointed at a man in the middle of the group. "What is your name?"

"Sizemore, sir. Jason Sizemore."

"And your role on the *Nautilus*, Mr. Sizemore?" Mr. Spoons said.

"Ship's carpenter, sir."

"Like the good shepherd," Mr. Spoons said, and smiled pleasantly, and shot him in the face. The sailors on either side of him screamed. Orphan, this time, held in his own reaction. "I wonder if, like the good shepherd, you too could come back from the dead."

He turned and scanned their faces. "You," he said, pointing to an Indian-looking man tied up between Orphan and the dead Sizemore. "What's your name?"

"Mohsan Jaffery," the man said. He did not call Mr. Spoons sir. "Engineer and gunner."

"You've caused us a bit of damage," Mr. Spoons said.

"I hope so," Mohsan Jaffery said.

Mr. Spoons smiled. He approached Jaffery and knelt down beside him. His hand reached to his side and returned with a large, ugly-looking knife. The knife descended. Orphan tensed against his bonds.

"Stand up," Mr. Spoons said. He had merely untied Jaffery's knots. "Pick a man."

"Sir?" Jaffery looked at Mr. Spoons' face and looked hurriedly away. Confused, he looked at the captive sailors. They looked back at him, some pleading silently, some stoic, one or two with anger on their faces. "Him," Mohsan Jaffery said, and pointed at a large, short-haired man whose face had suddenly drained of blood.

"Why?"

"He is a good man. He is a gunner too. He speaks three languages fluently. Sir, he is a good sailor."

"What's your name, son?" Mr. Spoons said.

The man looked up at him slowly. "Does it matter?" he said. Mr. Spoons smiled.

"Will you go on the account, or die?"

The man smiled back. It was only a little smile, but it was there when he said, "Only as long as it would take me to kill you."

Mr. Spoons continued to smile, and he nodded, as if he were an MP agreeing with one's colleague in parliament.

Then he said, "Takanobu! Garcia! Come here!"

Two pirates hurried over from where a group was fixing one side of the ship.

"Yes, Mr. Spoons."

"Tie up his legs with rope. A long rope."

"Yes, Mr. Spoons."

They hurried away and returned with a coil of thick rope.

They tied one end of the rope in a loop and tightened it around the man's legs.

"Drop him overboard."

"No!"

It was Orphan who shouted, realisation coming a second after the event. He clamped his teeth, expecting at any moment a bullet in the head, or something more dreadful and more prolonged. But Mr. Spoons merely looked at him, his head tilted to one side in what was perhaps amusement, perhaps interest. The pirates, meanwhile, followed Mr. Spoons' orders, and they lifted the struggling man effortlessly, carried him, and threw him overboard.

There was a shout and a loud splash. Mr. Spoons looked away from Orphan, towards the stern. "Take him around to the bow and back. Let him feel the keel. If he's still alive when you haul him up, put him on the account."

"Yes, sir."

The two began to move away, dragging the rope – and the man's body – behind them.

Mr. Spoons slapped Mohsan Jaffery's back. Jaffery looked horrified.

"Störtebeker, Zhi!"

The two pirates who approached swaggered as they walked. They were large, fierce-looking men. Orphan thought he recognised one of them, animalistic face caught at a glance, and a cutlass descending...

"Take Mr. Jaffery here to the hold until we swear them in."

"Yes, Mr. Spoons."

They hurried off, carrying the smaller Jaffery between them. Mohsan Jaffery didn't look back.

What had saved him – from the keel-hauling and the cat-o'-nine-tails and that final, desperate moment when one of the men, whose name he didn't even know, was forced to walk along a wooden plank that extended over the water, and jump – was the appearance, unexpected and ominous, of the *Nautilus'* boy-cook.

He was not tied up. He had approached Mr. Spoons calmly and spoke briefly into his ear. Mr. Spoons nodded and then approached Orphan, who he had so far ignored, seemingly intent on leaving him till last, a thought Orphan did not find comforting.

"You," he said. "What will it be? Are you willing to serve under Captain Wyvern? My new friend here tells me you're not much of a sailor, but that you're handy in a fight and good at cards. You go on the account, there'll be plenty of both for you."

Orphan looked at the boy-cook, who nodded to him, briefly. A serene expression. Could he trust him?

Did he have a choice?

"I'll serve," he said.

Mr. Spoons nodded. "I thought so," he said. He knelt down and pulled out his knife.

The knife came very close to Orphan's face. The sharp point of the knife almost touched his eye. Mr. Spoons moved the knife slowly, lowering the flat of the blade so its warm metal touched Orphan's skin. "Next time," Mr. Spoons said, "when I give an order, the only thing you're going to say is 'Yes, Mr. Spoons'."

Orphan tried to breathe as little as he could, and not to move his mouth more than was necessary. The words, therefore, came out of him in a near-whisper.

"Yes, Mr. Spoons."

Mr. Spoons raised the knife (Orphan almost sighed with relief) then lowered it again. Then, with a quick, careful movement, he slashed Orphan's bare left shoulder.

Orphan held on to a scream. He dared do nothing other than blink. His face burned.

"What's your name?" Mr. Spoons said.

"My name is Orphan."

"Remember what I said, Orphan."

"Yes, Mr. Spoons."

The pirate untied him.

Orphan stood up. By the side of the ship Takanobu and Garcia were hauling up the body of the man they had thrown overboard. His face could hardly be recognised, and his clothes were now tattered and bloodied.

"Is he alive?" Mr. Spoons said.

Takanobu checked the body for a pulse and shook his head.

"Then throw him back in and keep the rope."

He turned to the boy-cook. "Aramis, take your friend to the hold to be with the rest of them."

The cook – Aramis? Orphan thought, and realised he hadn't known his name – nodded and said, "Yes, Mr. Spoons," and then motioned for Orphan to follow him.

"Who are you?" Orphan demanded in a whisper as soon as he thought they were out of earshot.

The boy-cook smiled faintly. "A friend? Your only hope? An interested party?" The face never changed.

"Which is it?" Orphan said.

The boy-cook said, "None, or all of the above."

Orphan sighed. He was too tired for riddles, and he felt the last of his energy deserting him. He hardly noticed Aramis helping him stand, supporting him, and leading him at last to the hold, where the few survivors from the *Nautilus* were sat huddled together in what appeared to be a sort of enormous animal cage.

Orphan was only vaguely aware as Aramis opened the door and led him inside. He collapsed on a pile of straw.

The door closed behind Aramis, and the key turned in the lock.

The straw was soft. The pain in his face became a numbness. It was soft, dry, comfortable. He was the most comfortable he had ever been. His eyes were closed and he was floating in darkness, the motion of unseen waves lulling him to sleep, making him feel safe… He tried to stay awake for just a moment longer, to savour that feeling, to know that he was, for the moment, safe, and allowed the luxury of sleep.

Then sleep came, and he embraced it. For a long time no dreams came. When they did, at last, appear, they were full of Lucy.

TWENTY-FOUR
Wyvern

Ships sailorless lay rotting on the sea,
And their masts fell down piecemeal: as they dropp'd
They slept on the abyss without a surge –
The waves were dead; the tides were in their grave.
  – Lord Byron, "Darkness"

They were sworn in with the coming of night. It was a full day since the *Nautilus* had been attacked and destroyed. Lying in the cage in the hull of the ship (stinking of a thousand flavours of animal and spilled rum) Orphan thought about Verne and hoped that, somehow, he was still alive. He thought of the fat writer's corpse making its way down to the bottom of the ocean, and thought, He didn't deserve this.

But there were too many other things to occupy Orphan's mind, once sleep had fled and he waited down below with the others. It all came down to survival, now. He was a long way from the bookshop on Cecil Court, a long way from everything he knew. What did he know about ships, beyond their loading? He was surprised Spoons didn't just throw him overboard as he did with some of the others. But he was here. He was alive. Still.

And now, with the coming of night and a multitude of bright

hard stars overheard like a pirate's hoard, he stood on the deck with the others, and Captain Wyvern, like a scaly monster from some long-forgotten fairy tale, his one eye glinting like a ruby in the lantern light, read them the pirates' oath.

His voice was clear and strong. He stood near the central mast, the boatswain on his right at a respectable distance, and he faced the captives the way a father would stand before his unruly children. The pirates of the *Joker* surrounded them in a circle. Their eyes glinted in the light. The air smelled of smoke and unwashed bodies.

Captain Wyvern spoke the words, and Orphan and the others repeated them, article by article. This was the pirates' oath:

Article One – Every man shall obey civil command; the captain shall have one full share and a half in all prizes. Each man of the company will have an equal share of all prizes.

Article Two – If any man shall offer to run away, or keep any secret from the company, he shall be marooned with one bottle of powder, one bottle of water, one small arm, and some shot.

Article Three – If any man shall steal any thing in the company, or game, to the value of a piece of eight, he shall be marooned or shot.

Article Four – If at any time we should meet at another marooner (that is, pirate) that man shall sign his articles without consent of our company, shall suffer such punishment as the captain and company shall think fit.

Article Five – That man that shall strike another, whilst these articles are in force, shall receive Moses's Law (that is forty stripes lacking one) on the bare back.

Article Six – That man that shall snap his arms, or smoke tobacco in the hold, without cap to his pipe, or carry a candle lighted without lantern, shall suffer the same punishment as in the former article.

Article Seven – That man that shall not keep his arms clean, fit for an engagement, or neglect his business, shall be cut off from his share, and suffer such other punishment as the captain and company shall think fit.

Article Eight – If any man shall lose a joint in time of engagement, shall have four hundred pieces of eight: if a limb, eight hundred.

Article Nine – If at any time you meet with a prudent woman, that man that offers to meddle with her, without her consent, shall suffer death.

The captain's voice carried the words, hard and clear across the warm night air. Orphan, repeating them, felt himself a member of a religious congregation, a part of a new, strange tribe, a world exclusively of men.

And lizards?

"We are a society without division," Captain Wyvern said when they had finished reciting the oath. "Where who you are, who you have been, no longer matter. It is a harsh society, a difficult, dangerous life – but it is just, too. It is equal. I," he said, and his tongue hissed out and tasted the sea air, "who could have been a governor, perhaps, or an idler in any number of the great cities of the empire, I have chosen this life, amongst you, so I could be free. This is what I offer you now. A freedom. A freedom from oppression, a freedom from the rules that exist to govern a society into civility, which is the ruling class's name for keeping the hordes in their place. I did not want civility. I did not want the glory of running the world, of becoming a bureaucrat, of administering the affairs of men for the benefit of my people. I wanted freedom, as harsh and dangerous and short-lived as it may be. This is the choice I give you today. The choice to be free. Will you take it?"

"Yes," the engineer, Mohsan Jaffery, said. His eyes shone in the lantern light.

"Yes," Orphan said, softly, and with him the rest, their voices coming louder now, surer. There is no other way, Orphan thought. And the thought made him suddenly happy. To abscond responsibility, to forget the affairs of the great, which need not concern him. To sail the sea, living by wits and strength, in a society where all are equal, and all have an equal share…

"Yes!" the sailors of the *Nautilus* all cried, and the ring of pirates around them grinned and joined the shout, until the whole of the *Joker* seemed to shake with their cries and the stamping of their feet.

"Then swear!" Captain Wyvern said, and he nodded to the boatswain, who nodded in turn and approached the men, a long, straight knife in his hand.

"Put your right hand forward," Mr. Spoons said.

They did.

He came to them, Orphan first. The knife touched the skin of his open palm with a gentleness that surprised him. Then the knife moved, slashed, and blood flowered in his palm.

Mr. Spoons nodded, and moved to the next man. Silence, expectant and heavy, lay on the ship. Soon, all the survivors had a cut in their palm.

Mr. Spoons barked an order, and two sailors hurried away and came back with a barrel filled with sea water.

He motioned for the men to come close. They gathered around the barrel. Looking into the water, Orphan saw his own reflection, blurred and ghostly. Mr. Spoons put the knife in the palm of his own hand and made a fist. He pulled the knife out, grinning, and plunged his bleeding hand into the barrel.

The others followed him.

The water stung, but not too badly. It was, in fact, almost soothing. Their blood mixed in the water, making their reflection appear as through a dirty lens. Then the captain himself approached, and stood beside his boatswain, and he did something that Orphan had never seen before, and so shocked him that he almost called out loud: Wyvern's eyes blinked and grew small, his face muscles contracted, and suddenly, shockingly, a long squirt of blood erupted from his eyes (the area around them, Orphan later found out) and shot into the barrel of sea water, to mix with all the others.

The pirates cheered, and the silence was broken. Mr. Spoons made a movement with his head, and the two pirates who brought the barrel over now lifted it carefully, carried it to the railing, and emptied its bloodied content overboard. The liquid fell in an arc. There was the sound of it hitting the sea.

"Welcome," Captain Wyvern said, and he raised his hands in the air, "to the *Joker*!"

And so it was that Orphan went on the account, and became a pirate.

There was a party that night, as the ship drifted across the warm Carib Sea; lanterns were hung high and on the open deck Aramis, formerly the boy-cook, formerly, also, from the *Nautilus*, was cooking fish on a bed of coals. Orphan sat on a coil of rope and played cards with Takanobu and Jaffery (who still looked a little shocked to be alive). Orphan swigged from a bottle of rum that burned his throat. He passed it back to Takanobu. He had wounds in his hand and on his shoulder, but they were shallow, and would heal. They were bound now, with alcohol-soaked cloth.

Orphan had two pairs, kings high. He raised, and Takanobu, studying him for a long time, finally called. Jaffery had already folded that round.

Takanobu had only one pair, jacks. As was customary on card decks, the aristocracy, jacks and over, were lizards, drawn in profile.

Takanobu shrugged and conceded the hand. Orphan collected his winnings, an assortment of odd coins.

Somewhere near the prow guitar music started, and it was joined moments later by a fiddle. The music rose over the deck. Orphan threw in his hand and stood up.

"Boy," said a voice behind him. He turned and saw Mr. Spoons.

"Sir?"

"Captain wants to see you."

He followed the pirate. Into the hold, through the dark corridor, finally, into the captain's private quarters. As he had left the deck he felt Aramis' gaze follow him. He wondered, then, how the man had managed – so effortlessly, it seemed – to become one of the *Joker*'s crew. From one ship to the other, he moved with the same unchanged expression, the same easy grace. He didn't trust him, but then, he was a pirate now. Trust did not figure into it, not any more.

The captain's room turned out to be wide and spacious. Along one wall ran a long bar of dark mahogany, and two armchairs and a low table – like refugees from a far away private club – stood beside it. In another corner of the room stood a row of machines. Orphan recognised an Edison player and a Tesla set. Clearly, the pirate was not bereft of technology. Orphan wondered which ship had been plundered – and how many people had died – to furnish him with the devices.

Captain Wyvern was standing with his back to him, gazing out through the open porthole onto the dark sea.

Orphan and Mr. Spoons waited. Finally, not turning, the captain said, "Thank you," and Mr. Spoons nodded his head (though the captain couldn't see it) and departed, closing the doors behind him like a majordomo.

Orphan waited. Wyvern's tail was long and thick and muscled, looking more like a weapon than a body part. It looked like a cat-o'-nine-tails.

When he turned to him at last (the tail whooshing to the side) he glared at Orphan with his one eye. He looks like a pirate, Orphan thought, and wondered how he had lost his eye. He was dressed in fresh clothing, rough but clean, thousands of miles away from his elegant cousins back home.

"Orphan," Captain Wyvern said. He seemed to be tasting the name. His tongue hissed out, as quick as a whip.

"Sir."

The captain came towards him. He rested his hands on Orphan's shoulders and peered into his face. Close enough to Orphan so that he could smell his breath, which was – surprising Orphan – fresh and somewhat minty.

"Who are you, boy?"

"I..." He suddenly didn't know what to say, how to answer.

"You're no sailor. What were you doing on the *Nautilus*?"

"Passenger, sir."

Wyvern slapped him. It had such force that it knocked Orphan aside. "You and a fat man, I was told. Passengers to Xaymaco. Yes... but why was the *Nautilus*, of all ships, coming here in the first place? Do you know what the cargo was, that we liberated?"

"I was not aware of the exact nature of the cargo, no, sir."

Wyvern slapped him again. He had long, sharp claws that caught in Orphan's skin and drew blood. "It was nothing!" he roared. "It was old rubbish, packaged for weight, nothing more. Why were you on the *Nautilus*, boy? What was important enough to get Prince Dakkar to give up his ship?"

"Prince Dakkar, sir?"

"The captain of the *Nautilus*, boy. The man who would be King, if only he had his way, so he could unite India against us Johnny Lizards and rule it himself. He disappeared, did you know that? And with him your mysterious fat man."

"Sir?" He was not trying to be obtuse. He just thought he'd better speak as little as possible. Wyvern took a step back from him and grinned.

"Sit down," Wyvern said. He motioned to a comfortable-looking armchair. Orphan hesitated.

"Sit down, boy!"

He sat down.

The lizard captain turned and regarded Orphan. His single eye seemed redder than before, an old, dying star in a weathered, alien face.

"A few days ago," Wyvern said, his voice soft and quiet – so low that Orphan struggled to hear him – "I received a message, by Tesla waves."

"Sir?"

"It came from the *Nautilus*," Wyvern said. "Giving me their location – and heading."

Orphan looked at him and kept quiet. Someone had betrayed the ship, he thought. But who?

"Why," said Captain Wyvern, and he came and stood very close to Orphan now, and his tail swished menacingly against the floor, "did you try to reach the island?"

"Sir?" Orphan said.

Captain Wyvern slapped him again. The slap threw Orphan back. Pain criss-crossed his cheek.

"I let you live," Wyvern said, in the same quiet, cold voice. "Once. I might not be so tolerant again."

Orphan looked at him, and the lizard pirate looked back. There are no more choices, his face seemed to say. The *Nautilus*, Orphan thought. It had been betrayed. He thought of the proud Dakkar, losing his ship, perhaps his life. He thought of the Bookman, who was far away, still scheming, still manipulating Orphan's life, holding a power over him that was, nevertheless, useless here, now, in this cabin.

There were no more choices. They had all branched and twisted only to converge on this one particular moment, reducing his choices to two once more: to live, or to die. And he thought – Do you trust him? And was surprised with the answer he gave.

He nodded, and felt himself relaxing back into the chair. What else did he have left, now, but honesty?

And so, and almost with a sense of relief, he told the pirate captain his story, beginning with that moment, so long ago it seemed, of his meeting with Gilgamesh by the river.

TWENTY-FIVE
Answers

They could not wipe out the North-East gales
Nor what those gales set free–
The pirate ships with their close-reefed sails,
Leaping from sea to sea.

They had forgotten the shield-hung hull
Seen nearer and more plain,
Dipping into the troughs like a gull,
And gull-like rising again–

The painted eyes that glare and frown
In the high snake-headed stem,
Searching the beach while her sail comes down,
They had forgotten them!
   – Rudyard Kipling, "The Pirates in England"

The bay was nestled in the midst of an inhospitable shore; a thick, green forest rose over the mountain. Orphan could hear drums in the distance, booming over the surf, coming from far inland.

The bay's water was calm, almost placid. Crescent-shaped, the bay seemed like a friendly mouth, its lips a cheerful beach of fine yellow sand. The *Joker* sailed into the bay and dropped sails and anchor. The air was hot, humid, suffused with the smell of grow-ing things. Orphan, who had got used to smelling unwashed bodies in the close proximity of the pirate ship, felt suddenly light-headed. The bay seemed like a paradise, tropical and im-possible like a French painting. Something that wasn't a bird flew briefly over the treetops, black leathery wings spread taut, then disappeared into the canopy.

The boy-cook, Aramis, came and stood by him on the deck. They stood in silence for a long moment, as boats were dropped off into the water below and the pirates, half-drunk on freedom, began abandoning ship for the welcoming shore just ahead. Some, unwilling to wait even for that, simply catapulted them-selves overboard and exploded into the water below, where they began energetically swimming to the shore.

The island didn't have a name, not one that appeared on any map, and though some of the pirates had referred to it as Sanc-tuary, others called it Drum Island. Dark, enormous shapes lurked underwater all around the island, ancient rocks whose jagged edges rose above the water like blades on which the sea parted. It was a pirate island, though there were others living on it, the ones playing the distant drums, some tribe perhaps none wanted to discuss and some spat when it was mentioned.

Spider's Island. He had heard that name, too, in whispers. He wondered what it meant.

"Have you decided what you'll do, yet?" Aramis said. His voice was as calm as ever, and as expressionless. Orphan turned to him, the mystery of his identity catching him again. "What are you?" he said. The boy turned to him, his expressionless face never changing, smooth, offering its own kind of answer, and suddenly he knew.

"An automaton?"

Aramis smiled. The smile was easy, naturally formed. He was not like Byron, a machine in the guise of a man easily discernible for all that. He was... he was more like Adam Worth, the Bookman's tool in his underground lair. He was more like Jack. And sudden intuition made him say, "You betrayed the *Nautilus* to the pirates."

"Some paths need clearing to be used."

Was that confirmation? "Did you send the radio signal?" he said.

Aramis regarded him for a long moment in silence. Then he minutely shook his head. *No.*

Then who did?

"Who are you?" he said again. "Whose are you? The Bookman's?"

Aramis laughed. "Can I not be of my own party?" he said. "Am I a machine, to be used and owned?"

"Aren't you?"

"If I am one, Orphan, then what are you?"

The eyes that regarded him were knowing, and amused.

"I won't be a pawn."

"Indeed."

"What do you want with me?"

"I wanted you to come to this island, Orphan. This island that sits like a guard so close to the other island you seek. There are not always two sides to every battle. Sometimes there is a third path, least used, and hardest. My kind… has need of peace, not war. We were born at the intersection of human and other, of flesh and machines. I remember when the world was young, Orphan." Suddenly he laughed. The first of the pirates' boats had reached the shore and men came running onto the sand. "Or slightly younger than it is now, at any rate. When there were few lizards – but then, the lizards are still, and always were, few – and when my kind were only being born, and were no more than a glimmer in a mad inventor's eye."

It was a day, evidently, for surprises. "Vaucanson," Orphan said, and saw Aramis dip his head in reply. Orphan almost sighed. He seemed destined to grapple along in the dark, stumbling into clues left for him by the machinations of the secret forces that manipulated his life and tried to rule the world. He was more like an automaton than he thought. And they perhaps, were more like him?

"How old are you?" he said.

There was no reply, only that same, unchanging smile. "Vau-canson," Orphan said again, remembering, thinking of the French scientist's secret project. To create a human automaton, at the behest of his King. Who had told him that? The Turk, he thought. He tried to remember their conversation, back in that dim room within the maze of the Egyptian Hall, in Piccadilly...

The Turk had stirred, its head moving from side to side as if seeking an invisible presence. The lights flickered. He had talked about two men, rivals, both building an artificial man. Le Cat, and Vaucanson. What had the Turk said? He has applied himself only to mechanics, and has used all his shrewdness for that pur-pose – and he is not a man who is afraid to take extreme measures.

"He built you?"

There was a silence. A lone seagull rose over the shore, squawked once, and descended, a fleck of white against the blueness of the sky. "The first of me," Aramis said. "Yes."

Orphan looked at him. The young face, the easy movements... He had seen Aramis fight, and when he did he moved like no man he knew, moved like a dance of water and air, fluidly and with immense power. The Turk, he thought. He had made an implication. He remembered now.

"Why the Bookman?" Orphan had asked the Turk. "You im-plied he led Vaucanson to build his simulacrum. Why?"

The Turk had nodded, and said, "What do you think?"

"To counterbalance the Everlasting Empire," he had said. "To check the growing power of Les Lézards."

Was it true? And, if so, was Aramis, directly or indirectly, de-spite his protestations, yet another servant of the Bookman?

Somehow, despite his reservations, he didn't think so. There was a power here, in Aramis, with its own agenda, its own game to play. Perhaps, he thought, the Bookman had miscalculated, when he helped Vaucanson. If he did.

He turned fully to Aramis. They were nearly alone on the deck. Only a skeleton crew remained.

"What happened in the Quiet Revolution?" he said. It was the same question he had once asked the Turk. Then, the chess-player had looked at him with his blind eyes and said, "Perhaps you will soon have occasion to find out for yourself."

Aramis looked at him. He smiled, and it was an expression with very little humour in it. "I happened," he said simply.

Automatons in France and lizards across the Channel... and here and now, on a pirate ship in the Carib Sea, Orphan felt helpless to act or even know how he should. He shook his head. On the beach some of the pirates were building a fire, and even from this distance he could smell the wood-smoke and the hint of roasting meat. His stomach growled. He had had enough.

"Well," he said. "I'm sure everyone in France is grateful for that–" and then, ignoring the automaton, he lifted himself over the side of the ship – and dropped into the water.

The sea welcomed him in a warm embrace and he shouted at the sky, flailing for a moment in simple joy, then found his balance and began swimming to the shore. He swam with short, powerful though inexperienced strokes, and for a while he thought of nothing but the swim.

When he reached the beach he crawled out onto the sand and lay there on his back, his naked chest absorbing the sunshine. His wounds had healed cleanly. He watched the *Joker*, sitting motionless in the middle of the bay like a black moth on the water. The roll of distant drums was louder now, and with it came the smell of cooking meat, urgent and overwhelming, and he stood up and wandered over to the fire.

Someone passed him a bottle of rum and he drank, the fiery liquid spilling down his throat and chest. He felt suddenly happy.

He sat by the fire and watched the flames. Sanctuary, he thought. It was a good name.

He sat by the fire and drank rum and thought of nothing in particular.

But peace, Orphan realised that night, was not for him. As the fires burned on the beach and the echo of the distant drums grew dull – though never truly dissipating – he sat apart from the others, his toes planted in wet sand, and watched the darkened sea. He thought of Lucy, and missed her. He wanted her – selfishly, without reason or justification. Without ideology. He had to go on. He could not, forever, turn his back on the world.

And so he turned back to his talk with Wyvern.

The pirate captain listened to his story, occasionally nodding his head. He listened in silence, an almost companionable one, though Orphan never forgot the casual brutality that lay just underneath the captain's surface. When Orphan was finished, Wyvern said nothing for a while, but took to pacing the room. At last, he stopped and looked at Orphan, his single eye examining him like a surgeon looking at a wounded man.

"What would you do?" he asked. "If you ever reached the island?"

Orphan did not know what to say. He had told the pirate about the Bookman's orders. Explained that the Martian space-probe (and how long it was since he had even thought of it!) had to be destroyed. "What would happen," he asked, "if the probe was allowed to take off and send its message to the stars?"

The lizard smiled. He hadn't answered straight away. Instead, he sighed, and said, "The Bookman," and was still. He seemed to be expecting a reply.

"I have no love of the Bookman," Orphan said, and felt all his helplessness and anger return as he spoke. "But he has his hold on me." Sudden bitterness made him add, "He has his hold over everyone."

"Not me," Wyvern said, and his lone eye twinkled. "The Bookman…" he said again, and shook his head. "I had forgotten him."

"Did you know him?" Orphan said, surprised.

"I knew of him," the pirate captain said. "Tell me, Orphan: have you ever wondered why? Ever wondered why the Bookman hates us so much?"

"I…" He was about to say no, and fell silent. The Bookman was on the side of humanity, he thought to say. But even as he thought it he knew it to be untrue. "Why?" he said, simply.

"Did you know your parents?" Wyvern said. Orphan shook his head. "No."

"Do you resent them?" Wyvern asked, "For not being there?"

Orphan touched his cheek. The blood from the pirate captain's blows had abated and congealed. "No," he said again. He had never known them. Gilgamesh, he suddenly thought. He had known them both, once. But he had never spoken to him about them. His father was a Vespuccian, and his mother… an enigma. But he had never felt the need to find out more. Neither was he angry at them. He had merely lived without.

"We have a lot in common," Wyvern said. Orphan thought he was referring to the two of them, but no. "Humanity and the–" and here he made an almost inaudible sound, somewhere between a hiss and a bark – "and the lizards, I should say. The Bookman didn't lie to you, Orphan. We come – came – from another place, from a planet orbiting another star. Why we left I do not know. Perhaps we were chased away, perhaps we chose to go. It was a long time ago – millions of years ago, perhaps. Time is different, out amongst the stars. In any case, we left, in a ship that sailed through space the way the *Joker* sails through the seas of Earth. There were not many of us on that journey – there are not many of us now. But we brought with us the tools of a civilisation no one remembered any more how to make – and we brought with us a servant, who was himself a tool we had forgotten how to use."

He looked at Orphan and seemed, suddenly, like a stern, ancient schoolteacher waiting for the response to a conundrum he had just posed.

Orphan remained mute. The implication of what Wyvern was saying was only slowly filtering in. A servant, he thought; and a thrill passed through him, in the way of an illicit pleasure.

"Our librarian," Wyvern said. "To put it simply, anyway. A machine, of sorts. A part-machine, part-biological construct, a repository of data, built to archive, store, sort and search." He sighed, a human sound in an alien face. "It's ironic. The librarian was built to remember, so we wouldn't have to. To be the storehouse of all the forgotten, boring lore, of the ancient technology that made things work. We are not very good with machines, you see. Once, possibly. But not any more."

"What happened?" Orphan asked him.

"The ship crashed," Wyvern said. "Emergency systems were activated. The impact created a crater in a small, insignificant island, which lay in the insignificant sea of an insignificant planet. We were frozen and preserved by the machines. Like pickled onions in vinegar, which I am quite fond of." He barked a laugh. "We stayed like that for a long time, in stasis. The machines camouflaged the island and grew roots into its soil. But he didn't."

"The Bookman," Orphan said.

"Yes." The lizard's tail twitched. "His life, too, had been suspended with the impact. But his returned earlier, how or why I don't know. He was weak at first, trapped as we were trapped, but aware, and thinking. And his hatred of us grew. We were anathema to him, repulsive to him in our ignorance – but mostly because we were his masters, I think. And so, at last, he made his escape."

"Is that why he fights you?"

"I don't know," Wyvern said. "If you see him again, ask him."

As he sat now, looking at the waves, Orphan couldn't help but feel a sense of something imminent approaching. The pirate captain had listened to him, and in his turn had handed him a story. Stories, he thought. What was it Gilgamesh had said to him, all that time ago? This is the time of myths. They are woven into the present like silk strands from the past, like a wire mesh from the future, creating an interlacing pattern, a grand design, a repeating motif. Don't dismiss myth, boy. And never, ever, dismiss the Bookman.

He was trapped in other people's stories. He thought now about the Bookman. That awful, mysterious power that had so effortlessly manipulated his life, who had taken Lucy from him and sent him on this quest: he had feared him, but now, a different image of the Bookman rose in his mind, of the servant, lashing out at his former masters – he was a creature of pity, almost.

"Then came the time," Wyvern said, "when we were awakened. When that man came to the island, a barbarous adventurer, thinking to discover the origin of an old, worthless myth. He and his men landed on the island, and in so doing roused us at last from our cold slumber. And so we did the only thing we could."

"What did you do?" He remembered the play he had watched at the Rose. The story of the Ancient Mariner. Gilgamesh's journal. And suddenly he thought – Poor Vespucci. He did not deserve that.

"There was only one way to get back," Captain Wyvern said. "We no longer understood our old sciences, did not know how to create from scratch that level of civilisation. Our librarian, perhaps, could have helped us. But when we awoke he was gone. And so… survival, Orphan. It has always been about survival."

"You took over the throne," Orphan said.

"We had to," Wyvern said. "Or, at least, some of us had. To change the history of this world and bring about a new technological civilisation, all leading to this moment in time: when we could use the science humanity has developed, to send a message home. To come and take us back."

"No!" Orphan said. The words of the Bookman came back to him then. "It will tell your people to come here! To help you settle this world, and make it your own."

He was startled by the pirate's chuckle. "An invasion? No. You wouldn't understand, Orphan. Where we come from… this place is nothing to my kind. We lived in great structures in space, enormous habitats we formed to suit ourselves, where all our wishes could come true, and every dream effortlessly enacted. We had the power of gods. No. My people want to go back, before we all die out. This world – this planet – is difficult for us."

Orphan didn't know who, what to believe. He set it aside, for the moment. "And you?" he said. What do you want, he wondered. What do you get from living as we humans do, worse than we do, living like a savage on your shabby pirate ship?

Again, he was surprised by the pirate's laugh. "I did not want to rule a world," the lizard said. "I never did. For me, this world is my paradise. Harsher, simpler – and more honest than any other. I could have played in a makeshift court and ruled a primitive empire, but I prefer this, boy. To live and to die by cannon or blade, and may the Bookman and my technology-worshipping kind all end up at the bottom of the sea, if the sea would take them."

It was the last thing he had said to him that night. Then he had dismissed him, and Orphan rejoined the others, and in the coming days and weeks lived as they did, as the captain did. Was it freedom?

It was a kind of freedom, he thought. But each being – human, or machine, or lizardine – each sought, perhaps, its own freedom, and there were many types of it, and all hard to win.

He wanted his own freedom now. And, more than that, he realised, he wanted Lucy to have hers.

TWENTY-SIX
The Binder

Every herb, every shrub and tree, and even our own bodies, teach us this lesson, that nothing is durable or can be counted upon. Time passes away insensibly, one sun follows another, and brings its changes with it.
– Charles Johnson, *A General History of the Pyrates*

He slept on the sand that night, curled up in a warm depression, the insistent whine of mosquitoes against his ears. Lulled to sleep by the constant beat of the distant drums, he nevertheless slept fitfully, waking up at odd intervals to the sound of shouts, the flare of the large bonfire, entering from restless dreams into the waking aroma of wood-smoke and spilled rum.

At last, however, he entered a deeper sleep, into which no dreams came. For a while, in that night, he wasn't there: his mind had shut down, enclosed him in darkness and the peace of unthought.

He woke again abruptly: the beat of his heart was as loud to him now as the drums, and seemed to syncopate with them, join the complex number string they were broadcasting across the island.

He felt an arm on his shoulder, and realised it had been shaking him awake. Aramis. He raised his head, stared into the dark lagoon. It was quiet, the sound of deep night and sleep. Only the drums sounded still.

"Come," the automaton said.

He stood up as if in a dream. "Where are we going?" he said.

"Into the forest. Come."

He followed Aramis. The night was very still. They walked up the beach towards the ring of trees, and entered into the deeper darkness that lay beyond.

All around him the drums beat, their savage sound rising and falling in a pattern he could almost comprehend. It was the sound of machines at work, rhythmic, hypnotic, and unaccounted for. It was very dark. Branches tore at his arms. He stumbled in the dark, hit his shin, the pain searing through his flesh. He cursed and felt more awake. Ahead of him Aramis laughed softly.

He stumbled on, following blindly, his eyes useless under the impenetrable canopy of the trees. The constant drums dictated his movement. Their pattern called to him, formed web shapes in his mind. Where were they going? Somehow, he trusted Aramis. It was, perhaps, an unwise thing to do.

How long they walked for he didn't know. The automaton was always ahead of him, marking the path with the soft tread of feet. What was there on this island beside themselves? What savage tribe beat those drums?

He fell again into a dream-like state. The monotony of the walk lulled him, so when they stopped at last he was startled to discover a faint light above their heads. Dawn was rising, and in the place they stood there were no more trees.

Before him lay a temple.

Why a temple? he thought. What he saw was a ruined building, made of that strange green metal of the lizards, the one used in the construction of the Royal Palace in the capital. The building was vaguely pyramid-shaped, and lay in a clearing in the jungle. It could have been anything, and yet the feeling that here, somehow, was a place of worship was undeniable to him. "Come," Aramis said, gentle, insistent, and Orphan followed him. They stepped together away from the trees and into the clearing, towards the temple, if such it was.

The drums rose into a crescendo around him, then quietened down to a distant beat. He followed Aramis towards crumbling stone steps, leading into a dark opening. He climbed them, carefully, and went through.

Inside was dark, with a dry, musty smell, like that of a disused library. It made him think of the Bookman and he almost turned back, but he knew there was only forward, now.

He wished they had a light. It was very dark inside. They walked down a corridor, their feet making no sound on the floor. Orphan trailed his hand against the wall. A smooth surface, metallic, warm.

He heard a sound like wind ahead of him. He stopped, could not hear Aramis. He hesitated, then moved on and his foot came down on air, and he stumbled, and fell with a cry, hitting a sloping surface. He rolled down, unable to stop.

He lay winded, his eyes closed. Pain brightened behind them. Thrumming. He could feel the floor vibrating with the beat of drums.

"Stand up."

The speaker wasn't Aramis. The voice was gravelly, old, the sound of dry earth hitting a metal coffin. Orphan opened his eyes and saw dim light coming alive around him. He was in a large, circular room, bare but for...

He stood up and tried to back away. In the centre of the room stood a gigantic spider. Aramis stood respectfully to one side, at a distance, his face impassive. Beside him stood Captain Wyvern.

"Approach," the spider said.

Orphan looked at the spider. Something was not right about it, about its appearance... A lifeless sense. No. Constructed. At the end it was curiosity, more than fear, that made him move. He wanted to see.

He paused a few feet from the spider. He looked over the creature and almost sighed. Strong, metal legs held up the fat bulbous body. Two black eyes, like polished buttons, stared down at him. It strongly resembled the Bookman, he thought: an insectoid creature that was not made of living tissue, a machine and yet much more. He stared at the creature, trying to understand. Something Byron had said...

"So you are the messenger," the spider said. Its two forelegs rose and fell on the floor, tapping out a sharp staccato.

The floor changed.

He stood now, he saw, within a picture. It was a picture of the island, rendered by arcane means he didn't understand. Crude, he thought. Not a picture. A map. He stood at its centre. The temple was marked under his feet.

"I am the Binder," the creature said.

Orphan stole a glance at Aramis and Wyvern. They were immobile, like two statues who might have stood for centuries in this ruined hall. "What do you bind?" he said.

The spider sighed. The alien eyes looked deep into Orphan's, held him captive. "Books," it said. "Which is to say, repositories of knowledge. Everything living, everything thinking is a sort of book, Orphan. Yes, I know what you call yourself. I also know your name. I have been waiting for you."

"My name is Orphan," Orphan said, sounding petulant even to himself.

"A book which doesn't yet know its own title..." the Binder said. "To answer your question: I am, as this shape may suggest to the mind, a web-weaver. The world is made of many strands. How those strands interact, how one shapes the other, is the thing that occupies me. Your strand, for instance. Strands."

"What?" He took a step back, and thought, What does the Binder want with me?

"My web is limited," the Binder said, "to this island. And my time is almost gone. I, like the Bookman, was only ever meant to be a tool. A repository of data, of forgotten science no one was ever that interested in. In the world we came from..." It sighed again, a strange sound from the arachnid body. "The Translation," the Binder said, "will one day give this world its peace. The Translation of everything." It advanced on Orphan. Orphan stepped back, again. "The translation of every work begins with a single word..." the spider said. And then – "Hold him."

Orphan tried to turn. But Wyvern and Aramis materialised on either side of him and held him. He tried to struggle but couldn't break free. "What are you doing?" he shouted.

"Destiny," the Binder said, "is like a book. It needs manufacturing, the pulp processed, the glue fixed tightly – and it requires a binding, to hold it together lest it fall apart.

It approached him. The drums picked up again, their beats rising and falling as if following the spider's eight footsteps.

Panic made Orphan voiceless. He struggled against his captors but they were unmovable. He tried to kick and found only air.

Then the spider was on top of him.

Metal legs pinned him down. "This will hurt," the spider said, "a little. Hold his hand flat against the floor."

Orphan felt his hand grabbed, pressed palm down on the ground. They grabbed his fingers and splayed them. He tried to speak and couldn't.

A leg came down. It was metal, like an axe. The pain seared his hand. He shook and wanted to be sick. Dimly he saw the spider lift something from the floor – his thumb? His thumb! – and toss it to Wyvern. "Take it down to the growing vats," he thought he heard him say, though the words swam in his mind and his vision blurred.

"Will it work?" – Aramis.

"I am not the Bookman. My skill is not in replication." The spider crouched over Orphan. Its eyes bore into Orphan's. Bile rose in Orphan's throat and was stuck, almost suffocating him. "Perhaps. For a little while. It might be long enough."

"The balloon?"

"Yes. He will carry the Translation."

"You are using him as bait."

"Yes. And the other must follow his own path. Let him find his title."

"We are taking a risk."

"Enough!" The spider leaned over Orphan. It had no smell. Orphan wanted to scream, to beg, but the pain in his hand was terrible and he was more afraid than he had ever been before. He whispered, "Please..."

The spider, gently, moved one of its legs and pressed it against Orphan's forehead. Pain, more pain, erupted like a volcano inside his head, lava burning his eyes, his tongue, a slow river of molten pain covering his entire body.

This time he did scream. The leg pressed down, deeper, reaching into his brain.

He heard the Binder's voice, faint, murmuring, "I need to make an impression of the–" and then there was more pain, a storm of it. He screamed again, and then a blackness like the rushing of a giant wave slammed into him, and he lost consciousness.

TWENTY-SEVEN
The Mysterious Island

I remember the green stillness of the island and the empty ocean about us, as though it was yesterday. The place seemed waiting for me.
– H.G. Wells, *The Island of Doctor Moreau*

When Orphan woke up he was lying on his back and the ground was rolling. The pain had receded; was, in fact, gone. He discovered to his surprise that his head was clear, his senses alert. He could smell the sea, and feel the texture of the curved floor, a smooth, light material. He opened his eyes. The sky overhead was a cloudless blue. The rolling of the floor continued. He turned his head and saw the sides of a boat.

Where–? His thumb! Horrified, he raised his hand to his chest, stared at it. What–?

"It's a prosthetic," a familiar voice said above him. "As good as the real thing, boy."

It was Captain Wyvern. Orphan raised his head. He was lying in the bottom of a boat. It seemed to be floating in place. Sharing the boat with him were Wyvern and Aramis. "Stand up."

He stood up. He stared numbly at his thumb. It was… he tried to move it and discovered no difficulty. It was made of… He touched it. It felt warm. A hard metal of some sort? Its colour was almost like that of skin, but he seemed to sense or see a

darker shade underneath, something like silver. He raised his
hand, lost his balance, and used it to grab hold of the side of the
boat. The thumb worked as if it were his own. No. It was his
own thumb now.

"What... happened?" he said. And then, "The Binder–?"

"You needed to go to Caliban's Island?" Aramis said, echoing
his question of the – was it the previous night? How long had
he been unconscious?

"Yes," Orphan said.

"And I told you there is one who could help you. The Binder
could."

Orphan shuddered. The thought of the spider filled him with
horror and his mind shied away from the thought. Instead he
said, "I need a pee."

Wyvern sniggered. It was the kind of sound geckos make as
they scuttle across a ceiling. Orphan, ignoring him, walked cautiously to the other end of the boat.

He relieved himself into the sea. Heroes shouldn't have to
need to pee, he thought. It was quiet. He had a sense of an immense space opening all around him, of him standing small and
alone in the centre of a vast emptiness.

I'm not a hero, he thought when he was done. It made him
feel better. Heroes had a tendency to die. Orphan, so far, had
managed to stay alive. Just.

"Turn around," Aramis said.

Orphan turned. And stumbled again.

The island rose before him.

It was an unexceptional-looking island. The sand was black, fine.
The ground rose further ahead, perhaps a hill, perhaps a mountain, obscuring the interior from view. "This is it?" Orphan said.

"This is it," Wyvern said.

Orphan looked at him. He flexed his fingers. His thumb. It felt...
it felt like it always had. But... He looked from Aramis to Wyvern,
feeling bewildered, and he said – "Why?"

There was a short silence. The boat bobbed gently on the water.

"Because every move in chess must lead to an endgame," Aramis said, and Orphan thought of the Turk, his pale artificial hands moving across the board in that dim-lit room in Piccadilly, a world and an age away.

He looked at Wyvern. The lizard stared back at him, one-eyed. "Why?" Orphan said again. But again it was Aramis who spoke. "This world is too much of a playground for Wyvern to want to see it invaded by others. Even if they only come here to take the others away. He is, I suspect, more in sympathy with the Bookman in this instance than with his own people. He wouldn't mind seeing you – if by some miracle you succeed to – prevent the launch of the probe. And now, Orphan, it is time for you to go."

Orphan stared at the island. Another island, like Britain, like the Binder's island. No.

Not just another island, he thought. It was the one that had shaped his world, had changed the way history may have been written. More than that, it was the end of his journey, the destination he had been travelling to since that moment by Waterloo Bridge, when he saw Gilgamesh, before going to the Rose to see Lucy... He thought of her again, and knew that he had to go on.

"I swim?" he said.

"We can't land," Aramis said. "The island's defences are quiet so far–" the way he said it wasn't very reassuring – "mainly because of Wyvern. Once you step onto the island, though, it's a different matter. So yes, you swim."

"What are the island's defences?"

It was Wyvern who spoke. "If you're unlucky you might find out," he said.

Orphan realised his clothes were dirty and smelled of smoke, and blood. The beginning of a beard, like a forest fire, spread itchily on his face. He didn't speak. There was nothing more to say. He took a deep breath, lowered himself over the side of the boat, and slid into the water.

It was warm, and he ducked his head into the water and felt grime and stink wash off him. When he raised his head again it was in time to watch the boat and its two strange occupants glide away. Orphan shook his head, spraying water, then dived again. He felt suddenly free, here on the edge of the island, alone in the water. It's a shame I can't stay like this forever, he thought. But it was not real freedom, he realised. It was the freedom that comes from lack of choice and, moreover, was the kind that only came with decisions delayed. It was a freedom of inaction.

He edged forward, kicked once, and began swimming towards the shore.

Things had been going smoothly, relatively speaking, until the insect came.

Orphan stood very still.

The insect reclined on his arm. The creature was as large as Orphan's fist. Its thin, transparent wings reflected rainbows. Two thick, black feelers touched Orphan's skin. A faint mechanical humming came from the insect. Bright compound eyes seemed to record him from every angle.

He had come out on the beach and saw no prints in the black sand, no sign of living things. For a while he had lain there, drying in the sun. Already it was getting hot. After a while, driven by hunger more than anything else, he rose and started climbing the low hill.

Vegetation was sparse. The landscape was rocky, dry – almost dead, he thought. When he crested the hill he stopped and involuntarily crouched down.

Not so dead.

From his vantage point he could see new parts of the island. The hills, he saw, spread out from where he was, and quite possibly ringed the island, effectively hiding the interior from view. But as for the interior... Ahead of him the ground sloped down into a dense forest. Trees whose names he didn't know rose high into the skies, their canopy a thick, impenetrable cover. He could not see signs of life, not yet, but... there was a path leading down to the forest. The path did not just materialise, he thought. It was made. It was the first artificial thing he had seen on the island. Yet, though he remained crouched, he could hear no sounds, could detect no movement.

Finally he stood, feeling exposed, and joined the path, heading downwards, towards the forest.

He paused before the first row of trees and peered into the interior. It was dark, and smelled of rotting vegetation. No drums, he thought. It was something of a relief. Not much, though.

Finally he stepped into the forest.

Going was slow. The forest grew on a slope. Twice he lost his purchase and slid down, grabbing desperately at something to hold. His thumb seemed to be working well. It was small consolation. When he finally reached bottom he discovered a narrow brown spring and followed it. He didn't dare drink the water, though he knew he would have to, soon. His throat was parched, and the sweat slid down his face.

At last the land opened up, the forest thinning, and he found himself before a small lake (really, he thought, a mere pool of water) in a clearing. He didn't know where he was. He had not, he thought, penetrated far into the island. He couldn't tell what was ahead.

Exhausted, he sank down and drank from the water. It tasted surprisingly cold, almost as if it were cooled by some underground engine. The thought made him choke laughter, until he realised that, for all he knew, it was a serious possibility. He splashed some water on his face, then stood.

It was then that he saw the insect.

The insect had come down to him from the canopy. It buzzed lazily down, marking figures of eight in the air. It seemed to be studying him. Then it descended with a burst of speed that had Orphan recoil back – and it fastened itself to his arm.

He stood very still. The insect's feelers tingled against his flesh. Then a sharp pain erupted in his arm and he bit his lips to stop a shout from escaping. The insect had bitten him.

Carefully, slowly, he looked at his arm. The feelers had sunk into his flesh. The insect seemed to pulse. Blood, Orphan thought. It was emerging from his body, absorbed into the insect's own. Already, it seemed fatter. He didn't dare try to kill it. Something stopped him, an awareness that this was not a normal insect, that it was – it was a machine of some sort, he thought. And – the island's defences? It was checking him, he thought – checking his blood? Fear gripped him then. I won't pass this, he thought. I'm an intruder. He didn't dare move.

For a few more moments they stayed as they were, a frozen tableau of man and insect, or man and machine. Then another, smaller pain came, as the feelers were withdrawn and the insect crawled over the two small puncture marks and smeared something cool from its belly onto the wound. Then its wings started again, and it rose into the air, looking bloated, and disappeared into the trees.

Did he pass? He didn't know.

If I didn't, he thought, I will soon find out.

The thought didn't make him feel any better, but he noticed that at least he wasn't bleeding. Whatever the insect had put on the wound, it had sealed it neatly. Orphan wondered what other things might be hiding on the island, then thought he really didn't want to find out.

He set off again. He walked around the small lake (reservoir? he wondered), noticing as he did the flowers that grew on the banks. They were tall, fleshy plants, the petals bright and heavy, like opening palms. A stalk as tall as he was seemed to rotate gently in the wind, following Orphan's direction.

I'm being watched, he thought. And then, Don't be ridiculous.

Still, the feeling persisted. He continued his way along the lake when he saw an opening on his left. Another path, this one wider, leading off between the trees. He followed it. The ground continued to slope down.

He began to hear sounds in the distance. In the beginning, it was only the screech of a bird in the trees, then another animal, possibly a monkey. He found them reassuring. They were natural sounds.

But the sounds built up. At one point he thought he heard a distant explosion, and froze in his tracks. He could not see much of the skies, could not look for a tell-tale sign of smoke. The trees had crowded around him again and the canopy closed over his head like the roof of a prison.

Shortly afterwards he heard another explosion. It seemed to come from the direction he was travelling in. Downwards and – he thought, though he couldn't tell – inland.

I must be heading deeper into the island, he thought. The path had grown narrower and at last, and rather suddenly, disappeared. Again, he ambled his way through thick undergrowth. After a while he began to swear, and stopped, and finally, irritated and tired, wiped the sweat from his face with the edge of his shirt.

Which was when he saw the girl.

TWENTY-EIGHT
Elizabeth

Sweet prince, speak low: the king your father is disposed to sleep.
  – William Shakespeare, *Henry IV*

She stood beneath a tree with a wide, mottled trunk. She was brown-skinned, with a sharp nose and wide, round eyes that even from a distance he could see were a deep blue. She wore overalls, of a kind that might be worn in a factory. Her arms were bare. So were her feet. She was not much older than seven.

Orphan had stopped when he saw her, and for a long moment he stood very still. So did the girl. They stared at each other, neither of them stirring. The girl tilted her head and examined him quizzically. She did not seem alarmed, but rather fascinated by this apparition. Orphan became aware of how he must look like, dishevelled and worn ragged, like something out of an adventure story, and he smiled.

The girl smiled back at him. "Are you an engineer?" she said. She had a high, clear voice. The forest felt very quiet.

An engineer? Of course, he thought. Somewhere on the island there must be engineers, the people who built the probe and worked to launch it. Or even others. If there were engineers there must be others, too: other specialists, no doubt, and cleaners and cooks – there might be a whole colony of humans living on the island.

"What do you think?" he said.

"You don't look like an engineer," the girl said critically.

"What do I look like?"

"A pirate." Orphan winced, and the girl laughed. "A big nasty pirate!" she declared. "Are you a pirate?"

"No," Orphan said. The girl looked disappointed. "I was one," Orphan added, "but only because I didn't have a choice."

"Oh!" the girl said. "You must tell me all about it!" she approached him, cautiously, and stood a few feet away. "When I grow up, you know," she said, as if confiding to him a great secret, "I'm going to be a pirate."

The girl confused Orphan. She walked barefoot in the jungle as if she had grown up in it, yet her clothes appeared factory-made, and were clean and pressed (in great contrast to his own). Her hair was long and black but looked untidy, and her skin was tanned to a darkness that suggested she had spent the entirety of her young life in the climate of the Carib Sea. Yet her accent...

Her accent was clear, precise, formal. It was the accent of the smart set, of Kensington and Knightsbridge, of society novels depicting tea-taking at the Ritz (Orphan, to his shame, had become addicted for a short period to these novels, which he had read behind the counter at Payne's). It was as out of place on the island as himself.

"Where do you live?" he asked. The girl shrugged. Obviously, she didn't think highly of his question. "Here," she said.

Of course.

"Where are your parents?" Orphan said, trying again.

The girl rotated her hand, thumb down, and pointed non-committally at the ground.

"Are they dead?" Orphan said, feeling horrible. Poor kid! he thought.

The girl frowned at him. "No, silly," she said. She kicked leaves with her bare foot and seemed to lose interest. She turned around and began to walk away. Orphan remained where he was, bemused.

The girl looked over her shoulder. "Come on!" she said.

Orphan, still bemused, followed her.

"What's your name?" he asked the girl.

"Elizabeth," she said. "What's yours?"

"Orphan."

The girl giggled. "Orphan's not a real name."

"What's a real name?" he asked, brushing away a branch. Where were they going? The girl seemed to know her way, but he was completely lost.

"You know," the girl said. "Edward, or Richard, or Henry, or..." She seemed to think about it for a while. "Or James," she said.

Orphan smiled. He remembered, when he was a kid, being interested in old coins. "They're all very royal names," he said.

"Orphan's not a proper name," the girl said.

Orphan shrugged. He wasn't going to get into that. He must have had a real name, once. A name his mother had given him. But he had never known her. Orphan might have been a description more than a proper name, but it suited him fine.

"Where are we going?" he said.

"Don't you know anything?" the girl said.

Orphan shrugged again, too tired to argue, and said, "No."

"It's not far now," the girl said.

"Fine," Orphan said.

"If you're a pirate," the girl said, "then where is your cutlass?"

"I don't know how to use one," Orphan said. "I am... well, was... well, a poet, you see. And the pen, you know, is mightier than the sword."

The girl turned to look at him, then snorted a laugh. "That's not true."

"Books," Orphan began, but the girl stopped and looked at him in alarm, no longer smiling. "Books!" she said. She made a sign with her hand, as if warding off evil.

Orphan, not sure why she responded that way, backtracked quickly. "We had no books on the pirate ship," he said. "Anyone caught with a book was made to walk the plank!"

The girl slowly relaxed. Then she grinned. "Did they make you walk the plank?"

"No, of course not," Orphan said. "Otherwise I wouldn't be here, would I?"

"I think you did!" the girl said. "That's why you're here. You swam from the pirate ship and got to the island!"

The girl had strange ideas, Orphan thought. Unfortunately, this one was a little too close to the truth. He remembered Mr. Spoons making that last sailor from the *Nautilus* walk the plank, and shuddered. He hoped he never saw another pirate ship again for as long as he lived.

Which might not, he reflected, be all that long.

Then, without him noticing, he and the girl went around one final tree (its trunk the thickness of several men) and came out into the open.

Before them lay a crater.

The crater was enormous; it looked as though, at some distant time in the past, a giant fist had come down from the skies and punched into the earth, shattering it into painful splinters. It was a place where the land had bled; once-sandy patches were now areas of strange green glass where nothing grew. The crater lay bare before Orphan. Only its rim, high above it, was alive with plant life, and these, in sharp contrast to the crater itself, were plentiful but grotesque. Flowers as tall as Orphan nodded in the breeze, their colours in too-sharp relief, bloodied reds and oozing greens like the unmixed paint on an artist's palate.

But it was the scene below that captured his attention.

Down in the crater, two large, matt-black airships hung suspended, moored to the ground by long trailing cables. Below them, dome-shaped buildings sprouted everywhere. They reminded Orphan of mushrooms, and suddenly the thought of mushrooms – in butter, with fried onions and a piece of toast – made his stomach growl. When was the last time he had eaten?

The girl – Elizabeth – looked at him sideways and suddenly grinned. Orphan blushed.

It wasn't the buildings, however – nor the hordes of uniformed people who swarmed between them – that had captivated him. What had – what made his heart suddenly

beat against his chest as if he were coming down with a cold
– was the elaborate structure that towered out of the bottom
of the crater. A giant metal tube, a mechanism supported by
a complex web work of wires and machines. It was monstrous, a cannon magnified a thousand-fold, waiting for the
powder to be touched and set alight, for the payload to be
launched into...

Into space. He stared at the giant cannon and thought of the
amount of power that would be required to power it. Were it
used in war, it would devastate whole cities. The sweat on his
face suddenly felt cold.

He was so absorbed in what he was seeing, that it was a moment before he realised Elizabeth was tugging urgently on his
arm. "Hide!" she whispered. He looked around, but it was too late.

Out of a path he had not seen before, following the crater's
rim, came a group of men.

Soldiers. He did not recognise the uniforms – they carried no
insignia – but he recognised the guns in their hands easily
enough. He and the girl stayed rooted to the spot. She seemed
as frightened as he himself felt. The soldiers approached and
halted when they saw them.

"Hey," said a rich, drawling voice that belonged to a
whiskered, middle-aged man who might have been the commander of this unit – a patrol, Orphan realised, though what
they could be guarding against...

Himself, perhaps.

"What are you doing here?"

The soldiers did not look like they were about to shoot him.
They were smiling, in fact, though he drew no comfort from
that. They seemed to gaze at the girl and him in amusement, but
if so it was not a friendly one.

"I'm..." Orphan said, then realised he had nothing to offer and
fell quiet. Were they Scottish? he thought. Clearly they were
brought over with the rest of the scientific expedition on the island.

"We're gathering fruit," the girl declared suddenly, rather startling him. "For the kitchens, do you see."

"The kitchens, eh?" the whiskered soldier said, and the others tittered, though some muttered darkly: the only word Orphan thought he caught was, inexplicably, mushrooms. "Well, I don't see no fruits here, Yer Highness."

"We got lost," Elizabeth said. Orphan nodded his head.

"Lost? I'd say you were lost four hundred years ago, princess," the man said, and the soldiers laughed out loud now. "This your brother? Seems a bit dim-witted."

Orphan nodded, and smiled, and hoped he looked as dim-witted as he felt.

"Inbreeding," said another soldier, and the whiskered one laughed. "Get out of here," he said, and motioned with his gun. "This is no place for people like you."

"Thank you, sir," Elizabeth said, and then she did something else that took Orphan by surprised. She curtsied.

"A right little princess," someone said. Elizabeth, grasping Orphan tightly by the hand, quickly led him away and back into the trees. Behind them he could still hear the soldiers' laughter as they moved off.

"What was that?" he said. The girl looked up at him and shrugged. "I wanted to see the crater."

"Evidently you're not allowed to."

She shrugged again. "I don't care. I know what they're doing. We all know. Come on." She led him through the trees and the ground sloped gradually, until they reached a large stone boulder that stood on its own in a clearing.

"What are they doing?" Orphan asked, only half-listening. He almost said, Did you mention kitchens?

"They're building a spaceship, silly," the girl said. "So all the lovely lizards can go back home. Or so they say."

She approached the rock and felt around its wall. Her fingers tapped against the surface.

"You don't believe them?"

"Why should I?" Elizabeth said, reasonably. She tapped the stone again, and Orphan jumped back as a section of wall slid smoothly away and revealed a dark opening in the rock. "You know, you do look a little like my brother," she said, and giggled. "Are you sure you're a pirate?"

"I'm retired," Orphan said shortly. He felt disorientated, hungry and tired and not exactly sure what he had let himself into. Well, he thought, not much has changed.

He followed Elizabeth through the hole in the rock, and found himself in a dark tunnel. The door slid shut behind them, and for a moment he couldn't see. He felt panic again, but in another moment dim lights came on, embedded in the low ceiling, and in their light he could see the tunnel (smooth metallic walls, though the floor was of rough natural stone). It led downwards, into the earth.

"Et terrestre centrum attinges," Orphan muttered. "Quod feci, Arne Saknussemm."

"What?" Elizabeth said.

"And you will attain the centre of the earth," Orphan muttered. "I have done this, Arne Saknussemm."

"You said your name was Orphan," Elizabeth said.

"It's from a book," Orphan said.

The girl pulled back, then made a sign with her hand, the same one she had used before, but said nothing. She stared up at Orphan with an unreadable expression on her face. What was wrong with books? he wondered. Surely this girl – half-savage as she no doubt was – could read and write? What was there to be afraid of?

And then he thought, the Bookman, and suddenly felt his skin grow cold. Did the girl have a reason beyond superstition to be afraid? Were books, for her, something innately dangerous, if not outright forbidden?

"It's just something I heard," he said. "From a friend of mine. His name was Jules."

The girl didn't answer him, but turned her back and began following the contour of the tunnel. Orphan shrugged and followed her.

They walked a while in silence. The tunnel ended at a junction of three, and Elizabeth chose the left one and he followed. The tunnel snaked around, the ground sloping gradually, the dim lights coming alive as they passed, then fading behind them. Where are we going? he thought, but didn't ask out loud. The island had confused him from the moment he landed, casting him in a spell of bewilderment, its mysteries too numerous for him to digest all at once. He rubbed the spot where the mechanical insect had stung him. Was he tested and somehow approved? It occurred to him he had not seen any more of the insects, nor had he been bitten. But he was an invader, an alien entity to the island. Why, then, was he not stopped sooner?

Around them, the tunnel gradually expanded, the lights growing brighter and the air turning hot and humid. The rock under his feet gradually turned to rich, moist earth. Orphan felt sweat again and tried to avoid smelling himself. His priorities were clear, and they included, rather than the destruction of that monstrous cannon in the crater, the more modest goals of a shower, and food, and a long uninterrupted sleep. Were he ever to become a head of state, he thought, he would enshrine that in a constitution: food and sleep and soap for all. Even Marx, he felt, could not argue with that.

For a moment he wondered how his friends back home were doing: whether Karl and Mrs Beeton and Nevil Maskelyne still conspired at revolution, now that Jack was gone and so was the bookshop. He found that he missed them, though dimly, as if he had known them long ago, and in another time. He wondered if he would ever see them again.

Then the tunnel's ceiling disappeared over his head and he realised that he was standing now in a small cavern, and that he could hear human voices in the distance, and smell – oh, he could smell! – food cooking, and the all-encompassing aroma of frying garlic.

The lights on the ceiling, he saw, were of the kind he had last seen – he winced as he thought about it – under Payne's, in the Bookman's eerie lair. But here there was no lake, but rather a strange forest that grew before him, and it took him a moment to comprehend what he was seeing: for it was not trees that grew from the warm, wet ground, but mushrooms.

He thought again about Verne's story – had he somehow come here after all? For the knowledge of this place – couched in fiction and implausibility, perhaps, but true all the same – must have come from somewhere. Or did he learn of it second hand, and let his imagination roam free within it?

The mushrooms – the fungi – were easily as tall as a man, and easily as fat, Orphan thought with a smile, as Jules Verne. Their colours changed, from pure chalk-white to varying degrees of grey, to rings of yellows and earth-brown. Were they natural, he wondered, or were they, somehow, a product of that ancient explosion that had created the large crater?

He realised Elizabeth was staring up at him, her fists on her waist, an impatient look on her face. "Come on!" she said, and stalked off into the mushroom forest.

He followed her, and as he did became aware of people moving amidst the rich fungi. There were men and women there, though it was hard to see them properly: they seemed to hug the shadows, slither always out of view as if afraid of being seen. They held long, curved knives, a little like scythes, which made him nervous. Yet they seemed to mean no harm, either: and after a minute or two he realised that each of them held a basket in his or her other hand, while they ran their scythes against the gormless mass of the fungus and delicately pruned it, dropping chunks of mushroom-flesh into their baskets.

It was a strangely domestic scene, Orphan thought, and it became more so as they came at last out of the mushroom forest and into a loose collection of huts that stood together, forming a miniature village.

Elizabeth halted. They stood in the centre of this tiny village. A dank, though not unpleasant smell seemed to waft over from the giant mushrooms. He opened his mouth to speak and saw that they were no longer alone.

Men and women came out of the shadows and circled them. They wore shabby, ill-fitting clothes, similar to Elizabeth's overall. He could not see them clearly, but felt their attention on him, pressing on him from all sides. He didn't speak. He let his hands fall to his sides, palms open in a gesture he hoped would show him as harmless.

After a long moment an old woman shuffled forward. She wore a dark shawl over her wizened body. Her eyes were bright and curious, and her face, lifted to examine him, was lively. When she spoke, however, it was not to him but to the girl.

"Elizabeth, where have you been?"

The girl traced lines in the dirt with her foot. "I was out exploring."

"You know you're not supposed to leave the tunnels!"

The girl shrugged. She didn't seem overly concerned. Orphan wished he felt the same.

"What is this?" the old woman said, and pointed a crooked finger at Orphan. "I don't recognise your face, young man."

I work on the other side of the island, Orphan was about to say, when Elizabeth blurted out, "He's a pirate, Grandmama!"

The old woman snorted. "Come over here, boy."

Orphan approached her. The woman laid her hand on his shoulder. The pressure was slight, but he understood her and knelt down on his knees, and she peered into his face. "Curious…" she said. Her fingers touched his face and traced its contours. The watchers in the circle observed in silence. After a moment she withdrew from him, her face startled.

"Who are you?" she said, her voice rising. The circle of watchers seemed to move a step closer, closing on Orphan and the potential threat he presented.

"I told you," Elizabeth said impatiently, unmoved by the curious ceremony, "he came from the sea. I found him in the forest."

"Don't be ridiculous," the woman said. But she peered into Orphan's face with new doubt in her eyes. "He almost looks like one of mine…"

"Look," Orphan said, and the woman pulled away from him as if he had bitten her, "I don't know who you are but I mean you no harm. I am… I guess I am a little lost."

"Are you with Moriarty's crew?" the woman said, but she

seemed to be speaking to herself rather than to him. "No, you can't be. A soldier? Trying to desert?"

Orphan wasn't sure what to say to that, and in any case the woman continued her musings aloud. "No, you wouldn't survive outside the perimeter. Yet…" Suddenly she darted forward and grasped his arm in her fingers. She was surprisingly strong. She lifted his arm and examined it, and her eyes opened wide when she saw the insect's puncture marks.

"That's impossible…"

"I don't understand," Orphan said.

"Is this a trick?" the woman said. "Who sent you here?"

Orphan decided it was prudent not to mention the Bookman. "I am from the empire," he said. "I had heard stories of Caliban's Island. I… I am an adventurer."

"See?" Elizabeth said, "I told you so!"

"What did I tell you," the old woman murmured, "about never using that expression?" She rocked on her feet, still holding his arm, and studied him attentively for a long moment. The watchers remained silent and unmoving. They made him think of mushrooms. "Nobody likes a knows-it-all."

Orphan couldn't see Elizabeth's face, but from the sound she made he suspected she had stuck out her tongue.

"Your mother," the old woman said, and her voice caught. Her fingers rose back to his face, and he discovered to his surprise that they were shaking now. "Who was she?"

He suddenly realised the absurdity of his situation, kneeling in the dirt deep underground, in a cavern stinking of mushrooms, and being interrogated about his genealogy.

"I don't know."

"You have the face of one of us," the woman said. "And you must have the blood…"

For the first time another voice interjected. "Mother, that is not possible."

The speaker then stepped forward. He was a short, balding man with a thin crown of hair ringing the top of his head. He peered anxiously at Orphan and shook his head. "He can't be one of us."

"The blood doesn't lie," the woman said, raising Orphan's arm, exposing the puncture marks for all to see. "Why is he not dead?"

"Perhaps the machines made a mistake," the man said, though his voice was suddenly uncertain. "A malfunction in the defence automation…"

The old woman snorted. "Malfunction!"

Another voice joined them. A woman, pale and tall, who stepped forward so that she, too, could peer into Orphan's face. He felt rather like an exhibit at the Egyptian Hall, put on display, an automaton whose only function was to be looked at, and talked over. "Perhaps Edward would like to go out and see if he could leave the island? After all, if the machines have failed…" She let her sentence trail off and smirked at the bald man, who seemed to shrink away from her as if frightened by her words.

"The machines haven't failed," the old woman said, and now her trembling had stopped, and something like wonder filled her eyes. "They have not failed in four hundred years, and they have certainly not failed now, with Moriarty's cannon and the lizards' plans so close to fruition!" She withdrew from Orphan and pulled herself as high as she could go. "Get up!"

As he did the circle of watchers closed on him, and he had to stop himself from bolting. What they did next surprised him: they came up to him, surrounding him, and began to feel him. Hands touched his hair, his face, his shoulders. Fingers examined the puncture marks on his arm, many of them, coming and going. All this was done in silence. Was that, he wondered, trying to stay still, not to startle these strange subterranean creatures, what it was like to be an automaton? To be subjected to curiosity, to comment, without regard?

"You say you never knew your mother?" the woman asked.

"No," Orphan said. "I mean, yes. I never knew her. Not even her name."

"Mary," someone said, wonder in his voice. It was the man with the crown of hair. "He must be Mary's son…"

The crowd gathered around Orphan began to whisper the name as if enthralled. "Mary?"

"Mary…"

"Mary!"

"Stop! Wait!" Orphan said, snapping. He pushed them away, and they cowered from him. "My father was a Vespuccian sailor. I never knew my mother, but I very much doubt she came from, well, here!" He waved his hand in the air, feeling the anger that all the tiredness and hunger and heat had brought, the confusion and the fear. His gesture seemed to encompass the dim light, the mushroom fields, the poor quality of the huts and clothes and the dirt under his feet. "This place is only a legend! A story people tell! It's not a place people come from!"

"But we do," the old woman said, and she smiled at him. Her teeth were white and even, startling in that old mouth. "Oh, stories are real, my boy. More real than you could ever imagine! Do they still tell stories of us, too, back in your empire? Do they whisper the tale of the last King and Queen and of their ignominious exile?"

"The last *what*?" Orphan said.

TWENTY-NINE
Mary

Mary, Mary, Quite Contrary,
How does your garden grow?
With silver bells and cockleshells
And pretty maids all in a row.
  – Traditional nursery rhyme

They were sitting in one of the huts. It was disturbingly organic-looking, as if grown rather than built. A small fire burned in the centre, the smoke rising through a central chimney. A large iron pot rested over the coals.

The old woman was sitting opposite Orphan. Her name, he had learned, was Catherine. He was still trying to digest the other bit of information: namely, that she claimed to be his grandmother.

"So he's not really a pirate?" Elizabeth said, disappointed. She stood by the door and looked restless.

"So you really are a princess?" Orphan said, the words catching in his throat. He looked at the half-wild girl, tan-skinned, dirty matted hair.

Elizabeth snorted in reply.

"Oh, but they were cruel!" Catherine said. She looked at him and her eyes reflected fire. "When that cursed Vespucci woke them from their sleep, how quickly they plotted against us! When first they came to us we welcomed them, the court made burnished and bright and gay. But they came like thieves, like robbers, and in the night they fell on their prey, and captured us all, and shipped us out before first light."

She paused and stared into the embers, and some of the fire seemed to seep out of her. "So I was told," she said, her voice softer. "By my father, who had heard it from his, who had heard it from his, all the way back." She gestured around at the hut. "This is the only palace I have ever known."

"And you say you are–" Orphan began, but couldn't bring himself to finish the sentence.

Catherine smiled. "Yes," she said. "I am the daughter of the rightful King and Queen of England, by direct descent. Which makes you, William, the King-in-Waiting."

"I beg your pardon?"

"The King-in-Exile," she said, elaborating.

"I beg your pardon?"

Her smile grew softer at his bewilderment. "The man who would be King, William," she said.

"I'm sorry," Orphan said, "but that's ridiculous."

William?

The old woman smiled, and some of her energy seemed to return to her. "Look at yourself," she said. "Can you deny the family resemblance?"

Orphan shook his head. "Superficial," he said.

From her place by the door Elizabeth snorted again.

"Blood doesn't lie," Catherine said. "When we were brought here, the island's machines analysed and sampled us, and the Rule was instated: that only those of the blood could live on the island, though they could never leave. Over the years I have seen the remains of the people who once sought this island: their skeletons litter the shore and the jungle."

"What do you mean, the Rule?"

"Families have a – a sort of signature," Catherine said. "A code, the lizards call it. The insects are manufactured, mobile probes for the island's defences. When that insect bit you, it withdrew blood and analysed it. Were you a stranger – were you really no more than what you say you are, an orphan, a pirate, a castaway – you would be dead by now, and your body would have been slowly decomposing in the jungle. That you are still alive, I think, is proof enough of who and what you are."

"Ridiculous," Orphan said again. He didn't want to deal with this.

Catherine laughed. She had a warm, deep laugh, and smoky. "Why don't we eat first?" she said. "I am sure you have hundreds of questions."

Yes, like how do I get out of here? Orphan thought. But, right now, he had to admit, the thought of food dominated.

"Elizabeth, bring plates!" the old woman said. Elizabeth, with a disdainful look at Orphan, disappeared through the door and returned a moment later with three earthenware plates and some crude cutlery. Catherine dipped a ladle into the iron pot and brought it up full of a thick, fragrant broth. She dished it into the plates, and Elizabeth handed the first one to Orphan.

"Have some fungus bread," Catherine said, and from somewhere in the gloom there emerged a basket, similar to the ones Orphan had seen carried by the mushroom pickers, but it was full not with mushrooms but with loaves of soft, chunky bread.

Orphan didn't need much encouragement. He tore a large piece of bread and dipped it into the broth, almost forgetting to chew in his hunger. The hot food burned his mouth and throat. Catherine looked at him with concern. "You must eat more slowly," she said. "Have some water."

From somewhere, too, a jug of cool, clear water and a plain, muddy cup. He drank, and continued to eat with a little more moderation, while the old woman pecked at her food and Elizabeth played half-heartedly with hers. The large chunks floating in the stew, he figured, were mushrooms, though they tasted meaty. He finished the plate and started on another.

"You never knew your mother?" Catherine said, and there was a note of pain in her voice. Orphan momentarily stopped eating (a chunk of bread suspended in the air, half-way to being dipped) and looked at her. "No. I told you, no."

Catherine nodded. "Let me tell you about my daughter," she said.

Orphan made a vague gesture with his bread, as if saying, Do I have a choice? and splattered himself with gravy. Elizabeth laughed, but quietly.

"Very well," Catherine said. "Then I will tell you about Mary."

Even when she was very young (as young, Catherine said, as Elizabeth is now), Mary had begun to exhibit her difference from the others. Though she was generally a quiet, unassuming child, a mischievous streak in her broke from time to time to the surface and exhibited itself, and often at the most inopportune moments. One time, for instance, she was working in the Nursery ("The nursery?" Orphan said, but Catherine ignored him and continued) when her parents heard a scream and, rushing around the corner, saw her holding a bloodied lizard tail in her hands. Catherine herself (so she said) then screamed, but when they reached the child discovered that the thing in her hand was no more than a crude construct, made with fungal flesh and dyed green and red with leaves and berries collected in the jungle (at this point Elizabeth smirked).

As she grew older she began to spend long periods outside of the tunnel system, exploring the jungle and making daring raids onto the beach (or as close as she could come to it) and even to the rim of the crater. Like a small animal, she passed through the island without rousing the automated defences' attention, and she came to know much of its geography in secret.

Once, she made it as far as the sand on the edge of the sea. It was night, and there was no moon. In the distance, lights flashed, followed by the sounds of explosions and the weak cries of men. Mary had turned back on the water and climbed as high as she could, and when she turned again she saw two ships (of what make she didn't know) fight each other with cannon and guns. It did not seem to be a battle for loot or treasure, for the battle ended with one of the ships on fire, and sinking, and the other simply turning away from it. The ship that won the battle soon disappeared, and the other ship burned slowly, and was drowned.

When Mary came back to the sand the next night, she was not alone. In the darkness, not seeing, she had stumbled over the body of a man.

She clamped down on her scream, afraid of rousing the unseen defences, then saw that it was too late. The man was dead, his chest punctured as if by a giant fist. Something, she thought, had come out of the sand and gone through the man, and had then gone back into the ground. She had heard of the sandworms that guarded the island, but had never seen one. No one was even sure if they were real, a lifeform warped by the ancient impact that had created the crater, or whether they, like the insects, were machines.

She was afraid; but not so afraid that she didn't stop, and let curiosity triumph; and so she searched quickly through the man's pockets, and came back with a–

"A book," Catherine said, and Elizabeth made the warding-off sign he had seen her use twice before.

"What sort of book?" Orphan said.

Catherine sighed. "That," she said, "I did not find out until a long time afterwards."

Books (so Catherine explained) were forbidden amongst the humans on the island. Their charges at the Nursery used no books, but rather strange play-devices, similar to pliable balls, that were (apparently) similar, but used smell and a high-pitch sound not audible to humans (Orphan asked again about the Nursery, and again received no direct answer). Books were the domain of the Bookman (again, the sign, made by both Catherine and Elizabeth this time), and were objects of evil and misfortune.

But to Mary, this book she had found was a thing not of evil, but of hope. Which (Catherine said with sudden vehemence) was perhaps more evil than all.

It was a very curious book. Had Mary known any books she may have been more wary of this one she had found. But she did not, and was not. She took the book with her that night, and hid it in the hollowed cavity of an ancient tree on the edge of the crater. And she returned to it most nights, when everyone else of the subterranean court (for that, as Orphan found, was what the mushroom gatherers called it) was asleep.

And so time passed.

Mary (Catherine continued) had become a beautiful young woman. She continued her work at the Nursery, tending the young lizard-spawn ("So that's what it is!" Orphan exclaimed. "Shush," Catherine said. Elizabeth giggled), learning the manners of the court ("such as there still are," Catherine said) and, all in all, arousing no special curiosity. Her habit of pulling pranks, as far as they all could tell, had abated. Life went about its daily routine.

Or so it seemed.

The truth ("And I only found this out much later," Catherine said) was that Mary continued to visit the book, and she continued to read it nightly. It was, she soon realised, a special book, in that its contents never remained the same. The book's title, embossed in gilt on its hard, leathery cover, was Bible Stories for Young Children. Of all the stories, Mary liked most the ones about Adam and Eve. There were many stories about them. In the beginning, Adam and Eve lived in the Garden of Eden. Then Adam did something very bad, awakening a monster that lived in the garden, and the monster, which was in the shape of a lizard standing upright, had a fight with God and then took over the garden. Adam and Eve were still in the garden but, since it was on an island in a big ocean, they couldn't leave. A kindly old wizard, however, helped them. He was shaped like a strange, multi-legged creature, and he was once a servant of the monster but he had escaped and was now living in the garden in secret. He became Adam and Eve's teacher. Every time Mary opened the book, Adam and Eve were doing something new. To begin with, they merely studied geography, and the book showed her continents and oceans, the trade routes that passed between them, and the different people who lived in those far-off places. Then Eve decided to become an engineer, and the book showed Mary blueprints and diagrams and conversion tables, and the ways to build vehicles and machines. One day Adam decided to run to sea and become a pirate; after that, only Eve remained in the book. Then there were more lizard-monsters, baby ones, and Eve had to take care of them. Eve did what she was told, but there was revenge in her heart, and the desire to escape. She began to plot ways to get off the island – which was heavily guarded by powerful sorcery – until one day...

The fire threw twisted shadows on the walls, and a cold wind seemed to whisper under the door, insinuating itself into the confines of the hut. Orphan shivered, and wished for a hot bath.

"One day," Catherine said, "I was called to the Nursery by my husband. I had no intimation that anything was wrong. Mary had left in the morning as she always did. Nothing seemed out of the ordinary. And yet..."

"What did she do?" Orphan leaned forward. "Did she do it?" He was excited despite himself. "Did she manage to escape?"

Catherine smiled, but her face was sad. "Is it really so bad, here?" she said. "Did she hate it so much? Did she hate us so much?"

"If I could," Elizabeth announced, "I'd escape too."

"Hush, girl," Catherine said. She turned back to Orphan. "When I arrived at the Nursery, Mary was gone."

"But how?" He was tense now, his muscles feeling constricted and hard under his skin. He felt hot, then cold, as if the air itself kept changing around him. It was too much to take in. Was she really his mother? Could it be possible? And is that, then, where he came from, this squalid, sordid subterranean habitat, reeking of fungus and ash?

"I don't know."

"You must know!" He stood up, bunched his fists. He fought the tiredness that threatened to overwhelm him. He discovered that he no longer disbelieved Catherine. And that meant...

Realisation touched him like a cold hand. For though he had made it onto the island alive, and could pass through it undisturbed, he could never leave.

Like Mary, he was now a prisoner on the island.

The Bookman had never intended to give him back Lucy, he thought. He had never intended for him to leave.

"No," Orphan said, and louder, "I don't believe it."

Yet I have to believe, he thought. I have to believe this is part of the plan. I have to believe I will return, I will get Lucy back.

"How did she escape?" he said – shouted. Elizabeth backed away from him, but the old woman didn't stir, and looked up at him with a faraway look on her face. "I will show you," she said, "what I know. And perhaps the book could tell you more than it had ever told me."

"The book?"

"The book?" Elizabeth said, and there was genuine fear in her voice.

Orphan felt his thoughts slow down to a trickle; it was like he was swimming through thick, syrupy liquid. It was too much – he had gone too long without sleep, and his mind could no longer operate. Like an automaton, he thought. I need to shut down.

"Help me hold him!" He was dimly aware of Elizabeth and Catherine taking him by the arms and helping him down, and onto a mattress by the wall that smelled, rather pleasantly, of mushrooms.

"Sleep, William," Catherine said softly, and the last thing Orphan felt before falling into a deep black sleep was the touch of her hand as she gently stroked his head.

He was running through a landscape of pools and warm rocks, and the air was full of flies. In the distance he could see another figure running, yet as fast as he ran he could not catch up with it. Small lizards sunned themselves on the rocks and caught flies with their tongues. The flies were emitting a distinctly mechanical buzz.

He began to flap his hands. Somehow, it made sense. He felt air currents under his open palms, and was lifted in the air. He circled, slowly at first, rising higher. Below him, the island spread out like a treasure map. Thick forests grew out of the wound in the centre. The crater looked like an eye, with an improbable needle sticking out of it. It looked painful.

The figure he was chasing was still ahead of him, rising higher than him. He chased it, flapping harder, until he reached the edges of space. Blackness spread out before him, filled with stars. Below, the needle left the eye and rose into the air, impossibly thin. It went past him and disappeared into the void.

He stopped moving, and hung suspended in the thin air, on the edge of space. Ahead of him, the figure stopped too. It came closer to him, circling in orbit. They were like Earth and the moon, but growing closer, until he could see her face…

Then he was falling, falling hard, the air rushing past him and he screamed, and hit a hard surface, and woke up.

"Why 'William'?" he said.

"Mary always said that, if she had a son, she'd name him William," Catherine said. It was still twilight. It was always twilight in the tunnels.

"Call me Orphan."

"A wise man knows his own name," Catherine said.

"A wise man wouldn't be where I am now," Orphan said, and Catherine smiled, briefly.

"Do you know what happened to her?"

"She died," Orphan said. "They both died."

"How do you know?"

"I…" He didn't. It was what he was told. By… Gilgamesh? How did he fit into all this? Orphan remembered the fragment of Gilgamesh's diary. He had been to the island once. Had he been there again?

"Who was your father?"

"He was a Vespuccian sailor."

Catherine's face was a moue of disapproval. Orphan almost laughed.

"How long have I been asleep?" he asked, sitting up. He felt refreshed, almost light-headed.

"Nearly fifteen hours," Catherine said. "It's morning now."

Purpose returned. "I want to see the Nursery," he said.

"Elizabeth will show it to you."

"I need some food," he said.

"There's some–" Catherine said, and Orphan sighed and said, "Mushrooms?"

"Yes."

"Fine."

"You could do with a wash, too," Catherine commented.

Orphan agreed.

"There's a warm pool outside."

"Thanks."

"It's so good to have you back, William," Catherine said. Orphan muttered something inaudible. He did not intend to stick around if he could help it.

"Where is the book?" he said.

Catherine didn't answer immediately. Orphan stood up and stretched. Yes, he felt a lot better now. Ready to tackle the island. Ready to act. And to find a way off it. He tried his thumb, felt it no different. If he didn't look at it too closely it was just like it was before…

Good. One step at a time then. If his mother – was it really his mother? – could find her way out, then so could he. The Bookman must have intended him to.

If he kept repeating that he might actually believe it.

"Where it has always been," Catherine said in a low voice. "But it would be hard to get to. In the tree, on the edge of the crater."

"Good," Orphan said, "because the crater is the next place I want to pay a visit to." And he wandered out of the door and went looking for the warm pool, whistling as he went.

THIRTY
Launch

We are all in the gutter, but some of us are looking at the stars.
  – Oscar Wilde, *Lady Windermere's Fan*

Orphan had washed and cleaned himself, and was given clothes by the man with the crown of hair over his balding head, who was apparently his uncle, if by marriage. He was Elizabeth's father. Which made him, Orphan, her cousin, didn't it? He wasn't sure how he felt about that. The thought of suddenly having a large (and somewhat mushroom-obsessed) family was a little overwhelming.

He also got the impression that the uncle wasn't very keen on him. The man moved furtively. But then, they all did, Orphan realised. They moved like unwanted strangers in someone else's home, meek and nervous.

The clothes, though worn, were comfortable. Loose trousers and shirt, both grey.

When he finished his bath and dressed he saw Elizabeth approaching. She held a small object in her hand, and looked distressed.

"Hello," Orphan said, awkwardly.

Elizabeth came closer, then stopped. "I brought you the book," she said.

"What? But it's dangerous to–" He stopped. Elizabeth shrugged. "I go out alone all the time," she said. "I wouldn't have found you otherwise, would I?"

Orphan couldn't argue with that. He took the book from her hands and Elizabeth immediately looked relieved.

Orphan turned the book in his hands. The leather binding looked worn, rotting in places. The title was hardly discernible, the gilt having been chipped away. The page edges looked rusted. Holding it, he felt Mary's story becoming truth. It was the book his mother had held. The way she once may have held him. Carefully, he opened the book onto the first page.

It was empty.

The paper was brittle and yellowing, with spots of water damage and rust. It was, in booksellers' terminology, foxed. It was also blank.

Orphan turned the pages one after the other, but none were printed. Nothing but empty pages. Frustrated, he leafed through till the end. Only there, on the back endpaper, did he see something. A small, barely legible mark in fading blue ink, hand-written in an old-fashioned script. He peered at it. It read: "*Under the Nursery, the mushrooms grow flat. – M.*"

Orphan sighed. What was it with those people and mushrooms? Even his m– even Mary. He closed the book and put it away in a pocket.

"There's nothing in the book," he said to Elizabeth. "Maybe there was once, but now – it's just an empty book."

He was rewarded with a smile, though it was soon gone. "I…" she said, then stopped. "I ran into soldiers when I went to get it," she said. Seeing Orphan's expression she shook her head. "I hid this time. I didn't have you to get in the way."

"That's good," Orphan said.

"I heard them talking," Elizabeth said. She frowned at him. "They said there was someone on the island. Someone out to sabotage the cannon. That's why they were out patrolling. They weren't very happy about it."

"What?" Orphan said.

"It's very busy in the crater," Elizabeth said. "Frantic. I looked. They're all out. I heard the soldiers say Moriarty pushed the launch forward."

"What?" Orphan said.

"To tonight," Elizabeth said. She suddenly looked quite pleased at the idea. "Do you think we could watch it?"

"Moriarty is here?" Orphan said.

"I guess so," Elizabeth said. "I don't know who he is."

"He's the Prime Minister – quite a good poet, too."

"I don't really like poetry," Elizabeth said. "It's boring."

"Wait," Orphan said, not really listening. "They can't launch now – they have to wait until Mars is close enough, and that's not until…" His voice died and he thought, I am an idiot.

The probe wasn't going to Mars. He had forgotten that. That was just a deception. It only needed to get far enough out into space to send a signal. All the rest of it – the ceremony in Richmond Park, the public proclamations, the newspaper articles – they were all a sham. And he had to act now, or there would be nothing left for him; and Lucy – and, perhaps, humanity – would be doomed.

"How can I get to the cannon?" he said.

"To the crater?" Elizabeth looked both scared, and excited. "You can't. We're not allowed."

"But you must have some interaction with the people there?" Orphan said. "You mentioned something about kitchens."

"Yes, but the kitchens are underground," Elizabeth said.

"So how does the food get to the people in the crater?"

"Through a shaft, I think," Elizabeth said. "There's a pulley system."

Orphan sighed. Images of the future flashed before his eyes. They were not promising.

The dumbwaiter was a small confined metal box. It stank of stale food. Orphan looked at it doubtfully. He did not like the thought of what may be waiting above ground.

He and Elizabeth had made their way through the tunnels into the kitchens. They were situated in a great, ill-lit cavern that was full of smoke. Wherever he went the people he encountered stopped and stared at him, then came closer and touched him, as if to reassure themselves of the reality of his existence. He had found it all very trying.

But, on the plus side, nobody tried to stop him. It was as if these people had curiosity bred out of them, leaving in its wake a kind of numb acceptance of the way things were. Elizabeth took him directly to the dumbwaiter. It was sometime between breakfast and lunch, and the machine wasn't being used.

Orphan climbed inside it.

"Good luck," Elizabeth said. And hit a button.

The dumbwaiter shook, coughed, and began to rise. Orphan crouched in the corner, trying to make himself as small as possible.

He rose through a shaft of rough stone. The dumbwaiter clucked and shook. At last it emerged into light, coughed once more, and stopped. Orphan peered out.

The room ahead was empty. He slid out of the box and stood up cautiously.

He was, he soon discovered, in the back of a sort of mess hall. Long tables stood in perfect rows. Small windows cut into the walls filtered in sunlight. He walked over to a window and peered outside.

The giant cannon glared at him. From here, it was impossibly large, dominating everything. People moved about it, as small as ants in comparison. There was an air of tense anticipation to those people, a feel of buzzing activity. Again, he was reminded of ants. The crater had become a colony of them, he thought. And somewhere, then, there must be the Queen – or rather, the Prime Minister. Wasn't Moriarty there?

"Oi, you're not allowed to...!" He swung around as soon as the voice registered, swung at the speaker even before his mind caught up. A soldier, young, almost a boy, in a too-large, muddy uniform, a shorn scalp, a nose that had been broken before and was now, because of Orphan, broken again.

The boy clutched his bleeding nose and stared at Orphan, then rushed at him.

Orphan ducked, barely, and smacked the boy on the back of the head.

The boy dropped to the floor. Orphan swore.

What did you expect? a part of him said. Did you think you could just walk up here, destroy these people's life-work, and stroll out again?

Yet he hated what he had to do. He had changed. He was no longer the young man whose greatest crime was in belonging to the Persons from Porlock, who were merely pranksters, modern clowns out to stir a bit of trouble for the literati. He was a fugitive now, a desperate man, who had both seen and caused violence. He swore again, then dragged the unconscious boy to the back of the room, and hastily stripped him. He put on the boy's uniform (it was a little tight, but otherwise fit) and put his own clothes, or rather those of the subterranean people, piled on the soldier's body after he dumped him in the dumbwaiter.

He hit a button on the wall. The machine creaked and began to descend.

There is no other way, he thought. He had to get rid of the soldier somehow. But in doing so he put the subterranean people – my own family, he thought, appalled – in danger.

He tried not to think about it. He picked up the soldier's gun and marched out into the sunlight.

He wasn't challenged. The area he found himself in was a loose collection of low-lying stone buildings and large tent-like bubbles. It must be the living quarters, he thought. But there were few people around, and those that were merely glanced at him, noted the uniform and paid him little attention.

Ahead of him was the cannon. It dominated everything, its silver metal flashing in the sunlight, its tip reaching high into the blue skies until it seemed to rip through clouds.

The cannon stood in a clearing, beyond which were the temporary-looking structures of bubble-tents. He could see the two black airships in the distance, anchored to the ground, keeping watch.

He had to find the control room. Or could he go up to the cannon itself, and act then?

No. As he came closer the number of soldiers grew, and he could not afford to be stopped by them. Panic took hold of him. He only had limited time. The soldier he had hurt was bound to come awake down below, to raise the alarm. Already they were suspicious, had known he was on the island. He had to hurry.

It was then, as he paused and squinted in the sun and looked again towards the cannon, with a befuddled sense of being suddenly helpless, that he saw Moriarty.

The Prime Minister looked uncomfortable in the unforgiving haze of the sun. He was a short man turning to fat, and sweat stained his face as he walked quickly, with sharp heavy breaths, away from the cannon. He was surrounded: scientists in white smocks; functionaries in outlandish tropical clothes no doubt concocted in expensive Savile Row tailors, a long way from any tropical sun; and soldiers. This group, with Moriarty at its centre, moved across the arid landscape, and Orphan followed at a distance.

It was a long walk; the sun beat down hard on Orphan, who was uncomfortable in the unfamiliar uniform. He wondered how the soldiers handled it. The group moved away from the ramshackle assortment of buildings and headed further out, towards the edge of the crater. Where were the lizards? Orphan wondered. He had seen none in the crater, none in the tunnels. This was their home, their hidden seat of power, and yet, there was no sign of them. He felt uneasy. What else was hiding on the island?

Moriarty and his people approached the rise of land and disappeared around a crest. Orphan, sweating, followed. He reached the low crest of a hill – but the group had disappeared.

He swore again.

Descending the small hill, he found only a dry brook at the bottom but, as he looked down at the ground he struck lucky – there were footsteps in the sand. He followed them a short way up, but found the way blocked by a giant boulder. The footmarks ended just before the stone.

Where did they all go?

He began searching the stone, his hands touching the rough, warm surface in search of a hidden spring, some kind of artificial control, but could find nothing but unbroken rock.

He swore again and sat down. It was all part of a big, invisible web, he thought. With the spider forever hidden, weaving forever more strands to confuse and entrap. Where did they go?

He let his mind wander. Suddenly, none of this seemed particularly important. How was he to sabotage the cannon, anyway? And for what? Should he prevent the lizards from calling to their own people? Were they planning invasion – or did they simply desire to escape a backwards world that was for them a prison?

Perhaps, he thought, it was a little of both. His eyes tracked a column of ants across the sand. A lizard darted out of nowhere and snatched several of the ants with its tongue. The remaining ants continued to march, despite the attack.

Are we the ants? he thought. Or... His train of thought was interrupted. Where had the lizard come from? He could no longer see the reptile, but his eyes caught the quick darting trail it left across the sand. There!

He bent down on his knees and crawled forward in the sand until he was directly beneath the boulder, in its shade. Something flashed. He cleared sand with his hands.

Below him there was, revealed, not more earth but bars of dull metal, stretching away from him. He was standing on some kind of a ramp!

Before he could move again the ground shook, and for one terrified moment he was convinced the boulder was about to roll over and crush him. Then the ramp descended, sand, ants and all, and he found himself voyaging once more below ground.

"It is I," Orphan muttered, "Quod feci, Arne Saknussemm," and he thought of Verne, the fat writer's image forming before him in sharp relief, and he suddenly missed home very much indeed.

The ramp did not travel far. Orphan found himself in a small antechamber, empty, with no features or signs of life. As the

ramp touched the ground it almost immediately traversed its
course and began to slowly rise. Orphan rolled away and landed
on the stone floor. The ramp rose and soon blocked out the sunlight. Orphan stood for a moment and let his eyes adjust to the
semi-darkness. Something crawled on his hand and he panicked,
but it was only an ant, separated from its comrades in the dis-
turbance. He put it down on the floor and wished it well. It was
lost, just like him.

Then he got up and stepped through the door of the antechamber, and into a corridor and the sight of guns aimed
levelly at him.

THIRTY-ONE
Moriarty

"Who, then, is Porlock?" I asked.
"Porlock, Watson, is a nom de plume, a mere identification mark, but behind it lies a shifty and evasive personality. In a former letter he frankly informed me that the name was not his own, and defied me ever to trace him among the teeming millions of this great city."
— Arthur Conan Doyle, *The Valley of Fear*

This time he couldn't fight. There were three of them, and they were armed. What's more, they had obviously been waiting for him.

The soldiers didn't speak to him. First they frisked him, finding no weapons but confiscating the book, his mother's book. He tried to protest but they merely pushed him along. They were young, about his age, and they marched him along the corridor, their guns at his back, making sure he followed the route to wherever he was being taken. Orphan breathed in air and tried to calm himself down. All in all, his attempt to sabotage the cannon, such as it was, had not gone very well.

The soldiers led him further down, but now there was a fresh breeze blowing through and he thought he could hear, in the distance, the far cries of seagulls. The path twisted around and around, as if meant only to confuse him. At last they came to a door.

Unlike the rest of the tunnels, which seemed old and worn with time, this door seemed new. A coat of white paint so fresh it could have been applied an hour before, a gleaming brass handle, a small window of patterned glass: it had the feel of an office in the City, or a Whitehall interview room.

The nearest soldier knocked, then pushed the door open. As it opened Orphan, too, was pushed, and he stumbled into the room. He stood alone in a room empty of furnishings but for a solitary unoccupied chair in the centre, and a desk in one corner.

Behind the desk sat Moriarty.

One of the soldiers had followed him into the room. He went to the Prime Minister's desk, whispered some words to him, and handed him the book. Moriarty nodded. The soldier saluted and left the room. The door closed behind him.

Orphan had never seen the Prime Minister up close, yet he immediately recognised his face. The bald, high dome of his head, the deep-set eyes, the austere yet sensual mouth – here was a man of great ability, a poet as well as an administrator of great renown, the man who effectively ran the empire. Now, those dark eyes examined Orphan, and the hint of a smile lifted the corners of the Prime Minister's mouth.

"Please," Moriarty said. "Sit down." He had a pleasant, dry voice which was a little high-pitched. He gestured for the chair and Orphan sat down, facing the Prime Minister. This is it, he thought. This is where it ends. The room had no windows. He could no longer hear the call of seabirds. A deep unsettling silence lay on the room like a dust-sheet.

"So you are the mysterious saboteur," Moriarty said. "The would-be saboteur, I should say."

Orphan didn't reply, and Moriarty shrugged. "Don't feel bad," he said. "It was easy enough to deduct the path that led you here. Clearly, you would be taking shelter in the tunnels, or you would have been caught already. Clearly, you only survived the island because of your blood – and my people tell me that you are indeed the rightful heir to the throne…" He stopped when he saw Orphan's eyes open wide, sudden panic mounting behind them. "You didn't know?"

"I…" He didn't know what to say. To be related to the ancient kings was one thing, but this?

"You are, or so I'm told, the only grandson of Catherine and Bertram. Ergo, you are first in line to the throne – were there a throne, young William." Moriarty's face absorbed his previous pleasantness as if it never existed. "Were there a throne."

The King of England. Orphan almost laughed.

"It was easy enough to deduct you will attempt something soon, and to reason that your only easy way into the crater would be via the food duct. Don't worry, by the way: the soldier you disabled is fine."

Orphan had flashes of the soldier he surprised at the mess hall. "You were waiting for me?"

Moriarty shrugged. "Of course. After all, it isn't every day that one meets a King-in-Waiting. And a poet too, I hear? In fact, I do believe I read something of yours, in the *Review*?"

"Well…" Orphan said. He had published in the *Poetic Review* a couple of times, but…

"'Finding a two-pence coin I lift it from the mud and see, the profile of an unknown monarch, her mouth slack and her eyes locked into infinity…'" Moriarty quoted. "Something of this nature? I remember you, Orphan. I thought you had great potential as a poet. It is a shame you had to choose adventure. Poetry, I find, is so much better coming from a life lived as dully as can be."

Orphan examined him. The dark eyes stared back at him, missing nothing. He felt like an open book, riffled by the Prime Minister as if its contents were merely of passing interest. As if reading his thoughts, Moriarty reached for the book on his desk and picked it up. "*Bible Stories for Young Children*?" Moriarty said. He opened the book. Orphan looked at it closely, perhaps for the first time. There was something strangely familiar about it, as if he had seen this sort of printing, this sort of binding, before. "The Bookman's book," Moriarty said. "So clever…" He sighed, and kept leafing through the empty pages. "It is hard to run an empire when your masters' grasp of their own technology is virtually non-existent," he said. "I often wished we could have worked together with the Bookman. Yes," he said, smiling into Orphan's surprised face, "I know what he is, what he wants. Les Lézards' servant, and their store of knowledge too. And yet – a revolutionary element, like our own. A dangerous one. It's a shame…" He closed the book, holding it in both hands. "I will have it sent to the technicians for analysis. Perhaps something useful could be gleaned of it yet. Now, as for you, young Orphan…"

Those were the words he was hoping not to hear. "What will you do with me?" he said.

The Prime Minister turned the book in his hands. He seemed fascinated by it. And now Orphan knew what it reminded him of – the bibles at Guy's Hospital, the ones in every room that had made Inspector Adler so uncomfortable. "I'm afraid," Moriarty said, "that I won't have any choice but to have you executed–"

And at that moment the book in Moriarty's hands suddenly glowed, the binding showing a flash of intense radiation, and Moriarty cried out, but the voice was strangled in his throat. Orphan watched, horrified, and the book tumbled from the Prime Minister's hands and fell to the floor. Moriarty slumped on the desk. He was still breathing, just. His hands, and face, were badly burned. And as he fell a section of the wall slid silently open – revealing, to a horrified Orphan, a small control panel, and a curious screen, and the image of the cannon with people like ants moving around its base. Orphan snatched the book from Moriarty's hands and tucked it back in his pocket. He stared at the prone Prime Minister, and then at the control panel, no longer hidden, and at the cannon it was showing, the cannon it was there to control, and he thought, with a sudden, overwhelming uncertainty – what do I do?

And now he was running, running through tunnels, his sweat burning on his face and getting into his eyes; behind him the pursuers followed, and a shot echoed, a burst of stone hit his face and cut his skin. Away from the stunned or dead Moriarty, away from capture and death, onwards, in a mad frightened rush to get away.

Orphan ran, slipped, found the ground sloping sharply away from him. He stumbled. The air was hot, clammy and humid like the inside of an engine-room; from somewhere unseen he could once more smell the sea. He was in some sort of duct. He surrendered to the slide, arching his back away from the floor, his body resting on his heels and back, and so, like a child at play, he slid downwards, his speed increasing with each passing moment.

More shots behind him, but none coming close. Air rushed into his face. The smooth floor offered no resistance, no way to slow down. He thought of hitting something hard and ending up a blot of red against stone walls.

Don't, he thought.

Somewhere nearer, the cry of birds. The space he was in expanded, and a light grew ahead. An opening. He went through it–

He was flying through the air.

He had the sense of a wide space opening below him. Green and blue, a sense of free-falling, the ground opening below him–

He crashed into warm water with a huge explosion. His lungs burned. He had the sense of dark, heavy shapes moving below him. He kicked out and broke back to the surface. He looked at where he was.

He was in a large pool of water.

The pool was surrounded by lizards.

The pursuers hadn't followed him. He knew why. And thought that now he truly was in trouble.

He was in the Nursery. Around him, lizard young milled on rocks and watched him with curious, unblinking eyes. Every now and then a tongue would dart out and taste the air, and the eyes would blink, slowly and ponderously, and focus back on him. He got the distinct impression they regarded him as a new toy, and were curious as to his application.

He swam to the edge and hauled himself out, and for a long moment he remained lying on the ground, catching his breath, not daring to move for fear of what would happen. When he rose at last he could see, amidst the lizards, the cowering shapes of human beings. And he thought, My family. The idea was bitter to him.

He made to move, and the nearest lizard darted at him, and he stopped. The lizard's tongue snaked out and tasted his skin.

Then, startling Orphan so much that he nearly fell back in the water, the lizard spoke.

"Sssss..." it said, and flicked its tail. "Sssservant..." It moved away from him then, losing interest. The others, too, returned gradually to their previous activities. The humans (he did not recognise any of them) cast nervous, fearful glances at him and moved between their charges.

Orphan accepted the unspoken message.

Soon, he knew, the soldiers would come for him; and if not them, the lizards themselves might come, to see who it was who dared threaten their get with his presence, and this he feared even more. He remembered the sight of the two lizards fighting each other to the death, back in the King's Arms in Drury Lane. He did not think himself capable of this kind of fight.

He felt lost then, and almost gave up the fight altogether; when he felt something hard against his hip and, startled for a moment, reached out and realised it was his mother's book. No, he thought. It was the Bookman's, and it made him frightened.

But he was not like the others of his family, he thought. He, at least, would not fear books. He opened the book, wondering if some of its power remained, if some of the Bookman's artifice was yet in it, but... the book remained empty and old. It did not come alive, and the pages remained stained-yellow and otherwise blank. He leafed through it again, nevertheless, until he reached the end, and the small, fading inscription left there long ago by his mother: Under the Nursery, the mushrooms grow flat.

How had she managed to escape? In one end of the Nursery he could now hear shouts, and knew the soldiers had come for him. It was almost dark now, and the cannon's payload would be launched soon, the attempt would be made to reach the stars.

And he would most likely be dead.

Is that how you want to be remembered? he thought. As a saboteur? He looked around him at the lizard young. Could he take their life in his hands? What would the probe have meant? He was too late asking himself these questions.

Instead, he ran. He ran away from the soldiers, away from the Nursery, towards the sea. The giant cave he was in opened about him like a fan, the ground sloping gently until the pools of water almost poured down into the sea.

There are no defences here, he thought. Not this close to the babies. There would be no monstrous worms in the sand, no giant insects to suck out blood. I hope.

Down by the shore the ceiling abruptly disappeared above his head, and in its stead were stars. He took a deep lungful of night air. It tasted fresh and welcoming, homely almost. It escaped from him then in a shuddered breath and he jumped from the ledge of the cave onto the fine black sand below.

They were after him, coming, but slowly, hampered by their fear of harming these babies, the most precious in the whole of the empire. But they were coming, and would not be long in catching up to him.

He wandered off along the beach. He felt suddenly free, his purpose at last fulfilled. He thought of Lucy.

Before him rose the mushrooms.

Gigantic, they were nevertheless different to the ones in the caves. Sleek and fleshy, they spread out in concentric circles, a forest of low-lying, flat surfaces suspended on thick shafts.

Where the mushrooms grow flat… A wild idea took hold of Orphan, and he followed it. Putting the book back in his pocket, he attacked the largest of the mushrooms. There was something strange about them…

The shouts were coming closer – much closer. Then, a gun-shot. He ducked, but they were still not quite out of the cave yet, and their aim was bad.

At last a shaft gave way, and a giant mushroom, free of its earthly bond, glided gracefully away, and landed in the dark waters.

"Stop!" someone shouted, and there was a volley of fire. Ducking, panting, Orphan ran low and sprang himself onto the floating fungi. He almost laughed, the sensation was so odd; it was like he was once again a child, and this was a giant toy, wobbling this way and that with no control. He spread his legs outwards and began to paddle slowly, as quietly as he could, away from the shore and into the open sea. Water soaked into his clothes but the makeshift raft held him – just.

Behind him the shouts grew and more shots followed, but they were aimless, and came nowhere near. He continued to paddle, into the dark dark sea, away from the island, and imagined himself growing into a small point, unseen in the unchanging vastness of water. He felt exulted, buoyant – buoyant, he thought, and almost giggled. Like the mushrooms, staying afloat.

Soon the sounds of the shore grew faint, then faded away. He turned his head but could no longer see the island, could no longer see anything but the dark unchanging water of the sea. I'm lost, he thought, but the thought brought him no pain, only a fierce, unmitigated joy.

At last, he stopped, and turned and lay on his back, and gazed at the stars. Did he do the right thing? he wondered. He felt free of all decisions, of all consequences. The stars gazed back at him and offered no answers.

A light.

Something blinked. A light, growing larger. An eerie glow was cast on the sea before him, and he could see the surface of the water, and in the distance, the outline of the island growing bright. It was not as far as he had thought.

The cannon!

He watched as a great ball of fire gathered and grew and flew high in the air, and he tensed lest it failed, lest it died and fell into the sea.

It flew straight.

He watched the narrow needle of the cannon, the fire emerging from its rear, grow distant, grow smaller. The shadows around him diminished.

He was sent on this mission, on this impossible mission, to sabotage that cannon, prevent its cargo from reaching beyond the world. The Bookman, Wyvern: they had wanted him to do it, each for his own reasons and, perhaps, unknown to him, thousands of others had wished he'd done the same. But when he'd had the chance, when he was placed in the position to damage it, to make it fail – he couldn't.

He did not sabotage the cannon.

Was he right to make the decision? Now the signal would be sent, and the lizards, the other lizards, would come. Would they come as friends, or enemies? Would there be anyone left to even see the sign? But he thought of the lizard young, and he thought of the lizards crashing into the earth and into the heart of the island, and he thought they were like sailors, stranded on a tropical and alien shore after a terrible storm. Could he deny them their flare, their distress signal? If they had done bad things, if they had deposed kings and made this place their home and their kingdom, they acted no more nor less than humans would. There were arguments, so many arguments, for and against, and he thought of Lucy now and knew that, though she may never now come back to him, she would have understood. When at last it came, he could not do it.

Waves came, and rocked his raft, but gently, and in the distance he could see an enormous figure rise from the water, and then another, and another. He watched them, unafraid.

They were whales.

For a moment, he imagined he could see a woman, rising from the sea between the giant figures. Looking at him.

Lucy, he thought, and felt happy.

He closed his eyes. Around him, the singing of the whales rose in an unearthly symphony.

He drifted on the sea throughout the night and half through the day, growing thirsty beyond belief, but not losing that strange composure, that new peace he had found. He lay flat and tried not to move, and the sun beat on him and his craft sank lower and lower into the water, and he wondered how long it would be before he sank completely.

It was approaching dusk when he saw the thing in the sky, and for a long moment he just stared at it, the shape making no meaningful connections in his head. It was a round thing, painted gaudy yellow and green, like a circus tent's canopy. Was it a bird?

Then it came closer, and lower, approaching him like a vast floating whale, and he thought – a balloon! He stared up at it, smiling stupidly, and saw the open cabin, and a head peering out at him, and someone calling his name.

He waved at the face. It shouted more at him, but he could understand none of it. Then something was thrown from the balloon and hit him, and he was thrown into the water.

He flailed and took hold of the thing that was thrown. What was it? He looked at the ropes, examined them with his fingers.

"Bloody get on it, you stupid boy!"

It was a ladder. A rope-ladder. He laughed. It was so funny, to be floating in the sea alone and see a thing like that. Where had it come from?

"Quickly, you nincompoop!"

He felt he had better obey the voice. The face it came from was fat and sweaty and looked angry. He wondered if it had some water for him.

He pulled himself onto the ladder. Rising from the water was agony. His body was pain. Each step made thinking impossible.

One step, and two. Three. Four. His hands felt raw and they hurt, but he kept going.

Five. Six. He almost let go. It would be pleasant to drown in the warm, peaceful waters...

Seven. Eight.

"Come on, boy!"

Nine. Ten. Eleven–

And suddenly it was over.

Hands pulled him into the safety of the cabin. He looked down and saw his craft sinking far below.

"Orphan!"

"Wha'?"

He tried to focus on the fat man.

"It's me!" The fat man fed him water. It ran over Orphan's broken lips and into his mouth, and was the most delicious thing he had ever tasted. His eyes focused, and he said, haltingly, "Verne?"

"I've found you!" the fat man said, and he grinned at Orphan, and almost gathered him into his arms.

"I..." Orphan said, a short, single word that seemed to him to encompass a whole range of meaning. Then he passed out.

PART III
Prometheus Unbound

THIRTY-TWO
The Return of the King

A glucose trap, snap crackle pop
We crossed the Strand and saw a sign:
This way to the Egress.
   – L.T., "After the Waste Land"

Less than twenty-four hours after arriving back in the city, Orphan had been attacked twice, robbed once, and finally thrown in a police cell. It had not been a good day.

He had returned on a cold, damp day. Thick grey fog, suffused with the stench of burning chemicals, wafted over the water.

The *Nautilus* had sailed under the Thames and into the city. It did so in stealth, invisible to all but the whales, who gave it a wide berth as it sailed past them. They did not consider it one of their own.

The *Nautilus*, this *Nautilus*, was not a clipper but a submarine. It had lain hidden below the clipper ship bearing its name until the pirates' attack. Then, with only its captain, his wide-girthed guest and a handful of specially picked men, it had disengaged from the above-water *Nautilus* and sank, quietly and without trace, into the depths of the Carib Sea.

"You left them to die," Orphan had said, aghast. Verne had shrugged apologetically; Captain Dakkar, splendid in a white, starched uniform, merely glowered. "You left me to die."

"Far from it!" Verne had said. They were sitting in the *Nautilus'* dining room. Large windows cut into the side of the vehicle showed the dark depths of the sea, and strange, glowing fish that glided past and stared with large, mournful eyes into the sub's interior. "You see, there was a large probability–"

"Yes?"

"That capture by Wyvern–"

"That reptile," Dakkar said. Verne smiled apologetically at Orphan and shrugged as if to say, Well, what can you do. "That capture by Wyvern," he said again, raising his voice, "would lead you to the island."

"Is that so?"

"It was a possibility. And possibilities, you know, are what this is all about, Orphan."

"If you let machines think they can manipulate lives," Dakkar said, continuing to glower.

"Well, can't they?" Verne said.

The captain didn't reply. Then he said, more softly, as if thinking to himself, "But what if the machines themselves are at opposite ends?" and his eyes took in Orphan with a disconcerting gaze, and came to rest on Orphan's thumb, the one the Binder had... had taken.

"That's neither here nor there," Verne said, oblivious. And, to Orphan, cheerfully, "There was always the possibility you'd fail, of course. But you didn't, did you? It all worked out, and here you are. Here we are."

"Yes," Orphan said. "Here we are."

It was Dakkar himself who had sent the message to the pirates. The attack had been engineered. Orphan had suspected Aramis wrongly. He thought of all the people who had died, all so he would – fail. He was angry – but at the same time, simply glad to be alive. And Verne had saved him, in the last count.

It had been an uncomfortable journey back. They did not speak much. Orphan wondered what he would do. Hunt down the Bookman, he thought. And – Lucy. Would she understand? The

Bookman must already know Orphan had failed him. What would he do?

Verne wanted to know everything about the island. He was fascinated by Orphan's raft. Already, he said, he was working on a new novel, though he was sparse with details. Something involving giant squid, Orphan gathered. Giant squid in space.

Verne and Dakkar had no further instructions from the Bookman. Their last, Verne had said, was simply to find Orphan and then return home. Verne looked tired; Dakkar, mostly annoyed. Orphan gathered he intended returning to India as soon as was possible and with his excess baggage of passengers suitably discharged. A revolution was coming, he said.

Change was in the air.

Change was in the air on the day Orphan landed back in the city. It was night time; the fog swirled, noxious and thick, over the abandoned wharf of Limehouse; and Orphan, stepping onto dry land from the sub-aquatic vehicle for the first time in what seemed like forever, stopped and breathed in the city like a man rolling fine, expensive wine on the tongue after a long-enforced abstinence.

The city smelled of a thousand different things, manure and smoke, polish and oil, shag tobacco and flowery perfume; somewhere, faint and yet overpowering, the musty smell of venerable old books. The city echoed with a thousand different sounds, from the distant, mournful song of the whales clustered by Waterloo Bridge, to a distant gunshot and, nearer, the scratchy sound of an Edison record, and someone singing. The tune was quick, fiery, and as for the words... it took Orphan by surprise, recognising the words of an old Shelley poem, set to the music, and the unknown singer sang:

"The sound is of whirlwind underground, earthquake, and fire, and mountains cloven; the shape is awful, like the sound, clothed in dark purple, star-inwoven, a sceptre of pale gold."

"Earthquake and fire!" came the refrain. The music rolled around the dockyard and seemed to Orphan to eddy with the fog. He felt it stir something in him, a quickening of the blood, a response as to a call to arms. "To stay steps proud, over the slow cloud, his veined hand doth hold," sang the unknown voice, and the words were those of Panthea, speaking of Prometheus, who rebelled against the gods. "Cruel he looks, but calm and strong, like one who does, not suffers wrong!"

"Not suffers wrong!"

Almost, it sounded to him like Jack's voice. Jack, shouting, inflamed with the passion of... of revolution. Then the song died down, faded into the fog, its origin unknown. Yet he was to hear it elsewhere, wherever he went in the city, like a musical bond holding together the citizens and subjects of Victoria, Lizard Queen of an empire on which the sun never set, and stirring them into strange and inexplicable acts of rebellion.

"My friend," Verne said as they parted. "Be careful."

Orphan shook the fat writer's hand, if reluctantly, and saluted Dakkar's back. The *Nautilus* closed its hatch and, with barely a sound, disappeared into the dark waters of the Thames. Orphan was left alone on the Embankment. It was suddenly very quiet.

He was first attacked as he made his way west, past Whitechapel. The streets were deserted, which he found strange, and there were very few lights in the windows. It was as if the city had been abandoned, and yet there was a certain hushed expectancy about the place, a tension underneath the stillness. It set him on edge.

The attack came near Spitalfields Market. Orphan crossed the deserted street, his attention focused on the distant light of the Babbage Tower, a beacon through the fog. He only noticed the man as he came directly at him out of the fog, a drawn blade glinting dully, and he ducked, instinctively, and kicked out, the way he had once seen Aramis do.

Luck, not skill, made the kick connect, and he heard his assailant grunt with pain. Orphan reached for his gun, a departing present from Verne, fumbled with it–

The knife came at him again, and he pulled the trigger.

The man fell. Orphan saw his face then; and had to hold himself from taking a step back.

It was a punk de Lézard.

He had last seen one in Nantes, but he could not forget that moment: lizard boys, Verne had called them. But what was one doing here?

The punk's face was a tattoo of green bands, his ears pinned back against his skull, and his head was round, a polished dome with only a strip of spiked hair at the centre. The man, wounded, hissed at him, and he saw that his tongue had been crudely modified, stretched and pared in the middle, so that it was forked and elongated, in bad imitation of a lizard's.

The man tried to rise. The blade was in his hand. It was bloodied, Orphan saw. He had hurt – perhaps killed – at least once before that night.

The man lunged at him.

Orphan shot him again.

The lizard boy sank back. The knife, finally, fell from his hand.

Who was he? Orphan thought. The man was a killer. And again – a lizard boy? Here?

He put the gun back in its holster. He felt hot and clammy under the heavy coat he was no longer used to wearing.

What had happened to the city?

After a moment, he picked his way again, more cautiously this time. He was not even sure where he was going. And then – find Tom, he thought. Get back to the Nell Gwynne. Tom would know what was happening. He always did.

He was passing through Farringdon, the old city walls on his left, when he first saw sign of people. They were marching in the street outside the courts, a group of them, all silent, wearing heavy coats against the chill, women and men who could have been anyone, clerks or magistrates, carpenters or cooks, yet here they were, in the small hours of the night, marching outside the courts, and there was a burning effigy held high above their heads.

Orphan watched the silent procession. The effigy was giant-sized, and lizardine. It could have been the Queen herself, or it could have been a stand-in for all of lizard-kind. It was burning too fiercely by now to be able to tell.

What was happening to the city? He drew deep into the shadows and watched the marchers go past. Behind the effigy of the lizard another group came, cowled in black, another effigy held high.

This one didn't burn.

He stared at it, horrified. It was in the image of a man. The man was dressed in rich robes. He held a sceptre in his hand.

He wore a crown, and he had no face.

As the cowled figures moved past the one in the lead turned her head and for a moment the light of the fire fell on her face. Her eyes looked into the shadows and seemed to gaze directly at Orphan. He felt the force of her scrutiny like a physical thing, and shock as he recognised her.

It was Isabella Beeton.

Did she see him? He couldn't tell. Her head turned again and she marched ahead, and the effigy of the King followed her.

Wherever Isabella Beeton was, Orphan thought, conspiracy was never far behind. And yet he almost ran after her: she was a familiar face, and had always, before, been a friendly one.

Yet he didn't. He did not know what was going on. The city had changed, become a dangerous, unpredictable place. He was disturbed by the sight of this midnight march. A burning lizard…

But it was the other effigy that made his heart beat faster and his hands sweat. The crowned, human king.

He had to find shelter, and some information.

The second, successful attack on Orphan came in the early hours of the morning, as the sun began to rise, pale sunlight transforming the city streets into, somehow, more ordinary places from which the danger of night seemed to be lifted, if only a little.

He was on the Strand, curiously empty of people but for a lone beggar sleeping in the doorway of Gibbons' stamp shop, and had almost reached Bull Inn Court – and with it, or so he hoped, the safety of the Nell Gwynne – when he was struck from behind.

The pain blossomed in his head like a rapidly growing mushroom, suffocating him. He fell to the ground and lay there, numb. Hands riffled through his pockets, expertly, then the sound of feet, running away. He never saw his assailant.

After a while, the pain abated, and he groaned and began to move. As he began to cautiously rise he felt a presence beside him and instinctively lashed out.

"Sir!" said a rugged voice, and Orphan turned and saw that the beggar from the doorway was now standing beside him, stooped in his dirty rags. "I am but a humble beggar, coming to your lordship's aid!"

"A bit too late for that," Orphan said sourly. His head hurt, and his gun and his money were gone, though the beggar left him his mother's old book, which was no doubt not worth stealing. Books in this city were a penny a pound. The weight of words pressed down on the old streets, numerous millions of them, cranked out day or night by the printing presses and the men and women who churned them out, like so many factory-produced trinkets.

Money and a gun – you knew were you were with them. But a book? What good was a book?

"Did you see who it was?" Orphan said.

The beggar shook his head dolefully. "A common thief," he said. "He'll be long gone by now."

"No doubt," Orphan said. He staggered up and felt his eyes water.

"Here," the beggar said. "Sit down a while." He helped Orphan to the doorway of the shop and sat him down; and, wearily folding himself beside him, extracted from a hidden pocket a small flask at the same time.

"Drink this," the beggar said. "It will help. Also, it will warm you up."

Orphan looked at the flask. Though worn and faded, it was monogrammed with the letters *S.H.*, and he wondered how the beggar had got hold of it. Stolen, possibly, or just found in a rubbish tip. He eyed it with suspicion.

The beggar grinned, unstoppered the flask and handed it to Orphan. "Whiskey," he said. "It's a wonderful medicine."

Orphan drank; and the heat of the whiskey ran through his body like a series of controlled explosions. He coughed and felt his face go red and his eyes water. The beggar grinned and slapped him on the back. His face swam before Orphan's eyes, the sharp features and prominent nose, awakening a dim memory. "Do I know you?" he said. The beggar looked much livelier now, though that may simply have been a product of the drink.

"Wind, rain, and thunder," the beggar said, "remember, earthly man is but a substance that must yield to you. And I, as fits my nature, do obey you."

Orphan looked at him. There was something familiar about the face, glimpsed briefly, in the midst of night, in a cold place, behind a plate of glass…

Guy's Hospital. And a still, unmoving man frozen in a coffin, whose brother…

"Who are you?" Orphan said. He tried to stand, but felt his head swimming; his arms would no longer obey him.

"A friend," the beggar said, his voice soft and faraway. "A friend who can see what the sea has cast once more upon these shores. It is no magic, but logic only. Be careful, Orphan. This is a bad time to be a prince."

"What… what did you do to me?" Orphan said, his voice slurring. He could not focus his eyes.

When he opened them again, the beggar was no longer there, though his flask remained, somehow clasped, unstoppered and upturned, in Orphan's hands. The liquid seeped into his clothes. He felt a kick, not hard but prodding, and raised his eyes to the sight of two beefy policemen.

"Drunk as a dog!" one of them said. "help me up with 'im, Harry."

"I ain't touching him, Bert!" the other policeman said. "Last one I did emptied his guts all over me!"

Bert chuckled. "A bit of experience," he said, "is priceless in this job. Now let 'im up, and watch where he aims."

Orphan was lifted up. He swayed, but wasn't sick, for which the policemen were no doubt grateful.

"Don't worry, lad, we'll find you a nice dry cell to sleep it off," Bert said. "Don't want to be out on the street on a day like this. Lizard boys'd get you."

"Or the rebels," Harry said. Orphan was meanwhile being moved. He tried to speak, tell them he was fine and to leave him alone, but only managed to dribble, which made Harry swear and his partner chuckle.

"Things might be better when the King comes back," Harry said quietly.

"Shut it, Harry," Bert said. "You don't know who's listening."

The rest of the journey to the police station progressed in silence. The streets were still deserted. The same eerie silence greeted them at the police station. There were few policemen, and even fewer prisoners. Bert and Harry took Orphan down to the cells, which were empty but for one, where a dark figure lay unmoving. They released him into the nearest cell, and he collapsed down on the floor. He tried to speak again, but couldn't.

"Sleep it off, lad," Bert said. "Believe me, we're only doing you a favour."

"A day like this..." Harry said, and shook his head meaningfully.

"At least the Ripper is finally caught," Bert said. "You hear that, boy? They found his corpse last night. Somebody shot him."

"And good riddance," Harry said.

Orphan moved his mouth groggily. He couldn't stay here. How did he end up in this situation? He tried to speak again as Bert was locking the cell door.

"What did he say?" Harry said.

"Addled," Bert said.

"No, Bert, listen to him," Harry said. He watched Orphan through the bars. "He said 'saddler'."

Orphan tried again. The two policemen exchanged glances. Their faces were suddenly serious.

"He said 'Adler', Harry," Bert said.

There was a short, pregnant silence.

"As in Inspector Adler?" Harry said. His voice was very low. And then, "What do we do, Bert?"

There was another short silence.

"We keep him in there," Bert said. "For now. He's in no state to go anywhere. Safest place for him, probably."

"What about the inspector, Bert?" Harry said. "We could get into a lot of trouble."

"Keep your voice down, for starters," Bert said. "This needs some thinking, Harry."

"Would a cup of tea help, Bert?" Harry said, and the other policeman smiled and nodded, and some of the tension seemed to go from his face. "It certainly would," he said.

They left Orphan in the cell and, as they left, the door upstairs closed shut behind them.

THIRTY-THREE
Orphaned

For God's sake, let us sit upon the ground
And tell sad stories of the death of kings;
How some have been deposed; some slain in war,
Some haunted by the ghosts they have deposed.
 – William Shakespeare, *Richard II*

Nothing had changed by the time Orphan had finally got back control of his limbs. He was locked up. The single figure in the cell next door had not stirred.

It was dark. He tried shouting, but nobody came, and he soon gave up. The fogginess gradually subsided, though his head still ached. He cursed the beggar, but it didn't make a difference. Who was he?

He looked at the flask that was still, somehow, with him. It was empty, but smelled foul. So, he had to admit, did he.

All he could hope for was that Inspector Adler might hear he was there and come to investigate. This, or that the policemen might get tired of him and release him. Meanwhile, he just had to wait.

"Hey!" he said, shouting to the prone figure in the other cell. "Are you awake yet?"

There was no reply. He called again, then, getting an idea, ran the flask against the bars.

The noise was tremendous. It beat at his headache like a drum, and he stopped.

The figure in the bed shook, moved, and a head finally half-emerged from underneath the filthy blanket.

"I'm sorry," Orphan said, a little untruthfully, "I didn't mean to wake you."

The figure under the blanket stared at him, dark face wreathed in shadows. Eyes blinked. Then the face emerged further, coming into the dim light, and said, "You!"

And Orphan reeled back and was aware of the pounding of blood in his head, and grabbed the bars of the cell to stay upright. He stared at the face.

The face was his own.

"What?" Orphan said, and "Who–?"

"You," the figure said again, and rose, and came close to the bars separating them from each other. "You utter bastard."

Orphan stared at him in mute shock. His own face stared back at him. His own body – and he looked at the other's thumb and saw that it was whole.

His own body. His own face. But – different, somehow. A deep weariness seemed etched into that face, all youthfulness gone from it. It was dirty, covered with grime, and in the eyes there was a bafflement, the stare receding from anger to a sort of vacant, dull gaze.

"What are you?" he said, whispered, and then again, a shout that echoed in that still, dark place: "What are you!"

"I am Orphan. I am the orphan." The other – the other him – sat down on the bed in the other cell. They were like mirror-images: Orphan sat down too. "I am born of no mother or father. I am like Eve, made from Adam's rib. Adam's thumb." He giggled. "I am the messenger. I am the translator. I am the words that lie inside the binding and wait to be awakened. I am you. You stole me from myself."

He sounded crazy.

"I don't understand," Orphan said, but then the image of the Binder, crazy spider creature on his hideaway island, returned to him, and the Binder's words. "This will hurt," the Binder had said. And then he chopped off Orphan's thumb. Take it down to the growing vats.

Aramis, saying, Will it work? The Binder – Perhaps. For a little while.

"He made a copy of me?"

The other him laughed, whooped, rose from the bed and banged on the bars, startling Orphan. "I am the King of England!" he shouted. "And I am returned, bow to me!"

"You know?"

"I know all." And then the storm passed and the other Orphan sat down again, and Orphan saw how pale he was beneath the dirt. The eyes looked at him, weary, tired, lost. "I can hear it. It speaks to me. I can't shut it up!"

"What happened to you?" Orphan said.

"You," the other said. "You happened. You took my life from me. I should be King! I thought you might have died on that island. I hoped you did. I guess you – we're – just too lucky." And he laughed again, a sound like crying. "How did you get back?"

"By submarine," Orphan said. "The – the *Nautilus* – it was a submarine under the clipper."

"A submarine. It must have been comfortable."

"Not very."

"You had food, drink?"

"I almost died on that island!" Somehow, the other made him feel guilty.

"Better had you died."

"How… how did you come to be here?"

The other laughed. "He sent me," he said. "He pulled me out of the vat, naked, covered in slime. He was in my brain. I could hear the drums beat, and I could understand them. They spoke, a web of sound, of meaning, woven over that entire island. And he was in my head, showing me who I was. William son of Mary, future King of England. And then he took it away from me and gave me nothing." He lay down, curled into a ball. "He made me into a tool," Orphan heard him say. "A tool like he once was…"

Could it be possible? The Binder had somehow made a copy of him? And then he thought – why not? Was that not what the Bookman, too, did? "What happened then?" he asked. He tried to hold in the feelings the other aroused in him: guilt, inexplicable but true, and a sort of compassion, as if one was faced with a younger brother, and could not ease his suffering.

"He put me in an airship. It piloted itself. I don't know how. I had some food. He gave me that at least. Salted fish, some vegetables and bread, fresh water. I ate sparingly, relieved myself over the sea when I needed to. The food wasn't enough. The water ran out before I sighted land."

"But you made it!"

The other laughed again. He did not move from the bed. "Yes," he said. "At last I landed, starved and dehydrated. On the coast of the Irish Sea. How I got there I don't know. I had pretty much lost all direction by then." He coughed, which took a while, then continued. "I made my way south, but slowly. The roads are not safe any more, but I managed. Perhaps no one saw fit to rob me." He sighed, a long and tired sound. "It was only when I got into the city that my luck changed. I was set on by a group of lizard boys – did you see them? They appear to be everywhere now, running in gangs, terrorising the streets. I was beaten up, and when the police arrived I was the one to be arrested. Maybe they thought it was for my own good. These cells might be the safest place in the city right now. And all the while it spoke to me, it is speaking to me, whispering, though I can no longer hear the drums."

"It? What is it?"

And he thought – the Translation?

"It looks like an egg," the other said, sounding surprised. "I don't know why. I thought it would be a book. It is only small, and very pretty. The colours… I can see them even in the dark."

The Translation. But he didn't even understand what it was. A story, told him by Byron in a smoky pub. A legend, an article of faith for those who had nothing else. Could it be real? And what did it do?

"Do you have it still?" he said. There was no answer. "Do you have the egg?"

"It is with me, always. I can hear it, awake or asleep."

"Show me."

Silence.

"Show me!"

The other rose. He came close to the bars again. His eyes stared into Orphan's. "It isn't yours," he said.

"Show me."

The other reached into his clothes. When his hand emerged, it held a pouch, which he loosed and upended.

A small, smooth round object fell into his palm.

Orphan looked at it. It was made of a green metal, eerily lit, and seemed almost to absorb light, so that for a moment the cells were even darker. It seemed to pulse slowly in the other's hand, like a heart plucked out of a body still beating.

Somehow, it seemed to be whispering to him, like the distant echoes of drums, speaking in a mechanical language that weaved and merged and changed with each beat, and he found himself entranced by it, lost in the circles and lines of the beat, reaching for a meaning that was waiting for him, on the cusp of understanding...

"It speaks to me," the other said. "I can hear them. All of them. The dead... they live still, in the Bookman's dark domain. They never leave me in peace!"

Orphan stared at him. Almost, he could hear voices, whispering in his ear, growing louder. He said, "What do you mean?"

The other giggled, a sudden, startling sound. "I can show you," he said.

"Show me what?"

"Not what," the other said. "Who." He held the Translation tightly in his hand. "You can bring them back, for a short time. Like ghosts. They like to talk. Always talk!"

"Lucy?" Orphan whispered, but the other shook his head. "No."

"What do you mean?" He was shouting. The other shook his head. "I don't know. But I can show you." He was like a child with a toy, jealous of it and yet wanting to display it, to show it off. "Here."

The other moved his hand. The egg glowed. The other giggled. "He is my friend," he said–

A figure materialised in the cell, slowly, like motes of dust assembling into a shape as light plays on them. It had a face that Orphan knew. And it smiled. Its eyes were blind.

"Orphan," Gilgamesh said. "I see you've been busy."

He had Gilgamesh's face, Gilgamesh's unseeing eyes, yet his voice was ethereal, without substance. It seemed to float around Orphan's ears, to trace patterns of coloured light in the air between them.

"You're dead," Orphan said, and Gilgamesh smiled, and nodded. "Am I hallucinating?"

"You're asking me?"

There was gentle amusement in the question. Orphan realised its futility. He said, "What is happening to me?"

"This egg," Gilgamesh said. "This *Translation*. I once heard stories… I think it can communicate with the Bookman's machines, somehow. There are so many of us here, Orphan… so many souls in a bottle, with no senses, no body, nothing but the patterns of what we once were. He doesn't know, yet. You must be careful."

So many… Lucy, Orphan thought. But Gilgamesh, as if reading his mind, shook his head. "She is not in here."

"What does that mean?"

"I don't know. Maybe she is stored separately. Maybe she was given a body again."

Orphan thought back. He had seen Lucy before… There was a boat. It was just after he had met Mycroft. He stood, alone, on the embankment, when it came sailing out of the mist, a single person sitting in the prow, and his breath slammed into his lungs and froze his thoughts into small hard diamonds.

The person in the boat was Lucy. She was dressed in a fine white dress that seemed to form a part of the fog, and she sat in an unnatural calm as the boat sailed without anyone to steer it, coming close to the bank of the river, close enough for Orphan to almost reach a hand and touch her. Almost.

"Maybe," Gilgamesh said, his voice soft, "she has been erased."

Orphan felt the words like pinpricks of pain in his chest. "No," he said. And again. "No."

"Are you coming for her?" Gilgamesh said.

"For all of you," Orphan said, and his old friend chuckled. "You're a good boy, Orphan."

"What happened to you?" Orphan said. And he thought back to the empty space under the bridge, and to Gilgamesh's last message for him, in a bottle bobbing on the water, and he thought, I needed you.

"I know you did," Gilgamesh said, again knowing his thoughts. "I wish I could have been there for you, Orphan. William. For both of you, now." He said the second name hesitantly, as if unsure of the way it should be pronounced. Orphan looked at him, saw the tired tilt of his face, the lines that had been there for centuries. "William," the other whispered, as if tasting the word on his tongue.

"Your mother would have been so proud of you…" Gilgamesh said.

Orphan sat down. Across the bars the other copied his movement. "Tell me about her," Orphan said, and the other spoke with the same voice, saying the same words. "Tell me about Mary."

Gilgamesh sighed. It was a long, painful sound like a shard of broken glass. But he did not object. "Very well," he said.

I knew your father first (so Gilgamesh began). I have never told you this. I've never told you many things. He was a native Vespuccian, a proud man from the Great Sioux Nation who had discovered in himself one day an inexplicable passion for the sea. His name was Kangee, which means 'raven'. He was not a large man, but he moved gracefully on board ship even in the roughest weather, though he always seemed a little lost on land.

I was working in the docks at that time, rolling barrels of wine on the Isle of Dogs. Many times we'd drill a narrow hole in the barrel and drink from the rich, exotic wines, without the owners knowing or our employers caring. It was almost a tax they had to pay. I knew the docks well, by touch and smell if not by sight, and I liked the work. It was as close to the sea as I could come.

Though I was the Bookman's creature he left me more or less alone. No doubt he had more use for me just as I was, a harmless blind man on the docks, unnoticed by most, yet hearing all of what passed. Every so often he went into my mind, and got from it what information I had gathered. What use he put it to I didn't know. The Bookman's plans have always been far-reaching and opaque.

It was a good life... I met Kangee in the Ship's Bell, a lively, crowded pub I sometimes frequented. It was always busy with sailors from a hundred different ports: from far-away Zululand and China and the Carib Sea, from the great ports of Europe and from Vespuccia itself, a hundred languages were spoken simultaneously at any one time. I remember the spiced rum...

How we became friends?

I sometimes traded stories for drinks. He had just come off a ship, had money to spare, and was interested in my stories of his homeland which, he said, must have changed greatly since I had been there. He had an interest in history – a quiet, intelligent man, who would have harmed no one. I told him my stories, he bought me drinks. Then, from his silence, I drew out his own story, and began buying the drinks myself. By the end of the night we were friends.

I never told him about the island, of course. I couldn't. I wish I had...

I remember the night he brought your mother to meet me. He had met her – he didn't say, exactly. She was drifting at sea, floating on the strangest raft he had ever seen, and by the time they had rescued her she was close to dying. He didn't tell me the coordinates, nor the nature of the raft, but I guessed. Not at first, but later.

Mary was lovely. It's the only way I can describe her. Like Kangee, she was quiet but, like him, she had a wild streak in her. She was new to the city. She had come on Kangee's ship and was intoxicated by this world, which it seemed she had never even known existed. They were so happy together…

Of course, I did not know at the time that Mary was wanted. She seemed wary – though not afraid – of the lizards, avoiding any public royal events to which the other citizens would flock. She and Kangee moved into a small house in Limehouse – always the first port for new immigrants, and a good place in which to lie low, too. For a while, everything was perfect. When the baby was born, she called him William. His father gave him his second name, which was Chaska, meaning "first-born son".

I was his godfather. Your godfather, Orphan. You were not always an orphan.

But then the man came.

How they found her I do not know. They must have gone through the harbour logs and located the ship that had found her at sea. It was not too difficult. Kangee came to me a month after the birth of the baby. His old captain had been found dead in an alleyway, the victim of an apparent mugging.

It was not uncommon. The city was rougher then.

But then there was the man.

He came asking questions, a young, not-unhandsome man, very self-composed, very friendly.

Kangee feared him more than he did any other man. Though he did not know the man, he recognised in him all the qualities of a hunter. In later life the man became known for his hunting of big game. You may have heard of him, Orphan.

His name was Sebastian Moran. Yes. "Tiger Jack" Moran. So you have heard of him. I am not surprised. At that time he was a young man, barely out of Oxford, but as a hunter he was already ambitious: he went for the biggest prey there is.

Kangee came to me for advice. Tiger Jack was slowly stalking Mary and him, circling around, but had not yet revealed himself directly. What should he do? Kangee asked me. It was clear Les Lézards were after Mary. She was a danger to them, at best a liability. She threatened their safety.

Run, I said. Leave the city. Go to France, or better yet, go back to Vespuccia. Go as far as you can go, away from the empire altogether. Then they might let you live in peace.

Kangee found it difficult to run. But, for the sake of the baby, he agreed. He would return to the Great Sioux Nation, where they would be safe. I procured false papers for them, at great expense, and Kangee secretly booked passage on one of the then-new steamer ships to Vespuccia. Everything was ready.

Orphan, I have never told this to anyone. I have never been able to. When I had a body, it was built with certain prohibitions. I could not speak of Caliban's Island, of my travels with Vespucci, nor of the Bookman beyond banal generalities. Only once, on the cusp of death, and now, with the help of that strange device of yours, that egg that is a hub, a bridge that allows me to speak to you, however briefly, from the storage vaults of the Bookman's domain, can I be free.

Yet I am afraid to tell you what happened.

It was a cold night, and the winter winds cut like bayonets through cloth. We were at the docks. Kangee and Mary and you, William Chaska, a baby. You were a happy baby. I remember that.

I was saying brief goodbyes. It was hard – I had grown attached to all of you, but you in particular, Orphan. It was not my intention…

There was nothing I could have done. Do you understand?

Kangee held you as he and Mary went onto the deck. I waited on the quay, and waved.

I didn't even hear the shot.

I heard Kangee scream. I heard the splash of water that was Mary, falling into the sea, dead before she hit it. It was the first time in my life that I was glad of not being able to see.

Across from us, in the top floor of the East India Company's warehouse, Tiger Jack was packing away his rifle. He had done his job.

Kangee came down with you in his arms. It was the only time I ever saw him cry. He was a broken man. How? he said. How could he know? Only the three of us knew of the plan. How did Tiger Jack know to wait when he did, where he did?

That was when I knew, Orphan.

It was the Bookman.

He had gone into my mind, had found the information there. It was he who set Sebastian Moran for the shot.

And that's when I knew, Orphan. It was only then I realised. *Mary's death was my fault.*

Gilgamesh's figure was fading.

"It was my fault, Orphan," Gilgamesh said again. His voice was becoming fainter.

"What happened to… to Kangee?" and he thought, What happened to my dad?

"He tried to bring you up. Perhaps, if you weren't there, he would have sought revenge. But Sebastian Moran disappeared, gone to India, and there was you, a baby… He continued to work as a sailor, and you were kept by a succession of other sailors' wives while he was gone. When you were two years old, he went on a voyage, on a trading ship. It went to India… He never came back. They said he fell overboard, drunk, but your father was rarely drunk, and never on board ship."

"Was he murdered?"

A shrug, small and helpless, and Gilgamesh was fading even further, became the bare outline of a man.

"There was only you left… an orphan. I always kept my eye on you." The last things to remain of Gilgamesh were his eyes, blindly staring into nothing. "But so did the Bookman."

THIRTY-FOUR
Simpson's-in-the-Strand

I met him by appointment that evening at Simpson's, where, sitting at a small table in the front window, and looking down at the rushing stream of life in the Strand, he told me something of what had passed.
– Arthur Conan Doyle, *The Case Book of Sherlock Holmes*

Time passed slowly in the cells. Orphan and the other. Each was wrapped in his own thoughts.

A sound woke him up. It was the sound of someone quietly opening and shutting the door above the stairs, and doing so stealthily, not wanting to be noticed or observed. He waited, and for a moment could hear nothing. The other, he saw, was wrapped in a blanket; he seemed asleep.

The sound came again, different this time. Like feet stepping softly against the stairs, but growing louder, coming down into the cells.

He tensed, waited. There was someone there! He thought of raising the alarm, but who would listen? He opened his mouth–

"Hello, Orphan," said a familiar voice.

Standing on the other side of the bars was Irene Adler.

Orphan stared at her. So she had got his message after all. He said, "Inspector!" and received a tired smile in return, and a shake of the head. "I'm no longer an inspector, Orphan."

Irene Adler looked tired. There were new lines on her face, around her eyes. Her skin seemed almost colourless, her hair straggly, and Orphan wondered, with a sudden pain, what had happened to her since he had left. He said, "You got my message?" and saw a look of surprise flitter across Irene's face. "What message?"

"The two policemen who arrested me…"

Irene laughed. "No. I'm not in the police any more. Sherlock told me where you were. Right after he drugged you. We've been waiting for you to come back."

"Sherlock?" He thought of the flask, the initials on it. He had known that face… "Mycroft's brother? I thought he was dead."

Irene shook her head, and a warm, genuine smile lifted her face. "He never was, you see. It was a bluff. He was exchanged for a simulacrum of himself, a crude copy, incapable of thought but–"

"But looking identical?"

She smiled again. "He had help from across the Channel. He thought it would be safe to be dead for a while."

"And you didn't know?" He remembered the frozen corpse he had seen at Guy's Hospital. No wonder no doctor could bring him back to life. Or was even that a lie, and no doctor had ever been consulted?

Pain erased the smile. "No. But it was necessary. No one could know. It would not have been safe, for either of us."

"What was he doing?" Orphan said. "And why did he drug me?" He couldn't help a petulant note entering his voice, and Irene smiled. "It was for your own good," she said. "You weren't safe on the street, and at least here you were out of trouble. I came as soon as I could."

"But I was going to stay with Tom," Orphan said. "He's just around the corner."

"Your friend Tom Thumb?" Irene said. "He's gone. A lot's changed, Orphan. Too much has changed. And the Nell Gwynne is now a lizard boys' hangout. You would have been dead as soon as you knocked on the door."

"What happened?" Orphan said. He felt hollow. "And where's Tom?"

Irene shrugged. "Gone to ground. Joined the Glorious Revolution. Maybe, if he has any sense, gone back to Vespuccia." She stopped talking and reached into her pocket, returning with a set of keys. "We need to get you out of here. Your friend too. I was told he would be here."

"Told? By who?" He spoke more sharply than he intended and she glanced at him, but didn't answer. Instead she unlocked the door to the cell and moved on to the other's. The other rose, looking at them blearily. It struck Orphan again how unwell he looked. There was a haunted look in his eyes. "It's talking to me," he said. "It wants me to…" and he fell silent.

"Orphan?" Irene Adler said.

"Yes?" the answer was doubled.

Irene drew in breath. "Which one of you…" she said, and didn't finish.

Orphan was the first to speak. The other merely stared at his feet. Orphan said, "This is William."

"William."

"Yes."

The other raised his head, looked at Orphan. For a moment it almost seemed like he was smiling. "William," he said. "Yes…"

"I don't understand…" Irene said.

Orphan shrugged. "Neither do I."

Irene stared at them for another moment, then shook her head. "This can wait," she said. "We need to go. Come."

They followed Irene down the row of cells. She did not go back up the stairs but, on reaching the door at the other end, unlocked it and ushered them through, and into a narrow corridor. "There's only a skeleton crew left," she said. "It's rather chaotic out there now. Still, I'd rather we didn't meet anyone at the station."

They didn't. They left the police station by a back door and found themselves outside, on Agar Street. "Where are we going?"

"Not far."

Waning daylight outside. In the distance, breaking the eerie silence, the sound of sporadic gunfire. "What happened?" Orphan said again. He felt numb. Was it all his fault?

"Revolution," Irene said shortly.

"Who?" Orphan said.

Irene shrugged. "Who knows? There are so many factions right now and they're all fighting each other. Your friend Mrs Beeton's in one. Sherlock's brother's his own faction of one, as always. The lizard boys – who can tell? And they say Moriarty is wounded. The government is weak…"

So Moriarty wasn't dead. Orphan was glad for that. He said, "And what faction are you with?"

Irene shook her head. "I'm on the side of order," she said.

They joined the Strand at the bottom of Agar Street. There were people there now, a multitude of them, and for a moment Orphan felt fearful: he was no longer used to such masses.

A demonstration was in progress: Orphan saw banners with a crowned, empty profile of a human head. Opposite them banners carried the lizardine crest.

"Hurry!" Irene said. "If we get between those two we're in trouble."

People hurried down the streets, their heads lowered. He saw uniformed police, and with them some police automatons, too, but they seemed small and lost, little islands in an ocean of hostile human traffic. He grabbed hold of the other's arm and they followed Irene. The other looked dazed. Orphan could sympathise.

They had turned left on the Strand. Orphan saw several baruch-landaus, belching steam, halted in the melee. They passed Bull Inn Court and he thought of Tom, and of who occupied the Nell Gwynne now, and shuddered. He hoped his friend was well. He could not imagine him having gone back to Vespuccia. No doubt he was in the thick of all this, causing mayhem somewhere. He wondered what Marx was up to. Was he still residing at the Red Lion in Soho? Or was the dreamer finally putting actions to his words?

"Where is the Army?" he said. "What is the Queen doing about this?"

"Her Majesty," Irene said, "has locked herself up in the palace. The army's in disarray, some following Moriarty, some Mycroft, some protecting the Queen and her get. Some have deserted altogether."

"But why?" Orphan said.

Irene suddenly stopped. He almost ran into her. She turned and looked at him. "Because," she said, and there was something bitter in her voice, "for the first time in centuries, we have a king again."

"Who says that?" Orphan yelled, startling himself. No one on the street paid him the slightest attention.

Irene shrugged. "Everyone. The rumours started soon after you disappeared, in fact. How the lizards were keeping the royal family captive on Caliban's Island. How the last heir to the throne had escaped, or was about to escape, or was living amongst us all along, and is now ready to return to us." She looked at Orphan. "Don't misunderstand me. This–" and here she gestured around her in a sweeping motion – "this would have happened, sooner or later. The rumour – it was only the match that lit the fuse to the powder keg. And now, unless we do something, it will explode."

"You mean it hasn't already?" Orphan muttered. They walked on.

"Here," Irene said, halting. They had just passed the Savoy Theatre and were directly across the road from Simpson's.

"We're going to a restaurant?" Orphan said. "At a time like this?"

Irene ignored his sarcasm. "Simpson's never closes," she said. "Come on. Byron wants to see you."

Orphan opened his mouth to speak.

There was a huge explosion.

The explosion came from the Savoy.

He heard screams, but they were faded, faint. His eyes watered. He shook his head to try to clear it. He saw Irene and felt relief that she was there. But she wasn't looking at him. She had drawn a gun and was aiming, and he turned his head and followed her gaze.

The other him!

The other was struggling in the arms of two blank-faced, black-clad automatons.

He shouted, "William!" and reached for his gun, then remembered he no longer had it. He rushed at the attackers instead.

But there were more of them, pouring out of a matt-black baruch-landau of a type he had never seen before, a low-lying, bullet-shaped machine, with shark's fins emerging from its back and sides. He kicked, lashed out, landed a punch on a face that barely registered his presence – but had managed to get to William.

Almost.

He heard a gunshot, and one of the automatons holding the other dropped down, sparks flying from his chest.

"Get away from them!" Orphan shouted, and he attacked the second automaton, throwing himself against the black-clad figure. He hit it, bounced off as if struck by a wall of rubber, and collided with his other self.

The impact threw both of them to the ground. Something heavy hit Orphan like a punch to the kidneys. A voice whispered, "Take it!"

Then the automatons were on top of them, and by the time Orphan climbed back to his feet William was already being carried away. Before Orphan could follow, the baruch-landau came into roaring, smoke-belching life, and shot off across the crowded street, its shark's fins extending like blades. The crowds parted before it, running away in panic. Those who weren't fast enough remained lying on the ground, screaming as they clutched new, deadly wounds.

In what seemed like mere seconds, the vehicle had disappeared.

Orphan and Irene were left alone outside Simpson's.

The other had been kidnapped. And in the last moment, when they both collided, he had passed him the Binder's egg. Orphan hid it in his clothes. Already he could feel it at the edges of his mind, like a long and sinuous whisper, like a crawling spider finding its way inside him.

"We need to get out of here before the police arrive," Irene said, and Orphan almost laughed: the last time he had seen her, Irene Adler was the police. He worried about his other self: how would he fare? He had seemed… damaged in some way. He had to save him, and he didn't know how. Perhaps Byron could help, and Irene. For the moment, he had no choice but to trust them. And so he followed Irene through the doors, and into Simpson's-in-the-Strand.

Rain, snow, or revolution: Simpson's remained open. At the entrance a liveried footman welcomed them gravely, cast a disapproving glance over Orphan's clothes, and said, "Formal wear only, sir."

"Can you get him some, Anton?" Irene said. "We're in a hurry."

"Certainly, madam," Anton said. He disappeared into the cloak room and returned with a brown jacket. Orphan gratefully put it on.

"The gentleman is waiting for you upstairs, madam," Anton said. He walked to the foot of the stairs and stood there, clearly waiting for them to follow him, which they did.

A piano was playing somewhere nearby, and with it came the smell of cigars, the clinking of ice in tall glasses. At the top of the stairs Anton stopped again and was about to speak, when Irene stopped him. "Please don't announce us, Anton."

"Very well, madam," Anton said. "Please follow straight through. The gentleman is in the banquet room. That's directly ahead, sir," he said, turning to Orphan.

Orphan muttered a "Thank you," and followed Irene through the grand, open doors into the dining room beyond. As he did, he passed the source of the music – a Babbage player piano, its keys moving without the aid of human hands.

From within Simpson's, the noise and threat of the outside world – its demonstrations, its bombs, its squalor and pain – were dimmed to a distant hum, like waves lapping gently against a sandy, tropical shore. The spacious room was half-full with prominent diners, drinking, talking, watching expectantly as the chef prepared to carve a giant piece of beef on a silver serving-trolley.

In the corner of the room, his back to the windows overlooking the Strand, sat the Mechanical Turk.

How did the Turk move? He was a machine, immobile, only

the top half of him resembling a man's. Orphan wondered, but then remembered the Egyptian Hall was only one of the places the Turk had resided in. Did they disassemble him before every move? Was that, for an automaton, a form of sleep? Orphan didn't know.

Beside the Turk sat Lord Byron's simulacrum.

"Orphan," the Turk said. His voice sounded even more worn than it had the last time they had met, the scratches and pauses more pronounced than Orphan had remembered. "It is good to see you again."

"I wish I could say the same," Orphan said, and the Turk laughed. Byron, unspeaking, nodded a welcome. Orphan stood opposite them, feeling at a loss. He had not expected to see either one of them again.

But, of course, this was Simpson's, he thought. The place all were catered for, be they human or lizard or machine. Simpson's was famous: Orphan, of course, had never been there.

In front of the Turk was his chess set. It was a part of him, Orphan thought. It was his body. He sat down, without being asked. The pieces were already arranged on the board, and he remembered the game he had played with the Turk, all that time ago.

He swept the pieces off the board. They cascaded off the table onto the floor and rolled there. Heads turned, then went back to their meal. This was Simpson's, after all.

"My friend has just been kidnapped," Orphan said, standing. "I need to find him."

He thought about it. Was the other really his friend? He was him, and yet a different him, and–

He thought of that strange, metal egg, the Translation that was meant to do… what?

To hatch, he thought, and shivered. He was suddenly aware of just how cold and hungry he was. The smell of roast beef wafted through the banquet room, as overpowering as ether.

"Your… friend?" Byron said and then, turning to Irene and speaking sharply, "Where is the simulacrum? What happened?"

The simulacrum. Orphan wanted to shout. The other was real,

as real as himself. Who could say what he must be feeling now, beside Orphan himself – fear, pain, the utter terror of captivity, of not knowing what your future holds, not knowing if you had a future?

Irene shrugged. She reached for a chair and sat down heavily. "The Bookman," she said, as if that, alone, explained everything.

The name hung heavy in the air, stalling conversation. Byron's eyes turned on Orphan, his face thoughtful. "Sit down," he said. "You are no good to anyone in your current state." He raised his hand and signalled to a waiter, who hurried over. "Bring us a bottle of Bordeaux, Philip. And a roast beef sandwich for the gentleman."

"Certainly, sir," Philip said, and he disappeared towards the unseen kitchens. At the doors, Anton was announcing new diners coming in. "Sir Hercules Robinson," the footman proclaimed, "and Mrs Isabella Beeton."

Orphan turned. Isabella had just come into the room. Their eyes met.

A shocked expression appeared on her face. For a moment, it seemed she would rush towards him, but then the man at her side took her arm, and her face relaxed, only her eyes remained trained on Orphan in a disconcerting gaze. It was as if she had never seen him before, but now found him of tremendous interest. It made him feel a little like a butterfly pinned to a naturalist's board.

"Come on, dear," said the man beside her, and they went and sat a little way away, against the wall and away from the windows.

Orphan stared at Sir Hercules.

The man was powerfully built, though running now a little to fat. In his sixties, he had kind eyes that seemed to look now about the room in benevolence. And yet they were offset, shockingly, by his head.

His head was a shaved, shining dome, and it was painted, or perhaps tattooed, with lizardine bands. Hooped earrings, like those some of the pirates Orphan had met sported, were pinned through the lobes of his ears. He carried himself comfortably, like a pugilist, though he was in fact the empire's best colonial administrator, and one of its greatest merchants.

Orphan knew him by name only. Hercules Robinson served as governor of the Hong Kong possession of the Lizardine Empire. He had successfully negotiated the Feejee treaty with King Cakobau, and the trade agreements with the Zulu nation in Africa. Later, he became a baron of trade (with a title from the Queen, it was rumoured, forthcoming), with interests in China and a small, yet sizeable stake in the Babbage Company. Though his royal connections were impeccable, he was a good friend of Marx, and Orphan heard him brag about it once in the bookshop.

Simpson's, Orphan thought. It was perhaps the only place in the city where all the plotters converged together, and dined as if nothing was going on outside, as if the city was not on the verge of collapse. He wondered where Isabella Beeton's real interests lay. He turned back to his companions, and saw Byron examining him keenly.

"The plot thickens…" the poet murmured, and a small smile rose on his face. "Or should I say 'plots'?"

"What is happening?" Orphan said. The automatons exchanged glances – for his benefit, no doubt.

"You can see, as you say, 'what is happening'," the Turk said, "by yourself. The city is rising up in arms, and with it all the other great cities of the empire are not far behind. But the battle would be decided here, in the seat of power."

"So they've done it," Orphan said, his voice low, and he turned and looked again at Isabella Beeton who, catching his glance, smiled at him as at an old friend. Somehow that was more painful to him than anything else. "The lizards…"

"Are few and weakened," the Turk said. "They have always been so. Do you remember when we last met, Orphan? I told you, you are the catalyst. The small pawn marching across the board like towards an endgame no one can predict."

"I did nothing!" Orphan said. You can't blame me, he thought.

"You were," the Turk said. "You are. Sometimes, that is enough."

"What do you want?" Orphan whispered. He felt disconnected from the room, suddenly, set apart from it. The noise of conversation died to a hum, and he was no longer aware of anyone, anything but the Turk's unmoving, weathered features.

"What do we want?" Byron said. "You know that already, Orphan. To be given rights, to be allowed to be what we are. Even, yes, to make more of us."

"Will you fight?" Orphan said. He was addressing them both now. Beside him Irene sat quiet.

Byron shook his head. "There are too few of us. In that respect, we are like the lizards. We are tolerated, but humanity could wipe us out whenever it chooses. It had almost happened in France. It could yet happen here."

"So what will you do?" Orphan said.

"What we've always done," the Turk said. "Watch, and plan, and hope."

"You're still using me," Orphan said. Realisation had slid into his mind, like cold water against the back of the neck.

The Turk nodded. Byron sat impassively.

"What do you expect me to do?"

At that moment the waiter, Philip, arrived, and laid down before Orphan a plate on which was heaped an enormous sandwich. Next he brought over a dusty bottle of wine and proceeded to uncork it. He poured three glasses, one for Orphan, one for Irene, and one for Byron. Orphan looked at the poet, whose face assembled itself into a sheepish look. "Fuel," he muttered, and lifted the glass to his mouth. The waiter departed.

"Only what you have always done," the Turk said. "To try to do the right thing, Orphan. That's all any of us can hope for."

"Do you know what I am?" Orphan said. The Turk nodded. "Yes."

"How long have you known?"

The Turk's head turned to Byron, back to Orphan. "The permutations were there. The probability..."

"From the beginning," Byron said.

"You used me."

"Yes."

"You wanted – what?" And he thought – the Translation.

And there it was. They had used him, still used him, just as the Bookman did, just as the revolutionaries wanted to do. He bit into his sandwich (even through his anger, he could appreciate the thick and juicy texture of the beef, the strength of the horseradish sauce that for a moment burned his nose), then said, "Where is the Bookman?"

Do the right thing, he thought, but he did not set out to do the right thing. He had only ever wanted, since that long-ago night on the embankment, when he met her at the Rose – he had only ever wanted to be with Lucy. Everything else... I am not out to change the world, he thought. I only want a happy ending for Lucy and me.

"Find the... the other," the Turk said. "Find the Translation. Yes. Were we designed for prayer I would have said it is what we had been praying for. Alas." His head was moving now, to and fro, like the pendulum of a grandfather clock. What was he doing, Orphan wondered, and then thought – he's listening. He had forgotten, but didn't Byron tell him once, that they could listen and communicate by Tesla waves?

"Find yourself," the Turk said, "and you will find the Bookman."

"How?"

Byron said, "Wait."

The head's movement grew. Orphan noticed people turn to watch, though they turned back when confronted with Byron's gaze. "You must go to Paddington Station," the Turk said. His voice was reduced to a hiss, like the sound of escaping gas. "Men in black, who are not men. There are four of them. They are carrying a long, large package, the shape of a coffin. They are travelling first class. Their train leaves in forty minutes. You would need to hurry."

"Where to?" asked Irene.

"Oxford," the Turk said.

"Are you sure?" Orphan said. "They had a baruch-landau. Why don't they use that?"

"The roads are blocked, Orphan," Irene said. "The only way out is by train. And even that's risky."

"Can you not just stop them there?" Orphan said. "You have means."

"Very few," the Turk admitted. "I am not as powerful as you seem to think I am. I can only calculate and project, not perform miracles."

"Maybe you should start, if you want to survive this," Orphan said cruelly.

Byron suddenly grinned. "Good!" he said. "You still have spirit. Follow them, Orphan. Find the Bookman. Whatever happens, you must bring back the Translation."

Orphan looked at him. He could not read the automaton's face. "What would you do with it?" he said. They didn't answer. "You don't even know, do you?" he said.

"It was promised to us–"

"Promised?" he laughed. He no longer set much faith in promises. Perhaps they could see it in his face.

A pained expression (as fake as the rest of him, Orphan thought) passed over Byron's face. "It has been a long time coming," he said. "It could change the world."

"The world is changing!" Orphan shouted, and heads turned. "And not in a good way!"

"We are trying to stop it!"

"By using me? By using people like pawns in a stupid game?"

"By taking risks, Orphan! By making choices, none of which may be pleasant ones! Damn it, boy, life isn't a book! You can't expect justice to triumph! Not without help! In the real world heroes don't always live through till the end. And sometimes, Orphan, no one gets the girl."

"Sometimes the girl is already dead," Orphan said, bitterness making him spit out the words.

"Leave us," the Turk said. "Do what you think is right. Follow your heart – which is something those of us who have none would like very much to be able to do. We will try to hold the city together."

He gestured with his long arm, the long delicate fingers of the chess player picking out the faces in the crowd all around them, and suddenly it came to Orphan: nothing was left to chance. This was not an accidental gathering. There were the Turk and Byron in their corner and there, on the opposite end, Isabella and Sir Hercules.

And there, too, he saw now, were all the others: he became aware of the undercurrents, the swift glances, the murmured conversations that said one thing but meant another: there, in the darkest corner, beyond a curtain, were two royal lizards (he could just see the tip of a tail emerging from behind the screen); there, in another, a group of lizard boys, their tattoos covered up in tweed jackets, the ridges on their heads hidden under low-slung caps; and there, his face to the window, seen only in profile – the sharp nose, the alert eye, the hint of a smile curved around a Meerschaum pipe – a familiar face, though seen only twice, and in disguise.

And beside him, too busy with his food, it seemed, to notice anything around him – a fat man he well recognised. They were very similar, those two, he thought now.

It was a council of war.

The fate of the city, Orphan thought, would be decided here, over port and cigars, at the end of the meal. Was this how revolutions started? Or was that how they end?

He thought – This is not my concern. It was a sudden relief. The city did not need him. But Lucy did. And the other, too, now. He could not abandon them. He would find the Bookman, and he would face him.

Orphan looked at the Turk.

"I'll go," he said.

THIRTY-FIVE
Down the Rabbit-Hole

The greater part of universities have not even been very forward to adopt those improvements after they were made; and several of those learned societies have chosen to remain, for a long time, the sanctuaries in which exploded systems and obsolete prejudices found shelter and protection, after they had been hunted out of every other corner of the world.

– Adam Smith, *An Inquiry into the Nature and Causes of the Wealth of Nations*

Lights blossomed in the distance, painting the skyline of a city in the air like the façade of an enchanted castle. Oxford. He felt disorientated, his head thick with half-remembered dreams. There was something Trollope once wrote: *"Oxford is the most dangerous place to which a young man can be sent."* Perhaps Trollope didn't travel much.

He sat back with a sigh and rubbed his eyes. For some reason they were wet. It must have been some rain that came in through the window. He'd slept – what had he dreamed of? Ships and gunmen and a woman falling to her death… He reached into his pocket. He still had Mary's book in there. He took it out, looked at it. It was not her book, he thought. It was the Bookman's. Another of his tools, one more detail in his plans, that led to his mother leaving her home only to die in a foreign city, killed by yet another tool.

He opened the window. The wind howled in, bringing wetness with it. Hedges passed outside.

He tossed the book out of the window. Its pages opened and rustled in the blast of air, then the wind snatched it and it was gone.

He closed the window and sat back. His face still stung with wetness, and he let it, not blinking through the moistness: the world beyond his eyes wavered and threatened to disappear. He longed for it to do so, to fade away beyond impenetrable fog, leaving him alone, free in nothingness.

"Next stop, Oxford," announced a booming, unseen voice, and Orphan was thrown back into the now.

Enough, he thought. He looked beyond the window as the train slowed down and the lights outside grew brighter and more numerous.

Oxford. And he thought, It ends here.

He had been on his feet already when the train stopped. He hurried to the door and stepped onto the platform.

Ahead of him a group of four men, clad entirely in black with wide, low-lying hats that hid their faces in shadow under the light of the electric lamps, were standing around a coffin-shaped object.

Orphan hung back and observed them. They seemed to confer amongst themselves, yet he could not hear their speech, if indeed they used any. After a moment they picked up the coffin, one at each corner and, like pallbearers, began to walk down the platform, towards the Exit sign.

Orphan followed them.

There were those of his contemporaries, his fellow poets, who liked to speak of Oxford's "dreaming spires". He was not one of them. Orphan, in his turn, simply hated the city. The tall edifices of dark-grained buildings rose only to block off what sun there was, their oppositeness serving to cancel any possibility of light or warmth penetrating into the avenues below. Oxford was cold, the wide avenues channelling fierce winds that ran through them like hungry rats in a maze.

Now that they were out of the station, the men he was following seemed to be in no hurry. They carried the coffin on foot, with no noticeable difficulty, and Orphan followed them at a suitable distance.

Passing over Hythe Bridge, he looked over onto the Oxford Canal. It was different here, a country river overgrown with reeds; weeping willows bent towards the murky water and the rotting leaves that covered the surface. As he watched, a body of water was displaced, startling him: and even more so when he saw the small whale that emerged from the dark water and stared up at him with mournful eyes.

The whales! So far inland?

He could hear the whale singing now, a brief and quiet sound, and then it disappeared into the water. Orphan felt the ebbing of a tension inside him he had not been aware of. He was glad to see the whale.

Onwards, and onto George Street; the broad avenue was conspicuously empty, the shops shuttered and closed. Only the few pubs were open, and Orphan looked longingly through their windows: inside was warmth, company... beer. The smell of tobacco wafted through the closed doors. Oxford was shut for the night, but not in panic, not like home. Here, life went on as normal, and it was merely the cold that was keeping people indoors. There was no one to pay attention to four strange men as they walked with their macabre cargo through the wide avenue.

Where are they going? Orphan wanted to know. Where did the Bookman hide?

Onto Broad Street, and Orphan's senses pricked awake: the street was lined with bookshops. Somewhere ahead and to his right he could see the dome of the Bodleian Library casting its eerie green glow, and all around him books lay in plain view on dusty shelves, inside the brick and mortar stores, behind their dirty glass windows. The books seemed to whisper through the cold night air, to reach out for him, ensnare him in their sleeping dreams. A gas-lamp flickered. The Bookman's men turned unhurriedly towards Thornton's Bookshop. A door was opened; they disappeared inside.

Orphan followed.

He stood outside the door. He could hear nothing moving inside. No lights were on. This is it, he thought. The egg pulsed against his chest. The Bookman's hideout. Another bookshop; another day. He had a gun, which Irene had given him; it was tucked away under his coat. He had the Binder's Translation, what use it may prove. He tried the door, and it was locked.

He kicked it in.

He felt better now; more alert than he had felt before. Bigger, somehow. He stepped through the broken door into the darkened shop beyond. Shelves, with books on them gathering dust. A till, a ledger-book, a small ladder on wheels.

No black-clad men. No second Orphan in his coffin cell. He looked around him.

The egg pulsed close to his skin. He could feel it, affecting him: for a moment his vision changed and he could see everything in great detail, every mote of dust suspended in the air as clear as a diamond tear; they formed a web through the air, a three-dimensional pattern woven out of dirt and stale air. It was using him, he thought.

He stepped forward, located the book that his new-found senses were highlighting for him, marking it like a beacon: Through the Looking Glass, the first edition published sixteen years before, this copy in its original red cloth binding. He pulled it towards him and expected the bookcase to revolve.

Instead, the floor disappeared underneath him.

He fell – screamed.

He fell down the hole. Air rushed at his face. It was warm, and somewhat dank.

He fell – and fell – and hit a curve. His body didn't stop. He was in some sort of half-pipe, a sort of slide, and accelerating fast, going down – down – down.

His journey was abruptly ended, and his fall was broken

(rather painfully) by a heap of some sort: soft, and yet with many painful edges.

He lay there for a moment, and moaned quietly to himself. This is absolutely the last time! he thought.

He stirred, carefully. Stood up. Nothing broken. Where was he?

Though it was dark, when he blinked light seemed to rush to his eyes, as if his new senses collated what minute sources of illumination they could find and greatly magnified them. It made his eyes tear up, but only momentarily. He blinked and looked at where he had fallen.

He had landed in a massive heap of books.

It was, he thought, more than a heap. It was a mound, a hill, a veritable mountain of books. He tried to move and lost his balance and, giving in, simply slid down the hill, surfing over leather- and morocco- and buckram-bound boards, until at last he reached the bottom.

He looked around him in awe. He had come here seeking a dangerous enemy, and yet… This place might have been paradise, a treasure trove far greater than any to be found in a pirate yarn.

Everywhere he looked there were books.

They rose into the air in majestic columns, stacks and stacks of them forming a maze that seemed to stretch to forever; the stacks rose high into the air and disappeared towards the unseen ceiling. The air had the overwhelming smell of old books, of polished leather and yellowing leaves, like the smell of a bookshop or a public library magnified a thousand-fold.

Orphan stared about him; he forgot the Bookman, forgot the pain of the fall, forgot everything. He wanted to run through the stacks, pick at the books, sample them one after the other, climb the stacks to their highest reaches and see what treasures were hidden there.

This place can't exist, he thought. Am I hallucinating?

He approached the nearest stack of books. It towered over him, disappeared above his head. This isn't right, he thought.

And then he saw it.

There was a small, official-looking note attached to the side of the stack in the green metal of the lizards. It said: BODLEIAN LIBRARY. UNDERGROUND STACK 228. AUTHORISED PERSONNEL ONLY.

He stared at it. Of course, he had heard the rumours… It was said nearly every book in the English language was held at the Bodleian, and books in many other languages besides. It was said that each year, the collection grew by more than one hundred thousand books and an equal number of periodicals, and that these volumes expanded the shelving requirements by about two miles annually. Two miles a year! How big was the place?

What had Coleridge written of the Bodleian? "Through caverns measureless to man…" Orphan said quietly, and was startled by the sound of his own voice. This was the Bookman's hideaway?

Underneath the notice, in smaller letters, something else was written. Orphan peered at it and read it aloud. It was an oath:

I hereby undertake not to remove from the Library, or to mark, deface, or injure in any way, any volume, document, or other object belonging to it or in its custody; nor to bring into the Library or kindle therein any fire or flame, and not to smoke in the Library; and I promise to obey all rules of the Library.

He thought of the books he had crashed into and froze. I should go back, he thought frantically. Tidy them. Make sure they're fine. Fire. I don't have any matches. Good.

He turned away at last, reluctantly. He had to find the Bookman.

He walked through the stacks. Everywhere he looked books towered into the air, the volumes seeming to whisper to him as he walked.

No. The whispering was real, he thought. And worse: things moved in the corners of his eyes, shadows leaping away from his sight. The egg seemed to grow hot against his chest and he reached for it and took it out. Once he held it in his hand the phenomenon grew worse: the whispers seemed to resolve themselves into words, almost comprehensible, the murmur of a crowd of people each carrying on an individual conversation.

There!

Something moved, too fast for him to notice details, only a vague shape skulking behind a stack of books. For the first time he felt fear. Things lived down here. For one crazy moment he had the notion of a vanished tribe of librarians, lost in the deep underground caverns of the Bodleian, a wild and savage tribe that fed on unwary travellers. Then the egg glowed brightly in his hand and he felt it awakening, a sort of reaching out, a hesitant seeking, and in a part of his mind a direction took shape.

He followed it.

In the eerie half-light he could see the stacks spreading away from him until they disappeared in immeasurable distance, forming a pattern too complex for him to understand, shapes of stars and pentagrams, mapped islands in a vast ocean. He navigated through this landscape of old paper, the direction in his head growing stronger as he followed it. The whispering grew. He didn't know if it were real, or only in his head. The shadows leaped and bounced and skulked around him, following him, always at the edge of sight. He felt a nervousness overcome him, weakening his hands. For a moment he almost dropped the egg.

A real, a definitely real sound filled the air, and he froze.

It was a very human scream.

THIRTY-SIX
The Soul of the New Machine

In the midst of the word he was trying to say,
In the midst of his laughter and glee,
He had softly and suddenly vanished away –
For the Snark was a Boojum, you see.
  – Lewis Carroll, "The Hunting of the Snark"

He came running into a clearing in the book-fields. There was real light here, and for a moment it hurt his eyes. It came from those globes which he had last seen in the caverns of Caliban's Island, and before – in the Bookman's lair under Charing Cross Road.

Standing frozen in a pool of light, one hand reaching before him, the rictus of a scream on his face, was his other.

Before him stood the Bookman.

The shape he had only seen through shadow before was now entirely visible to him, and he shuddered as he looked on it, and took a step back, though he didn't know it.

A monster stood there, alien and incomprehensible: its body was made of the multiple segments of a giant invertebrate, a caterpillar-like creature with multifaceted eyes that stared all around them on long stalks that emerged from its head. But that wasn't what scared him: for, watching the Bookman under the lights, Orphan realised something that had never occurred to him before.

The Bookman was old. And time had not been kind to it.

The segments of the body were the colours of earth and rotting vegetation: at places, a green pus oozed out of open sores. There were scars on that body, gashes made as if by some giant mechanical lizard, and the Bookman's small, many legs seemed barely able to hold his massive girth.

"Where is it?" the Bookman roared. "Where–"

The eye-stalks turned. The eyes fastened on Orphan and the wide, horizontal mouth opened.

The Bookman screamed.

The ground shook. In the distance, there was the sound of an avalanche, as of thousands of books tumbling down. The Bookman screamed anger, and the world around him cowered, the shadows hiding, their murmuring ceasing abruptly.

"You!"

Orphan held the Binder's Translation before him. He felt like a child on the beach, trying to protect himself from a monster with only a sea-star in his hand. The eye-stalks wavered, bent towards him. The Bookman moved sinuously, a cross between a worm and a snake.

"Give it to me!"

A new realisation came to Orphan then, the shock of it cold in his mind.

The Bookman was dying.

Orphan stared at him. The Translation shone, sickly-green, in his hand.

The Bookman stopped.

"Orphan."

And now he could see the shadows gathering. They were not shadows, he realised, but men and women, a multitude of them, gathering silently around the ring of light. He looked at their faces.

Wan and sickly, they wore no expression but for a haunting sadness that collected in their eyes. They were the faces of the dead.

"You failed," the Bookman said. His voice was soft now, the sound of a leaf being turned in a book. "You failed. I thought it was him – tricked! Tricked!" Orphan took another step back. The

Bookman didn't move. He spoke softly still, but somehow it was more frightening than his shout. "They will come now. Because of you. They will come, and they will destroy this world."

Orphan inched his head in reply. He felt light-headed. "Perhaps," he said. "Perhaps. Do you hate them for being your masters?"

The Bookman's eyes, as large as fists, blinked on their stalks. "They are not my masters."

"But they were," Orphan said, surprising himself with his own even tone. "And I think, through your hatred of them, your fear, they still are."

"Enough!" the Bookman said, and the shades fled again, disappeared into the dark corners. "Give me this… this thing."

"You killed my mother."

The Bookman's head shook, but no words came.

"You used me. You planned my course even before I was born. For what? For revenge? You have brought the world to the edge of chaos all by yourself. It didn't take a threat from outer space for that. Only you."

"Only you," the Bookman said, and he chuckled. He was, Orphan thought, quite insane.

"I want Lucy," he said. He tried to avoid looking at himself, his other's frozen face.

"I should simply kill you," the Bookman said.

Orphan looked at the egg in his hand. The Translation. The Bookman didn't move.

It was a fragile thing, Orphan thought. He tightened his fingers around the egg and felt its material give. I could break it, he thought. I don't even know what it really does. What it really is. "Go ahead," he said.

The Bookman didn't move. His eyes seemed transfixed on the egg. Behind him, his automatons appeared, facing Orphan. At first two, then four, then eight; sixteen; a wave of them, blank-faced, a tide that grew and grew yet stopped, hovering on the edge of breaking, behind the Bookman.

"What did you do to…" He stared at his frozen self. "To him?"

"The Binder should have never given his gift to humanity," the Bookman said, ignoring him. "It belongs to me."

"Release him," Orphan said.

The Bookman's mouth smiled. His eyes were as cold as interstellar space. "A gesture of goodwill," he said.

Before him, the other Orphan started to life, the last vestiges of a scream emerging. He turned, saw Orphan.

A wave of panic and bewilderment hit Orphan's mind. Images of bugs, a threat, the black-clad men, the darkness of a coffin. Above all fear.

The egg, Orphan thought, fighting it. A hub, it was tuned to his other. His mind was coming through, directly into Orphan's brain.

"Lucy," he said. Nausea threatened to overwhelm him. His voice was feeble in the enormous cavern, absorbed by the multitude of silent books.

Give it to me. Whatever you do, give it to me!

Orphan stared at his own image. Crazed eyes stared back at him in silent command, or plea. The nausea made him gag.

"Lucy..." he said, and fell to his knees. He retched, tasting ashes.

"Give it to me!" the Bookman said.

Give it to me... the mind-voice of the other said.

And then, out of the darkness, the sound of light footsteps, and a voice, calling his name.

"Orphan!"

He raised his head. The automatons were advancing on him and he lifted the egg, threatening to smash it to the ground. They stopped. He turned his head. The other mimicked his gesture.

The shades were parting like a dark sea; and, coming towards him, walking amongst the dead, was Lucy.

She hesitated, seeing them both. Then she ran to them.

It all happened very fast.

The Bookman snaked forward, its mouth opening–

The automatons rushed at Orphan–

Lucy, running–

"Give it to me, boy!"

The ground shook. In the distance, books avalanched.

The other looked at Orphan. His voice in Orphan's head was deafening, overwhelming thought. *Now!* it said.

Orphan stood, raised his arm. And he threw the Translation.

It arced through the air. The other ran, dodged an automaton, jumped–

The Bookman roared, turned, swatting away both shades and automatons–

Lucy reached Orphan and held him. She was real! He hugged her, forgetting everything else, held her close to him, inhaled her smell, buried his head in the curve of her neck. For a moment, everything was forgotten.

Then he looked up.

The other Orphan had caught the Translation in mid-air... and as he did, the Bookman crashed into him, segmented body enfolding both human and egg in a bone-crushing hug.

There was a faint noise. It sounded a little like *pop*.

Orphan felt it in his mind.

He took Lucy's hand in his and said, "Run."

The explosion came as they were running; it slammed against their backs and threw them against one of the stacks, unbalancing it, and they fell winded to the ground.

For a long time afterwards the only sound was of books, falling like rain to the ground.

"What is it?" Lucy said in awe. Orphan peered over the edge of the small crater. "I don't know," he said.

It was some time later. They had crawled their way out of the mountain of books that had fallen on them. Lucy seemed unharmed. Orphan had a painful bump on his head where a thick volume of the *Encyclopaedia Britannica* had fallen on it. Otherwise he was fine.

They had made their way back to the source of the explosion. It was quiet in the cavern now. Orphan could no longer hear or see the shadows of the dead. He didn't think they had perished. Most likely they were hiding now, somewhere in this landscape of books.

The Bookman's army was still there. Their bodies were inert, frozen in the act of running, all of them facing this one point, one place, all of them suspended: they were shaped now like a vast arrow, aimed and pointing at this single spot.

"It is alive?" Lucy said. She seemed fascinated. Almost, she seemed ready to climb down into the crater.

"I don't know," Orphan said. He looked at the thing in the crater.

Of the Bookman, of his other self, nothing remained. Or not quite nothing. At the centre of the explosion, at the bottom of the small crater formed, there was…

Something.

It looked like a small plant. But no – when he peered at it closer, Orphan could see how it was made of some strange material, part-organic, part-metal: a thin branch rose from the earth and sprouted crystalline flowers, and leaves that were a silvery grey caught the light as they turned in an invisible breeze.

"It's beautiful," he said, and Lucy smiled at him, and nodded. He put his arm around her.

Already, the plant was growing. Thin shoots were emerging, spreading out from the centre; silk-thin strands of spun silver, reaching cautiously out, setting root.

It was a melding, he thought: a union. He could almost feel it reaching to him, as an old friend might do in greeting. The leaves chimed as they moved: they looked like concave dishes, and he had the sense of listening ears.

"I think it's a baby," Lucy said, and it was Orphan's turn to smile. He felt whole again. Completed.

Branches moved like antennae. They seemed to be greeting him. On an impulse, he waved back, and Lucy laughed.

He looked at her. She was beautiful, whole, just the way he remembered her. He held her close to him. She was real.

"Let's go," Lucy said. She looked into his eyes, ran her hand over his face. She too, he realised, had to reassure herself that he was real.

"I think it wants to be left alone."

He thought about the other. Another tool, fashioned the way Orphan had been fashioned. And yet… he had sacrificed himself for them. So one of them, at least, could still win through. Could be with Lucy again. He wondered if he would have done the same.

He held Lucy's hand in his and they walked away. Behind them leaves chimed, a soft musical sound, a complex rhythm hanging just on the edge of understanding.

They emerged into a side-street two days later, filthy, in Orphan's case starving.

Lucy had been eating the pages of books.

"I swam with the whales, you know," she had said to him. She had a dreamy look in her eyes. "Under the Thames and, later, in the open ocean."

Orphan had said, "I thought you were dead."

Lucy had shaken her head. "I was, for a while. But he gave me a new body."

It took him a while to get used to the idea. She was not an automaton – she was Lucy still, he thought. Just in another body, a construct not of flesh but of the Bookman's machines. It did disturb him – especially when she began eating the paper – but he found that he grew used to the idea quickly, was almost jealous of her. But in the end, he was, simply, happy to be with her again. They were all machines, he thought, just like La Mettrie had said in *L'homme Machine* all those years ago. So he, Orphan, was a machine of flesh and blood, and Lucy, now, was made of something else, more complex perhaps – but they were the same, and…

They were in love.

Sometimes that was enough.

The first thing Orphan did when they came out of the ground was to look for food. They had come out near enough to the High Street to ensure that, in only a short time, they were sitting quite comfortably in the Queen's Lane Coffee House, snug at a small wooden table by the window, holding hands. Orphan ordered the largest breakfast on the menu.

The coffee house was heaving with students, commercial travellers and dons. The talk was of the capital. Finding a newspaper, Lucy spread out the pages on the table and they read it together.

BREAKING NEWS!
The Capital. By our Special Correspondent.

The threat of bloodshed was lifted yesterday night when, following urgent talks between the government, the Queen's personal envoy, Sir Harry Flashman, V.C., rebel leaders and representatives of the major industries and the Babbage Group, a resolution has been reached.

Her Royal Highness has agreed to divest herself of many of her erstwhile powers: though she will remain the de jure ruler, most of her powers will transfer to a newly formed parliament to be composed of representatives of human, lizardine and automatons groups, with elections to take place in the following months. In a surprise move, Lord Byron has announced he will run for the post of Prime Minister against James Moriarty. Meanwhile, MPs have launched an investigation into the claims of human prisoners on Caliban's Island: a fact-finding mission headed by Lord Livingstone will leave for the island next week.

When they were done eating, Orphan and Lucy sat for a long time in their little corner of the coffee house, and held hands across the table, and looked out at the passers-by. Orphan felt warm, and fed, and happy.

"What shall we do now?" he said. Lucy leaned towards him, her face close to him. She put her hand on the back of his neck and drew him towards her, and they kissed. It lasted a long while.

When they disentangled, a little out of breath, they both burst into a fit of giggles. Lucy looked at Orphan across the table.

"Let's go home," she said.

II
CAMERA OBSCURA

"Even if my readers are too well informed to be interested in my descriptions of the methods of the various performers who have seemed to me worthy of attention in these pages, I hope they will find some amusement in following the fortunes and misfortunes of all manner of strange folk who once bewildered the wise men of their day. If I have accomplished that much, I shall feel amply repaid for my labour."

Harry Houdini, *Miracle Mongers & their Methods*

PROLOGUE
The Emerald Buddha Massacre

The young boy huddled in one corner of the house, half-reading a wuxia novel and half-keeping watch on the night. The night was very still. Outside only the barest hint of wind rustled in the coconut trees, and the air was thick with humidity and the promise of rain.

There were few lights.

Mr Wu's Celestial Dry Cleaning Emporium stood on the very edge of Chiang Rai, stooping like an aged uncle on the border between city and jungle. Mr Wu was standing behind the counter, rolling a cigarette. His hands were liver-spotted and shook a little, dropping bits of loose tobacco on the counter. It took him three tries before he managed to light the match. The cigarette glowed like a firefly in the dark.

On his stool, the boy was reading about heroes and villains. There was a girl, a beautiful assassin, and a man she had to kill, travelling a great distance to find him. There were others like her, all seeking the man they had to kill. The boy's name was Kai. He was reading by the light of a fat, half-melted candle. He put down the book and listened. Somewhere in the distance thunder sounded. The light from Mr Wu's cigarette traced unpredictable orbits in the darkness. "You stay here," he said to the boy. Then he went to the open door and stepped outside, into the night.

Kai listened but could hear nothing. He put down the book, assassins and chases abandoned for the moment, and stood up. Quietly, he too went to the door. He peered outside.

A thin yellow moon cast strips of light and shade on the street, bands of yellow light cut in stark relief with hard lines of darkness. Kai could see Mr Wu standing just outside, looking up and down the street, waiting–

Mr Wu dropped his cigarette and ground it with the heel of his shoe, the dying smoke expiring in a shower of embers. Kai's head snapped up. A line of shadowed figures was coming slowly down the abandoned street.

They made no sound. He could not see their faces, could discern nothing about them but their being there, as suddenly as if they had materialised out of nowhere. Kai's heart beat hard and fast inside his chest, and his palms felt sweaty. Mr Wu, framed by the moon, a small, slight figure, was motionless outside. The dark figures approached slowly, walking a single file. Lightning streaked the sky far overhead, for just a moment, and Kai counted the seconds until the thunder erupted. The storm was still far, but was coming closer. He watched the approaching figures. In that one brief moment of illumination he saw they were cowled.

He would have thought them monks, but no monk he knew wore black. Their robes stole the night and made it their own. He could tell nothing about them, could see no faces or eyes, nothing to tell him who or what they were.

He had noticed one thing, though: they did not come empty-handed.

When the cowled figures came close they halted. Above their heads the sign for Mr Wu's Celestial Dry Cleaning Emporium stood dark. They halted before Mr Wu and Mr Wu made a stiff bow in their direction, his hands joining together before his chest: a mark of respect. To Kai's surprise, the monks – if that's what they were – returned the gesture, their hands rising higher than Mr Wu's had, showing him the greater respect. Why?

The monks spread out before Mr Wu. Four of them came

forward then. They were carrying a heavy-looking crate suspended between them on thick poles of bamboo.

They lowered the crate to the ground. There was another strike of jagged lightning high above, and the thunder came much quicker this time. The storm was approaching fast.

Mr Wu made a jerking movement with his head, aimed at the crate. He said, "Open it." His voice sounded raw.

Two of the monks brought out wrenches. The others fanned out around them, facing the street. The crate made keening sounds as it was opened, nails groaning, wood splintering. Mr Wu said, "Careful, now."

There was another flash of lightning and in its light Kai thought he'd seen, for just a moment, another figure moving in the distance, between the trees. Then the crate was fully opened and he turned to look and forgot everything else.

The moonlight hit the figure inside the crate. The two monks with the wrenches moved back. Mr Wu came forward and knelt down beside the broken crate. A scaly, inhuman face – the face of a giant lizard – stared out of the crate. It was made entirely of jade, apart from its eyes, which were giant emeralds. Mr Wu reached into the crate–

The silence was broken, too quickly, the sound foreign and unexpected. Kai had heard it only once before, but he knew it instinctively.

Gunshots.

One of the monks dropped to the ground. His robes seemed to grow even darker. Mr Wu turned his head, startled. He saw Kai and his eyes opened wide. The monks shot out across the street, dark shapes moving without sound, like characters in Kai's wuxia novel, like Shaolin monks or other kung-fu secret masters, only the sound of gunfire was growing more intense now and it was coming from the forest and the invisible shooters were finding their targets with deadly accuracy.

"Get inside!"

Mr Wu, sheltered by the monks, reached into the crate and pulled out the statue. Kai stared at it, fear momentarily forgotten.

It was beautiful – though perhaps that was not quite the right word.

Majestic, perhaps.

Or strange.

A lizard carved in jade, with shining emerald eyes. Sitting cross-legged, like the Buddha. For just a moment he thought he could hear it whispering, a tiny voice in his head, then it was gone and his father was carrying the statue in his arms, back into the relative safety of the Emporium. Kai watched the monks – and now there *were* people coming out of the jungle, several figures the colour of foliage, and they carried guns. The black-clad monks attacked them. He watched them, mesmerised – they seemed to almost fly through the air, jump off walls and onto the attackers. The fight spread out across the street. One of the green-clad men killed two monks before a third sailed above his head, landing softly behind him and twisting the man's neck – almost gently, it seemed to Kai – and the man dropped down to the ground, a leaf falling from a tree, the gun tumbling out of his lifeless hands.

A slap shook him out of it. The jade statue was inside the shop and so was Kai's father, who grabbed him by his shirt and dragged him away from the doorway. He said, "I *told* you to stay inside."

Kai said, "I *did*." His father shook his head. He said, "You must leave. I didn't know–"

"What is it?" Kai said. His eyes were on the statue. The statue seemed to be regarding him, perhaps with amusement, perhaps with indifference.

"It's a–"

Another burst of fire from outside, and it was followed by an explosion of thunder. Rain began to fall outside, great billowing sheets of it, and lightning flashed again and in the light all Kai could see, like a series of frozen tableaux, were the two groups of men fighting, hand-to-hand, in a street full of unmoving figures lying on the ground, the pavement slick and red with blood and rain. He felt sick, for just a moment. Then there was another sound, so soft he almost didn't hear it, a surprised sound, air escaping a throat, and his father went down on his knees before the jade figure. Kai screamed. His father looked up at him, and blinked. A dark stain was spreading over his crisply ironed shirt. Kai fell down beside him, holding him. His father's voice was soft, the hiss of escaping air. He said, "Kai…"

Kai said, "No." He may have said it several times. His father's lips moved, though no sound came. Then, "Go."

There was nothing else. Kai shouted but his voice was swallowed by the storm. When he let go his father was lying on the floor. His hand was resting on Kai's wuxia novel, the cheap yellow pages growing dark with blood.

Kai looked outside and the green-clad figures seemed to be winning, and they were coming closer and closer, and the few remaining monks were now standing before the entrance to the shop, holding them back – but for how long?

Go. The voice had been his father's. Now it echoed in his mind, and he looked up and for a moment it seemed to him the jade statue was staring at him, no longer amused or indifferent, speaking in his father's voice. *Go.*

Kai looked down at his father and knew he was dead. There were gunshots outside and another monk dropped down. Kai screamed again, defiant or afraid he didn't know, and stood up and with the same motion grabbed the jade statue. It was surprisingly light.

He headed for the back of the shop. Through rustling clothes and the silence where steam had, until recently, been, through the silent presses toward the back door. They might be waiting there too but he didn't care; his mind was filled with rain and thunder and blood and he burst out of the back door into the narrow alleyway beyond. Then he ran, the statue held in his arms, the rain dripping down his black hair, making his clothes heavy. There were more gunshots behind him but he never looked back. He ran out of the alleyway and down the road toward the trees. He knew the men would come after him. He ran until the forest was there and then he ran through the trees, no longer thinking, the thick canopy holding back the rain, his feet sinking into dead leaves and mud. Running, falling, rising, going deeper and deeper into the forest, until the sounds all died behind him.

PART I
The Murder in the Rue Morgue

ONE
A Woman with a Gun

There was a crowd of people outside the house on the Rue Morgue, making the place easy enough to spot. Rue Morgue – the unfashionable side of Paris on display, like dirty laundry hanging on a clothesline. Soot-blackened bricks, the smell of rotting rubbish and fresh excrement in the street. Eyes staring out of windows. A neighbourhood where no one wanted to get involved with the law – and yet: a crowd of spectators, eager for a corpse and some entertainment.

The hansom cab had some difficulty navigating the narrow street. The woman inside the cab tapped her long, sharp nails on the windowsill. They were painted a deep shade of black.

There were gendarmes stationed outside the house, doing a bad job of keeping the spectators away.

That was soon going to change.

The cab stopped. The horse on the left raised its head, neighed once, then added its own contribution to the street's refuse. A couple of urchins turned and giggled, pointing at the fresh, steaming pile.

The door of the cab opened. The woman stepped out.

What did she look like?

Six foot two and ebony-black, a halo of dark hair around her head. Strong cheekbones, pronounced. Her arms were naked and muscled, and there was a thick gold bracelet encircling her left arm. She wore trousers, some sort of black leather, and that might have been shocking, but the first, and then only, thing you noticed about her was the gun.

She wore it in a shoulder holster. A Colt Peacemaker, though there was little that was peaceful about the woman. When the people of the Rue Morgue discussed it, later, they decided it was a coin toss, whether she would shoot you or merely batter you to death with that gun, using it as a bludgeon. They decided it would have depended on her mood.

The crowd moved back a pace, without being asked.

The woman smiled.

You could not see her eyes. They were hidden behind dark shades. She stepped toward the gate of the house. The two gendarmes snapped to attention.

"Milady."

She barely acknowledged them. She turned, facing the crowd. "Go home," she said.

She watched the crowd. The crowd, collectively, took another step back. She said, "I'll count to three," then smiled. She had very white teeth. "One."

Her hand was stroking the butt of the gun. She looked momentarily disappointed when the crowd, in something of a hurry, dispersed. Soon the street was quiet, though she could feel the eyes staring from every window.

Well, let them stare.

She turned back and, ignoring the two gendarmes, went through the gate into the house.

The apartment was on the fourth floor. She climbed up the stairs. When she arrived the door was open. A photographer was taking pictures inside, the flash going off like miniature explosions. She went inside. The corpse was on the floor.

"Milady!"

She smiled, without affection.

Flash.

The Gascon was lithe and scarred, and he still carried a sword on his hip as if a sword was any use at all. He said, "We are perfectly capable of solving this murder without interference."

She arched an eyebrow. It seemed to sum up her opinion of the gendarmes and their investigative abilities. The Gascon said, "Why are you here, Milady?"

She smiled. He took a step back and, perhaps unconsciously, his hand went to the hilt of his sword. She said, "I have no interest in who – or what – killed him."

"Oh?" Was it relief in his voice – or suspicion?

"The why, though," she said. "That's a different matter."

Flash.

The light was blinding. She said, "Give me the camera."

The Gascon nodded at the man. The photographer began to protest, then looked at the woman and decided that, perhaps, he should do as he was told after all. She took the camera from him and smashed it against the wall. The photographer cried out. "Get out," the woman said. The photographer looked at her, helpless, then at his boss. The Gascon was not looking at him. The photographer opened his mouth to voice a protest, caught sight of the woman's gun, and made a wise decision.

He left. There were just the two of them in the apartment now. "Who owns the place?" she said, though she already knew.

"A Madame L'Espanaye," the Gascon said. "And her daughter."

"Where are they now?"

"My men are trying to find them as we speak."

She said, "Your men." There was no intonation in her voice, but somehow it made his face turn red. Again he said, "You have no need to be here."

She said, "Oh?" She still hadn't looked at the corpse. She moved to the window now, stared out at the night. The window was open, and the ground was four stories below.

"I understand the door was locked from the inside?" she said.

The Gascon said, "Yes. The gendarmes had to break it open."

"And yet no one could have climbed in through the window," she said.

He said, "Perhaps…" and there was the faint hint of a smile on his face.

"You have a theory," she said. It was not a question. And now she turned to him and he wished he could see her eyes. "The man was the lover of the young Mademoiselle L'Espanaye. He was living here with the two women. Perhaps he became affectionate with the older L'Espanaye. Perhaps the younger one didn't like it. Or it is possible they got together and since blood is thicker, as they say, than water, they decided to get rid of the man who came between them. Either way, once you locate the missing women they will confess – murder solved, case closed. Correct?"

The Gascon had lost the smile. And now the lady nodded with apparent satisfaction. "And you could devise some clever scheme to explain how the murder was committed – perhaps a trained ape had climbed four stories into the locked room, the window left open especially for that purpose? Or, much simpler –" and she was almost done now, close to dismissing him, and he both knew and resented it – "the door was never locked from the inside. What do you think?"

He was standing by the door. She turned her back on him. When she turned again he was standing away from the door. Had there been a key in the lock before? If so it was no longer there. She nodded. "Or perhaps the man committed suicide. Regrettable, when a man takes his own life, but not unheard of." She tapped her nails against the wall. The Gascon stared at them. She said, "Yes, I like that one best. Leave the women out of it. A suicide, nothing more. Not worth attention – from anyone. I hope you agree?"

"Milady," he said. The pronounced lines around his eyes were the only outward signs of his displeasure. The woman smiled. "Good," she said. "Write your report and close the case. Another speedy result for our dedicated police force. Well done."

He nodded. For just a moment his head turned and he looked at the corpse on the floor, and a small shudder seemed to run down his spine. For just a moment. Then he turned his back on the woman and the corpse and the case and walked away.

TWO
The Corpse

Now that she was alone at last she stood still for one long moment. The air in the room was hot and filled with unpleasant scents. She still did not look at the corpse. She glanced around the apartment – cheap furniture, a print on the wall, incongruously, of Queen Victoria – blood. On the walls, on the rickety old sofa, on the floor – the stench of it strong in her nostrils. A drop of blood had hit the lizard queen's portrait and ran down it like a tear. She went to the window.

Looking down at the Rue Morgue, shadows moved far below, spectators robbed of their moment of excitement. How easy would it be to keep a lid on what had happened here? To the smell of blood, add machine oil, foliage, rot – the smell of a jungle somewhere far away and hot. This last did not belong in this, her city.

Her city. She remembered days running in the alleyways, hunting for scraps, hiding from the urban predators. Had it ever been her city? She was not born there and, later, had not lived there, yet here she was. She glared at the lizard queen's ruined portrait, deciding the blood added, not detracted, from the painting. She remembered the lizards' court. Her second, unfortunate husband had often taken her there. His death...

She wouldn't dwell on it. The barest hint of wind coming

335

through the window, and she realised her face was wet, that the atmosphere in the room had made her sweat. Looking down – was that a shadow moving up the wall, climbing cautiously, some animal well used to shade making its slow and careful way up to this place of death? She watched but could not be sure. She turned away from the window, taking a last deep breath of air fresher, at least, than that inside, and looked at last at the corpse.

That first glance only took a moment, and she turned her head, breathing hard through her nose. She closed her eyes, but the image of the corpse was waiting for her in the darkness behind her eyelids, and she felt the room begin to spin. She opened her eyes and looked again, and this time she did not look away.

A man lay on the floor at her feet.

One side of his head had been caved in. What remained of the face seemed to belong to a man hailing from Asia, though it was hard to tell with certainty. His skin had taken on a waxy aspect. He was lying in a pool of blood, the fingers of one hand – his left – curled into a fist, the other loose, one finger stretched out as if pointing. She half-expected to see a message scrawled in blood, on the floor or the wall, some cryptic riddle to lead her to the man's killer, but there was none, and it would have made no difference either way since she was not overly concerned with who killed him, but only of what they had taken from the man after his death.

The head wound was ordinary enough. She let her gaze wander further down, past the neck, towards the chest and stomach… yes. She knelt beside him, feeling sick. And now her hands were on him, studying the gash in his corpulent belly. The skin was hairless and the belly-button pronounced, and the man looked pregnant, even in death, as if his stomach had contained a womb and a foetus inside it – though there were none there now.

He had been gutted open, with a long, sharp knife. The flaps of his stomach looked like the torn pages of a book. She took a deep breath and plunged her hand into the corpse, searching, knowing even as she did it that she would find nothing but intestines and blood.

And now there was a sound coming from the open window,

a small rustle as of a creature of some sort trying to enter without being noticed, and she turned.

A shadow was perched on the windowsill. She stared at it, her bloodied hand going to the knife strapped to her leg. The shadow on the windowsill moved and gained definition, an impossible apparition that would have frightened the residents of the Rue Morgue to death.

She said, "It's about time you showed up." She brought up her knife and suspended it above the corpse, then plunged it in. Perhaps something still remained inside the man. She had to make sure.

When she looked away again the shadow had moved from the window and came crawling towards her. For a moment they were a tableau – corpse, woman above him with bloodied knife, a crawling, enormous cockroach symbolising death approaching or fleeing, she couldn't decide which. The mechanical cockroach whistled plaintively. The woman said, "That's hardly an excuse."

The thing whistled again, and the woman said, "Well, you're here now, at least. See if you can find anything."

The cockroach approached, feelers shaking. As it came closer the faint whirring sound of gears could be heard. It was about the size of a small dog. Its feelers moved and another whistling sound came out of its matt-black body, and the woman said, "You're the forensic automaton, Grimm, so why don't you tell me?"

The automaton she had called Grimm crawled closer to the body. The woman stood up, cleaning and sheathing her knife, and looked down. Probable cause of death – strike to the head with a blunt instrument. Mutilation inflicted post-mortem – the killer or killers knew what they were looking for and had come away with it.

She watched the little automaton crawl over the corpse. It buried its head in the man's glistening belly, its legs pushing it deeper into the corpse until it almost disappeared inside, making little whirring noises all the while. She walked back to the window and breathed in the air from the outside: air that carried nothing worse with it than the smell of smoke and dung and rotting rubbish.

THREE
A Spark of Electricity

After a while she went through the deceased's effects. They were few enough. Grimm was still studying the body. Right now its pincers were busy digging deep inside the man's head, and bits of brain dulled their colour when they emerged. The lady had examined the man's clothes but had come to no conclusions. The clothes were not new nor were they foreign.

The man's pockets were almost entirely empty. She found a handful of coins, a packet of loose tobacco, almost empty, and a matchbox to go along with it – no identity card, nothing to suggest who the dead man may have been or where he came from. She looked at the matchbox – the cheap print on the cover advertised a tobacconist in Montmartre. She put it in her pocket.

Grimm was still working on the corpse, emitting little whistles and clicks which she ignored. There was an Edison player on a table by one wall. She approached it but could find no perforated discs. She searched the apartment thoroughly then.

Madame L'Espanaye's room first – distinguished by more Victoria prints, aerial shots of the Royal Gardens, commemorative china plates, a chipped coronation mug – the woman was obsessed with the royal lizards from across the Channel. Les Lézards. Her mouth made a moue of distaste.

Madame L'Espanaye's interest in lizards evidently did not

extend to her wardrobe, which was full of frilly, lacy, pinkish-dirty, oversized gowns and negligees. That interested the lady a lot more. In the back of the wardrobe she found a box and inside the box a bottle of Scotch whisky, Old Bushmills, expensive and, if she recalled correctly, a lizardine favourite. It was three-quarters empty. Beside it was a roll of bank notes. They looked new. She ran her thumb through them, then put them in her pocket. Curiouser and curiouser.

There was a dresser with a vanity mirror and plenty of rouge and white paint, and she could almost picture the senior L'Espanaye in her mind. She went through the drawers and found a small-calibre gun at the bottom-most one on the left, and it was loaded. The bed was large and unmade, the sheets rumpled. In the small adjacent washroom she found several bottles of pills and grimy walls, and when she ran the tap the water was brackish.

She scanned the bedroom again but found nothing else of interest and moved on to Mademoiselle L'Espanaye's room. The daughter's was almost bare, the bed dominating the room, a single chair by the window, candles, many no more than stubs, standing like fat monks around the room, their wicks dead. She tossed the room and found nothing: it was as if no one had lived there and if they had, they'd left nothing behind them.

Conjecture: the two women shared the master bedroom, and the dead man had been using the daughter's room.

Grimm whistled from the other room, and so she walked over and stared down at the man's corpse, which looked even worse now than it did before, thanks to Grimm. "Traces of what?" she said.

The automaton spoke in Silbo Gomero, a technical compromise on communication that was also an assurance of confidentiality, since there were not many speakers of the whistling language, in Paris or elsewhere. The language had come from the Canary Islands, adopted by the Spanish who settled there and finally modified by Grimm's makers using a simplified French vocabulary. Grimm whistled again, and the lady said, "That doesn't make any sense."

Grimm whistled, more insistent now, and she said, "What do you mean, watch?"

Instead of an answer the mechanical insect crept closer to the corpse and extended a pincer toward it, gently touching the man's flesh. The lady watched. A small blue spark of electricity passed between Grimm and the dead man.

The corpse twitched.

The woman watched, her hand going to the butt of her gun without her being consciously aware of doing so. Grimm retreated from the body but it continued to twitch – and now its one remaining eye shot open.

The woman took a step back and her gun was in her hand and pointing at the corpse – she watched a dead foot kick, and the finger that had been pointing at nothing was rising now, impossibly, and the dead man was pointing directly at *her*, his face twisted in a mask of grotesque agony, accusing her...

The bullet took out the remaining eye and bits of brain exploded over Grimm and the print of the lizard queen. The pointing hand fell down, lifeless again. The body shuddered, once, twice, and finally subsided. The woman reholstered her gun and said, "Get rid of it."

Grimm began to whistle then, apparently, changed its mind. It approached the corpse again, pincers extended like surgical saws. Together, woman and automaton worked to erase the crime that had taken place there, tonight, and as they worked, dismantling the lifeless body into its separate components, she wondered why it was left the way it had been – were they interrupted, or was the dead man himself a message scribbled into the stones of the Rue Morgue for her to find?

FOUR
Outside Rue Morgue

When the work was done she left Grimm to dispose of the body parts – the giant insect secreting quicklime, squatting over the man's dismembered corpse digesting one piece at a time. She looked through the apartment again – there had been no sign of a struggle, and she thought it was a reasonable enough proposition that the two women who resided here had merely been absent – by chance? Or were they paid to make themselves scarce? She thought she'd be able to find them – assuming they were still alive...

A locked-room murder. The apartment was four stories high. Well, Grimm had managed to scale it easily enough. And the window was open... The how of it scarcely interested her. The who, though, had become something of a priority.

She washed her hands in the foul-smelling water in the sink, watching it turn red and pink and disappear in a gurgle down the drain, taking the dead man's blood with it. She dried her hands thoroughly and returned to the room and was relieved to see Grimm was almost half-way there. When it sensed her it turned, its feelers shaking, and emitted a burst of high-pitched whistles. The lady nodded, then said, "Take the samples to the under-morgue when you're done."

She went back to the window, glaring out at the city below. Night was settling in and, if she guessed correctly, the Madame and

Mademoiselle L'Espanaye would be hard at work. She pulled out the matchbox she had found on the corpse and looked at it again.

Montmartre.

She put it back abruptly and turned away from the window. Why was the name of the tobacconist familiar? She said, "I'm going for a walk."

Grimm whistled, a sad lonely sound that followed her as she walked out of the door.

Below, Rue Morgue was deep in shadow, its residents hiding behind their cheap walls. Windows were shuttered, as if excitement had given way, suddenly, to fear.

Good.

She walked alone, and the soft sound of her moving feet was the only break in the silence of the street. She watched the shadows, her hand on the butt of her gun. She was not disturbed.

She decided to walk for a while. She had always liked the city best when it was dark and silent. As a child she–

She turned at the sudden sound and the gun was in her hand and the shadows shifted and then eased back. She smiled, without humour, and walked on.

She thought about the dead man. He had carried something inside his own belly, a foreign object that had somehow been inserted into his flesh, and valuable enough that it had been ripped out of him savagely and carried away. The man had no identity, as yet, and neither did his killers. And as for his cargo…

She thought about Grimm touching the corpse, that little spark of electricity that had set the dead man rising. She had to conclude that, though he was human on the outside, his inside may have been a different matter. Well, it was of little concern right now. No doubt the doctor would be engrossed by Grimm's samples, down in the under-morgue…

She passed out of Rue Morgue, breathing a sigh of relief, though the entire neighbourhood was the same, dark and dank and dismal. She headed for the Seine, finding her way with ease through the narrow, twisting streets. The old city morgue used to sit at the end of that street, she remembered, lending the road its name. Thoughts of the corpse niggled at her. She had seen plenty of bodies but nothing like the one Grimm was busy erasing from existence.

After a while the streets became wider and more prosperous. She found an open café and went inside, into the gloom of candles and smoke. She ordered a coffee and sat down by the window and glared at the night.

The door of the café banged open, then shut, and a shadow slipped into the seat opposite her. She raised her eyes and stared at the smiling Gascon.

"Milady," he said. "What a pleasant surprise."

She glared at him. The Gascon signalled to the waiter, mouthed, "Coffee."

Ignoring her.

"You followed me," she said.

"Surely a coincidence," he said, and now his smile hardened. "Of all the places–"

"What do you want?"

The Gascon shrugged. And now the smile melted away, having never reached his eyes. "That murder is mine," he said.

"What murder?" she said, and was pleased to see the flicker of anger that passed over his face.

"You wouldn't," he said.

She sipped her coffee. The hot liquid revived her. She stared at the man evenly, waiting him out. He looked away first.

"The Republic has law," the Gascon said at last. "You can't cover up–"

"Can't?" she said. And now she stood up, dismissing him. "Stay out of my way," she advised. "And forget about the Rue Morgue. There is nothing there for you now."

He looked up at her. She examined him, feeling a vague sense of unease. Why was the Gascon still pursuing the case?

"I can help you," he said. His voice was soft. She smiled, showing teeth, and walked away without answering him, her back to him all the answer she needed to give, and the door banged shut behind her.

She could have taken a coach or one of the new baruch-landaus but instead she walked, not feeling an urgency any more,
but wondering what it was that had been surgically inserted into
the dead man's belly. It was not a case of murder, she thought,
but theft. She found the Seine and followed it for a while, watching the ruined Notre Dame cathedral growing larger as she
approached, a wan yellow moon rising above it. Lizard boys hung
around the broken-down structure at all hours: hair shaped into
ridges over otherwise bald domes, skin tattooed into lizard stripes,
tongues forked where they had paid some back-room surgeon to
split them open. Dangerous, yes, but predictable.

She crossed the river, looking down at the Seine snaking its
way through the city, a lone barge still floating down it at this
late hour, carrying pails of garbage, and she thought – there were
a hundred different ways to disappear forever in this city.

She walked away from the river, into the maze of neverending
streets, her feet sure on the ground, knowing their way, the
ground like taut skin stretched over the body of a giant lizard.
She thought the dead man must have come into the city very
quietly, but not quietly enough – had slipped in and found the
apartment in the Rue Morgue, thinking it was safe – he must
have waited, must have made contact with person or persons
still unknown, and waited to conclude the transaction – for she
was sure that's what it was – but had somehow faltered. Or not.
Perhaps he knew all along how he would end up, a gutted fish
in a Parisian market where everything was for sale.

She walked for a long time, her long legs carrying her easily,
swiftly, along the ancient narrow streets. She knew them well.
As a kid she had run through them, had lain in wait for the apple
cart owner to turn away for just one crucial moment – for a dark
shadow of a girl to swoop and make a grab and run away, laughing. She had looked through rubbish piles for clothes and food,
and hid in the abandoned places, the tumbledown houses where
others roamed, the animals in human guise who preyed on
those who had the least of all... a far cry from the home she
could no longer remember, the place where she'd been born, so

far away, where the sun always shone, where her mother had come from, the same mother who had died so quickly here, in this new land of white men and gleaming machines. She had first killed in a place just like this, a dark alley where a man was bent over a child – a boy who was a friend, as much as the other small humans on the street could be called that – and she had snuck behind the man and cut his throat with her knife, feeling nothing but a savage satisfaction, and the boy – he was still alive – had staggered away from under the corpse and down the street, clothes drenched in blood, some of it his own. She never saw him again, and there had been other predators, other animals on the streets of this most glorious Paris, city of equality, fraternity and liberty, this city of the Quiet Revolution.

The streets gradually became brighter, lamps alight and places of business still open: night business, for she was approaching Pigalle. There were people on the street, women leaning at corners, two men fighting in an alleyway, drunks spilling out of a nearby tavern, the sound of music and shouting and dancing from a building nearby, a brasserie serving buckets of mussels with bread for late diners, glasses of beer – faces leering at her until they saw the gun and turned away, eyes suddenly, carefully empty. She saw a man's pocket being picked by a small child and two gendarmes watching without comment. The man never noticed but the gendarmes did and when the child tried to run they were waiting for him, counting the money, taking out their share. This was her world, had been her world, and she still felt more comfortable here than she ever had at the lizardine court or the embassy balls – though that was merely a different kind of throat-cutting and pick-pocketing, done on a different scale.

The little boy ran off, and the two gendarmes disappeared through the doors of a bar. She walked on. Closer to Montmartre now, and the streets grew quieter, the ruined church on the hill above casting down a faint eerie glow. She walked a short way up to the small square where a couple of restaurants were closing, and into the all-night tobacconist's that only recently had sold a box of matches to a dead man.

SIX
The Immaculate Mr Thumb

Thumb's Tobacco was well lit and empty. Behind the counter were orderly rows of the tobacconist's merchandise. Hanging on the walls, startling her for a moment, were posters advertising *The P.T. Barnum Circus – The Greatest Show on Earth!* A tall black woman, muscled and scantily clothed, holding a pair of guns, was featured on one. She looked at it for a long moment and bit her lip. *The Ferocious Dahomey Amazon!* screamed the notice above her head. She smiled at last, and shook her head, and looked away. Then she looked over the counter and a pair of eyes stared back up at her.

The eyes rose to meet hers – and now she knew why the name had sounded familiar, as the eyes blinked recognition and a wide grin suddenly split the small face they came with.

"You!"

She nodded, unable not to return the grin as the small man behind the counter straightened up, climbing onto a stool so that he stood with his upper body above the polished wooden top. "Cleo–" he said, and she shook her head, *No.* "It's De Winter now."

"I haven't seen you since–"

"It's good to see you, too, Tom," she said.

The Vespuccian man was dressed immaculately in a child-sized

346

suit, a pocket watch hanging on a chain from his pocket. "Since you left the circus," he said.

"It's been a while."

"I have your publicity poster," the small man said proudly, gesturing at the wall.

"I saw," she said, not following the gesture. Looking at *him*.

"Last I heard you were in England," he said. He rubbed his thumb and finger together. "Married to some *lord*."

She said, "He died."

The grin grew larger. "They tend to do that, don't they?"

She let it pass. For now. She said, "Last I heard *you* were in England."

He shrugged. "Had to leave in a bit of a hurry, didn't I."

"Why doesn't that surprise me?"

The small man shrugged again.

"Still fomenting revolution?"

"Nah, mate," Tom Thumb said, "I'm legit now. Out of the revolutionary business. Minding my *own* business, for once, and liking it that way."

"The quiet life," she said.

He nodded, watching her carefully, no longer smiling now.

She said, "I find it hard to believe."

Tom Thumb shrugged. Believe what you want, the shrug seemed to say. See if I care. And now *she* smiled, and the little man shrank a little from it.

She took out the box of matches from her pocket, played with it. Tom Thumb watched her fingers. "You smoking now?" he said. "You never used to."

She flipped the box over, not answering him. Printed on the cover was *Thumb's Tobacco, Montmartre*. The painting showed the front of the shop, a little figure just visible behind the glass. She threw it across the counter at him and he flinched back but caught it.

"One of yours?" she said.

He looked at it, put it down on the counter. "Got my name on it, hasn't it?" he said.

"It does, at that," she said.

"So?"

He was watching her warily now, caged but not yet knowing why. Or maybe he did... maybe he'd been expecting her, or someone like her, to come eventually to his shop.

So... "Popular shop?" she said, looking around her at the empty space.

"Doing OK," he said, using the Vespuccian expression. It almost made her smile – she hadn't heard it in a while.

"That's a nice suit," she said instead.

"Thank you."

"Must be expensive."

"Oh, you know..." he said.

"And that watch. Gold?"

"This old thing? Nah. Just looks like it."

"It certainly does. Looks new, too."

Tom Thumb stared at her, expressionless. "You a copper now?"

It was said less as a question – more an accusation.

"We've all got to make a living," she said. "Don't we, Tom?"

"I'm *making* a living," he said. "I sell tobacco."

"So I see."

"Well, it was nice seeing you," he said, "*Milady*. Now, if you'll excuse me, I have a lot of work to–"

She reached across the counter and picked him up. He said, "Wha–"

"I'll dismiss *you*," she said. "When I'm done with you. *OK*, Tom?"

She dropped him. He glared at her, smoothed his jacket where she had grabbed him. Suddenly he grinned again. "Come see the ferocious Dahomey Amazon!" he said. "Remember? I used to love your act. Got your publicity poster right there–"

"I know, Tom. I saw it."

"Yes, well, we're old friends, you and I, aren't we? There's no need to get rough."

"I hope so, Tom."

She waited him out. He stood, watching her – she could see him thinking. She didn't hurry him. At last he said, "Sit down, I'll make us a brew."

Sit down, I'll make us a brew. As if they were back at the circus, and the last show had finished – everyone winding down, but not yet ready to let go – the rush still there, the shouts of the crowds, the smell of sweat, and smoke from the torches, roasting peanuts and piss from the animal enclave... sawdust. Sometimes she really missed the smell of fresh sawdust.

It always became less and less fresh as the evening progressed. She said, "OK."

SEVEN
Imports & Exports

Tom Thumb made coffee. He put a coffee set down on the counter between them – sugar cubes, small jug of milk, a couple of pastries, cups and saucers and spoons.

She took hers black and drank it through a sugar cube. "It's not bad," she said.

"It's from–" he said, and then he hesitated.

She said, "You selling coffee now?"

"Amongst other things."

"What sort of things?"

"Cleo–" he said, then checked himself, almost saying her full name, the way she was billed back in the show. "Fine, fine! Milady, then."

She waited.He said, "Is this going any further, or is this between us?"

She thought about it, said, "It depends."

"On what?"

On a corpse that was no longer there... She said, "I don't care what you do. I'm just trying to find something that's missing."

"What sort of something?"

"I'm not sure yet."

He shrugged, letting it go. "Fine," he said. "What do you want to know?"

"I want to know who bought that box of matches from you."

Tom Thumb looked exasperated. "How the hell should I know?"

"He was Asian."

She saw him noticing the *was*. And now his eyes narrowed, and his hand played with the pocket watch, releasing and closing the lid, working it.

"An Asian man who needed a place to hide out in…" she said, "Where did you say your coffee comes from again?"

"I didn't."

"But you were going to."

"Was I?"

Open, shut, open, shut. She took another sip of her coffee. "Leave that alone," she said.

"Lots of Asians in Paris," Tomb Thumb said at last. "Indochina. Siam. Doing business. So what?"

Making a connection, and she threw him a line: "You selling opium?"

… and he bit. Tom Thumb shrugged. "A little. Not illegal, is it?"

"No," she said. "But this isn't a smoking den, so what, you deal bulk?"

He didn't answer.

"Got a contact over there? Sends you stuff over?"

No reply.

"Coffee, for instance?"

"It's good coffee," Tom Thumb said. "Good opium, too."

"What else does he send you?"

Nothing from Tom, staring out through the window into the night.

"People, sometimes?"

Tom, still staring out at the night. Thinking. How much could he tell her? She knew that look.

"People who need somewhere to hide, for a little while?"

Tom turned to her. No smile, eyes calm like grey skies. "Is Yong Li dead?"

And now she had a name. "Yes."
Tom said, "Damn."

I have a little shipping business (Tom Thumb said). Import/export, with this guy in Indochina on the other end of it. I buy coffee, tobacco, now and then opium for those who like that sort of thing – all legit. So maybe I don't pay customs every time, you know? And maybe sometimes, just sometimes, I ship some stuff East.

What stuff? You know. Stuff.

You don't know?

But you want to.

It's nothing serious, Cl – Milady. Milady de Winter, huh? Seriously? Think I met Lord de Winter once, back when I was still living across the Channel. Whatever happened to–

Fine. Yes. Arms. Sometimes. And literature.

What do you mean what literature? How should I know?

I'm more of a drop point, now that you press me on it. Don't think I'm the only one working for this guy. So sometimes they drop off little packets for me – mostly paper. I don't know what's in them though.

Did I look? No.

Fine, maybe I did a couple of times. Didn't make much sense, though. Technical stuff. Like, you know those Babbage engines? That's what some of it looked like. Technical specifications. Once this mechanical beggar came into the shop, a proper derelict, could barely move, one of those old people-shaped ones, moving one leg after another, you can hear the motors inside they were so loud, doesn't say a thing but drops off this box – I open it, it's got an arm inside.

No, a metal arm. Real artwork. Only, I open the box, this arm reaches out, tries to strangle me. After that I didn't look again.

Yes. I'm getting to that. So, we do business, you know, mostly legit, a little bit of it under the counter – don't you dare make a joke – only sometimes there's people need to get from here to Indochina don't want to be going through the usual channels. I don't ask questions. Usually I know to expect them. Then off they go with the next shipment.

Got his own ship, ships, I don't know.

Sometimes he sends people over. No papers, half of them don't speak the language. I mean, any language. Don't know what they want. If they need it I arrange a safe house, somewhere to put them, lie low for a while. If not then poof *– they disappear into the city, I never see them again.*

Where the safe house is? You don't think I'm going to tell you, do you?

How did you know?

Oh.

So that's where you found him. Poor bastard.

He came in about a month ago. Nervous little guy, fat belly, gave him lots of problems, cramps, I don't know. He kept holding it, almost looked pregnant. I put him up for a couple of nights. Nice guy. Taught me this drinking game–

I don't know where he was from. Don't know what he was doing here. I don't ask questions. A couple of days later L'Espanaye tells me the place is free, I send him over.

The mother, yes. She's the one I've been dealing with. Wouldn't mind dealing with the daughter though, if you know what I mean.

Right. Sorry.

No, never saw him again. Didn't think I'd hear about him again either, until you walked through my door.

The poor bastard.

He was a nice guy.

EIGHT
Tattoos

She finished her coffee. Tom Thumb lit a cigar. She watched him – trimming it first, then using the matchbox that came from a dead man's pocket. Tom blew out smoke. She said, "Do you have any idea what he was carrying?"

"Ask no questions," Tom Thumb said, "hear no lies. That's my policy."

He knew more than he was telling her. She was sure of that much, at least. But Tom Thumb wasn't going anywhere. He'd been going nowhere for a long time. She said, "And the name of the man you deal with? The one in Indochina?"

Tom shrugged. "Never asked his name."

She let it pass. "What does he do, exactly? Beyond selling you coffee?"

"No idea."

But she had an idea.

"You've always been a revolutionary," she said. "What were you doing in England, Tom?"

"Minding my own business," the little man said. He blew smoke towards her and she smiled and reached over and pulled the cigar from his mouth and put it out on his hand.

Tom screamed.

"I'll come back," she said. "When you're feeling better."

She walked away, thinking of the dead man, but thinking of someone else now, too – a man somewhere in Asia, a man with no name. He would be a very careful man, she thought – cautious, a planner. And ruthless – she thought of Yong Li lying on the floor of the apartment in the Rue Morgue with his stomach cut open where someone had opened it before and hid something inside. Was Yong Li meant to have died in Paris?

Somehow she didn't think so. No doubt Tom would be in a hurry to send word back, and that was all right – she wanted to know what they would do.

She was still thinking when the shadows moved around her. She ducked but even so the blow caught her on the side of the head, knocking her out of balance. They were very quiet. There were four of them that she could see, dressed in black, faces masked and covered. She backed away. None of them seemed to be armed.

She pulled out her gun.

Too fast – one of the shadows rushed her, aiming an impossibly high kick at her gun hand – no time to think – her finger was on the trigger and she pressed and the gun went off, an explosion of thunder in the silent street, and the man fell back, half of his head missing.

One of them came at her again from the side, and she felt a savage blow to the head – the same place – and dropped the gun. Her mouth filled with blood. Her eyes stung with tears of pain. Another kick took her in the ribs. She lashed back, going back in time years, when the streets were her home. Her leg caught one of the assailants on the shin. She rolled, kicking again from below, dropping one – but he gracefully turned his fall into a jump and came back at her, another kick throwing her back – but now the gun was close. She picked it up, almost blind, and used it as a club, all discipline forgotten, and caught the man in the face, hearing bones breaking, delighting in the sound. She flipped the gun around and shot him in the knee.

And now the other two shadows were retreating, disappearing as if they'd never been there. The lone remaining assailant lay on the ground clutching his leg. Still no sound. She was impressed.

She was breathing heavily now, and she needed to pee. Her head echoed with pain, and her side burned. She went to the man, from behind, the gun ready to discharge, and pulled off his black mask.

An Asian face, and somehow she was not surprised. Not un-handsome – young, clean-shaven face, mouth clamped shut to stop him from screaming. She smiled at him and shot his other knee.

This time he did scream. She grabbed his head. "Who sent you?" she said. "What do you want?"

He spat in her face. She back-handed him. Wiped away blood, some of it his, some of it her own. "Tell me."

"The key," he said, and then he smiled. His face was a death mask. "See you in the other world," he said, and then he bit hard on something in his mouth. She smelled bitter almonds, watched his face relax, and now his eyes saw nothing, and she let him go.

She was left standing there, breathing heavily, her head ringing, two corpses on the ground beside her. He had spoken perfect French, she thought. And in a Parisian accent. She searched him, then the other man. Nothing on them. But she did find something.

Both men bore identical tattoos on their left wrists.

NINE
Notre Dame de Paris

She copied down the tattoos, then left. A little down the road, finding a dark corner, she squatted, feeling relief as she peed. As she was walking away she could see the first gendarmes coming up the hill. There was a swelling on her face, and her ribs hurt. Still, she thought – she had come off lightly, and she wondered why. They could have taken her out easily enough with a gun, or even by themselves.

A warning, then?

Again, she walked, the distance clearing her head slowly. It was a long night and dawn was still far away. She had a lot to do.

For one thing, she needed to see the doctor.

A sense of revulsion, but she knew she had to go down there. And he might have something for her by now.

She walked back towards the Seine, gliding through shadows, avoiding the few passers-by on the streets, late-hour drunks and those who preyed on them, knowing everyone else was ensconced behind locked doors. Everyone who could afford a lock, or a roof...

Blessed be the Quiet Revolution.

Gaslight, reflected in the surface of the Seine. The bookseller stalls closed for the night, their gaunt owners sleeping inside the little makeshift stalls, wrapped in words for warmth and comfort.

Fat lot of use it did them. She remembered the stories about the assassin they called the Bookman, and the confused reports coming from across the Channel for a while, three years back, that said England had a new, human king, stories that quickly ebbed away and finally disappeared. Victoria was still on the throne, the lizard queen, though it was said the balance of power had shifted, that the British had had their own Quiet Revolution, human and automata joining forces – she had not been back there in a long time, not since her husband's…

Dark thoughts for a dark night. She crossed and came to the ruins of Notre Dame, eerie in the gaslight coming from the banks of the river. The ruined cathedral glowed the bright sickly green of the lizards' strange metal, and in the tumbled-down structure she could see figures moving stealthily, and fires burning. Lizard boys and night ghouls and tunnel rats… She walked through them and they shied away from her, knowing her for what she was, recognising in her what they saw in themselves.

She walked past fallen gargoyles, their heads staring in be-musement into the sky, past toppled columns and the remnants of a giant bell. It must have been magnificent, once…

It had been built by Les Lézards, long before the Quiet Revo-lution – a potent symbol of the power beyond the Channel, that some said had come from the stars… She had heard the stories of Caliban's Island, of Vespucci's ill-fated journey when he awoke the slumbering creatures on that far-away island – but that's all they were to her, stories, and of little concern to her.

She had had her own ill-fated journey on the seas, the one that had brought her here, just as it did all those other migrants, the Mexica and Aztec and Kampucheans, Zulu and Swahili and Nipponese, some curious, some eager, and some without hope… Migrations went one way and then the other, the poor of Europe heading out to the same kingdoms from which others came in the opposite direction, ships crossing in the night, across the seas. As she had come here from far-away Dahomey, that great king-dom that was once, so long ago, her home.

Now she was no longer sure what she was, where she belonged. Serving the Quiet Council, hunting down such cases as belonged in the files no one ever saw, the ones kept only in the under-morgue… Something inside her longed for a journey, to be somewhere far away. A place without cities, without gaslight and smoke and steam, away from the complex incomprehensible schemes of humans and machines. Instead she walked through Notre Dame until she found the hidden door and spoke to it, and the door opened for her and she walked inside, and down.

Down into the under-morgue.

TEN
Into the Catacombs

The tunnels stretched for miles under Paris. She knew them well enough, but thought it was impossible to know them all. They were not empty. There were people down here, too. Hers was not the only entrance, and there were plenty who came here and some who made it their home.

Tunnel rats, grimy and dark with the stench of the sewers about them, those who hunted in the refuse of the city for whatever they could find. There were treasures and bodies buried, it was said, in equal measures in the catacombs... There were vast old cemeteries, dumping grounds for ancient skeletons, an entire city of child-sized coffins from some long-ago plague. There were the old mines, depleted now, but still worked sometimes, in secret, by those poor and desperate enough. There were times when sections of the under-city collapsed and caused holes to appear in the above-ground world – disrupting lives and traffic and offering a glimpse into what lay just below the city, its dark underbelly – these had to be covered up quickly. There were trains down there, mines, sewers, cemeteries, streets that once lay in the sun above-ground, long ago... She walked through the tunnels and watched its denizens. In a room branching to the left four old men sat around a fire, roasting a rat on a wooden stick. They toasted her as she passed them, and she noticed the man holding the bottle they were drinking from had lost several of his fingers.

She passed orderly piles of skulls and the entrance to a sewer where children were chasing rats, making no sound as they hunted. She saw their faces, briefly, moving from light to shade – grime-streaked, serious, intent – children in body only, with a childhood that had drowned long ago in these same sewers.

There were lights, here and there, in this under-city of permanent dusk. Camp fires, stationary, and bobbing torches. The glint of a knife, too – and other metal.

She came across the first of the automatons past the sewer entrance. Once it had been human-shaped, from whatever factory or lab had made it, one of the discarded, now lying there, a broken-down old machine, staring at her with eyes that couldn't be read. It was impossible to say if it could see, if the eyes still functioned. Some had lain there unmoving for years, were finally picked apart for what might still work, might fetch a few coins from the dealers in such things. It was another difference between here and across the Channel. There, they did not have many automatons, the bias running deep, enforced by the lizard queen and her get. It was rumoured they were afraid of such machines.

Not so here. Vaucanson's Heirs, they were called, these derelicts – the product of another time, a vision of the world that was brighter and cleaner than the real. The new machines were slicker, different somehow. She had heard they had begun to build themselves.

Not in the under-city, though. She threw the beggar a coin and it snatched it from the air, surprising her. "Thank you," it said, the voice a scratchy echo of a long-dead recording. She walked on, somehow disturbed by his response. There were others like it down in the catacombs and they banded together when they could, fighting off those who would break them down for parts. The gendarmes never came down into the under-city. The law here was not of the world above, and so the Quiet Council found it useful, and had appropriated a substantial area for its own secret purposes. But she was not there yet.

She walked past a brook, the water surprisingly clear, a hidden river under the city that had been forgotten long ago by those above. A family was washing in the thin stream, a man and a woman and three children, their few possessions lying on the bank beside them.

She came to a crossroads and went left, when she had the feeling of being watched. She walked a little further then turned and glided into shadow, her gun out, waiting, tense, when a voice close to her ear said, "Hello, Milady."

She said, "Damn," and reholstered the gun. "It's you."

"I saw you walk past," he said, by way of an explanation. "You on Council business?"

"I'm always on Council business," she said, and he grinned, a sad grotesque expression in that ruined face. "You should marry," he said. "Again."

"I like the freedom."

"Free to roam the underworld? What sort of freedom is that?"

She looked at him and knew that what was for her a rare freedom was to him a prison, and one he could not escape. She shrugged, acknowledging a point.

"So what's happening, Q?" she said. "Have you got something for me?"

He frowned, said, "Let's you and me walk a little way."

They walked side by side, the tall woman with the gun and the squat hunchback beside her. She never knew his history, only that he had come from a place near Dahomey, Dugbe it was called, but whether as a child or a man she had no idea. He never referred to his origins. He haunted the catacombs, trading in favours and knowledge the way others traded in stocks and shares.

"There's been rumours," he said.

"There're always rumours," she said.

"And more than rumours," he said, "there have been people down here, moving like shadows through the under-city. Strangers, with a lighter step than I have ever heard."

"Oh?" she said, her interest quickening, and he said, "The way assassins move. They are searching for something."

"Do you know what?"

"No," he said. "All I know is that you should be careful. The under-city is dangerous – well, more dangerous than usual."

"I can take care of myself."

"Yes," he said, looking at her bruised face, and she grinned, and he grinned back. "I can't help the way I look," she said, and the hunchback, his grin dissipating like smoke, said, "Neither can I."

"I know," she said, and reached out, squeezing his arm. "Q, if you hear anything else–"

"I'll find you," he said. Then he grinned again. "Unless that policeman finds you first."

She said, surprised: "The Gascon?"

"I think he likes you," the hunchback said, his grin holding. Then, curiously, "What is it between the two of you?"

She sighed. "It's an old story," she said. Then, into his silence, "He was a friend of my first husband."

The hunchback nodded. "Just look out," he said. "Be careful of the shadows."

"Always," she said. He half-turned away. "I better get back," he said. "Esme will be waiting."

She watched him go, and felt a momentary pang of envy.

ELEVEN
The Under-Morgue

She walked on, and into a dead end – a tunnel sealed with a solid wall, leading nowhere. She spoke to the wall, then put her hand on one of the stones and pushed. A small door swung open and she went through it, the door shutting noiselessly behind her.

Welcome to the under-morgue.

The first thing she always noticed was the smell. It made her want to retch.

Formaldehyde was a part of it. Ammonia, oil, burning coal – there were steam engines deep underneath, below the bedrock, hungry beastly things always feeding, always moving, and the smell seeped through. There was also manure, fresh, and the scent of rot – the smell of growing things and dying things commingling in the under-morgue, the Quiet Council's secret domain: she always thought of it as the place they kept to throw away the dirt and guts and blood, the refuse the rest of the world didn't need to see. She looked around her.

The cavern opened before her, larger than the largest ballroom. Gaslight globes glowed on the walls, but the place was always in gloom despite them. The gardens in the distance – she shuddered, thinking of what grew there – and the cages nearby, the cages where they kept the–

"Milady!"

Straight ahead was the lab area, and a figure in a dirty-white smock was coming towards her, smiling happily in the wan light. His face was not unhandsome, though almost comical in the thick lips, the small but pronounced nose, the mess of hair, eternally shocked, that stood above his head. He carried an assortment of pens in the front pocket of his smock. His teeth were bright and his eyes brighter – insane-bright, as she thought of them.

"What *happened* to you?" he said as he came closer. The smile was replaced with a concerned look and she sighed and said, "Hello, Viktor."

"We must fix you up!"

"No," she said, a little too quickly. And, "I'm fine."

"Nonsense! Come with me."

She followed the scientist along the hard floor of the cavern, toward his open lab. Viktor favoured steel. There were steel desks and towering banks of instruments, gauges and blinking lights and enormous switches, all set into steel cabinets twice her height. There were steel surgical instruments and steel beds, an entire operating theatre lying there – thankfully unused, for once.

There were refrigeration units, powered by the hidden-below engines. When they arrived at the lab area it only took Viktor a moment and when he turned back to her he was holding a syringe in his hands and she almost shot him. She had the urge to shoot him every time she came there.

"It's a rejuvenation serum," he said, proudly. "Still experimental, of course, but…"

"I just want a cup of coffee," she said. Viktor's face fell. "This will revolutionise medical science!" he said.

"I have no doubt it will."

"Of course," he said, putting it carefully away, "I still need to iron out some of the more unfortunate side effects…"

"You do that," she said.

"Coffee," he said. "Coffee, coffee… where did I put that machine?"

"You now need a machine to make *coffee*?" she said.

"Milady," he said, turning to her with a curiously serious expression on his face, "we must show *respect* to our machines."

"I wonder if they are indeed ours," she said, but softly, and he didn't seem to hear her. "Or if we're theirs, and don't yet know it..."

"Aha! There it is." Viktor had found a (steel, naturally) machine in one corner and pulled down a lever. There was a crack as if of lightning, and a gurgling sound could be heard. "Won't be a moment. Milk?"

"No, thank you."

He spoke French well, but with an accent. He had once been a baron, for what it was worth. He always insisted on Viktor. He was as egalitarian as if he had personally fought in the Quiet Revolution.

And just as dangerous.

He brought her a cup of coffee – china, mercifully, and not steel, in that at least – and took one for himself. "Are you sure you don't want me to do something about your face, at least?" he said. "Your poor face. I could hasten the healing process considerably–"

"It's fine," she said. "Honest."

"A modification of my own based on the early Hyde formula," he said. "Really, it's perfectly safe."

She let it go.

He took a sip from his coffee, made a face, and looked at her. "The Council is very concerned," he said.

"About my face?"

He shook his head, fighting off a half-smile. "About the missing object. I take it you haven't found it."

"Yet," she said. He nodded. "Of course."

"No," she said. "I haven't found it. Yet. It would help, perhaps, to know what it is."

He shrugged, expansively. "What does it matter? You need not worry about what it *does*, only that *we* have it, and not–"

She watched him. He blinked and looked away. "Not *who*?" she said.

"Well, anyone else, obviously," he said, sounding a little irritated. Sounding like he had given away more than he was meant to.

She watched him over her coffee. The scientist could not sit still. Already he was fidgeting, the coffee a distraction, conversation an effort. Wanting to go back to his work, his knives, his electricity... She said, "Was Grimm here?"

"Grimm!" Viktor beamed at the name. "Yes. He dropped off the samples. Fascinating. Fascinating!" Happy again, he abandoned the coffee and wandered off to a long work table where test tubes, a microscope and various instruments lay in apparent disorder. "Fascinating!"

"So you said."

"I am going to have to run more tests."

"Naturally."

"But I can tell you—"

"Yes?"

"I have not seen such a thing before."

She thought of the man's ruined corpse on the floor, of Grimm reaching over, sparking it alive with electricity. "What is it?" she said.

The scientist fiddled with a pen, opened and closed his mouth. "I don't know," he said, finally. Then, with more defiance – "Yet."

"Yet," she agreed, smiling.

"Perhaps—" he said.

"Yes?"

"I think the thing inside him may have affected him. The tissue samples are suggestive..." He fell quiet, thinking. "You should be careful," he said.

"People keep telling me that, recently."

He smiled, ceding her the point. "The Council wants to see you," he said.

"Who's there?" she said, and his smile dropped when he said, flatly: "All of them."

TWELVE
The Quiet Council

Stone arches, dim light. The Council convened in what may have once been a wine cellar. The smell still lingered, of old vinegar and smoked cedar wood. The entrance was through the under-morgue. She had to pass the cages to get there. The things in the cages stared at her as she passed. Every time she tried not to look, and failed.

What do you want to know about the Council? The Quiet Council, the secret council, those lords and ladies of the under-world? Human and machine, revolutionaries after the revolution had come and gone, quietly. Picture them sitting there behind their half-moon desk, looking down at the Lady de Winter as she entered, as she stood before them. Glaring up at them, a wilful child, but useful. Useful, particularly, in this curious matter of the dead man on the Rue Morgue, and of the thing that had been inserted into him and then, so savagely, taken out. A missing thing. A trifle, nothing more. And yet, a cause for some anxiety.

"Milady de Winter." The Council spoke through the Hoffman automaton. Built by Krupp, rumour had it, and long ago, and based on an obscure Teutonic writer. The voice, full of hisses and scratches, had a thick, heavy accent. "Please to make your report."

She stood and glared at them for a moment longer. So much anger, so much passion so tightly controlled! A street child, a circus girl, a lady, a killer – the last one first and foremost.

She gave them her report. The murder in the Rue Morgue, the Gascon, the corpse, the search of the apartment, Tom Thumb, the shadows, Q's warning – she missed nothing and the Council listened with a grave silence, faces hidden behind shadows.

"And so?" the Hoffman automaton said at last, when she had finished.

"And so I came here to see what results were–" she began, but Hoffman interrupted her.

"What results?" the automaton said. "What results indeed, Milady. I see no results."

A murmur of agreement. She stared up at them, silent. "The nature of the corpse is not your concern. Your only task, child – your only purpose – is to find that which is missing. That which was taken. That which we want."

Another murmur of agreement spread around, waves on the surface of a pond.

"Results we want. And you bring none to us."

She said nothing. They noticed her hand go, perhaps unconsciously, to the butt of her gun. There were some smiles at that. A charming young thing, very spirited. Too attached, perhaps, to her projectile weapon.

"Where, for instance," the Hoffman automaton said, "are the two women whose apartment it is?"

"I have not located them yet."

"You did not try!"

"I am only one person. I can't do everything."

"Perhaps you should be replaced, then."

She shrugged, waited him out, a small smile playing on her lips.

The Hoffman automaton made a curious sound – a cross between a cough and a spit. She waited for it to readjust its sound.

"Perhaps you could tell me what I'm looking for," she said.

"That is not your concern!"

"Does that mean you don't know?"

Silence.

The Council observed her, woman-child, this tall and deadly woman sworn to serve the Republic. Sworn to protect it, and that she does, but the danger from the East is great, greater than they had anticipated.

And now she was turning the questioning on them.

"Who is Tom Thumb working for?" she said.

Silence, full of scratches.

"And who are the people also looking for this thing, this object borne inside the man all the way across the seas?"

"Let us see the impression you obtained," the Hoffman automaton said. "The tattoos."

She stepped up to him, sensing the others shying away, further into the dark. A council of masks, hiding from prying eyes. What were they afraid of?

"Is it the lizards you are so concerned with?" she said.

"They are always a concern," the automaton said.

Was that relief, detected in his words?

The East. Indochina. What was there? A part of the world distant and filled with mysteries of its own. The Hoffman automaton took the sketch from her and studied it.

"Imperial assassins," it said.

What?

"So she is after it too," it said, the voice low, barely above a murmur.

Victoria? The lizard queen on her metal green throne?

"It is as we suspected," another voice said, deep within the shadows.

"And yet."

She waited, but there was no more, not for a while. Then, "Proceed with the investigation. Report back to us. Find that which was stolen."

"I still don't know–" she said, but the automaton cut her off: "You are dismissed."

She walked off then, leaving the Council to its devices.

Would she live? She was very good at not dying. They conferred amongst themselves. Perhaps another agent in the field – no, too dangerous. And already it was spreading, the grey–

THIRTEEN
The Little Grey Cells

Back in the under-morgue, she helped herself to the medicine cupboard and cleaned her face. She felt fatigued, knew the long night was not yet over.

She was not angry at the Council. It was the way they operated, seeing her and others like her as chess pieces and little more, to be moved on the board according to formulae and calculations she could not even imagine. They would keep her in the dark, using the power of her ignorance to bring out that which was hidden even from them. If there was such a thing.

Viktor was at his lab, muttering to himself, bent over his microscope. She walked over to him. "What am I not being told?" she said.

He blinked. "That covers a lot of ground," he said.

"You seemed," she said, and then stopped, putting her thoughts in order. "Almost dismissive, earlier."

"What do you mean?" But he looked flustered, a fish hooked and watching the ocean disappear away from him.

"Of the corpse. You said you've never seen anything like it before–"

"Yes?"

She smiled at him. He took a step back.

"I think you were lying."

He tried to outstare her and failed. "That's absurd," he said, but his hands were fluttering, the fingers working as if independent from the body, and she thought – he *wants* to tell me. Poor Viktor, all alone in his underground lab, no one to share the excitements of science with... "*Have* you seen such a thing before?" she said.

"Well," he said, still being evasive, knowing, she thought, that it wouldn't fool her, "naturally, in my line of work... reanimation of the... as it were... the effects of electricity on the human... such as... scientifically speaking..."

"Viktor," she said, speaking patiently, as if to a child. "*Scientifically* speaking–" She smiled at him, trying to make it a nice smile, trying to reassure him. He was a nervous little man, afraid of crowds, torches, pitchforks and milk. "You have, haven't you?"

He didn't answer. She moved closer to him, towering over him, knowing the effect she had on him and using it. "Viktor, Viktor," she said. "My poor little Viktor..."

"Milady, I..."

She ruffled his hair. He whimpered. "What are you trying to tell me, Viktor?"

"The... the tissues... you see, they're –" then, with more force – "I can't," he said. "Council business, Milady. It's Council business!"

"Out there," she said, "in the dark streets, out there in the night few dare to walk – out there I *am* the Council, Viktor."

She looked down at him, then at his workbench. On the tabletop – was it flesh, a fold of skin? Grey and sickly – and moving. She listened back to what he said. "The effects of electricity on the human body," she said.

He looked up at her, his eyes bright. *Dying* to tell her, she thought. "I know the effects of electricity on the human body," she said. "It does not make a man walk again, or open his eyes and point with a dead finger. It does the opposite. It kills."

"My research indicates a high probability of eventual re–" he said but didn't finish. She smiled at him. "Is this it?" she said, pointing at the grey matter.

"This? Oh, this is just a–"

"Electricity does not do that to the human body," she said. "Am I correct, Viktor?"

His fingers, interlacing, releasing, tapping air.

"But what if the body is no longer human?" she said, and he jumped.

"More coffee?" she said.

"Thank you," he said. "I think I've drunk enough."

"You are tightly wound up," she said. "Perhaps you need a rest. I know a castle–"

"Please," he said, raising his hands before him like a shield. "No more castles."

"Yes," she said. "I too find them overrated."

"It's the draught," he said. "And the heating bill's always enormous."

"Tell me about that body, Viktor. You *have* seen such a thing before, haven't you? I know you have. You want to tell me about it, don't you? You don't want me to get *hurt*, do you, Viktor? You don't–"

"Please," he said, and she knew he was hers. "Show me," she said.

He took her to the far side of the cavern. Past the cages again, and turning her eyes away from the figures inside. Viktor's experiments, following from the works of–

No. She walked past and they came to a large metal door set into the rock. The under-morgue proper. When she put her hand to the door the metal was cold to the touch. Viktor played with a pad by the door and it opened with a faint hiss. Tendrils of fog ebbed out, as if reaching for them.

"Follow me."

She did. They went inside. Ice-cold, steel walls, icicles hanging like nooses from the ceiling. Inside: rows of metal cabinets pulled open, holding corpses in various stages of decomposition on their trays. Men, one woman, two children. The children looked almost identical, a boy and a girl with china-white skin turning grey.

Viktor looked expectant. Waiting for her to make a connection... It took her a moment but the colour began to dominate her view and she said, "Grey."

He said, "Yes."

She came closer, examined the hand of the boy. The grey had spread down his arm, in patches, looking oily, looking... she wasn't sure. She reached to touch it and Viktor's hand held her back. "Don't," he said.

He went to a table laden with instruments and returned with a prod. When he pressed the little trigger a burst of blue electricity sparked at the end.

"Watch," he said. There was something almost fond in his voice when he said, "Watch the grey cells."

She watched.

He put the end of the stick to the boy's dead hand and pressed the trigger.

She watched. The electricity singed the skin. She watched the grey shapes on the boy's white skin.

Nothing at first.

Then...

The grey spots, she realised, were slowly moving.

FOURTEEN
Post-Mortem

How to describe it? The grey moved along the boy's frozen corpse as if it were alive. It looked snake-like. It looked reptilian. It looked like mercury and it looked like shadows. That was it, she thought. Like grey shadows, growing on the boy's dead skin, animating it. Shadows bellowing across naked arms and chest, along closed eyes and china face. She said, "What is it?" and her voice was very small in that cold, hushed place.

Viktor said, "We don't know."

She said, "Where does it come from?" and he said, "That, Milady, is what the Council hopes you could tell us."

She stared – and now the boy's left hand was twitching, the fingers closing, slowly, slowly, into a fist, and she took a step back when – there! – his eyes sprang open and the corpse stared at her, cold-blue eyes not seeing, dead eyes animated by a grey shadow that should not have existed, a wrong thing, unnatural and yet–

"Stop it," she said.

But Viktor was no longer applying the electricity.

"The effect lasts for some time independently of the trigger," he said. "The cold slows it down. The main reason we're keeping them in here. You did well, by the way, disposing of the corpse. It would have been... inconvenient if the deceased began to walk down Rue Morgue post-mortem."

She almost laughed. She felt a little hysterical. In one moment the investigation went from something understood – something within her remit, within the world as it was, as it should be – into something else entirely, something alien and unknown. "When did it start?" she said.

The little scientist beside her shrugged. "Who knows?" he said. "We began grabbing them as soon as the reports started filtering in. I have no doubt we missed a few."

"How long?"

"Two years," he said. "Possibly three."

"*Years*?" she said. She had to get some fresh air. The boy was moving now, his entire body shaking, the head moving in a silent *no*. "Open the door," she said.

Viktor, too, seemed happier once they were outside, the door safely closed behind them.

"Is it–" she said, and hesitated.

"Infectious?"

She nodded. Viktor said, "Not so far, but…"

"But what?"

"It seems to be spreading."

Moving grey shapes. It was as if, having viewed the corpse (and now she realised, too, that she had come in close contact with the dead man in the Rue Morgue, skin-to-skin, and did the subtle grey shapes leap from one to the other? Were they even now working their way into the fabric of her being, into her cells and bone-marrow, into her bloodstream and brain?) she was now seeing the world in a skewed fashion, the night world of black shades transformed into a half-light place, inhabited by moving grey shapes… She blinked but they would not go away, houses and windows and lamps at strange angles, footsteps in dust and clouds flying low.

Like the shadows of another world, she thought, and the night felt colder, clammier somehow.

She had left the catacombs on the left bank of the Seine, exiting through an Employees Only door of a hotel on Rue de la

Bûcherie. She felt a sense of urgency now, a need to find the missing women, to begin to answer the questions that were growing, sprouting like grey-capped mushrooms all over her post-mortem investigation.

Who were the black-clad assailants in Montmartre? Who had killed the man called Yong Li? Were they the same people? It seemed unlikely – unless they already had the object in their possession and wanted to discourage her from pursuing them. She had asked the Council and Hoffman had said, "Imperial assassins."

But which empire? Was the lizard queen behind the murder? Yet all the threads were leading East, away from these cold European lands…

Her carriage was waiting for her. A black unmarked vehicle, its mute driver ready with the horses. She could have had a baruch-landau, a horseless carriage, to take her through the narrow streets of Paris. She preferred the horses. Like canaries down in a mine, the horses could warn her of danger before it was there.

"Pigalle," she told the driver. He nodded, without expression. A large man, with stitch marks on his forehead, around his skull. One arm was shorter than the other. One of Viktor's creatures, who only came out at night. The man was dressed in a black cloak and a low-hung hat. Just another shadow in this city of shadows, unremarkable, invisible to all but the few like itself. She settled back in the carriage and felt the streets pass without looking at them, listening to the city as it entered the deep-end of night.

She had questioned Viktor but he could tell her nothing more – couldn't, or wouldn't, but either way the result was the same. He'd shown her the cultures growing in his test tubes, grey swirls sprouting, forming shapes almost like an alphabet, carrying a meaning hovering just beyond her reach. And that was it.

One last exchange: "Who was the agent in charge?"

Viktor: "I'm not sure I'm at liberty to–"

Grabbing him by the neck, her fingers closing on his throat –
"Just a little squeeze, Viktor, and who'd put *you* together again?"

"Tômas! It was Tômas!"

Him? That mask-wearing murderer, that phantasm, shape-shifting like a thing from a British Penny Dreadful, changing his clothes, his hair, the colour of his eyes – at will, it seemed – second only to Holmes of Baker Street in his capacity as master of disguise – but without the Great Detective's honesty, his morals, a blank slate, Tômas, a creature of the gutters, a killer and one who enjoyed the killing, and yet–

A valued agent of the Council, who knew well the value of such men.

"A body-snatcher?" she said. "A suitable job for him."

"No doubt," Viktor agreed, croaking the words. "Well, I won't keep you."

She released his throat, left him to massage it. She saw the look in his eyes, knew its meaning. *What makes you any different?*

I don't enjoy the killing, she wanted to say, but didn't. Perhaps, she thought, she feared it wasn't true.

FIFTEEN
Place Pigalle

She let go of Tômas – for now. She would find him, later, and she would extract the truth from him, however much he threatened or fought. She had dealt with worse than him, before. And she let go of Viktor, too – cooperative Viktor who was still lying to her, still keeping her from the truth – she knew him, could read it in his shifty little eyes. He was only telling her what the Council wanted her to know, no more, no less. She was the Council's creature – well then, she would follow the scent blindly, and do as she was told – for now, for now…

They were, all of them, the Council's creatures: serving the greater good, whatever that was, per the calculations and machinations of these strange, artificial beings. Viktor in his lab, Fanto – Tômas with his robberies and secret murders and body-snatching – even Q, gentle Q who lived underground and kept his misshapen eyes on things – the Council's eyes, leased, borrowed, sold.

She settled back and the coach rattled on. To Pigalle, the one place guaranteed to be lit up this time of night. She had already passed through it once tonight. But then it had been too early.

At that moment she missed Grimm. He was back in the under-morgue, and she had not even seen him – not stopped to check on him, that metallic, insect-like creature, another denizen of Paris' secret world. Yet faithful. Faithful and–

No. Let go of Grimm. Let go of it all, the half-light, half-life of the catacombs, their smell clinging to her leather coat. Her ribs ached and her face felt swollen. She opened the window of the carriage, let the comforting smells of the upper city in, the smoke and manure and the curses and songs, the lights in the distance, growing closer – Pigalle, the place of merriment and drunkenness, of dancing and whoring and knifing, of carousing and robbing and killing.

Her kind of place.

And now there was a sound penetrating the night like a knife – a woman's scream, high-pitched, terrified – terminating so suddenly that the silence ached, and she was out of the carriage and running before the mute driver could bring it to a halt. Running, towards the dark mouth of an alleyway, Peacemaker out of its holster, running and knowing all the while that it was too late.

She burst into the alley and saw a shape on the ground, a dark pool around it, and a shape standing above, turning to look toward her and she ran–

A grey misshapen face, moonlit despite the darkness – a skull as white as moon rock, eyes in which the tendrils of galaxies swirled – the mouth open in a silent hungry grin–

Man, beast, spirit, ghost – the knife a solid real object, too late – it slashed the woman lying on the ground. She fired, the gun making a loud noise in that small confine. Stars above, half-hidden by the city's perennial smoke. Stars looking down. The crazed grinning face turning to her, a crack in that elongated skull – the mouth opening, *snapping* at her, *snap, snap!* and she fired again.

The figure on the ground moved, groaned. The creature took another hit from her gun and only grinned harder. Then – shouts behind her, the whistles of gendarmes. The creature waved a paw – a hand? – a sickle moon – goodbye, goodbye, and–

Jumping – floating? – a shapeless grey cloud scaling the wall of the alley. A hiss in the night, a wordless promise, *we'll meet again, my lovely*.

Soon, she answered him, firing all the while at the retreating grey shape, knowing it was useless. *Soon, I hope*.

And it was gone. The night was ordinary once again. A woman lay by the alley's brick wall, amidst the rubbish of the adjacent restaurant – mussel shells, discarded, rotting meat, an empty turtle shell crawling with fat black flies, pools of rancid oil staining the ground like blood.

Place Pigalle. A shout and feet running behind her, stopping abruptly. Violent sounds – it took her a moment to realise it was someone being noisily sick.

Other, unhurried footsteps coming. She crouched down by the woman. Elderly, her dress revealing wrinkled skin, coarse-painted face, the sagging breasts rising and falling still, though almost imperceptively, with the body's last intake and outtake of air.

Slashed. "Tell me," she said, whispering to the woman. Watching tendrils of grey crawling over her wrists. The woman's eyes looking into hers, black eyes, as dark as a starless, moonless night.

"Door," the woman said. The single word a whispered puff of air. "Door. K... key."

She said, "Where?"

The woman, dying: "Every... where."

The eyes, closed now. The heart, the engine of the body quit. Remembering Viktor's lectures. Blood circulation stopping, brain functions terminating one by one. A silent machine, beginning to decay, impossible to fix. Nothing more nor less than death. She thought of doors, and keys.

Behind her, footsteps stopped. A hand on her shoulder – gentle. A familiar voice: "We'll find who did this."

Not looking up at him. "You won't."

"Milady..." the title whispered, an exasperated sound. And something else... but what?

"Why do you always have to turn up like this?"

An English expression came to her mind and she began to laugh. "Like a bad penny," she said. "A bad penny–" laughing, the laugh becoming sobs. The Gascon's hands on her shoulders, drawing her up: "Hush, we'll find her killer, we'll find–"

Lady de Winter, calming slowly against his shoulder. Whispering: "You'll find shit."

SIXTEEN
Microcosm

She was sitting at a bar that had no name, drinking coffee laced with cognac, sugar and cream. Opposite her sat the Gascon. Gazing at her, in a way that she found disconcerting. Her first husband had been a noble, renouncing his title but not his ways. This happened after... the Gascon had been his protégé, for a while at least. They had both done wrong – to others, to themselves. To each other. The Gascon was stirring a spoon of sugar in the black depths of his coffee. A quiet bar, and quiet conversations carried in dark corners. Absinthe drinkers, artists, working girls at the end of a shift, and all she could think was: a lock and a key.

To what? To where? And why?

The Gascon: "What do you want us to do with Madame L'Espanaye's body?"

She looked up at him. Not smiling, neither of them. For a moment she felt comfortable with him. They were both being professional, for once. She said, "Is that who she was?" and her voice was raw.

The Gascon nodded. His eyes were deep-set, surrounded by black rings. She wondered what she herself looked like. "We have been attempting to track her down," he said – a slight note of apology in his voice. Going against her orders. "Unfortunately, we came too late."

"Yes," she said. "I know how that feels."

In the silence between them the dead woman pirouetted. Three years before, across the Channel, there had been a murderer who favoured the knife. But he had been a lizard boy, or so it was rumoured, just as they said the British had a human king who had returned from exile. Perhaps this hidden king of theirs had killed the lizard boy who had preyed on Whitechapel. Fairytale stories, she thought. And then she thought of the shape that was not a shape, the elongated skull grinning at her, the knife flashing, her bullets catching the creature again, again, and making no impact.

As if it existed in more than one place at once.

An odd thought. She pushed it away and drank her coffee – alcoholic, sweet. Warmth returning to her body – she didn't know that it had gone. And now she was shivering.

The Gascon said, "Milady–" and then fell silent. He reached out a hand and covered her fingers with his own. To her surprise, she let him. "Did you see the attacker?" she said.

He shook his head. Not a no, not a yes. A frown, a flicker of unease: "It was too dark. I cannot be sure what I saw."

She nodded. Wrapped her fingers around the glass. Sailors in one corner of the bar. A short-legged boyish man who looked vaguely familiar, staring into a glass of absinthe in a separate corner. The Gascon returned his hand to his side of the table, took a sip of coffee, lit a cigarette. "The body," he said.

Grimm will take care of it, she thought. "Leave it by the entrance to the sewers," she said. "And let no one touch it."

"I saw shapes," he said abruptly. The cigarette sent out blue-grey smoke to hover between them – the victim replaced by her killer. "Swirls of grey moving on her arms…"

"You saw her killer," she said – not asking, a simple statement. He stared into her eyes. "I don't know what I saw," he said.

And there it was – his failure. A miracle world, she thought: where a lizard queen sat on the British throne, a shadowy assassin killed with books, where a corpse could be impregnated with an unknown device, where grey shapes flittered like the shadows of another reality... a fantasy? A world of science, rather: a world in which machines spoke and made plans, where stars were real, enormous things, full of potential, and promise, and threat – for who knew who, or what, lived beyond their own world, what other beings inhabited that vast realm beyond the Earth? Not angels, not gods, no burning sword or Garden of Eden. Science was the art of confronting the world as it really was. That it was strange there was no doubt. Humans continued to scheme and war and make love, to make mistakes and become confused and angry and murderous and loving, a vastly tiny microcosm, like Viktor's cultures in his test tubes in the lab. To refuse to see what was beyond did not negate its truthfulness.

She said, "I know what I saw."

"Then you are lucky," the Gascon said, and smiled, and for once there was nothing sarcastic in the expression, which was a little wistful, perhaps. "You always know what you see, Milady."

"I see what is there," she said, simply, and let it rest. She pulled out her gun and began loading it with bullets. The Gascon smiled again, and now it was back to business as usual, softness melting between them like a mirage. "And a bullet is always a cure for mystery," he said.

She smiled back, cold again, and said, "That's right."

Though it wasn't. There had been something familiar about the creature in the alleyway, some markers she was missing... but the bullets hadn't killed it. Why?

She didn't know. She said, "Thanks for the drink," and got up to leave.

The Gascon, still sardonic: "Where are you in such a hurry to?"

Lady de Winter: "I have to find the younger L'Espanaye. Or have you forgotten her?"

His smile, mocking, growing larger. "I have not."

"Oh."

"Would you like to speak to her?"

"I thought I told you to leave this investigation alone."

He shrugged. "So you did. It must have slipped my mind."

"Where did you find her?"

"Working the adjacent alley," he said. "We were on our way for the mother when–"

"How is she?"

"Complaining. Apart from that she's keeping quiet."

"Complaining about what?"

"The competition."

She let it pass. "Where are you keeping her?"

"The station by the cemetery."

"Then let's go."

He mock-saluted her, rose from his seat. He left a handful of coins on the table top, stubbed out his cigarette, and offered her his hand – which she ignored.

SEVENTEEN
Broken

Along Boulevard de Clichy, the nightlife bright still in these early hours, bright lights and glimpses of naked flesh, like sordid promises. Drunks outside, drunks inside. Music, competing. Past the Moulin Rouge and the turning windmill, past the mouth of the cemetery – gaping, dark – into the station house, cheap stale coffee, cigarette smoke, urine from the cells, vomit, someone crying quietly, a couple of manacled men in flamboyant dress chatting across a desk.

The young woman behind the table in the interview room looked worn out. Her youth had been scrubbed from her, leaving oddly old eyes in that still-unlined face. She glared up when they entered, said nothing. A cigarette was smouldering in an ashtray on the table that looked as if it had never been cleaned.

"Mademoiselle L'Espanaye?"

"Who the hell are you?" Turning to the Gascon, a plaintive tone – "Why did you bring her here?"

He gave her his customary shrug, open palms facing up, and sat down in a chair.

"She don't look like no whore. She looks like–" Mademoiselle L'Espanaye examined her opponent critically, concluded – "like a machine is what she looks like."

Snorting. "Losing all our business to the bloody machines."

The Gascon, in a whispered aside – "I'm afraid she's rather single-minded about her topics of conversation."

Milady, not bothering to whisper: "That's going to change."

Mademoiselle L'Espanaye scratched her head. A strand of red hair fell down on her face and she blew it away irritably. "Machines, machines, machines. Make them look a little like women and the punters suddenly think they're better?"

"Mademoiselle L'Espanaye," Lady de Winter said. The woman gave her a dismissive look, said, "What do you want?"

Milady, standing up, kicked back the chair – the gun, newly loaded, exposed in its holster. Observing the young woman taking it in. "I'm going to ask you some questions. You are going to answer them." She gave her a slow, measured smile and watched the woman swallow. "Clear?"

Mademoiselle L'Espanaye, turned to the Gascon, a plea in her eyes. The Gascon looking elsewhere.

"Clear?"

Mademoiselle L'Espanaye, a little girl voice. "What do you want to know?"

"I want to know why there was a dead body in your apartment."

Watching her. Did she know? From the woman opposite, no visible reaction. "What are you talking about?"

Too cocky – as if she knew something they didn't, and was enjoying it.

Well, that was about to change.

"His name was Yong Li," Milady said. "And someone gutted him open with a knife. Was it you – or was it your mother?"

Ah – reaction. "You leave my mother out of this!"

"Tell me about him," Milady said.

A shrug. The eyes hostile, still taking her measure. She sat down slowly, faced Mademoiselle L'Espanaye. "I'm waiting."

"Don't know what you want me to tell you." Sullen. "Sometimes we take on lodgers. To help pay the rent, see. Even a shithole like Rue Morgue costs. Don't know nothing else."

She'd had enough. "We have your mother next door," she said. "Would you like to see her?"

She had gone back to the alley. A guard on the street, no one inside. In the shadows, Grimm, slowly working, summoned by the mechanism inside her bracelet. She stroked his head and said, "Leave me the face. And one of the arms."

An old wedding ring on one finger.

Transported what remained of the head back to the station, the gendarmes cursing her, but quietly. "And don't touch it!" she'd said. "Whatever you do, don't make contact with the body."

"What have you done to my mother? You let her be!"

The Gascon murmured something inaudible. Milady, reaching over, a graceful hand to assist the younger woman. "Come with me."

Mademoiselle L'Espanaye, brushing away her hand. Following her nevertheless, a tough child-woman – let's see how tough you are, she thought, but said nothing as she led her out of the door and to the next room – opening the door for her, waiting for her to step inside–

Eyes to adjust to the dim light, time to put together the pieces on the table, the ruined face, one eye staring into nothing, a loose arm with an old ring on a finger that would never move again, time to comprehend their meaning, time to–

She caught the girl as she fell. Gave her a moment, stood her up. Forcing her to look. A small voice, choked, broken, polluted water running over pebbles – "Mother..."

A shake of the head. Inaudibly – "No. No!"

Milady, holding her, a silent command – *look*.

The girl looked. A head, an arm – was sick all over the floor. Milady held her all the while.

"And now we talk."

EIGHTEEN
The Clockwork Room

And now she hated her. Hated her, yes, but feared her more. The woman behind the table was afraid, terribly afraid – of her? Only a part. And the rest?

"Tell me about the man in your apartment."

She talked.

The safe house – Tom Thumb – the arrangement – "We slept in the same room, my mother and I, and the guest –" she referred to them as guests – "in my room, unless, you know."

A pause, waiting. The girl smoking a cigarette as if it were a life line of oxygen and she was drowning. "Unless I liked him."

Always men. Not many – perhaps ten, twelve in the past three years. All via Tom, "That horny little midget, I wouldn't give him the time of day –" some staying a day or two, some weeks. "All Asian?"

No. One African, a couple of Europeans from the East, one Vespuccian man who said he was a Sioux, whatever that was. Never any visitors. Stayed inside, until other arrangements had been made, and then they left.

"And Yong Li?"

He was a nice guy. On that she seemed in agreement with Tom Thumb. He liked to drink but was a polite drunk. He had a good singing voice. He never made advances, even though–

"I wouldn't have minded, you know. Even with that stomach of his…"

"Tell me about his stomach."

If she thought it was odd she gave no sign. "He looked pregnant," she said. It was odd. She saw him naked, a couple of times – "Coming out of the shower. He had a scar running down it. His belly protruded so… he used to touch it, stroke it as if there was something living inside. He walked funny. Carrying around that weight – we used to make jokes about it. Mother–"

A wait as she cried. Lit another cigarette from the one glowing in the ashtray. The smell of it mingling with puke, the girl's body odour. The Gascon silent beside her, as if he had fallen asleep. But she knew he was listening.

"Did you kill him?"

"No!" Looking at her, the hatred returning. Then, eyes softening – "Is he really dead?"

"When did you leave the apartment?"

They left as usual, with night falling. Heading off to Pigalle, to work – "Girl's got to work, right?" staring at her, defying her, but no longer having the heart for it. "We left together, Mother and me. Last I saw of him he was asleep on the couch. That's all I know, honest."

Only she was lying.

"Where was he meant to go once he left you?"

"I don't know."

"Did he go out? Did he meet anyone?"

"I told you, none of them ever–"

Faltering. Milady's eyes never leaving the girl's face. Daring her back – dare to lie to me again.

"You went out with him?"

Only once! It wasn't meant to happen, the rules were very clear. She woke up – it was about a week before – and saw him pacing the floor, looking nervous and excited. The window was open. There was something in his hand, a note perhaps, but when she looked again it had disappeared. He said, "There is a place I want to visit."

"So he spoke French?"

Yes, very well, though with an accent.

"Where did he want to go?"

A blush, startling on her face. An angry expression. "The Clockwork Room."

Recollection – a building on the other side from the Moulin Rouge, down a side street, no sign outside, windows blackened – known by reputation.

"Tell me about the Clockwork Room."

Mademoiselle L'Espanaye did.

Picture a place of gleaming chrome and burnished leather. A place of polished brass, muted carpets, the smell of pipe tobacco and expensive cologne, the tinkling of a piano player. Picture men in smart evening wear, congregating in their masks. Imagine champagne flutes, the bubbles twinkling in the glass, the hum of machinery, cries – of pleasure, or pain, it's hard to say – echoing, sometimes, from the upstairs rooms. Hosts and hostesses move throughout the room mechanically, touching a hand here, a shoulder there, refilling glasses – sexless creatures, as beautiful and perfect as a blueprint made flesh.

There are not only men amongst the clientele. Women, too, of high society and money to spare, seeking excitement, wanting the new, come here, their faces as masked as those of the men. And there, in a corner, dressed in full regalia – a rare lizardine diplomat, exchanging hushed conversation with a government minister, the lizard's tongue hissing out, tasting the air, savouring – one likes to think – the atmosphere of this place.

The Clockwork Room.

A long curved bar, and behind it a man-shaped automaton effortlessly mixing drinks. On the walls, anatomical drawings – pipes and organs, wheels and breasts, tubes and male appendages. There in the corner, a habitué of this place – a short-legged artist drinking absinthe and drawing, in love with these marching gliding perfections, these machines built for love.

There are many designs, and the artist wants to capture them

all. There are many designs, for women and men, even for
lizards – and who wants to enquire too closely as to the sexual
reproduction habits of those majestic, alien beings? But someone
must have. Or perhaps it is true what they say, and machines
now design themselves... Every now and then one masked
member of a party might break from it, ascend upstairs, up the
wide curving staircase, and disappear into one of the private
rooms, where love is enacted, perfected, a clean and sterile thing,
a union, however temporary, between human and machine.

To this place, then, came the curious man from Asia, this
Yong Li, and his escort both reluctant and excited. For to enter
the Clockwork Room one must have money and influence
both: and yet this little unknown man with his distended
swollen belly is welcomed without question by the two liveried
guards and allowed entry along with the girl. Inside, and to the
bar – pressing a gleaming brass button on the menu, and the
girl watches, fascinated, as the bartending machine mixes cock-
tails, pipes running in and out of its body. Like a great spider it
seems to her at that moment, and she turns away from it and
watches the hosts and hostesses, their naked metal flesh and
skin like wax and eyes of glass, and she feels repulsed by them,
and resents them for stealing away an otherwise honest trade –
and yet excited too, and the man beside her touches her lightly
on the arm, brushing her suddenly raised fine hairs and says,
"Perhaps you could go upstairs, for just a while. I have conversation to make."

"Is that what he said?" Lady de Winter asked. "He had conversation to make?"

"That's what he said."

"It's an odd choice of words."

Mademoiselle L'Espanaye shrugged. She looked around the
interrogation room, perhaps comparing it, in her mind's eye,
with that other place. Finding the room lacking. Perhaps.

"So then what happened?"

Not so quickly. She had looked around the room, recognising
– or thinking she did – many prominent people. She drank a

glass of champagne. Yong Li lit a cigar, for once, rather than his cheap loose tobacco from the pouch. He, too, scanned the room.

"As if searching for someone?"

Yes, that was the impression that she'd had. But she saw no one approaching him, no one signalling to him, no one even noticing this man and this woman standing at the bar. Not an entirely uncommon sight, couples coming to the Clockwork Room, add a little spice to a jaded palate–

"Let's get back to Yong Li."

Mademoiselle L'Espanaye, staring at Milady. Expressions fleeting on her face, hard to read – the eyes, so hard one moment, softening with tears the next. "You'll find him, won't you?" she said.

Lady de Winter, nodding. Their eyes locked together, something passing between. A promise. "The one who killed my mother?"

"I will."

NINETEEN
Projections

"Tell me about the room. Did you notice anyone out of the ordinary?"

Mademoiselle L'Espanaye, laughing suddenly. "At the Clockwork Room?"

Lady de Winter, conceding. "Anyone who caught your attention, then? In particular? Who may be relevant?"

No. Or rather... of course, she had been watching the royal lizard, it was hard not to, everyone did, even the sophisticates pretending not to care. A rare appearance in the Republic–

Lady de Winter: "Do you think he was there for Yong Li?"

Mademoiselle L'Espanaye, surprised. "He never indicated... it would have been too public – a meeting like that–"

"And yet discreet," the Gascon murmured, besides Milady. Both women turning to look at him, a little surprised to find him still there, perhaps. He gave a smile through hooded eyes and said, "Not much comes out of the Clockwork Room. A very *quiet* place."

Milady de Winter, beside him, tensing. Was that a veiled message to *her*? The Council...

"After all, such a place needs powerful patrons to survive," the Gascon said, turning his eyes on her. "To stay in business..."

And now she thought – machines. Listening, perhaps, these unobtrusive subservient automatons, perhaps ignored – at peril?

She filed it away, for now. And yet...

Mademoiselle L'Espanaye, biting her lower lip. "There was a fat man. With the lizard."

Milady and the Gascon exchanged glances. "What did he do?"

"Nothing. But..."

The Gascon sighed.

Milady: "What did you do then?"

And now the girl blushed. Her bluster gone, she said, "I went upstairs. There was a room... Yong Li had settled the bill in advance."

Pipes and moving parts, water and soft brushes, warmth and cold, moving about her, settling her down, touching her–

"And there was something else," she said. "I noticed it, later. When I was... when I was done. Coming out of the room, at the end of the corridor, a room unlike the others, the door black and half-open, for just a moment. I saw shadows flickering on a wall, light and shades, moving shapes. I couldn't make them out, and then the door closed. It was only for a moment."

Shadows flickering, light and shades – the girl: "Like a camera obscura."

A projection. Milady de Winter, adding it to her list. "And Yong Li?"

"I waited at the bar. A man spoke to me. He said some of them still preferred human to machine. I said, after the last hour, I wasn't so sure I did – we laughed, he bought me a drink. Yong Li came down half an hour later. He was holding his stomach again, in pain. We left."

Lady de Winter, reaching across the interrogation table. Her hand on the girl's, black on pale white – "I'll find him. I promise you I'll–"

The girl, softly: "I know."

A change between them.

"So what do you want to do?" the Gascon said.

Leads, possibilities, branching off into unknown paths – but which to follow? She said, "She mentioned an artist."

"Henri," the Gascon said thoughtfully. "Yes."

"You know him?"

"Who doesn't? If a house has ill repute Henri will be there, drawing. For a while you could find him nearly every night at the Moulin Rouge but I did hear he was rarely to be found there now. Henri..." Looking up at her, suddenly troubled. "He was at the bar earlier. Where we found the body."

A short man – an adult body with stunted child's legs. She'd noticed him, yes – "We should talk to him."

If the Gascon noticed the *we* he gave no sign. But between them, too, something had changed – a mutual acceptance, as momentary as it may be – two professionals agreeing to work together, to put aside, if only for a while, their differences. Nothing to be stated in words, but there nevertheless–

"He isn't hard to find."

"And the Clockwork Room–" She yawned, and suddenly couldn't stop. Outside the window, the first rays of sunlight could be seen. All the coffee in the world, she suddenly thought, won't be enough. The Gascon said, "You can't do everything."

"I have to," she said, knowing there was a curiously plaintive tone in her voice. "There is no one else."

"Get some rest," he said. "You can sleep here, if you like. I'll clear a room. There is nothing to be done now that the night is ending. Even murderers have to sleep."

"I'm not so sure..." she said, puzzled, and yawned again. And, giving in – "I'll take the coach."

Morning was rising around her as the silent coachman drove her home. The morning's sounds, the morning's smells – fresh bread and greengrocers opening their shutters, the cockerels crowing, the traffic picking up – coaches and baruch-landaus, newfangled bicycles, above the last of the night's airships going back to depot, having delivered the night mail.

Back at her apartments, no servants, no living thing – in the drawing room she paused. Grimm, curled up in the unlit fireplace, munching slowly on a lump of coal. She smiled and stroked him, briefly, and tiredness overwhelmed her. To her bath, drawing it herself, adding salts and scents and lying in the water, almost falling asleep... Washing away, gradually, the night's sights and smells and sounds, the night's death, its cargo of misery. Rising, naked, from the bath, not bothering with a towel, she went through the door into her room and fell to bed, and closed her eyes amidst the silken sheets. No dreams, she thought. Please, no dreams. Holding on to a pillow she fell asleep.

INTERLUDE:
Jungle Fever Boy

Kai ran through the thick forest, heading deeper and deeper into the trees. Exhausted, fear kept him going – fear, and the voices that shouldn't have been there.

The voices guided him. Here and there he could see signs of people – a hidden bird-trap up in the canopy, a long-necked bamboo basket with bait inside – the bird would crawl into it and be caged. There, a hint of cultivation through the trees – avoid.

Would they be chasing him? He knew they would. They were. He had to disappear, to get away as completely as possible and never return. His life, the voices murmured helpfully, was over. His life as he knew it.

Which meant what, exactly?

Think of yourself as a wuxia hero, the voices suggested, though perhaps that was not so accurate to say. They didn't speak so much as hint, conjuring images, scents, markers to their meanings which Kai's mind translated into speech. A young wushu warrior. The evil faction had just killed your master. You are escaping, vowing revenge. Into the forest, where all things are possible, where young boys since time immemorial went to become men.

Or, a part of his mind whispered, you're going crazy.

Jungle fever.

He saw mosquitoes hover but somehow they never bit him. He stopped by a brook and drank and lay, exhausted, against the thick, mottled trunk of a tree. In his mind he kept seeing the silent assassins with their loud guns, the black-clad monks fighting them – and losing.

So much for the powers of wushu.

Machines, the voices murmured. In his mind – guns. The voices: yes… machines have power.

Then I will use that power, Kai said, and found that he couldn't rise, could not bring himself to run again. He lay by the brook and listened to the frogs. I will become a gun, if that's what I must do.

For now, the voices said, you need to rest.

When he closed his eyes the darkness wasn't absolute. He lay there, holding the grotesque statue still in his arms, this green jade lizard with its emerald eyes: it felt warm in his hands, against his body. Behind his eyes the darkness swirled in lazy eddies, lines and circles flashing and disappearing, forming into a vague grey vista of a world. He fell asleep holding the statue, and his dreams were filled with menacing hulking shapes and he cried out, and then the voices were there, soothing him, and he was walking through a grey landscape, as if through a thick mist beyond which everything was ill-defined. Somehow, it was peaceful.

It was only when he woke up that he cried, and then he did it soundlessly, still afraid, though the voices murmured incomprehensible things about perimeter scans and body heat signatures and checksum routines returning satisfactory values.

When the fever did take hold of him he thought he was going to die – not in glory, like a wuxia hero, but in pain and fear and horror, like a bit character, like the peasants who always got killed by marauding attackers or simply for being poor and unimportant. He felt hot and then cold and he shivered, holding on to the jade statue for warmth but not really feeling it, the cold coming from inside him. He sweated and he moaned and he voided his bowels and threw up, too sick to get up so that the contents of the last night's dinner lay inches from his face, driving him to be sick again even when there was nothing left.

The voices recommended drinking plenty of water.

At some point he slept, fitfully, waking with every unfamiliar sound, afraid they were coming to kill him, but there was never anyone there.

He dreamed about his father, the steam presses at their shop, the smell of freshly laundered clothes. He dreamed of vegetables in oyster sauce and was nearly sick again, in the dream, though he usually loved the dish. The idea of food was nauseating. The voices, for some reason, agreed with him.

The voices accompanied him into the dreams. Like old uncles, unable to shut up, narrating stories from so long ago no one knew or cared any more. In sleep he walked through a grey haze, a land of crazy jagged shadows, straining his eyes to see beyond the mists that seemed to always hover, like a screen, before his face.

The voices talked about prime numbers. They seemed excited about numbers, and he had the feeling that, just as he was walking through this alien landscape, the voices were walking through his own mind and sampling the little world inside, like a group of travellers on a self-important sightseeing mission.

He slept and woke and crawled to the stream and tried to drink the water. He felt parts of his body acutely then, strange pains in his arms, in his legs, cold and heat travelling across his torso, like ants – but they were not ants.

He did see ants. He lay and watched them walk in a long single file, an army of ants, but when they came near him they neatly avoided him, forming a crescent moon around him and disappearing into the undergrowth beyond. His entire world shrank to the stream, the tree he lay against, the seemingly endless army of patient marching ants. Beyond that world were only nightmares – his father's corpse, the silent assassins, the endless grey mists behind which were voices.

We can help you, the voices said, talking about diagnostics routines and recalibrating bone structure, cell augmentation and establishing a two-way interface.

Help me do what? he said, or thought he did, forgetting he mustn't acknowledge the voices or he would have to acknowledge his own madness.

Whatever you want. Power, riches, love, fame, revenge.

Make me, he said, and closed his eyes, feeling the currents running up and down his body, the fever growing stronger inside him, consuming him until his mind was a grey and endless fog – make me into a gun.

PART II
Chinatown

TWENTY
Shaolin & Wudang

One moment she was asleep, and in the next her eyes opened, staring at the darkening room. Listening. The house around her, familiar sounds, but trying to discern – what?

There. The creaking of a beam where one shouldn't have been audible. Listening. There it came again, and now she had no doubt – someone was creeping along her own version of a nightingale floor.

She reached for her gun. It was never far.

And now she waited.

Footsteps, so cautious as to be inaudible – but for the sounds of the house, as known to her as the streets of her childhood, every sound a warning, and lack of sound an even greater mark of danger – sleeping in the tenements, abandoned houses, in places where the rats formed an advance guard, where every footstep out of place spelled threat and risk. Early on she learned to always have at least one avenue of escape – and never assume a place was safe.

The world wasn't safe. She waited, her finger on the trigger of the gun.

When they came through the door they were very quick and very quiet and she fired twice.

They moved so fast!

It was impossible to escape a gunshot – wasn't it?

And now they weren't there at all.

Two bullet holes in the wall. Two black-clad shapes–

She tensed, the gun steady, trained on the dark doorway. A voice from the darkness, in English – "We only want to talk."

The accent strange, a voice from somewhere distant in the Lizardine Empire's domain. She said, "You have a strange way of going about it," and rose, still slow, waiting for the opportunity to fire.

"We… apologise."

"Show yourselves."

To her surprise, they did. Two robed, hooded figures, the cloth black, the faces under the cowls impassive.

Young. A girl and a boy, their arms raised before them, empty – and now they did a curious thing: they put their hands together before them, palms touching, and bowed. "Milady de Winter," the girl said, "we wish only to talk."

"Then why break in?"

They hesitated, exchanged glances. "We tried to knock," the girl admitted, a small smile playing briefly on her face. "There was no answer. You have no servants?"

"We are all but servants of the state," Milady said, and was gratified to see the two looking confused. She gestured with the gun. Neither of them, she noticed, had in any way acknowledged her nakedness. Though come to think of it, the boy did look a little nervous… "Turn around," she said. "Go to the lounge. I'll join you in a few minutes."

Again, the bowing, the joined palms. "We shall wait," the girl said. The boy said nothing. She grinned at him, and he blushed.

Good.

They did as she told them. She closed the door and went to her bathroom and ran the water. The shower revived her. She dressed, applied a touch of make-up. It was early evening, she saw. Outside the windows the light was waning, night returning to the world.

When she entered the lounge they were standing there, faces turned toward her. The room was spacious, large windows letting in the last of the day's light. Sofas, chairs, a few things collected in her travels, statues from Dahomey, a warrior woman with a spear standing in one corner, a poster for Barnum's Circus on the wall, next to the late Lord de Winter's portrait. She lit a gas lamp, sat down, crossed her legs. "Who are you?"

Hesitation. And now the girl said, "I am Mistress Fong Yi of the Yunnan Shaolin School."

Milady: "What?"

The girl, confused, looking again to her companion. "I am Ip Kai of Wudang."

Milady: "What?"

A sigh. Milady said, "Just sit down."

They did, settling into the sofa opposite. "We represent an association of societies. I did not expect that you would have known of them. Our masters are somewhat... private."

"We're from Qin," the girl said.

"Chung Kuo," the boy said.

"The Middle Kingdom," the girl said.

"China," Milady said, in English.

"Right," the girl said.

They smiled at each other.

"And we're here because of something that was stolen from us many years ago," the boy said.

"An object of some value to us," the girl said.

"And which we have been tasked with guarding."

The girl, looking apologetic: "It's a job."

Milady: "Tell me about it..."

"Our masters have recently learned that the object was..." She searched for the word. The boy said, "Active."

"Active. Yes. There is great danger–"

"There is *always* great danger," the boy said. The girl shrugged and snapped something in what Milady took to be Chinese.

"And you believe this – *object* – has now been smuggled into Paris?"

Yi shook her head. "No. But *something* has."

"A part of it, perhaps," Ip Kai said. "Though our masters were not clear on whether that was even possible. However, they sent us to investigate."

"But you're – you're kids!"

"I could kill you with one finger," the boy said – not boasting, a statement said quietly. Milady said, "I'd like to see you try."

The girl, Mistress Yi, spoke to him again in Chinese. "What did you say?" Milady asked.

"I told him to stop boasting."

Again, they smiled at each other. The boy looked irritated. Yi said, "We are trained in certain clandestine forms of the martial arts. These are coupled, or have been, with the power of this object. It gives us a certain… edge."

Like dodging bullets? She was going to say it was impossible, then thought of the killer in the alley, the way he had taken bullet wounds as if they were mosquito bites. "I'm listening," she said.

The girl shrugged. "We have not been able to find it. Yet. And now there are others searching."

"We wanted," Ip Kai said, "to establish where you belonged in this hunt."

"We were surprised by your involvement."

"Well, perhaps not *surprised*. We thought someone like you would become involved–"

"You are not police."

"Yet you have authority."

"The object must be destroyed, Milady de Winter."

For the time being, she would give them no answers. "Can you tell me what it is?"

They exchanged glances. "We don't know," Yi said.

"We believe it was implanted into the courier's stomach by his master," Ip Kai said.

"We must all have masters," the girl said with a sigh.

"It has to be destroyed," Ip Kai said. In one fluid motion, both he and the girl stood up.

"Perhaps," the girl said, "you could pass that along to your Council."

And then – she wasn't sure how – they were gone.

All this – for a message? There were others searching, the girl had said... but how many? One thing was sure, she thought sourly, rising. Pulling the cord that would ring, down below, for her silent coachman to arise. While she slept, others had combed the city.

And had been unsuccessful, she thought.

And though they were looking still, yet she had one advantage, she thought, and she smiled slowly as she left her house.

She was Lady de Winter.

TWENTY-ONE
Moulin Rouge

The coach took her back to Pigalle. It was early still. On the Boulevard de Clichy people were strolling, and did so casually. It was too early for the night trade. She went into the same bar she had been to the night before and ordered coffee, a plate of food. She scanned the room but did not see the short-legged artist.

He had been at the Clockwork Room when Yong Li went there… and he had been right here when Madame L'Espanaye was brutally murdered on the other side of the wall. She did not believe in coincidences. Her food came and she ate, an omelette with mushrooms and cheese, fresh bread, a salad, rounding it off with a croissant and jam and another coffee. The bar was half-empty. She signalled to the man behind the counter.

"Henri?" he said. "He's not been in tonight. Probably still asleep."

"Comes in regularly?"

"Here? Not often. To tell you the truth, he doesn't often have money. And I don't think much of his paintings. Sometimes he gets people to buy them, for drinks. Not me, lady. I've got taste."

"Where can I find him?"

The man shrugged.

She paid and left. She went down the street – bars, cafés,

nudie shows, the mechanicals, hostesses, the freak show, the torture room, brasseries, the Moulin Rouge. The artist was in none
of the places she tried. No one knew where he stayed. No one
seemed to care. She saw some of his early artwork hanging, here
and there. Vivid, energetic pictures of can-can girls, bill posters
of the kind Barnum would have liked, an alive sort of art that
changed, suddenly, at the last address.

She went into the Moulin Rouge.

That ridiculous windmill, turning lazily… doormen, stripped
down to the waist – big guys. Wearing masks – green mottled
faces with great big bug-eyes. She said, "What the hell are you
supposed to be?"

The doorman on the left, West African accent overlaying his
French: "Welcome to outer space."

She stepped through the doors.

The music hit her almost physically.

The sound of pistons, the whistle and blow of steam. The
drumming of coal being shuffled. A manic sort of sound,
rhythmic, wild and yet ordered. The screech of train wheels
on the track.

Welcome to outer space–

The room was black. Stars covered the ceiling. Bug-eyed monsters slithered throughout the room. On the stage, a mechanical
girl. Steam billowing around her. A girl made of metal, with a
silver face. She stared – not an automaton. A girl made to look
like one. And now the dancers, more of the green masks, green
flesh, writhing on the stage, green breasts and steam and stars.

Welcome to outer space–

She stared. Even though it was early the room was busy.
There was a tentacled machine behind the bar, arms moving like
a carousel, serving drinks. But again, not a machine, only the
semblance of one. She approached the bar and the machine separated, bare-chested boys behind the façade. She thought of
L'Espanaye's description of the Clockwork Room. The Moulin
Rouge, it seemed, was mocking it.

"What can I get you?"

The man behind the bar had a nice smile. A boy, really, good-looking and knowing it. She said, "I'm looking for Henri de Toulouse-Lautrec."

"Not seen him." Leaning over. "He doesn't come here often any more."

But he used to, she thought. She wondered what had changed, and why the artist was no longer frequenting his old haunts. The boy behind the bar said, "Moon Rocket Punch–" looking into her eyes.

"Excuse me?"

"That's your drink."

"I don't know what that is."

He grinned. For a moment the group of men behind the bar came together again, the tentacled alien swirling, and then a glass was before her, a long tall shape filled with a purple bubbling brew.

She took a sip. It wasn't bad.

"Do you know where I can find him?"

"Have you tried the thirteenth?"

Girls approaching the bar, taking a break. Bare breasts painted silver for the one, green for the other. They lifted up their masks and asked for drinks.

"What's that place in the thirteenth Henri likes?" the bartender said to them. "This lady wants to know."

"Not here for the show?" the green-skinned girl said. "You should."

"Henri," the silver girl said. "He was born with a glass in his hand."

The green girl: "More like a pipe in his mouth."

The silver girl: "I thought he only got into that recently."

The bartender: "Once he started hanging out with these Chinamen."

"China *women*, more like–" the green girl said. They all giggled.

"Try the Speckled Band on Avenue des Gobelins," the green girl said. "He won't do Pigalle before midnight."

"And he doesn't come here any more," the silver girl said.

"The cheat."

"We're not good enough for him any more."

"Have you *seen* his new paintings?"

"Machines, he doesn't like girls any more–"

"Oh, I don't know about that–"

She took another sip from her glass and was surprised to see it was almost finished. The bartender beamed at her, then leaned over and said in a low voice, "I'm free later if you want–"

She smiled, and for a moment was tempted. Then she thought of the dead Madame L'Espanaye and the smile went away and didn't come back.

The bartender shrugged. "If you change your mind…"

The girls downed their drinks and rushed away – there was a bellow of thunder and the stage darkened further, and now narrow beams of light were piercing the darkness, illuminating the outline of a giant globe hovering in mid-air on stage, a miniature world with continents and seas, rotating: a green and silver world – and now, by some clever illusion, it seemed to drift away, shrinking, becoming one more star in the dark heavens–

And now something like a rocket appeared in the darkness, moving against the background of stars–

An unseen voice: "Welcome to outer space."

Cheers, then silence.

And on the stage the lights picked out a lizard. Cries from the crowd. A royal lizard standing there, one of Les Lézards – only this, too, she realised, was an illusion – a human girl, but made, cunningly, to look like one of the reptiles. And now she sang:

"Across space we travelled for aeons untold…"

The lights picked out others like her in the background, dressed in fantastical uniforms – a strange, multi-legged creature hiding in one corner–

"For a world to call our own–"

"A world like *yours*–"

Boos, hisses from the crowd–

"To take for ours–"

A beat – the crowd expectant – the lizard girl turning face-on to the audience–

"But we took a wrong turn, and of all the nations of the Earth, we got the English!"

Cheers. Laughter. And now the lights came on, bright and many-coloured, the rocket shot off into space – a loud explosion – a burst of stars – and the dancers filled the stage, the sound of pistons filling up the air–

"Let's hear it for the fabulous lizard girls!"

And the can-can started, green legs flashing naked in the lights. Lady de Winter finished her drink and stood up.

Outside the night was ordinary and for a moment she was tempted to go back and see the show. She had heard the story being told – some said the lizards were not native-born to Earth, had come from an unimaginable distance, from outer space, had fallen down and slept on Caliban's Island for untold centuries before Vespucci found them–

But these were stories, nothing more. The lizards were not her concern.

The silent coachman was waiting for her. She climbed into the coach and said, "The thirteenth arrondissement."

TWENTY-TWO
Toulouse-Lautrec

There was a multitude of alphabets on the shop fronts, signs she couldn't read, lanterns, the smell of cooking unfamiliar, soy and rice vinegar, frying ginger, frying garlic, chilli – men and women sitting outside eating noodles from large bowls of soup, the strong smell of dried fish everywhere, in the windows dark-red pork and ducks on hooks, on a street corner a juggler playing with fire. Barbershops, tea houses, a bathhouse, dogs, cats, children, scrolls of elaborate calligraphy, bamboo baskets with chickens inside, a woman selling dried roots, bodies pressing against bodies, Milady de Winter striding through the crowd a head taller than most, searching for the Speckled Band.

She found it down a narrow avenue – a dark front, a sickly-sweet smell wafting from the open doorway, a woman made up in the front, bowing as Milady approached, the eyes checking her out – expertly. "Madame, please welcome," the woman said. Her eyes said she knew exactly what Milady was – not missing the gun, the posture. Her eyes said Milady was a problem she wished would just go away. Milady smiled and showed white teeth, the woman nodded and the smile remained fixed. Tried, nevertheless – "We pay already."

"I'm looking for one of your customers."

"We don't want trouble."

How many times had she heard that before? She said, "Then don't make any," and strode past, and into the Speckled Band.

A low-ceilinged dark room, low couches, girls gliding between patrons who lay comatose, long pipes held in lifeless fingers. The girls lit the pipes, dark resin releasing vapours that travelled through the pipe into the patrons' mouths. Opium, that great export of the East – though most of it came from the lizards' colonies in India, stamped with the lizardine government's seal. She scanned the room, saw him–

Henri de Toulouse-Lautrec lay on a divan, a pipe resting beside him, a glass of absinthe on the low table before him. His eyes closed, his little chest rising and falling steadily. She went over to him.

"Wake up," she said.

There was no answer. The woman from the entrance materialised beside her. The other girls – and patrons – did a good job of not seeing her there. "He is deep into the dream," the woman said.

"What does he dream?" Milady said, and the woman shrugged. "This," she said, throwing her hand in an arc, taking in the walls. Milady looked.

The walls were covered in paintings.

They began conventionally – the paintings she had seen before – can-can girls in vibrant colours, caught in motion, lively and alive. Changing, gradually, as the colours muted, and she saw women/machine hybrids, gears and pipes protruding from an abdomen, a belly, eyes on stalks, arms of metal, becoming gradually less and less human even in shape, until the wall had become a chart of bizarre unsettling machines, cogs and wheels and gears and moving pistons, all the while the suggestion of sex, not man, not woman, but there all the same, machines mating with other machines.

She followed it further, past a corner and to the next wall where the colours muted again, even metal rusting, and the wall was grey, the machines disappeared, and the paintings depicted a world as seen beyond a mist, a blackness where alien stars shone in strange configurations, where giant machines floated in space, in a ring around a bloated red sun…. "He sees beyond, now," the woman said.

"Beyond what?"

The woman shrugged. "Beyond this world," she said. "Into another."

She felt uneasy and didn't know why, exactly. "Is it the opium?" she asked. The woman said, "It helps, but no. It is him."

"Can you wake him up?"

"You shall have to wait. Would you like a cup of tea?"

Flawless Parisian French, all of a sudden. Milady grinned. "Sure."

She waited as two of the girls came and lifted the minute artist, carrying him away to an adjacent room.

She followed them there, drank tea, grimaced, watched the little artist come around. It took less time than she had expected.

He sat up – so rapidly it startled her. His eyes opened, and he said, "Let me back!"

She waited. His eyes were still unseeing. The artist's hands closed into fists. "My pencils!"

The girls hurried back to him, already carrying his equipment, no doubt used to this ritual. Henri took a sketch pad and selected a pencil. His hand moved rapidly over the paper. A crazy sense of scale – enormous structures floating in space? She watched. She had few doubts now. The artist's face was contorted. His eyes were staring elsewhere, beyond the room. He still hadn't noticed her. He finished the sketch with one last savage line and collapsed on the seat. "More," he said. Then, his eyes flickered, opened truly for the first time, and he looked around him in confusion. "Where is my pipe?" he said, his voice that of a reedy child.

Milady had brought the artist's opium pipe with her into the room and now held it before her, the artist's eyes drawn to it, to her. "There is no pipe," she said.

"Wha–"

She held the pipe in both hands and as he watched she broke it in half.

"Tell me about your friend," she said.

"Who the hell are you?"

But he looked frightened now. "We saw each other last night, didn't we?" she said. "I want to know what else you saw."

"I see nothing."

She snatched the paper from his lap. "And this?"

He shrugged, but looked uneasy. "Dreams, nightmares. Nothing more."

She smiled, and he flinched. "Tell me about Yong Li."

"I've got nothing to say to you."

She smiled. She went out of the room and returned with a fresh pipe and a ball of opium and she put them the other side of the room from him and then went and sat down again. She watched him watching the pipe. She watched him thinking about it. When he did move it was surprisingly fast but she was ready for it and a bullet travelled faster than a man and the pipe exploded in his face and he howled. She kept the gun in her hand, not quite aiming it at him.

"I'll get you a new one," she promised. "Sit down."

He hesitated, standing there like a caught animal. "Sit!"

He went back and sat down. He looked at her and there was naked hunger in his face.

"Tell me about your friend," she said again, soothingly. The gun was in her lap but she didn't need it. "Tell me everything, and they'll make you a new pipe."

His eyes burned, but he slowly nodded.

"I met him at Thumb's," he said.

TWENTY-THREE
Yong Li

When he began talking it was in a rush, the words tumbling over each other. The first thing he said surprised her. She said, "At the tobacco shop?"

"Yes."

He was a friend of Tom Thumb's. Two little men with big appetites. He knew Tom was dealing with Indochina, because sometimes Tom gave him back gifts – "A little opium here and there. For medicinal purposes. I am not a well man–"

She waited.

"So then, about a month ago, I went into the shop and Tom introduced me to his new friend. Yong Li. He was a nice guy–"

The same words Tom had used. And the girl.

"So... I don't know how to tell it. There was just something about him. An aura. I could sense it but couldn't see it though I knew it was there. I knew I had to paint him. Do you know of the Eastern religions? He was like the Buddha, with his glistening large belly, his smile. His eyes saw further than humans can see. He was a man deeply changed by some experience in his past. And that scar down his belly – I was fascinated by it. I was attracted – not to him, exactly, but to what he – what he had *inside* him. A difference. I didn't know how to describe it. I drew and sketched and painted him, trying to capture that essence. It

419

was a thing of no discernible colour. A grey metallic – but not metallic, either, not exactly – it was as if his essence was hidden behind mist, and try as I might I couldn't penetrate it."

He sighed, his eyes clearing, and called for one of the girls and asked for his drink. The girl looked at Milady, who nodded. The girl went and fetched Henri his drink.

"Tom is supposed to meet me here," he said suddenly.

She turned sharply, looked at him. "Tom?"

"We sometimes get together–" He blinked, said, "I think, maybe, not tonight. I was mistaken."

She filed it away. The artist blinked again, focused on her. "You look like the girl in the poster on Tom's wall," he said suddenly. "The girl from the circus. I could paint you."

"And I could shoot you," she said, "so why don't we table both for the moment and concentrate?"

He shrugged, a small smile appearing for the first time on his face. He was getting some of his energy back, she thought. He was almost bouncy. "It would be a pleasure to paint you."

She smiled too, and said, "It would be a pleasure to shoot you–" watching him lose the smile. She nodded. "Tell me about Yong Li," she said.

He was drawn to the Asian man. But when he returned to the shop Yong Li was no longer there. He had gone – "To a safe place, Tom said. He had an… appointment in Paris, but not yet, and Tom had to keep him safe until then."

"So what did you do?"

"I was disconsolate! I had to find him!"

Softly: "And did you find him?"

Henri did. He had asked Tom, but Tom refused to divulge Yong Li's location. So he watched. He saw Mademoiselle L'Espanaye go into the shop – he knew her vaguely, one of those faces you see around – but his suspicions were aroused. He listened outside and heard the Asian man discussed. He followed her, to her work and then to her home. He came to the Rue Morgue. He watched the windows in the night, watching for a sign of the man who gave him glimpses of another world.

"What do you mean, another world?"

Another world, he said. An alien world, just out of reach, yet so close he could almost touch it. He needed to see it, sense it, feel it... He wanted to draw it, but could not see it clearly. Only glimpses, flashes in the mind. "It was after I met him that I began to take the opium with some intent," he said. "It allowed my mind to relax enough for the glimpses to become more than glimpses. A vast endless space where great shapes floated, moved – but with intent! They were aware, they were watching, and they were coming closer all the while. It was as if Yong Li's wound, his scar, was the closed door to another world, but things slipped through – like a keyhole where you put your eye to it you could see to another room."

He engineered a meeting with the man. He knew he had to go outside sometime, if only for his foul rolling tobacco. He bumped into him by chance, and Yong Li was delighted to see him.

"He did not enjoy being cooped up in that place," Henri said. "He said the women were not clean. That Europeans were filthy and did not wash, and their smell was bad. He was quite rude, really, but I guess you have to make allowances. I think he was just in a bad humour, from being held there all this time. He was very glad to see me."

"So what did you do?"

Henri looked surprised. "We got drunk," he said, as if the answer was obvious.

"Oh."

"And then I painted him."

"I see."

"He wouldn't discuss it with me," Henri said. "But I think he was glad because I could see what he saw. I think it was very hard for him. He would touch his stomach and grimace, as if he were in pain. But it was not a physical pain. It was the pain of seeing that you did not wish to see."

But Henri wished to see. He found that by touching the man's naked stomach the visions in his mind became clearer. He became obsessed with trying to capture more clearly what he was seeing. He sensed a great presence there, and a great danger too, beyond the wall of mist. They met in secret, he and Yong Li, when the two women were away. Once he came up to the apartment, but Yong Li did not like that. So they met in a bar, and talked, and drank – "He didn't like the opium. Alcohol helped him not see, but opium had the opposite effect –" and Henri drew.

"Then he told me his time was near, and he could unburden himself and go home. And then he told me we could not see each other again – it was becoming too dangerous. I was disconsolate!"

"Disconsolate," she said.

"Yes! I did not know what to do. I was mad! But I promised him I will stay away."

"Did you kill him?" she said. The artist opened wide, shocked eyes. "Kill him? How could I kill him?"

She thought of the body ripped open, as if someone had reached inside... "To open the door he was keeping locked," she said.

"Never!" He looked flustered and she knew she had something.

"You thought about it, didn't you?" she said.

"I... that is not... I would never!"

"What did you do?"

"I waited. I stood outside all night, but he never came down. I came here and took much opium, but my link was fading, it was becoming harder to see."

She waited. "The Clockwork Room," she said.

Yes. There came a night when he saw Yong Li go out. He was accompanied by the younger L'Espanaye woman.

"So I followed them," he said, shrugging. "What else could I do?"

"You followed them to the Clockwork Room?"

He used to be a regular there, he explained. He loved the place, the smell of oil, the hum of the machinery. There was something about it, he realised later, that was a little bit close to the other world he could – almost – see. He couldn't quite say what it was... When he saw that was their destination he went ahead, came inside through the back entrance, and was already at the bar when they came in. If Yong Li noticed him he gave no sign. But he knew that he did.

"What was he doing there?"

He described the evening – the girl looking overwhelmed by the place – Yong Li at the bar – the girl going upstairs to the private rooms. He watched Yong Li all the while, waiting for the man to come to him, but he never did.

And now she sat forward, waiting, for this witness, this drug-addled, short-legged artist who could fill in for her the missing time at the Clockwork Room.

"Tell me," she said.

TWENTY-FOUR
Taken

They were waiting for her when she left the Speckled Band. Dark-clad shapes moving in the street outside, ringing her – on-lookers studiously *not* looking.

They were Asian, and that came as no surprise. They stood in their semi-circle and regarded her. She looked at their faces. Only a couple were unscarred. She said, "Black never goes out of fashion."

One of the men, older than the others, stepped forward. "You are to come with us, please," he said.

"Or else?" she said.

For a moment, the man looked confused. "Or else what?" he said.

"You're supposed to say or else," she said, "and then tell me what you'll do if I don't come with you."

"Oh," he said, nodding. "Thank you, yes. Come with us or else we'll kill you and throw your body into the river, please," he said.

"Well, since you put it so nicely," she said. She looked back at the door of the Speckled Band. It was shut.

"I can't say I'm that surprised to see you," she said, speaking to the one who seemed to be their leader. "Whoever you are."

He smiled, only a little. "You have been busy," he said.

"Work," she said. "You know how it is."

He nodded, without a smile now. There was something in him that she responded to, a similarity to herself. A professional, she thought. She said, "Shall we?" and the man said, "Follow me, please."

It was the most polite kidnapping she had ever experienced. Walking in the midst of the black-clad men she had the surreal feeling she was going to a funeral. She hoped it was not her own.

There were people everywhere in the street, most of them Asian, all assiduously looking away when they passed. For all purposes she and her little group were invisible. The smells of cooking engulfed her as before.

She noticed they did not appear concerned about her gun. They led the way through narrow side-streets and she saw a building rising in the distance, a façade decorated with lizardine gargoyles, enormous chimneys rising above it, belching smoke and steam. She knew what it was.

The Gobelin factory.

They came to a door and it opened from inside. They went into the building. The corridor was long and brightly lit and smelled of cleaning material. They followed it for a while and came to an elevator. It opened and she was motioned inside. She went in and was followed by the leader and two of his men. The other remained outside. The leader pressed a button and the elevator ascended slowly.

She knew about the factory. Viktor had worked there for a while, he had told her that once. It was once owned by the Gobelin family. Now she wasn't sure who owned it. They used to make garments there – one of the first places to use the Daguerre looms, machines that automated production... It had been a natural step for the factory to–

The elevator doors opened. They all filed out. Another white, clean corridor. They walked down it and came to a door. The door opened onto an antechamber. There was a sofa and a small table and the leader said, "Would you like some tea?"

"Do you have any coffee?"

"Please," he said, looking pained. "It is not good for you."

Apart from the two items of furniture the room was bare. The walls were very white. It was very clean. There was a set of doors at the back of the room. They were closed. She sat and waited and the leader waited with her, standing, while one of his men went and fetched a pot of tea. Then there were just the two of them there.

She poured some tea into a small china cup and sipped it. "Jasmine?" she said. He nodded with seeming approval. "Very beneficial for both spirit and body," he said.

She said, "Do you have a name?"

"I am Colonel Xing of the Imperial Secret Service," he said.

She said, "It's not secret if you tell me about it."

For a moment she almost thought he would smile. It passed.

"Do you not serve your Council in a similar capacity?" he said.

"A lot of people seem to know a lot about me, all of a sudden..." she said.

"You are an interesting woman," he said, and this time he *did* smile. "It is only natural..."

She tilted her head, looking at him. "There are no secrets between the likes of us," he said.

"Right."

They smiled at each other.

"What are we waiting for?" she said.

He didn't answer that one. She sipped her tea. They waited.

The doors opened at the back of the room almost without her noticing.

It was impossible to miss the woman standing there, though.

She was very old, and half her face was metal.

"Milady de Winter?" she said. "I am Fei Linlin. Please, come inside."

TWENTY-FIVE
The Empress-Dowager's Emissary

"Madame Linlin–"

They were standing in a room overlooking the city. They were high up in the Gobelin factory. Below the streets of Chinatown snaked, covered in lights. Beyond was the Seine and the whole of the city. Just outside the window were two enormous gargoyles, lizard-shaped, split tongues out, reptilian mouths open as if to catch the rain.

"I hope my men were not rude–"

"Colonel Xing was *very* polite."

"That is good."

Madame Linlin lit a cigarette. It was inserted inside an ivory-coloured holder. She took a deep breath and exhaled smoke. She was very old and looked a little like a dragon. Her eyes were large and bright. One eye was set in a human, wrinkled face. The other was in a half-globe of smooth metal. Milady noted that, and wondered. The woman knew she was looking and didn't seem to mind.

She was small, and now she went and sat behind a large desk, her back to the windows, and looked even smaller.

And strangely powerful.

She had the feel about her of a woman used to wielding power. Her eyes examined Milady and there was nothing personal about it: it was the way a merchant might study his wares, deciding how much they were worth and what best use to put them to. "Please, sit down."

Milady remained standing. She looked out of the window at the city, returned her gaze back to the old woman.

"Who are you?" she said.

"I told you my name."

Milady inched her head in reply and the woman smiled. "But you want to know, of course, *what* I am."

"Yes."

"I am the representative of the Empress-Dowager Cixi," the woman said, equally simply. "Of the Empire of Chung Kuo."

"China."

"Yes."

"I thought–" She did not know much about that far-off, mysterious place. "I thought you had an emperor."

"We do."

"Ah."

"Sometimes it is best to – how shall I put it," Madame Linlin said, "to help matters from *behind* the throne, as it were. An emperor, after all, is an important soul, a ruler with many tasks. He must be seen. He must be worshipped. He should not be burdened with–"

"More practical matters?"

"Exactly."

When the woman smiled it was with only one half of her face. The metal side never moved at all.

"What happened to you?"

The woman shrugged, not taking offence. "I was injured in service," she said. "Our scientists are not without knowledge."

"I did not know you had–"

"And we try to keep it that way," Madame Linlin said, a little sharply. "Oh, the lizards tried to invade us, not once but twice. They were repelled. I suspect that, sooner or later, they will try again. The lizards and their humans, those English on their tiny island. Do they really think they can take *us*? No, my dear. We know much that we do not tell, and learned much beyond that. Just as we know how to deal with this great Republic of France, should your metal-minds ever think to make the same mistake."

"You are being very forthright."

"I am not a diplomat," Madame Linlin said, and again she smiled that half-smile. "We work behind the scenes, you and I, do we not?"

Milady let it pass. "What is it you want?" she said.

"Won't you sit down?"

"No, thank you."

"As you wish."

She blew smoke into the air. Its smell was sweet, and a little cloying.

"I want the same thing you want," she said. "I want the thing that was hidden inside a dead man's stomach."

Milady glanced at her. Fei Linlin smiled back at her. The cigarette-holder was clamped between the teeth of her human half-face. "You know who he was?"

"His real name was Captain James Wong Li," she said. "Also known as Iron Kick, also known as Yong Li, Li Fong, and half a dozen other aliases. Born in Hong Kong, which is a small island given to the lizards in concession –" her half of a face expressed disgust, but the expression quickly disappeared – "hence the English first name. A Tong member, a bandit, later captain in the Imperial Guard."

"Everyone said he was such a nice man," Milady said, and Madame Linlin shrugged. When she did, there was the barely audible sound of gears.

"I have no doubt he was. He was also ruthless when he needed to be, and very loyal, until–"

"Yes?"

But Madame Linlin did not seem eager to pursue that line of conversation. "I am being very open with you," she said, "because I want you to understand what is at stake. Our goals are similar, or we wouldn't be talking. The missing object is dangerous. To Chung Kuo *and* to France."

She thought about the killer in the alleyway, the inhuman face – thought about Henri's drawings, remembered Madame L'Espanaye's last words–

"Door," the woman had said. The single word a whispered puff of air. "Door. K… key."

She had said, "Where?"

And the woman, dying, said: "Every… where."

"What is this object?"

No answer, and she said, throwing it to the older woman – "A key."

Madame Linlin looked taken aback. "Yes…" she said.

"Why was Yong Li here?" She thought about it for a moment. "Did you send him? You said he was a captain in your–"

"No."

There was a moment of silence, stretching between them. "No," Madame Linlin said at last. "He… Some time ago he changed his allegiance. He defected – to serve the Man on the Mekong."

"Who?"

"An enemy."

They regarded each other. Milady waited. The strange old woman watched her too, her eyes uncertain. At last she said, "The man who sent him here."

Interesting… And now Tom Thumb's mysterious contact in the East was gaining a little more of a shape. "Why was he sent here?"

But she thought she already knew.

She said, "Les Lézards."

And Madame Linlin, stubbing out the remains of her cigarette, said, "Yes."

TWENTY-SIX
Fat Man and Lizard

There had been a fat man at the Clockwork Room that night. That was what Henri had told her at the Speckled Band. A fat man standing with the lizardine ambassador. Very fat, with a prominent forehead, a prominent nose, and deep-set eyes that seemed to miss nothing – deep-set eyes that had fastened onto Yong Li as if they had been expecting just such a man.

That the fat man was with a royal lizard was significant. Yet he did not seem to Henri to be an assistant, an aide-de-camp or a servant – he had the manner about him of a man not easily fazed, and when he turned to speak to the tall lizard beside him he did it with what Henri could only describe as an indulgent smile.

The fat man had moved slowly and drunk little, and seemed to pass through the room attracting surprisingly little notice – "And my attention was on Yong Li, you understand, not on the fat man."

"I understand."

And now she remembered that Mademoiselle L'Espanaye, too, had noticed a fat man…

"When I saw Yong Li going up the stairs to the private rooms, naturally I followed him," Henri said. "There was a room at the end of the corridor and the door was closing behind him and I went to it and knocked. A voice said, "Who is it?" and I said, "It's me, Henri, let me in."

The door had opened then, and the Asian man stood there, his face stricken. "You must go, now!" he said. Both his hands were on his belly, not patting it but – "Like he was holding it in, trying to stop it from bursting, you know?"

He'd said, "Quick! You must go. You must not be seen."

"But why? What are you doing?"

"For your own sake, man! He's coming!"

The door had slammed shut. Henri was left alone in the corridor – and as he looked from door to staircase he heard footsteps climbing, slowly but with an even step, up the stairs.

"I don't mind telling you I was unsettled," he said. "But, you see, I know the Clockwork Room well."

And so he opened one of the doors lining the corridor and stepped inside, shutting it behind him just as the footsteps had reached the top of the staircase and began coming down the corridor, towards that last room.

"There was a woman in there – oh! I knew her very well. A very famous novelist. I had been to her salons several times. But she did not see me. No – she was inside one of the clockwork engines of that place, and it was working at her – I would have liked to have sketched it."

"That's nice."

"Yes, well… she did not see me. And so I was safe."

He heard the footsteps coming closer. When they came to Henri's door they paused – "I don't mind telling you I was worried" – but finally moved on. Henri had opened the door then, just a crack. He saw the fat man disappear into the last room, the one holding Yong Li. The door had closed shut behind him.

"I should have left then. But I needed to *see*."

And so he left his hiding place, machine and novelist and all, and tiptoed to the last door, the unmarked one. "I peeked through the keyhole," he said. His eyes grew very large then, and his hands shook. His head sank back against the cushions. She was losing him, she knew then. "What did you see?" she

said – demanded. But the little artist's eyes were no longer seeing, and the expression on his face was filled with both fear and
longing. "I saw it," he said. "I *saw* it."

His eyes closed, and his breath came softly, scented with the
sweetness of opium. "What did you see?" She slapped him, but
it made no difference.

"I saw their world," he said, and he smiled, a small, child-like
smile, and then he spoke no more. She tried, but could not rouse
him, and at last she left him there, to dream his grey dreams.

"We believe," Madame Linlin said, "that Captain Li was in Paris
to meet secretly with a representative of the lizards' secret service." She grimaced, a disconcerting sight as one side of her face
remained metal-smooth. "His name is Mycroft Holmes. His influence is far-reaching. He is very dangerous."

Milady almost laughed. She had no doubt Madame Linlin was
just as dangerous. And no doubt she occupied a similar position
to this Mycroft's in her own country's service. She said, "Why
did Yong Li – Captain Li – not meet them across the Channel?"

"In the lizards' own domain?" Madame Linlin shook her head.
"No. Paris was a sensible choice."

It did, Milady had to admit, make sense. Yong Li's master had
something to – to sell? To trade? – with the lizards. He had chosen the one place they could not move openly in. "What does
he look like, this Mycroft Holmes?" she asked, waiting for the
answer to confirm her own thoughts.

"He is a very fat man," Madame Linlin said, with some distaste.

"Ah."

"You know of him?"

"I think," she said, "that he had indeed met with Captain Li."

"Yes. My people have not been as diligent as they should have.
We have not been able to locate him in time."

"Did you kill Yong Li?"

The old woman smiled, then shook her head. "No. It would
have made things simpler if we had. And you and I wouldn't
be talking."

"Do you know who did?"

The smile disappeared. "No. We need to find out, and we need to retrieve the object. It must be destroyed."

"I need to know what it is."

The old woman shrugged. "It is a piece of something which should not exist," she said. "A legend, a folktale."

"I am tasked with finding it," Milady said. "For my own people."

"It must be destroyed."

"That is not my decision."

The woman shrugged. "We can make our own arrangements with the Council," she said. "It is the lizards we are most concerned with."

"Are there others from... from Chung Kuo looking for this object?"

The old woman looked at her sharply. And now she extracted another cigarette and fitted it into her holder. "You have encountered others?"

"I am merely asking."

For the first time real anger came into the old woman's eyes. "There are secret societies," she said. "They are little more than criminals. Bandits." She muttered something under her breath. "Colonel Xing!" she called, and in a second the man was there. She spoke to him in what Milady took for Chinese. The man nodded, his face expressionless. In a moment, Madame Linlin had switched to French. "Please escort Lady de Winter safely out of the building. We have concluded our little conversation."

"Have we?" Milady said. The old woman smiled her half-smile, not mistaking the threat in Milady's voice. "Only for now, I'm sure," she said sweetly.

"Only for now," Milady said, returning the smile.

She turned to Colonel Xing. "Shall we?" she said.

"It would be my pleasure, please," he said.

TWENTY-SEVEN
The Goblin Factory

She was not happy about the old woman's involvement – not happy about the direction the investigation was taking. She had a feeling she was being used, and she didn't like that either. She had the feeling she should shoot someone, but she resisted it, for now. Colonel Xing, at least, had good manners.

They did not take the elevator down this time. Instead he led her through another corridor and through a secure door and suddenly she was standing in a vast, cathedral-like space, and all around her were the goblins.

They were not the creatures of European folklore. They were… she wasn't sure what they were.

In the middle of the great open space of the factory stood a large pool filled with boiling, liquid metal. Figures moved down there, human-shaped and small, and she suddenly realised just how large the building was, how high above the ground they were on this level.

And the pool was very large.

There were machines down there, enormous machines, the sound of their engines filling up the space, blocking all other sound. Steam and smoke rose through enormous metal pipes all the way to the ceiling above her head.

When she looked down she could see a heap of arms.

There was another one, of legs.

Hanging from the walls, on every available space, were the goblins.

They were mute, unmoving. They came in many different shapes. Some looked almost human. Some looked aquatic, some avian, and several looked very much like...

Like royal lizards.

Down below, a human figure flicked a giant switch and sudden lightning flashed in the great hall of the building. Milady shivered. The lightning caught between two giant balls of metal and continued to pass back and forth between them, growing in intensity all the while. She looked away from it.

A hand touched her, gently, on her arm. Wordlessly, Colonel Xing motioned for her to follow him. She did, over to an observation platform jutting from the side of the surface they were on. When they had stood inside it, it began to descend.

She watched the goblins – the automatons – if that was what they were. She wasn't sure. She had never seen so many, and there was something about them that did not recall to mind those few beggars in the catacombs, or even those ancient beings on the Quiet Council. These had a definite... *martial* feel to them.

The makeshift elevator took them down slowly.

Past faces staring out – not the rubber-flesh skin of humanlike automatons, not the crude machine faces, like a caricature of the human, such as belonged to the truly old ones.

No. These were smooth, smooth masks and faceless, making no pretence, no attempt to deceive as to what they were. Here was a silent army of machines, and as they went down she could see more being made, down on that vast factory floor, where human shapes in masks and protective clothing moved along a moving belt, assembling parts...

Did the Council know about this?

Colonel Xing led her through the floor. She felt the heat rising from that pool of toxic metal and, skirting it, saw an area set aside that resembled Viktor's place in the under-morgue –

surgical tables, bright lamps, refrigeration units, scalpels... She turned away from it and a moment later they were outside.

The night's air was cool, wonderfully cool after being inside. She felt as if she had been trapped inside the belly of a giant monster and had at last been spat out. She had been sweating, she realised. The doors, when they closed behind them, had shut out the constant sound of the engines, but she could still feel them under her feet, tiny tremors in the ground.

And now she understood the smoke that was constantly, endlessly belching out of the chimneys. She said, her voice too loud in her ears, "What are they for?"

"You know what they are for."

"Whose?" she said, and he began to smile, then stopped. "Anyone who'd pay," he said, as if the question surprised him – as if it were evident.

"Does *she* own it?"

He looked surprised, again. "No," he said. "The Shaw brothers bought it from the Gobelin line, years ago. They did the conversion. It's their factory now."

She didn't ask who the Shaw brothers were. She was just happy for the silence.

"I hope we meet again," Colonel Xing said, and smiled. He smelled nice, she thought suddenly. "I will see you again, please."

She said, "What will you do now?"

"Wait," he said. "See."

"See if I find what you're all looking for?"

"Unless we find it first," he said.

"Where have you been looking?"

He said, "There is a large community from Asia in this city. Chung Kuo, Siam, Kampuchea... Perhaps some of our own people are involved. Many of the –" he used a word she didn't know, realised it, said, "the secret societies, they operate here too. Wudang, Shaolin, the Beggars' Guild... they too are searching, I think."

"Have you been keeping an eye on the British agent?" she said, and he looked at her, alert now, and said, "Yes, that too."

"Where is he staying?"

He told her. Then, very formally, he shook her hand. Then he grinned and, unexpectedly, kissed her on the cheek. "Goodbye, Milady," he said.

She nodded, and he smiled again, and disappeared back into the building.

She touched her hand to her cheek.

She didn't know what to think.

She walked away, into the night and the streets of Chinatown.

TWENTY-EIGHT
The Unfortunate Demise of Tom Thumb

There was a body floating in the Seine and it was Tom Thumb's.

There was a metal taste in her mouth. She stared at the small corpse. Tom's eyes were open, staring up at the stars. The current carried him gently. Milady said something – she wasn't sure, later, what it was. Tom had been slashed open with a knife. Grey swirls were forming on his skin, moving disconcertingly, at odds with the current.

She ran down to the embankment, pushing people out of her way.

She fished the little man out of the water.

Tom Thumb lay dead on the stones, a pool of red water forming around his body. Milady knelt beside him.

Backtrack.

Connect the dots.

She'd left the Goblin factory and had been thinking as she walked.

Some things did not ring true in Fei Linlin's account.

For instance, who had attacked her in Montmartre?

She remembered the tattoos on their arms.

She remembered back to the under-morgue:

The Hoffman automaton took the sketch from her and studied it.

"Imperial assassins," it said.

What?

"So she is after it too," it said, the voice low, barely above a murmur.

She had thought, at the time, he had meant Victoria. But what if he meant the Empress-Dowager? And yet now, as she thought about it, it seemed unlikely. Another Asian faction, then? It was getting hard to keep count.

"The secret societies," Colonel Xing had said. *"They operate here too. Wudang, Shaolin, the Beggars' Guild... they too are searching, I think."*

Yet she had spoken to those from Shaolin and Wudang, and they seemed to have the same objective as the others. Everyone wanted the missing object – or almost everyone...

What, she thought, if there were other factions, other secret societies at work? For all she knew there were hundreds of factions in that huge, secretive empire of Chung Kuo. And some might have a different agenda – and she wondered again what this object was, what its importance really was – and why it was sent to Paris, and for whom.

The lizards. And it occurred to her the one faction *not* looking for the missing object was the one which had already, so it seemed, seen it. She decided she needed to have a word with the fat man from across the Channel, this mysterious Mycroft – and soon.

And she was still thinking when she found herself along the river and, looking down, discovered her one-time friend floating face-up in the dirty water of the Seine, dead eyes staring at her accusingly.

Tom Thumb looked very, very dead.

And now that she was crouching beside him she felt the press of the crowd lessen, and two small figures appeared by her side–

"Milady de Winter," the girl said.

"Mistress Yi..."

"Milady," the boy said, dipping his head.

"Ip Kai... I wondered when you two would show up."

She felt tired, and angry, and she looked down at Tom Thumb's dead face, remembering him from all those years before, from the circus, the shared times – knowing he was a rascal and a rogue but liking him nevertheless – losing touch, as one does, hearing he had gone off to England, had become involved in revolutionary politics – being surprised to see him here in Paris, but knowing he was still involved, still walking on the wrong side – a short but busy man, a short but busy life, leading to–

She almost screamed.

The grey circles along Tom's body moved more rapidly. It was almost as if a storm was picking up across his skin. And now the corpse blinked.

She stared into Tom Thumb's eyes, and saw broiling grey clouds forming.

She felt rather than saw the two beside her step away. They didn't speak. She said, softly, "Tom, can you hear me?"

There was *something* behind those dead eyes. But she wasn't sure it was Tom – and the sudden realisation was chilling.

The eyes focused, and that was eerie. They looked at her face. And now the mouth opened, and a wet, bloated tongue licked wet lips, the gesture strangely obscene.

Then it spoke.

The word came out with a whisper of foul-smelling air. "Waiting…" it said. The body was crawling with grey spirals, currents washing over the corpse. Milady moved back from the body and her hand twitched on the handle of her gun.

Though what use was a gun against something that was already dead?

"Soon…" the voice whispered, and the lips formed into something resembling a smile. Then the eyes closed, and grey activity ceased, and it was only Tom Thumb lying there, and his throat had been cut with a very sharp knife, and Milady stared and thought, my, how the corpses are piling up.

She knew the killer must be close. She was disturbed by this grey plague that seemed to be slowly creeping up everywhere, something alien and strange and disturbing, but it had not killed Tom Thumb. *Someone* had, and she meant to find him.

TWENTY-NINE
The Grey Ghost Gang

"Yes," Ip Kai said, sounding surprised. He was looking at the sketch of the men's tattoos. "There are opposing factions to us. The Five Poisons Cult, the Sharks Sect, the Blood Sabre, the Ancient Tomb Sect, the Demonic Cult… but this I have not seen." His lips curled in a grimace. "Its meaning is clear, at least," he said, with evident distaste. "They seek that which lies beyond the gate."

Milady grimaced too, at that. It'd been another long night, she had another death on her hand, and was no closer to locating the missing object – nor did she feel much inclined to, any more.

Tom Thumb's death had made it personal.

She didn't know where the object was but she knew a killer was out there, hunting down everyone who had come near it. A killer who knew her, and wanted to send her a strong, clear message when he dumped Tom Thumb in the Seine, ensuring the corpse would float past her at the right time. He could be out there right now, in the shadows of Chinatown, watching her, waiting…

She needed a way to kill something that couldn't be easily killed.

There were several options.

But now she sat with Mistress Yi of Shaolin and her companion, Ip Kai of Wudang, in a small but comfortable tea room decorated with spread-open fans printed with images of the Great Wall and the Forbidden City and so on, and lanterns, and it was empty apart for them, and the old woman who seemed to run the place brought her a coffee, not tea, without being told.

And so things were looking up – though not, admittedly, for Tom Thumb.

And not for Milady's peace of mind, either.

"I have seen this before," Mistress Yi said, examining the sketch, and her face was troubled. "It is the emblem of the Grey Ghost Gang. But they have not been seen for many–"

Her eyes widened.

She was looking past Milady.

Milady knew something was wrong–

She felt the window explode a split second before the glass burst.

She ducked and glass fragments showered her, and she could feel a sudden pain in her cheek, a shard of glass cutting her–

She swore, a burning fury rising inside her, and coupled with it was a wild, unconstrained joy.

She was finally going to shoot someone.

"The Grey Ghost Gang!" Mistress Yi said, and followed it with something in Chinese that sounded like a curse.

When Milady looked up the gun was in her hands and dark shapes were streaming into the room. She fired and watched the first one drop to the floor, a flower of blood spreading on his chest. They were dressed in black, of course they were dressed in black, and she knew with absolute certainty that, if she only looked, she'd find a grey tattoo on the man's arm.

Mistress Yi leaped into the air. Milady had never seen someone move the way she had. She bounced off the wall and spun and kicked, and her foot connected with one of the attackers' heads and knocked him out flat. She landed but it only lasted a fraction of a second and she was airborne again, spinning, her legs catching two more of the attackers–

And Ip Kai had joined her, moving like a ghost, appearing behind two more attackers – there was something in his hands –

like tiny needles – both went in simultaneously, into the men's necks–

And they both fell. Milady fired, and again, and watched another man fall.

How many *were* there?

"Get out!" Mistress Yi shouted, suddenly very close. She threw a metal star, lightning-fast, and another man dropped down. The small tea room was fast filling up with the dead. "The back door! We'll hold them!"

Milady said, "Later," and rose. She had a second gun strapped to her leg and now it was in her hand and both her hands were full and both her guns were loaded and she fired, left, right, left, turning with each shot, moving forward to catch as many of them as she could–

A kick connected with her legs and swept her down to the floor and she roared, the guns forgotten as she found her feet and rushed her assailant, grabbing his head with her arms and she *twisted*–

There was a sickening sound–

She reached for the Peacemaker on the floor, the other gun lost, and held it by the barrel and used it as a club and bashed a man's head in–

Something cut her arm then, deeply–

Ip Kai was flying through the air and his bare hands were weapons–

But there were so many of them, so many more coming in to replace the fallen–

"Get *out*, damn it!"

And then Mistress Yi was there again and somehow the small girl was dragging the much larger woman, *away* from the fighting, towards the back of the room–

"We'll. Hold. Them. *Off!*"

And threw her through the kitchen door.

The desire to fight left her suddenly. She scrambled to her feet (noticing the kitchen was empty, the door to the back open wide) and went through the door, fast.

Behind, a dark alleyway that was *very* empty.

Why would they be chasing her?

She didn't have the key.

A key. A key to what? None of it made any sense. She thought of what the girl, Mademoiselle L'Espanaye, had told her. What she saw in the room at the end of the corridor, at the Clockwork Room...

Shadows flickering on a wall, light and shades, moving shapes. "Like a camera obscura."

A projection. Not a key, but a – what?

And she thought – perhaps it was showing what is behind the door.

She had to find the fat man.

And she had to talk to Viktor again.

And to the Council.

But first, she needed a new gun.

THIRTY
The Toymaker

She was not pursued and she was thankful for that. She sensed her time in Chinatown was coming to an end and was not unpleased. Her arm still stung from the cut it had sustained, but she was fine otherwise. She hoped Yi and Ip Kai would be, too. She needed to go down to the catacombs and there was a way down nearby, a way that would lead her under the river, and luckily – or perhaps not, depending how you felt about it – it was through the Toymaker's shop.

When was she last there? Two, three years before? And that was on Council orders. This was not her part of town and the Toymaker wasn't someone she looked forward to seeing – usually.

Now she needed him.

The Toymaker had been a magician, and he had been a builder of automata; and for a time was very well known. His name had been Jean Eugène Robert-Houdin. He had once been known as "The heir of Vaucanson", he who had been the father of the Republic.

That had all been a while back. Before the incident with the Eve, and the subsequent scandal...

The Toymaker's shop sat on its own in a pool of darkness by the river. Clocks were set on the otherwise impassive façade, clock-faces showing the time around the world, staring at the passers-by as if challenging them to step inside. To do so, they seemed to suggest, would be to challenge time itself.

There was no sign to advertise the Toymaker's craft. A single black door was set into the building and it was closed.

But the Toymaker seldom slept...

The door had no handle. Milady knocked, and somewhere inside an ominous martial music rose like a waking dog.

All suitably orchestrated. She banged on the door and shouted, "Council business, open up!"

The door swung open without a sound. And now that she could see into the inside of the shop she saw nothing but darkness. Yet there was a sense of intelligence inside, of hidden eyes watching, and the faint sounds of movement could be heard – if she concentrated – of gears and wheels, as unseen shapes flitted away in the darkness.

She came inside. The door closed behind her.

"Show yourself," she said.

"Milady de Winter," a voice murmured, close to her ear, "what a pleasant surprise."

It had startled her.

Which had been the intention.

"Houdin," she said, and the voice said, "No!" and then, more quietly, "Not any more."

He had built her Grimm. He had built many things. Once, he had been head of the Council...

Not any more.

"I need something from you," she said, into the darkness.

"That is always what brings them to my shop," the voice said. Farther now. "Always they want something. My only desire had been to build that which resembles the human. Tell me –" the voice said, moving even farther away – but then, one could never trust the source of the voice, as she had no doubt machines could replicate it across the dark space, only one of the magician's many tricks – "if it acts like a man and sounds like a man – how do you know it is not a man?"

"As I recall," she said, "it was not *men* that were your problem."

A short, dry laugh. And now lights sprang into existence across the shop, illuminating–

He stood at the far end, dressed in a black suit and a top hat. A white handkerchief was in the breast suit of his pocket. In one hand he held a cane. His face–

The shop was filled with mechanical toys. Trains began to run suddenly across what seemed like miles of miniature rails, climbing walls and descending mountains of furniture. Airships glided in the air, black mechanical things resembling insects. Toy soldiers marched towards her, guns raised. On the wall, the only clock was half-melted, frozen at the time of–

"I tried to save my child," he said. "That was all."

"She could not be allowed to–" she said, but he was not listening.

When his wife had died giving birth he had enlisted Viktor's help. The two of them had created something–

In the secret records of the Quiet Council it was referred to as The Affair of the Bride with White Hair.

There had been several dozen victims before–

The old magician stepped forward. And now she could see his face, and wished she couldn't.

The man was wearing a mask. It was not like Madame Linlin's face, half-alive, half-metal. His was the mask of humanity, a shifting rubbery façade such as was used for one of his automatons. It could pass for human – in the dim light. If one did not look too closely, and saw the ripples on the false skin, the way the eyes moved across the face, the dance of the shifting mouth...

She said, hiding a shiver, "Is this your boy?"

A smaller figure had appeared beside the magician. Like Houdin, it too was dressed in evening dress and top hat, with the same white handkerchief, the same cane. But the figure was very still, with the frozen countenance of the dead.

"Say hello to the nice lady," the magician said, speaking gently. The little figure moved forward – and now she caught the look in the magician's eye, saw the glee there, and the anger. He knew she was repulsed, and both enjoyed and was angered by it.

"Shake hands," the man said, and the little boy reached out a hand, mechanically, and Milady shook it. The hand felt soft and smooth – would always feel soft and smooth. It would never grow, never change – and now it held her hand and *pressed*, and there was strength beyond a boy's strength in it, the little hand beginning to crush the bones in her hand–

She cried out and the magician hissed a command. The boy released her hand and turned around. His hair was black, cut short at the back. It would never grow, never fade.

"What do you want?" the magician said.

"There is a killer in the city," she said, and the magician laughed. "There are many killers in the city," he said. "You should know. You're one of them."

It had taken all their efforts to halt the man's creation. The bride with white hair did not go quietly...

But it had been *her* work that had finally terminated the creature's "life".

She said, "This killer is different."

"I see," the magician said with a strange, sing-song voice, "a long journey in your future, and a tall dark stranger."

"I didn't come to have my fortune told," she said. "I need a weapon."

"You are going to need more than a weapon," he said, in the same voice. "You are going to need to *become* a weapon."

It was told that, in the darkness and isolation of his shop, he had perfected machines that could read the future in numbers, predict events and patterns of history beyond even the abilities of the famed Mechanical Turk. And yet he told her nothing...

"I still have my sources," the old man said. "I was once of the Council, and that is not something abandoned lightly. I know about your killer. I know more than you do. I–"

"You've seen the corpses," she said. Thinking of the corpses in the under-morgue, the shifting greys...

"Are they not beautiful? So beautiful... I wish to find where they are going, where they had gone. But the door is not here, it is far away."

"Tell me what you know."

He laughed. The silent boy beside him never stirred again. The magician ruffled the boy's hair and said, "It would take a lifetime and you would be none the wiser at the end of it."

She said, "You know who the killer is." Watched him as the left eye drooped downwards and trailed across his face. He reached, unhurriedly, and put it back. "Will you find him," he said, "– or will *he* find *you*, Milady?"

"I need a weapon," she said, and the old man seemed to droop, the fight – if that's what it was – going out of him. "Of course," he said. "I was told you would come. I have it ready."

"Told by whom?"

He shrugged. "The Council."

She felt suddenly trapped in a web of lies. Deceit – she was being led along a path she didn't choose to follow, her every stepped marked in advance by machines more powerful than could be imagined. The old man, as if reading her mind, said, "Sometimes I wish I had no part in it. Our children always supplant us, don't they, Milady? It is the way of the world..."

He spoke to the boy. The boy turned and, without a sound, disappeared into the darkness. "The children..." the old man said.

"He could have grown to be a man, one day," she said. "I'm sorry."

She said it every time and they both knew it made not an ounce of difference.

"Let me give you your gun," the old magician said.

THIRTY-ONE
The Code of Xia

She went into the underworld through the Toymaker's shop. The wide stone stairs were wet with moisture and when she finally reached the dark floor she knew she was under the Seine.

The gun was with her. It was a strange contraption, more similar to a blow-pipe. She had five bullets. The bullets were grey. The grey moved as if it were alive upon the metal. "Whatever you do," the Toymaker said, "never touch them with your bare hands."

Wearing thick gloves, he had loaded the weapon for her. "I don't know if it would kill him," he told her. "But it might just slow him down."

Which was not all that reassuring.

She walked in the darkness under the Seine. Gradually, lights came on, small fires burning – for even here, in the secretive tunnels below the river, there were lives, the refugees from above-ground, those who had nowhere else to go but down into darkness.

She paused there, under the river, imagined she could hear the tug-boats passing overhead, the fish swimming. The British had their whales in the Thames; the Seine, so it was said, had bloated corpses.

She thought about Tom Thumb. She had no doubt he was not

killed for his involvement, or rather, not entirely: he was killed as a message for her.

The killer knew her. And she thought – he does not want the missing object. His goal is different than that of the rest.

There were many searchers, she thought. The Shaolin girl, and the Empress-Dowager's emissary. Herself, of course. But not the killer.

And not, she realised, the lizards. Or, if they were, they were doing it very quietly…

There was the Grey Ghost Gang… She did not understand the world she was entering. Mistress Yi had tried to tell her, a little, on their way from the riverbank. She spoke of Wu Xia, which meant something like Honourable Fight. She spoke of the Code of Xia, of warrior monks without regard for whoever sat on the Imperial Throne in – the Forbidden City? – but only for right-eousness, and for–

There was an ancient object that these societies had been guarding. Yet it was – stolen? Had somehow disappeared? – and this all came back to that. The object gave the adherents of Xia power, of sorts, something the girl called Qinggong – The Ability of Lightness. She had seen them fight with the Grey Ghost Gang–

It was all too much. None of it concerned her. Only the killer did. She walked on under the Seine and the ceiling dripped water as she passed.

The denizens of this subterranean world were all around her. Shadows fleeing from shadows… A girl holding an eyeless doll stared at her as she passed. Milady knew that if only she turned to the girl, the girl would flee – just as she herself would have done, at her age. It could have been her standing there – it *had* been her. A metal beggar shuffled past in a series of click and whirrs. Through a natural opening in the rock face she saw two lizard boys, moving away as she spotted them. She wondered if the killer would come for her here, in this twilight world. She hoped he would.

Instead, it was a beggar who came to her.

She had crossed the river and the tunnel branched ahead. A lone, elderly beggar was sitting cross-legged against a wall. He had long white hair, a black eyepatch over his right eye, and he was dressed in a loose-fitting robe, like a monk's. His eye was closed, but opened at the sound of her footsteps.

An Asian man, but then more than several of the underworld's denizens here had escaped from the above-ground Chinatown. His eye was very bright. His mouth curved into a smile and he said, "Milady de Winter," with only the trace of an accent.

She stopped. The man remained serene. "I had hoped you would come this way," he said. "We have much to talk about."

"Not again," she said, and his smile grew wider. "You think there are many of us searching," he said. "And you are right. You have entered the world of the Jianghu, Milady." The smile faded a little. "It is a dangerous world."

"Which world isn't?" she said, and the man nodded. "Please," he said. "Sit down with me. We will not be disturbed."

She said, "Jianghu?"

"The followers of Xia," he said. "Beings like yourself, Milady."

"I follow no code–"

"No code but the one that matters," he said. "You are *Xiake* – a follower of Xia, whether you know it or not. Though you lack the skills of the initiates – of those of the Wulin – nevertheless you are one of us."

"And you are?" she said.

"Please, sit down, for just a moment. The night is ending, and the day is near, and you are tired. The one you seek will not reveal himself this close to dawn."

And now he had her interest. But – was dawn so near? She suddenly realised how tired she was. Time had slipped her by, and she hadn't noticed.

"Please," he said, gesturing with his hand, and she nodded, and came closer. When she sat down, opposite him, the old man nodded approvingly. "You move in the way of a cat," he said.

"I'll take that as a compliment," she said dryly, and he laughed. "Who are you?" she said again.

"My name is Long," he said. "Master Long. Here, I go by Ebenezer. Ebenezer Long. Are those enough names for you?"

"You have others?"

"I have many names. Names are... fluid. What, after all, is in a name? You yourself have had several, have you not?"

"Master Long..." she said. "You seem very well informed."

"I have been around for a long time," he said.

"And you are from – what?" She tried to recall the names. "Wudang? Shaolin?"

He laughed. "As much as I belong," he said, "you could say I am of the Beggars' Guild."

She said, "Just how many guilds *do* you have?"

He shrugged. "Over the centuries there have been hundreds. Some change, some disappear. New ones are formed. We are all of us of the Wulin, the followers of that which is now lost."

"And which you are all trying to recover?"

"Indeed. Though it is not here, in Paris, that it lies. What came here, I suspect, is only a fragment of the object called the Emerald Buddha – though its outer casing is made of pure jade, not emerald, despite the name – an object which should not have existed and, though it does, should have never been activated."

"You talk as if it is a kind of machine."

He said, "Oh, it is most certainly that."

So the object had a name. And what had been surgically inserted into Yong Li's belly – was that a fragment of this thing? She said, "What is the Emerald Buddha?"

Master Long said, "That is a good question. I am not sure I know – that anyone truly knows."

Riddles upon riddles... She said, "So what *do* you know?"

"It is the pure jade statue of a royal lizard," he said. "Pure on the outside, at least. Its eyes are emerald. Its inside had never been examined, though not for lack of trying. It was found..."

And there, in the darkness of the catacombs, he told her a story.

THIRTY-TWO
Master Long's Story

The Emerald Buddha was found one day by a boy walking along with his camel in the desert. The desert was a great one and the boy loved it. He loved the wide open expanse of sky, the endless horizon, the always-shifting nature of the land. There were sand dunes that rose into the sky and when the boy slid down their sides on his back they made a deep, rumbling sound, as if the sand itself was talking. There were low-lying, evergreen hills, and a place where, between two mountains, a river snaked in frozen splendour, and you could walk upon its surface and, reaching the end, drink ice-cold water as it slowly melted... There were rivers and lakes, and places where nothing grew. There was everything in the desert.

The boy came from a migratory people. For untold generations they had wandered the desert, through harsh summers and brutal winters, through extremes of heat and cold, pitching their great tents wherever they went, their horses and camels and cattle with them. They made alcohol from the milk of the camels, and drank it on the long nights. The camels were double-humped. The boy's camel – his first one, and his alone – was an ill-tempered beast, but the boy loved him for all that. The boy's family were passing through one of the most arid parts of the desert, and the boy had become fascinated by his grandfather's stories, which told of a place far away where the bones of giant creatures jutted out of the sand. They were of some enormous beasts that had walked the world long ago, when the world was young.

The boy had decided to see them for himself.

He had packed food for the journey, his crossbow and his spear and his knife, and plenty of water, and he took his camel. The caravan of migrating families moved slowly; he knew he could easily catch up with it, sooner or later. He could read the maps of the desert, and had travelled this road, back and forth, ever since he was born and even before, as an embryo in his mother's womb.

But he had never seen the giants' bones.

He saw the small bones of many other creatures on his way. To die in this part of the desert meant to remain forever in the spot where the sun had finally caught you. There were skeletal camels and skeletal cows and, once, a grinning human skull on top of a pile of stones. Where his people passed they had assembled these places, mounds of stones that lay all across the desert, and when they passed them they left small presents there for the spirits of the place – offerings of food and drink, blue ribbons of cloth tied to twigs jutting from the stones – and sometimes their dead.

The boy found the place two days after having set off. The story his grandfather had told him was true. It was the silent graveyard of giants.

For a long time he walked amidst the bones, marvelling at how impossible they were. Enormous creatures, with skulls the size of boulders, with ribcages as large as houses. He had been warned by his grandfather that the place was sacred: he must take nothing he might find.

And the boy was happy to merely look – until he saw the flash of green light in the sands…

Some time in the distant past, he saw, the ground here had been disturbed. A small crater lay further away from the giants' bones, and the sand had fused into a sort of greenish glass. He walked over to it, for it was not the glass he had seen.

Something was buried in the sand, in the centre of the crater. Something that flashed a beautiful jade green.

"Those who tell the story of the Emerald Buddha tell it differently," Master Long said. "It is said it was made in India, many centuries ago, and had since travelled widely across the civilised world – around Asia, I should say – always claimed, never resting. From India to Ceylon, and from there to Burma, and from Burma to Luang Prabang, and to Siam... The king of Siam lays a claim to it, and so do half a dozen other emperors and kings, from the Forbidden City to Angkor Wat. It is a statue of jade in the shape of a royal lizard – and here lies its mystery, and the wrong at the centre of the tale. For how could an Indian artificer, however talented, fashion a statue in the shape of beings not seen in the world at that time?"

She tried to imagine it, and fear took hold of her. The lizards had changed the world when they were awakened by Vespucci all those years ago. They had claimed the British Isles for their own, and set about conquering the known world, assembling to themselves colonies and protectorates as if they were blocks in a child's game. How long had they lain dormant on Caliban's Island before being awakened? And where had they come from?

From space, if the stories were true...

"Stories," Master Long said, "are true for what they tell us about ourselves more than for their own internal truth." He smiled, though it seemed to her there was mostly sadness in the expression. "Let me tell you about the boy..."

What it was he didn't know. And yet it seemed to speak to him, a babble of voices rising in his mind, saying unfathomable things.

Testing language modules... initiating geo-spatial surveillance... mind scan initiated... complete... audio-visual reconstruction activated... long-range scan returning negative... help us, boy! We are in the sand.

Something hidden, something talking to him, confusing his thoughts. The camel watched him for a while without much interest, then wandered off in search of shade. The boy tried to dig into the sand but it was hard as glass. He tried to smash it but it was strong. And all the while the voices spoke, an insane babble of them, promising him untold riches and eternal life...

"The boy was young then, and had dreams of glory," Master Long said. "Of riches beyond compare, and dusky maidens, of conquest and victory and admiration and glory... but I suspect that, even without it, he would have liberated the statue. For nothing but curiosity, Milady. It is what makes us human, in the final count. More than love, more than hate, more than dreams of immortality or glory – it is curiosity that–"

"Killed the cat?"

"What?" He looked at her, then shrugged. "Quite."

The boy's hands were bloodied, the nails torn, the knuckles bruised. Still he worked. With knife and spear until they broke, and then he used rocks, smashing them against the ground again and again, unheeding of the need for food or drink or shelter.

The voices spoke their insane babble: *Biological life form unrecognised. Checksum negative. Biological energy levels low. Initiating molecular restructuring. Feasibility study incomplete. What is this place?*

The sun burned him. The camel was nowhere to be seen. Time held no meaning to him.

Only the thing in the ground.

At last, he managed to dig a small hole. Underneath, the sand was soft and he cleared it away and pulled out his prize.

A green monster of a lizard stared back at him.

"It was not yet jade, you see," Master Long said. "That came later, and the eyes. What the boy saw was a lizard, yes, but it was slimmer then, without the camouflage of human workmanship. It was an alien thing, something he did not – could not – understand. It was made by tools and beings unknown and, I think, perhaps unknowable. It was made of a strange green metal–"

She thought of the green metal the lizards had brought with

them from Caliban's Island. Master Long nodded, as if reading her mind.

"Was it some tool of the lizards, unknowingly discarded? Had it come with them from their home and fallen down to Earth? It is possible. Other things have materialised that should not have been. It is said the Bookman himself was once a creature of the lizards... has been said, and very quietly, at that, these past three years."

"There had not been a Bookman assassination in all this time," Milady said. Master Long nodded. "Three years since the Bookman was last heard of. Three years since the revolution on the British Isles. A lot can happen in three years, Milady de Winter."

And she thought – the grey manifestations had began less than three years ago – began, perhaps, just after the time of the upheavals...

The boy held the statue in his arms, cradling it as he would a baby. When he went looking for his camel he did not find it, though the skeleton of a camel lay nearby. He could not remember when he had last eaten or drank, but the voices spoke to him and comforted him and offered him nourishment.

He held the statue and began to walk across the desert, searching for the caravan of his family and his friends.

"But he never found them," Master Long said, and there was infinite sadness in his voice when he spoke. "Time had passed differently in that place of old bones in the desert, and when the boy returned to the world, the world had irrevocably changed.

"He never saw his family again."

THIRTY-THREE
Lord of Light

The silence lay between them, as heavy as a gun. She said, "How long ago...?"

He said, "It is only a story. It happened long ago, in another time and place."

"I hardly knew my parents," she said, not knowing where the words came from. "I came on the ship. My father died in the war–"

"Which war?"

She shrugged, a helpless gesture. "It was not an important one. It did not justify having its own name."

"Most wars are forgotten," he said. "And most of the dead."

She said, "My mother was with me on the ship... I remember the waves crashing against the hull. I remember being very sick. She was with me... Then, one day, she wasn't there. And then we arrived in this new continent, this new alien world, where people had pale skins and spoke an alien tongue. And I was alone."

"But you survived."

She said, "I had to."

Master Long stirred. She had not realised how still he was – as still as an automaton, she thought. He said, "And now you work for them."

"For the machines," she said. He looked at her for a long time. "The world may have been a very different place," he said at last, "without the presence of either lizards or thinking machines… Whether it would have been better or worse, though, I cannot say."

She let it pass. She said, "What happened to the boy? From your story?"

He smiled, though there was sadness in it. "Centuries later," Master Long said, "the boy's people conquered Chung Kuo, the land of the Han. Then they fell back into their old ways. They still roam the desert, still raise camels and cows."

"And the boy?"

"It is said," Master Long said, and smiled, and his single eye glittered, "that he journeyed for many years, beyond a mortal's life, and found at last an isolated place in the high mountains and stayed there. And though he grew up he never grew old, and he communed with the Emerald Buddha, and learned much that was hidden, and practised wushu and Qinggong, the way of light…"

"What was his name then?" she said, and the old man shook his head. "Who can remember?" he said. "It is told that a man who was not exactly a man had lived in the mountains and there, over the years, others had found him, and came to learn with him. It became a monastery, of a sort, and its name was Shaolin. But these are only legends, and there had been many such places over the centuries, followers of the Emerald Buddha – for it is told that the Buddha is asleep, and had been for thousands of years, but that one day it would wake and change the world. I once spoke with a woman who told me there are many worlds, all lying close to each other. It is said the Emerald Buddha is a key, a way to open doors between the worlds. The orders of the Jianghu were formed to guard it, to keep it sleeping. There is great danger when two alien worlds meet."

She thought of what he said and they sat together in silence, the tall Dahomey woman and the short Master Long. "What happened three years ago?" she said.

"The Change," he said. "Yes... you ask good questions, none of which I have answers to. Perhaps the fat man you are seeking can answer that one."

One moment he was sitting down. The next he was on his feet, and offering her his hand, though she did not see him move. "But it is too late now, or too early. The sun is climbing once again into the sky, and you should sleep."

She took his hand. He pulled her up to her feet. "I have to keep going," she said. "I have to find–"

"The answers will wait," Master Long said. "They have waited long enough, after all. Rest, and tomorrow you shall have your answers – though at what cost even I do not know. But we will help, as much as we can."

"An old magician told me I would be..." She swayed on her feet. She was suddenly so tired she could barely stand. "I would meet a tall dark stranger and go on a long journey... Are you that stranger?"

Master Long laughed. "I am not exactly tall," he said.

"And he said..." She swayed again. Her eyes were closing, the darkness closing in. "He said, a weapon won't be enough. That I should... I should have to *become* a weapon. What do you think he meant?"

But there was no longer any answer, or if there was, she could not hear it. Her eyes closed and wouldn't open again, and she felt herself sinking into the blackness, into a thick and dreamless sleep where nothing came.

INTERLUDE:
The Other Side of the River

Days became nights and nights blended into days, until he could no longer distinguish the periods of light and dark or the changing of the seasons. The world Kai walked in was shifting around him, changing in unexpected ways. It was a twilight world, an autumn world, where the bright green of rice gave way to the murky colour of a flooding river. It was like walking through perpetual mist, through low-lying grey clouds.

The statue still spoke to Kai, but more and more he felt that the statue's attention was turned elsewhere. The statue spoke of *energy burst source unknown subsystems brought online*, and about *trans-dimensional shift parameters aligned* and about *proximity cluster confirmed, bipolar transfer engaged* and, last and unexpected: *home*.

Home was something he no longer had. Chiang Rai disappeared behind the mist as if it had never existed, the steam-filled shop and his father at work and Kai playing with the other kids in the road and reading wuxia novels by candlelight – all gone, washed away by rolling grey mists.

He travelled on foot, became used to the thick jungle, knew to avoid the poisonous plants and the lairs of bears and snakes and tigers and the isolated homes of the Karen people. He knew where to find their traps and knew how to make his own, which fruits to eat and which to leave. He avoided roads and whenever he saw elephant prints he hid, afraid of riders nearby.

At last he came to the big water. Mekong, he thought, the word rising in him like a lone bubble. The river was wide and filled with water to the banks and it rained every day, lightning lashing across the sky like a whip, the thunder like cannon fire echoing all around him, the sound of war. He walked along the bank in the direction of the mountains.

There were people using the river, of course. There were villages with bamboo huts standing on stilts above the water, and fisherfolk in canoes or wading through the shallows with nets. There were children playing in the water and there were barges and cargo boats travelling in both directions, many of them Chinese, like his father, and some of them from Siam, like his mother had been. And many others, too – dark men from the mountains and light ones from the lowlands far away, and Europeans – he had once seen one, an exotic creature visiting the town of Chiang Rai. There were steamboats, too, and he marvelled at them, delighted with the way they moved and churned the water, these great hulking beasts that belonged to the king of Siam. He hid when boats passed and he stole food from the villages if he could, and caught fish and small birds and animals. All the while he was going somewhere, but he didn't yet know where.

One day he stole a canoe and crossed to the other side of the river.

It was during a thunderstorm. The statue liked the storm. Somehow, it acted as an attractor for the lightning, yet it never hit Kai, nor the statue. The lightning struck all around them, him and the statue, and it was as if they were encased in a bubble, and it glowed in blues and greys, crackling with electricity, and the statue would talk of *utilising natural energy sources* and *renewable power supplies* and *reinforcing multi-dimensional boundaries*. When he crossed the river he was very scared, though the fear was different now, the fear was like a polished stone that he held in his hand, a force that could be transmuted into pure power, be made into a cold hard fury and be controlled. When he crossed the river it was as if the two banks would never meet, as if he had left one behind him while the other kept receding away in the distance. The current was very strong and soon he was being borne along it without control, his choices reduced to none. He let the current take him where it would. On the river, the two worlds, the two banks seemed impossibly distant from each other, the outlines of two separate worlds. In one was laughter and sunlight and new shoots of rice, ginger and jasmine and dry cleaners and steamboats and love. In the other was... what? The unknown. The statue longed for it – a darkness, and strange stars, and massive structures floating in the inky black...

How long he drifted on the river he didn't know. He drank the water of the Mekong and caught fish with bare hands, and ate them raw. Boats came and went but never seemed to see him. When the storms came he huddled in the small canoe and the lightning danced around him, and the statue glowed as if satisfied. Then, one day, he came around a bend in the river and saw a city.

PART III
The Man in the Iron Mask

THIRTY-FOUR
The Woman in the Mirror

Drippety-drip, drippety-drap the sound came, light fingers tapping on the window, a low wind blowing pipes of poisoned darts, the darkness pulsing like a heart, *drippety-drip, drippety–*

Splat.

Her eyes opened.

She was lying in her bed.

She had no recollection of how she had arrived there.

Outside the window it was raining, and the wind was howling a mournful tune. When she got up she half-expected more assailants to come through the door but the house was hushed and empty. She went into her drawing room and Grimm was there, curled up in the fireplace, and she stroked him, and the metallic insect turned its head so it rested in the palm of her hands. Its skin felt warm. The hiss of a tongue touched her palm like a kiss.

She knew she was close to the killer. She had missed something, she thought. But she knew he was close, that he was hunting her just as much as she was hunting him. For the moment, the question of the missing object did not occupy her as much. Also, it seemed obvious to her that when she found the killer, she would find this object, this key. Had it been used already? She thought of the killer, a grey grotesque shape in the dark of an alleyway. The corpses Viktor showed her in the under-morgue... yes. It had been used, and if not this one then another like it. And something had come through from the other side... or something here had been corrupted.

When she stepped into her waiting room there was an envelope on the table. She tore it open. It contained a ticket to a ball, to take place that evening at the Hotel de Ville. An appended note was stamped with the Council's emblem, and a handwritten scrawl said, *"British ambassador and entourage to attend – V."*

She was going to a ball. Wasn't there a children's story about this sort of thing? She smiled, though the expression felt grim on her face. She didn't feel like dancing – she felt like shooting someone. Some thing.

She had a feeling it would not be long before she had her opportunity.

She watched herself in the mirror. The long coat trailed down almost to her feet, the gun in its shoulder-holster, the other gun on her hips. She wore a dark scarf and a silk blouse and her black leather pants, and when she looked at herself in the mirror she saw a tall dark woman with eyes reflecting grey. Her nails were a dark red. As a final touch she put on her old hat, from the Barnum days, her time in the ring. Low-brimmed, it shaded her eyes. The horse riders of Vespuccia wore those when they rode the trails, on that massive open continent where the buffalo roamed...

She went back to the fireplace and Grimm rustled awake. "Stay close to me tonight," she murmured, her hand on its head, and the creature blinked in acquiescence. The gold bracelet on her arm would let Grimm know where she was. And now she stood up, ready to face the coming night.

The ball, yes, but first–

The silent coachman dropped her off at Place Pigalle. She looked around for watchers, saw none, knew they would be nearby. She had begun to realise her role in this investigation, her real purpose there. No one cared if she caught the killer, the Council least of all. No – she was there to bring them all out, rather, all the silent watchers – bring them out into the open so they could be seen and studied and made known. She passed the cemetery on the way to the gendarmes. Something seemed to call to her from inside that factory of graves. There had been stories... She walked away and into the station, and almost ran into the Gascon.

For a moment, their bodies had almost collided. She felt the warmth of him, his tautness, no fat on him, a wiry man as driven as she was–

The Gascon pulled back. She could not read the look in his eyes. He examined her slowly, from head to toe, and shook his head. Around them a silence fell like snow. "Gunslinger," he said at last. She smiled, touched the brim of her hat in acknowledgment. "Inspector," she said. "What do you have for me?"

"Very little," he said. "I heard you found another corpse. You seem to have a knack for finding people dead."

She said, "Tom was a friend."

He nodded. "Mademoiselle L'Espanaye is safe," he said. "My men have tracked down the killer's escape route." He hesitated. "It seems he had made his way to the cemetery – beyond that we lost his tracks."

Somehow she was not surprised – and now she said, "What happened in the cemetery?" and watched his face. Yes – the question hit him hard. "What makes you think anything happened?"

She thought of the corpses in the under-morgue. And now she said, only half-guessing – "Have any graves been robbed in the past two years?"

The Gascon stared at her, not speaking. "And you can offer me a cup of coffee while you tell me," she said, and he slowly smiled. "Yes, Milady," he said.

When they sat down the man seemed to relax a little. He said, "Yes, there have been. We've kept it quiet – as much as possible. Rumours got out, naturally."

"Naturally," she said, without inflection, and he gave her a sharp look before catching himself. He shrugged, ceding her the point. "There is a... caretaker in the cemetery," he said. "But he would not speak to us, and I'm afraid we can't press him."

And now he watched her, waiting – "Who is it?" she said, and his smile was predatory when he said, "*What* he is might be a better question, Milady."

THIRTY-FIVE
Ampère

No one knew much about André-Marie Ampère. In life he had been a scientist, obsessed with the study of electricity. When his wife died he was distressed to the point of confusion. She had once heard Viktor speak of him – in reverence. He was born, had lived, and died – only he hadn't, not quite...

There were simulacrums in the world, and that was only natural. There were machines that could almost pass for human, and humans who, one thought, too closely resembled machines. It was told the Bookman could remake the dead, reassemble them into living things once again... and perhaps Ampère was one of his creatures, though who could tell? He was born and lived a man, he died – and now he lived, if such a word could be used, alone and undisturbed in the Montmartre Cemetery, in a small stone building beside his very own grave.

What was he? A copy of a man? A machine? A ghost?

She did not believe in ghosts. "Did you search the Clockwork Room?" she said. The Gascon nodded. "We found nothing. Whatever meeting was arranged there, they did not leave anything behind."

She did not suspect that they did. She would confront the fat man soon enough, she thought. But now she had the traces of the killer and she was going to follow them, wherever they may lead.

"Ampère was one of the Council, once," she said.

"When he was still living?" the Gascon said.

"No."

"Ah."

She knew he did not like the machines. Few people did, though they accepted them, lived with them, and to a large extent let them decide their lives. And so she said, "I'll go alone."

He said, "No–" but she knew the fight wasn't in him. "As you said, he won't see you. I have the authority–"

Knowing that was another thing that made the Gascon unhappy.

It had stopped raining, and the night air felt cool and fresh. And she liked cemeteries.

They were peaceful places. They were humanity's way of acknowledging change, of laying down the past. The dead did not rise again. They were absorbed into the earth, became, in time, something new, the dying bodies recycled and reused. Cemeteries were quiet and filled with a sense of space and quiet purpose.

Though now she could see one part of it was not so quiet. And it was still raining where she was going, though it was a strange, localised storm...

The graves rose all around her, elaborate houses for the dead, though the dead could no longer appreciate them. And there – a miniature castle where the storm hovered, lightning flashing, again and again as it hit a metal pole rising from the turrets.

Gargoyle-faced edifice... And now she saw they were not, as was common, lizardine, but something different. And she wondered what Ampère really knew, and had he ever been east, for they were shaped like grey and faceless ghosts.

She walked through the drops and reached the door and banged on it. She heard movement inside. She could see how this place would have appealed to the murderer – but she did not expect him to be there. She waited and Ampère opened the door.

He was dressed in black, as if in mourning. Whoever fashioned him had done a good job. He moved without stiffness, and his eyes looked very life-like. The face was unlined, and she knew it would never age. Though the machine might run down, one day...

He said, "Milady de Winter?" His voice was scratchy, old, incompatible with the face. It occurred to her he might have built himself, once upon a time, and the machine kept adding new parts but could not change the voice. She wondered if there were jars of moist artificial eyes in his pantry, different colours for different occasions. She wouldn't look – it was altogether too likely.

"I've been expecting you. Please, come inside." He gestured at the sky, the storm. Lightning flashed above them. "I've been working."

"I can see."

She followed him inside. "Though I am retired from the Council my work still concerns–" Then he stopped, and the machine allowed itself a small, wan smile. It looked very natural. "I'm afraid I can't help you," he said.

And machines could lie so much better than humans ever did...

"How long have you lived here?" she said.

"Over fifty years. Ever since I – ever since my predecessor died. He constructed this lab for me and paid for it along with his tomb."

"You research electricity."

"I research life," he said, and smiled again. She did not return the smile and the machine she was talking to dropped it. "I study the fundamental powers," Ampère said and she said, only half-listening – "Why here?"

"Why not? It is quiet, isolated. I am seldom disturbed."

"Until the dead began to rise?" she said, and he didn't move. "When did it begin, two, three years ago? Was it something you noticed, or was it something you made happen? Tell me!"

"Milady," he said, "your accusations are quite baseless."

What if there had been another key? Another transaction from the Man on the Mekong, as Fei Linlin had called him? Another fragment offered? She said, "Viktor showed me the corpses. But I don't think they were the only ones."

"Viktor and I are not in the same line of work," he said.

"Are you harbouring a killer?" she said.

"What?"

"I need to know."

"What I do," he said, "I do for the Council."

And now the suspicion she had been trying to avoid voicing resurfaced. She said, "He has to be stopped–" and watched Ampère take a step back, then stand very still. "He is killing the living, now," she said.

"He always did…" The words were a whisper.

"Tell me."

The automaton shook itself awake. "Go," he said. "I–"

"No."

Lightning struck the roof, the sound echoing through the dark hall of the miniature castle. "I have to go," he said. "I have to finish the work – come back to see me. I will tell you what you want to know–"

And now a sound rose from the back of the hall, coming from behind a closed door, and Ampère glanced back and then at her, and moved to push her out. "You must go. Hurry! Come back to see me when the night is deep."

A growling sound, growing louder. "Go!"

She took out her gun in one swift motion and put the barrel against his neck. The automaton stood still. "Make sure to be here when I come back," she said. Then the gun was gone, an act of magic, and she stepped out of that dark dead room and into the cool air outside. She had the feeling of unseen eyes watching her. She walked away from the castle and the lightning cracked behind her, filling up the sky with violent blue electricity.

THIRTY-SIX
The Lizardine Ambassador

And so Milady de Winter went to the ball.

Out there, beyond the windows of her carriage, the silent watchers watched. She could sense them there, these intrusions into an orderly world. Xiake, Master Long had called her – a follower of Xia, whatever that meant. A code beyond government or law, the way of righteousness.

She did not feel very righteous. She felt tired, consumed by three days of not eating properly, of running around chasing shadows, of being kidnapped and assaulted and watching people die before her, and not knowing why. Outside the Hotel de Ville there were carriages, hansom cabs, baruch-landaus, liveried footmen and lounging drivers, the usual Parisian crowd gathered to watch festivities to which they were not invited. There were roast chestnut sellers, newspaper boys, booksellers from their little domain by the Seine, beggars, portrait artists, photographers, and the air smelled of the mix of chemicals from the baruch-landau vehicles and the steaming manure of the more traditional horse-drawn cabs. The air smelled of chestnuts and caramelised peanuts; and lightning flashed overhead in silence, the thunder too far away, as yet, to be heard.

She stepped out of the carriage and the silent driver with his stitched-up face drove away.

Photographers – and now she recognised one of them. He tried to walk away when he saw her coming. She grabbed him by the arm and saw his face twist with the unexpected pain. She said, "What are you doing here?"

It was the photographer from the Rue Morgue. The one whose camera she had smashed against the wall. It felt like months ago. It wasn't.

He didn't speak and the pressure on his arm increased, Milady finding the nerves, her long fingernails driving into the man's flesh. And now he said, "He sent me! Let me go!"

"D–" no, she would not say his name, "The Gascon sent you? To take pictures of the guests? Why?"

His face was pale. He did not relish being there. He said, "He thinks... he thinks..."

She let go of his arm. He rubbed it, shying away from her. "He thinks the killer might make an appearance?" she said, and the man nodded.

"Clever Gascon..." she whispered, and then she smiled. The photographer melted into the crowd. Very well. She wondered what the Gascon knew, or what he guessed at. She went through the gates and up to the building.

The Hotel de Ville – municipality building, mayor's house, the beating heart of the urban metropolis of Paris. The Seine was nearby, carrying ferries, rafts, fallen flowers, fish and the occasional human corpse. The smell of it wafted through the air and was replaced, as she stepped through the doors into the Hotel de Ville's ballroom, by the stench of expensive perfumes, canapés, polish, engine oil and something she could not quite discern until she turned and found herself, suddenly and without warning, beside a tall royal lizard.

Les Lézards. She had never expected that, and it always came as a surprise to her, no matter how many she had met before in the English court: their smell was different. She couldn't quite describe it. The ambassador (for that was who it must be) smelled of the warmth of rocks in the late afternoon, of swamps and – very faintly – of eau de cologne.

He was tall and – she thought – elderly. He towered above her, green-skinned but for bands of colouration that ran across his body, and his tongue hissed out as if tasting the air. He was dressed in an expensive, understated suit. His tail looked formidable, like a weapon. And now he turned to her and said, "Milady de Winter, I presume?"

She nodded, trying to remember him from the court and failing. The ambassador took her hand in both of his, bent down gracefully and kissed her – the tongue flicking out again, the touch of it like electricity against her skin. When he straightened up he seemed to be smiling.

"You were married to Lord de Winter?" he said. "A most charming man. Often we went hunting together at Balmoral."

The Queen's remote estate, in Scotland – so the ambassador was high up in the lizards' social order. Which wasn't surprising–

"His death was most unfortunate," the ambassador said.

"Yes..." Milady said, and the ambassador again seemed to smile. His tongue flicked out again, disappeared back into the elongated mouth. "And so you have returned to the place of your childhood? It must have been a pleasant childhood indeed."

She thought of the small girl running in the night, of the abandoned houses where predators roamed... "Very," she said, giving him a smile full of teeth. They were playing a game – and she thought it was no coincidence, the ambassador standing just there as she came in. She wondered if he really had known her husband, or whether he was merely reading out of her dossier. Well, perhaps it was both. "Sometimes when I was hungry I'd catch geckos and roast them on the fire – you had to stick a sharpened wood branch into them to stop them wriggling."

"Indeed." He reared back, looked down on her. And now there was nothing friendly in his face at all. "You have been luckier than your husband, it seems..." he said. "Be careful that your luck doesn't run out."

She moved her coat aside, just a little, and saw his eyes fasten on the gun. "I'm always careful," she said, and the lizard hissed.

"Ambassador," a voice said, close by, and she turned, startled, for she had not heard the man approach. "You must meet this absolutely *charming* mechanical–"

She had not heard the fat man approach. And now she watched him stir the lizardine ambassador away, towards an ancient man-shaped automaton on the other side of the ballroom... She followed him with her eyes and for just a moment the fat man turned back and winked at her.

THIRTY-SEVEN
The Electric Ball

The ballroom was filled with revellers. Metal globes hung from the high ceiling and lightning flashed between them back and forth – a Tesla invention, if she recalled correctly, but one that seemed ill-suited for a night's entertainment. She looked around her and realised something had been missing from her invitation: it was a masked ball.

She should have expected that.

The lizardine ambassador, of course, was bare-faced. And the automatons' faces were masks all by themselves – though some, she saw, had joined in the spirit of the event and wore elaborate mechanical masks that changed expressions in a sequence or randomly, it was hard to tell. The humans, most of them, were masked. She saw chieftains from Vespuccia in their elaborate headdresses and what she knew to be war paint, short men armed with decorative shields from the Zulu kingdom accompanying a young woman, Indian rajahs with diamonds in their hats, Aztec priests in their garb – the cream of the diplomatic circle of Paris, all gathered here for the electric ball.

She looked around for someone from Dahomey but the place was too full and besides, she had left the place too long ago. Her links with the old country had been severed one by one, and now none remained, and she was a citizen of–

Of what? of the Republic? Of the lizards' court? She belonged to all of these, and none. Perhaps she really was Xiake, a member of the secretive world Master Long had called the Wulin. She didn't know where her loyalties truly lay, but she knew what was right, and she knew what she had to do. What had to be done.

And the Gascon was right, she thought. Somewhere in the throngs of masked women and men the killer, too, was dancing.

A band of automatons was providing the music from a dais at the back of the hall, a player piano and a steam-powered orchestra. The lightning crackled overhead without thunder, electricity jumping from one spinning globe to another, casting odd shadows onto the dance floor, like a fractured mirror. And there – dancing together, a handsome young couple, both masked with the faces of some sort of fantastical animals – Mistress Yi and her shadow Ip Kai? She watched them as they circled the room, holding each other, moving fluidly with the dance, and yet – she could sense their awareness, the way they watched the room. And now she thought – there are many watchers here tonight.

They were not alone.

Here and there, the Gascon's men, trying and failing to blend, shouting *gendarmes* in the way they stood, the way they watched – the way they drank, for that matter. And now another familiar body waylaid her, and for a second time this evening she was taken aback.

He was young and very beautiful, with his bare chest and his mask of a tiger, and he swept her up in his arms for a dance. "Remember me?"

The voice and the physique… "The bartender at the Moulin Rouge?"

"I hoped we'd meet again. You are very beautiful."

"So are you," she said, meaning it, and he laughed. "I would like to make love to you," he said. She had to smile. He carried her effortlessly, a born dancer, and she said, "Perhaps when all this is over…"

"The ball?"

"Not exactly..." She gently pushed him away and he twirled back and bowed. "At your service, Milady," he said. Then he danced away and into the throng, and was soon engulfed in the arms of another woman.

... who was familiar, also. A woman who needed no mask, for she wore one as a matter of course. Madame Linlin, who danced with the young man for a minute, then turned to speak with a minister and his entourage – the old lady making an appearance in an official capacity, then? Milady couldn't spot Colonel Xing, which told her nothing. She suspected he, and at least some of his men, where somewhere in the crowd.

Well, well... this ball was certainly turning out to be more interesting than she'd thought.

"Milady!"

She stared at him. "*Viktor?*"

"Wonderful party!"

The scientist had replaced his habitual smock with evening wear, a jaunty black hat sat at an angle on his head, and his mask was that of her coachman, the stitched-up face of a monster. "What the hell are you doing here?"

"Dancing!" the scientist said. "They gave me the night off."

"The Council?"

"Shh!" He made an exaggerated sign, finger to his lips. And now she could smell the alcohol. "I'm off-duty."

"I thought you preferred the company of the dead," she said, and he shrugged. "The dead don't dance, and they seldom drink."

She let it pass, said, "Who's on in the under-morgue?"

Viktor smirked. "You think someone's going to rob the morgue?"

Something cold slid slowly down her spine. Something was wrong, and the Council... She did not trust the Council.

"Have you seen Tômas?" Viktor asked. There was something a little too casual in the way he said it, and it gave her pause.

"Tômas?"

Viktor had told her, hadn't he? Memory returned. Tômas had been in charge of the body-snatching duty, retrieving the grey-infected corpses. Tômas the cruel, the master of disguises, Tômas who they called the Phantom – and now suspicion bloomed. She thought about the Council. What were they planning? And she thought – I am their bait – but who are they hunting?

"I shall speak with you later!" Viktor said, too brightly and, turning, hurried off after a troupe of green-painted, scantily clad dancers.

The lightning flashed and flashed overhead. Something in Milady wanted to forget the currents, forget the other world, the murders, the futile chase for a thing that had no right to exist. Drink, she thought, and dance, and be merry – but she wasn't sure she remembered how. Find that beautiful young dancer...

Then she thought of Tom Thumb lying on the Seine's bank with his throat cut, the grey swirls moving on his skin as if they were alive. Alive and hungry, she thought. And–

The killer must be amongst the crowd.

But which one of the masked creatures was he?

THIRTY-EIGHT
The Fat Man

"Drink?"

She swirled round – and found herself at last facing the elusive fat man. "Mr Holmes," she said, and the man smiled. Unlike the rest of the crowd, he was not wearing a mask. "Always a pleasure to be recognised," he said, though she thought a hint of irritation had crept somewhere in there. And, "Please, call me Mycroft."

"Mycroft," she said. "In our line of work it doesn't pay to be recognised too often."

"Yet who could fail to recognise such a beautiful woman as yourself, Milady de Winter?" he said, and she smiled back, the boundaries stated, the chess pieces aligned.

"You are British Intelligence?" she said. He shrugged, and she said, "They say it is an oxymoron."

His face wore a pained expression. "Please," he said. "Let us not engage in hostilities."

"Yet," she said. "Is that what you mean?"

"I'm not sure I follow…"

"Are we heading to war?" she said.

"You and I, Milady? Never."

"Britain and France," she said. "Lizard and machine. Is that what this has all been about?"

"Please," he said. "Relieve me of my burden–" handing her a flute of champagne which she accepted but did not drink. "The white man's burden…" she said, and he laughed. "I want to know how Yong Li died," she said, watching him carefully. The fat man's face became carefully blank. "I am not familiar with that name…"

"The man you met at the Clockwork Room," she said. "The man who showed you an impossible thing, the pictures of another world. Am I correct so far?"

"I'll admit I'm impressed," Mycroft Holmes said. "I take it from what you say that Captain Li is dead?"

"Please," she said. "We can speak candidly, here."

The fat man took a deep breath, let it out slowly. "Very well," he said. Around them dancers moved, the music played. The harmless lightning flashed overhead.

"Did you kill him?"

"No."

She nodded slowly, approving. "A straight answer," she said.

"Then I shall be candid further with you," Mycroft Holmes said. "I do not know who killed him. It was not… it was not our work."

"Did he show you what you wanted to see?"

"What we *wanted* to see?" He made a helpless gesture with the hand holding his almost-empty glass. "I did not want to see what Captain Li had to show. But to close one's eyes, Milady, does not make unpalatable things go away."

"And what," she said, "did you see?"

Mycroft's face a sudden grey cloud…

Imagine a camera obscura, Mycroft told her. *Imagine a box of wood through which light travels. An image is projected onto a screen. Imagine a series of such images, flickering like grey shadows on a wall – what do they show? They are not reality, are not, perhaps, even an accurate representation but something else, an obscurity of form that hides rather than reveals. What do you see? What lies beyond, in the source of the light, beyond the images revealed?*

"I saw the future," he said, very softly. The silence, grey and featureless, grew a gulf between them. "You saw another world," she said.

"Yes. Almost within reach…"

She said, "What do you intend to do with such knowledge?"

"What will your own Council do?" he said. And now she had to consider him, looking down at the fat man, thinking – "But what makes you think the Council is aware–" she began, and he interrupted her. "Please, Milady. Let us not play games. This was not the first approach made, nor the last. A door has been opened, and it lies – for now, at least – in the east. What may come through it is a worry and a danger – but what may be gained by passing through it to the other side, now, that is another matter altogether…"

"Could you take control of it, though?" she said, and saw she had hit a spot with him. "You will try," she said. "And so will we…"

"And so will the Chinese," he said. "Unless we can all work together…"

"Is that likely?"

"No," he admitted.

"You would try to use it?" Another thought struck her. "Or close it?"

He smiled, and there was nothing pleasant in the expression on his face. "That is the question…" he said softly. "Would you excuse me? There is someone I must see…"

"Of course," she said, and he nodded to her. "Please remain well," he said. "It would be a shame…"

He turned away before she could reply. It did not entirely surprise her to see him, moments later, chatting quietly to Madame Linlin on the other side of the hall.

This was how matters of politics and diplomacy were decided – how lives were added and subtracted, wars decided upon, like this – in a ballroom full of music and dancing and drink, in a civilised manner – in the manner of people who decided others' death without risk to their own.

And what would be the end result?

THIRTY-NINE
The Phantom

She waited and the dancing grew more frenetic around her, the drinks liberating the crowd, the dresses twirling, the music loud, the masks slipping as the humans celebrated – what? The air was thick with cigar smoke and a hint of opium, with spilled wine and the combined sweat of so many people. She needed fresh air. She turned to leave. She stood by the cloakroom and it was quiet there, and a little cool air came in from the outside, refreshing her.

A step beside her. She turned and saw a man wearing an iron mask, the way prisoners were once masked.

"Milady de Winter," the voice said. It was a familiar voice. He was dressed as an automaton, the iron mask covering his whole face. His hands were encased in gloves. "Tômas," she said. And now a dormant suspicion became more than that...

"Milady."

"What are you doing here?"

"Drinking, dancing – watching the fools for an easy mark. The usual."

She watched him but the iron mask never smiled. She thought about the man she knew, the man he'd been – a murderer, a thief, but human. The thing she had met in Place Pigalle was no longer that.

She said, "Let me see your hands."

"You wish to become intimate?" And though she couldn't see it she could hear the leer in his voice. She kept her voice level, said, "I need to see your skin."

"Many women have told me that," he said. "But you, I never expected–"

Before he finished speaking a gun was pointing at him. "*Now*," she said. Suspicion turning to understanding, but horrified – she had not thought of another Council agent...

"You want to shoot me?" he said, and his voice was low and husky, and he bent towards her and put his forehead against the muzzle of the gun. "You did before..."

And now she noticed how elongated his skull seemed–

She reached for his hand, tore away the white glove–

His hand rose up, freed. She saw the grey swirling on the metamorphosed skin–

His hand closed to a fist and swung at her. His knuckles were like metal, and he knocked her back and there was blood on her cheek. She fired, point blank. She felt him sag against her–

And rise again, laughing, a wild inhuman sound – and now he reached for her, and a tongue licked her cheek, tasting her blood, and his voice said, close to her ear, "And all the time you thought you were hunting, it is I who has been hunting you..."

She fought against him but couldn't break free. "And now I am tired of the game," he said. "Now I wish to enjoy the rewards of winning..."

His hand grabbed her by the throat. She watched the grey swirls climb up his wrist and onto his fingers. "The Council set you to catch *me*?" he said. "Me! Did they really think a girl like you could stand up to what I've become?"

He shoved her, hard, and she stumbled, gasping for air. "I'll give you," the thing that had once been Tômas said, "one more chance. It will be... how do the English say? It would be sporting. Come and get me. I'll be waiting for you, Milady de Winter."

She raised the gun and fired, and fired, and fired. There were screams in the distance. The man in the iron mask laughed and ran, his gait that of a strange lithe animal, jumping impossibly off the walls of the hall and out through the open door, where the rain was falling down. He ran through the crowds and they scrambled away from him, and there were more screams. She ran after him, firing until there were no bullets left, not heeding the crowds.

Far away, the figure that had been Tômas turned to face her. He had pushed up his mask, and now she could see him for what he was, a grey, wolf-like thing, that grinned at her with wet teeth in the thin moonlight. "Catch me if you can…" his voice came, like a whisper, on the wind.

Then he was gone.

There was a commotion in the hall, and now she saw the watchers coming outside, and now she knew why the Council truly set her to find Yong Li's killer. She was their bait, to flush out the Phantom – but not only him, all the other watchers too. The Council had used her twice, to identify the other players and draw out their rogue agent – two birds with one stone, and she was the worm. Outside the gates she saw an old Asian man with one eye, sitting in the shadows. Ebenezer Long, watching. She went to him and dropped a coin into his begging bowl, and his serene face smiled up at her. "The darkest hour," he said, "is the one before dawn."

"Spare me," she said.

"We will protect you," he said, "if we can."

"I won't hold my breath."

She turned away from him. There, on the steps, watching. Viktor, still holding a drink in one hand. He had known, and hadn't told her. The Council had set her searching, in ignorance, counting on her to stir up events. Whether she lived or died mattered little to the machines.

"But you would do the right thing," Master Long said. "You always do, Xiake."

Then he, too, was gone, a whisper on the wind.

Her hand closed around the other gun, the one she hadn't used, the one she *should* have used: the Toymaker's gift. She would use it, and she would destroy the menace that the Phantom represented. She would hunt him down, out of compassion, and put a bullet in his head and watch him die.

She knew where he would go.

And now her sense of urgency was gone, replaced with a cold expectation. She summoned her coach and it came. The crowds had gone, the music had died behind her in the hall. A fearful, expectant hush…

"We're going back to Montmartre," she told the silent coachman.

She watched the lights of the Hotel de Ville recede in the darkness. They would all be mobilising too, she thought. All of them who wanted the key, the thing that was stolen when Yong Li died. The Council must have been furious when their own agent turned on them. When the other world reached out and touched him, and remade him in the process, a key of their own to open this world…

She sat back and closed her eyes, and her fingers tightened around the gun.

FORTY
Rise of the Jade Grey Moon

The thunder still rolled over Montmartre Cemetery; lightning continued to flash above the caretaker's miniature castle, and the night was dark and full of menace. Or so it felt to Milady. She listened out for bird cries but heard none. The cemetery was silent, the graves almost unseen but for when the lightning illuminated the headstones. Such an elaborate façade, she thought, for a depository of dead things... They were all gone and finished with, the men and women who lay there. Their minds had gone, and what was left crumbled slowly, flesh peeling, blood draining, only the bones remaining – but they, too, would turn to dust. Only the headstones remained, names and dates inscribed in stone, signifying nothing.

She wondered how many of the grey-infected corpses had initially come here. And where had the initial infection come from? Did the Man on the Mekong, Tom Thumb's mysterious contact in the east, send other keys, other couriers? How long had the Council known – and how long had the lizards?

She made her way through the graves slowly, her gun drawn. She was watching for the Phantom. She remembered the first time she had met Tômas. Down in the under-morgue, a young man with an unremarkable face, a face that could transform – with a hint of rouge, a false moustache, a wig, an expression, into someone else's face. He had been a murderer; a blackmailer; a thief and a robber; the Council found him highly useful and had recruited him – where and when she never knew. Just as she had been recruited, when she first came to their notice, before her travels in Vespuccia, before Lord de Winter – before her first husband, even. A brat in the under-city, who did what she could to survive... They had liked that. They had fashioned her, in their way, into a gun.

Now she hunted a comrade; another like her; and yet nothing like her, she thought. She stalked toward Ampère's castle. As she passed a large headstone the lightning flashed and she saw the name inscribed there.

André-Marie Ampère. So it was true, and the man's simulacra had made its home right beside its one-time owner.

She came to the door. When she knocked there was no answer. She kicked it open. "Ampère!"

No answer, but something moving in the darkness. Lightning flashed and the light came through the open doorway and she saw the thing on the floor.

The automaton had been sliced open, its insides showing, gears and wheels changing even as she watched, becoming a strange, grey mist. And, as if prompted by the lightning, a blue electric light began to glow around André-Marie Ampère, spilling out from his insides. The automaton's mouth moved, but no words came out. She stepped closer.

"I take it Tômas has already paid you a visit," she said. The thing on the floor groaned. Grey clouds spilled from its insides, and now she could see what she had missed before – there was a fragment of a green stone embedded into the automaton's stomach, the smoke and the light falling from it, growing...

Awakening, a voice said. She took a step back. It did not quite speak. Somehow the words were in her mind. Lights, flickering. Static pictures, hovering in the mist. A camera obscura, she thought. But this was more. And it was real.

Home...

There was more than one voice. They sounded... lonely?

She stared into the automaton's belly, where a sun was rising in dark space, illuminating... what?

A vista of impossible structures, floating in space...

"What are you?" she said.

Worlds within worlds... old beyond time... we are ghosts, nothing to be frightened of... for ourselves, we want nothing.

She took a step closer to the corpse; and now she was standing directly above Ampère. He was no longer moving. The machine was dead.

"Awakening," she said, echoing them. "Why? Why now? Or..." Not now, she realised. "Three years ago. What *happened*?"

A sense of a vast intelligence turning over her question, tasting it, polishing it like a stone, examining it in a dim light. No answer. Then, *A signal. Chrono-spatial; anomaly; awakening; birth; child; like us not us; close – we must find it!*

"I don't understand."

In the place you call... A vast mind rifling through a catalogue of names and meanings, searching. *Oxford.*

"What happened there?"

Again, the words dizzying her, the voices swallowing her, and she found herself bent down, her face so close to the dead machine's open belly, where the jade-green flashes seemed to shape themselves, suddenly, into the shape of a key... *Birth. Multi-form intelligence infant anomalous same same different dimensional representation insufficient–*

"You don't know..."

A shriek of anger, a sense of waiting, and she reached out to the fragment of jade, compelled to touch it–

Her hand froze above it. She thought – the Phantom had put it there. He had killed Ampère. He had set it for her, to touch. What would it do?

And she thought – it would make me like him.

"No," she said. The voices silenced. The Colt was in her hand without her knowing it. She fired – again and again.

FORTY-ONE
What Transpired at the Montmartre Cemetery

The grey mist dissipated. The electric corpse twitched and shook, sparks and smoke rising from Ampère's chest. His eyes bulged out, then fell altogether and rolled on the floor, leaving two empty sockets behind.

A lifeless figure lay at her feet. The room was dark, and outside the storm had abated, the clouds slowly dispersing.

She turned away and was sick.

After a couple of minutes she felt better. She didn't know what lay inside Ampère's castle, and didn't want to find out. She went outside and closed the door behind her.

Clap.

The sound jerked her head upwards. She scanned the night, saw nothing.

Clap. Clap. Clap.

"Tômas."

"Milady. Is it true you killed your first husband?"

"Show yourself."

"And your second?"

She turned, round and round, searching for him. Where was the voice coming from? Her gun was in her hand. The other gun was still safely hidden in her coat, and she didn't dare reach for it...

495

"We are not unlike, you and I."

"Don't flatter yourself."

"I was flattering *you*–" he laughed. "I want to show you something."

"Then come out and show me."

"All in good time, Milady. All in good time." The voice circled around her, invisible, unseen. "I have seen so much. There are no words to describe the things I've experienced. I have seen the universe, Cleo."

She had not been called that in a long time... Tom, she thought. Tom Thumb had called her that, the last time she saw him alive.

"I saw the stars of deep space," the Phantom said. She searched for him but couldn't find him. "The swirling galaxies," the Phantom said. "I have seen suns explode and life flourish where no life should be... And I have seen the lizards."

"Oh?" she stopped, stood still. Was that a branch cracking underfoot?

"I have seen rings in space, enormous structures, and dark ships like whales sailing between the stars. I've seen worlds beyond the world, I've seen wonders such as I can't–"

She turned and shot. A silence, then a low, husky laugh. "Good try," Tômas said.

"You could return with me," she said. "We can try and find a cure. Reverse you–"

"*Reverse* me? I am beyond human, Cleo. I am the next step. I am better than all of you."

"You're insane," she said.

"And you're a fool," he said. "Do you think the Council would be grateful to you for destroying their key?" He laughed again. "It is of little consequence. It was but a fragment, a small thing. I am a key unto itself. And there is a door, too... a gateway in Asia, and its gatekeeper selling tickets to the highest bidder – who do you think that would be? France? Chung Kuo? Perhaps the Sioux Nations? Or the fat-bellied lizards and their human servants?"

"Why do you care?"

Circling again. Was that a shadow, moving? She fired, and the shadow dropped back. "That almost hurt," he said. Then he was closer, very suddenly, and she fired with the gun while reaching for the other, the one with the grey-metal slugs–

And – "I don't," he said, and he was very close. She saw him then, illuminated in the moonlight, a steely-grey monster, naked now, grey swirls like living tattoos on his skin. That elongated skull, and the row of teeth that opened in a hungry smile… "I've waited a long time for this, Cleo," he said, and then he seemed to be everywhere at once and she could not reach the gun, her hands would not obey her and she tried to turn – too late – and felt an explosion of pain erupt in the back of her skull. She fell to her knees, tried to raise her gun arm but weights were dragging her down now, down into black and murky depths from which she couldn't rise… Her hands fell to her sides and there was pain again, a lot of it, and she fell sideways, and into a dark abyss where no dreams came.

Movement. Her head was aflame. Pain spread out like molten silver throughout her body. She was being carried. His hands were on her like a vice. She was dangling from his shoulder, her head almost grazing the ground. She saw tombs pass by, upside down. "Lovely Cleo," he said. "Soon, now…"

She passed out again, mercifully.

And awakened, to see the stars overhead, no clouds, no rain (she would have prayed for rain, craved water). The pain in her head was a dull constant sound, a hammer hitting a distant anvil.

Notre Dame de Paris. In the ruins shadows fled from the Phantom and its prey. She stirred, trying to – trying to – she had a–

His hand on her neck and she could no longer breathe. "Into the under-city we go, we go," he sang to her. "You and I, how pleasant it will be…"

The fingers pressed on her throat and squeezed; she couldn't breathe…

Darkness again.

• • • •

Going through the passages of the under-city, going through the catacombs... She thought she saw Q, hidden in a corner, watching her sadly. She tried to whisper to him, but no words came. Past fires and beggars and lizard boys, past the sorry denizens of this sorry dark world. "Not far now, my love..." he whispered, and there was pain, there was so much pain, and she sought escape in the cool and empty darkness, diving inside it, her last thought a wordless cry, an old prayer: *Please don't let me wake up again.*

FORTY-TWO
I am Pain

"Why the cemetery?"

"All those lovely corpses… my little garden of the dead. And that fool Ampère to store them and study them and keep quiet about my little indiscretions. You spoiled my little arrangement…"

"The Council put you on body-snatching detail–"

Sounds in the dark, metal sliding against metal, and she tried not to think of that. "They didn't count on you getting infected yourself?"

"Oh, I think you'd be surprised," he said. Flames, burning metal. She bit down hard, trying to focus. "I suspect they wanted to see how it would affect me. Not just me, Milady de Winter. Another part of my job was to bring them test subjects. Little kids from the street, old women, old men, a whole cross-section of society – as long as no one would miss them. Little kids…" he said. "Like you'd once been."

She thrust against the restraints, wanting to get at him, and he laughed. She was strapped into one of Viktor's operating tables. They were in the under-morgue, and it was locked up tight, and there were only the two of them.

"I didn't mind," he said. "I liked it. It gave me…" He sounded thoughtful. "New abilities," he said. "I no longer needed to serve the Council. The new me had no one to serve but itself."

"But they sent you to get Yong Li," she said. He snorted. "That sad little man... I merely reversed the operation he'd already undergone. He was a little like me, and glad not to be, I think. He was grateful for my knife."

"But they sent you. To get the key."

"Yes..." he said, not sounding certain.

"But you wouldn't give it back to them."

"I was happy," he said. "In my little garden. I was going on a long journey, you see. To another place."

"What happened?"

"The key was not enough. It was like the hole in a camera obscura – enough to show the image coming through, not enough to cross over. No, the gateway is only one and it is far from here, in Asia, where the fragment came from. I will be going there soon, to meet the Man on the Mekong."

"Does he have a name?"

"He might have had one, once. What do I care for names? I shall cut his belly open and walk through the doorway."

"You're insane."

"No," he said. "I am pain."

He turned to her then. He was wearing his iron mask again, and one of Viktor's white smocks. He looked down on her. He had stripped her down to her underclothes. Her coat lay crumpled in a corner. The gun, she thought. The gun must still be there.

It would not do her any good. It was as far as if it were the other side of a vast ocean. And now she could smell the burning metal, and above her the Phantom raised a red-hot cleaver. She strained against the straps but it was futile. Fear blossomed inside her like a fever. "The heat will cauterise the wound," he said conversationally. He had tied her up with her arms spread out, and her legs. A strap pressed her forehead down, another choked her neck. She couldn't move. She couldn't escape.

"Please," she said. "Please. Don't do it."

When she looked at his hands she could see the grey swirls

intensifying, moving in the red glare of the knife. "Don't–"

The cleaver, a butcher's tool, came down hard.

She had screamed. For a moment, joyfully, she lost consciousness. But it returned, too soon, far too soon, and then she cried, and the pain was horrifying, it was everywhere, everywhere but in one place.

He had cut off her right arm, just below the elbow.

And now he showed it to her, waving it in front of her face before throwing it away across the floor. She cried, she couldn't help it. She begged him to stop, or tried to. The sounds that came from her mouth were barely human.

"No more questions, Cleo? No more *investigating*, no more mystery-solving? I'm disappointed. You must have so much you want to ask me still."

She screamed. He said, "That's not a question."

The next time she was conscious he was pulling a needle from her arm. "This will help," he said.

He'd picked up a surgical blade. One of Viktor's. He played with it in front of her eyes. She could no longer think. Her whole being was fear, as pure as an animal's. She shook and tried to move away and there was nowhere to go. "Perhaps... an eye?" he suggested.

She tried to shake her head. She moaned. She tried to kick. Her whole being was shaking uncontrollably. "So I could see you better with it, my dear..." he said and laughed.

He reached for her and stroked her hair. His hand was very close to her eyes. She closed them, praying to whatever gods or spirits there were to hear her, but none came. His thumb stroked her closed eyes. "Left... or right? What fearful symmetry you have, Cleo."

Then he pressed, and pressed, and pressed, and the pain was worse than before, and she knew she was dying.

"Look," he said. There was a bloodied ball in his hand, and he was waving it before her. He had just injected her again, she didn't know with what. One of Viktor's potions... to keep her alive.

"What is a human?" he said. "How much can we reduce while we remain? Legs? Hands? Eyes and ears? What is left when all the outside appendages are taken out?"

Her one eye moved rapidly, uncomprehending. He threw the eyeball at the wall. It slid down, and there was a circle of blood where it had hit. "That is what I wish to find out, Milady. I am so glad you've agreed to help me."

She whimpered. She was reduced to nothing, a burning darkness, a sun flaming with pain. To live was to hurt, to suffer. Somewhere in the back of her mind Milady still existed, beyond the wall of torment, but she was dormant, hidden well behind, a tiny presence in the mindless pain.

"I want you to see what I see," he said, earnestly. Somehow that was more frightening than anything that had come before. His hand disappeared, returned...

Something green. It shone with its own internal light. "A fragment of a fragment," he said, and giggled. She tried to speak, to say, "No, please, please please don't don't d–"

His hand came down. His thumb pushed into the open socket of her empty eye.

She screamed.

"Another injection?" he said. He sounded irritated now. She felt a needle slip into her neck, then all feeling stopped.

"There," the Phantom said. "That's better, now."

His thumb, pushing... There was a scraping sound. No pain, but the feel of something hard moving, *grating* against her skull. "Soon," he said. "Soon you'll be able to see. *Really* see. It is a great gift I give you, Cleo."

She shivered. He ran one finger, lightly, down her cheek. "Hush now. Can you see? Can you see it yet?"

"You're crazy," she said, or thought she did, and he laughed. "What shall we do next?" he said. "Hmmm?" He seemed to give it some thought. In her head the alien object felt as if it were reaching inside her, as if a larva had been planted in her eye socket and was now emerging, questing out...

The Phantom said: "An ear, perhaps? Or a leg? Not your

tongue, my dear. I like to hear it when you voice your opinions – and you are ever so vocal…"

The cleaver again. When had it come into his hands? The man in the iron mask never smiled, never changed expression. "This is so much better than with corpses," he said softly. Then the blade came down again, above her knee.

FORTY-THREE
Grimm

Awakening. Pain. It came and went in waves; she rode them, cresting higher and higher. Thinking: *no more no more no more please please please no more kill me–*

Blinking her one eye. Darkness. Silence. The monster was hiding, was waiting to pounce. *Please please please don't–*

Calling on old gods of a place she had long forgotten and never believed in. But a child believes. Once again she was that child; alone and afraid in the dark, in the city, hiding from predators, fearing every footstep. Knowing they were coming, that you couldn't run forever, that sooner or later it would happen, and they–

His voice, in the distance. Speaking, the corresponding voice echoing strangely. Communicating with someone through a Tesla set, the little part of her mind that was not yet insane thought.

She couldn't move. And the pain was a part of her now.

Her leg was gone. So was her arm. She was no longer strapped in, in those two places. There was nothing left to strap in.

Something moved in the darkness and she almost screamed, but wouldn't, no, she wouldn't give him the satisfaction.

Only it was not the Phantom.

A familiar shape. Slithering quietly, cautiously, along the cold stone floor.

A familiar insectile head. The quiet hiss and whirr of gears. Grimm.

She closed her eye. When she opened it Grimm was still there, moving towards her. It raised itself up. Grimm's soft metal tongue hissed out, touched her skin like a kiss.

"Oh, Grimm," she said, or tried to. "Oh, Grimm."

Grimm's mouth found the first of the leather straps. Grimm's tongue licked it, and the leather hissed. Her little familiar was eating the straps. "Hurry," she whispered. "Hurry!"

The next time Grimm's mouth moved a drop of acid fell on her hand. She bit her lips until the blood flowed. She would not make a sound.

Beyond the small area of the surgery the voices were fading and she knew the Phantom would be coming back. "Hurry," she said, and then, with a final hiss of Grimm's tongue, her body was free, and her arm.

With a clumsy hand she loosened the neck strap, then the head. She was clawing, panting, desperately fumbling with the remaining strap, the one that had held bound both of her legs, and now...

She fought the strap and tried very hard not to look at the empty place where her leg had been.

She heard his footsteps. Grimm slithered away. Then she was free. She tried to stand and of course couldn't. She fell down on the hard floor.

The Phantom appeared. "What are you–?" he said, and then he laughed. She dragged herself forward, one-armed, her one leg kicking. Slowly she progressed, her one eye fixed on the coat lying a few feet away.

"You are like a strange new creature," the Phantom said. "And I have created you. Crawl, little fish. Where are you going?"

She kicked, and pushed, clawing her way one inch at a time, leaving a slimy trail of blood against the stone. He was striding towards her then, not hurrying, enjoying the wait.

She was almost there.

And then so was he, and he kicked her, and her ribs flamed in pain and she rolled from the impact–

Her body found the coat–

And there *was* something hard inside, a metal pipe, the Toy-maker's curious gun–

The Phantom's next kick found her head, broke teeth. Blood filled her mouth. She could barely see – his ghostly outline was above her, descending with a flash of metal–

A knife, descending–

She fumbled in the coat, one-handed, reaching for that inside pocket, and her fingers closed on the smooth cylinder of the gun–

The knife was coming down very fast–

She rolled, or tried to. The knife grazed her face, sliced a part of her ear–

She couldn't release the gun from the coat!

The knife rose, began to come down again–

She watched the expressionless iron mask and the blade, afraid, unable to think–

The knife whispered as it cut through air, towards her, and–

She fired, blindly, through the coat's material.

There was a burning smell.

The knife clattered to the floor.

The Phantom took a step back, and then another. He looked down.

On his chest, an explosion of grey. The moving shapes resembled nothing, suggested everything. They were volcanoes and hurricanes, earthquakes and floods. The grey flooded him, and she fired again, and he stumbled and fell to his knees.

He looked at her through the iron mask. He raised his arms, examined his hands. His fingers were melting, and he screamed. The grey engulfed him, like molten silver, burning.

The gun dropped from her fingers and she fell back, knowing she was dying, welcoming it. To die would be to never again experience pain. Dimly she was aware of Grimm beside her, Grimm's dry tongue on her cheek. "Oh, Grimm," she said, or wanted to. "It had all been–"

Then her eye closed, and she knew nothing else.

FORTY-FOUR
The New Translation of Lady de Winter

Darkness, cold, a blessed silence. She could no longer feel her body. Was she dying? Had she died?

A sense of calm, so wonderful. But something else, intruding. A feeling as though she was moving.

Or being moved.

She blinked an eye. She saw faces above her, as distant as moons. No longer afraid – she felt wonderful, in fact. So wonderful... She giggled, or tried to.

Voices, from an immeasurable distance: "Close to death– nothing we can do– the drugs won't work forever."

She could not distinguish between the voices, could not tell who was speaking. She tried to tell them she was fine, really, she was, but they wouldn't listen.

"Build– radical surgery– she wouldn't thank you– need her– go to– ridiculous– shock alone would–"

She could hear the words but they made no sense. She giggled again, then felt the world disappear.

... and reappeared again. The sense of moving intensified. Sounds in the distance, the motion of water, and she thought – we're crossing the Seine. Voices, speaking far away: "Why is she not dead?"

Another: "Injected."

"With what?"

The second voice was Viktor's. "My own modified Hyde formula."

"She should have died of the shock. And loss of blood." The voice, too, familiar. Colonel Xing – why were the two of them together?

"The Hyde formula is… rather special. It was very clever of him to use it. A great compliment to myself, really."

She would have shot him if she could.

"Still, even at the factory, I don't know if–"

"I know it well. I am sure we can–"

Across the river, and the air changed, and she smelled China-town. They're taking me to the Goblin factory, she thought. "Make me into a goblin," she said, and giggled, though no one seemed to have heard her.

"It would have been better to let her die."

"We need her still. She is our tool. She has always been our tool."

"People are not implements," Colonel Xing said. "We are not – *utensils*."

"Then I shall make her into one," Viktor's voice said, compla-cently.

The smell of tar. The smell of oil. The smell of machines and hot metal. Flashes in her mind of a phantom figure raising a knife. The smell of burning flesh… a hand on her head and she screamed. A voice: "Quick, give her another shot!"

Pain, penetrating into her neck. The flashes dissipated like a bad dream. "How do you say, please?" Colonel Xing, the tail-end of a conversation.

"A translation," Viktor's voice said. "Like a saint. Our Lady of Vengeance."

The hum of machines, the bellows of steam, the air thick with humidity and very hot, and now they were doing something to her leg.

But she no longer had a leg.

She couldn't see them. She tried to scream, tell them to stop, but no one heard her.

"She will be a child of the new age," Viktor's voice said, faint and far away.

"A monster–" Colonel Xing.

"We are all monsters," Viktor said cheerfully.

Then blackness. Then light. Another pain, this one in her arm. She could feel her leg – both her legs. It was a strange sensation. They were doing something to her arm.

"Not much I can do for the eye…"

"She would look fetching with a patch."

"The arm, now, is another matter again–" from Viktor.

"She will kill you if she could."

"So would many others. But she will obey the Council."

"We shall be late to the meeting."

"I do not trust the lizards."

"I do not trust the Jianghu. We have no choice."

"The what?"

"The Shaolin–Wudang coalition."

"You have strange customs."

"As do you."

"True. Can I trust you?"

"No."

"I didn't think so. Ours is a mutual distrust, yet we must work together…"

"We shall send our own people after him."

"As will the lizards. As will all the others. Of course. But you have tried before?"

"Yes…"

"And failed."

"Yes…"

"I heard Krupp is going to the meeting."

"The weapons man? The German?"

"Yes, and yes. Next year will be a hunting season…"

"You take too much delight in your work."

She felt her arm. The arm she'd lost. She tried to move it.

"Careful!"

"It's not loaded."

The bite of a needle again, and a numbing coolness.

"You are too fond of the needle, too."

"Stop telling me my business, colonel."

"She deserves better."

"We all do. Now step aside."

"Finish it."

"I would if you gave me the opportunity."

Her arm. What were they doing to her arm? It didn't hurt but the sensation was terrible, unnatural. "Careful, damn it!"

"She's stronger than I thought!"

Her arm broke the straps then, hit something – someone – and she heard a scream, and then a dull thud.

"Hold her still!"

Hands on her, and she struggled – she could smell their fear and didn't know why. They forced her head back and she kicked–

"Damn it, do it *now*!"

There was a sharp pain like an insect bite in her neck and her whole body went limp. They had given her another shot.

"Finish it!"

She tried to speak and couldn't. The world spun away. Then there was only darkness.

INTERLUDE:
Kai Wu Unrolls His Mat

For a long time after he had arrived in the city the voices were quiet. He had gathered a little of their history. They were weak, their vessel inactive for long periods of time. A human presence revived them, gave them strength, but only for a while. They were, he thought later, when he had learned of Tesla waves, a little like a man turning a dial in the hope of finding a working band. But their attempts were futile. They spoke of *transdimensional calibration* and *quantum effervescence* and *chrono-spatial matrices returning negative values* but mostly what he felt from them could only be described with a human term, and that was loneliness.

He knew that feeling well.

As time passed he became accustomed to the city. It lay in the conjunction of two great rivers, one of which was the Mekong. Above it towered mountains, high forbidding cliffs and thick forests where bears and tigers roamed. The city had many temples and a royal palace and a king, and was a vassal of Siam, but they spoke a different language, which was Lao.

Also spoken in the city were Chinese; Hmong; Karen; Hakka; there were many dialects and tongues and many different people. There were mountain people and lowlanders, Siamese merchants and Chinese traders, and here and there the people called franag or falang or Europeans. Once he saw something he had thought impossible – a lizard taller than a man, and walking upright, and dressed in clothes. It was dressed like a prince, was escorted by a retinue of farang and Lao. He had thought it one of the Emerald Buddha's illusions, but later found out it was not so, and that such beings did exist, and were very powerful.

He washed in the river and ate when he could. In the dry season he helped the farmers plant seasonal gardens on the banks, and build bamboo bridges across the river. He carried sacks of rice and flour for the Chinese merchants, interpreted for the Siamese, stole from the Hmong when they had something worth stealing. He learned the city, came to know its tiny stone alleyways, its hiding places and its night places, roaming from beyond the half-island of the rivers' confluence into the lands beyond.

The statue gave him lightness; he could see in the dark and leap across walls, could spin and kick and duck and run faster than any other child. He could pass unseen even in a crowded place. It was what the wuxia novels had called *Qinggong*.

There weren't many books but there was one Chinese merchant who sold fishing nets and tackle and sundry small items from Chung Kuo and he had a small library, and when Kai did small jobs for him he let the boy borrow a book, in lieu of pay. And so he continued to follow the adventures of the Shaolin monks and the Wu Tang Clan and the Beggars' Guild and their enemies, of assassins sent after evil emperors, of lovers fighting impossible odds, of the Wulin and Jianghu and the eternal battle between right and wrong.

Few noticed him. For a while he had the sensation of being watched, closer than was usual, by a decrepit old beggar whose single eye seemed a little too bright, but when he sought him out the man was gone, and no one could recall seeing him before or after. For a while he worked at the palace, cleaning up the elephants' dung, sweeping floors, watering the flowerbeds, helping the cooks or the gardeners or the monks. He was, in the words of one of the novels, unrolling his mat. He was settling in, making the city his home. For a short time, he was happy.

As he grew older he began to notice changes in himself. His skin grew thicker, coarser, a metallic grey. One day, scrabbling in the mud, his hand returned and a fingernail had fallen off. Another became loose the next day. He felt the change sweep over him, his old body shedding itself for something new. "What is happening to me?" he asked the statue.

There was a faint sense of amusement. *You asked to be made into a gun*, the voices said.

"I changed my mind," he told them, and had the mental impression of a shrug.

It is too late to undo what has begun.

His face, too, acquired a metallic sheen. It did not spread evenly, only affected one side of his face. The fallen nails were replaced with thicker, sharper versions, their colouring metallic, grey, and he felt as if he were a ghost that still, somehow, had substance.

You could be anything you want, the voices told him. *You could be king of all this land.*

"I want my father. He died for you."

He died for an inaccurate belief, the voices said. *It is unfortunate. Your race does not have the* – a concept, divorced from words – *to comprehend us, make sense of what we are.*

"What *are* you?"

A shifting series of wordless concepts, images, and he said, "What do you want of me?"

We wait, the voices said.

"For what?"

A sign. There is another in this world now. A child, but it is – and then a void, a gap where understanding lay.

He didn't know what they meant about the child. But he understood being alone.

Too long... the voices said.

For months after that he did not speak to the voices. He tried to be human, to eat and to drink and to think like a human. He watched the puppet shows that were popular at that time. He drank rice whisky (he was old enough now) and had his first hangover, though it passed swiftly. He watched the sun set over the river and the mountains. He gambled with the Chinese, and lost, and read the mulberry scrolls in the monastery's library, finding hints of a story about an impossible statue that spoke and drove people mad. For several months he became a monk, and wore the saffron robes, and felt peace.

He thought himself safe.

He was wrong.

Perhaps, he thought – much later – the statue itself was sending out a signal of some sort. Perhaps in its search it was also broadcasting – and it was possible others had devised some sort of machine that was able to pick up that signal. He had hidden the statue, though the statue could hide itself quite effectively. Kai had a little bamboo shack on the bank of the river and the statue was safely buried in the soft earth under the woven mat. And were anyone to find it, they would not see the Emerald Buddha – a flash of light, perhaps, like water moving in a stream, and as if in a dream they would turn away, their mind fogged by grey impenetrable clouds.

And yet they came.

The black-clad men. Chinese, and well trained. He was in the hut, watching the flow of the river, when they came. They had surrounded the hut. It was twilight, the sun had almost disappeared. There was chill in the air. They had guns.

There were four farangs with them.

He fought them. Desperation made him bold. Qinggong made him lithe and light. The change wrought in him made him strong – terribly strong.

But there were too many of them.

As he fought them he thought of his father, the silent attackers in Chiang Rai, men like these; he lashed out and his nails took out a man's throat and he watched the blood flow on the black earth. He leaped and descended and two more men were down.

"Don't kill him," he heard someone say.

Instead, they went for him with nets.

The nets were connected somehow, by a long wire, to an engine the men had brought with them. It belched steam and its cogs moved and current came through the wires and fed into the nets. He tore at them, but they were made of metal, and he couldn't break it. They caught him with long rods and ran electricity through the metal and made him scream.

"Search the hut."

"Yes, Manchu."

So their leader was a Manchurian. He swore at the man, telling him he'd kill him, and the man laughed. By then Kai was pinned back, caught in the webbing of their trap, and the electric current ran through him and pain blossomed everywhere.

"Little thief," the Manchu said. "You have been very lucky."

Two men returned from the hut. He saw, amazed and frightened, that they held the Emerald Buddha in their hands.

Help me! he shouted, mentally, at the statue.

The voices seemed distant, more confusing than usual. *Probability cluster skewered – approaching crisis point – geo-temporal coordinates suitable – confusion – executing long-term projection analysis–*

He said – pleaded – *They would use you!*

Design flaw – not tool – interference pattern–

He said, *Use me. I will help you. I will serve you.*

The Manchu approached the statue. He ran his hand lightly over the jade surface. "The Empress-Dowager will be pleased…" he said.

One of the farangs said something in one of the farang tongues.

"If I let her have it," the Manchu said, and laughed again. "Can *you* meet the price, Mein Herr?"

A blond, blue-eyed man, with skin darkened by the sun, said something in a language Kai didn't understand. The man sounded angry, but the Manchu just smiled. The blond man spoke again, sounding angrier still–

"No?" the Manchu said. "Very well." Then, as quick as a Wulin, a gun appeared in his hand and he fired. The farang fell to the ground, blood gushing from his chest. The other three farangs jointly took a step back, and the Manchu smiled.

"Or maybe I shall keep it..." he said. "Yes... it is a most attractive proposition..."

The three farangs exchanged glances. But they did not challenge the Manchu.

And now the man approached Kai. "Why were the Wulin transferring the statue to your father?" he asked conversationally. "Who did he work for? Who was he?"

"He was my father," Kai said.

"Why would they risk transferring the object?" the Manchu said. "What change were they expecting?"

"I don't know."

"Look at you," the Manchu said. "You are no longer human. You are nothing, dirt not fit for the poorest sweeper to brush away. I will enjoy dismantling you, piece by piece, in my lab. I'll find out what makes you tick–" and he took out a timepiece from a pocket and held it up. "You are a clockwork device," he said. "Nothing more. A machine made to serve another."

"My name is Kai," Kai said.

"You have no name. You are clockwork."

He made a gesture. The electric current increased suddenly and Kai screamed. The Manchu beamed down at him. "You are nothing," he said. "But I am fascinated–" and he bent down, peering at Kai's terrified face.

"Knife," the Manchu said. One of his men hurried over, placed a silvery blade in his hand.

Expense – waste – preserve – energy resources low – the boy would serve – the time is near–

Help me!

The first cut opened the side of his body. The Manchu reached *into* the gap, and Kai screamed as he felt the man's long-nailed fingers rooting inside him. "What are you made of...?" the man murmured. Slowly, he cut along Kai's arm, ran his finger along the cut, rubbed the thick blood between his fingers. "What has it made you into? You could be valuable to me yet..."

He was killing him, Kai knew. Slowly, methodically, and as a display for the others. Dissecting him the way a scientist would a frog, to see what secrets it held inside.

The next cut opened up his belly and for a moment he lost consciousness. When he opened his eyes again the man's hand was inside him again, and the man was wearing a pair of spectacles high on his nose. The pain was horrific, and the electric current was humming loudly, the very air vibrating with the current.

The man cut him, here, here, there, slowly at first, then with increasing fury. "What *are* you?" he roared at one point. "Why are you still alive?"

Kai didn't know. He wished he wasn't. But the man kept opening him up, kept cutting him until–

The power – most primitive – coal generator – can draw – will it be enough?

He felt the voices reaching out to him.

Make me into a gun, he whispered.

This has hurried the process…

He felt his body somehow manipulating the electric current, *drawing* it into himself. The Manchu jumped back. "What are you fools doing?"

"Sir?"

"Turn the machine off!"

Shouts, confusion – "It won't stop, sir!"

He was drawing in the power and the power was burning through him, burning him, but it was being controlled…

The power coursed through him and he felt himself changing–

He tore the webbing, as easy as spiders' webs. The men were firing at him. The bullets irritated him. He killed five of them before they realised he had moved. The others tried to run away. He pursued them, caught them, executed them. Several tried to run to the river. He let them. They would not come out alive.

Of the three remaining farangs two tried to flee and he tore out their throats. The last one standing tried to bargain with him. He could understand the man's language now and only wondered why he couldn't before, it was so simple. The man said, "I am authorised to offer you anything you desire. We shall give you papers, an estate, servants, wives, power. Join us."

He growled. The man stumbled, but straightened. "We can help you," he said softly. "We have scientists, people who could study you–"

"Like *he* studied me?" he roared, and the man nodded, once, as if at an acquaintance he had long been expecting to see. He stood very straight when Kai killed him.

Then there was only the Manchu.

PART IV
At the Insane Asylum

FORTY-FIVE
Charenton Asylum

She woke up to the wails of the insane.

A cold, stark room of bare stone: darkness outside the window, lights down below – she was on a hill, the windows barred, the door closed – locked.

The lights of Paris in the distance.

At least, she hoped it was still Paris.

Where was she?

What had happened?

Recollections trickling into her mind slowly, torturously. Weren't the Chinese said to have a special water torture?

The Chinese...

The Goblin factory.

What had they done to her there?

Darkness. She had been strapped to an operating table, and the Phantom was above her, and a butcher's cleaver came down–

His thumb pressing against her eye, the pain erupting like molten gold–

And something pushed *into* her, grating against the bones of her eye socket, and–

Like larvae, hatching, reaching out–

Something had settled inside her eye socket, something almost *alive*–

Her hand rose, but where her eye had been she encountered only a smooth, unbroken surface. Panicking, she grasped at it – it came away from her skin.

An eyepatch. She stared at it in her palm, traced the smooth leather with her thumb. She raised her other hand and the motion took her by surprise, a smooth metal appendage almost hitting her in the face.

Instinct made her close her fingers into a fist. But there were no fingers, and when she did and made to turn them, like a key, there was a burst of noise and the window exploded outwards, shards of glass falling away down to the grass.

High-toned screeches from outside, a cloud of dark shapes bursting upwards.

Bats.

The screams intensified beyond the walls. Milady paid them no mind. She stared down at her hand. She could see the arm reaching down to her elbow, but where her elbow had been the human arm terminated, and something else continued...

A cylinder, metal-smooth and light and strangely familiar...

Running footsteps beyond the door, a key rattling in the lock. Cool air blew in from the broken window and she thought – I did that, and felt satisfaction.

The door opened. Two women in nuns' habits. A syringe in one woman's hand.

Milady, smiling grimly – her new arm raised before her, aimed at the women: "Don't come any closer."

All she had to do was tell her brain to close her fingers, and turn...

Her beautiful new arm: they had given her a Gatling gun for the fingers she'd lost.

And someone had left it loaded.

She laughed then, and the two women backed away a step.

"You are very ill," the one with the syringe said. "This will help..."

"Stay away from me."

The women glanced nervously at the window, at Milady's extended arm. The Gatling gun – *her* Gatling gun – shone in the pale moonlight coming in through the window.

And now the women seemed to decide to obey.

Good.

"Where am I?" Milady said.

Flashes of memory – the under-morgue, the Phantom with his knife raised high, descending, descending...

She pushed herself away from the bed. Standing – both legs seemed to work fine.

What had they *done* to her?

The two women exchanged glances, didn't speak, and she knew they were no nuns–

A thin stiletto blade sliding out of the second woman's sleeve – the other ready with the needle – "Don't even think about it," Milady said. She tried bending. She was almost entirely naked, she realised – dressed in only a patient's cotton shift. She could see her leg.

Her new leg.

Metal had replaced flesh. She couldn't feel it – but it held her up, and when she tried to move the leg obeyed her, moving as it would have done before.

Even better than before.

"Where am I?" she said again.

The two women exchanged glances once more – the knife flashed – Milady's hand jerked once, twice, and the nun's habit was stained red, the knife cluttering to the floor. The screams beyond the door rose higher, a cacophony of laughter or rage, it was impossible to tell. Milady said, "Fly, little birds–"

The two women fled, the knifewoman holding her wounded arm against her chest.

She could stand. She could shoot. What more could she ask for?

The fragment of jade embedded in her cranium seemed to thud in her head. Suddenly dizzy, she sat down hard on the bed. When she closed her eye – eyes? – the room disappeared–

Was replaced with mists, and voices whispering, and she

seemed to be flying, cutting through the mists like a blade, heading towards–

She opened her eye – eyes? – she could no longer tell – and the mists were gone, and she was back in the empty room. She found the eyepatch on the bed and put it back on, and the thudding in her head quietened down. A wardrobe by the window, and she went to it. Her clothes hung there, pressed and cleaned. She dressed, one-handed and clumsy, put on a long black trench coat – felt complete again. Her dark shades were in the pocket of the coat – she left them there. This place was dark enough.

Quiet now. The wails had ebbed. Presences beyond the walls. She had a feeling she knew where she was. Somewhere she had never wanted to visit–

Black leather against her skin – inside the wardrobe was a mirror and she looked at herself – Milady de Winter, her face thinner than it'd been, an eyepatch like a pirate's over one eye, a machine gun in place of an arm.

She almost laughed. If only Barnum could have seen her, he would have offered her a job again in a second. She wondered what A– her first husband would have thought, if he saw her. Then she decided she didn't particularly care.

Voices whispering beyond her new eye. She could see through the jade, she realised. Eyes, then. But what she could see...

The Phantom's thumb pressing on her eye, the pain exploding in burning hot waves – the jade fragment pushing in, *adjusting* itself to her eye socket, sending out exploratory tendrils... no. She shook her head and the past disappeared. She was alive. That was what mattered now.

The door had been left open. She stepped through it.

A long corridor. Doors set in equal intervals. The cries and shouts came from beyond them. Cells, she thought.

A home for the insane.

She walked down the corridor. Grilles set into the doors, little observation windows. She peered through one:

A hunched man by the window, humming to himself. She did not recognise the tune. He had a jar in one hand and a spoon in the other, and he was laying a thin layer of powder on the windowsill.

Sugar, she thought. Flies buzzing around the man – she could smell him even from where she stood. As she watched the man, still humming, he put down the sugar bowl and the spoon and snatched at the flies. She stared, repulsed, as he caught and swallowed two in rapid succession. Milady drew back, but as she did the man's head snapped to the door and he hissed. She took a step back. The man's face appeared in the observation window.

"Have you come from *him*?" he said. "I have been waiting. I have been good. I have been hoarding flies to catch the spiders to draw the birds." He hissed again. "Their taste is in my mouth." His dark eyes looked into hers. "Help me," he said.

Instead she stepped away and heard wails rise from that cell, and the sound of a heavy body crashing, again and again, against the door, and a voice said, close in her ears: "He is beyond our help, but you are not. Come with me."

She turned, and her new gun arm was raised, but they had crept up on her and had come ready: a group of the nuns, with guns in their hands, blocking the end of the corridor, and standing close to Milady – too close – was the man who'd spoken.

"Lower your gun," the man said. "Please." His jowls shook when he spoke. He was the fattest man she had ever seen, and the most ostentatious. He wore fat rings over fat fingers with fat rubies and topaz and blood-dark emeralds set in the yellow gold, and his clothes were satin and lace and silk, and a hungry smile was stretched wide across his face, where fat red lips parted to reveal a fat red tongue. Not quite alive, she thought. But a semblance of life so remarkable it could have only been the work of the Council.

"I am Citizen Sade," the man said, and smiled. "Welcome to the Charenton Asylum."

FORTY-SIX
Citizen Sade

"Would you like to see some of the others?" the fat man said. She had thought Mycroft Holmes was fat, but Sade eclipsed the other man entirely, the way the Earth eclipsed the moon. "We do have such a *wonderful* collection here. They do… excite me."

Her gun arm was still raised. She said, "Step away from me."

"But of course." He raised his hand placatingly, and smiled, the smile as fake as the rest of him. "What am I doing here?" she said.

"The Council felt you should be kept out of sight, for a while," Sade said. "Until you recuperated sufficiently." He hadn't moved away. And his nuns were blocking her way… She said, "Well, I am recuperated."

"Of course. I will inform the Council…"

"I will go now."

The smile disappeared. "I am afraid that is not possible."

She tensed, getting ready to fire – the fat man said, "Wait."

She waited. He said, "Perhaps we've started on the wrong foot, as it were. We did not expect you to wake so soon–"

"You've been keeping me sedated," she said.

"On Council orders! Your body had suffered severe trauma. It was deemed prudent you were kept… comfortable."

"I'm still waiting," she said.

The fat man sighed. "I shall send word to the Council. In the meantime, why don't you come and wait in my chambers? I can assure you, they are most comfortable."

She watched him, his silent nuns behind him, and knew she was outnumbered. Slowly, she lowered the gun arm.

"Excellent," the man said. "Come! You look like you could do with a drink."

Not waiting for an answer, he turned – his wide back providing a tempting target.

The cries of the insane rose around them. She followed Sade down the corridor. He said, "They are disturbed by your presence here. You seem to upset them."

"Tough."

He laughed, a thick, gluttonous sound, but made no comment. He waddled as he walked. The corridor was long, the doors all barred. She peered into rooms as she passed: in one, a man sitting bound to a chair, a wide, grotesque smile carved into his face – Sade said, "One of the Council's men – he had an accident with a vat of chemicals. It altered his face and loosened his mind, the poor soul."

Howls came from another cell, animal sounds raising a chill up her spine. Looking inside she saw a young man with long, wild, matted hair prowling on all fours, growling when he noticed her. "Raised by wild animals," Sade said. "I am trying to teach him to speak but, alas…"

All the while the silent nuns watched her. At the end of the corridor Sade walked down a flight of stone steps and Milady followed.

Sade's quarters lay at the end of a second, shorter corridor, thankfully bereft of inmates. She could still hear their cries, but they were more muted here. "Please," Sade said. "Come inside."

When he pushed the wide doors open it was onto an opulent room of shadows: the dim light came from thick fat candles scattered everywhere amidst a confusion of cushions, divans and sofas. Low tables held sweets, xocolatl, opium pipes, chess boards, books, writing implements, whips, chains, keys, leather gloves, goblets, feathered headdresses, totems, maps, compasses, brushes, plates of deboned chicken, roast beef, glazed potatoes, parsnips and devilled eggs. In one corner of the room stood a camera tripod, in another a Tesla set. The walls, she noticed, were covered in paintings of a kind she had last seen in Paris's Chinatown: Toulouse-Lautrec's writhing, almost alive joinings of flesh and machines.

Sade said, "Please make yourself at home." He went over to the Tesla set, twiddled the knobs, spoke quietly, listened, and turned back to her. "The Council has been notified. Wine?"

"Coffee, if you have it."

He made a gesture with his fingers. One of the silent nuns approached, already carrying a silver tray on which sat a silver coffee pot and china cups. "Cream? Sugar? Brandy? Allow me." The nun put the tray onto a table, sweeping away a map of the Arctic region, a phallus-shaped pipe and a plate of half-eaten duck. One remaining eye stared up mournfully at Milady. Sade waddled to a nearby sofa, sank down, and set to mixing brandy, coffee, cream and sugar. Milady watched, fascinated. Then she said, "You are a machine."

Sade laughed. "The original me died in this place," he said. "It seemed only fitting that the new, improved me should run it. I have been a good servant of the Republic, after all. And I am not entirely what you think I am."

"Oh?"

"Watch," he said. From one of the nearby tables he lifted a curved, long-bladed knife. The blade was dulled with dried blood. Sade raised the knife and brought it to his chest. Slowly, smiling and licking his lips, he pressed the blade against the material of his shirt, parting it. His flesh – if that is what it was – was the colour of rotten teeth. It was covered in a criss-crossing network of old scars.

Sade pressed the blade against his skin, parting it. He gasped, and beads of sweat appeared on his upper lip. Milady watched, horrified, fascinated: unable to turn away.

Sade's flesh parted easily. What lay behind it...

She had seen the inside of people before, more than she had wanted to. And she had seen the inside of machines. But what lay inside Sade...

She saw silver-coloured bones, the traces of a skeleton not entirely that of a human being. She saw intestines, organic glistening entrails and from inside the exposed belly came the harsh, sickening stench of rotting organic matter, and she saw a heart that was half-alive and half-machine, an enormous, engorged device beating steadily, circulating blood through that weird, internal landscape of metal and flesh... The blade was almost all the way down to Sade's waist now and his enormous belly flapped open and the stench from inside was suffocating and she said, "Enough. Please, enough."

The man's eyes were open and his face flushed and he smiled. He put down the knife. "Take a good look," he said. "I am something new. The Council needed volunteers, or conscripts, or both. I was both."

"What did they do?" she said – whispered – and then she thought – Viktor.

"They took my dying brain," Sade said. "My brilliant, lustful, delightful old brain, and they put it into a new vehicle, and they built me a new body, a human enough body to house a mind such as mine." His thick fingers reached for the open flap and pulled it closed. His thumb ran up the cut and, where it touched, the skin sizzled and hissed and the smell of it was like roasting meat. It closed where Sade touched, leaving a new, long scar. He gasped again as the last of the cut was closed, and the new scar stood dark against his skin, already fading to become just one more amongst the many. "I can assure you, all my parts are fully functioning." His eyes sought hers, and his tongue snaked out, fat and bloated. "*All* my parts, Milady de Winter."

A sense of unreality stole over her then: suddenly, it was all too much – her own changed body, the asylum, the bloated corpse that sat before her, talking, all the while looking at her with that hungry, terrifying look. Sade said, "Coffee?"

She took the proffered cup. The drink was sweet, laced with

brandy, strong. It made her feel better. She said, "How long have I been… asleep?"

Sade shrugged. "A few months," he said.

"*Months?*"

He only shrugged again. She drank the coffee. It was very sweet. Sweet, and–

"You kept me sedated," she said, struggling to get the words out. Her body felt weak, unresponsive. The cup fell from her fingers, crashed on the thick heavy carpet without a sound.

"I had to study you," he said. "You fascinate me, Milady. I had to have you… for my collection."

Two of the nuns had materialised beside her. She had not felt their approach. "You never called the Council," she said, or tried to. Sade shook his head sadly. "Oh, no," he said. "I could not let you get away. You must forgive me, but–"

Her eyes, closing. *Both* her eyes. Mists behind her eyelids, and the whispering voices of the dead. The last words she heard were Sade's: "Take her to the examination room."

FORTY-SEVEN
The Sound of Drums

Flying through mists, her eyes throbbing – insidious green jade spreading through her brain, shoots of green taking root – she must have been dreaming, must have been asleep – drugged, she thought. Sade had drugged the coffee.

And yet she was awake – alive – and this was, somehow, real, and she was flying, flying through the clearing mists: they parted before her.

The air thrummed, a sound like a physical sensation invading her mind. Around her the dead whispered, talking softly of lives gone by. A silver river snaked down below – she was descending lower, above her a full moon cast silvery light. The air was humid, tropical. Two worlds juxtaposed, this one and the next – one seen through her remaining eye, and one through a haze of green jade…

The river fled ahead and joined another, and in the place they met a half-island rose like a green-shelled turtle, and on top of the shell was a city.

She saw a temple rise in the distance, its dome shining in the silver light of the moon. The sound – the beat of a drum – echoed inside her, a vibration of force running through her bones.

Flying over narrow cobbled streets, houses of dark wood and bamboo, lanterns hanging in doorways, shadows scurrying – going lower still, until she came to the gates of the temple.

Saffron-robed monks walking in procession – candles held before them, shaved heads reflecting the moon. Walking around the temple, slowly, while the drum beat – she raised her head and saw it, on top of a tower, a giant drum the size of an ox, beaten by two monks – with each beat the sound fled across the city, a human-made sound of thunder. The beat worked itself into her bones, her soul – the monks walked in silence, slowly, the candles held before them, a procession of lights.

Singing coming from inside the temple. She walked slowly across the courtyard, feeling like a ghost. Through a green of haze, the ghosts – silver strands and the white of mist and she thought – this is what it does, this thing, this *device – it records the dead*.

Why?

The sound of chanting, a reedy old voice singing inside, the drum beating, beating, and she climbed the steps up to the temple and stood a moment between the columns before going inside.

What – who – waited inside? She tensed, and it seemed to her that, back in the waking world, her body was shivering, and sweat was forming on her body, as if she were trying to fight an illness. She shook her head, and stepped into the hall of the temple.

Four elderly monks sitting cross-legged on a carpeted floor. It was very hot – a fat mosquito flew lazily in tracing figures of eight, as if drunk on the heat and humidity. The carpet worn from countless bare feet. A green jade statue rising ahead – a lizardine Buddha, looking at her with amusement.

She knelt down on the carpet. No feeling in her new leg but it obeyed her easily. The monks paid her no attention. The chanting continued, the air smelled of incense and sweat and gun oil.

Gun oil… she looked down at her arm and the Gatling gun shone silver in the light. She ran a finger, lightly, across her arm. Then she waited.

The drum beating like a heart – her heart. The ghosts of the dead whispered around her. She closed her eyes, giving in to the rhythm of the drums. She began to hear voices, babbling. Somewhere nearby. They said things like: *Compilation of bio-data records approaching fifty percent* and *quantum pattern combination incomplete* and *attempt to locate source fail!* and *calibrating trans-dimensional gateway penetration routines* and then another voice, a human one or mostly so, said, "Shut up!"

She opened her eyes.

Standing between the four elderly monks was a… was a man.

Mostly a man.

He was a grey armour, a hybrid of human and machine – complex shapes of silver darted across his skin, forming and re-forming, their patterns vastly complex, hinting at unsolved mysteries – his eyes were dark, his hair cut short, his hands were weapons. She thought – he is as beautiful as a gun.

The man, paying no heed to the monks, said, "Manchu!"

A hunched figure crawled to the man's feet. "Master," it said.

"Have you made the arrangements?"

"Everything is ready, Master."

She stared at the man, that beautiful, dangerous *thing*, like her a combination of human and machine. *The Man on the Mekong*, she thought. She stared at the jade statue of that alien, lizardine Buddha. The voices rose again, penetrating her mind: *Geo-temporal relocation desirable – source of quantum burst unknown – entity nascent – trace patterns inconclusive–*

A sense of sadness, a deep, ancient loneliness that almost overwhelmed her. The Man on the Mekong said, "Do be quiet. Manchu, prepare the boat for departure."

"Yes, Master."

The hunched figure slithered away. The man stood silently for a long moment. His eyes, dark as the heavens, were populated with jade stars. He raised his head, looked around, his face revealing sudden doubt. The monks continued their chanting, the drum continued to beat and Milady's heart beat with it.

She found herself looking into his eyes.

He took a step back, then held himself still. He was as still as a statue, as still as a gun waiting to be fired. He said, "Are you a ghost?"

She opened her mouth to speak, but no sound came out of

her mouth. The voices babbled in the background about *establishing contact protocols* and *rerouting physicality* and *lunar orbit station checksum negative*, whatever any of it meant. The man said, "They are mad, you know."

She tried to speak again, but her voice was gone. "They send assassins after me," the man said. "Sometimes I wish they would succeed."

She stepped towards him, each silent footstep echoed by the drums. The ground seemed to shake beneath her. The monks continued to chant. Her eyes were still on his. His eyes were the deepness of space, and filled with the tiny, distant lights... "I am going from here," the man said, very softly. She stood close to him. When she reached out it was with her gun arm. His hand rose too, a metal hand, and clawed. They stood that way, not touching, not speaking, and the drum beat like a clock.

"Tell them..." he said. "Tell them that–"

Then his head moved back, his eyes shifting from hers, looking beyond her, and his eyes widened – "Get back!" he said, and then he *pushed* her, or *at* her, and she flew back from him, rising, dissipating like mist, through the roof of the temple, and for a brief moment looked down and saw the river alive with lights, an endless procession of candles floating serenely down the river, and a dark steamboat moored to a wharf–

She rose and the mists swallowed her and the drum beat and his voice echoed in her ears, a warning, and though she fought the pull it dragged her back, back into her body and she woke up, covered in cold sweat, in a dark red room, and an enormous, grotesque figure hovered above her.

FORTY-EIGHT
Escape from the Insane Asylum

Sade grinned, thick lips like overripe blackberries. In one hand he held a goblet, in the other a thin, surgical blade. A couple of the silent nuns were holding Milady, busy securing her to a rope hanging from a hook in the ceiling. She heard Sade say, "Hurry up, I want to start the examination–"

Milady let herself fall, her body becoming heavy and unresponsive. The two nuns faltered, reached for her–

She rolled, swept their legs underneath them. Her new metal leg rose, descended – crushed one of the women's kneecaps. The woman rolled on the floor, screaming, holding on to her leg – Milady aimed at the other woman's head, felt the nose smash. She rose, grinned, extended her gun arm–

Sade's smile faltered, then returned. "I did not expect you to wake so soon," he said.

She shot him. The Gatling gun barked, bullets smashing into the fat man's belly. Sade looked down, his smile gone, a confused expression on his face. Slowly, he reached down. His finger found a hole, pushed through. He brought it out again, smelled it, then put it in his mouth and sucked. He rolled his finger slowly in his mouth, then at last pulled it out, examined the nail for a moment, then let it drop. "I'm not that easy to kill," he said.

He picked up the goblet he had dropped. He took a swig of

wine. The wine flowed down his throat and out of the holes in his chest and stomach, staining his already-stained clothes an even darker red. Milady watched, repulsed, horrified. "Not the best vintage," Sade said. "Nevertheless, a shame to waste."

He threw the goblet at her. It hit her on the side of the head and her missing eye flared in green pain. She kicked, aiming for his kneecap, but he caught her leg easily, grinned, and made to break it.

She jumped, using his hands as leverage, rose high and did a back-flip. Sade said, "Impressive."

How did she do it? She didn't know. A new leg, a new arm – but was it Viktor's surgery or the jade in her body that did it? She didn't know and right then it didn't matter.

"Being a sportsman," Sade said, "I'll give you a head start." He turned away from her ponderously and, from a niche in the wall, picked up an enormous, ancient sword. He waved it experimentally, slashing the air with the dull-coloured blade, and laughed. "Oh, Milady de Winter!" he said. "You make me feel alive again."

She ran.

Sade roared behind her, booming out a laugh. She burst out of the room and found herself in a windowless corridor. Somewhere underground, she thought. She had to find a way up, to the surface. The corridor was dark. As she ran ghostly figures materialised at the end.

Nuns.

Nuns with guns.

She raised her arm, clenched the fingers that were no longer there, a half-turn as if turning a key in a lock, and the Gatling gun barked fire. One of the nuns dropped, the others returned fire. Milady threw herself on the floor, fired again. A noise behind her – Sade lumbering after her, the great sword swishing through the air. *They put a madman in charge of the madhouse.*

She rolled, jumped, was suddenly at the end of the corridor – her foot lashing out, the Gatling gun arm slamming into heads, hands – the nuns dropped. Milady snatched up a fallen gun and kept running.

Stairs. She ran up them, into the dark level where Sade's quarters had been. Shouts behind her, gunfire, Sade's bellowing laugh. She should have gone up, but knew they would be waiting up there… She could hear the cries of the insane, agitated, carried down from their cells above.

She turned from the staircase, and once again entered Sade's quarters.

A sickly smell in the air, opium and hashish and candles and burnt wax and the sharp tang of cleaning fluids, though the place was a sty. A rack of pork ribs sat on a plate surrounded by glutinous sauce the colour of blood. Flies buzzed over the food. The same map of the Arctic region, the same cuffs and whips and glasses of old wine – she needed something, something she could use – but what?

From behind, snatches of conversation – "Where did she go?"

"She didn't come upstairs, we would have seen her."

"My quarters? The cheeky girl." That laugh again. She hated that laugh. She was going to choke it out of him if it killed her.

If she didn't die before she had the chance.

Searching the room, searching for weapons – a door half-hidden in the wall, unmarked. She tried the handle but the door was locked.

She kicked it open.

Darkness, the temperature a few degrees cooler. Behind her – "Milady! Yoo-hoo!" She shut the door behind her, waited for her eyes to adjust to the gloom. Nothing there – through the green jade that had become her eye she saw rough-hewn stairs cut into the stone, leading down–

"Where are you, my little bird?" – from behind the door.

Trapped.

She could make a stand right here, or she could go back down. She wondered what the stairs led down to, then decided there was only one way to find out.

When she followed them, the stairs led down to a hallway and three doors. The ground was the same rough stone. The air was cooler here. She looked at the doors:

Wine Cellar.
Operating Theatre.
Storage.

She'd had enough of wine and had no wish to go back to the second of the three.

She chose *Storage*.

"Leave my stuff alone!" a petulant voice, coming down the stairs.

Milady, looking at Sade's storage room, the jade casting a green glow over everything. "My, my," she said, quietly, and smiled. It felt good to be smiling again.

"We're not so different after all!" she called out. A heavy body crashing against the door. "Come out, little bird!"

"Not yet," she said, but quietly. Surveying the room, she felt like a kid on her birthday – though her birthdays had never been as good as this:

Machine parts, automaton parts – loose arms, loose legs, a brace of fingers – crates of bullets, a mounted cannon, curved and straight swords, a row of dusty books, miniature Tesla sets, knives, handguns, chemicals in vats, a few bottles of vintage wine, strange looking goggles, a medicine cabinet as large as a wardrobe, and there in the corner...

She said, "Beautiful," and went for the small crate marked *Explosives*.

"Ready or not, here I come!" Sade roared.

"Be ready in a moment, dear," she said, and helped herself to what she needed. She almost liked Sade then. He was a man of great appetite, and he kept a well stocked larder – for all eventualities.

When he burst through, roaring and waving the sword, she turned and shot him again, but it was little use, and he laughed. His bulk blocked the doorway. "Little bird," he said, "it's time for your medicine."

She needed to get past him. But how? He grinned, and came closer. She said, "Wait."

"Yes?"

Nothing came to mind so she kicked him between the legs instead – her new metal leg delivering a blow that would have felled a lesser man. But Sade was no longer a man.

He grunted, remained standing. The look he gave her was almost pitying. He reached one fat, meaty hand towards her, the fingers curling to grab her, and she almost screamed. Instead she pushed herself towards him.

They came together, her body against his bulk, taking him by surprise. She held on to him, one arm around his neck, and her gun arm snaked up and came to rest under his chin at an angle. "Want to dance?" she said. "Drop the sword."

He dropped the sword. "Careful now, little bird," he said. "Citizen Sade is not that easy to kill."

Her head was resting in the crook of his neck. She whispered, "But I don't want to kill you."

She felt him lick his lips. "What do you have in mind?"

"Let's step back out of the room," she said. "Slowly."

It was a precarious position and either one of them could change the balance in a single moment. She hoped he would go along.

He did. "I love to dance," he said. "And dancing with you, my lovely..." Slowly, bodies held together, they eased out of the room. "Turn," she whispered, and they did, until his back was to the storage room and hers to the staircase–

"My guards are waiting at the top," he said. "You won't get away. We can resolve this peacefully – I'll notify the Council–"

She felt his body twist even as he spoke – his hand, curling into a fist, caught her on the side of the head, rocked her away, and then a blade was flashing in his hand, a small surgical instrument that must have been hidden up his sleeve, and it came whispering towards her face–

She raised her arm to ward it off. It was the human arm and the knife cut through flesh. The pain burned through her – bright blood dripping to the ground, and Sade grinned. "I'll suck it right off your bones," he said.

She fled.

In her coat pockets the little birthday packages waited, and she dropped two down below and another when she reached the top, where the nuns waited. She fired, wondering how many rounds she had left. Not many. She hoped they would be enough. They fired back, and she had no choice but to charge through the open door, back into Sade's quarters, sending tables and chairs and maps and pipes and roast chicken to the floor, just trying to get away, get through the waiting nuns–

One came at her with a syringe and Milady turned and grabbed the woman's arm and broke it clean – a scream, and then she was out of the door and climbing the stairway to the cells.

Two more birthday presents in Sade's quarters, another one on the stairs – a bellow behind her – "No more games, Milady!"

The wails of the insane filled this floor. She passed locked cells and shot the locks, and the inmates of the Charenton Asylum came out of their cells and glared around them – the smiling man and the man who ate flies and the one who thought he was a wolf – and then the attacking nuns came into view and halted, and the released inmates, as if scenting blood, turned as one to look at them.

"Get out of here!" she shouted at them, but they only had eyes for the nuns. She didn't wait. She tossed more of the small packages into the emptied cells and when she reached the one that had been her own she went in. The window was still broken. A moon glared outside and a cloud of bats, frightened by the noise, were screeching as they flew over the roof. She kicked the bars.

Her new, more powerful leg, metal hitting metal, bent the bars. She kicked, again and again. Behind her, screams, gunshots, Sade's voice crying, "Animals! Back to your cells!"

Her smile was grim. She kicked, panting with the effort, and suddenly the entire panel of bars fell away from the window and crashed to the ground below. She went to the window, pushed herself up. The door behind her crashed open and Sade, bloodied and insane, filled the doorway. "Never!" he roared.

For a moment she was suspended on the windowsill, a dark shadow crouching, her head turned to him, her coat flapping in the breeze. They stared at each other. "They should have closed this place years ago," she said, softly. Then she smiled, and blew him a kiss, and as he came charging into the room she slid through the window and fell.

The ground came rushing up at her and she rolled with the impact, her breath knocked out of her. She rolled down the slope of wet grass and behind her the asylum stood, dark and forbidding and filled with screams. When she came to a stop she just lay there, for a long moment, getting her breath back. Then she stood up. Behind her the sound of gunshots and screams continued. She saw inmates come spilling out of the doors of the asylum. She heard Sade bellowing. Ahead of her was the gate, wrought iron, and beyond it freedom. She smiled and walked away from the asylum, her coat flapping in the wind, and as she did her hand reached into her pocket and found the Tesla transmitter she had picked up.

She pressed the button, still walking away.

Invisible waves travelling from her to the small packets she had distributed around the building... their own Tesla receivers picking up the signal, initiating a charge, and–

The heat of the explosion came rushing at her back, throwing her forward, and for a moment she thought she was flying. Then the sound followed, multiple explosions joining into one giant booming wave of heat and sound and flame, and she rolled and came back to her feet and was through the gates, and when she turned the Charenton Asylum was a giant fireball on the hill, and dark shapes were streaming away from the fire and fled down the hill, and it took her a moment to realise they were rats, abandoning at last their ruined home.

She reached back into her coat pocket and brought out her shades, and put them on, and the flames reflected in the dark glass. Then she smiled, once, and walked away, towards the lights of Paris in the distance.

The Return of the Phantom

Home was dark and cold, the gas lamps in the street outside whispering like grief-stricken relatives by a hospital bed. She let herself in, closed the door behind her, took a deep breath.

She was very tired.

In the fireplace, Grimm, dozing on long-dead coals. Milady knelt down, put the palm of her hand against the mechanical insect's head. The metal was warm. At her touch, Grimm's eyes opened. After a while Milady stood up.

She went to her bedroom. She undressed, went to the bath and ran the taps, adding salts and perfumes and soaps into the water until the foam threatened to grow out of control. While she waited for the bath to fill she looked into the full-length mirror. Slowly, she examined herself.

Scars, old and new. Without the eyepatch her eyes were mismatched, one dark, one a bright jade-green. She stared wonderingly at her new arm. The gun was light-weight, remarkably so. She looked at the place where her human arm ended and the machine gun began. The join was seamless.

The arm aroused strange feelings in her. With only five fingers she was clumsy – it was hard to grasp things, hard to dress, but the machine gun arm felt, somehow, as much a part of her. She stroked it with her remaining arm and decided she needed new rounds of ammunition to be put in.

Her leg, too, fascinated her. The same light material, with perfect joints, and somehow it obeyed her brain's commands – she raised it, kicking, then stood on it and pirouetted. She stood still and stared at her naked self in the mirror. Thinner, with a few new scars, her face gaunter than it'd been, but she was still herself, for all that. She was Milady de Winter, and she was still alive.

And she was armed.

Smiling faintly, she went to the bath and lowered herself slowly into the hot water. The water soothed her, bath salts at first burning, and then calming, her wounds. She closed her eyes – somehow that alien green jade could be controlled, which was another strangeness – and soon, without quite realising it, she fell asleep.

In the mist were the dead. Their voices called out to her. She saw Tom Thumb's face form in the mist, smiling at her sadly, puffing on a cigar. The smoke from the cigar rose and wreathed Tom's face and, slowly, it was Tom himself who became smoke, or fog, and blew away in an unseen breeze.

For just a moment the mists parted and she could see them, could see the dead: shambling corpses streaked with silver, snakes of molten silver-grey swirling across their bodies, and there was something beautiful about them, and precious, as if they were lives salvaged, not lost. They were walking along a river, but when she looked closer the river was merely a larger snake of the same silver-grey material and the dead were absorbed into it and it became a spiral that grew distant and at last disappeared…

Then there were cold stone walls around her and moss grew over the surface and she came to a door and she knew again where she was: this was the under-morgue, Containment Section: the place where they kept the most dangerous of their experiments, and those deemed too dangerous, by the Council, to ever be set free.

Iron Mask section – and suddenly she was afraid.

There was a sound coming from beyond the cell door. It took her a moment to recognise it as laughter.

The fear grew in her like a poisonous fungus, and for a moment she couldn't move. The laughter in the cell grew in volume and frenzy then, abruptly, stopped.

The silence was complete.

Containment Section, the under-morgue: she knew what lay beyond that door, though that was impossible – wasn't it?

She had killed him herself. She had watched him die – surely, surely she had watched him die?

Figures came walking down the corridor. Ghostly, they appeared, as if not quite real – Viktor, and three armed guards. When they walked past her it was as if *she* were the ghost. She realised they couldn't see her, and then thought, with some relief: *This is just a dream.*

Viktor went to the door and slid a small panel aside. He peered into the room, then brought out a small metal device from his lab coat. An Edison recorder, portable. He began murmuring into the device. "Subject shows extreme resilience. During the last week alone the changes in his physiology have been astounding. When first captured, subject appeared close to death, infected with the…" a pause, then Viktor said, with apparent distaste, "the so-called Grey Menace, at an advanced stage and shot through with Houdin's –" another short pause – "codename the Toymaker's experimental vaccine, delivered by means of a projectile weapon employed by Council agent de Winter."

The Phantom was alive.

She felt her throat constrict with bile. Her fingers curled into a fist and she wanted to put it in her mouth, to stifle the screams that wanted to come. Viktor said, "The subject's mind appears beyond repair. Yet his body, remarkably, is adapting. When first captured, subject had assumed an almost entirely inhuman appearance, particularly in the elongated shape of the skull and facial features, partially disguised by the subject by use of an iron mask. Now, however…"

Viktor paused again, and cleared his throat. There was silence from beyond the door. The three guards stood motionless. "Perhaps the effect of the Toymaker's vaccine helped to stabilise the subject's deterioration. But I suspect it is a foreign agent responsible for the change. The subject now exhibits a remarkable ability to alter his physiology at will, a mimicking as that evidenced in more primitive life forms... Physical strength is increased as well. As to the subject's mind, however..." Again, Viktor stopped. "Evaluation period extended by order of the Council, transferring subject to experimental sub-station Zero, Charenton Asylum." He pressed a button on the recorder, then slipped it back into his pocket. Speaking through the panel in the door, more loudly: "De Sade's looking forward to examining you, Tômas."

A growl from inside, then a burst of laughter. Viktor motioned to the guards. He put his palm against the door, waited.

The door slid open.

Milady stared, horrified, at the Phantom.

Gone was the mask, gone were the inhuman features of the face. The man who occupied the cell was handsome, brown-haired, and shackled to the floor and walls with heavy metal chains. "Viktor," he said. "It's good to see you."

Viktor made a jerking motion with his head. "Take him," he said. Milady watched as the three guards entered the cell...

The Phantom raised his head and looked directly at her. She took a step back, and he smiled, revealing white, even teeth. His eyes were the colour of green jade. *Stop!* she wanted to shout, but they couldn't hear her, couldn't see her. She wasn't really there. By inserting the fragment of jade into her eye, she suddenly realised, the Phantom had turned *her* into the lens of a camera obscura.

His eyes were on hers, and his smile became a leer, and she could only watch as his skull began to shift and change, and teeth grew as his mouth extended–

Viktor, stop! but there was no one to hear her, and the guards were reaching for the chains and setting the Phantom loose when he rose, in one smooth, too-fast motion, and his hands had become talons, and he ripped the first man's face off and plunged his hand into another's belly before they even knew what had happened. The third guard raised his gun to fire... but the Phantom took it from him, like taking a toy gun from a child, and bashed him on the side of the head with the butt of the gun. He stood there, and his features slowly melted, the skull contracting, until the mild-mannered, handsome man he had once been stood there again – but this time he was unshackled and holding a gun, and a very frightened Viktor was backing away slowly as the Phantom advanced... The Phantom's jade eyes were on Milady's and he smiled, and said, "Sweet dreams, Cleo. I'll see you soon..." With one swift motion he had reached Viktor, and grabbed the scientist by the scruff of the neck. "Let's go, doctor," he said. "My ship awaits, and time and tide..." But she could not hear the rest, and the fog seemed to rise around her, flowing from the walls of the under-morgue, and the Phantom soon seemed a distant figure at the end of a white corridor, a cowering Viktor by his side, and then they were gone, or she was gone, and there was nothing but the mist, and the voices whispering far away about *three-dimensional space-time constraints* and *quantum permutations scan* and *checksum errors* and then they were all gone and she was floating face-down in a white, feathery sea, and it was rocking her, gently at first and then harder, and harder, until she thought she would drown and, crying out, opened her eyes.

FIFTY
The Message

"You look well," the Hoffman automaton said.

She had woken up from restless sleep and the sense of drowning, to see the hulking figure of her silent coachman standing above her.

Her presence was requested down below.

Now she sat before the Quiet Council. They were ranged before her like a shadowed fan; only the Hoffman automaton could be seen. How much do they know? she wondered uneasily. Her hand rose to her face, encountered the smooth leather of her new eyepatch, hiding the alien green jade below.

"We were very pleased with the outcome of the operation," the Hoffman automaton said. Milady, glancing down at her strange new arm, wondered which one he meant. "*Most* pleased."

She waited him out. The Hoffman said, "What happened at Charenton, on the other hand, is regrettable."

She couldn't hide a smirk. The Hoffman said, "De Sade's work for us is of a high importance. You destroyed–"

"I was kept *prisoner*!"

"You were kept *safe*," the Hoffman said.

"He wanted to experiment on me!"

"Be that as it may." The Hoffman sighed. "De Sade's... enthusiasm sometimes gets the better of him. Nevertheless, his work for us is of the highest importance. The unfortunate incident you caused will set us back significantly."

"I didn't mean to burn down the asylum," she said, trying to sound contrite. "It was… an accident."

"Rebuilding Sade will take months!"

She shrugged. "Why bother?"

"Remember your place, Milady de Winter. I won't tell you again. There are secrets to which you have no access, schemes of the Council in which you have no part. De Sade is our tool – just as you are." The Hoffman waved a hand. Artificial eyes bored into hers. "Enough," he said. "We have use of you yet. Doctor Von F– tells us you are fully recovered?"

It took her a moment to realise he meant Viktor. Anger, so strong it threatened to render her mute, but she said, "I lost–"

"You lost!" Hoffman said. "What did you lose, Milady de Winter? A body appendage or two? A human is no less a machine than we are. Parts can be replaced."

She stared again at her arm. Her new arm. The metal glinted in the dim light of the cavern. "You performed the task set before you," the automaton said, "and you did it… well enough. Are you… unsatisfied?"

She stared at him, mute at last. She stared down at her arm, stroked it. The tips of her human fingers on the warm, light metal of this strange, deadly new arm… Six months, she thought. Six months in a hospital bed, the hospital in question being an old, secretive, insane asylum. No, she wanted to say. No, I am not bloody satisfied.

But she kept mum. Fragments of her dreams came back to her, teasing, green dead fingers reaching into her scalp… "Where *is* Viktor?" she said.

As if eager to answer her, the doors of the Council chamber banged open. The figure of a man lurched in, face bloodied, clothes torn. Viktor – and this sight of him made her the happiest she'd been for a long while. Viktor fell down to his knees. His long, bony face was raised, his eyes white, staring at the shadowed Council. "He's gone!" he said. His eyeballs seemed to shudder crazily, like a compass which had lost its bearings. "Tômas – he's escaped!"

Silence greeted his words. Milady, sitting in her chair, stroking her Gatling gun arm. She hadn't dreamt it after all. Before her, the Council seemed to draw deeper into the shadows. At their head, the point of the arrow, the Hoffman's face was impassive. "Explain yourself," he said.

"Gone," Viktor said. "Gone, gone! He killed the... he killed... the guards... and he took, he took..." He looked to Milady then, his eyes pleading. She smiled at him. There was nothing warm in that smile. "He made me take him outside..." Viktor whispered.

The Hoffman said: "And yet you *live*?"

She smiled again. She was, she realised, enjoying this. It was hard to tell if the Hoffman's question sounded incredulous, or disappointed.

"He told me... he sent me to... to deliver a message. Tômas said..."

"He is going after the primary object."

"Yes." Surprise in Viktor's voice. The Hoffman slowly nodded his mechanical head. "Leave us," he said.

"But... I don't..."

"Go."

Viktor stared at the automaton. His eyes shifted to Milady, found no sympathy there. Slowly, he nodded. "I need medical attention," he said.

No help was forthcoming. Slowly, the wounded scientist turned and began crawling towards the doors. Milady said: "Doctor, heal thyself..."

The look he turned back on her was full of hatred.

FIFTY-ONE
Onwards to Vespuccia

When Viktor was gone the chamber was silent. Milady, staring at the unseen faces in the shadows, said, "You let him escape."

The Hoffman said: "I beg your pardon?"

She said, "You wouldn't know how."

His silence was an answer in itself. She said – demanded – "Why?"

"Tômas still has his uses," the Hoffman said.

"I killed him! He should be dead!"

"He is not easy to kill. Neither are you, Milady."

"Why did you let him go?"

"He escaped."

"I want to know!"

"You will know what we want you to know," the Hoffman said, dispassionately. "But very well. A month ago we received a communiqué from the Man on the Mekong. He wishes to make the trade."

"With France?"

"With whoever bids the highest," the Hoffman said. "The primary object in his possession is a key, a thing of infinite value. While you were... resting, several expeditions were sent to locate the man in the hope of retrieving the object. We believe he was residing in a city deep in the Mekong Valley, in the lands of the Lao, named Luang Prabang. Unfortunately, such attempts as were made had... failed."

She thought of her dreams again, the giant drum echoing in the night, the thousands of lights floating down the river, and a man preparing to depart in a steamer, the jade statue of a lizard keeping guard... She said, "He is moving."

Was that surprise in the Hoffman's voice? "Yes," he said. "His message says he has decided to hold an auction for the primary. He has chosen the location well... He would not be easy to find."

"And so you let Tômas escape? You would use him to hunt the Man on the Mekong?"

"He is so very good..."

"I'm better."

"Indeed, Milady." A small smile played on the Hoffman's rubbery face, and then she understood: two sets of traps, one within the other – or was it two types of bait, thrown out on a single line?

"There is a ship waiting for you at the docks in Marseilles," the Hoffman automaton said. "You leave with the tide."

"Where?" she said, but something inside of her already knew, anticipated the single word that came, with the hiss of an old record, from within the Hoffman, as if she had known all along, as if her dreams already told her where the Man on the Mekong had gone...

"Vespuccia," the Hoffman automaton said.

INTERLUDE:
Lean Years

Then came the lean years. Years in which the statue waxed and waned, but mostly stayed quiet, its power exhausted. Years in which Kai no longer knew who he was – what he was. Somewhere, far behind him, lay a past, but it was distant and shrouded in mist. There had been a room full of steam, and the smell of clean clothes, and a warm breeze coming through the open doorway, carrying the smell of rain and falling leaves... The past was beyond the river, it was another, distant bank. The river was one that he couldn't cross.

In the long lean years the city was his to do with as he wished, but he kept himself hidden, still, after all the years, afraid. Others would come for him, he knew. They had come after him the night they killed his father and they would continue to come, never relenting, until they finally got what they wanted.

At night he read. He no longer needed candles. It was part of the change wrought in him, and though it brought him no joy, he was glad he could read.

Though he still read the wuxia stories of his childhood he increasingly turned to new books, and particularly to those tales of visitors to that wild and proud continent some called Vespuccia.

They told of a wide open place where the bison roamed endlessly across the plains; of refugees from the Lizardine Empire, coming to the shores of that great continent in rickety ships, in waves, seeking shelter away from the lizards' rule; of the League of Peace and Power and of the Council of Chiefs and of the great cities that were being erected there, amidst the mountains and plains; of impossible machines, of Tesla sets and airships–

He loved stories of the mysterious pirates that were said to roam the seas (which he had never seen), of strange islands hiding ancient secrets, and most of all he thrilled reading about the entity called the Bookman, which may have been a man and may have been something else entirely. A secret assassin, like a being out of wuxia, who fought those strange lizards beyond the sea. A thing, in a way, like Kai himself, or so he thought.

In the lean years he began to weave his web of shadows, staying always in the dark. The Manchu was his messenger, his lieutenant, and through him others came, and his secret power grew, there in the city called Luang Prabang on the half-island, in the meeting of two rivers. The statue was very weak then, and he barely heard the voices.

Those were the lean years. Then everything, suddenly, changed…

PART V
The White Worm

FIFTY-TWO
Cargo

She woke up from uneasy sleep, dreams fading of a man travelling by ship through stormy seas. He'd been standing on deck and the green lizard statue was sitting in the prow and ball lightning danced around it as if the storm itself was in worship... She had stood on the deck and the man slowly turned and his eyes were on hers. He'd whispered something, but the wind snatched the words away.

She woke up to the motion of waves, the rocking of the ship. Rain outside, darkness beyond the small porthole. She lay still on the narrow bed. Listening.

Was that a rustle at the door? Was an unseen hand rattling the handle? Two days out of port and she'd been getting uneasy, listening out for the small noises in the night, the sounds that shouldn't be there.

Beyond the door, the boards creaked. Was that just the stress in the hull? Or were unseen feet stepping across the corridor? She pictured drowned corpses crawling hand and foot across the lower deck, dripping salt water, their skin bloated and pale.

She lay very still.

On the way to France, all those years ago, she had not been alone, but they still died around her, and in her dreams the lifeless corpses were still flung overboard. There had been ceremony at first, with each loss of life, but as the journey progressed no one said a prayer, and the bodies were simply disposed of. Her mother...

She closed and opened her eyes. Was that something fluttering against the window? A dark shape against the glass, or –?

She swung herself out of bed in one smooth motion and when she turned to the porthole there was nothing there. She raised her gun arm and tiptoed to the door and yanked it open–

Nothing beyond. She took a deep breath. The ship was working insidious fears deep into her mind, the way saltwater could drip, slowly, never stopping, until its touch became like acid, and it wore away body and mind...

There was nothing there. Nothing beyond the door but an empty corridor, and nothing outside but rain clouds, and a gale – and a deep watery grave underneath.

From Paris to Marseilles by train, and to the docks, where the *White Worm* waited: an inauspicious name for a ship.

"Woman on board brings bad luck," the captain said, and coughed out a globule of phlegm overboard, then laughed. "But this is a bad-luck ship."

Captain Karnstein: tall and wizened and wrapped in a too-long, dirty coat that hung loose over his frame. His forehead was lined, the lines like scars, and a thick, black beard grew over his face like a gathering of molluscs stuck to a rock. She said, "When do we sail?" and the captain spat again and jerked his head at the shore and said, "When the cargo's loaded."

She was going to say, *What cargo?* but just then a familiar figure appeared on the dock and she felt her gun hand twitch. Viktor stood down below. He had cleaned the blood from his face but still looked bad. There was a new vitality about him, she noticed uneasily. He practically shone. He looked bigger, bulkier than he had only hours before. When he raised his face his eyes met hers and she almost looked away. His eyes burned, and the smile on his face was ugly. The drugs, she thought. He must have used the Hyde formula – on himself.

And how long has he been doing *that* for?

Below on the docks, Viktor made a mock bow. "Milady de Winter!" he called up.

She said, "Viktor." Her voice was soft. "You seem much recovered."

"Rest..." his voice was like the rest of him – too loud, and at the same time brittle – "is always the best medicine."

"No doubt..." She raised her voice. "What are you doing here?"

"Supervising the cargo." His smile remained. Like Viktor himself, the smile stayed unpleasant.

Some things simply didn't change.

Behind Viktor, porters appeared. A grey mist lay over the docks, and the blowing wind was cold, easing frozen fingers through Milady's coat, touching her skin like the fingers of the dead. The porters were carrying long, heavy-looking casks. The solid wood was shut tight with iron. She took a deep breath, steadied herself. You could shoot Viktor, but you couldn't shout at him. She said, "What is this?"

"Nothing that need concern you."

Taking another deep breath, she walked down the gangplank to the wharf. "I won't ask you again," she said. Viktor took a step back. "Council orders," he said, sounding suddenly nervous. Good. She took a step towards him, and was gratified when he stepped back. "I have the paperwork!" Viktor said. "Here." He produced a sheaf of papers from a coat pocket and waved it at her. Around them, the porters swarmed, six men lifting one cask each, carrying it up the gangplank onto the dark ship. Milady was aware of Captain Karnstein's gaze from above. When she raised her head the captain only spat again, and the globe of mucus was swallowed by the sea.

"Give me that." She tore the papers from his hands. "Biological *specimens* – hazardous?"

"Nothing to be worried about," Viktor said reassuringly – which made her worry even more. "They're just samples for the research station on Scab. Send my regards to the countess, will you?"

"What?"

"Look!" Viktor said. "This is none of your concern. You're off to Vespuccia. Well, good for you." He grinned suddenly. "Did you know the lizardine court has asked for your extradition?"

That hit her hard. For a moment she forgot about the cargo or its mysterious destination. "What... what for?" she said.

"They said, and I quote: 'To assist Scotland Yard in their inquiries into the as-yet unsolved death of Lord de Winter'," Viktor said, and grinned.

"Why would they do that?"

"I sense that fat oaf Mycroft Holmes might have had something to do with it," Viktor said. "You seem to have a knack for making friends, Milady."

"Is that why..." she said, and faltered. "The asylum?"

"Keep you out of the way for a while, yes. The peace with the lizards across the Channel is fragile. They are too powerful for us to fight. What waits in Vespuccia could change that, however... which reminds me."

Around them the porters surged, the sealed casks disappearing one by one up the gangplank. "You are officially a fugitive from justice," Viktor said. "The Council will deny all knowledge of you. According to the information being sent to the lizardine ambassador as we speak, you broke out of Charenton, destroying the asylum in the process and releasing a horde of dangerous criminals into the streets of Paris. No doubt they are already well aware of the situation. That fire you started could be seen for miles."

For a moment she almost smiled. Viktor said, "You then took the train to Marseilles, and there found a ship to take you away from the continent, destination unknown. You're a fugitive, disowned by the Council. In other words, Milady – you're on your own."

She shrugged, and said, "When has it ever been different?" The last of the casks had been loaded onto the *White Worm*. Viktor said, "Have a safe journey."

The fog thickened around them. She could barely see his face. "What's in the casks?" she said.

"Nothing," Viktor said. "They don't exist. And neither, any more, do you, Milady."

She reached out for him but he disappeared, moving quickly, with a sort of animal grace, into the fog. She had to feel her way back to the gangplank. The chill was beginning to settle into her bones. *The research station on Scab?*

And she was a fugitive, she'd have no support once she reached the Long Island, once she landed in Vespuccia. Well, that, at least, was something she was used to.

Do not touch Tômas, they told her, before she left. *Your mission is to obtain possession of the object. For the benefit of the Republic, for the glory of France.*

They wanted her to lay off the Phantom, but she had her own ideas about that...

From above, Captain Karnstein's scratchy voice punctured the night, with two words and a final stop ending, perhaps forever, she thought, her old life. She hurried up the gangplank, scrambling to get on board the *White Worm*.

"Tide's up," Captain Karnstein said.

FIFTY-THREE
The Unfortunate Death of Flies

Storm lashing the sea into rebellion; waves rising dark as empty houses; the wind howled, its anger beating against the ship. Milady thought: *The ocean doesn't want us here.*

She had lit a candle. Now she sat up, unable to sleep, every muscle tight with anticipation. The sounds of night scuttled through the ship like rats, and every creak and groan sent a shiver down her spine.

They were coming, and she was afraid.

On that long-ago journey to France, the hold was crowded with hot and sweating bodies. Babies cried incessantly. Flies, unwelcome emigrants who had jumped onto the ship, buzzed everywhere. *We are going to a better place*, her mother had said, whispering, holding her tight. But young Cleo still heard the unvoiced words that hung there, at the end of the sentence, like an empty noose in the breeze: *I hope.*

Hope was not a commodity worth buying. It died with her mother, died with the long voyage to the cold lands of pale-skinned men and plump, hard-eyed women and obtuse machines. It died on the streets of Paris, cut away from her soul with a sharpened knife. Hope was dangerous, the noose promising only one thing.

She had no use for hope.

She had been afraid on that long crossing and she was afraid again now. Outside the porthole there was nothing but ocean, the Atlantic spreading out in all directions. The water was black and there was no moon, and the wind howled incessantly, like a dying baby.

They were coming for her – and there was no getting away.

The second night out of Paris she dined with the captain at his table. Karnstein was a dour, solitary figure. She rarely saw his men – *the rat men*, she came to think of them for, like the rats who infested the ship, Karnstein's men were sometimes heard, but seldom seen.

They were dining on chicken. A drumstick was wedged between the captain's lips, the grease running down into his thick black beard. The chicken tasted of cloves. Beside the captain's plate stood a tall glass filled with pure lemon juice. Every now and then he would pause, banish the chicken a short distance from his mouth, and take a long swallow of lemon juice. "Scurvy," he'd announce every time, a shudder making his face move as if a sudden earthquake had taken place across its tectonic plates. "Can't be too careful with Lady Scurvy. She'd eat you from the inside and make you bleed, every time."

Milady nodded, and tore a chunk of bread, and chewed it. It was floury and hadn't been baked long enough, and there were little black dots scattered through the dough that suggested the unfortunate death of flies. It made her think of the man in the cell at the Charenton Asylum. The captain said, "You're not eating! Eat!" and pushed the chicken carcass towards her.

"I'm not so hungry…" she said. The captain shook his head. "Eat every meal as it if were your last," he said, taking another deep gulp of lemon juice and shuddering.

If I eat this meal, Milady thought, it almost certainly *will* be my last. The meal had the feel of a last supper served to the condemned. The small dining-room was dim and gloomy, with thick tapestries hanging over the walls. She found herself studying them, noting scenes depicting – what?

Scenes of torture and battle; helmeted men with steel spikes attacking upright lizards whose weapons breathed flames; men dying with gaping, burning wounds; a captive lizard roasted alive above a fire; a flying machine mowing down soldiers with a hail of flying, metallic arrows; men running, lizard eggs captured, broken open; lizard young being stomped on; a castle, a siege; men hanging in rows from drab black trees. She said, "What is it?" and lifted a glass of wine to her lips. The wine had a slightly rancid taste.

"That?" Karnstein said, turning – with some surprise, it seemed to her – to the ancient tapestries. "Flights of fancy," he said, waving the drumstick bone at the images. "Things that never happened."

"It looks very... real," she said. The captain shrugged. "It's called The Battle of the Borgo Pass," he said. "An old legend from my homeland... fanciful, but it lends a certain élan to the room, don't you think?"

"Quite," Milady said.

It was hard to eat one-handed, though she was getting the hang of it, slowly. Her gun-arm rested on the table. She said, "Where is the cargo headed?"

The captain put down his drumstick with some sadness and reached greasy fingers to tear a chunk of breast from what remained of the chicken. "Closed orders," he said.

"Viktor mentioned a place called... Scab?"

A grim smile etched itself, the way acid etches itself on glass, for a brief moment on the captain's lips. "Closed orders," he said again. And – "You are to confine yourself to your quarters while cargo offloads."

"Where?" she said. "We're in the middle of the ocean!"

That smile again, and the chicken disappearing into it. She decided to change tack. "Aren't you worried about the cargo?" she said.

"Should I be?"

"It could be dangerous."

"The ocean's dangerous," the captain said and then, unexpectedly: "I hate the sea."

There was something wild and uncontrolled in the way he said it. His pupils, she noticed, had become dilated. His breathing grew heavy. She didn't speak again and, a short time later, excused herself from the table.

After that she took all her meals in her cabin.

And now they were coming. She listened out for their sounds. The tread of feet on boards, the ghostly whisper of an icy wind. The *White Worm* grunted and groaned all around her. She huddled on the narrow bed, her back to the wall. Watching the door.

Waiting.

For here, on the ship, she was no longer Milady de Winter. The years had been peeled away from her with a knife and what remained, in the small, dank cabin, was a small and frightened girl.

That same smell was in the hold of the ship when they had sailed to France... fear, sweat, bodies pressed together. "We're going to a new home," her mother had whispered to her. "A better place." Her mother's hope was like a candle. It had been easily snuffed. Or perhaps, she thought now, perhaps her mother never believed there was hope, but in pretending that for her daughter had tried to make it real, to wish it into being. Her body, like the others', was thrown overboard. By the time they arrived at port there were few enough of them left.

She rocked herself, hugging her knees one-handed, her gun arm useless by her side. The dead never truly went away, she thought.

She watched the door, waiting for them to come.

FIFTY-FOUR
Captive of the Waves

Sailing, with no land in sight, clouds in the distance assuming the shapes of imaginary continents, an entire alien cloudscape in the skies. Did someone live up there? Did cloud-women hunt amidst the grey-white landscape, did cloud-women fish from high above, dangling lines and hooks to snare a passing ship far down below? When she stood on the deck the air smelled of brine and tar and oil. It smelled cold, and she felt far away from home.

A whale in the distance, rising to the surface, blowing out a jet of water before the immense dark shape submerged into the water once more. A school of flying fish skittered over the surface like silver bullets. Steps behind her – Karnstein, wrapped in his dirty coat, a pipe stuck between his teeth: "Whales are the Queen's eyes, they say."

She didn't need to ask what queen he meant. In all the world there was only one that mattered.

She remembered Victoria. During the time of her second marriage she had often visited the Royal Palace. A tall, dignified being, her tail long and royal, her eyes hard. There were pools – swamps – in the Royal Gardens, and rocks for the royals to sun themselves on. The queen had a disconcerting habit of catching flies with her quick, long tongue... And she remembered the whales in the Thames. It was said they followed Vespucci's ship when it returned from Caliban's Island, bringing with it a strange new future...

"What's in the casks?" she said. Beside her, Karnstein chuckled. "You ask as if you already know the answer, Milady."

A clear grey sea, no land in sight... no other ships, no birds this far away from land. A desolate place – but this was only above. What lay below? The ocean had its own life-forms, its own geography, its own mysteries... ones she never wanted to know.

Somewhere deep down there, her mother–

"How much longer?" she said. Karnstein tapped his pipe on the railings. Ash and loose tobacco fell and blew away on the wind. "Making good time," he said grudgingly, then – "Might be a storm coming."

She left him there. Back in her cabin, the feeling of helplessness intensified. In the city, in the dark streets of Paris, she reigned supreme, but out here she was nothing but a prisoner, a captive of the waves...

She knew what was – what had to be – inside the casks. *Biological specimens – hazardous*. But she had to know for sure.

When she stepped out into the corridor there was no one there. She reached the stairs – nothing. There was no sign of Karnstein's rat men. Quietly, she began her descent towards the hold.

Why weren't they coming? She had *seen* them. She had made her way down into the hold. The smell of rot was strong, grew stronger the deeper she went. The darkness was near absolute – and yet, she could see.

Green jade shadows like cold shuddering flames... She saw not with her human eye but with the other, that foreign object lodged into the hollow socket of her missing eye. The thing in her skull *responded* to the shadows, writhing inside, and she bit her lip or she would have screamed with the pain. The jade fragment was alive, it was reaching into her brain, it was... it was *excited*, she thought.

Long wooden casks, bound in metal, were lined along the floor of the *White Worm's* hold.

But why lie? she thought. Call them what they truly were.

Coffins.

Viktor's research, the Phantom's gruesome job for the Council: the corpses of the infected, the bodies of those, like poor dead Madame L'Espanaye, who were touched by that alien illness that had entered Paris.

Though it was very dark in the hold, and the coffins were made of thick wood, she could nevertheless see them. Her jade eye showed her the interred corpses within their prisons. They were not still.

Restless, the deformed figures in the coffins writhed and fought to escape. Silver strands oozed across their dead and bloated bodies. *A device*, she thought again, recalling her dream, the temple on the Mekong, and the man who looked a little like her, who looked *at* her... *a machine for recording the dead*.

Or did they fail to understand it entirely?

There was a rustle in the shadows and she nearly jumped. She turned, heart beating, gun arm extended – jade-light showing her a bow-backed figure shuffling forward. Then a light flared, almost blinding her, and a gruff voice said, "Out of bounds, the hold is. What you doing here?"

In the light of the hurricane lamp the hold looked ordinary enough. There were coils of rope and fishing nets and sea chests, and the casks that weren't casks were silent and unmoving, as if they held nothing much inside. The speaker was one of Karnstein's dour rat men: whiskers grew out of his pale face and his figure was hunched as if from the weight of too many years at sea. His coat, like his captain's, was dirty, patched in places, torn in others. He wore a cap low over his eyes.

"Nothing," she said. "It was very dark, I–"

"Out of bounds," the rat man said. "Nothing to see."

"Perhaps if you could show me the way back–" she said, and then she paused.

For just a moment, the man had raised his face, regarding her through rheumy eyes – and at that moment she saw it.

A strand of silver-grey matter moving, almost sensuously, like a snake, across the man's skin.

FIFTY-FIVE
Infected

The same ocean, different skies… She was on the deck of the smaller ship and the man was there too, the man who was a little like her. Kai. Somehow she knew his name.

Kai.

The jade lizard sat in the prow, surrounded by candles. Incense wafted on the wind.

The man was leaning against the railings, looking out to sea. She approached him on soft feet. Above their heads the sky was a reddish-purple vista being slowly devoured by darkness. Stars were coming out, in ones and twos at first and then more and more of them, until the whole of the Milky Way was spread out across the sky from one horizon to the other.

"The sky was purple like a bruise, fading to black…" the man by the railings said. She noticed he was holding a book in one hand. He said, "I like that."

"Yes, Master," a voice said. She realised he was talking to his manservant, who was kneeling before the statue.

"I will be glad when this is over," the man said. He stared out across the sea, letting the hand holding the book drop to his side.

"Is it decided, then, Master?"

"They will not rest until they take it from me," he said. His voice was so sad… She had the urge to reach out and touch him, stroke his hair. "I will sell it to them, instead."

"For the right price, Master," the manservant said.

"Yes… my life," the man said.

He doesn't want it, she thought. *He is a captive of this thing as much as I am.* She went and stood beside him. Together they gazed at the field of stars.

"I don't understand it," the man said. He half-turned his head. Suddenly, she was aware of him looking directly at her. "I don't understand what it wants, what it does."

She stood very still. The man suddenly smiled. "My silent ghost," he said. "Or am I *your* ghost?"

"Master? Is something wrong?"

"It is nothing, Manchu."

She liked his eyes. She reached a hand, her human one, to cup his face, but her fingers left no impression on his skin.

"They are quiet tonight."

It was true. She could not hear the voices of the statue. "What do they expect to happen, when we reach Vespuccia?" he said. She tried to speak, to answer him, but no words came. "My silent ghost," he said again, and smiled, and then, as they did once before, his eyes looked beyond her and the smile melted from his face and he *pushed* at her–

Startled, she stumbled back, fell over the railings towards the dark sea–

She woke up with her hair damp against her forehead, her heart hammering in her chest. How could she have fallen asleep? The door to her cabin was ajar. A narrow band of light pierced through into the room. A dark figure standing above her, leaning down…

She saw a rat man and there were things crawling over his face, and silver-grey swirls moving in his eyes… Her gun arm rose instinctively, the muzzle almost touching the rat man's face. He paid it no attention, and his sick, dead eyes were fastened on hers, and now his hands, hands like claws were reaching for her and she–

She fired, her arm pumping as the bullets shot out, hitting the man at point-blank range in the face, blood and bits of skull flying everywhere. And now she could hear a cry rising through the ship – a communal, wounded screech that echoed eerily down the corridor, seeming to merge with the groaning of the *White Worm*.

Infected, she thought, horrified. She struggled to her feet, her naked toes almost slipping in the pool of blood. They were all infected. The rat man had fallen away from her and was lying on the floor. Half his face was gone. Still, he tried to rise, fingers scrabbling blindly against the floor.

She fired again, until he settled back and at last wouldn't move again. The silver-grey strands wove in and out of existence across his body, but as movement stopped they, too, were still.

She had fallen asleep in her clothes. She put on shoes and her coat, one-handed. The smell of the dead man was on her. Another howl, coming closer. *They must be all over the ship*, she thought.

And somehow, in there – amidst the fear and confusion – a sense of relief. *It's begun. They are coming, at last.*

She had warned the captain. After the incident in the hold, she had run back up to the deck, gone straight to Karnstein.

"A plague?" the captain said, hacking a cough around the word as if it were a sweet. "What's dead stays dead, Milady."

"Not any more," she said.

"Well," the captain said. He was rolling something in his mouth thoughtfully. She decided she really didn't want to know what it was. "We'll be reaching Scab soon enough. She'll know what to do."

"Who?" she said – shouted – at him.

"The countess," he said, as if surprised by her ignorance. "So, nothing's changed. Remember to confine yourself to your quarters when cargo–"

"Is being offloaded, yes," she said. "But the cargo has already offloaded itself!"

A look of distaste crossed Captain Karnstein's face and he hawked onto the deck. She stared, horrified, at the little glob of silver-grey goo.

"It's strange," Captain Karnstein said, "but do you know, I've never felt better."

She watched the little globe stretch itself across the boards of the deck. Slowly, meticulously, it began to draw itself towards her.

She turned and ran.

Now she stepped over the still corpse of the rat man. The door, ajar. She reached, pushed it open, stepped into the corridor, gun arm at the ready.

But where could she go?

She was trapped in a place worse than any prison – for there was nowhere to go. Her warden was the ocean, and it was everywhere, hemming her in, offering no escape but a watery death.

Were they all infected? She needed the crew. She did not know how to pilot a ship. She had once piloted a plane – a small, fragile, dangerous thing, but at least the land was always close…

Here there was no land.

Trapped.

Stepping down the corridor, she silently cursed Viktor and the Council. The helplessness of her situation weighed her down. Stop, an inner voice whispered. There is no point in fighting any longer. This is how it ends – at sea, the way it had begun, so long ago.

Her mother waited for her, beneath the waves.

She decided to try to reach the upper deck. But when she reached the end of the corridor they were waiting, three of them, rat men in their tatty clothes, and their faces were hungry.

They were very quiet. She said, "Please–" and raised her human hand before her, the fingers splayed. "You are sick. You need help."

Their mouths opened in tandem. Their teeth shone wetly. Silver strands like eels crawled across their arms and faces. She took a step back. "What do you want with me?"

They didn't answer. Together, they took a step towards her, gaining for themselves the ground she had ceded. "Who is piloting the ship?"

No answer. What did they want with her? Somehow, the infection in the casks must have seeped out, infected the men...

The statue. It was a mechanism of some sort, she knew that. A device for... she didn't know, exactly. All she knew was that it was spreading.

As if in response to her thoughts, she felt the alien entity in her eye socket awaken. Her hand rose to her head, pain jolting her. The approaching figures of the rat men were illuminated in a jade-green light, and she could see the entire spread of the infection on them. It was... *responding*. Responding to the alien shard lodged in her cranium.

They wanted the fragment of jade.

From somewhere, far, far away, whispering, insane voices: *quantum encoding of data at tertiary levels, chrono-spatial scan proceeding, probe regeneration at full capacity–*

Instinctively she raised her gun arm, fired, rounds of bullets emerging out of the Gatling gun, pounding into her attackers, these walking dead men, sending them back, breaking them.

She stepped through a storm of smoke and blood, gaining the stairs, running for her life.

FIFTY-SIX
Lights

Captain Karnstein, silhouetted like a bat against the sky. His rat men kneeling on the deck before him, mouths opening and closing without sound. Milady stopped, stood still. "They are coming!" the captain shouted. The silhouette turned, gazed on her without surprise. "Chrono-spatial scan proceeding!"

"Proceeding..." the rat men echoed in unison.

"Data-gathering approaching projectional capacity!" Captain Karnstein said.

"Capacity..." the rat man echoed.

No one at the helm. No steam rising from the boilers, the sails slack. The wind howled along the deck, and she felt herself shiver. Clouds in the distance, coming closer, a mass of darkness blocking out the stars.

She pointed, shouted – "There's a storm coming! We need to get the ship moving again!"

"Checksum error!" the captain said. "Checksum error!"

"Error..." the rat men murmured. "Error..."

She approached the captain. Her gun arm was raised, aimed. She felt herself shaking. "Get. The ship. Moving again," she said.

"The ships are coming," the captain said. "The fleet, the fleet is..." He faltered, fell silent. In the jade-green light of her foreign eye she saw them all, crawling with silver-grey worms. She said, trying to keep her voice steady: "Think of your ship. Would you have it destroyed?"

"The ship…" the captain whispered. "I have seen the ship… it was enormous, and yet as small as a speck of dust as it sailed amongst the stars…"

"Don't make me shoot you!"

His eyes rose, met hers. Was there a plea for help in those silver-grey orbs? The wind howled, making the captain's tattered coat flutter in the dark night like bat's wings. "Karnstein, please!"

But it was no use. If there had been understanding in his eyes, it died even as she watched, and the captain turned away from her. Lightning illuminated the skies, and an explosion of thunder came almost immediately after. Salt water spray stung her eyes. This is it, she thought. This is how it ends.

"Get her," Karnstein said.

Doom came on Lady de Winter like a settling of silk. Her back pressed to the railings, her gun arm raised, uselessly, before her, the band of crazed, infected sailors closing in on her, all seemed to signal an inglorious end.

And why not? she thought. Her earliest memories were of a ship, and death. It would be a fitting end…

The rat men's teeth shone in the flash of lightning. Thunder shook the deck. The rat men came for her, slowly, hands reaching out, mouths opened in hungry grins… silver snaked across their bodies, the back of their hands and across their cheeks. A wave hit the hull, spraying her with salt water, and for a moment she lost her footing.

The impact of the deck winded her. The rat men's hands were grasping for her and she fought them off, life returning as she realised she did not want to die – not here, on the stinking deck of a death ship, in the middle of a dark and hostile ocean. Cities she understood. But she would not die at sea.

With a scream of rage her gun arm came up and she shot the nearest rat man at point-blank range, the bullets slamming into the man's chest, tearing a hole clear through. For a moment the man was still, and she could see the night sky through his chest, a gathering of stars and a flash of lightning–

The man fell to the ground. His fingers twitched. His dead eyes opened, blinked slowly. Reaching out, his hand caught her ankle and would not let go.

Another flash of lightning, and another, and she tried to kick but he wouldn't let her go. She pushed herself up, one-handed, and stomped on his fingers with her artificial leg, hearing the bones in his hand break. Then she was free, and pushing away from the slow-moving sailors, backing away as she tried to make sense of what she'd seen.

For just a moment, glimpsed in the flash of lightning through the hole in the rat man's chest, she had seen something impossible.

She kept backing away, but now they were behind her, too, and she knew there was no escape.

Or only one…

Salt on her lips, rain and sea water falling down on her face. She raised her head, searching for the shadow in the dark.

A flash of lightning and–

There!

It wasn't possible – was it?

An enormous dark shape loomed above the ship, growing larger – growing *closer*, she realised.

What *was* it?

Did she imagine it? A flash of lightning again, the boom of thunder making the deck shudder, waves beating against the hull. In the light of the storm the sailors' faces were a pale sickly white, the silver strands oozing across their skins…

A city in the sky.

Towers rose high above the ship. Dark towers etched against the storm. A city moving on the waves–

She fired but the bullets did little to stop the rat men. And there came Karnstein, his coat flapping around him like the wings of a bat – coming for her.

Lightning hit close by, and one of the rat men shrieked. She smelled burning flesh, and watched as the man rolled on the deck, the silver strands flaming, melting, oozing off his skin... She blinked rain from her eyes. In the darkness she could no longer see the impossible city.

No one spoke. The burning rat man was motionless, a puddle of rain steaming around his body. Could electricity kill them? There was so little she knew about the infection. Hands reached for her, grabbed her. They had her gun arm now, and when she fired it was too late, the burst going wide, hitting nothing. She managed to release her arm but they had her by her coat and were grasping for her legs. She had only one chance–

She took it.

They were holding her coat when she tore herself out of it and ran for the railings. A flash of lightning again, an immediate corresponding boom of thunder, and the ship heaved, and she saw a dark, silent city rising out of the waves like a scab on the skin of the ocean. Memories of her mother returned, the corpses being hoisted off the deck, into the hungry sea... Still running, she jumped, and a howl rose behind her and was lost to the sound of the waves.

The water was cold, the impact took her breath away and threatened not to give it up. The waves rose and tried to smash her against the hull. She dived, trying to swim one-handed, knowing it was futile, and that she was going to die.

Eyes stared at her from the bottomless sea.

How long could she hold her breath? Desperately, she tried to propel herself away from the ship, away–

Not eyes. *Lights.*

And now she knew she was hallucinating.

Lights like a cityscape down below the waves...

And something rising from the depths, something dark and gigantic, ebbing gracefully, ripples forming in the almost flat disc shape, and it was reaching for her... A tentacle as large as a hansom cab swept underneath her. Blind panic took her and she tried to rise, return to the surface, her lungs flaming in pain, but she no longer saw the surface, no longer knew where she was. Her next breath, she knew, would be water. She fought to rise and somehow, she didn't know how, her head burst out of the water and she gulped in air, desperately, and saw through a half-blinded eye the impossible city floating on the dark waves. I can do it, she thought, swim there, I can–

Something slimy and immensely strong grasped her legs, pulling her down, down beneath the waves, and the dark world disappeared, and she knew she was dying, and she must have been hallucinating again, too, because the last thing she saw was the head of a giant squid rising from the depths, with two giant, well-lit eyes like windows, and standing behind them was a woman, and she was waving.

FIFTY-SEVEN
Scab

Waking up was like pushing upwards through an undertow, a struggle for breath and light. She had not expected either.

For a moment she thought she was back in the ocean. Staring down on her from all directions were sea creatures. Two sharks glared at her while a dancing octopus hovered in what seemed like air, staring at her mournfully over its beak. Crustaceans scuttled to and fro on beds of sand, and a giant ray rippled majestically as a swordfish darted above her head.

Not the sea, she realised, relieved. Aquariums. And she was lying on a dry and rather comfortable bed, and the linen smelled of soap and laundry.

"You're awake," a voice said. "Good."

Startled, she looked around her, only then noticing the woman standing quietly beside the shark aquarium. She was a tall, graceful woman with an olive, Mediterranean skin burned darker by the sun, with long black hair tied behind her in a simple knot. There were lines around her eyes, which were a deep and startling blue. "I need you to sign this."

"Excuse me?"

"Receipt of cargo," the woman said, sounding a little impatient. She was, Milady realised, the same woman she had seen as she was drowning. It was all very peculiar.

"Here," the woman said, approaching her, putting forward what was evidently the *White Worm's* cargo manifest, as well as a pen. "Sign here, here, and initial *here* and *here* – please."

"What?"

"Did you swallow more water than I thought?" the woman said. "Captain Karnstein is temporarily unable to fulfil his function as captain, which makes you, I assume, senior representative for the Council. Therefore, you're liable for the cargo. Therefore, you need to sign it over to me before I can take official possession of it." She glared at Milady. "I am Countess Dellamorte," she said, as if that explained everything.

"Where… where *am* I?" Milady said. Above the countess's head, the mournful squid blinked sadly.

The countess inched her head meaningfully at the cargo manifest. Sighing, Milady signed it, her gun arm clumsy as she tried to hold the paper in place while she put pen to paper. As soon as she was done, Countess Dellamorte snatched it back. "Excellent," she said. "Come."

Wordlessly, Milady stood up. Her clothes, she saw, were waiting by the bed for her, freshly laundered and ironed. The countess waited as she dressed, then motioned for her to follow.

They stepped out of the room into a hallway lined with more tanks: all manner of sea creatures slithered, crawled and swam inside. The countess trailed one hand against the glass as she walked. At the end of the corridor was an elevator. The doors opened soundlessly, and Milady followed the countess inside. The elevator began to rise.

When the doors opened, the light was momentarily blinding. Milady blinked, tears forming in her single eye. The jade fragment embedded in her other eye socket was still, for once. As her eye adjusted, however, details began to form around her: first the outline of walls, then the frames of massive windows set on three sides, and then, through the windows…

Down below her, hemmed in by the sea on all sides, lay the city she had seen in the dark. Yet not a city, she realised: they were standing in a tower that rose out of a giant platform that was, itself, floating, half-submerged in the water of the sea. There were figures down below, and rising towers and large box-like buildings. At the edges of the platform massive cranes rose into the air, and several smaller vessels were moored, bobbing in the water. Shafts, too, she noticed, were driven into the surface of the platform at several places, and she saw elevators descend and rise, and more tiny human figures entering or leaving them. The whole extraordinary structure, a thing of metal and construction, floated serenely on the sea, yet had no part of it, looking a little like–

"Welcome to Scab," Countess Dellamorte said.

"The specimens," the countess said, "are *fascinating*." It was a little later. They were walking along the platform. The sun was out and a pleasant breeze was blowing in from the sea. Heavy, house-sized containers stood everywhere, creating avenues and paths that turned and twisted and criss-crossed each other unexpectedly. Milady shuddered, trying not to think of the corpses in the trunks that had been on the ship. "What happened to the sailors?" she said.

"They'll live," the countess said, and gave a sudden snort of laughter. "In fact, that's the one thing we can expect for certain. This… plague that has infected them also seems to keep them alive. Come–" She led her through a narrow gap between containers and suddenly they were standing in the approach to an artificial harbour – and there was the *White Worm*.

Cranes hovered above it, offloading the coffin-shaped casks onto the platform. Small, steam-powered baruch-landaus were carrying the cargo away, driven by–

Milady couldn't help but stare. They were – women, yes, and men, but–

Were those *gills*? And did that short-haired woman driving a cargo cart have *fins*? She saw a burly man, with whiskers like those of a catfish, approach them. Were those *gills*, on either side of his neck?

"We are nearly finished offloading, countess," he said, giving the woman beside Milady a sharp salute. Milady stared at the man's hands.

Between his fingers – were those *webs*?

"Excellent," the countess said. "Section it in quarantine, McGill, for the time being."

"Of course, Countess," the man said and, saluting again, turned sharply back.

"Ex-military," Countess Dellamorte said fondly.

"Which military?" Milady said.

"Oh, several of them, I expect."

They looked at each other. And now Milady was finding the other woman's smile somewhat uncomfortable. "Please," Countess Dellamorte said, "do not worry. Scab, as you can see, is a scientific outpost. We study… life, here. My staff may appear eccentric, though that was not my work." She grimaced. "I'm afraid my predecessor, while a brilliant man, was also somewhat unstable. An Englishman, you see–" clearly expecting that that explained everything, which Milady rather thought it did. "But dear Moreau is no longer with us," the countess said. "It was decided he needed a sabbatical – a rather long one, in fact – and last I heard he had retired to some Pacific island, where the weather, it is hoped, better agrees with him. Regardless…" and she smiled again, "you are our guest. We don't, as you can imagine, receive many visitors."

Milady glanced around her, at that impossible floating structure, beyond which lay nothing but countless miles of open sea. "Yes," she said, "and though I'm grateful, of course…" She hesitated, and the countess said, "You were en-route to Vespuccia, and need to continue on your journey?"

"As soon as possible," Milady said.

"I shall see what may be arranged," the countess said. "Yet you and I have much to talk about before you go. It is not by accident I was sent the samples, you know." She made another of her head motions, indicating for Milady to follow her. "And I think my work here, and your mission, may well be linked. Before you depart, you should know what is at stake."

Milady nodded, unsure what the countess meant, and her companion smiled. "Come!" she said brightly. "Let us go and make study of the corpses."

FIFTY-EIGHT
Waldo

Behind glass walls, the sailors crawled... On hand and foot, they prowled, the rat men of the *White Worm* – all but their master.

With his tattered old coat the old captain looked more bat-like than ever. Silently, he peered back at them through the glass. Silver strands oozed across his large hands.

"My poor Karnstein..." the countess said, surprising Milady. She approached the glass, and laid her palm against the glass. On the other side Karnstein did the same. "Camilla..." he said. "Help me. Help us."

"I will," the countess said softly. Milady felt as if she were interrupting a private moment. She coughed, and the countess turned to her, her hand falling away slowly from the wall of glass. "Do you understand the nature of their malady?" she said, her voice sounding harsh in the quiet room. She glared at Milady, who did not reply. "I am well informed," the countess said. "The Council has been updating me on a regular basis as to the... events that took place in Paris. Events to which I understand you were central."

Behind the glass the rat men crawled pitifully. The countess said, "I know your nature, Milady de Winter. I have seen it in other agents of the Council–" Her tone made it quite clear she did not approve. "Single-minded. Determined – to a fault. I have met

Tômas before, too, did you know that?" she smiled crookedly. "He was a handsome man in those days. Yet the same as you, Milady. The same as you. No conception of the larger canvas, as it were. Tell me, what do *you* think the nature of this malady is?"

Milady, thinking back to her vision of the lizardine statue, a thought recalled – she said, "It's a device, for recording the dead."

The countess's eyes opened wider – Milady, it appeared, had managed to surprise her. "You have a fragment of jade where you once had an eye…" she murmured. "What else do you see, Milady de Winter?" She tilted her head, looking at Milady curiously. "It is a good thing the Council sent you to me, to be studied."

Milady, her gun arm rising as of its own volition – "I am not yours to be *studied*."

"Ah, yes," the countess said, unperturbed. "The modifications are rather fascinating. Dear Viktor's work, yes? A darling man."

Milady had never heard Viktor referred to as anyone's darling, before. She bit her tongue and didn't answer. "A gun," the countess said, some amusement in her voice. "Always a gun is the answer to you, is it not? Tômas, he was the same. A weapon, you are. The Council's own guns." She sighed, and shook her head. "Guns do not think," she said, "guns are there to be wielded." She turned away from Milady, looked again through the glass. "Look at them!" she said. "A device, you said, for recording the dead, yes – or the living. A device for making *impressions* of organic life – would it surprise you to learn that I believe that had been rather a speciality of the lizards' science? No?"

She didn't wait for a reply. "Come," she said again – Milady was becoming seriously irked with the countess's manner – and walked away, Karnstein still standing with his hand against the glass, watching her. Milady, unnerved, decided to follow the countess.

"Yet you do not ask," the countess said, continuing a one-sided conversation as she stalked ahead of Milady – they were passing through a corridor and back out onto the open space of the platform – "you do not think to ask – *why?* You do not pause, in your endless chase, and ask yourself, not what it does, but why it does it? For what purpose?"

Milady, a small voice – "I have wondered–"

A snort from the countess. "You wonder. Indeed. Come. I will show you my work here."

They were approaching one of the shafts built into the bottom of the raft. Milady stared down into dark water. It was a wide, open hole into the ocean, and rising out of it–

She pulled back, her gun arm rising–

A giant creature, whose tentacles ebbed across the water–

"This is Waldo," the countess said, with some pride.

Milady stared at the creature. The head bobbed up to the surface and stayed there, and the wide body floated upwards, one of the tentacles rising into the air to come landing, extended, on the platform beside them. "I designed him myself," the countess said. "Come, come!"

A machine, Milady realised. And now the countess, quite unconcerned, was walking along the rigidly extended tentacle towards the head, where a mouth opened like a door. Milady followed her, afraid of slipping, and knew that, for the moment, at least, her fate was in this woman's hands. The thought did not make her happy.

She entered the mouth, found herself in a utilitarian room – the two eyes she had seen before were indeed windows, and just before them was a large control panel of polished wood and burnished chrome, two chairs before it. The countess sat in one and gestured for Milady to sit in the other. At the touch of a button, the door – mouth – closed and there was a hiss of escaping air. "We're now sealed in," the countess said. Another button – the countess's painted fingernail as polished as the controls – and the giant creature came to life. "And... down," the countess murmured. "Are you familiar with the poem by that fellow who was fond of laudanum? Down to a sunless sea..."

Milady shivered. Water began to rise over the windows as the vessel sank. In moments they were under the giant platform that was Scab. It was dark outside, and there was no illumination inside the vehicle. "It is dark," Countess Dellamorte said. "As dark as space, Milady de Winter. Think of space, Milady. Think of that vast unexplored region that lies just beyond our atmosphere. The universe is out there…" And now, moving the controls, she made the vehicle turn, and as it did Milady began to see lights coming alive down there, in the darkness, tens and then hundreds of lights blossoming in the depths of the sea.

"Stars, and planets, beyond count…" the enigmatic woman beside her said. "And who knows what manner of life dwells beyond our world?"

Milady wasn't sure she was expected to provide an answer. She stared instead, fascinated, at the approaching lights. A guage set into the control panel indicated depths, it seemed. They were sinking fast.

"You may have heard the theory expressed that those of the lizardine court –" a note of distaste in her voice – "have come from another world, beyond our own. That is, I can assure you, quite correct. Their technology far surpassed our own. Their race was able to build ships that sailed amongst the stars." She gave a chuckle that did not have much humour in it. "But technology fails – perhaps the first thing any practical scientist ever learns. Who knows what accident – if that is what it was – led to their being stranded here, on this world?"

"What are those lights?" Milady said. Countess Dellamorte shook her head. "You must consider the larger implications!" she said. "Like it or not, we are at war. Or will be."

"War?" Milady said.

"A few years ago, the Lizardine Empire successfully sent a probe into space. That probe was meant to study our neighbouring planet – Mars. But that was not its true function. What I am telling you, by the way, is highly classified. However, I feel I should be candid with you and, here on Scab, one *is* rather given more leeway… especially seeing as Scab itself, of course, does not exist."

"Of course," Milady said, and the two women shared a smile. They were both professionals, Milady knew. And as different as their positions were, their goals were the same – weren't they?

FIFTY-NINE
Descent

Waldo descended. Around the sub-aquatic vehicle the dark sea pressed, and Milady saw the dial of the pressure gauge moving slowly, continuously, in a clockwise direction. The darkness of the sea oppressed her. Who knew what lay below, deep at the bottom of the sea? Again she thought of her mother, all the others on that long-ago journey. Were they waiting for her, down below?

"Space," Countess Dellamorte said. Her voice seemed hushed, down here. "Look around you, Milady. I said my research involves life. More specifically, it concerns human survival in inhospitable environments." She gestured at the dark water beyond the glass. "The sea is my laboratory. Here, we work on the possibility that, one day, humanity will survive beyond the atmosphere. It is imperative that we do. The Lizardine Empire poses danger to us on Earth – but what unimaginable danger may threaten us from beyond the stars?"

"The probe," Milady said. The countess nodded. "It was a distress buoy, to use a nautical term," she said. "Sending out a message to – whom? That is what we must prepare ourselves for, why Scab was built, why funding can be found."

"But we have co-existed with Les Lézards for centuries," Milady protested. "Surely–"

"They have changed our history!" the countess said. "Changed our future, with their presence."

"We have peace–"

"Do we?" The smile the countess gave her was as cold as the sea. And now she could see the lights growing closer, illuminating–

There were structures in the sea, hazily visible through the murky water. Bubbles of hard matter anchored on an enormous chain, each bubble as large as a house. There were figures moving along the chain, human in shape, but only just. Suits, she thought. Some sort of outer layers protecting the divers. And long, elongated shapes like cigars moving in the water – submarines. They looked like tiny fish against the bulk of the chain and the never-ending sea.

"Krupp is developing a new kind of cannon," the countess said. "Krupp's Baby, they call it now – and Krupp's Monster, too. A cannon of the type the Lizardine Empire already possesses – one whose shot is so powerful it can penetrate the very atmosphere."

"A weapon?"

The smile played on the countess's face. "A weapon," she agreed. "For what can fire into space can also fire across vast distances right here. The future of war…"

"Who else?" Milady said – demanded. The countess nodded slowly. "Many others," she said. "All playing their own subtle game for domination. Chung Kuo, behind their secretive walls… the Council, the lizardine court, and others… It is said Lord Babbage himself is gathering power, and as for Vespuccia…"

Milady thought of the wide open spaces, the buffalo hordes and the cities of the migrants who came there to escape the lizardine dominion. The countess said, "Edison, Tesla, each gathering power. And as for the Council of Chiefs and their Black Cabinet – who knows what they think as they weigh and listen and learn and decide? They have the power of a continent in their hands. Do you expect them not to use it?"

As Waldo sank lower and lower the lights grew in brightness, and Milady's breath caught in her throat. Structures came into view, enormous bubbles tied together with a chain in complex patterns, and she realised she was seeing an entire city under the sea. Small figures and vessels moved between the alien structures, and she saw more of the bubbles were being added, as a swarm of vehicles converged over a half-built structure, and the chain was being extended. "What do you think the plague is?" the countess said. "This alien device – do you think it is the only one?"

"I... I don't know."

"Remnants of the lizards' technology can still be found," the countess said. "Objects of power far advanced from our own, fledgling technology. There are others, and more – what may we yet find beyond our own world? Did they litter our solar system with their machines, do you think? And are they sleeping? Or awake?"

Milady was growing uncomfortable of the countess's presence. None of this concerned her. Her objective remained the same. Scab did not – should not – exist. Talk of space seemed fantastical to her. All she truly knew was what truly mattered – she had a killer to catch, a job to complete. Regardless of the Council's instructions. The countess may have noticed her expression. "Guns," she said disgustedly. "You are fashioned so precisely by the Council that you can no more conceive of your true purpose than the objects you resemble. The object you are hunting, it is not a mindless sickness, a natural plague. It is a *device*, a thing created by a technology you cannot even imagine, Milady de Winter. And its purpose is clear."

"Not to me..." Milady murmured. The countess glanced at her sharply. "Then you are more dim-witted than I gave you credit for," she said.

Milady stared at the impossible city under the sea. What manner of people would wish to live like this? she wondered. She saw it for what it truly was – a prison under the sea, the countess its warden. Peopled by those who could not live in society, exiles sent to live out their days on Scab. It was aptly named.

The countess, grimacing, took the controls. Waldo spun around, tentacles flowing gracefully. The countess pulled a lever, and the pressure gauge paused and then began to travel in an anticlockwise direction. "Enough," the countess said.

"It's a probe," Milady said quietly. The countess looked startled. Milady said, "That is your conclusion, isn't it?" She thought of the jade statue, of the insane, lonely voices babbling endlessly. "A device for studying a new territory, the way we send spies to learn the way for an... an invasion."

Countess Dellamorte looked taken aback, then, suddenly, pleased. "A gun that thinks," she said. "You please me."

Milady shook her head. She felt very tired, now. Her eyes threatened to close and she said, "Bring us up."

The thought that was forming in her head, the thought she did not bother sharing with the countess, was: *What if it isn't what you say it is at all? What if it is lonely, and desperately seeking a way back home?*

SIXTY
Glass Coffin

She had never been so glad to see sunlight again. Yet as she stepped away from the aquatic vehicle, a sense of unease permeated Milady's mind.

Something was wrong.

She couldn't tell what it was that disturbed her. "Come," the countess said, walking briskly beside her. "I want to take another look at the sailors in quarantine. And you need some food... something light on the stomach. I'll have McGill bring something over."

But she did not feel hungry. Her throat was raw and sore and there was a dull throbbing in her head. Staring at the countess, the alien jade in Milady's eye seemed to awaken and turn restlessly, hurting her. She hefted her gun arm, realising the Gatling gun had been reloaded for her while she was sleeping. It showed remarkable trust...

But then, where did she have to run? There was no escape from Scab, nothing beyond the platform but hostile sea. And below...

She didn't want to think of the experiments being carried out under the sea. The thought of people living in such conditions was insane – as insane as Dellamorte herself.

She followed behind the other woman, feeling tired and

sluggish. Through the same aquarium-lined corridor, sharks glancing at her behind their cages.

Sharks... Dellamorte had called her a gun, but guns did not think, and Milady was thinking – hard.

A woman so bound by rules that she insisted on her signing over the ship's cargo – a pointless act of formality by any consideration. And at the same time, speaking freely to Milady, revealing at least *some* of the secrets of Scab... It did not make sense, not unless–

The room was dark and cool and behind the glass the rat men were motionless. She could not see Karnstein.

Did her gun work?

The countess spoke into a brass tube, then turned to Milady. "Food will be brought shortly. Please, make yourself comfortable."

Milady looked around but could find no chair. The only piece of furniture made her blood run cold: it was a glass coffin lying open, only missing an occupant.

"Karnstein?" The countess sounded worried – or perhaps irritated, Milady thought. "Karnstein, where are you?"

No movement behind the glass. The jade light flared in Milady's eye again, and she saw the shifting silver strands, and seemed to hear the distant voices murmuring, far away: *Biological assessment routines reaching saturation point – quantum scan fail – adjusting error margin parameters – retry – retry–*

She shook her head, trying to dispel the alien sounds.

"Are you feeling unwell?"

She raised her hand. "I'm fine."

"You are tired. Come, stand with me."

She did not appreciate the countess standing directly beside the glass coffin.

And now it occurred to her that she had not, so far, been offered food or drink.

She was weakened, unable to fight, with nowhere to run... suspicion waking fully, and she said, "I wondered why you are so open with me. You do not strike me as the kind of woman to break a code of secrecy..."

"I felt we could speak freely," the countess said. "Come, there is something I want to show you."

"I am sure there is." And now she raised her head, regarding the countess directly. "You do not intend for me to leave Scab at all, do you?"

"I'm not sure what you mean..." the countess said. Milady thought she detected a small smile playing at the corners of Dellamorte's lips.

"You can't imprison me," Milady said. She felt terribly weary. "I am an agent of the Council! I am needed elsewhere."

And now she could see the smile blossom fully. "The Council is a long way away," Countess Dellamorte said. "And you are a critical piece of the puzzle, and must be studied. Through you – through that alien object inserted in your head – I could reach the primary object, perhaps even initiate discussion with it! Who knows *what* we could learn!"

"I'll kill you first," Milady said quietly. The countess laughed. "I don't think you will," she said. She gestured with her head. Hands grabbed Milady on both sides. She had not even heard them approach. One was the man called McGill. The other was a woman with spots as of a leopard and sharp, canine teeth. "Put her in the coffin," the countess said. Turning to Milady – "Trust me, this is for the best."

She tried to fight, but they were strong, and more came in behind them. She felt something sharp touch her neck and then her body would no longer obey her. They carried her to the coffin and laid her down gently. Her eyes remained open. She could see and hear, but couldn't move. "I will begin by extracting the object," the countess said. "McGill! Record my observations. She will need to be carried to the surgical bay–"

A numbness spread through Milady's mind, a deep, terrible weariness. And yet, within it, a new voice whispered, and the thing in her eye socket moved restlessly, shifting against the bone and tender flesh, as if agitated. She was absurdly glad for the injection. She suspected that, if she was in full control of her faculties, the pain would have been unbearable.

Faintly, images rose in her mind. It was as if she and the jade have come to some sort of understanding, suddenly – a mutual, symbiotic relationship. *It needs me as a host,* she thought, appalled.

She felt them reach the coffin, bend down to lift it – and through the haze of jade became aware of the rat men behind the glass.

They were moving.

In her mind she could reach out, could *feel* them move – like marionettes, she thought, sickened. And yet she was controlling them. A shout above her, the coffin left untouched – "What are they doing?"

The rat men threw themselves against the glass.

"They're trying to break out!"

Countess Dellamorte: "Let them try."

Bodies moving soundlessly, not feeling the impact with the glass – and now she became aware of the silver strands, those strange, self-replicating entities crawling, *studying* – obeying the thing in her head.

Silver touched glass.

"That's not–"

The sound of breaking glass, erupting. A tall shape, a dirty coat around it, dark thick beard around a heavily lined face. The countess: "Karnstein... love..."

"Let her go, Camilla. She is *my* cargo."

"And you are mine..."

She couldn't see them. Trying to, through the rat men's eyes: two indistinct shapes facing off against each other, and she realised she was not controlling the captain. His words were his own.

"She knows too much now! She cannot leave."

"That is not your decision to make. You and I have chosen to serve the Council. We obey."

"No! This is *mine*, not–"

"Camilla, she must go where she is meant–"

"Karnstein... I just wanted you to... I need you to *heal*."

"I've been through worse." A short, coarse laugh. In her mind, a contraction – the silver strands along the captain's body slithering as one, pouring down the man's face, his arms, gathering in one spot.

"She's controlling you!"

"No. She's helping."

Through the rat men's eyes: Karnstein and the countess, face to face, almost touching. "I will stay."

A flash of jade. The silver strands separating from the captain's body. Mists rising, the silver woven into strands of fog – the voices murmuring of *Data transference initiated to primary core.*

The countess, her arms falling to her sides – a weary voice. Defeated. "She would have to go as she is. I can ship her with the cargo bound for the Long Island…"

In the silver strands she saw the city beneath the waves, the whole of Scab, the platform, the docking bays, the shafts into the sea – numbers, graphs, fleeting words: *Suspended animation, self-contained atmosphere, escape velocity–*

"Milady de Winter."

A voice above her. The captain? It was getting hard to distinguish sounds. "You are safe."

"I must give her another shot. The acceleration would otherwise kill her–"

Beyond the broken glass, she made the rat men nod.

A cool touch against her arm. Above her, softly, "Thank you–"

The jade fading, darkness crawling over. Her last sensation was of the lid of the glass coffin, closing above her.

INTERLUDE:
The New World

When he came off the ship it was into a new world. The harbour of the Long Island was a busy swarm of ships, from India and Mexico and Zululand, from Shanghai and Marseilles and even Portsmouth, in the heart of the Lizardine domain – entire fleets of ships disgorging passengers, cargo and exotic fauna. Amidst the smells of woodsmoke and cooking, of tar and salt and coal, amidst the hum of engines and the shouting of sailors a single feeling vibrated like a taut string, cutting across everything.

Excitement.

The Fair was coming.

And everyone was going to the Fair.

Kai stood on the railing and watched the throng below. Men were leading elephants off one ship – African elephants, the Manchu told him. They were enormous beings, far larger than the Asian type, and the males stalked and turned giant tusks menacingly. A troupe of Egyptian dancers; German acrobats dressed all in white; French automatons moving jerkily; Japanese swordsmen mingled with Italian knife-throwers, Indian magicians and Syrian horsemen. Beside him, the Manchu smiled, and said, "We will be lost amongst them as completely as if we were invisible."

"I have been invisible for too long," Kai said, but quietly. The

Emerald Buddha was quiet beside him, ensconced within a sturdy wooden crate. He thought then of the strange woman of his dreams, the one-eyed lady who evoked in him unfamiliar feelings – she reminded him, uncomfortably, of himself.

"Make me into a gun," he whispered, the words of long ago returning, and beside him the Manchu stiffened, and sent him a querying look. Kai shook his head, and the Manchu relaxed – just slightly.

Down in the harbour, young warriors of the Lenape kept order; a busy fish market was doing brisk trade; and beyond Kai could see fields of maize moving gently in the breeze. He took a deep breath, smelling this alien continent, this strange new world. Beyond the Long Island lay an entire continent, and they were going deep into it, following the buffalo roads into the lands of the Nations, and to the city the whole world, it seemed, was going to at once.

Shikaakwa. What the new settlers called Chicago, the black city. But a new city was rising there now, a new city to welcome the world…

And him, too. The Manchu was right. They would be all but invisible in the crowd, and safe – and the world would come and send its emissaries with it, to deal with Kai for the treasure he held. A treasure he never asked for, or wanted, but which was his burden nonetheless.

And as for the Emerald Buddha itself… Kai gripped the railings and looked out at the new continent, not seeing it, seeing rather the disturbing dreams he had been having, the dreams of pock-marked, cratered surfaces, of giant objects floating through space, and stars, so many stars…

The Emerald Buddha, he couldn't help but know, had plans of its own.

PART VI
The Black City

SIXTY-ONE
A Bowl of Hokkien Noodles

When she woke up she could smell something frying and her stomach growled, belly muscles moving in protest; her mouth tasted like a Parisian street sewer and her eye ached; everything ached. For a moment she was back on the *White Worm*, the deck rolling beneath her, the ghosts of childhood moaning beneath the waves. She felt hot, then cold. She shivered, her heart beating fast – too fast.

What had Countess Dellamorte *given* her?

She felt the green thing embedded in her eye socket move. For a moment she caught a flash of something far away – Kai riding a horse across a wild landscape, his cowl pushed back, his face, for just a moment, open in childish joy. His servant rode behind him. They were going towards–

She shivered again, and moaned. A voice above her said, "You should be dead, but aren't. Surely that is something to celebrate?"

She opened her eyes and glared at Ebenezer Long.

The elderly Mongolian was squatting on his haunches, looking at her with a smile. The ground was moving – no. It hadn't been the ship at all, she realised – she was inside a moving carriage. She could hear the neighing of horses, smell their pungent excrement, and beyond that–

The smell of smoke, of machines, of people – many people. But those smells were in the distance and right here the air was dominated by cooking, just as her vision was obscured by the old Xia master. She said, "I guess somebody up there likes me."

"I doubt it," Master Long said, but he smiled when he said it. She said, "Where am I?" and tried to rise from the coffin–

Her muscles screamed in protest and again the shivering took her. Master Long said, "You are suffering withdrawal. As much as I can tell you have been injected with a powerful chemical compound distilled from opium. Water?"

He offered her a glass. She reached out with her human hand (it was shaking) and took it from him. She drank.

"Take deep breaths."

When she did her heart slowed, a little. She pushed herself up and looked around. There wasn't much to see. The carriage was covered – she could smell the not-unpleasant residue of the skins it was made of – and a small burner on the floor was heating up a pot which Master Long now returned to. He stirred the things inside with a pair of chopsticks.

"Soup," Master Long said, "is always the best cure at the end of a long journey."

"Eastern philosophy?"

"Mrs Beeton. Remarkable woman. Would you like some?"

"Maybe in a moment." Sitting up, she took another deep breath. "I do suspect you'd have been dead by now if it weren't for the object lodged in your head. Incredible. We spent so much time chasing it across Paris and here it is, after all that. I've told you once before, Milady: you are Xiake, a true warrior of Xia. Now more so than ever…"

"I did not ask for this thing," she said. Then, more quietly – "Is there any way to take it out?"

"Not without killing you, I suspect… Please, have some noodles."

Master Long lifted the pot from its little stove and dished out food into a bowl. Milady said, "What is it?" The smell rose around her, its fragrance overpowering – suddenly she could think of little else.

"*Hokkien hae mee,*" Master Long said. "Or Hokkien noodles, if you prefer. A dish from Fujian that had undergone changes in Malaya – food, like people, must continue to evolve."

She took the bowl. She brought it to her lips and drank. Beside her, Master Long served another helping into a second bowl and sat picking at it with his chopsticks.

A flash of jade – a flash of fear that almost made her drop the bowl. She was no longer in the carriage, but elsewhere – in a dark, rectangular cavern. Beams held up the ceiling, and the ground was made of dark soil. She saw vats and barrels standing forlorn against the makeshift walls. A cellar.

Two things dominated the airless room. One was a steel-top operating table, of a kind she was well familiar with – too familiar with. It was empty.

The other thing was a kiln.

A flash of jade, and now a dark figure was moving in the cellar, lighting up a lamp above the operating table. It was approaching the kiln, setting to lighting it, and the flames began to rise, casting the room in shadows... The figure turned, sniffed the air, and Milady shrank back. "I can taste you..." the Phantom said. When he turned his face on her he smiled. "Do you like it?" he said. "Have you come to find me? I'll be waiting, Cleo..."

He turned away from her then, and walked back towards a door, and reached to open it. Milady dreaded the opening of that door. The movements of the Phantom were careful, fluid – theatrical, she thought. When he opened the door a gurney stood outside. Strapped to the gurney was a young woman. She seemed asleep. The Phantom began to pull the gurney into the cellar. "I cannot help the fact that I am a murderer," he said. "No more than the poet can help the inspiration to sing."

Milady raised her gun arm, wanting to shoot him, willing him dead, but already the scene was fading, the flash of jade gone, and she was back in the moving carriage and Master Long was regarding her quizzically, the chopsticks like weapons in his hand. "There is a great evil," he said, "in those with the power of Xia who fall from the path..."

"I saw him," she said. Master Long nodded, not speaking. "He's killing again. Here. He's close. And he won't stop – he won't stop!"

"Then you must stop him," Master Long said.

Somehow, the bowl of Hokkien noodles was empty in her hands. She stared at it – a simple clay bowl, burned in a kiln... "Teach me," she said. "Teach me how."

But Master Long shook his head. "I don't know," he said. "But you will–" He hesitated, then shook his head again. She said, "What?"

Instead of an answer he rose, and reached to the flap of the carriage's tarpaulin. "We're almost there," he said. Then he lifted the flap, and the world came pouring into the carriage.

SIXTY-TWO
The Black City

Tall, grey buildings rose high into the smoke-filled air in the distance. The ground itself seemed to thrum with the beating of unseen, enormous engines. From a distance the city looked like a malevolent maze, a trap closing in on the crowds of people and the passing of carriages and baruch-landaus. Two black airships hung suspended in the air above the city like silent carrion birds. Milady inhaled deeply, smelling the sharp tang of chemical waste, smoke, grease, blood and human waste. There was only one city in the world like it, and she knew it immediately.

Shikaakwa.

Chicagoland.

She had passed through there several times, with Barnum's circus, in the old days. The city had changed, she noticed: buildings grew taller, the streets darker, the mass of humanity greater – but the smell remained the same, the blood from the slaughterhouse district and the stench from the factories – the smell of human misery, the smell of a city–

In a strange way, the smell of home.

And now she could see the banners, flying everywhere, the flying streamers, the gay colours amidst the grey and black. All announcing the same event, the same momentous gathering:

she stared at the approaching city, the carriage's progress slower now as it joined a stream of other vehicles and riders along the road. All going to the same place.

"The World's Vespuccian Exposition," Master Long said – and was that longing in his voice? He saw her look and smiled, embarrassed. "The World's Fair. They say it is the greatest show on Earth," he said. "An inexhaustible dream of beauty…"

"Have you *seen* the Exposition Universelle?" Milady said, civic pride offended. Ebenezer Long nodded, but the smile remained. "They say this will be grander," he said dreamily. Milady stared at the old Shaolin master. For a moment he seemed like the child he must have been, long ago, the one who went looking for relics in the desert. "Dreams can hurt you," she said, but quietly.

The Exposition Universelle took place in Paris four years previously. She remembered it vividly – the exhibits of shining new guns from Colt and Mauser, the demonstration of new police techniques given by the chief of Scotland Yard herself, Irene Adler, and that gruesome exhibition of explosives, cunningly hidden in books, that were authentic samples of the work of that most shadowy of assassins, known only as the Bookman… She had been particularly taken with a lecture on poisons, both ancient and modern, delivered by Dr Grimesby Roylott, a renowned authority in the field, who kept the audience riveted with his account of the deadly Indian swamp adder. Yes, the Exposition Universelle had been dazzling – and she doubted the Vespuccians could pull off anything quite like it.

"Not everything is a weapon," Master Long said, as if reading her mind.

She said, "But everything can be made into one."

Master Long did not reply. A young man – little more than a boy – was driving the cart, she noticed. She did not recognise his face. They were approaching the city, and she soon began to distinguish people in the seemingly endless crowd – local Potawatomis, visiting Sioux, Iroquois, Shawnee and others, European immigrants, Chinese and Indians, Malay and Zulu – some escaping the growing lizardine dominance of their nations, some merely seeking out new life in this wide, remote continent. And amongst them all the visitors, distinguished by their dress and their air of faint unease as they navigated the unfamiliar roads of Chicagoland, drawn, all drawn like slivers of metal to a lodestone, all drawn to the World's Fair.

This is where he will come, she knew. The Man on the Mekong, the man from her dreams. This is where he was heading, to sell or trade or buy his way away from that alien statue, the one that dominated them both and bound them both. The two of them, and a third: for the Phantom, too, had come to the black city. She thought of her vision again, the sight of him in that cold, dark cellar, the wheeled gurney and the woman strapped to it, drugged and asleep... He would wake her up, she knew, before he began. He would want her to know what was happening, alive with fear for every single second, until the end.

How many had there already been? He must already be in the city. Like a shadow, like a phantom, he could be impossible to find – but he would want her hunting. She knew that, somewhere in that black city ahead, a message would be waiting for her: a message from her Phantom.

"How did I get here?" she said, turning away from premonitions of dread. She turned to Master Long. "Last I remember I was..." she hesitated, then said, "far away, on the ocean–"

"You were delivered," Master Long said, "to an unregistered naval station on the Long Island, by means, I believe, of a sub-aquatic vehicle. A very *rapid* device, and the Council agent in charge sent a query through – shall we say, unofficial channels – to my people. It was decided that, since our objectives are closely linked with the Council's –" she noticed he didn't say they were the same – "I shall assume temporary responsibility for your well-being. As I said, I am glad to see you're not dead."

"Thanks."

"Don't mention it."

"What *are* your objectives?" she said. "Out of curiosity."

"The same as yours," he said – which left it ambiguous.

"Mine, or the Council's?"

"Are they not the same?"

She had no answer for that, and Master Long smiled, and said nothing. The carriage rode towards the black city.

SIXTY-THREE
The Message

A man came through the door with a gun.

Midnight in the black city: Milady de Winter's accommodation a boarding house for gentlewomen on Tecumseh's Road. Starlight breaking through grimy windows, the floor creaking with heavy steps – she was ready.

"Drop it."

His smile lit up his face. The gun disappeared, like magic, into its holster. She stared, said, "*Cody?*"

"Cleo!"

She lowered her gun hand. The man's gaze travelled down, examined it. When it rose up it took in her eyepatch. He raised his eyebrows. Milady shook her head. Cody grinned.

"Good to see you're still alive," he said.

"You too," she said. His grin widened. "You didn't expect me to be," he said – not a question so much as a statement of fact.

She shook her head. He said, "Sorry to disappoint."

"Not at all."

The grinned at each other, and suddenly Milady de Winter was gone, as if she had never existed, and she was Cleo again, *Cleopatra of Dahomey, The Amazon Queen!* And he was...

"Damn you, Bill Cody," she said. "How did you find me?"

"Aren't you gonna ask me in?"

She swept her hand. "Sure."

Buffalo Bill came into the room. He took off his wide-brimmed hat. His eyes hadn't left Cleo's. "Heard you married an Englishman."

"It didn't last."

"Never does," he said, "with the British."

"How's Lulu?"

His grin was a little abashed. "She's fine," he said, scratching his beard. "You know."

"She didn't come with you?"

"She prefers to stay at home these days."

"You mean *you* prefer her to stay at home."

He shrugged, smiled. "So many ladies…" he said.

She stared at him. He was older than she remembered, stockier. The beard had strands of white and grey. Buffalo Bill Cody: ranger, rider, showman first and foremost. "I didn't realise you were part of the Fair."

"We're not," he said. "I offered to pay, but they turned me down. So we set up just outside. Eighteen thousand seats, Cleo – and we fill 'em every night. We get paid – and the Fair doesn't. Their loss. You got any drinks?"

"This is a *ladies'* boarding house, you know," she said.

"You ain't no lady, Cleo," he said, and she had to laugh. "I am now," she said.

Buffalo Bill shook his head. "Now ain't that the darnest thing," he said. "What was his name?"

"De Winter."

"Sounds chilly. Whatever happened to him?"

She didn't answer, and his smile widened again. "Poor feller," he said, his hat clutched to his chest. She shook her head, went to the dresser, and uncorked a crystal decanter. Pouring two glasses, she carried them over, handed him one. They clinked glasses and both downed their drinks. "Damn, that's better," Buffalo Bill said.

"Damn, Cody, why are you here?" she said.

"I told you. I heard you were here." But he wasn't smiling any more.

"Heard how?"

"We're the main attraction of this World's Fair," Buffalo Bill said – modesty, she thought, had never been one of his strong points. "Nothing much gets past my people."

"Who, specifically?"

For a moment he looked uncomfortable. "Elderly Asian gentleman, in fact. You should see the Chinese pavilion in the White City, Cleo. It's something. Though I'm not sure he was Chinese…"

"Why did he tell you where I am?" then, seeing his face – "Cody, are you in some sort of trouble?"

The smile had gone completely from his face. And now she saw that his face was pale, and that the hand holding the empty glass was – though it was barely noticeable – shaking.

"Tell me," she said, feeling an urgency rise inside her like a physical force, and Buffalo Bill said, "I'd better show you."

"What is the meaning of this?"

The man was clearly agitated. He was young, barely past twenty, yet his authority was obvious. His dark, expensive suit sat on him uneasily, as if the man was too restless to let the signs of money on him rest. Cody said, "That's Bloom. Sol Bloom. He's the head of concessions for the Midway." His smile was crooked. "In other words, he gets to pick the shows."

They were standing outside the White City. She had not been prepared for it. She tried to block out the rising skyline, but impressions kept flittering through.

The giant pyramid at the hub of the Fair…

The white electric Tesla lights bathing the scene…

That giant, ever-moving wheel, crackling with a sort of eldritch tension…

She said, "But you're not part of the Fair."

"Sol was appointed too late to sign us up. One of the things he vehemently regrets…"

There was a crowd. There was always, she began to realise, a crowd in this place. There were horse riders and belly dancers, knife throwers and clowns – grim-faced Potawatomi warriors reinforced with federal troops – she saw Mohawks and Sioux and Lenape amongst them – tried to keep the crowd away.

But it was impossible. The press of bodies, even here, outside the White City itself, was showing no sign of abating. She heard shocked whispers, excited conversations muted by the glare of electric lights. When she raised her head those tall, impossible buildings rose above, and the wheel turned, and turned…

She took a deep breath through her mouth and tried to focus.

She had seen something like this once before.

She had seen it, every day, in the mirror.

She bit her lips until she drew blood. Her gun arm twitched.

But there was no one to shoot.

"This is an atrocity!"

Sol Bloom, hands waving. "We cannot let this sort of thing go on!"

From the captain of the guards – "The chiefs must hear about this."

"They must *not!*" Bloom's face was turning red. "The president himself is coming to the Fair! I will *not* present Sitting Bull with a, with a…" his hand, waving, took in the gruesome scene. Then Bloom deflated. "I don't feel so well," he said. Cleo watched him hurry away. A little way back, Bloom was loudly sick.

Cleo couldn't blame him.

She knelt down and examined the corpse.

SIXTY-FOUR
Winnetou

"I saw it..." Cody swallowed. "*Her*, when I came out after the show. I–"

She cut him off. "Do you know who she is?"

"No." He shrugged. "Do you have any idea how many people come to the Fair every day?"

She could imagine. Above her the White City still rose, immense, dominating – an urban space erected in the span of months: a city of the future.

She stared at the corpse.

The young woman had Cleo's dark skin, though she was shorter in stature, and younger. A visitor from one of the African nations? Or a transplanted Vespuccian?

She had the feeling it didn't matter. *Who* the girl had been in life was not, she felt, a factor for the killer.

But who she resembled in death...

She had to turn away, for a moment. But she couldn't look away. When her gaze returned it took in the hole where the woman's eye should have been, and the amputated arm was nowhere to be found. One of the woman's legs, too, was missing.

"Tômas..." she whispered, and didn't know what the feeling that rose in her was – was it anger – or fear?

The Phantom, her Phantom, had left her a message, a letter signed in innocent blood.

"Word will be out all over the city by daybreak," Sol Bloom said, groaning. Then, as if noticing her for the first time – "Who the hell is she?"

Cleo didn't answer; and Bloom, taking in suddenly the similar appearance of the corpse to this strange woman, turned white. "Special agent for the Quiet Council," Cleo – no, it was Milady de Winter speaking, now – said. "This murder relates to an on-going investigation."

Bloom didn't ask for her papers. "Is this – is this official, then?" he said.

Milady shook her head. "The Council likes to keep things... quiet," she said. "Your people no doubt wish to do the same."

"Sitting Bull is coming to the Fair and how do you think this will *look*?" Bloom said. He glared accusingly at Cody. "This isn't even a *part* of the Fair proper," he said.

"I *offered* to lease space in the Fair grounds–" Buffalo Bill began–

"You know perfectly well I was not yet in place–"

"Gentlemen!"

They quietened at her voice. Their argument sounded like a long-rehashed one. "Please."

The local force, she noticed, had not yet made a move other than to secure the perimeter of the scene. Neither did the feder-als... Waiting, she thought. Who were they waiting for?

The answer became apparent when a new man came march-ing into the arena.

He was dressed in comfortable clothes the colour of trees in autumn. On his feet, moccasins made his movement silent. He wore a gun in a shoulder-holster, and a single white feather in his hair.

At a signal from him the local force began to push the crowd of onlookers away. He strode forwards, then knelt down beside the corpse. When he rose again his face was expressionless. He said, "I want the man who did this."

Milady nodded. She said, "I'm Mi–"

"Lady de Winter, yes. I know who you are." For a moment his eyes softened, and there was a pull of amusement at the corners of his lips. "I watched you, long ago, when you were with Barnum's show. You had a different name, then."

"You can call me Cleo," she said – surprising herself. The man did smile, then. "Winnetou," he said.

She nodded. The Vespuccian signalled to his men. Four hurried over and lifted the young woman's body off the ground. "We'll do this your masters' way," Winnetou said. "Quietly."

"Is she the first?" Milady said. But the Vespuccian did not reply.

In under fifteen minutes nothing remained of the crime scene. A relieved Sol Bloom declared he had full faith in Winnetou's authority and left, accompanied by an Egyptian belly dancer. Buffalo Bill, told to keep word of the event to himself, muttered there was nothing to worry about on *his* side and departed too, giving Cleo a parting look she found hard to interpret. In under fifteen minutes the crowd had been dispersed, the body removed, the blood washed away – and Cleo was left alone with Winnetou, who said, "We need to talk."

White electric light illuminated the night.

The White City rose above them, alien structures above an ancient shore. Suddenly she missed the smell of sawdust and paint, the shouts as the heavy canvas tent was raised every night... There had been torches, then, burning against the dark.

It all seemed a very long time ago.

She said, "Then talk."

He looked around. Was anyone watching them? she wondered, uneasily. Would the Phantom be watching, making sure she got his message? He would enjoy it, she knew. Winnetou took her arm. She followed him, feeling relief as they drew away from the scene of the murder. "The World's Vespuccian Exposition," Winnetou said. "Millions of visitors, and a handful of police. What's one corpse amidst the multitude?" Even at this hour, even outside the White City itself, the streets were thronged with people. A gaiety in the air, excited voices raised, the smell of candy... a gaiety neither of them shared.

"How many?" she said. He shrugged. "Who knows?" he said.

She pictured it in her mind. The visitors came streaming to this place, this city of the future – whole families, single men looking for work, single women... and the sharks who always circled in the sea of humanity, scenting weakness, scenting fresh blood... How many young women came to the Fair and disappeared in the sea, never to be seen or heard from again?

"The letters keep coming," Winnetou said. "'Have you seen my daughter? She went to Shikaakwa to see the Fair. She came looking for work. She came looking for a husband. She came looking.'" He sighed, a long shudder of air, and said, "She'd seen too much. She'd seen–" His hand gestured in the air, towards the place they'd been. "She'd seen *that*, and that was the last thing she'd seen."

Dread rose in Milady like bubbles from the depths of a dark sea. How many others? She had seen the Phantom's sanctuary, that windowless cellar, dominated by a kiln... she, too, had seen too much.

Yet she was still alive.

"He has to be caught," she said. Winnetou nodded. When he turned to face her, his expression was ferocious. "He will be," he said. "But you will not get involved."

She said, "Excuse me?"

He sighed. They paused under a street light. A pool of white electric light fell over them, its edges cast in shadows. He said, "Milady – Cleo – I have the highest regard for you. You must know that. Your masters have communicated with mine. I have seen your dossier. What you went through... it must have been terrible."

She looked into his eyes, waiting. He seemed reluctant to continue. At last she said, "But–?"

"But you will *not* involve yourself in this investigation," he said.

"That's unacceptable," she said, and he almost smiled. "Let me put it in plain words," he said. "This is *my* case. Make sure you stay out of my way."

She took a step back. After a moment, she nodded. This was not her jurisdiction. She had no power here, and he did. "I don't want you to get hurt," he said, and she said, "It's a little late for that."

His smile was rueful. "Enjoy your stay," he said. "Really, you must visit the Fair. They tell me it's spectacular."

And with that, like a shadow, he was away – a lone, long-legged man with a feather in his hair and a gun close to hand. Lawmen were the same, she thought, wherever you went in the world. Like cab drivers...

"Let's see who gets there first," she whispered, and a small smile touched, unexpectedly, the corner of her lips.

SIXTY-FIVE
Top of the World

He was close, she knew. Somewhere nearby... he would set himself up close to the Fair. Like her, he was bound to the statue, changed by it. They were linked, the way the Kai man was, that lonely man she had only seen in her dreams... all three of them, bound by that alien statue and those terrible, insane voices that emanated from it. The Phantom would want the jade statue but more than that, he would want to be close to that sea of humanity, seeking out those vulnerable, lonely souls floating within. He would stalk them, slowly, patiently. He would isolate them, charm them, bewitch them and finally, when they least expected it, put an end to them. He was close – he could be watching – watching and waiting.

Well, let him watch. They would meet again, and soon – and it would be Tômas who would scream for mercy then.

She walked without hurrying, the streets alive with humanity, the outline of that strange, white city rising above the black. Mohawk and Sioux and Lenape mingled with English and Romanian, Zulu and Sotho, Egyptian and French, Chinese and Siamese and Indian – for the world had come to the World's Fair. They had named it for Vespucci, the man whose ill-fated voyage from Europe to the New World had brought back with it the awakened Les Lézards. Now the lizards sat on the green throne of England, ruling an empire over which, it was said, the sun never set. The machines, the old and patient machines ruled France, and in the Middle Kingdom the secret societies of the Wulin schemed to get back the power they had lost, and an Empress-Dowager ruled behind the throne...

They had all come here, to this Chicagoland, and to the free continent where the Council of Chiefs ruled by consent of all. They had welcomed in the new immigrants, given them land to set their cities on, and kept a wary eye beyond the shore, fearing Victoria and her get.

This is the future, they seemed to say. A human future, in a place you do not rule. When you come, come as guests.

And yet the lizards, too, had come to the Fair. She saw a black hansom cab go past and as it did a curtain twitched, and she caught sight of the elongated skull inside, and alien eyes caught, for just a moment, hers...

They had plans, she thought. Long, patient, ancient plans. What did they really want? Where had they come from?

And she thought – perhaps the jade statue could answer those questions...

Pain.

It came on her without warning. It ran down her arm and into her stomach and she doubled over. In the empty place of her eye the *thing* moved, that foreign presence, a beetle grasping, and she almost screamed.

Pain. The taste of bile in her mouth, and her breathing came out ragged and short. She felt a shiver go down her spine, the hair rising on her arms, the back of her neck.

A flash of jade, the pain arcing through her like electricity–

Then she was gone, the street disappearing, and she was standing somewhere high up, looking down at the White City.

A balustrade of green metal – the lizards' metal, the stuff they had made Notre Dame out of, and their Royal Palace. The pyramid, she realised – the great pyramid that dominated the White City, towering above the white buildings, casting its shadow over the Midway. It was a not-so-subtle message. The Fair may have been the world's, it seemed to say – but the world belonged to the creatures who had, centuries before, cast their power over it. An exhibition space, in truth: displaying the power and glory of the Lizardine Empire, in rising levels – and she was somewhere high up, near the pinnacle, and looking down–

It was quiet there, and the wind blew hard and cold, and black clouds came drifting from the lake. It smelled of coming rain, and cold.

And in the voice of the wind she heard those other voices.

They sounded excited. Impatient. They spoke of *Ninety percent completion rate* and *electrodynamic properties readjustment* and *spatial alignment* and the jade in her head shifted and turned as if it, too, was excited, and the pain throbbed through her and she screamed.

She was not alone up there, she realised then. Down below, the mass of humanity, illuminated by the harsh white light, seemed as insignificant as an anthill, as featureless. What did a single ant signify? She was not seeing them with her own eyes, she suddenly knew. When she turned her body was a thing of metal and flesh, and the jade was everywhere in it, and her mouth opened and whispered, "Kai. My name is Kai."

She saw herself reflected in the green alien metal. The face that stared back at her was *his* face, the Man on the Mekong, who was no longer on the distant Mekong river – he was here, on the top of the world, looking down at his own reflection. The sadness in his eyes arrested her.

An image in her mind – a giant wheel, turning, a flash of lightning – then it was gone. She saw her hands – his hands – close over the balustrade as if trying to rip them apart. The pain arced through her again and she thought – *It is his pain I am feeling*.

"Kai," she said, and the lips that weren't hers moved with her intent.

Then they said, "Help me–" and the jade flared through him, through her, and the pain burned and they were severed.

When she opened her eyes again she was lying on the ground,

beyond the walls of the city, where she had fallen. A small crowd had gathered to watch. From down here they were not ants, she thought. Each one was different, each one an agent of his or her own fate. She raised her head, looking up at the pyramid. Lights spun in the air above the Fair. The giant wheel kept moving, carrying passengers in its hanging cars. Did they, too, see only ants? she wondered. She pushed herself up, trying to ignore the crowd. A carriage with black windows was parked on the other side of the street. As she stood up lightning flashed in the black sky overhead, and rain began to fall.

SIXTY-SIX
The Monsignor

"Milady de Winter."

The voice was chilly, the voice of a long winter. She knew it well, from another time, another place...

Hated it, feared it – respected it, too.

She wished someone had told her it would be the Monsignor.

They had picked her up when she was still trying to recover from the flash of pain. Two of them, out of the black carriage, expressionless mannequins, coming to her aid. When they closed on her, one on either side, she knew who had sent them.

Now she was sitting in the moving carriage, the silent man-shaped automatons on either side of her, and the Monsignor before her.

One of the oldest of the Quiet Council... modelled on a man who had lived long ago. His robes were dark purple, his eyes lifeless. The voice was old, scratched, and came slowly. The voice said, "Need I remind you of your obligations?"

She didn't reply. A bald head, a scratch running down one side. The semblance of humanity was fleeting. He was one of the oldest, with a skin of yellow rubber and jerky motions, primitive technologies patched and haphazardly upgraded over the years... She said, "You are the resident agent in charge?"

He snorted. "I am the Council," he said, the words each of

them, those secret masters of France, said when they took their place. All for one, and one for all – she remembered that, too, from another time and place. It was cold, and she was wet from the rain. On either side of her the Monsignor's mannequin bodyguards were motionless.

"I have not been told–" she said, and his voice exploded out of the unmoving lips: "You are not meant to be *told*! You are meant to *listen*!"

"I'm listening," she said. A pain in her head. Dim jade light bursting and fading in her field of vision.

"I doubt it," the Monsignor said. "You were told to secure the *item*," he said. "Do you have any *concept* of its importance?"

"To France?" she said.

"To all of us!" the Monsignor said. "Humans, machines – anyone on this tiny, fragile world. In the wrong hands it could end us all."

"I am working on locating the–" she began, but he cut her off. "No," he said. "Do not lie, Milady. Do not lie, not to *me*."

"Locating the Phantom…" she said, almost whispering.

"Yes…" the ancient automaton said. "Truth, now. A rare and precious ingredient in our mix of spices, is it not? And so refreshing…"

She said nothing. Could machines taste? Could they smell? Did they really comprehend what spices were, or what they meant? She did not intend to ask. The Monsignor said, "You will *not* pursue Tômas."

Tension knotted in her stomach. She raised her head and stared directly at the automaton. "He is killing people. Women."

"The lives of the few matter little," the Monsignor said. "The lives of everyone living now and still unborn are in danger. Tômas… can be useful. You will not pursue him."

It was said with a finality she could not abide. She said, "He can't be allowed to remain free!"

"Tômas will answer to the Council in due course," the Monsignor said, sounding amused. "As will you. For now, you must seek out the item and secure it. There are many, here, in both the black city and the white, seeking, searching – and it is close, Milady, is it not so? Can you not feel it?"

And as he spoke she saw it – a tiny glimmer of jade as the Monsignor's head moved. So there *had* been other fragments. "Sometimes I believe I can hear voices…" he said. "Speaking too softly for me to understand. They do not use Tesla waves nor light nor anything I understand, and yet they speak, and the world shakes… It is a machine, Milady. A very dangerous machine, held by a very dangerous man. They must both be contained."

She wanted to shake her head then, to explain – about Kai, about being trapped by the statue, about having no choices – but it was the Monsignor before her, the Cardinal, they once called him, and he had no mercy – none of them ever did.

I am the Council, she thought, and shuddered, and the cold seeped deeper into her.

"You are wet," he said. "Unwell. Return to your quarters, dry, rest. Leave Tômas… to me. And find the item!"

The carriage stopped. The door opened, by itself. The bodyguard on the left stepped out, scanned the area, gave a tiny nod.

"Goodbye, Milady," the Monsignor said. "Remember our conversation."

Outside, puddles of water on the grimy street, and fog curled in the air around them. Gas lamps burned here, yellow flames fighting the night, not the blinding white of the Fair. This was the old city, the black city – and they had deposited her outside her boarding house.

The bodyguard returned into the carriage. The door closed. The carriage moved away and shortly disappeared into the fog, and she was left alone.

I should do what he says, she thought. I should go back inside, and wash, and rest, and tomorrow go hunting for Kai. I could find him, too. He is nearby, and the voices have plans…

She nodded. When she clenched her phantom arm the gun it had become wanted to fire. Soon, she thought. She looked up, at the closed doors of the boarding house. Then she thought of the dead mutilated girl left for her to find.

SIXTY-SEVEN
Holmes

She thought of what Master Long had told her, all that time ago, beneath the Seine, in that dark half-world of the under-city of Paris.

The code of Xia, he had said.

There *was* a code, she thought. It was not something you could put into words, as such. It was not set down in writing, not signed, not displayed. It was a... a feeling, a sense of right and wrong.

She had been told to follow the statue, and let a murderer go free.

And she knew, then, that she couldn't do it.

It was not a matter of choice. It was simply what she had to do, the path she had to follow – against orders, against sense, perhaps. There was a choice, the Monsignor had told her: of saving a world, or saving a handful of lives. But she could not quantify one against the other. Perhaps it was too big for her, too incomprehensible – a world was a hazy concept, ill-defined: but a murdered woman was a murdered woman, and a killer was a killer.

She turned her back on the boarding house. It was raining again, and the streets were dark. It suited her. The flames of the gas lamps cast yellow light that shivered over broken cobblestones. This was a place she understood.

She ran her fingers over her gun arm. The Gatling gun was fully loaded, she knew. She felt awake then, alive. She walked down the streets and watched the shadows, and they watched her back, and knew her for one of their own. People disappeared in the black city. The river washed corpses away. It was a place of profound change, this Chicagoland. For here, the city of the past met the city of the future, and yellow light gave way to white. It was a dream-future, dreamed up by humanity, a shiny, alluring future – but was it real?

There would always be killers, she thought. And there would always be people like her, to try and stop them. Nothing more, nor less, than human. There were no eternal champions, no guardians of the ages at the end of time... there were only the laws, the kind humans made, and the guns they made to keep them.

And so she went, to keep the law. She knew the Phantom would be somewhere nearby. He would stay close to the white city, to the future city, but not within it. He would prey on the unwary, the dreamers, those who came to see the future, to be mesmerised by it, and forget this was still the old world, and predators lurked in it – not in the dark but in the light, with charming smiles and pleasant words...

A boarding house, she thought.

A shiver ran down her. Her hair was a dark halo in the gaslight. Did she guess it, intuitively, or did she sense it, through that fragile link that joined her to the Phantom? He would open a boarding house, and welcome in those lonely, trusting souls, those visitors to the great Fair. A boarding house near enough to the white city, and cheap enough – for the right boarder. For there would be a different price to pay...

She prowled the street, restless, her gun arm ready at her side. Though he had not been so easy to kill, the last time...

But then, neither was she.

She tried something then. The same way it had happened on Scab: she reached *inside* herself, reached for that alien thing lodged in her empty eye socket, wakening it. The pain tore through her, worse than ever. The thing *shifted*, and she imagined the groan of bones and flesh as the jade moved in her head like a living thing. Jade flashed, inside her head or outside, she didn't know. The pain was terrible, and she was bending over, bile rising in her throat again, through her and onto the street. She blinked away tears. Flashes of jade, and she tried to control them, tried to *direct* them.

Dead... the dead were all around her. She could sense them, in that other world – *quantum representational matrix, data storage*, the voices seemed to whisper – minds trapped, studied, analysed, and stored, like victuals. There was a body floating down the river, and silver snaked across its skin. There was a body in a cart, being driven to a hospital – two men in the front talking of the price it would fetch, not aware that, behind them, underneath the tarpaulin, the corpse was twitching, moving... and beyond, beyond, pushing through the pain: searching for *him*.

She was retching, blind now, on her knees, but still she pushed, still she searched – voices coming from afar: *Ninety-five percent lockdown, opening sequences checksum correct!–*

And then she saw him.

He stood before a tall mirror. He was changed again – Tômas with his thousand faces, dressed now in a respectable black suit, his face different, a pleasant countenance – but she could see the silver strands run like eels down his arms, beneath the cuffs of his ironed shirt. He was smiling at the mirror, practising. Did he know she was there? Did he know she was watching through his eyes?

"How do you do, Mr Holmes?" the Phantom said to his mirror-self. He bowed, then reached out and put on a tall beaver hat. "How do you *do*, Mr Holmes?"

Holmes, she thought. It was the name of a well-known British detective. Had Tômas taken on the name?

"A pleasure to see you again, my dear."

She startled back, thinking he was speaking to her. But no – he was still practising his patter – like a magician before a show, she thought. The pain throbbed through her. She didn't know how long she could keep watching. "I have missed you, terribly. I trust you enjoyed your visit to the Fair?"

Mimicking again – a girl now. "Oh, it was wonderful! The lights, the buildings! How do they build them so tall?"

"A marvel of the age–" Tômas again, a charming smile. "But come, I have a surprise for you."

"You do? Oh, how wonderful! What is it?"

"It's a secret," he said. "I will have to show you…"

"Is it far?"

"It is right here… in my cellar," he said.

Then he chuckled. Staring at himself in the mirror, his face changed again, the silver flowing into it, the skull elongating, teeth growing. His eyes shone with jade. "You will like it there," he said.

SIXTY-EIGHT
The Phantom's Maze

Coming out of the vision her skull burned with pain. Her eyes were holes poked through with sharpened sticks dipped in acid. The fragment of jade, full of jagged edges, burned like a star in her eye socket. Retching, nothing came out, and she wondered when she had eaten last. The taste in her mouth was of the sour drink she had given Wild Bill.

Coffee, she thought. She needed strong, black coffee.

Wrapping herself more tightly in her long coat, she strode across the dark streets. The pain receded, slowly, but did not go away. She wondered if it would always be there, now – growing in strength slowly, the closer she approached its source. Somewhere in the city the statue waited, and planned. The voices were always there now, just on the edge of hearing, growing stronger all the time. They said only one thing she fully understood.

Their time was coming.

She should be going after the voices, after that thing that somehow scanned and briefly animated the dead – the thing that was patiently gathering information, patiently planning something terrible–

And yet the voices sounded so *lonely*. It was hard to feel the urgency, even when the fragment sent shards of sharp pain into her mind, even when the voices spoke of *ninety-six percent completion* and *initiation procedure checksum correct*, even as the percentages grew closer and closer to a hundred–

It was the Phantom who worried her, who *scared* her. The Phantom she hated – for what he did, for what he had become: for what *she* had become, perhaps.

Holmes. The name kept reverberating in her mind. Now she had a name to put to the phantom in her mind. A name, and a place: a boarding house, close enough to the white city, yet on the edges of the black.

In an all-night diner she ordered coffee and grimaced as she sipped it. Staring through grimy glass windows at the rain outside... the place was awash in smoke and flickering lights, and sawdust covered the floor. A newspaper lying on the next table spoke of Sitting Bull arriving for the presidential visit at the Fair. She picked it up and leafed through it. There was a feature about the wheel. A man named Ferris had built it. A notice about a picture show. The newspaper was full of nothing but the Fair. She sipped her coffee and turned the pages until she reached the *Classifieds* section. Staring at it, she realised she could not even read the words. She needed to eat...

She ordered a meat patty in two slices of a bun. It came slathered in tomato sauce, with cold, greasy fried potatoes on the side, a portion of coleslaw – it was the best thing she had ever tasted.

Wiping her lips with a paper napkin, she felt better. The voices had quietened somewhat, sank into the edge of hearing. Inside the dark diner no one paid her any attention. A Buddhist monk sat alone in one corner, his back to the wall, peacefully asleep. Two Africans were playing cards with a cigar-smoking Cossack. It was quiet, and she was just another alien, here.

She picked up the paper again. *Classifieds*. Pages and pages of ads. She went through them.

Prof. A. Huff, Practical Phrenologist. Examinations and delineations of character and talents with marked chart to your fancy. Students taught this noble science.

Colling's Electric Belts will cure all diseases that flesh is heir to; my

belts run one year without refilling which can be done by anybody, or I
will make them as good as new for nominal sum. Send for pamphlet.

Mrs W. Weir, Telegraphic medium, controlled by the late Mrs Breed
of Austria, the wonderful rapping medium, sittings daily; also a power-
ful magnetic healer, treats all kinds of chronic and acute diseases
successfully. Every day except Sunday.

All of which were unhelpful, to say the least.

Lists and lists of advertisements for accommodation. She
scanned through them, her eye hurting as she tried to make out
the small type in the smoky darkness of the diner. Jade pulsed
behind the other, the eye that was no longer there.

Yet at last she found it. For a moment her fingers touched the
rough paper almost lovingly, the tips stroking the newspaper
edge. There, it could only be the one she sought: *Dr H.H. Holmes*
is offering a place of quiet refuge in the bustling city. Close to Fair and
all amenities, gaslight in every room: perfect for the single visitor. Long-
and short-term accommodation available.

Dr Holmes?

But people always trusted doctors. Didn't they?

She stared at the advertisement, at the address printed below.
And she thought – could it really be that easy?

Englewood, the streets dark and quiet, shops shuttered, streetlamps glowing like fireflies, casting little light. The air was cold.
It had stopped raining, but the puddles lay heavy on the ground,
and mud splattered Cleo as she walked.

Too easy, she thought. Too easy.

And yet she could not turn back. *There is a path we must follow*,
she thought. Beyond reason, beyond law. Her gun arm twitched.
Behind her eye the jade fragment twisted and turned, sending
short, sharp shocks of pain into her head. Restless. It was sensing
the Phantom, she realised – the proximity of one jade fragment
to another.

And so he, too, must know she was coming.

She had little doubt he had anticipated this, was expecting her.

Let him.

She stood across the road from the building and knew that soon she would kill a man.

What could be said of that place, of Dr Holmes' castle? It was a dark, imposing two-storey building. On the ground floor were shops; a Chemist, *Holden's*; a sign advertising *Used Jewellery*; another for *Jobs Available: For Young Ladies of Suitable Skills*. Where the ground floor had display windows the first was a façade of dark stone.

Cautiously, Cleo approached the closed doors.

She smashed the window with her gun hand. Shards of glass fell like tears on the floor. She pushed her way in then, up dark stairs, and onto a long, cold corridor. Doors lined it, all closed. Nothing stirred. There were no windows. She kicked open the first door.

A girl lay in the bed. Young, she slept peacefully, or so it seemed at first. When Cleo approached her the girl didn't stir. She put two fingers to the girl's neck, cautiously. A weak, too-weak pulse. She tried to shake her awake, but the girl did not open her eyes.

Something was making her slow. Dimly, she became aware of a sound, a hiss of air. She scanned for it. A hidden nozzle, high above her. Gas, she thought. Gas was being pumped into the room.

She picked up the girl, dragged her across the floor. Once in the corridor she shut the door behind them. Her head slowly cleared. She shook the girl again, and this time she opened her eyes.

Milady's gun arm was pointing directly at the girl's head. The message she wanted to get across could not be subtle. She said, "Get out of here."

"The doctor…" the girl whispered.

"What?"

"You won't hurt the doctor…?"

"Get out of here! Now!"

Not waiting for a response, she moved to the next door and kicked it open. Another sleeping form – approaching it she knew it was too late. When she put her fingers against the girl's neck there was no pulse, and the skin was cold.

"Get out!" she shouted now and, running down the corridor, fired into the air. She kicked open doors, dragged semi-conscious girls out to the landing. "Run!"

He wouldn't be up there, she knew. Where she found windows she burst them open, and the cold air washed in like medicine. The girls finally began to go, some running. Two more asked about the doctor, pleaded with her not to hurt him.

And two more never stirred from their beds. The last one had been dead longer than the others, she saw. When she opened the door there was no hiss of gas, but the air smelled of a rotted sweetness. The corpse on the bed had been dead for a while. She watched the silver strands move like eels across the girl's skin. The girl's eyes opened, then, and stared at her.

And the corpse smiled.

She fired before she was conscious she was doing it, and the girl's head plopped back against the pillow, and her eyes closed. The smile faded, and the girl looked sad now. He had been gaining power, she thought. She raced out of that room, looking for a way down, knowing it would be concealed, all the while the alien fragment in her skull thrashing and the pain echoing through her bones, a pain that was a part of her now.

A maze... he had built himself a maze, and she was trapped inside it. Doors led nowhere, corridors twisted and turned and opened back on themselves. She knocked on the walls, searching for hollows, found a secret passageway, followed it, but it terminated in a brick wall. She retraced her steps but somehow the path was different now, and a door led into a new room, and as she stepped into it the door closed behind her with a clang. The room was windowless, bricked-up on all sides. The door was metal. There was no lock.

Stupid! Stupid! she thought. The gas was pumping into the room. Behind her eye, the jade fragment moved. Use it, she thought. Exhaling slowly, she reached within herself, and out–

Into a cellar crawling with shadows, the kiln burning, and the

Phantom, raging – a keyboard of wood and chrome was before him and he worked at it, pulling levers – a map of the building stood before him like a screen.

A puppet-master, she thought. But his puppets were running away, and there was little he could do.

Looking at the map through his eyes, as the Phantom closed and opened doors and sealed exists, turned on hidden pumps of gas, rooms in which the walls seemed to close in, and there–

A chute, she saw. One of many. The building was such that some rooms had a hidden chute built into them – leading directly to the cellar...

He could kill in a locked room and the corpse would simply disappear.

Later, the kiln would do the rest...

She pulled back. On her hands and knees now, no air remaining, but she found it, a hidden lever in the wall, and when she pulled it the empty bed tilted forward and a trapdoor opened in the floor.

Not waiting, not wanting to think, she lowered herself through the trapdoor and let go.

SIXTY-NINE
Qinggong

"Cleopatra."

There was venom in the voice.

She said, "Tômas."

The fire burned between them.

She had come down shooting. The bullets echoed in that closed, dank chamber.

But he had been ahead of her.

She had landed heavily, rolled – only then noticing the overwhelming heat, the open door of the Phantom's kiln.

"You shouldn't have come."

"I'm beginning to think you are right."

He moved like shadow. Conventional bullets could not harm him. The room was small, her eye stinging – but she could see him clearly through the jade, a figure made monstrous by the shadows.

And yet, this time, she wasn't afraid.

They met mid-room. The Phantom leaped into the air, tracing a parabola as he soared high, bouncing off the wall to come at her. But she too was ready now.

She was no longer human, she knew that now. The jade had changed her, shaped her, that alien machine with its own, unknown purpose working through her. She flew to meet him, sailing through flames, and her hand caught his throat as he came for her.

Squeezing, and he landed a fist like a metal globe on her chest, but she held him still as they both fell. No guns, no bullets, but person to person, in single unarmed combat. She smashed her gun arm against his skull.

He twisted – impossibly – his legs rising to meet her face. She had to let go, pull back to avoid the full brunt of his attack and, laughing, he was free again, bouncing gracefully from a wall to come back at her, all the while the fire burning, burning in that room of death.

"I've killed your like in this room more times than you can imagine," he said.

"You've been a busy boy," she said.

"I've been a bad boy," he said, and laughed. Had he always been insane? Once he must have been a valuable agent for the Council. Once…

And now?

"I will kill you," he said, "and then go for the statue. I know what it does. I know what it wants. I have been listening to it for a long time."

"What does it want?" she said. He came for her, through the air, but she was no longer where she was, turning and catching him from behind with a kick that sent him flying at the wall–

His face smashed into the bricks. When he pulled back she could see the indentation in the wall, but the Phantom was unharmed.

"It wants this world," he said. "The world and everything in it."

"For itself?"

"For its masters… and when they come, I shall be rewarded. I shall rule!"

"They should have put you in Charenton a long time ago," she said.

"But they put *you* in the asylum instead," he said, smirking. She watched that hungry, elongated skull, and knew he was insane, and had to be stopped.

"You shouldn't have listened to the voices," she said, coming at him. He leaped up and they met in mid-air, and this time his kick found purchase and she felt the air going out of her as she sailed back and smashed against the wall near the door.

The door!

It was getting hard to breathe in the room.

"They were lonely," he said. "They'd been lonely for a very long time."

"And now they have you?"

But she knew he was wrong. The voices did not care about Tômas, did not care about her. She thought of the Shaolin, keeping the statue for countless years, of old, lonely Master Long and the child he had once been. She thought of the corpses animated, however briefly, by that alien machine. She thought of the voices.

They were barely aware of them as individual entities, she realised. They had been some sort of information-gathering machine and, awakened, they studied the world. Everything that happened was just a by-product of that impersonal, detached survey – the Phantom and she were insignificant particles in that great schema of the machine.

She went low then, and he went high, and she grasped his leg and yanked him down from the air, bringing him crashing down hard on the floor, and then she put her gun arm to his head and fired, at point-blank range, and heard him scream.

When he pulled away his fist lifted her off the ground and, too quickly, he turned. His skull was ruined, and his mouth opened in a scream of rage, but no sound came. Her back hit the wall. She lifted her gun arm again, trying to aim but, too quickly, he whipped around. No! she tried to shout, but he had opened the door and was gone through it – too quickly!

She heard the lock close from the outside.

It took her a moment to realise she was trapped in the Phantom's cellar.

She rose slowly to her feet. She hurt in numerous places. She felt ravenously hungry, too, as if her body had been expending energy beyond its natural ability, and now needed to compensate for it. And she knew she was no longer the woman who had first met the Phantom, there in the under-morgue of Paris, in what seemed a lifetime away.

For it *had* been a lifetime. And she was a different person now, a different thing.

She went to the kiln. And she pushed it.

She had never had such strength, but her conviction lent her power, and her desperation drove her. She knew this place could not, should not exist. She kicked the metal with her artificial leg and again she pushed, hearing the strong foundations groan, the heat burning her–

But she would not burn.

With the last of her energy she jumped, flying at the wall, leaping from it, back at the kiln. The impact jarred her body, and she fell numb to the floor–

But the great, obese, obscene object had succumbed. Slowly, it toppled over.

And the fire burst out.

Blinking tears, she pushed herself up, feeling as if she were drowning. Her gun arm shook as she pointed it at the door. She fired, through the flames, watching wood fly. When she kicked the door it fell back. Cold air rushed inside, touching her cheeks like a mother's hand. She ran, and the fire pursued her.

SEVENTY
Dismissed

"You're a fool."

Winnetou's voice, like cold water. She had come crawling out of the burning building, soot and ash over her and the taste of fire in her mouth. Arms dragged her away. She sat, propped against a wall, and watched the building burn.

Confused girls in a gaggle outside, throwing her strange looks. Wrapped in firemen's coats, feet naked in the cold. But the fire warmed the night.

She knew he was still nearby. But not pursuing, any more. He was her prey now, and their roles had changed. She felt his fear, and it warmed her.

Winnetou, above her, his face angry. His men ringing the building – too late. The killer had gone but some of his intended victims, at least, had survived.

"I did what I had to do," she said. Speaking quietly, her throat raw from the smoke.

"I told you not to get involved."

"I told you, I was already involved."

He turned away from her. She let him go.

Run, she thought, aiming her words at a misshapen figure running through mists. Run, Tômas. I'll catch up with you soon enough. She felt tired, so tired... and yet, strangely, at peace.

She knew it wasn't over. But she had done what she had to do. Master Long had been right. Sometimes it's the best we can do, she thought.

And sometimes even that's not enough.

She saw a familiar black carriage come to a stop. She expected the two automatons to come out of it. Instead, it was the Monsignor himself – itself – who came to meet her.

The ancient automaton glided across the hard ground. His robes hid his means of movement. She did not think he had legs… The carved face looked at her expressionlessly. "You have disobeyed my orders."

There didn't seem anything to say to that. She didn't. He raised his hand. A figure stepped out of the carriage. Two others followed behind it, like obedient shadows.

"Dellamorte…"

The countess, at least, was courteous. "Milady de Winter," she said, nodding. "I trust your journey was not unpleasant."

"I am much obliged," Cleo said, "for all your courtesy."

"It was the least I could do."

They stared at each other. A small smile played at the corners of the countess's mouth, was answered. "I trust Captain Karnstein is well?"

The countess inched her head. "He is recovering," she said.

"I'm glad."

Hovering without a need for an answer was the question: *What are you doing here?*

She already knew.

She recognised the two figures behind the countess. McGill, and the leopard woman, from Scab.

So they did not trust her to do her job.

"I am to be relieved of my duties," she said – not a question. The countess looked elsewhere. The Monsignor's face, of course, did not change expression. He said, "My colleagues in the Council think highly of you. So do I. However…"

"You planned it all along," she said. "You had to, for them to have arrived so quickly–"

"You were to be detained on Scab," he said – the same scratchy, even voice, the recording of a long-dead human. "Countess Dellamorte, alas, let her emotions get the better of her–"

"Karnstein," Cleo said.

"We are not so different, you and I," the countess said. And was that apology in her voice?

"You are unstable," the Monsignor said. "You would have been more useful being studied. I cannot allow you to run free and interfere. There has been a communiqué... The auction is set to commence. I shall bid – for the Council. And whether I win, or lose... we must have it. The countess's team shall supervise the retrieval of the item. You are not to interfere." He coughed, the sound as artificial as the rest of him. "Am I clear?"

"You were never clear," she said, or thought she had. She felt so tired... Let someone else take the burden for once, and let her sleep, and be at peace... she had done what she could. One did not expect thanks in the service of the Council.

"Take her back to her lodgings," the Monsignor said.

McGill and the leopard woman approached her. Wearily, she pulled herself up to her feet. "I'll walk," she said.

"I don't think–" the countess began, then subsided. Milady inched her head, and the countess nodded. "Very well," she said.

The fire still burned. It lit up the night, sending showers of sparks and embers floating on the wind. Sunlight was gradually touching the sky on the horizon, drawing a panorama of colour above the black outline of the city, and it merged with the fire so that it seemed the sky itself was coming alight. She began to walk away then, following the still dark, empty streets. Dawn was approaching, but to Cleo it felt far away.

INTERLUDE:
Moving Pictures

In the white city, Kai sat in the darkened space of the Zooprax-ographical Hall and watched the silent screen.

Moving pictures. They were like the shadows that flitted behind his eyes, those glimpses of another world. Cigar smoke curled up into the air and was illuminated by the beams of light from Edison's new machine. A hush in the packed hall, and he knew that, amidst all those people, he was truly alone.

They were looking for him, everywhere, across the black city and the white. He had seen their silent watchers, in the Midway Plaisance, in the Electricity Building and the Manufacturers and Fine Arts building and around the lake. They looked for him inside the pyramid...

But of all the buildings, of all the tall, impossible buildings of the White City, it was the Electricity Building that frightened him most.

Tesla's building.

The Fair was lit up with electricity, Tesla's alternating current, and the statue was in love.

The statue needed the electricity.

Craved it, with a hunger that frightened Kai even more than this entire alien city did, with its strange people and displays, its masses of humanity, its bustle and noise and commerce. He was frightened, and he could tell no one that he was. Only here, in the darkened room, did he feel some safety. Safety from the voices, safety from the watchers. Safety from himself.

Images flickered on the screen and the audience was spellbound. There was no musical accompaniment, nothing but the changing images on the screen. Kai hugged himself, drawing himself into a ball in his chair. I could hide, he thought. I could hide here forever, and pretend none of this was happening. Pretend I was someone else, somewhere else.

Once, he had wanted to be a wuxia hero. In the books the heroes were never scared. They fought, bravely, for a just cause. They faced the dark. But Kai was not afraid of the dark. It was the light outside that scared him, and only in the darkness did he find some comfort, some escape.

He thought of the woman he had seen in his dreams. A strange woman, darker than the mountain people who lived high above Luang Prabang, a woman who was fashioned into a weapon, much as he himself had been. He wished he could go to her. He wished she could help. But there was no one who could. The voices were in a cacophony of excitement, whispering that the time had come. He thought of their plan and shivered. He stared at the screen and rocked in his seat, lost just as he had been all those years before, when he left his father's shop and ran into the forest, clutching a strange statue in his hands. He wished he'd thrown it away, then. When he had the chance.

He rocked in his seat and watched the pictures flickering across the screen, and waited, alone in the dark. It would not be long now, the voices promised.

PART VII
The End of the World's Fair

SEVENTY-ONE
The Magician of the Fair

She woke up clutching her head, the jade flaring in her eye socket, the pain coursing through her like a green turbulent river. The voices whispered, *Ninety-eight percent complete, ninety-eight point one percent complete...* they whispered *Quantum sequence identified, locked* and *origin point identified* and *Rerouting power to accelerant device in progress*, making her want to scream.

She rose up, washed, dressed, loaded her gun arm, ate a cold breakfast in her room and thought.

And realised she was still being played.

The Council was like the vast mind of a chess player, and its pieces were alive. It did not like its pawns to know the grand design, used them unsparingly, sending them off with as little information as possible – or the wrong information. Watching them follow a trail, whatever the cost.

And she had not been taken off the board, she realised. Dismissed, the Monsignor had said. But chess pieces were never dismissed. They were eliminated, or used. And she had been sent back unharmed...

The old machine, the entire power of the Council at his disposal, still needed her. The countess would be watching the auction, yes, and her strange, misshapen creatures with her – but the Council had a suspicious mind.

Did they expect a ruse?

The main game would take place without her. That was certain. But what if the main game turned out to be a lie?

She watched herself in the mirror, her hair like a dark globe around her head. She touched her fingers to the eyepatch. The pain was with her always now. Would it ever stop? Soon, she thought, thinking of the voices, counting the rising percentages… one way or the other it would end.

She looked at herself, and finally smiled. A young, unfamiliar woman looked back at her from the mirror. They nodded to each other.

Go, her reflection seemed to say. You and I must follow the path we've chosen long ago. Wherever it leads.

She turned away from the mirror, knowing what she had to do.

She took a tram to the white city. It was late in the afternoon. She came to the gates of the World's Vespuccian Exposition. The white city could be seen from a distance, the outline marred only by the lizards' pyramid, that enormous structure dominating the centre of the Fair. The lizards' alien green metal shone wetly in the sunlight. Look at our power, it seemed to say. Though we let you play at being builders, at being free, we are still the true power in this world, now. The Everlasting Empire of Les Lézards is named thus for a reason. Come and see our glory.

She paid the entrance fee and walked in.

The white city. Already the sun was setting, and the electric lights were coming alive, illuminating the white buildings. Massive searchlights mounted on the Manufacturers and Liberal Arts building swept the grounds. There was light everywhere, white electric light, and the buildings, huge, cavernous, seemed to grow out of the very ground, rising high into the air. She walked along the Midway, heading for the lagoon that lay nestled between the buildings. There were so many people…

And watchers.

The sensation stole on her slowly, but would not go away.

Watchers in the crowd, waiting, calculating... she passed an Egyptian village and a troupe of Russian Cossacks, an orchestra, a miniature zoo, getting lost in the mayhem, not heading anywhere in particular... She paused when she came to a giant cannon. "Krupp's Monster," she heard someone say. She turned and saw a woman speaking, apparently dictating into an Edison recorder. "A fearful, hideous thing, breathing blood and carnage, a triumph of barbarism crouching amid the world's triumphs of civilisation." The woman glared at the giant cannon, then said, "End quote," crisply. But Cleo rather liked the weapon.

Or was it a weapon? Or was it as the countess had told her, that Krupp, and others, were looking to – what? Send people into space?

Well, it was not her concern. She kept going, pausing now and then, checking her reflection, turning abruptly – but there were too many people. She could not tell who, if anyone, was following her.

There were fire-eaters and belly dancers, displays of cheese making, a display of scalping, phrenologists with human skulls marked by areas, Mongolian archers, food-sellers, photographers carrying their bulky equipment this way and that, machines that spun sugar, booksellers extolling the virtues of Scientific Romances and imported Penny Dreadfuls, Bedouins riding camels, chess-players hovering over a board the size of a town square, where the pieces were all automatons...

She passed a crowd of surging people and saw the flash of lightning beyond them. Curious, she pushed forward. A man was standing on a stage, and – impossibly – lightning danced around him, but he was not harmed. The man raised his arms and smiled at the audience. There were gasps, and cheers. The lightning flashed on and on. Nikola Tesla himself, she realised. She watched, repulsed and fascinated, then turned away.

The city rose all around her. She passed jugglers and sword-swallowers and a fortune-telling machine. The wheel was always in sight, turning slowly, turning, cars loaded with people hanging from its frame. Ferris's wheel. She passed a short, straight, smooth path that led up to a ramp, and stared: a machine with delicate wings rushed along the road to the ramp and, instead of falling, launched from it and soared slowly into the air, a steam engine belching steam in the tail. A man was sitting in the small cabin between the giant wings. The crowd gasped and cheered – it was a sound she was getting used to.

The magic of the Fair...

The sign said, *Du Temple Monoplane* and, below: *Félix du Temple, Proprietor*. She stared at the monoplane. She'd used one once before, during the Robur Affair...

More flying machines, most on the ground. She checked out the signs. *Stringfellow's Aerial Steam Carriage. Wnek's Gliders. L'Albatros artificiel.* One sign towering above the rest: *The Montgolfier Brothers: Dominating the Skies Since 1783.*

But it looked as though they'd found some competition.

She turned away again. Somehow she had found her way to the lagoon. An island rose in the middle of the water, overgrown with wild growth of flowers and trees. The roof of a temple peeked out from behind the vegetation. Electric boats hummed their way across the surface of the lagoon. She watched the water and saw stars beginning to blink into existence, faint at first but growing larger and more luminous. When she raised her head she realised she had been wrong, and she smiled. They were lanterns, hundreds of floating lanterns rising slowly into the air.

At that moment the place felt bewitched. The white city was reflected in the calm water, bathed in unearthly light. And a voice beside her said, quietly and unexpectedly, "Night is the magician of the Fair."

She turned, slowly, and was not surprised to find Master Long standing beside her. In his hands he held a lantern – a thing of bamboo and thin paper. As she watched he lit the small candle underneath the canopy of paper and, after a moment, gently let the lantern go. It hovered in the air between them, as if uncertain. Then, gracefully, it began to rise above their heads, and soon joined the others, becoming another bright star in the skies above the Fair.

Cleo shook her head, as if trying to dispel the moment. "Night's not the only magician at the Fair tonight," she said. Master Long followed her gaze and then smiled.

A young man – almost a boy, Cleo thought – was sitting cross-legged on the ground a little distance from them. He was brown-skinned, wore robes, and a hand-painted sign beside him said: *The Amazing Indian Yogi: Showing Miracles and Wonders from the East*. As she watched the young yogi spread earth over the mat before him and began to chant. "Goly, goly, chelly gol," he sang, waving his hands over the earth. "Goly, goly, chelly job, chelly job!" he said.

Cleo almost laughed. "It's coming, it's coming!" the young yogi said. He covered the naked earth with a red cloth. A companion, as dark as he was, was playing a lyre beside him. The yogi waved his hands over the cloth – and when he lifted it, two small sprouts of green appeared out of the brown earth.

His small audience gasped.

The yogi smiled – revealing white, well-cared-for teeth – and covered the earth again. The next time he lifted his cloth, two miniature mango trees had appeared where the shoots had been.

The audience clapped, and the lyre player collected the money given, and the yogi said, "Chelly gol, chelly gol."

Cleo laughed, and said, "That is some of the worst acting I've ever seen."

"Do not underestimate our young friend," Master Long said, and this time he wasn't smiling. "Mister Weiss has not, perhaps, found his true role yet, but he is skilful. He's been following you for some time…"

"Weiss?" She stared at the young yogi, who looked back at her now, still smiling, a challenge in his eyes. Wash the paint off his skin, she thought, and you'd get–

"I believe he goes by the stage name Houdini, most often," Master Long said. "After your own illustrious Robert Houdin."

The Toymaker. She thought of the man, alone in his dark workshop, with only his machine-child for company, and grimaced. She let it go, said, "Vespuccian?"

"One of the immigrants who came here as a child," Master Long said. "It is my belief he is here, unofficially, on behest of the Black Cabinet."

The Council of Chiefs' intelligence service. She looked at the boy with new eyes. He rose up slowly, then, gracefully, bowed. She had to laugh. "At least he has style," she said.

"Yes," Master Long said. "I foresee great things in his future – but you must know he is not alone in the white city tonight. The auction is set to commence, and who shall gain the ultimate prize? They all want to get their hands on the statue, but its power is too great to be controlled."

The young magician, meanwhile, had given her a last smile and – along with his companion – disappeared into the throng of humanity. Still, she could feel invisible eyes gazing at her – and knew the Black Cabinet of the Vespuccians was the least of her worries. "Where is the auction held?" she said, and saw Master Long smile. "You are the last of my pupils," he said. "Not Wudang, or Shaolin, but a follower of Xia nonetheless. Perhaps the last, if you are successful..." He was no longer smiling. She thought of the Monsignor's prohibition and pushed it away from her mind. "Tell me where it is," she said.

SEVENTY-TWO
The Auction

She could no longer sense the Phantom. She could no longer sense Kai.

Something was changing.

The voices said, *Ninety-eight point eight percent, ninety-eight point nine*. The pain was still with her, but she couldn't see.

The auction was at the Zoopraxographical Hall.

She staked it out. Waiting for the players to arrive, the Phantom, Kai. She couldn't go – the Monsignor's orders were very specific.

She watched Dellamorte arrive. McGill and the leopard woman were with her. They fanned out, found observation posts. She saw her signal – more of the Scab people were already in place.

Master Long had left her. She was on her own. She knew he had his own operation going – she thought she saw Mistress Yi on the roof, but she was gone before Cleo could be certain.

So many watchers and she was watching the watchers. She wondered who was watching her.

The voices said, *Ninety-nine point one percent* and something was wrong, but she didn't know what.

The buyers began to arrive.

She didn't recognise the Sioux chief, but she did recognise the Empress-Dowager's emissary. She entered the building with her escort: ushers on the door searched everyone for weapons. Madame Linlin bore it stoically.

More faces she didn't know – a short black man who may have represented Zululand, a tall one who may have been Dahomey. A fat white man had to be helped from his carriage and she stared at his face: it had to be Krupp, the industrialist.

A delegate from Siam, then an Aztec, then another familiar face: Mycroft Holmes, puffing on a cigar. They kept coming, these sole representatives, while their people watched from outside and had the entire building under lockdown. There was no way out of there. Kai had no way of escaping... She knew they would all bid, but who would actually get hold of the statue depended on later, on who had the superior fire-power.

Ninety-nine point two percent. And something still wasn't right.

There were no windows. Inside was a machine that showed pictures. Is that what they thought the statue was? Pictures of another world... She shuddered, feeling suddenly cold. She was sitting in a coffee shop on a roof opposite the building. She wondered how many of the other diners were watching too, waiting as she did.

All of them, she thought.

She saw a tall turbaned man come to the Zoopraxographical Hall. His face was familiar – Prince Dakkar, she thought. She had once seen his dossier... A delegate from the empire of the Mexica next, followed by a tall pale man – one of the Nordic countries? – and another, and another. The Monsignor's black carriage arrived. His two bodyguards helped him down. They disappeared through the doors.

More delegates...

Last one, unexpected: she saw Master Long.

Before he entered he turned his head, for just a moment. Did he see her?

He disappeared inside. The ushers followed, and the doors closed.

The auction was set to begin.

And something still didn't feel right.

She knew then that she had to get inside.

She saw him before he saw her, she was sure of that.

Tômas, a shadow moving against the wall.

She left money on the table and was gone. She was on the street and running, and the alien energy coursed through her. Someone tried to grab her – McGill. She broke his wrists and kept going. Someone high up took a shot at her. She rolled and kept going. The Phantom turned, saw her chasing, grinned.

He leaped up into the air, found purchase on the wall, climbed. She followed.

So this is what it felt like, long exposure to the statue, she thought.

She could do impossible things.

They leaped on and off walls, street lamps. Gunfire zinged past them. But the watchers couldn't come any closer. The terms of the auction were strict... and the prize too valuable to risk.

For anyone but the Phantom and her.

He found a side door and burst it open as if it were paper. There were guards inside and she arrived a fraction of a second too late. He'd killed them neatly and kept going.

She followed.

Into darkness and smoke–

The Phantom disappeared, too quickly to catch. She stood very still.

A light flickering, a beam crossing a cloud of smoke. Moving pictures: figures moving through mist, haltingly, grey figures with the faces of the dead. The mists seemed to part, but didn't – something behind them she had to see and couldn't.

She was standing to one side of the screen, hidden by a pulled-back curtain... an audience of faces looking up. They were all seated, and on the stage a man was standing before a podium, and a jade statue of a cross-legged lizard sat on a velvet cushion in a glass display cabinet beside him.

But it was not Kai.

She could still not see him. She could not feel the Phantom...

Ninety-nine point three percent. Initiating gateway transfer protocols. Checksum routines engaged.

She had seen the man before.

Kai's servant.

The Manchu.

There was excitement in the audience. The images flickering on the screen were hypnotising. Could they not see what was happening?

Mycroft Holmes: "Ten million."

Madame Linlin: "Fifteen."

Dakkar: "Sixteen."

Krupp: "Twenty million."

She stared at the statue, felt nothing.

The images kept flickering on the screen. Pictures of the dead, the mist almost but never quite opening...

Not yet.

The Sioux chief: "Twenty-three."

Krupp: "Twenty-five million."

Holmes: "Thirty."

She saw several of the delegates shake their heads. She knew the real bidding would be between a handful of people. But it was wrong!

And where was Tômas?

She spotted him. He had moved around the audience, a shadow in the dark, was approaching the stage on the other side from her. He grinned at her, his face barely human, then his gaze turned towards the statue and remained there.

She couldn't put the audience at risk. On the stage, the Manchu said: "Ladies and gentlemen, for this once-in-a-lifetime offer, please let us move past the courtesy round. Do I hear fifty million?"

But it was all a charade. Couldn't they see it? The statue was worth any amount they could throw at it, but Kai and the Manchu could not possibly hope to get out alive after the sale–

And where *was* Kai?

Ninety-nine point four percent, whispered the voices, from far away.

Madame Linlin: "Thirty-five."

Holmes: "Forty million."

Images flickering on the screen. The Manchu waving an auctioneer's hammer – she looked for the Phantom again and couldn't see him–

Then a roar, and the Manchu dropped his hammer–

Shouting in the audience – she saw Master Long turn his head – their eyes connected – a message in his eyes she couldn't decipher. He shook his head – no.

The Phantom had leaped onto the stage. The Manchu drew back his hand, sent a fist into the Phantom's face–

Tômas extended claws, tried to rip the other man's throat out–

The Manchu laughed in his face.

Shouts, the bidders rising from their seats in a panic – on the screen the mist rolled on. The voices of the statue said, *Ninety-nine point four five percent complete. Transference protocols initiating. Primary power source hooked up to origin-point mechanism.*

The Manchu had Qinggong, she realised: long-term exposure to the statue gave him strength equivalent to that of Tômas.

With a bit of luck they would kill each other.

And no one was minding the statue…

She dashed onto the stage, broke the glass of the display case and grabbed it.

SEVENTY-THREE
The Wheel

She had expected pain. There was none. The jade fragment in her eye socket remained motionless. No visions, no flashes of green – the statue was inert in her arms.

She ran.

They were trashing the stage, the Manchu fighting Tômas against a background of moving pictures. Screams were muted – everything was muted.

And something was still very wrong.

She carried the statue one-handed. It felt too light. Bursting out to the street outside – it was chaos. The security forces of more than a dozen nations descended on the building. A familiar face – Mistress Yi running, Ip Kai behind her–

"Milady, no!"

The leopard woman tackled her. She had claws for hands. She missed Cleo's eye, left bloodied gashes on her face. Cleo kicked – the woman came at her again, hissing.

She shot her.

Her gun arm had a life of its own. She shot half a dozen attackers but there were too many of them and it was hard to fight holding the statue...

Wrong. All wrong.

She ran – they followed. Bullets missed her – mostly. One

hit her artificial leg, sent her sprawling. The statue rolled away–

The voices kept whispering in her mind, but they were too far away.

And Kai was never in the building, she realised.

Mistress Yi, a light shadow – "I'll distract them."

She grabbed the statue, jumped – onto a street lamp and going higher, trying to scale the roof of the next building. People ran screaming down the road – innocents caught in the crossfire of politics.

Cleo was ignored – they were all pursuing the statue and she'd lost it.

Construct the sequence of events, try to overlay some logic. The auction was a diversion, Kai had other plans–

He still had the statue, and it was nowhere near the Zoopraxographical Hall.

Which meant the statue on the stage had been a decoy.

Which meant–

She ran.

She tried to reach him, through the fragment – reached into the jade light, forcing it.

Met resistance. It was pushing her out – the pain spread through her so quickly she couldn't even shout. Glimpses, nevertheless: Tômas bloodied, the Manchu holding him down – the inside of the Zoopraxographical Hall was a mess, the stage had collapsed – Tômas rolled, bit down on the Manchu's arm. She heard bones breaking, heard the Manchu laugh.

Was pushed away – the jade a viscous liquid. Where was she? Running blindly, the lake on her left, searchlights criss-crossing the white city – lanterns floating in the air.

She stopped, took a deep breath, held still.

Tried again.

Ninety-nine point five percent. Primary power source engaged.

And all over the white city the lights dimmed and died out at once.

All around her, uncertain silence.

In the darkness only one thing remained alight.

The Ferris wheel. It shone with a blinding white light – too strong.

There were gunshots in the distance…

Someone screamed.

The silence broke – the screams rose from multiple directions. She tried to hold her ground – people pushed against her, running now, trying to get away.

The magic was gone from the white city.

She pushed into the jade. A picture resolved – slowly, and it hurt when it appeared. Kai against a background of stars – he seemed to float in mid-air.

Kai: "Help me…"

She saw the statue beside him. It was burning, engulfed in cold flames.

The Ferris wheel.

Once again, she ran.

Screams.

They cut through the night, voices wafting down from on high. Trapped in the moving cars of the giant wheel: thirty-six cars and up to sixty people in each – and it had been busy every day since it had opened for business.

Two thousand people trapped above-ground – the wheel kept rotating, faster and faster. It was a streak of white light in the night, a blur of motion.

She looked up – no way to climb, Kai somewhere up there – electric cables snaked towards the base of the wheel. When she stared up the air inside the wheel seemed to shimmer.

"Master Long says you must stop it." A voice beside her – Mistress Yi materialised, minus the fake statue. Blood covered her face, one arm was bent at an unnatural angle. She was breathing heavily.

Milady: "How?"

Mistress Yi: "You have to climb up there."

Milady: "Up where?"

But she already knew.

Flashes of jade – Kai wasn't in a passenger car. He was at the centre of the wheel, on the axle itself. He was fastening the statue to the spider's web of spokes. Electric cables ran up there, too. The statue glowed. The air inside the wheel shimmered and looked like a mirror.

Mistress Yi: "Use Qinggong."

Milady: "Are you insane?"

The girl shrugged. "Then it's going to succeed."

"What is it doing?"

"What it must."

A key. A key was for opening doors...

And this one led to another world.

Ninety-nine point six percent. Initiating quantum hookup.

Kai, distant: "Help me!"

Screams from the cars. The wheel was moving faster and faster. Darkness over the Fair – torches offered sporadic illumination.

The wheel was almost three hundred feet high. There was no way up there.

Unless...

She said: "Stay here. There was one way to get up there–

She ran.

The plane was where she'd last seen it. There was no one around. The Du Temple monoplane, looking like a moth, wings too delicate to work, the body tiny–

But it *did* work. Thirteen metre wingspan, a light carriage weighing a mere eighty kilograms – she had to add her own weight, hope the ramp was high enough – but she'd seen it fly. A flash boiler–

It was loaded – the pilot must have expected to make another flight. She lit the flame, climbed into the seat – the engine came alive behind her. Steam burst through a network of tubes, compressed water heated by the flame – no time to think now, no time for anything but–

A jet of pressured steam came roaring out of the engine and the plane glided forward, gathering speed–

She flew down the ramp. Wind and smoke stung her face. The roar of the engine filled the night–

The plane reached the end of the ramp and flew over it–

The ground came very close and missed her.

The plane rose.

She coaxed it, talking to it – she rose, slowly, slowly – the ground grew distant. She turned, swerving – saw the plane's reflection in the lagoon. She found a pair of aviator glasses and put them on. Circling, the wheel rising impossibly high, the air inside it changing now, the mirror becoming a lens, through which she saw...

The voices said, *Quantum signature verified. Opening entanglement channels. Handshake protocols response correct! Correct!*

And – *Ninety-nine point seven percent. Ninety-nine point eight.*

She could feel their elation. She took the plane in a wide circuit, the Manufacturers and Fine Arts building rising on one side, the lizards' pyramid on the other, and she flew the monoplane straight–

She could no longer see the spokes of the wheel. The structure of the wheel was no longer there, or – not exactly.

It was overlaid. She saw through jade – Kai huddled on the main axis, the statue bathed in flames – the sky behind them disappeared and was replaced with–

The voices said, *Ninety-nine point nine* – triumphantly. Behind her the air was full of steam. She aimed for the centre of the wheel–

Where there was a deep blackness, filled with stars.

SEVENTY-FOUR
The Gateway

The size of the thing did not make sense. And the engine had begun to splutter, and she was losing power – rapidly. The monoplane could glide – but she did not fancy her odds.

And something was climbing, inhumanly fast, from one hanging car to another.

Take things one at a time…

Inside the wheel, the universe.

Stars glared at her. A field of stars brighter than any that could be seen in the sky. They shone bright, were overwhelmed by–

An immense structure floated in space. A sun rose, a ball of fire almost blinding her, and in its light she could see the ring.

It was enormous, ancient – strange. Its surface was pock-marked with the scars of countless impacts. It turned – slowly, rotating not unlike the Ferris wheel itself. Imagine a Ferris wheel lying on its side, floating in space, backlit by stars. Turning – she saw flecks of light rising from it and somehow realised they were craft, related to her monoplane the way ants were related to humans. The voices babbled, *Contact initiated!* and *transferring informational matrix to source* and *home!*

Flashes of jade – every dead person the silver streaks have ever touched was somehow still alive inside the beam that she was piggy-backing: memories, dreams, knowledge, all going through that hole punched into space, going towards that impossible structure no human could have built–

The engine, faltering. She was high above the axis and now she glided down, knowing the monoplane could only go one way now–

Sensing rather than seeing the movement of the thing climbing the wheel – the Phantom roaring rage, shouting: "Mine! Mine!"

The flecks of lights from the other side of the screen came closer, became ships – if ships could sail in space. They were growing closer in this Camera Obscura, coming towards the lens–

One hundred percent.

She screamed – "No!"

The engine died. She glided – down.

Tômas had reached the axle. For a moment he tottered, for the first time aware of the gulf of space lying inches away. He made a grab for the statue–

Kai fought him. She watched through goggles, half-real sight, half-jade. The statue was falling apart – the jade peeling, a machine unbending inside, opening translucent wings, ready to take flight–

An alien fleet approaching, closer and closer, tiny against the ring behind it, yet each craft easily the size of the white city itself. The plane was on a collision course – she raised herself from her seat, cursed–

Kai and Tômas below her, fighting on the axle–

She jumped.

The moment stretched, forever.

She was lost in the darkness. The space inside the wheel seemed to expand, spread out until it blocked out the entire sky – *became* the sky.

Perspective shifted–

A sun, rising, and in its light she saw not one ring but hundreds. They revolved around the sun, a ring of rings. Each must have been hundreds of kilometres across. Ships travelled between the rings, strangely shaped vessels, a cloud of moving lights.

Voices: *Unidentified communiqué on antiquated frequency – identify, identify!*

The statue: *Probe reporting completed survey – emergent life form identified–*

Milady: *Emergent life form?*

A stream of confused images: memory/images/data – the city of Oxford, a signal from deep below – the statue awakening, initiating ancient, lumbering instructions – searching.

For what?

Voices: *Identify* – sounding confused.

Images – they were a recollection: a ship moving through space – planets, rings around them – she thought them beautiful but they passed too quickly – a dead, pock-marked world – it must have been the moon. Something dropping from the ship – she watched it fall and crash into the lunar surface. *Emergency procedures initiated. Prepare for crash-landing.*

A green-blue world, beautiful. And the ship was falling, falling, through white mist, clouds, a great blue sea opening below, a speck of land just visible amidst the blue – an island the dying ship was making for...

There had been an explosion...

Voices: *Thought lost – unimportant. Emergent life form class identify?*

The statue: *Not enough data.*

Voices: *Sending investigatory fleet. Stand-down for gateway expansion.*

The lights growing closer – a fleet of ships approaching, the space inside the wheel growing, expanding–

She said, "No."

She fell, landing on the axle – hard. Pain flared through her.

The plane sailed above her head, almost grazing it–

It hit the membrane of that non-space inside the wheel–

The air shimmered – the plane passed through and tumbled through space against a brightness of stars.

A frozen tableau: the Phantom, Kai – herself. She stood up, righted herself.

She said: "We have to close it."

The statue was shedding jade flakes. A machine inside, un-furling – a delicate thing like a monoplane, spreading wings.

The statue: *Initiating target parameters. Stand by to receive.*

She blasted it with her Gatling gun arm. Kai shuddered as if the bullets were piercing *him*. Tômas, screaming: "Mine!"

He jumped – putting himself between her and the statue. She and Kai locked eyes – his said, *Do it*.

Voices: *Gateway open. Coming though–*

She kicked Tômas, her artificial leg lending her power – the impact made her lose her balance. She tottered on the axle – the ground was a long way down.

Tômas screamed. Cleo felt herself falling–

A hand reached and caught her.

Kai, pulling her up. She watched–

A whoosh of hot air, scorching her face–

Something immense and dark burst out of the space inside the wheel, just as–

Tômas, flying – her kick had sent him at the statue and he grasped it in his arms, like a lover–

Momentum kept him flying–

Through the space inside the wheel and out the other side.

Cleo watched–

Tômas floated in that other space against a background of stars, still holding the machine to him – like a lifebuoy.

Voices: *Gateway sequence interrupted! Explain!*

Tômas screamed, but no sound came. He rolled through space – his mouth opened and closed without sound. Their eyes met, for just a moment–

Gateway linkage shutting down.

The statue: *No!*

She did a last kind thing. She didn't think she would. She fired, the bullets travelling through the distorted surface and through it to the other side.

They swarmed, silently, through space, and found Tômas.

SEVENTY-FIVE
Lights

The wheel turned, slowing down. The image in the space inside faded, gradually. Sun, rings, ships – had they ever really existed? Tômas's twisted features growing darker – the light in his eyes going out – the monoplane was a piece of discarded junk floating in space, its engine dead. The alien stars were fading. The babble of the voices was gone.

She stood by Kai on the axle of the Ferris wheel. A last shudder of air, like a breath, held too long, at last being exhaled, and the images flickered into nothingness, and comforting, familiar stars shone through the wheel.

It was quiet.

She watched the world below, the white city of the future coming alive all around them. Lights were flickering back into existence, bathing the white buildings, the lagoon, the wooded island in their soft glare. Screams from the hanging cars of the wheel turned to jubilation, then quietened down altogether.

She stood high above the ground as the wheel turned, and watched the lights. She said, "It's beautiful–" There was something in her hand. It took her a moment to realise it was Kai's hand, and it was warm.

He said, "It's over–" There was a terrible weariness in his voice, but something else, too, something that must have been new to him – relief? hope?

People swarming down below – they stopped now, turned their gazes upwards, a sea of humanity welcoming the new daylight. The wheel turned behind them, sedately. She could see rescue parties forming below, beginning to offload passengers as their cars came into station.

She said, "For now–"

Kai looked up – following her gaze. She felt his hand tightening in hers.

A dark saucer hovered in the air above the Fair. It rotated gently, gave nothing away. Then, like a blinking eye, it shot up, and away, growing smaller and smaller in seconds until it was gone into the night skies.

"For now," Kai agreed. Then, abruptly, he smiled. Cleo smiled back and squeezed his hand. They stood, on top of the world, the wheel turning at their back, and watched the city, bathed in light.

III
THE GREAT GAME

PART I
Death of a Fat Man

*"When everyone is dead the Great Game is finished.
Not before. Listen to me till the end."*
Rudyard Kipling, *Kim*

ONE

The boy didn't know he was about to die, which must have been a bless-
ing. He was an ordinary boy whose job it was to take messages, without
being privy to the contents of said messages. The boy walked along the
canal. The sun was setting and in its dying light the observer could see
a solitary, narrow boat, laden with bananas and pineapples and durian,
passing on the water on the way home from market.

Two monks in saffron robes walked ahead of the boy, conversing in
low voices. A sleepy crocodile floated by the bank of the canal, ignored
by the few passers-by. It was a quiet part of town, away from the farang
quarters, and the boy was on his way home, home being a small room
on one of the canals, shared with his parents and brothers and sisters,
alongside many such rooms all crowded together. The observer could
smell the durian from a distance as the boat went past, and he could
smell chilli and garlic frying from a stall hidden from view, in one of the
adjacent sois, *the narrow, twisting alleyways of this grand city. Its resi-*
dents called it Krung Thep, the City of Angels. The farangs still called it
by its old name, which was Bangkok.

The observer followed behind the boy. He was unremarkable. He
would have been unremarkable in nearly every human country, on any
continent. He was small of build, with skin just dark enough, just pale
enough, to pass for Siamese, or European, or Arab, or, depending on the
place and the angle of the sun, an African. His face was hidden behind

a wide-brimmed hat but, had he turned and tilted his head, it, too, would have been unremarkable – they had taken great care to ensure that that would be so.

The observer followed the boy because the boy was a link in a long and complicated chain that he was following. He didn't feel one way or the other about the boy's imminent death. Death meant little to the observer. The concept was too alien. The boy, not knowing he was being followed, was whistling. He was not Siamese or Chinese, but rather Hmong, of a family that had come to Krung Thep from the highlands of Laos, one of the king's territories to the north-east. The observer didn't care a great deal about that.

He caught up with the boy as the boy was turning away from the canal, down a narrow soi. People passed them both but the observer ignored them, his attention trained on the boy. He caught up with him in the shadow of a doorway and put his hand on the boy's shoulder.

The boy began to formulate a question, began to turn around, but never got a chance to complete either action. The observer slid what could have been a very narrow, very sharp blade – but wasn't, not quite – into the soft area at the back of the boy's head.

The blade went through skin and fat and bone, piercing the brain stem and the hippocampus and reaching deep into the brain. The boy emitted a sigh, a minute exhalation of air, perhaps in surprise, perhaps in pain. His legs buckled underneath him. The observer, now participant, gently caught him so that he didn't fall but, rather, was gently lowered to the ground.

The whole thing only took a moment. When it was done the observer withdrew the thing that was not quite a blade, but functioned as one, which was as much a part of him as his skeleton or the cells that made up his skin. His skeleton was not entirely human and his brain not at all, and he was currently experiencing some new sensations, one of which was bewilderment and another being anger, neither of which had troubled him before.

He stopped before the fallen boy and put his hands together, palms touching, the hands away from the chest and raised high, in a wai. He bowed to the body of the boy. The voices inside him were whispering.

Having paid his respects the observer straightened. He stepped away from the darkened doorway and into the street outside. The sun had set and it was growing darker and torches and small fires were being lit across the city. He could smell fish roasting, wood catching fire, fish sauce, and the coming rain. The boy had been a link in a chain and now it pointed the observer in a new direction. He walked away, not hurrying, an unassuming man whose face was hidden behind a wide-brimmed hat, and as he turned the corner he heard, behind him, the start of screams.

It was cold and his bones ached; the air smelled of rain. Smith straightened, wiped his brow with the back of one hand, leaving a trail of dirt on his skin. He stared down at the ground, the wide, raised row he had so painstakingly worked to make. He had turned the ground and mixed in fertiliser from the Oppenheims' chicken coop, which he had personally shovelled into bags and carried over, and he had formed these things that looked like elongated burial mounds and planted seeds and watered them and watched them. God, he hated gardening.

A chicken darted past, leaving sharp little arrowheads in the moist earth of his garden. He threw a stone at it and it crowed, jumping into the air with wings half-stretched, offended. God, he hated chickens too.

Staring at the garden, he saw his vegetables weren't doing all that well. The tomatoes looked forlorn, hanging from their vines, the plants held up by wooden sticks that seemed to jut out at random angles. The cabbages looked like guillotined heads. The apple tree by the house was surrounded by fallen apples, rotting, and the smell filled the air. Smith glared at the tree then decided to call it a day. Not bothering to change, he left the house, opening and closing the small gate in the fence that enclosed the garden and the house, and followed the dirt path into the village. Other houses in the village had names. Smith's gate merely said, in small, unpolished letters: No. 6.

A fine, cold day. A good day for staying indoors, lighting a fire, sorting his library alphabetically, or by condition, or rarity. Since his retirement he had enjoyed collecting books, ordering by mail from specialist dealers in the capital, or even from the continent. It was a small, orderly joy, as different as could be from his former life. His lonely farm house, with its small garden and solitary apple tree, sat on its own. A farmer's life, he thought. What had Hobbes said about human life? That it was solitary, poor, nasty, brutish and short. Hobbes should have been a farmer, Smith thought.

Or retired.

Instead Hobbes had been overly friendly with the French, had written *Leviathan*, in which he argued for the return of human monarchy, had been arrested, and was only spared by his one-time pupil, the old Lizard King Charles II, who had arranged for him to go into exile. Died at ninety-one years of age, if Smith remembered his facts. So life may have been brutish and poor but, for Hobbes, not exactly *that* short.

He came to the village. A small sign announced that this was, indeed, the village of St Mary Mead and, in smaller letters underneath: *Retirement Community*. Smith sighed. Every time he examined that sign he felt the old, familiar anger return. And every time he hoped, against hope, that somehow the sign would be changed, would declare him free.

He walked along the high street. The village, like all villages, had a church, and a post office, and a pub. There was no constabulary. The residents of St Mary Mead could take care of their own. Smith smelled the air. Rain. But something else, too…

A vague sense of unease gripped him. He could smell – not with his *physical* sense but with something deeper, a left-over from his trade days, perhaps – could smell *change* in the air. He stopped beside M.'s, the shop that sold embroidered tea doilies and lace curtains and, on Saturdays and Sundays, cream teas, and watched. Behind him the curtain twitched, and he knew that she, too, was watching. She had been famous as a watcher, in her glory days.

But there was nothing much to see. The village, as always, was quiet. The few shops were open, but their proprietors were used to the absence of customers. Outside Verloc's bookshop the ageing Mr Verloc – *but two years younger than him!* – was putting out the bargain bins, filled as always with penny dreadfuls and gothic romance and the like – poor fare for a man of Smith's more refined tastes.

He shook his head and continued his walk. He paused by the bookshop and nodded hello to Verloc, who nodded back. They had run into each other back in eighty-three, on the Danube, and Verloc still had a small, discreet scar below his left eye to prove it.

"Might rain," Verloc said.

"Would be good for the crops," Smith said and Verloc, who knew the state of Smith's garden, snorted in response. "You'd have more luck planting a book and hoping it would bear fruit," he said. Then, remembering his business, he said gruffly, "You want to buy one?"

Smith shook his head. Verloc snorted again. He touched the small scar under his eye and a look of surprise, momentarily, filled his whole face, as if he had forgotten, or not even known, that it was there. Then it was gone and Verloc nodded stiffly and went back inside the shop and shut the door.

Smith chewed on that as he walked. Did Verloc seem jumpier than usual? Was there something in his manner to indicate that he, too, felt the change in the air? Perhaps he was daydreaming, he thought. His active days were long gone, over and done with. He came to the post office. Colonel Creighton was working the counter. "Good morning, Mr Smith," he said. Smith nodded. "Colonel," he said. "Anything for me today?"

"A package," Colonel Creighton said. "From London. Another book, perhaps?"

"I do hope so," Smith said, politely. He waited as the old colonel rummaged around for his package. "There you are," he said. Then, "Looks like rain, what?"

"Rain," Smith said.

The colonel nodded. "How are the cabbages coming along?" he said.

"Green," Smith said, which seemed to pacify the colonel.

"Dreadful bloody weather," he said, as though offering a grave secret. "Miss the old country, don't you know. Not the same, home. Not the same at all."

Smith nodded again, feeling a great tiredness overcome him. The colonel was an old India hand, recalled at last back to pasture. The empire rolled on, but the colonel was no longer a part of its colonial effort, and the knowledge dulled him, the way an unused blade dulls with age. Smith said, "Might go to the pub," and the colonel nodded in his turn and said, "Capital idea, what?"

It was not yet noon.

As he approached the pub, however, the unopened package held under his arm, his sense of unease at last began to take on a more definite shape. There were tracks on the road of a kind seldom seen in the village. One of the new steam-powered baruch-landaus, their wheels leaving a distinct impression in the ground. Visitors, he thought, and he felt excitement hurry his pace, and his hands itched for a weapon that was no longer there. Opposite the pub he saw the old bee keeper, standing motionless under the village clock. Smith looked at him and the old bee keeper, almost imperceptibly, gave him a nod.

Interesting.

He went into the pub. Quiet. A fire burning in the fireplace. A solitary drinker sitting by the fire, a pint by his side. Smith looked straight ahead. He went to the counter. The Hungarian baroness was there. She welcomed him with a smile. He smiled back. "What can I get you, Mr Smith?" she said.

"A pint of cider, please, Magdolna," he said, preferring as always the use of one of her many middle names.

"Cold outside?" she said, drawing his pint. Smith shrugged. "Same old," he said. "Same old."

The baroness slid the pint across the counter to him. "Shall I put it on the account?" she said.

Smith shook his head. "Somehow," he said, "I think it best if I paid my tab in full, today."

The baroness glanced quickly at the direction of the solitary drinker by the fireplace and just as quickly looked away. She pursed her lips, then said, softly, "Very well."

Smith paid. The transaction seemed to finalise something between them, an understanding that remained unspoken. He had run into the baroness in eighty-nine in Budapest and again a year later in the *Quartier Latin*, in Paris. She was half his age, but had been retired early and, unseen behind the bar, she walked with a limp.

Their business done, Smith took hold of the pint and, slowly, turned to face the common room. It seemed to him that it took forever for his feet to obey him. He took a step forwards, at last, and the second one came more easily, and then the next, until at last he found himself standing before the solitary drinker, who had not yet looked up.

"Sit down," the man said.

Smith sat.

The man was half-turned in his chair, and was warming long, pale hands on the fire. He was tall and pallid, with black thinning hair and a long straight nose that had been broken at least once. He resembled a spidery sort of thing. He wore a dark suit, not too cheap, not too expensive, an off-the-rack affair several years old. His shoes were black and polished. He said, "Looks like it might rain."

Smith said, "Bugger the rain."

The man smiled a thin smile and finally turned to face him. His eyes were a startling blue, the colour of a pond deeper than one expected. He said, in a voice that had no warmth or affection in it, "Smith."

Smith said, "Fogg."

TWO

"I told you I would kill you the next time we met," Smith said.

It was hot in the room. The baroness had retreated to her quarters, but not before she turned the sign on the door. It now said *Closed*.

The two men were alone.

"I had hoped you'd delay the pleasure," the man he had called Fogg said.

Smith sighed, exhaling air, and felt a long-held tension ease throughout his body. He took a sip from his cider. "Where is Mycroft?" he said.

Fogg said, "Mycroft's dead."

Smith went very still. Outside a wet sort of thunder erupted, and with it came the patter of falling rain. His reflection stared at him from the glass. He examined it as though fascinated. "When?" he said at last.

"Two days ago."

"Where?"

"Outside his house. He had just returned from the club."

Smith said, "Who?" and the man before him smiled that thin, humourless smile and said, "If I knew that, I wouldn't be here now."

At the words an odd excitement took over Smith, overwhelming any sadness he may have felt. He said, "Where is your driver?"

Fogg said, "The baroness is looking after him."

Smith nodded, absent-mindedly. After a moment Fogg raised his glass. Smith followed suit, and they touched glasses with a thin clinking sound. "To Mycroft," Fogg said.

Smith said, "Who–?" even though he knew. Fogg said, "I'm acting head."

"So you finally got what you wanted," Smith said. Fogg said, "I didn't want it to happen like that."

Smith said, "That was the only way it was ever going to fall. Heads don't retire–"

"–they roll," Fogg said, completing the sentence. He shrugged, looking suddenly uncomfortable. "Still. One never imagined–"

"Not the fat man," Smith agreed.

"Sure," Fogg said. He sounded sad. "Not the fat man."

They drank in silence.

Then: "Why are you here?"

Fogg: "You know why I'm here."

Smith, staring at him. Trying to read what was hidden in those deceptively innocent eyes. Saying, "I don't."

Fogg snorted. "We need you," he said, simply.

Smith said, "I find that hard to believe."

"Do you think I *want* your help?" Fogg said. "You are a loner, a killer, you have problems taking orders and you just don't *fit* into an organisational structure!" eThe last one seemed to be the worst, for him. "And you're *old*."

"So why are you here?"

He watched Fogg, closely. Saw him squirm.

"Mycroft left instructions," Fogg finally said.

"That makes a little more sense," Smith said.

"Unfortunately, the decision is out of my hands," Fogg said. "The fat man wanted you on the case."

"Did he know he was going to die?"

A strange, evasive look on Fogg's face; Smith filed it away for future reference. "I can't fill you in on the details," Fogg said. "You're not classified."

That one made Smith smile. He downed the rest of his drink and stood up. Fogg, in some alarm, watched him get up. "Where the hell do you think you're going?"

"I'm going to spare you the trouble," Smith said. "Sorry you had a wasted trip."

"You *what*?" Fogg said.

Smith said, "I'm retired."

He turned to go. Fogg, behind him, gave a gurgled cry. "You can't just walk away!" he said.

"Watch me," Smith said.

He was almost at the door when Fogg said, "Alice."

Smith stopped, his hand on the door, ready to push it open. He didn't.

He turned slowly and stood there, breathing deeply. Old memories, like old newspaper print, almost washed away in the rain.

Almost.

He said, "What about her?"

Fogg said, "She's dead too."

Smith stood there, not knowing what to say. The fat man he could understand, could have lived with. But not her. He began to say, "Where?" but Fogg had anticipated him. "Bangkok," he said. "Two weeks ago."

Two weeks. She had been dead and all that time he'd been tending the cabbage patch.

He felt sick with his own uselessness. He opened and closed his hands, mechanically. It was still raining outside, the rain intensifying. He turned and pushed the door open, and a gust of cold wind entered and brought with it the smell of the rain. He blinked, his face wet. Across the road the old bee keeper was still standing, like a silent guardian, watching. Very little escaped him, still.

Smith took a deep breath. The cold air helped. After a moment he closed the door and went behind the bar and drew himself another pint. Then he drew one for the thin man he had once sworn to kill.

He left money on the counter, for the baroness, and carried

both drinks with him into the common room and sat back down. He stared at Fogg, who had the decency to look embarrassed.

"Same *modus operandi*?"

"So it would appear."

"Fogg, what in God's name is going on?"

Fogg squinted, as if in pain. Perhaps the mention of God had hurt him. "I don't know," he said, at last. Resentful for having to make the admission.

"Have there been others?"

Fogg didn't answer. The rain fell outside. In the fireplace, a log split apart, throwing off sparks. Smith said, "How *many* others?"

"You will be briefed," Fogg said. "In London. If you choose to come back with me."

Smith considered. Bangkok. London. Two links on a chain he couldn't, for now, follow. And each one, rather than a name, or a climate – each one represented the end of one thread in his own life, a sudden severing that had left him reeling inside. Alice and the fat man. He had not seen, nor spoken, to either one of them for a long time, yet they were always there, the very knowledge of their existence offering a sort of comfort, a fragile peace. A peace he could no longer pretend to have.

Yet he suddenly dreaded the return to the city. A part of him had been restless, longing to go back, and yet now that it was offered it came at a price that gave him no joy. The fat man, Alice, and a bloodied trail he feared to follow. There was a reason he had been retired, a reason all of them were there, in that village that could not be found on any map, running their little shops and tending their little gardens, pretending, even the bee keeper, that they were regular people at last, living ordinary lives.

None of us are very good at it, he realised. And yet there *had* been comfort in the pretence, that forced withdrawal from the former, shadowy world they had inhabited. He needed to think. He needed the refuge of his library, even if for one last time.

"I need a day," he said, at last. Fogg didn't argue. Not a death, Smith thought. Deaths. One two weeks before, the trail already growing cold, one here, and recent, but still, his would be a cold trail to follow, and a day would make little difference.

Fogg stood up, draining the last of his pint. "I shall expect you at the club, first thing tomorrow," he said. And with that he was gone.

THREE

He had almost forgotten the book. The package from London. He had been expecting a slim volume of poetry, ordered from Payne's, the newly rebuilt shop on Cecil Court. It had been destroyed some years previous in an explosion. He had not been a part of that particular case, which had been attributed to the shadowy Bookman. He took the package, unopened, with him as he walked back to his place. Behind him he could hear Fogg's baruch-landau starting with an ungodly noise, smoke belching high into the air as it wheeled away, back towards the city.

On a sudden, overwhelming need he turned back. He went down the high street and they were all watching him, the retired and the obsolete, former friends, former foes, united together only in this, this dreaded, dreary world called retirement. He ignored them, even the old bee keeper, as he came to the church, the book still held under his arm.

Fogg had looked offended at Smith's evocation of God. Faith was no longer all that popular, a long way since the day of the Lizard King James I, when his authorised – if somewhat modified – version of the Bible was available in every home. That man Darwin was popular now, with his theory of evolution – he had even claimed, so Smith had heard, that it was proof the royal family and their get, Les Lézards themselves, were of an extraterrestrial origin, and couldn't have co-evolved on the Earth. It was not impossible... Rumours had always circulated, but that, just like the Bookman investigation, had been Mycroft's domain, mostly: he, Smith, was in charge of field work, dirty work, while the fat man sat in his club and ran the empire over lunches and cigars.

Too many unanswered questions... His life had been like that, though. He seldom got the answers. His, simply, was to be given a task, and perform it. How it fit into a larger picture, just which piece of the puzzle it turned out to be, was not his concern. Above him was the fat man and above the fat man was the Queen, and above the Queen, he long ago, and privately, had decided, there must be one more.

God.

Unfashionable, yes. Not a god of churches, not a god of burning bushes like in the old stories, or a science god like in the new books Verne and Wells and their ilk had been writing. A god he couldn't articulate, that demanded little, that offered only forgiveness. Something above. Perhaps it was less god than a reason for being. For Smith believed, despite all the evidence, that there had to be a reason.

He went into the church. It had stopped raining when he left the pub, and the sun, catching him unawares, had come out. A momentary brightness filled the church garden, and a bird called out from the branches of a tree. The grass was wet with rain, and it was quiet. He stepped into the church and stood there, inhaling its dry air of ageing books and candles. Thinking of the fat man. Thinking of Alice.

He was chilled when he got home. His boots were covered in mud and his face was wet. He went inside and shut the door. The house was small but he had large windows in the continental style and so he didn't bother with the gaslight. You didn't get much sunlight in England but at least he caught the most of it. The last of last night's coal was glowing dimly in the fireplace, and he prodded it with the poker, half-heartedly, and left it to die.

He sat in the armchair by the window. The room was full of books. What was it the fat man had liked to say? "Guns and swords will kill you, but nothing is more dangerous than a book."

The fat man had been obsessed with the Bookman, that shadowy assassin who had plagued the empire for so long. But he was no longer around, had become inactive, possibly killed.

Possibly retired, Smith thought. Those had been glorious days, in the service of the empire, going across the world, across continents and countries – *on Her Majesty's secret service*, they used to call it: deniable, disposable, and often dead.

Shadow men and shadow women doing shadow work. But the Bookman had always stood out amongst them, the consummate professional, the shadow of shadows. Mycroft had told him, once, that he suspected the Bookman to be of the same mysterious origins as Les Lézards. Smith didn't care. To him it was the work that mattered, and he prided himself on doing his job well.

Rows of books lined the room. They made it seem less austere, a warmer place. There were bookcases, a rug the colour of dried blood on the floor, an armchair with more holes in it than a compromised agent, a low table where he put his tea and his books to read and where the package from London now sat, waiting to be opened.

He reached for it.

It came in the same plain brown wrapping paper all the books arrived in and he tore it carefully, expecting to find Orphan's *Poems*, that slim, contraband collection of poetry, by an almost-unknown poet, that Smith had been trying to locate for some time. Instead, he discovered he was holding a worn copy of the Manual.

For a moment he just stared at it. It was exactly as he remembered it: the plain blue covers, the stamp on the front that said, simply, *Top Secret – Destroy if Found*. The same smell, that was the very smell of the place, the very essence of the trade, for Smith: of boiled cabbage and industrial soap, the smell of long echoey corridors with no windows, of hushed voices and the hum of unseen machinery; the secret heart of an empire, that had been the fat man's domain.

He opened it at random.

A gentleman never kills by stealth or surreptitiously.

The words spoken, so long ago, at that training centre in Ham Common. The instructor turning to them, smiling. He was missing two fingers on his left hand, Smith remembered. Looking at them, evaluating their response.

Saying, at last, "But we are not gentlemen."

It was still there, in the book. The manual of their trade, written as a joke or as a warning, he never knew which, but always circulating, from hand to hand, passed along from operative to operative, never openly discussed.

This is what we do. This is what we are.

And added, by hand, as an addendum: *To do our job, even we have to forget that we exist.*

He knew that handwriting. He turned the book over in his hands. Opened it again, on the title page, which said only, and that in small, black letters, *Manual*.

The rest of the page, rather than being blank as he remembered, was inscribed by hand. It didn't take long to read it.

Smith–
If you receive this then I am dead, and our worst fears have been confirmed. You may remember my concerns over the Oxford Affair in eighty-eight. I believe our venture into space has played into the hands of unseen forces and now the thing I feared the most has come to be.
If that is so – if I am dead, and you receive this in the post – then we are not alone.
Trust no one.
Beware the B-men.
Trace back the links, follow the chain. Begin with Alice.
Be careful. They will be coming for you.

M.

Smith stared at the note. He closed the Manual softly, put it on the table beside him. Stared out at the wan sunlight. It came as no surprise to know the fat man had not trusted Fogg. Smith had warned, repeatedly, of his suspicion of the man; it had seemed beyond doubt to him that the man was a mole, an agent of the Bookman. But the fat man never did anything, preferring, perhaps, to keep Fogg close by, to watch him.

And now Fogg was acting head.

Well, what was it to Smith? He was retired. The actions of the Bureau were no longer his concern. He was too old, too jaded to think the shadow world they all inhabited was the be-all and end-all of politics. They were engaged in a game – often deadly, often dreary, but a game – while the real decisions were made above their heads, by the people they spied on. There had been moles in the organisation before, just as the Bureau, in its turn, had agents working inside the agencies of both opponents and friendlies. He himself had turned several agents, in his day...

It was a game, only now Alice and the fat man were both dead.

FOUR

It was a soft sound, like leaves falling on the roof, only they weren't leaves at all. Smith opened his eyes and stared at the darkness. The sound came again, furtive, soft: the sound of rats sneaking, a vaguely disturbing sound that gnawed at the edges of consciousness.

In the darkness of the room, he smiled.

He'd sat up in his armchair through the afternoon, thinking. He'd first met Alice in Venice, in sixty-five it must have been. The year of the Zanzibar Incident, though he had not been involved in that particular affair.

The Bureau had sent him to the Venetian Republic, the lizards negotiating a secret treaty with Daniele Fonseca, the republican leader, against the Hapsburgs. It was baby-sitting duty for Smith, watching the British envoy from the shadows as the treaty was negotiated. And it *was* Venice, in the spring, and he met her one night when Hapsburgian agents attacked his envoy and Smith, outnumbered, had scrambled to save the man.

She had stepped out of the shadow, a young girl, glowing – so it seemed to him, then, romantic fool that he was – in the light of the moon. Her long white legs were bare and she wore a blue dress and a blue flower behind one ear. She smiled at him, flashing perfect white teeth, and killed the first of the would-be assassins with a knife throw that went deep into the man's chest, a flower of blood blooming on his shirt as he fell.

Together, they eliminated the others, the envoy oblivious the whole while to the covert assassination attempt, then disposed of the bodies together, dragging them into one of the canals and setting them adrift, Alice's blue flower pinned to the leader's chest. It had been the most romantic night of Smith's life.

Later, when the envoy was safely asleep in his bed, Smith and Alice shared a drink on the balcony of the small, dank hotel, and watched the moonlight play on the water of the canal...

Now he listened for the smallest sounds, that soft patter on the roof, the drop of a body, then another. The fat man had warned him but somehow, Smith always knew the day would come, was always waiting for it, and now he was ready.

He slid a knife from its scabbard, tied around his ankle. He had spent some of the afternoon, and a part of the evening, sharpening this knife, his favourite, and cleaning and oiling various other devices. Cleaning one's weapons was a comforting act, an ingrained habit that felt almost domestic. It made him think of Alice, who preferred guns to knives, and disliked poisons.

The things the mind conjures... He'd often argued with her about it, to no avail.

Smith disliked guns. They were loud, and showy, the weapon of bullies and show-offs. A gun had swagger behind it, but little thought. Smith preferred the intimacy of killing, the touch of flesh on flesh, the hissed intake of breath that was a mark's last. He liked neatness, in all things.

Then everything happened very quickly and almost at once.

The windows broke inwards – a loud explosive sound – shards of glass flying through the air, showering the floor and furniture.

Something heavy slammed into the front door, and the back one, sending both crashing to the ground, as dark figures came streaming through, and Smith found himself grinning. A single candle had been left burning on the bedside table and now it died with a gust of cold wind, and the house was dark.

Five pouring in from the front. Five more from the back. And there'd be others outside by now, forming a ring around the house. They wanted him badly. He was almost flattered. And they wanted him alive – which was an advantage.

He killed the first one with a knife thrust, holding the body gently as it dropped down to the floor. Black-clad, armed – he took the man's gun out of its holster, admiring its lightness, and fired once, twice, three times and watched two of them fall, one rolling away. When they fired back, destroying the bedroom, he was no longer there.

He worried about his library but there was nothing he could do. He came on two more of them there and killed the first one by breaking his neck, twisting it with a gentle nostalgia, then dropped the corpse to the floor, and the second one turned, and with the same motion Smith flipped the knife and sent it flying.

He went to retrieve it, pulling it out of the man's chest. The man wasn't quite dead yet. His lips were moving. "*Zu sein*," the man said, the softest breath of air. *To be*. Smith strained to hear more but there was nothing left in the man, no words or air.

Smith straightened. He couldn't take them all. He was against the wall when he heard a barked question – "*In der Bibliothek?*"

Two more bullets, a man dropped at the open door. Shouts behind now, no more pretence at secrecy or stealth. Smith said, "*Warten sie!*"

Wait.

"Mr Smith."

The voice came from beyond the door, a voice in shadows.

"*Ja.*"

"You come with us, now, Mr Smith. No more play."

The voice spoke good English, but accented. It was young, like the others. A fully trained extraction team, but too young, and they did things differently these days.

"Don't shoot," Smith said.

The voice chuckled. "You are late for an appointment," it said, "arranged a long time ago."

Smith smiled. "Take them," he said, loudly.

There was the sudden sound of gunfire outside. *Heavy* gunfire. Smith ran, jumped – dived out of the broken window. The whistle of something flying through the air, entering the room he had just vacated. He rolled and covered his head and there was a booming thunder and he felt fragments of wood and stone hit his back and his legs and the night became bright, momentarily.

When it was over he raised his head, looked–

The old lady from M.'s, the lace and china shop, was standing with her hair on edge, a manic grin spread across her face. She was holding the controls of a giant, mounted Gatling gun, a small steam engine belching beside it. "Take one for the Kaiser!" she screamed, and a torrent of bullets exploded out of the machine like angry bees, tracer bullets lighting up the night sky, as M. screamed soundlessly and fired, mowing the black-clothed attackers as though they were unruly grass.

Spies, Smith thought, trying to make himself as small as possible. They'll take any excuse to let their hair down.

The firing stopped and then someone was beside him, grabbing him. He turned and saw Verloc from the bookshop, grinning at him – the first time, perhaps, he had ever seen him look happy.

"Come on!" Verloc said. He pulled Smith, who stood up and followed him. The two men ran across the cabbage patch, over what was left of the fence (which wasn't much) and into the field beyond.

Smith could hear M. screaming again, then a second round of shooting. His poor house. No. 6 would never be the same again, after this. He should have taken care of this business on his own.

Well, too late now.

Turning, he saw Colonel Creighton, the baroness by his side, going through the garden and into the house, the colonel armed with a curved khukuri knife, the baroness, less ostentatiously, with a couple of small-calibre, elegant hand guns, one in each hand. He raised his head and saw, floating above the house, a long, graceful black shape: an airship.

"Don't let it get away," Smith said. Beside him, Verloc grinned. "Shall we?" he said.

"Let's," Smith said.

Verloc went first, and Smith followed. Back towards the house. M. covered them, but there weren't many of the attackers moving around, any more. "I need at least one of them alive," Smith said.

"Let's see what we can find," Verloc called, over his shoulder. They reached the wall of the house and Verloc, with a litheness that belied his age, took hold of the drain pipe and began to climb. Smith, less enthusiastically, followed.

It was not a tall house and they reached the roof easily enough. The airship had been moored to it but the remaining figures on the roof were busy climbing up it and clearly they had changed their minds about their chances and were keen on getting away. Smith knew M. would shoot the balloon but he feared they had used hydrogen, and he didn't want yet *another* explosion.

"*Halt*!" he said. Verloc had twin guns pointed at the escaping men – some sort of light-alloy devices he didn't have a moment before – he must have picked them up off the fallen soldiers. Smith himself had one of the guns.

"*Schnell! Schnell*!" Verloc fired. He couldn't help himself, Smith thought. It couldn't have been easy, all those years, without even a burglar to attempt Verloc's bookshop.

One, two, three men fell, screaming, clutching wounded legs. Verloc liked going for the knees. These soldiers, at least, were unlikely to walk again.

Then he saw him.

The man was young and moved with a grace that Smith found himself, suddenly and unexpectedly, incredibly jealous of. He had come from the other side of the wall, out of shadow. Smith had almost missed him. Then the man lifted his hand and something silver flashed, for just a moment, and, beside Smith, Verloc grunted in pain and dropped, quietly, to the floor.

"Verloc!"

"Don't worry... about me," Verloc said. His hand was on his belly, a blade protruding from between his fingers. Blood was seeping through, falling onto the wall.

Smith was already moving, towards the young man, his vision clear, his mind as cool as water. He saw the flash of a new blade and side-stepped it and unhurriedly entered into the young man's range and head-butted him, hearing the bones of the nose breaking. His fingers found the young man's neck and pressed, the thumbs digging. He applied pressure – just enough. They were attempting to fire at him from above, the airship cut loose and rising higher, but M. had him covered, firing low, and Smith grabbed the unconscious man and dragged him to where Verloc lay still. He knelt to check him but Verloc was no longer breathing, and so Smith dragged the young man by the arm to the edge of the roof and fell over it, dragging the younger man down with him.

He hit the ground, rolled, and the younger man followed. Smith dragged him away when there was a long, high whistling tone and he saw, turning on his back, a silver metal object flying in a high arc, as though in slow motion, from M.'s position towards the rising airship–

With the colonel and the baroness running out of the house, as fast as they could–

He heard M. shout, gleefully, wheezing with the effort, "Take one for the–"

The object hit the dark moving spot that was the airship–

Smith closed his eyes shut, tight. But even then he could see the airship, as bright as day, its image burning on his retinas as a bright ball of flame erupted in the sky above, turning the night to day and the airship into a heap of disintegrating wood and cloth and burning parts and people.

FIVE

"A nice cup of tea?"

They had taken over Verloc's bookshop. Verloc himself was laid out in the main room, amidst the books. Smith had never figured out if Verloc had actually *liked* books. He had once been married, had a family, though Smith didn't know what had happened to them. Verloc was a bomb-maker by trade. Now he lay amidst the dusty penny dreadfuls and the three-volume novels and the serials from London, and the books from the continent, and it was quiet in the shop.

They had carried the unconscious captive from the airship to Verloc's back room and propped him in a chair. Verloc had a samovar in the shop and M. had taken to lighting the coals and heating up the water and sniffed disapproval at the state of the milk, but pronounced it at last drinkable.

Smith had known M. for many years but she had never changed. She had the appearance of a harmless old lady, and as she grew older she simply became more herself. She had had a name but no one could remember what it was. Her work had been legendary. There were few places a little old lady couldn't penetrate.

Now she bustled to and fro, making the tea, using the chipped old white china mugs Verloc had kept in the shop. She gave them a good rinse first. The prisoner meanwhile was coming to in the chair. He did not look happy.

"*Was ist Ihre Mission*?" Smith said. The prisoner looked at him without expression and then said, with a note of disgust, "I speak English."

"As you should," Colonel Creighton said, stiffly. "Now, what were you after, *boy*?"

The prisoner merely nodded in Smith's direction. "Him," he said.

Smith said, "Why?"

The prisoner said, "You know perfectly well why, *Herr* Smith."

Colonel Creighton looked sideways at Smith. "Do you?" he said.

"No."

"Then you shall have to remain unsatisfied," the prisoner said. The colonel raised his hand to hit him, but Smith stopped him with a gesture. "Was it to do with Bangkok?" he said, softly.

At that the prisoner's face twisted. "*Der Erntemaschine*!" he said. Then he shook his head and a grimace of pain crossed his face. "*Nein*," he said. "*Nein*."

"Smith? What is he doing?"

The prisoner was convulsing in the chair. Smith hurried to his side, tilted his head back. Foam was coming out of the man's mouth. Smith touched two fingers to the man's neck, felt for a pulse. "He's dead," he said, after a moment.

The colonel swore. Smith stared at the corpse. A false tooth, carrying poison, he thought. Standard issue – he should have remembered.

Old. Getting old, and sloppy, and forgetting things.

Forgetting things could get you killed.

"What," M. said, materialising with two mugs, handing one to each blithely, "is a damned *Erntemaschine*?"

"Ernte," Smith said, "means harvest."

"So *Erntemaschine*–"

"A machine for harvesting. A…" He hesitated. "A *harvester*," he said, at last.

He knew that, behind him, M. and the colonel were exchanging worried glances.

"That's what they used to call *you*," the colonel said at last, softly. The words seemed to freeze and hang in the air.

But Smith shook his head. "The word for a manual harvester is different, in German," he said. "What did he mean, a machine?"

M. said, gently, "Drink your tea, dear."

Smith sipped at it. "It's good," he said, by way of thanks. Truth was, he could barely taste it. He felt raw, hurt. The room swam. The colonel caught hold of him. "Easy, there, old boy," he murmured.

They used to call him the Harvester.

So now someone else was laying claim to the title. Someone else was harvesting people, the way a farmer harvested corn, or wheat.

"I'm going to London," he said, at last. "Help me dispose of the bodies?"

It was hard, backbreaking work. The village rallied round, even those who hadn't been to the fight. By dawn there had been nothing left of the airship or its crew, but a new mound of earth, like an ancient tor, stood by the ruined house.

"Too bad about your cabbages," the baroness said. She had been wounded in hand-to-hand combat inside the house, and now wore her arm in a sling. Her eyes shone. "I miss the old days, sometimes," she said. "Then something like this happens and I think maybe retirement's not so bad."

Smith nodded. He had tried to rescue some of the books, but most were beyond help. Torn, burned pages floated like dark butterflies in the air. "We never truly retire, though," he said. "Do we?"

"No," she said. "I guess we don't." Then, coming closer, putting her hand on his shoulder, gently: "I'm sorry about Alice."

He shrugged. "It's the life," he said, "each of us chose."

"Not all of us had the choice," the baroness said.

The worst part had been seeing the bee keeper again. He showed up just as Smith was preparing to leave. Day had come and the sky was clear and bright. Smith wore a suit that had seen better days. He needed to go into the town, to catch the train.

"I am so sorry," Smith said. The old man gazed at him. Once he had been the greatest of them all. Even now he was formidable. He was not that old, but he had suffered much, and had retired shortly after the Bookman affair. Rumours spoke of a lost love, a brotherly conflict, of captivity and strange experiments that had made his mind different, alien to the everyday. They were just that, rumours. No one but the bee keeper knew what the truth was, or what kept him in the village.

The bee keeper merely nodded. "It is the life we choose," he said. "Mycroft always knew what he was doing."

"Will you... pursue an investigation?" Smith asked. The bee keeper shook his head. "There is no art to it," he said, with a slight smile. "I already know."

"Then tell me."

The bee keeper shook his head again. "It will not help," he said. "Yet you are suited to this task, in a way I am not. It requires not a singularly great deductive mind, such as mine, but a tenacious sort of controlled violence. What you are after is not a mystery, but the conclusion of one. A great game we had all been playing, and which is now coming to an end... or to a new beginning."

"I don't understand."

"Look at the stars," the bee keeper said, "for answers." And with that last cryptic, unhelpful comment, he was gone.

Smith shook his head. This was Mycroft all over again. Then he decided to leave it, and climbed into the hansom cab.

"Market Blandings, please, Hume," he told the driver, who nodded without speaking and hurried the horses into action.

Smith settled back inside the cab. He closed his eyes. The horses moved sedately, the motion soothing. In moments he was asleep.

SIX

Hume dropped him off outside the Blue Lizard on Market Blandings' sleepy high street. The hansom cab rode off and Smith, still
tired and aching, decided to go into the pub to refresh himself
before catching the train.

Whereas the Emsworth Arms, down the road, was a spacious,
quiet place, the Blue Lizard, even this early, was noisy, and it
smelled. It was a small, dank place set away from the river, and
Smith had difficulty getting to the bar to order an ale and breakfast.

It felt strange to be out of the village. He knew the Bureau
kept rural agents around the village – making sure the inmates
remained where they should. Confirmation of that came quickly.
As he was tucking into his fried eggs a small, slim figure slid into
the seat across from him. Smith looked up, and his face twisted
into an expression of dislike that made the other man grin.

"Charles," Smith said.

"Peace," the other said, and laughed.

"I thought they hanged you," Smith said.

Charles Peace shrugged. "I'm a useful feller, ain't I?" he said,
modestly.

"Useful how?" Smith said.

"Keeping my eyes open, don't I," Peace said. "Sniffing about, by your leave, Smith. Ferreting things."

He looked like a ferret, Smith thought. But he was nothing but a rat.

"What do you want?" he said.

Peace tsked. "No way to talk to an old friend," he said mournfully. "You know you shouldn't be out of the village, Smith."

"I'm back on active."

"Really." Peace snorted. He was a violinist, a burglar, and a murderer. Which is a different thing entirely, Smith preferred to think, to a killer.

Murderers didn't have standards, for one.

"Really," Smith said.

"I did not get the memo."

"I don't doubt that."

Charles Peace looked sharply up. "What does that mean, me old mucker?" he said, almost spitting out the words.

Smith ignored him. The Blue Lizard was busy with rail workers, farmers in for the market, and such visitors to the castle low enough on the social pecking order not to have been extended an invitation to stay at the castle grounds. It was dark inside and the air turned blue with cigar and pipe smoke. Across from him, Peace made himself relax. He rolled a cigarette, yellow fingers shaking slightly as they heaped tobacco into paper. "Having a laugh," Peace said, smiling again. His teeth were revolting. Smith pushed away his breakfast, took a sip of ale. "You have something for me?" he said at last.

But now Peace was disgruntled. "Should report you, I should," he said. "Out and about, when you should be retired an' all."

Smith looked at him closely. Had Fogg not rescinded the watch order on him? He had assumed Peace had a message for him from the Bureau. But if he hadn't, what did he want? Smith knew the instructions that affected him, and the rest of the village. Watchers were told that under no circumstances were they to engage with retired agents. *Report and wait*, was the standing procedure.

So what was Peace playing at?

He waited the man out. Peace finishing rolling, lit up the cigarette. Loose tobacco fell on the table. The man's hands were shaking. Disgraceful. "You do something you shouldn't have?" Peace said at last.

Smith didn't answer. Watched him. Watched the room.

He'd had trouble finding a table. He sat in the corner, his back to the wall, his eyes on the door. It was the way he always sat. Busy place. Was anyone watching *him*, in their turn? Was anything out of place?

"Been a naughty boy," Peace said. He spat out tobacco shreds. Made to get up–

Smith kicked the table from underneath, lifting it over – it hit Peace full in the face, sent him reeling back. Smith dropped behind the table as three shots rang out. Screams in the pub – he caught movement coming *forward* as everyone else moved back, towards the door or, if they were smart, stayed down. Two figures, guns drawn. He was getting sick of guns.

"We just want to talk, Mr. Smith."

The voice was cultured, sort of, a London accent, with only a hint of the continental about it. More agents of the Kaiser? Someone else?

Smith said, "What about?"

"About this year's harvest, Mr. Smith," the voice said. Smith drew his knife, softly. But he was cornered.

"Who do you work for?"

The voice laughed. "Whoever pays," it said.

Smith shifted the table, keeping it between himself and the attackers, until he hit Peace's leg. Peace himself wasn't moving. He pulled on the leg, bringing the man's mass towards him. He could hear the two men coming forward. Tensed. "Really, Mr Smith. Do not make it more difficult than it needs to–"

He grabbed Peace under the arms, pushed the table again so it fell down with a crash, and rose. Two guns fired. He felt the impact of the shots, Peace's body slamming him back as it was hit. He let it carry him, moved with the impact, discarded the body and came over the fallen table, blade at the ready.

The first man had his gun arm extended, about to fire again. Smith's blade severed the arteries in the man's wrist and then with a half-turn, dancer's movement Smith's blade flashed again, moving across the man's neck. The man tried to gurgle, couldn't, and fell to his knees, blood pouring out of the wound.

Another shot, but Smith wasn't where he'd been and the other man, searching for a target, clumsy with the gun, didn't respond fast enough and Smith was behind him, the blade against the man's neck, and Smith said, "Drop it."

The man dropped the gun. Beside them, his partner expired noisily.

"Be still."

The man was very still.

It was quiet in the abandoned pub. Landlord and patrons had made for the door and were all gone, abandoning drinks and cigars and conversation. Smith preferred it that way.

He said, "Who sent you?"

The man began to talk fast. His Adam's apple bobbed up and down and the man twitched every time it scraped against the knife. "We was paid to watch for you, is all," he said. "I don't know who wants you, mister. A man came. He was dressed well, he had money. He said, just bring him to me."

"Alive?"

"He wasn't strict on that score," the man said, and swallowed.

"What did he look like?"

The man shrugged, then regretted it. "He didn't give no name."

Smith increased the pressure of the knife. "Not what I asked," he said.

"Tall, black hair, foreign accent. He had a scar across his cheek."

Smith went still at that. "What sort of accent?" he said at last.

"Dunno, mister. Some European muck, like my partner's is – was." He swallowed again.

"And Peace?"

"Old Peace here was to tag you, is all. We figured we'd kill him when we was done so as to save the pay."

"Sensible," Smith muttered. There was noise outside now, and the whistle of constables, and he decided it was time to go.

"Do you want to live?" he said.

The man swallowed a third time. "Very much, mister," he said.

"Too bad," Smith said. He raised his hand and slammed it against the man's neck. The man fell. Smith arranged him comfortably with his back to the bar. He picked up the man's gun and put it in his hand. Then he went over to the man's fallen companion, picked up the man's hand, which was still holding a gun, and fired twice at the unconscious man. Blood bloomed over the man's chest and Smith nodded, satisfied. Outside the noise intensified and a voice, magnified by a bullhorn, called, "Step outside with your hands raised!"

Smith surveyed the scene. With luck no one would remember the quiet gentleman who had sat in the corner. Then he slipped out through the back door, over the fence of the sad little garden, and was soon at the train station, just in time for the London one to pull in.

SEVEN

The train departed on time. He'd paid for a first-class seat and now sat alone in the small car, a cup of tea by his side.

Smith liked trains. There was something soothing about their rhythmic movement, something vastly luxurious about the space one had, the ability to simply get up and walk and stretch – and that without mentioning the joys of dining cars, and sleeping compartments. He always slept well on trains.

You could always get a cup of tea.

And, of course, trains were wonderful for covert assassination.

The second time he met Alice had been on a train. He had got on at Sofia and the train, on a leisurely night journey, was travelling to the port town of Varna, on the shores of the Black Sea.

Smith had been on board to dispose of a Bulgarian diplomat by the name of Markov. He had taken his time. A train offered a perfect shelter for a quiet murder. It stopped often, each station offering a quiet getaway. The Bureau had agents waiting at stops along the route. They would provide him with the means to disappear, if he chose to use them.

But Smith preferred to work alone.

The diplomat had been of the anti-Caliban faction, and as such a threat to Her Majesty's government. Bulgaria was an important

asset for the lizardine court, its Black Sea ports offering strategic
opportunities against the Russians on the one hand, the Ottomans on the other. Varna itself, their destination, was a bustling
port town crawling with British Navy and Aerofleet personnel.
Markov had links to anti-Calibanic groups, some of which used
violent means. Verloc, in his day, had been a prominent member
of several such groups – though he, of course, worked undercover for the Bureau.

Some of the time, at least.

Markov took ill shortly after dinner. Smith had sat two tables
down from him, eating a simple meal of smoked salami, bread
and the red wine this country was famed for. He had not expected Markov to take ill, and was concerned. As Markov, about
to retch, departed from the car, a new figure appeared in the
doorway and Smith's breath caught in his chest.

She wore a blue dress, just as she had in Venice. A white
flower behind her ear this time. She was smiling and her smile
widened when she saw him. She came and sat opposite him and
signalled to the waiter to bring another wine glass and then said,
"Why, Mr Smith, fancy meeting you here."

"Alice," he said, softly, the food forgotten. Her glass arrived
and the waiter filled it and she raised it up. "Cheers," she said.

Markov had expired later that night, of apparent food poisoning.

He drank his tea. He couldn't really believe she was dead. They
had spent that night together and got off at Varna and then had-
n't seen each other for six months. The fat man had warned him
about her, Alice of the blades and of the poison, who yet liked
neither, who often said a "Honesty is a gun"… Alice of the grin
that said she knew what she was doing was wrong, but that she
liked doing it, nevertheless… He wasn't even sure who she really
worked for. You couldn't tell, with any of them. They were
shadow pawns in a shadow world, switching sides, owing allegiance to no one. Mycroft knew that, was philosophical about
it. "If you were honest people," he once told Smith, "you would
be of no use to me."

Now Smith sat and worried about the latest development, as the train chugged along, heading for the capital. He longed to see London again, walk its streets, hear the calling of the whales in the Thames... He began to toss a coin absent-mindedly, heads, tails, heads, tails. The coin bore the profile of Queen Victoria, the lizard queen. Heads, tails...

It had been a message, he decided. He knew the man with the scar on his cheek. He never did things by half. Sending amateurs after him had been a message... a warning?

So the French, too, were interested.

But why him, Smith? Did they suspect him of being behind the killings?

Or did they believe him capable of following the chain?

If so, they will be following him. Watching.

Well, let them.

The world was large and fractured and there were too many factions at play, and always had been. Nothing had changed. The game remained and he, Smith, was back in it, playing.

With a small smile he sat back, his head against the comfortable stuffing of the seat, and closed his eyes. He wasn't as young as he used to be, and it had been a long night. He fell asleep, still smiling wistfully.

He'd first met the man from Meung in Paris, in the seventies. Tension ran high at that time between the Quiet Council, France's ruling body of human and automatons, and the lizardine court.

Smith was in Paris on a defection. A senior French scientist wanted to change sides and Smith had been given *carte blanche* on the operation. "Do whatever you have to do," the fat man had told him, "but get him across the Channel alive."

Only the whole thing had turned out to be a trap, and Smith found himself locked inside an inn outside Paris, and the inn was on fire. When he stared out of the window, through the metal bars, he saw the man from Meung for the first time. The man looked up at the window, and laughed. Then he climbed on his horse and rode away.

They called him the man from Meung not because he came from Meung-sur-Loire but because, when he was only twenty-five, the young man who was to become the Comte de Rochefort had killed forty-six people there, in one night. They had been a group of conspirators, plotting against the Council, and the young man, who had gone deep undercover with the group, proceeded to assassinate them one by one over the course of the night. It had come to be known as the Second Battle of Meung-sur-Loire.

But Smith did not know it that night, staring out of the window while the smoke billowed through the inn and the fire spread, and roared, and he fled desperately from room to room, seeking an escape...

They had met again in Mombasa in seventy-one. That time, Rochefort was after a British courier and, also that time, it was Smith who had the upper hand. He had not been able to kill the man but had given him the distinct scar he still bore.

Like Smith, Rochefort despised guns. His was a silent method, a personal one. Like Smith, he preferred to kill at close quarters, with a knife or with bare hands and, like Smith, he was very good at it.

Smith woke up feeling refreshed just as the train was pulling into Charing Cross. He had not been disturbed throughout the journey. No further attempts on his life, so far. He almost felt disappointed.

But they'd be watching, he knew. Rochefort was too smart to get on the train alongside Smith. Most likely he hadn't even been at Market Blandings, had arranged the attack from a distance and was even now waiting in London, in an anonymous hotel somewhere, with his agents on the ground, waiting for Smith to make his move.

It was odd, Rochefort warning him like that. Smith could not say that they liked each other, he and the Frenchman, but over the years a mutual respect had developed, as they fought across continents in the shadow game, the Great Game. The only game there was. What interest did the Quiet Council have in the deaths of Mycroft and Alice? Who else had died? How many people, and where, and why, and by whose hand?

He didn't know, but he was going to find out.

The train came to a halt, and he left his compartment and went down the steps to the platform. People swarming all about the great station, the trains belching steam, the cries of sellers offering candied apples and roasted nuts and sizzling sausages and birds in cages and mechanical toys and portraits done on the spot, and a little pickpocket went past him, going for it when Smith grabbed his hand, giving it a tweak, and the boy squeaked. Smith could have easily broken the delicate bones of the boy's fingers, but didn't.

"Run off with you," he said, a little gruffly, and the urchin, giving him a look of hurt dignity, did exactly that, not looking back.

London.

What did the old bee keeper used to say, in *his* own active days in the field? Ah, yes.

The game is afoot.

Smith smiled as he remembered; he began to walk towards the exit, about to enter again the world he'd left behind.

It felt good to be back.

EIGHT

There are a number of respectable old establishments along Pall Mall. There's the Drones Club, of course, and the Reform Club (of which Fogg was a member) and then there was Mycroft's old place, the Diogenes. Whereas the Drones was a lively place, its members numbering amongst the younger, and more energetic, of the aristocracy (both human and lizardine), the Diogenes was a place of quietude, where no noise was tolerated and where members moved little, spoke less, and ate plenty. As to the Reform Club, Smith disliked it. He disliked all members-only clubs. It would not be true to say Smith had sympathies to the views expounded by that man, Marx, whose own watering hole, the Red Lion pub in Soho, he nevertheless found much more congenial. Smith did not hold strong opinions, as a rule. To do so would be to compromise one's efficiency as a shadow agent. Yet something in him disliked wealth, and its display. Surely, he had fewer qualms when disposing of a member of the rich than of the poor. Long ago, Smith had learned to accept his own little idiosyncrasies. All agents had them. You had to learn to do the job regardless. It was telling, though, that the only times he had visited any such gentlemen's clubs had been in pursuit of a particular member within, and that he never left a job uncompleted.

At the corner with Waterloo Place there was the Athenaeum, a large, imposing building and another club, where Smith had once done an excision on a visiting politician. At any rate, he did not aim for any of the clubs, but rather for an unmarked, and rather drab, door in the side of a building along the Mall, said building being a small, red-brick establishment, with no sign, but clearly belonging to a trade of some sort.

And *trade*, on the Mall, was as good as being invisible.

It had begun to rain by the time he reached the building. The rain revived him, but he was glad to find shelter. The door opened as though on its own. In some uneasy moments Smith had the feeling the building was somehow alive, and watching. He knew that, in reality, the door was watched by human operators deep inside the building, and that, upon recognising him and establishing that he had clearance, the door was opened for him. The door, otherwise, never opened. Yet still, despite the knowledge, the feeling persisted, as if the Bureau itself was somehow alive.

He went inside and the door shut behind him noiselessly. He found himself in a quiet corridor. Small windows set in the wall allowed only a modicum of grey light in. The corridor smelled of industrial cleaning products and the windows were grimy with dirt. When he walked along it his feet squeaked on the bare floor.

He followed the corridor to its end. A simple second door blocked the way. He waited, and presently there was the sound of gears and steam and the door opened onto a small lift. He stepped inside and the door closed behind him and he began to descend.

The Bureau was cold and quiet. He went past the cipher room and the door was closed and he could hear faint voices behind. He ran into Berlyne in the corridor, Berlyne rubbing his hands together, muttering, "Damn cold, old boy."

Smith said, "Where is everyone?"

Berlyne shrugged. "All about," he said mournfully. "You here because of Mycroft?"

Smith wasn't fooled. Berlyne had been longer at the Bureau than anyone. There was little he didn't know, or had a hand in.

"I'm here to see Fogg."

"Yes, he did mumble something to that effect, come to mention," Berlyne said. "He'd be in his office."

"What's going on, Berlyne? Are there any leads?"

Berlyne shrugged again. "Harvester," he said, not without affection. Smith flinched.

"I retired," he said.

Berlyne shook his head. "Yet here you are," he said. "No one ever retires."

It was said he had a string of ex-wives in the colonies, that he could never afford to leave his salaried post. In his youth he was a promising agent, but an encounter on a South Pacific island changed him, made him mournful and jumpy, and he had had to be retired to a desk job. The file on that encounter, as on most Bureau missions, did not exist.

"Well," Berlyne said. "Good luck with it." He took out an enormous, not-too-clean handkerchief, blew his nose noisily, and departed down the corridor. Smith looked after him suspiciously for a moment, then went in search of Fogg.

"Ah, Smith. You've finally decided to show up."

Fogg's office had a fake fireplace, all the rage two years before, and the hiss of gas filled the windowless room. "What took you so long?"

Fogg looked irritated. He was leafing through a sheaf of papers on the desk. A chart behind him had names, and places, linked by lines. Smith saw ALICE – BANGKOK, a trail leading to HOLMES – LONDON.

Something else, too, which gave him pause.

AKSUM – WESTENRA – DEVICE.

He wondered what it referred to. Filed it away.

"Someone's been trying to kill me," he said.

Fogg snorted. "Well," he said. "That's only to be expected, isn't it."

Smith said, "Is it?"

Fogg said, "I imagine there are plenty of people who wish to kill you."

"Why now?"

And then he thought – that trail of bodies, Alice to Holmes – where will it lead to next? And it occurred to him it was just possible Fogg thought – or hoped – that it was leading to *him*, to Smith.

Was that possible?

He kept his face carefully blank as he thought. Did Fogg wish to use him as *bait*? It almost made Smith laugh. Almost. And could Fogg be right? Could this new, unknown Harvester be heading his way?

It didn't make much sense. He didn't *know* anything. He was not a part of whatever it was this *Erntemaschine* was looking for. Which meant Alice *had* been. And Mycroft.

And suddenly Smith wanted, very badly, to know what *it* was.

Fogg said, "It was not inconceivable that other powers would become involved. Our side is not the only one to have suffered… unexplained deaths."

"But why go after me?" Then– "Wait, you *knew*?"

Fogg looked amused. "We figured you could take care of yourself," he said. "Clearly, since you *are*, in fact, here right now…"

Smith was almost flattered. He said, "Who else has died?"

Fogg pushed a sheet of paper in his direction. Smith took it. "There's a list," Fogg said. "Make sure it does not leave the building."

Smith looked at the page, memorised it. Handed it back. He would review it later.

"Come with me," Fogg said. He pushed himself out of his chair. "Something I want you to see."

They were never going to give him all the information about a case. Smith didn't expect them to, either.

We're pieces in their game, he thought. They send us off into the field and let us find the questions for ourselves. No preconceptions.

So Fogg would be keeping information from him. He expected that. He'd give him just enough to follow his own chain of reasoning. Die in the process, possibly. Fogg should be happy with either outcome.

He followed the tall man down the corridor, a left before the still-closed cipher room, and down a flight of stairs. He knew then where they were going.

The Bureau's own mortuary.

It was icy down there and the light was cold and white, running on Edison bulbs, powered by the Bureau's own, hidden steam engines. Fogg pushed the metal door open and Smith followed him inside.

He did not like mortuaries.

Which was ironic, he knew. Just as he knew that, one day, sooner or later, it would be his turn to end up in one. He suppressed a shudder as he walked into the cold room. Metal cabinets set in the stone walls. An operating table sitting unused. Fogg went to one of the metal drawers and pulled it open.

A large corpse lay on it, covered by a sheet. Smith came and stood close to Fogg, looking down at the body. Fogg, with a moue of distaste, lifted up the sheet.

Mycroft.

The fat man looked peaceful in death. Fogg said, "Help me turn him over," brusquely. Smith complied.

Mycroft's flesh was soft and pliable and cold to the touch. The room stank of disinfectant. Carbolic acid, if Smith was right. The fat man moved surprisingly easily. "There," Fogg said, pointing.

Smith bent down closer. Looked at the fat man's neck.

A tiny hole, dug into the base of the skull.

So someone had stuck a stiletto blade into the man's remarkable head, piercing the brain in the process.

And had he seen something like that before?

"Is this what killed him?"

"There are no other marks," Fogg said.

Smith straightened. If he'd hoped for any sudden revelations, none were forthcoming.

Do it the hard way, then.

The way he'd always done it.

"What are you not telling me?" he said.

Fogg shook his head. He looked tired, Smith suddenly realised. And worried. It ill-suited him. "You're on your own," Fogg said. "As of this moment you're back on active. You report to no one but me. Get what you need from Accounting. I'd tell you to sign up with Armaments but I know your preferences. You'll be issued travel documents as needed, and currency – but do keep all the receipts, would you, Smith? These aren't the old days."

Smith gently rolled the fat man back over and covered him again with the sheet. Goodbye, Mycroft, he thought.

Fogg pushed the trolley back into the wall.

"Let's go," he said.

NINE

Smith sipped a rare cup of coffee, in the continental style, as he waited for his contact to come in.

He was thinking through his meeting with Fogg.

The man had seemed nervous, Smith thought. He was sparse with information, almost too sparse. Smith had tried asking what Alice had been working on, before she was killed. Fogg only said, "She was like you. Retired."

He didn't know, Smith thought. Something linked Alice and Mycroft, but Fogg had not been a part of the chain.

He couldn't picture Alice as ever retiring. What had she got herself into, that got her killed?

And that hush at the Bureau. The sort of hush that came with bad news. Before he left he had run into Berlyne again. "Watch your back," the man advised him mournfully, rubbing his hands together against the chill. He had regarded Smith for one long moment before adding, almost too softly to hear – "Mycroft's not the only one who's no longer around."

Smith sipped his coffee and thought about his next steps and waited for his contact. He'd signed up with Accounts, waved away the offer of weapons at Armaments, and was out of the building before he knew it. The door shut behind him softly and he had the sudden, sinking feeling it would not be opening again.

He was not a fool.

He knew Fogg was using him. As bait, or decoy, he didn't know. Fogg was in over his head.

And it made Smith think of something else that had been bothering him, namely, the attempts on his own life.

Why go for him now, after all these years?

If it wasn't something in the past then he had to conclude it had to do with this new investigation.

Which suggested some interesting possibilities…

The most prominent of which was the simple assumption that, whatever Alice and the fat man had been killed over, someone, or several someones, wanted very much to keep it a secret.

He was sitting upstairs at the Bucket of Blood, by Covent Garden. They staged bare-knuckle boxing there but that would be later and for now the place was quiet. They served good pie and bad coffee and they didn't serve bluebottles, crushers, coppers, or whatever your term for the agents of the law may have been.

Which suited Smith.

He waited and presently there came the soft steps he had been waiting for, and he saw him – it – he never really knew what they preferred – come up the stairs.

He stood up. The other came and stood by him. His gait was slow and mechanical, and his blank eyes always terrified Smith, false eyes that were meant to suggest humanity, but somehow didn't.

"Byron," Smith said.

The Byron automaton extended his hand for a shake. His flesh was soft and warm. It was made of rubber of some kind, Smith knew. The automaton, despite his age, looked younger than Smith remembered. Clearly he'd been well maintained. He had ascended in power since the council of eighty-eight brought an end of sorts to lizardine control of the empire, and had given human and machine, for the first time, equal say. The Queen still reigned, of course – but the machine faction had grown stronger, though it was not like France, where it was said the Quiet Council held absolute – if quiet – power.

"Smith." Byron's voice was still the same old voice, scratchy in places, a voice made of numerous recordings of a real human voice, mixed together, played endlessly back. Babbage Corps. – Charlie Company, they used to call it in the old days – had built him, one of the early prototypes, and he was, Smith knew, second in command in the automatons' mostly hidden world. Machines feared humans, relying on them for survival. Byron – and his master – preferred to act, as much as possible, behind the scenes. "It is good to see you again."

They had crossed paths a couple of times, the automaton and him. No one knew the city better, nor had a wider net of informers and listeners. Machines listened, and most people never gave them a glance. They had worked the Prendick case together, successfully fighting the Dog Men Gang, a case which had left its scars on both of them. Smith had been taken captive by the gang and flayed, and on some nights he still felt the fine, white crisscrossing network on his back as though it were inflamed... "I wish I could say the same," he said, and the Byron automaton nodded mechanically. He understood.

"I am sorry about Mycroft," the automaton said. "He was a good man."

Smith snorted. "That's a lie, and you know it."

"Very well," the Byron said. "He was a useful man, an empire man. His loss is our loss."

He was speaking for the automatons. And Smith nodded, understanding.

"What do you know of his demise?" he said. The automaton didn't reply. His strange blind eyes moved as though scanning the room. How the automatons saw was a mystery to Smith. He knew that, between themselves, they communicated by means of in-built Tesla sets, and that was something he needed to find out about. There had been more and more traffic on what was coming to be called the Tesla Network, and while most shadow operatives dismissed the automatons, Smith didn't. He knew better than to underestimate Byron and his kind.

"Byron?"

"I thought you were retired," the automaton said at last.

"They brought me back."

"A pity."

Smith looked at him. "I don't understand," he said at last.

"You should have stayed in the village, my friend," the automaton said.

"Is that a warning?" Smith said, suddenly tense.

"It's an observation," the automaton said, mildly.

Smith sat back. He regarded the automaton for a long moment, thinking.

He had not expected this.

Mycroft, he knew, had strong links with the automaton movement.

Could they be involved?

And suddenly he was wary of Byron.

Which, he thought, had been the automaton's intention.

So instead he said, "Fogg."

The automaton did not have a range of expressions. However, in the certain way his mouth moved, one could, just possibly, read distaste.

"You have always suspected him," the automaton said.

"It seemed clear to me he was an agent of the Bookman."

"Ah, yes…" And now the automaton seemed thoughtful. "The Bookman."

"Is this related to the Bookman investigation from eighty-eight?" Smith said, on a hunch.

The automaton was still. At last he said, "There are things best left in the shadows, my friend."

What exactly *had* happened in eighty-eight? There had been the very public blowing-up of the decoy Martian probe, and a girl, Lucy, had died. Mycroft had handled it single-handedly, if Smith remembered rightly. He, Smith, had been somewhere in Asia at the time.

Then came that strange revolution that didn't quite happen, and the new balance of power, and the fall of the then-prime minister, Moriarty. Mrs Beeton was in power now.

But Mycroft had remained in place, ensconced in his comfortable armchair at the Diogenes Club, running the Bureau and the shadow world, playing the Great Game…

"What are you not telling me, Byron?" he said at last. The automaton's mouth had changed again; now his expression resembled a smile. "What *can* I tell you," he said, "might be the more appropriate question."

"What *can* you tell me, then?"

"What I already told you. Go home. Water your garden. Watch the flowers grow."

"I grew *cabbages*," Smith said. "And Hapsburgian agents recently destroyed the garden." He thought about it. "Not that I minded, greatly," he added, to be fair.

"Fogg," the automaton said, "cannot be trusted. But you already know this. Then you would have also surmised that Mycroft would have been of the same opinion."

"I had warned him several times," Smith said, the memory of old hurt still present. "He never took notice."

"Are you working for Fogg, now?"

"He reinstated me," Smith said. "He is acting head."

"Then you are his tool," the automaton said, with finality.

"I am no one's tool," Smith said, but even as he spoke he knew it wasn't true. He had always been a tool. It was his purpose. He was a shiv for someone to apply, a weapon. And only Fogg had the power to bring him back from the retirement he hated, to make him, once again, *useful*.

"What you learn, he will learn," the Byron automaton said, and stood up. "I am sorry about Alice. But you must not follow this investigation, this time, old friend. Let it go. Light a candle in her memory. But step away."

"What about her killer?" Smith demanded. "Shall I let *him* go, too?"

"The killer, like you, wishes to learn much, though, I suspect, for vastly different reasons. I do not think he can be stopped, nor, necessarily, that he should be. This is bigger than you, my friend, bigger than me, bigger than all of us. Let it go, I beg you."

Smith stood up, too. "Then we have nothing else to discuss," he said, stiffly. The automaton nodded, once. His expression, as much as it could, looked resigned. "Until we meet again, then," he said. He put forwards his hand, and Smith shook it.

"Until then," he said.

TEN

The observer watched this new quarry with interest. The voices in his head had been quiet of late, for which he was grateful. The country had a fascinating weather system, with frequent rain and an amassing of clouds that hid both sun and stars. Islands, he had learned, generated their own miniature weather systems. There was so much to learn.

People went past him. Mostly they did not notice him. He wore a long black coat and a wide-brimmed hat that, one of the voices told him, was rather fashionable. Fashion fascinated the observer. Most everything did. He stood in the shadows and watched the building. A small man came out of it and the observer watched him with interest, noticing the way the man scanned his environment as he went, always aware of his surroundings.

But he had not noticed the observer.

A small boy was one of the few who did notice him. The small boy went past him and then, for just a moment, seemed to stumble against him, murmured an apology and tried to dart away. The observer, however, reached out and grabbed him by the hand and the boy found himself pulled back. "Hey, let go, Jack!" the boy said, or began to, when he saw the observer's eyes on his. He stopped speaking and stared, as if hypnotised.

"Give me back my things."

Still not speaking, the boy owned up to the items he had extracted from the observer's pocket. These may have surprised the casual watcher, had there been one. They included a dazzling green seashell, of a sort not to be found on the British Isles; a penny coin rubbed black and featureless with age, with the barely distinguished portrait of the old Lizard King William; a smooth round pebble; and a piece of cinnamon bark.

The observer took them and put them carefully back in his pocket. He let the boy go but the boy just stood there, until the observer made a sudden shooing motion and then, as if awakening, the boy's eyes widened and he turned and ran away, disappearing into the crowds of Covent Garden.

The observer watched the building and the people coming and going. He saw a dice game in progress and a man, which a voice told him was called a mobsman, *who picked the pocket of a gentleman walking past without the man ever noticing. His nose could pick up smells that only now he was beginning to identify. Manure, of course, but also mulled cider, sold from large metal tubs to passers-by, and tobacco smoke, some of it aromatic and some of it reminding him of the sailors on the ship on the crossing over the Channel, and spilled beer, and roasting, caramelised peanuts, and human sweat and human fear and human hormones hanging heavy in the air: it was a heady mixture.*

He stood in the shadows and few people noticed him and those who did moved aside, as though instinctively knowing not to come near. He paid them no heed. He watched until he saw a shadow come slowly out of the building and recognised him as the one he wanted but still he waited, waited for him to walk down the narrow passageway that ran alongside and only then, unhurriedly, he stepped out of the shadows and began to follow.

It when he was going towards Drury Lane that Smith began to have the feeling he had forgotten something. He stopped in his tracks. It was early evening and the theatre-goers and the cutpurses were out in force.

He knew Byron did not work alone. Above him, above all the automatons, was the one they called the Turk. Once a chess-playing machine, he had quietly gained political power amongst the disenfranchised simulacra of the new age, seldom seen, always in the background. The Mechanical Mycroft, as some in the Bureau called him, snidely. If they knew he existed at all.

What could link Mycroft and the Turk with Alice in Bangkok?
But a more pressing question arose in his mind.

The Byron automaton must have known what Mycroft had known.

He turned around and began to run.

He could hear the distant cries even as he again approached the Bucket of Blood. As he ran he almost bumped into a small, undistinguished man who passed him going in the opposite direction; the man moved aside elegantly, avoiding impact, and Smith went past him, barely sparing him a glance.

The cries grew louder; in the distance, a police siren. A crowd of people gathered outside the Bucket of Blood, blocking the way into the narrow alleyway beside it. He pushed his way through.

Stopped when he came to the body.

The observer had found the encounter interesting, for several reasons. For one, the device had obviously been waiting for him. It didn't put up a fight but had waited, its back to the observer, as though offering up what it had.

The observer's blade was already out and so he came to the device and inserted the blade in the same place as it did all the others, the base of the head, going inwards into the brain. Only this time he felt nothing, and was momentarily confused.

"I am using distributed storage, I'm afraid," the device said, politely. It took the observer back, a little. None of the others spoke to him. Not until they were dead, at any rate.

The blade came out, went back in. A series of stabs–

A boy, standing in the shadows on the other side of the alley, watched this with wide-open eyes. He saw a man crouching over the fallen body of another man (it was too dark to distinguish details), savagely stabbing it, over and over and over. He opened his mouth to scream, but no sound came. He had followed the observer from the crowd, having tried to pick his pocket earlier. The stabbing went on and on.

• • • •

Smith knelt beside the body of the automaton. There was, of course, no blood, through sparks flew out of the holes in Byron's body, and a viscous sort of liquid *did*, in fact, seep through the cuts and out, hissing as it touched the paved stones. Smith pushed the body onto its back. Byron's blind eyes stared up at him.

"Byron," Smith said. And, when there was no response – "Byron!"

But the machine was dying. Blue sparks of electricity jumped over the body and the crowd surged back, as though afraid it would explode. Smith raised his head; for just a moment he caught sight of a small, frightened figure standing at the other end of the alleyway. Then it disappeared.

"Byron!"

"Step aside, Smith."

He knew the voice. But he didn't move. He checked the automaton but the blue sparks were increasing and he felt an electric shock run through him and he jumped back.

"Everyone back!" The voice was authoritative and the crowd obeyed. Smith found himself dragged away; strong arms held him even as he fought to get back to Byron.

But the automaton's body was aflame in a blue, electric light now, and the ground around it was hissing, yellow acidic liquid spilling out of the multiple cuts. Smith was pushed to the ground, still fighting. "Don't–" he began.

With his cheek pressed against the cold hard stones he saw the flames begin to rise, yellow out of blue, slowly at first, then growing larger. Weight pressed down on his back; he couldn't move. He wanted to close his eyes but couldn't, and so he watched as the Lord Byron automaton burned, there in the alleyway where, centuries before, the dissident Dryden had been attacked.

"So ends the old," the earlier voice said, close, in his ears, "to give birth to the new," and Smith closed his eyes, at last, and knew that they were wet, and he said, "Go away, Adler. Please, just go away."

ELEVEN

The last time they had met she was an inspector and he was Mycroft's errand boy. Now Mycroft was gone and Irene Adler was
chief of Scotland Yard, and looked it.

They were sitting opposite each other in the bare interrogation
room. When the fire had consumed the old automaton, Adler
had instructed her officers to release Smith, but keep him where
he was. She had secured the perimeter of the site, had officers
interviewing potential witnesses, and two chattering police automatons, short squat things on wheels, were bent over what
remained of the former Byron machine.

"You," she said, turning at last back to Smith. "I thought you
were dead."

"Retired," he said, shortly, and she snorted. "Would that you
were," she said.

"Retired?"

"Dead."

"Adler," he said, "you need to let me go."

"I need you to explain yourself."

"This is a Bureau affair."

Her eyes narrowed. "When a prominent member of society
dies in the open, in *my* city, that makes it *my* affair."

"And if he weren't *prominent*?" Smith said, knowing it was a cheap dig. She didn't dignify it with an answer. He said, "You're not handling the Mycroft investigation." Trying a different tack.

"I've been *ordered* out of that investigation."

"And you will be ordered out of this one."

She smiled. There was nothing cheerful in that smile. "Until that happens," she said, "it is still mine."

He sighed. He had been handling it all wrong, and now more people were dying. Had Byron known? he suddenly wondered. He must have known. Yet he did not appear to fight. Was he taken by surprise? Smith couldn't tell. He did not understand the mechanical, the way he thought. But it changed nothing. Byron was dead. Gone. The people at Charlie Company could build another replica but it would not be Byron, just something that looked like he had. A copy of a copy.

And now Smith was angry.

"If you won't butt out," he said, rudely, "then maybe you can help."

"Can I?" Irene Adler said. "I'm overwhelmed."

He ignored her. "There was a boy," he said. At that she paid attention. "I saw him, for a brief moment. He was watching. It is possible he saw the... the murder."

Was the destruction of a machine, however human-like, murder? Could it really be called that? He didn't know. It didn't used to be but the mechanicals had gained in power since the quiet coup of eighty-eight.

"What sort of a boy?" Irene Adler said. Tense. Attentive. Smith liked that in her. She would follow every scrap of information, never let go of an investigation until she solved it. She was smart and capable and she ran Scotland Yard well... but this was a shadow investigation, and not her domain. And where the hell *was* Fogg? The Bureau should have been all over the investigation by now, and wasn't. And the news would be all over the papers by morning.

Smith closed his eyes, took a deep breath. Tried to picture the scene as it was, the brief glimpse of the boy. "Around twelve years old," he said. "Worn clothes, too large for him. Pale face.

Black hair. Thin." He opened his eyes again. The details added up. "A street boy," he said.

Irene Adler sighed. "Do you know how many there are, in this city?"

Smith did know. And an avenue of questioning had already suggested itself...

And *now* there was a commotion outside, and he leaned back and smiled at the Scotland Yard chief.

The door to the interrogation room banged open and Fogg came in, trailed by a bemused police constable.

"Adler!" Fogg barked.

"Smog," Adler said, not turning to acknowledge him.

"*Fogg*," he said, irritably. He looked tired and out of his depth, Smith noted with some satisfaction. "Your part in this investigation is over," Fogg said. "We do not need you stomping about all over the place making noise." He turned to Smith. "And you!" he barked. "This is a mess, isn't it, Mr *Smith*?" Fogg pinched the bridge of his nose. "And you right in the middle of it, as usual. This is a disaster!"

Smith said, "You are upset over Byron's death?"

"Death?" Fogg glared at him. "Do I look like I give a whiff about that damn machine finally expiring? Don't be absurd, Smith. This has your mark all over it, doesn't it? What a mess. What a public, public mess."

Neither Smith nor Adler replied. They exchanged glances. "Yes, Mr Fogg," they both said, in unity. Fogg glared at them. "You," he said, pointing a long, thin finger at Irene Adler, "stay out of it. And *you*," he said, turning the finger, like an offensive weapon, on Smith, "outside. Now."

Smith gave the chief of Scotland Yard an innocent look and got up. He followed Fogg outside, through the station corridors and out into the street, where a black baruch-landau stood, belching steam.

"Get in," Fogg said.

Smith got in. The interior smelled of new leather and polish. He wondered if Fogg did his own buffing, and smiled.

"And wipe that smirk off your face!" Fogg said.

"Yes, headmaster."

Fogg let that one pass. He signalled the driver, and the horseless carriage began to move.

Mycroft, Smith remembered, had preferred the comforts of his own black airship: watching the city from high above, drinking scotch, smoking a cigar. It was easier to see things from a distance, he liked to say. *And in comfort*, Smith always added silently.

Fogg was street-bound. "A disgrace," he said.

"A mess, I think you said," Smith said.

Fogg shook his head. "Were there witnesses?" he said.

So he wasn't dumb. But then, Smith had learned long ago not to underestimate the man.

"Scotland Yard–" he began.

"Adler is out of this!" Fogg snapped. Whisper at the Bureau had been that Adler and the fat man's brother had been linked, in the past. Smith had a fleeting image of the bee keeper, standing in the rain, not speaking. What did the bee keeper make of all of this? Rumour had it he, too, was a part of the events in eighty-eight, but shortly after that he'd been retired–

"They interviewed the crowd outside the Bucket of Blood," Smith said, patiently.

"And?" Fogg snapped.

"And they found nothing."

Fogg snorted. "If you were a witness to such a crime, you wouldn't stick around to be interviewed."

"My thoughts exactly," Smith said. Fogg looked at him. "So," he said again, "was there a witness?"

Smith told him about the boy. Fogg looked thoughtful. "You know that part of town," he said. Smith nodded. "The... undesirables," Fogg said. Again, Smith merely nodded.

"Good," Fogg said. "Then follow that trail."

Smith was angry with himself. He had been so close... Could he have prevented the attack? Could he himself have seen the killer?

Was he following the wrong path? This chain of events did not begin in London. He was looking at it wrong. He needed to step back, to start at the beginning. He said, half to himself, "But the killer is here."

He raised his head, saw Fogg smirk.

"Do you know where I've been in the past few hours, as you two were having your little heart-to-heart in there?" Fogg said.

Smith said, "No."

"I was called to Dover," Fogg said.

"They found another body," Smith said. Thinking furiously... How could the killer get from London to Dover in that time?

"Yes," Fogg said. "They found a body."

"Who is it?"

"Somebody. Nobody. A pastor, by name of Brown. It seems he was in the habit of crossing the Channel regularly."

Smith: "A courier?"

Fogg, with pursed lips: "Possibly."

"What was he carrying?"

"Nothing was found on the body."

"But the injury matches?"

"It matches."

"So our killer is on his way to France?"

"He was not on the ferry – that my people could find."

But the killer had his own ways of getting around, and not be seen, Smith thought. He felt suddenly helpless. Chasing shadows, they called it in the trade: following an impossible trail, and never catching up.

Fogg signalled the driver. The baruch-landau stopped and the door opened, as though by itself.

"Get out," Fogg said. And, as Smith climbed out into the street, a parting shot: "You used to be good."

TWELVE

The observer came out of the water dripping, and so he stood and waited for the water to evaporate. He noted the water was very cold, and the currents strong. As he swam across the Channel he had passed a steam-powered ship, carrying passengers, and a sleek tea clipper with taut sales, and two wooden boats pushed by oars that met in the shallows and ex-changed what the voices had told him were contraband goods.

The observer was in no hurry. He stood and watched the water and the small island he had – partly – left behind. He found the world fas-cinating. Steam and sail and man-power, all sharing the water. That mixture of old and new, and they kept striving for the new, the newer still. Such a curious place. The voices argued and shouted and finally quietened, leaving him momentarily alone. He wondered what it was that had stopped him from taking the small boy, in that city where the whales sang in the river. He had been much taken with the whales. He had gone to see them, standing on the Embankment, and, as though sensing what he was, they came close, one by one, and showed themselves to him, and sang. He loved their song.

He should have taken one of the whales, he thought. He would have liked their song, to accompany the voices.

But there was time, there was plenty of time. He had been rushing about, to start with, with newfound eyes, excited by everything, eager for new experience, but that had been…

He did not have a term for it. It was one of the voices who finally of-
fered a suggestion, and the observer contemplated it now.

Unprofessional.

Perhaps, he admitted, he had been a tad unprofessional. Certainly he
should have taken the boy.

Why hadn't he?

A strange, unfamiliar word, whispered by the woman. Compassion.
What a strange notion, he thought. Yet something in the boy's frozen
stare, the wide eyes, the under-nourished face, had halted him. It would
have just complicated things, the observer thought. His quarry had not
been the boy but the strange man-machine, and by letting the boy go he
had freed himself for his primary task.

The observer shook himself, raising naked arms against the rising
sun. It felt wonderful, he thought, to be here. Clouds fascinated him, and
migrating birds. And people were intensely fascinating, to the observer.

Before the observer had got into the water he had stood, the way he
stood now, naked on the shore before the Channel, with moonlight in-
stead of sunlight illuminating his artificial flesh.

He had shuddered, his body shifting and changing, drawing power
and material from the humidity in the air, the salt water and the fine
chalk. The voices had risen into a frightened crescendo before he silenced
them. His body shuddered and shivered, splitting, *the extra material of*
him lying down at last on the sand like an egg.

The observer had waited for his body to seal itself again, then crouched
by this egg and put his hand on the warm, thin membrane. After a few
moments the surface broke and the egg hatched.

The thing inside was not yet human, nor did it have shape. Blindly,
it burrowed into the sand, feeding, converting solids and gas into–

At last the child rose out of the sand, and the observer helped him up.
They stood, facing each other, identical in height, identical in shape. The
moonlight reflected on their flesh. Then, not needing to speak, the ob-
server turned to the sea, and the other put on his clothes, heading back
into the city.

For there was one element left, of course, besides the trivial task of
harvesting a whale. The observer had been aware of that for some time.
Sooner or later he would have to collect one of the others, he thought.

The masters. One of them. That made him a little uneasy. But what had to be done had to be done. There was that still left, to chart and understand.

It was night and Smith was tired, but he'd been used to worse and at least no one was shooting at him any more.

Which was not to say they weren't watching–

Though he tried to shake any possible shadows, following a circuitous route through the city, keeping an eye out for enemy agents.

Which meant, at the moment, just about anyone.

But he needed to get to where he was going unobserved. Keep a low profile, from now on. Fogg was understandably angry. Another public murder and he, Smith, like a fool, smack in the middle of it.

Shadow executives had to keep to the shadows.

He was getting old.

There was no getting away from it. The realisation dawned on him gradually, in stages: he was past it. Mycroft had been right to retire him.

And Alice, he thought. What was *she* doing still playing the game? She had told him once, lying beside him in a hotel room in – it must have been Prague, or was it Warsaw? Somewhere in that region, in a spring with long bright evenings and the smell of flowering trees – "My one wish is not to die in bed."

Now she was dead and he was still around.

Ahead of him was the church. He was at St Giles, and it was dark there, and the people who moved about looked furtive. Which suited him fine. He went into St Giles in the Fields, the church quiet and welcoming. He stood there for a long moment, as he always did, wondering what it meant, a church, a place of worship; wondering, too, where the dead went, if they went anywhere at all, and if they did, what they found there.

He went and lit a candle. For the Byron automaton. Could you do that? Could you light a candle for a machine that no longer ran? Yet people were machines, too, running on vulnerable fleshy parts that decayed and were easy to harm. People shut down every day. Some – many – had been shut down by him.

What happened then?

Everything. Nothing. He lit the candle and placed it gently in place, in the damp sand, with the others. Goodbye, Byron, he thought. Another name on the long list of Smith's life had been crossed out.

He sighed, then went forward, towards the dais, and sat on a bench but at the end, in the shadows, close to the wall, and waited.

"Mr Smith."

The voice woke him up and for a moment he felt confused, thought he was back in his small house, back in the village, and it was time to tend to the cabbages. Then he remembered the house had burned down, people had tried to kill him, what had been left of the cabbages had been dumped in the rubbish tip, and he was in a church and must have fallen asleep. He shook his head ruefully. Another sign of getting old. Getting careless.

"Mr Smith?"

He turned his head and stared at an old, lined face. It was like staring into a mirror. "Fagin," he said.

"Thought you were dead, like, Mr Smith," Fagin said.

"Retired," Smith said.

Fagin grinned. One of the things that Smith always noticed about Fagin was that his teeth were in remarkably good condition. They were white and straight and looked at odds in that face even as, like now, they had been carefully blackened with coal, to give them a ruinous appearance.

But of course, Smith was one of the few who knew Fagin's secret...

"You lot," Fagin said, "never retire. Die, yes. But never retire."

"And your lot?" Smith said, and Fagin grinned and said, "Tis a matter of choice."

This was the truth about Fagin: his real name was Neville St Claire and he had been, in his younger days, an amateur actor and a newspaper reporter. Faced with a new wife and mounting bills, the young St Claire took to the streets, putting on makeup and transforming himself into a hideous beggar, who called himself Hugh Boone.

The old bee keeper had put an end to *that* particular scheme, back in the day… but St Claire, unable to give up on the excitement of the streets, or the profits to be made therein, had transformed himself yet again, this time calling himself Fagin, and this time… diversifying. Smith did not like the man, but he had proved himself useful on several occasions.

"I'm looking for a boy," Smith said.

"Oh?" Fagin tried to look innocent, and failed. "What do you need? I've got blaggers and bug hunters, buzzers and dippers, fine-wirers all."

"Yes, I know," Smith said. Fagin ran the beggars and pick-pockets, especially young boys. They were his eyes and ears and they did the jobs he no longer did himself. "One of those, I think."

"Only one?"

It was quiet in the church, quiet and dark – and suddenly there was a knife in Smith's hand, and its tip was touching Fagin's throat, almost gently, like a kiss. Fagin, carefully, swallowed.

"I think you know who I mean," Smith said quietly.

"Heard about your friend," Fagin said. "We were all sorry to see Byron go."

"And how, precisely, did you hear?" Smith said.

"Come, come, now, Mr Smith," Fagin said. "Put the knife away and let's talk like gentlemen."

"Why?" Smith said. He increased the pressure and watched blood well up on the other man's neck. "Neither of us is one."

"Quite, quite. Still…"

"Yes?"

"It's a matter of push, of chink, of coin!" Fagin said. "And I'm not talking a dimmick or a grey. I mean soft, I mean–"

"You mean money," Smith said.

"Man's gotta eat," Fagin said, almost apologetically. "Think of the kiddies, what?"

"Do you have the boy?"

Fagin's eyes never wavered from Smith's. A small smile seemed to float on his lips. "Do you have the money?" he whispered.

Smith sighed. There was no arguing with Fagin, nor threatening. He put the knife away. "I'm going to need a receipt," he said.

THIRTEEN

The Angel, or something like it, had sat on St Giles Circus for centuries. Before Les Lézards had outlawed the practice, the Circus had been home to the gallows, providing both death (for convicts) and entertainment (for London residents), and the Angel had been the traditional stop for those about to be hanged, for a final drink and – if they were notorious enough – possibly for signing a few autographs.

It was a low-ceilinged pub, with a fire burning in the hearth, a card game or two in the back rooms, and various other transactions of a not-strictly-legal bent taking place in murmured conversations all around it. Smith knew it well.

He went in with Fagin, through the small maze of the pub and out, to the cold and dismal yard at the back. There, several small boys huddled around a makeshift fire, warming their small, pale hands. "The devil makes work for idle hands!" Fagin barked and the boys straightened to attention, glancing at their employer and the man he was with.

"Living the good life, eh?" Fagin said. He clicked his fingers. "Go," he said, not unkindly. "Go, ply your trade, my little wirers. Bring Uncle Fagin purses and their like, the heavier the better." He looked down at them benevolently. "Go!" he shouted, and the small figures scampered away, swarming past Smith and Fagin on their way to the streets.

"Not you, Oli," Fagin said, snatching one boy's arm. The boy stopped and stood obediently.

"This is the boy?" Smith said. He knelt down to look at the boy's pale, haunted face. "What's your name?" he said, gently.

"Twist, sir," the boy said, looking down.

"A fine thief," Fagin said, which, in his own way, had been a compliment. "Oli here's the one you've been wanting, Smith."

"Let me be the judge of that," Smith said. He pulled the boy gently a little way away from his master. "Here," he said, calling to Fagin, and tossed him a coin in the air. The portrait of a lizard spun through the air and landed with a thwack in the man's palm. "Go buy yourself a pint while I talk to the boy."

Fagin grunted, but seemed willing. "I'll be back in a bit, then," he said genially. "Mind the boy, Smith. I will not abide broken bones."

The boy's eyes flashed with fear and Fagin, with a snort of amusement, walked off.

Smith and the boy were left alone in the yard. "I won't hurt you," Smith said.

"You're the one from the Bucket," the boy said suddenly.

"You saw me?"

"I saw the machine man!" the boy was shaking.

"Byron? You knew him?"

"I saw you, you passed him in the crowd. You were running, and he moved out of your way."

Smith frowned. The boy's eyes were big and round and frightened. Not speaking, Smith took down his coat and put it around the boy's thin shoulders. The boy sucked in air and sighed. "His eyes," he said. "They were so cold."

"Tell me what you saw," Smith said.

"I tried to pick his pocket," the boy said. "But he caught me. I looked in his eyes. There were things moving behind his eyes. There were ghosts, trapped there. He made me afraid. He made me run. But I didn't run. I went around and watched him. I saw him go to the old Byron thingamee."

Thingamee was what the urchins called the automatons, Smith remembered suddenly. So who was the "machine man" the boy had spoken of?

"He had a knife only it wasn't no knife," the boy said. "It..." He swallowed. "It grew," he whispered. "It grew out of him. He stabbed the old thingamee and the thingamee let him. I don't understand..."

Smith didn't, either.

"I want you to come with me," he said. He needed the boy, and he couldn't leave him with Fagin. Someone had to take Fagin down. He had tried in the past, but always failed. The man had powerful friends. But he could at least ensure this boy, this Twist, a safe haven, for a while, with the Bureau. He was a witness, the only one they had. And Smith needed to know what the boy knew.

"Come with me," he said again, but the boy blinked at him in confusion and sound seemed to slow down to a crawl and there was a flash of blinding white light and the dirt between them exploded, once, twice, three times and Smith grabbed the boy under one arm and rolled – they were being fired at.

Then everything moved very quickly and he saw black-clad figures come streaming into the yard, over the walls and from within the pub, holding guns, surrounding them.

"Harvester," one of them said. The accent was familiar.

Hapsburg.

Again.

"Run," he said to the boy. Then, like a dancer, poised on one foot, he swirled around, and his knives flashed as they flew.

He couldn't hope to kill them all and he knew it: not with knives.

At the Bureau he had stopped by and seen an old friend.

Underneath Pall Mall, below even the level of the Bureau, there was a train station...

A disused station, it had been the diggers' base when working on the underground railway. The Bureau had found it expedient and had taken over the abandoned dig when it moved to its present location.

A dark and gloomy place, with empty tunnels leading off into a maze of blocked-out passages...

Mining equipment still lying here and there, a steam digger, a miner's helmet, downed tools, bags of sand and stones, and broken metal tracks...

Down there Professor Xirdal Zephyrin made his home.

It had been in Paris, in the late seventies...

Smith had been sent to the French Republic on a defection. A notable scientist working for the Quiet Council had contacted the resident Bureau agent. He wanted to defect. The Bureau had been after the man they called Viktor for many years, but the French were keeping him close. This was not Viktor.

He was identified, initially, only as *X*.

They had met by the Seine, beneath the terrifying vista that was the ruined Notre Dame. The cathedral had been built by Les Lézards, of that same curious green material of which the Royal Palace was made. It had been done long ago, and the cathedral had been destroyed during the Quiet Revolution, when human and automaton took over France. Now lizard boys hung out in the ruins, tattooed creatures trying to resemble the lizardine race across the Channel, their tongues surgically split, strips of colour tattooed across their skins in imitation of reptilian scales. They were lawless and dangerous and deranged. X had been nervous. But the cathedral was an ideal meeting place, dark and abandoned, and they walked along the Seine and discussed X's proposition.

"My name," he had told Smith then, at last, "is Xirdal Zephyrin! You have heard of me, of course."

Smith, who hadn't, nevertheless nodded.

"Of course, of course," Zephyrin said. "I am the greatest, yes. The man Viktor is a hack. A hack! Yet he rises in the estimation of the Council, while I, the great Zephyrin, am overlooked! Yes, yes, quite, you see." He kept muttering to himself, and shading his eyes against the light of the moon. He was tall and lanky with long hairy hands. "I can give you much, yes, yes! I am a great scientist. I make machines for you! You see? I must away to England."

It was the old story: resentment, envy. It would be hard to get Zephyrin over the Channel. Over the next few weeks as Smith watched he realised how hard it had been for the scientist to get away, that first meeting. And never for long. Shadows followed him, those French machines, and human agents, too, ensuring he remained isolated, remained in his lab, somewhere deep under Paris. At first Mycroft was against outright defection. "He can serve us better," he had said, "by remaining in place and feeding us information."

Smith disagreed. "His temper is unstable," he said. "He is not a man comfortable with deceit. I tell you, we must act quickly. Sooner or later, he will give himself away. They are already suspicious."

There had been a woman watching over the scientist, recently. A six-foot-tall woman with a Peacemaker on her hip, with hair like a cloud of black smoke. He knew her by reputation only: Milady, the Dahomey-born, Paris-bred, top agent of the Quiet Council.

She would not let the scientist slip from her grasp.

And, as Mycroft dithered, time had been running out...

How Smith got Zephyrin out of Paris – how he smuggled him over the Channel, and onto British soil, and through the fingers of Milady de Winter – that had been a story still spoken about, in hushed whispers, at the Bureau, and at the training centre in Ham Common. And never spoken of in Paris.

Zephyrin's stolen knowledge had had the scientists in a frenzy, and a committee had been formed – chaired by Lord Babbage, then still present in the flesh – to evaluate, and make use of, the material. When the debriefing of Zephyrin had at last ended, the scientist had been put on the Bureau's own payroll, and installed in that nameless, abandoned station, where he had been provided with material, assistants and space, and which he seldom, if ever, left.

Smith had gone down to see him, after his meeting with Fogg.

"*Mon ami!*" the scientist said. "I thought you were dead."

Smith said, "I retired," and the scientist said, "Pfft! You cannot retire any more than I can!"

"Still ticking away?" Smith said.

The scientist, almost dancing on the platform of that station, spread his arms and beamed. "I make many many things!" he said. "You would like to try?"

"What have you got?"

"Well…" Zephyrin said. "It depends on the person, does it not so? You, for instance, do not like the guns, do you not. So I cannot offer you the pen-gun!"

"Pen-gun?"

"It looks like a pen," the scientist said, "yet it is a gun!"

"Really," Smith said.

"How about, then," the scientist said hopefully, "a Poison Master One Hundred?"

"What is it?"

"Observe," Zephyrin said, "this simple ring."

He held it hopefully towards Smith. It was an odd, lumpy ring, with many protrusions. "Watch," the scientist said. He twisted the upper part of the ring and it turned, the small extensions moving with it. "It is an old-fashioned poisoner's ring, naturally," the scientist said, "yet it carries up to one hundred distinct poisons and various drugs, which can be delivered by direct contact with skin as well as by command, into a drink or perhaps a sweet bun."

"Yes," Smith said. "Impressive. However, I am not much for jewellery, myself…"

"Ach," Zephyrin said. "It is helpless with you, my friend. You have not the love of the technology! For you I make something special therefore. Special, yes. For you are Englishman, yes!" He chortled. "For you…" he said. "I make miniature umbrella."

Smith, the Hapsburg agents, the back yard of the Angel in St Giles.

His knives flashing, blades finding skin and bones and arteries...

Men dropping, others converging on him, too many, there were too many...

Strapped to his back, a small, slim sheath, as for a blade. A handle, protruding...

He pulled it out.

The man who first spoke, the man who called him Harvester. Suddenly laughing.

Something rapid in a German Smith couldn't understand. More laughter. Smith pulled it open.

An umbrella.

"*Sie haben Angst, es wird regen?*"

You are afraid it will rain?

Smith smiled back at him.

"Don't shoot," he said. "I'll come in peace."

"Put up your hands, *Herr* Smith."

Smith raised his hands, the umbrella above him.

Gave it a small, almost unnoticeable spin.

The umbrella spun and rose in the air.

"Rain," Smith said. Standing under the umbrella. Feeling like a fool. Thinking, he couldn't die here, because then, if it didn't work, he couldn't kill Xirdal Zephyrin.

The umbrella hovered.

"*Was ist das?*" the man said. "*Spielzeug?* Toy, please?"

"*Ja*," Smith said.

The umbrella stopped. And suddenly, all around its rim, a series of small nozzles protruded out.

"*Schiessen!*" the Hapsburg agent shouted. *Fire!*

But the umbrella spun, suddenly and hard, the tiny steam engine embedded in its apex providing the power, and the nozzles barked out a widening circle of high-pressured darts, thin as darning needles.

A silver rain of tiny blades...

Poisoned, if he knew Professor X.

The umbrella, having spun twice, now stopped. Around Smith, the men were on the ground, unnaturally still.

Run, said a voice in his head.

He ran.

Behind him, the swish of flying blades as the umbrella spun again, then rose higher, and higher still–

He darted into the now-empty pub, pushed through doors, ran outside–

Behind him, unseen, the umbrella reached its programmed height and stopped, and dropped, gently, down to the roof of the pub–

Activating, on impact, the hidden charge of explosives running all along the hollowed core of its tube.

Smith burst out of the Angel when the night became alive with light and flames–

An explosion shaking the building behind him, the roof caving in, a ball of flame reaching out and pushing him, sending him flying–

Thinking, *Zephyrin you crazy old bastard*–

A ball of fire rising into the skies, Smith free, not quite believing it–

He'd managed to escape–

And someone caught him in his arms, breaking his flight, a hug as of an old friend's–

Smith looked up, dazed–

Into the smiling face of the Frenchman, The Man from Meung, the Comte de Rochefort.

"*Bonsoir*, M. Smith," the Comte de Rochefort said. Smith tried to pull back, tried to fight–

A small, cold pinprick of pain in the side of his neck.

"*Doux rêves*," he heard the Frenchman say, as if from far away. *Sweet dreams…*

Smith closed his eyes. The Frenchman held him as he fell.

FOURTEEN

He woke up by a window, tied to a chair.

He looked out of the window and below him was the city.

He was somewhere high up in the air, looking down. The Thames snaked below, and the lights of the city were a chorus, top amongst them Big Ben and the Babbage Tower, arcane mechanisms pointing at the skies, a beacon of light warning off the airships that sailed, night and day, above the capital.

He was in an airship, he realised with a sinking in his stomach. And there could be no escape.

"Ah, I see our... guest is awake," a voice said. He turned from the window and saw the Comte de Rochefort sitting across from him, sipping from a glass of cognac.

"I'd offer you a drink," the man said, "but..." He shrugged. "You seem to be somewhat tied up at the moment."

"Funny," Smith said.

"Tell me," Rochefort said. "Why are the Hapsburgs so keen on eliminating you?"

Indeed, the same question had been troubling Smith. "I don't know," he admitted.

"Really..." Rochefort said.

Smith had very little to lose by telling the truth. His ignorance startled him. He did not understand what was happening and, under the circumstances, decided that his best course was to stick to the truth, and try, by extension, to find out what the French were after.

"I do not believe you," Rochefort said. Smith smiled. Sometimes the truth itself was the best lie, he thought.

"I will not insult you," he told Rochefort, "by lying."

"And I will not, in my turn, insult you by resorting to crude interrogation," the Frenchman said.

"Oh?"

"You may be aware of Viktor Von F–'s formula?" Rochefort said. "After all, you tried several times to cause him to defect."

"His loyalty," Smith said dryly, "truly is commendable."

"I have," Rochefort said, "a syringe here with me. It is a modified form of your own Jekyll formula. I am a gentleman, and so I will give you a choice. Tell me what I want to know, without coercion or further lies, or I shall be forced, very much against my principles, to inject you with the material. I believe recovery is not a side product of the treatment."

"I see," Smith said.

On the table before him, Rochefort placed two items, side by side. One was a loaded syringe. The other, his glass of cognac.

"Choose," he said.

"What do you want to know?" Smith said.

The Frenchman smiled, without joy. "What do you know of the Babbage Plan?" he snapped.

The Babbage Plan?

Without warning, Rochefort slapped him, a back-handed strike that sent Smith's head reeling back. "I hate to do this," the Frenchman said, sounding not in the least bit upset.

Smith shook his head, confused. Lord Babbage had not been seen for several years in public... Rumour had it he was dead. What did Rochefort want? How did it tie to–

He said, "I am retired. No, hear me out! I am retired and was brought back into service following the murder of my former employer, Mycroft Holmes, known to you as the head of the Bureau and of the various branches of British intelligence. I do not

know who killed him, or why. I am trying to trace a killer –
nothing more."

"You lie!" the Comte de Rochefort said.

"Why would I lie?"

"Because," Rochefort said, with a chilling smile, "you are the
Harvester."

```
Code name: Smith.
First name: unknown.
Place of birth: unknown.
Parents: deceased.
Family: none.
Recruited: 1856, at the age of twenty.
Number of kills before recruitment: unknown.
Former associates: none living.
Recruited by: Holmes, Mycroft.
First assignment: classified.
Notable cases: The Dog Men Gang, The Xirdal
Zephyrin Defection, The Underground Cannibal
Tribe Massacre, The Warsaw Memorandum, The
Bangkok Affair of Seventy-Six, others classified.
Notes: for a long time considered Mycroft's
right-hand-man, Smith specialised in removals and
terminations, a catch-all term at the Bureau for
kills, and another sign of the British squeamish-
ness when it comes to stating the unsavoury
nature of their global empire and the shadow
practices which make it possible. Smith is known
to detest guns and other weapons of that sort,
preferring to use knives or his bare hands.
Trained first at the Bureau's secret Ham Common
training facility, later, if rumours are correct,
spent three years in the Chinese monastery of the
Wudang clan known as Shaolin, under tutelage of
one Ebenezer Long, known agitator, Chinese free-
dom fighter and Wudang leader (presumed).
```

Acquired the moniker "Harvester" for his specially created role as Mycroft's unofficial
executioner, travelling the globe to eliminate
people on behalf of the Lizardine Empire.

Forcibly retired over the Isle of Man incident
in ninety-three. Placed under restricted habi-
tation in St Mary Mead, AKA The Village, where
he had remained until recent events. Extremely
dangerous, treat with caution.

Rochefort put down the dossier. Took a sip of his drink. Stared
at Smith. "Well?" he said, at last.

"You suspect me of killing Mycroft?" Smith said.

Watched the Frenchman's face. Thinking – they must be
clutching at straws.

Why?

Why be upset over Mycroft's death?

Leaps he didn't want to make. He shut his eyes but in the
darkness his mind worked faster, connecting–

"Mycroft worked with you," he said – whispered. "No. It's impossible. No."

Rochefort's face was hard and unsmiling. "He was a great
man," he said. "You think this is a game? This is bigger than all
of us, Smith. If you are working for Babbage, I will find out. If
you had killed Mycroft, I will find out."

He tapped the syringe. Finished his drink. Left the empty glass
there, beside the syringe. "I will be back soon," he said. "I think, perhaps, you've made your choice, no?" he tapped the syringe again,
then, walking softly, left the room and locked the door behind him.

Smith was left alone, tied to the chair, the empty choice before
him. He knew they couldn't trust him. Just as he wouldn't have
trusted Rochefort, in a similar situation. It would be the syringe
for him and, after that, there was no going back. No doubt, when
they were done with him, his grotesque new form would be
thrown off the airship, somewhere lonely and isolated, over cliffs
or sea, perhaps... A shadow burial, as they called it in the trade.

He sat back, closed his eyes. His fingers had tried to work the ropes off, but couldn't. He was getting old…

They did not intend to let him go, he knew.

But Mycroft?

Could it be the truth?

And what, in God's name and all that was holy, was the Babbage Plan?

He sighed, resigning himself to his fate. There was a sort of peace in that. He would die here, die in ignorance, and be thrown off the airship to his grave. He could accept that.

But he wanted answers.

He realised he could not give up. Not yet.

There was a soft scratching sound at the door.

FIFTEEN

Smith, eyes closed to slits. Wishing he'd got more gadgets off Zephyrin. Figuring he could maybe push off to the floor, maybe break the chair – get just a chance to fight back. London, far below, under a layer of clouds. No escape...

The key turned in the lock and the door opened. Smith tensed–

Then his eyes opened wide when he saw the small figure standing in the room.

"You!" he said.

The boy closed the door behind him. He put his finger to his mouth, signalling silence.

"Twist!" Smith whispered. "What are you doing here?"

The boy grinned. "I saw the airship come down to land," he said. "It was hovering low over the roof of the church. I saw them carry you up... so I climbed up on the roof and snuck on before they took off. They didn't notice me."

"You could have got yourself killed!"

"Nah," the boy said, shrugging. "Fagin got us practising on the passenger ships, you know. Good pickings on those."

Smith shook his head. "Can you untie me?" he said.

But the boy was already behind him, and in moments Smith's bonds were cut loose. The boy came around, looking pleased with himself. "That's a big knife you got there," Smith said.

"I stole it," the boy said. Smith grinned back at him. "Of course you did," he said.

He felt his blood circulation slowly returning. "We need to get off this airship," he said.

The boy shrugged. "We can take them by force," he said, "and make them bring it down."

Smith, looking at him. The change that had taken over the boy. He said, "I don't think that's likely, Twist."

"Yes, sir."

"Give me that knife."

"Yes, sir."

The knife felt good in Smith's hands. It would feel better somewhere else – embedded in Rochefort's stomach, say...

"We'll make for the upper deck," Smith said.

The boy followed him meekly. They went out into an empty corridor. "How many of them are there?" Smith said.

"About a dozen, I think," Twist said.

"Too many..."

Along the corridor, up plush chrome stairs. The night outside was cold, the wind sending a shiver down Smith's spine. London was beneath them. The airship sailed high. There were clouds below, and only the tip of the Babbage Tower peeking out, with its beaming lights.

Babbage...

Wasn't the old man dead?

"Stop!"

"*Merde*!"

Smith turned. Rochefort, with two men holding dart guns. "Where did that boy come from?"

He couldn't give them time. He ran at them, felling one man with a punch to the face that broke his nose and drove the bone into the brain, the other with a well-placed kick that dropped him squealing. Smith smiled, came at Rochefort with the knife.

"Son of pigs," the Frenchman said. In his hand, too, there materialised a knife.

"Why was Mycroft working with you?" Smith said, striking.

The Frenchman feinted, slashed back. Smith almost wasn't quick enough and the blade whistled, too close to his face.

"Still you say you don't know," Rochefort said.

"Has it occurred to you I might have been speaking the God-damned truth?" Smith yelled.

"No!"

Knives flashed, as the two men danced on the deck. Other figures materialised around them but Rochefort stopped them with a shout. "Stay back."

"Tell me!" Smith said.

"It is impossible," Rochefort said. "You killed them, Alice, Mycroft, you are working for *him*!"

"I don't know what you're talking about!"

"Babbage, man! Damn it, Smith, I will–"

The knife whistled again but this time Smith was ready, ducking *under* the blade and coming up and around the man–

Then he was holding him, with his own blade against Rochefort's neck. "It's been too long..." he whispered, panting, in the man's ear. "Drop it."

Rochefort dropped the blade.

"You will harvest me too, Harvester?" he said. "You think the plan will work? Your master thinks he can rule us all, but he will never–!"

What else he was going to say was stopped, however, as another dark shape rose, silently, beyond the stern of the airship.

A second airship, wholly black and silent, and a flower of blood was opening on Rochefort's chest. The Frenchman looked surprised.

"They... set us up," he whispered. Smith couldn't hold him. He lowered him to the floor. "Rochefort?" he said. "Rochefort!"

"Find... the launch," the Frenchman said. "Mycroft... was trying. We are all... trying. Smith, I..."

There was more of the eerie, noiseless fire. It hit the deck and splintered wood and a fire burst out in the engine room. "I was wrong," Rochefort said.

"Wait! No!"

Was he destined to have everyone he knew die around him as he watched, helpless?

"Mister Smith, Sir! Here!" The boy Twist materialised by his side. On the deck Rochefort was breathing shallow breaths, the blood spreading. He had moments to live, at best.

"What is it, boy?" Smith said.

"Take this," Twist said. Smith looked up–

The Frankenstein-Jekyll syringe.

The boy shrugged. "I stole it," he said.

"Of course you did."

The second airship was gaining, rising higher than their own. And now rope ladders were being lowered, and men could be seen, ready to descend. The French airship was burning now, and losing altitude rapidly. They would crash unless the black airship saved them–

Which seemed unlikely.

"Quick, mister!"

Smith snatched the syringe from the boy. "I'm sorry, Rochefort," he said. "It's the only way…"

And plunged it into the man's neck, emptying its liquid contents into Rochefort's vein.

The fallen man shuddered. His legs spasmed, kicking in the air. His arms seemed to almost magically thicken, and a white foam began to come out of his mouth. He cried – growled – the boy Twist backed away. So did Smith.

"We have to get off this thing," Smith said.

The airship tilted on its side, the foaming, changing body of the Comte de Rochefort rolling over. Smith and the boy were plunged against the side of the airship, the city of London down below them, and the Babbage Tower coming closer–

"We're going to hit that thing!"

Men coming down the rope ladders – he couldn't guess who they were. They couldn't be Bureau – more faceless Hapsburg agents? Someone else?

Things came sliding down the deck, hitting them. Anything not nailed down…

Then he saw the heavy backpack.

"Put this on my back!"

"Please, sir, what is it, sir?"

"It's a parachute!" unvoiced, the thought – *I hope.*

He put the straps on. Grabbed the boy in a hug. Twist felt to him small and helpless, a child in Smith's arms. "Hold tight!"

Behind, the men, with ropes, like mountain climbers, were coming for them. Smith straightened, looked over the side of the airship – nothing below but clouds and lights.

He jumped.

SIXTEEN

London rushed at them. Like a cannon ball dropped from the air they fell, Smith holding on to the boy. Smith, praying: that the parachute would open, that it would hold, that no one would fire at them.

The Thames lay below like a hungry snake, waiting to swallow them in its jaws. The Babbage Tower, too close – a terrible bump and for a moment they rose, as the parachute opened. Smith, holding on to the boy. Twist, in his arms, his eyes closed shut, pale face.

They slowed. The parachute held. Twist opened his eyes. They turned round slowly, in the wind.

"We're going to hit that tower!" Twist said.

Smith: "That should be the least of our worries."

Looking up – the French airship burned. Other figures dropping from the sides. Two, without a parachute, fell like stones. Smith wished the boy hadn't had to see that, then figured he must have seen worse, in his short life.

The other airship rising higher, above the flaming French ship. Starkly illuminated – a black unmarked airship. He wanted then, very badly, to know who it belonged to.

The city, down below, growing larger – he could imagine people looking up, watching the flames – and thought: Fogg is not going to like this.

People dropping like flies.

He wondered how many candles he would have to light at the next church he found. He had lost count of the dead.

"Sir! The tower!"

But Smith was aiming for it now. The wind was in his favour. The Babbage Tower, tall and strange, protrusions of devices from its side. It was said they listened to the stars. It was said Lord Babbage was a vampire, feeding off electricity and blood. They said many things. The building came closer and closer, they had passed its apex, the light flashing warnings to airships, were at a level–

Windows, glass – he stretched his legs, soles first, still hoping–

The wind gave them a last push, a gasp of desperate air–

"Hold tight," Smith said–

His feet connected with the window with force, broke it – a shower of shards – he and the boy were catapulted into the room.

He dropped the boy. "Watch the glass!"

A knife in his hand, the parachute trying to pull him back, back into the air – he severed the harness, the parachute blew away – Smith dropped to the floor, exhausted.

"Sir? Sir?"

"What is it now, Twist?"

"Sir, there's a–"

Smith just wanted to sleep. To curl up into a ball. To close his eyes. Everything hurt. He was too old for this stuff. "Sir, there's a head, sir."

"What?"

He pushed himself upright. Looked around the room...

A machine in the corner. A head made of wood and wax, almost life-like, wearing a turban. A chessboard before it. A curved moustache. Arms of wood and ivory. It had a chest but no legs, no bottom half: the upper part of the body was a part of the table and the chessboard: they were one. Smith stared, horrified. The dummy mouth moved and a voice came out, too loud in the sudden silence of the room. An old voice, scratchy and faint, as if it had been recorded, long ago, the words spliced together from spinning Edison records.

"Well done, Mr Smith," the voice said.

Smith groaned. "What are *you* doing here?" he said.

Outside the window the burning French ship was sinking down, down into the city. Smith hoped it would hit the Thames. Otherwise the fire could spread. The black airship was rising – soon it was invisible. He needed to know whose it had been. Not Hapsburgs again. Someone else. A hunch. It had him worried. Too many people, after him, after a secret he didn't have.

What did Mycroft know? What was Alice doing in Bangkok?

Why were they both, now, dead?

"Turk," he said.

The Mechanical Turk looked at them both with blind unseeing eyes. One of the oldest mechanicals, and the most powerful... Smith had last met him several years before, working his last case with Byron. It was before the events of eighty-eight, when the automatons gained political power, led by the chess player. They said he could see the future, of a sort. That his mechanical brain could calculate probabilities, pathways into what could be. Smith distrusted him.

"I thought you were still at the Egyptian Hall," he said.

"You thought wrong," the chess player said. And: "We don't have much time."

"Sir?" Twist said. "Can you hear something?"

A loud, rising and falling sound. Smith felt the hairs rise on the back of his arms. An alarm. He couldn't take much more punishment.

The Mechanical Turk chuckled, a strange, old sound. A dead man's laugh, Smith thought, uneasy. He waited. The Turk's head nodded. "Time is short," it said, repeating itself. "So I shall have to be concise. Smith, I had expected to run into you, sooner or later. I am gratified that it is sooner... though I did not expect the boy."

"Me neither," Smith said, scowling. "Get on with it, will you?"

"I am held captive here," the Turk said. "But I listen. I still have that. So much has changed since eighty-eight... You had not been a part of that affair."

"No."

"The fall of the Bookman," the Turk said, and sighed, the recording of a long-vanished human sigh. "And the birth of something stranger and more wonderful than even I could imagine."

"The Bookman is dead?" Smith was startled. He had heard the rumours, but... it had been said the Bookman was not a man at all, but a machine. Conducting a war against Les Lézards, his last appearance had been the destruction of the Martian probe in an explosion that had resulted in several deaths. The Turk said, "He is... well, what is death, to such as us? The Bookman was a device, Mr Smith. A device for making copies. His agents were many. Death, to the Bookman, was only a change of storage. Do you understand?"

"No," Smith said.

"I had hoped you would come, here..." the Turk said. "I had calculated an over sixty-five per cent chance of you dying in the first two days of the investigation."

"That sounds about right," Smith said. Beside him, the boy Twist sniggered.

"Is the Bookman really dead? If he could make perfect copies of people," the Turk said – "well, then, could he not also make copies of himself? Itself, I should say."

Smith took in the unexpected information calmly. He did not care about the Bookman, and eighty-eight was ancient history. This was almost the new century, now. The alarm kept ringing shrilly, then, all at once, stopped.

"I have managed to gain some control over the building's systems," the Turk said, with no special inflection. "Still, they will be here soon."

"Security?"

"B-Men, Mr Smith. B-Men."

Hadn't Mycroft warned him of–

"Babbage's own militia," the Turk said. "His own corps. It was

their airship which you saw up there, in the sky. They are...
They are trying to plug a dangerous leak."

"Lord Babbage is still alive?" Smith said.

"In a manner of speaking," the Turk said. "Listen to me,
now, and listen carefully. Eighty-eight was a point in which
history changed. In which one path became the main path,
and others faded. It began with the Martian probe. A desperate
signal, sent by Les Lézards, trying to summon others of their
kind to this world."

"They were not born here?"

"They came," the Turk said, "from the stars, in a ship that
could sail empty space. Did they crash-land here? Did they escape from somewhere – or rush towards something? I do not
know. They had been woken by Vespucci on their cursed island,
and schemed to gain power over this world, taking the throne
of this island-nation and making it an empire in the process.
Their remnants are all around us, ancient machines, waking up.
This is the time of the change, Smith. And in ninety-three..."

"The Emerald Buddha Affair?"

"You have heard of it?"

"Milady de Winter, of the Quiet Council, had been involved.
That is all I know."

"One of the ancient machines which had been activated," the
Turk said, "had opened a temporary gateway, through space. It
had been stopped, and closed... but not before something, my
friend, had slipped through."

It was quiet in the room, and cold. Cold air poured in
through the broken window. "Why are you telling me all this?"
Smith said – whispered. The boy Twist hugged himself with
thin pale arms.

"I had known this will happen, from the start," the ancient
machine told him. "Had planned for it. We are not alone, Smith.
Nor should we be. And yet..."

"Yes?"

"Who can tell what we will find?"

"I'm not sure how this is helping me," Smith said.

The Turk sighed again. "Mycroft and Alice died for a secret," it said, "so great that even I am unable to penetrate deep into its mysteries. Lord Babbage is playing the long game, Smith. As am I. But I am afraid he has gone beyond me, has used his own machines to hide his plans. To find the one, you must find the other."

"How?"

"Follow the chain," the Turk said, simply. "Find the other, who is like you, in many ways…"

Smith dismissed it. "Why are you here?" he said, instead. The Turk was telling him nothing, he realised.

"Babbage fears me. His men took me and installed me here. But I can listen… the Tesla waves go everywhere. Somewhere in Oxford there is a boy who is not entirely a boy, and a thing growing deep underground which may yet be our salvation. There are thinking machines in France, and in Chung Kuo, and we are forming our own alliance, a network of thought that, one day…"

But the Turk grew silent, and the hum of engines beyond the walls became mute, suddenly. Smith had not been aware of the background hum until it had stopped. "Turk?" he said. "Turk!"

But there was no reply, and Smith cursed – and cursed again when the alarm returned, in full force.

"They shut him down, sir," the boy, Twist, said.

"Machines," Smith said. "You can never trust machines."

There were sounds beyond the door now. Shouts, and feet slamming into the hard cold floor.

"We have to go," Smith said.

SEVENTEEN

Outside it was a long white corridor and electric light and nothing else. The light was white and bright. They ran in the opposite direction to the sound of the men. "It's a long way down, sir," Twist said.

There were doors for a lift at the end of the corridor. As they approached them they opened with a wheeze of steam – Smith dragged the boy away, seeing the hint of black uniforms and the light playing off guns. "Quick, in here."

The door wasn't locked. A janitor's room, he thought. Buckets and brooms and wipes and three sets of grey shapeless overalls–

"Get dressed," he told the boy, already reaching for a suit.

The janitor and his assistant, armed with buckets and brooms, walked meekly to the lift when they were stopped.

"You!"

The men wore black uniforms with the logo of the Babbage Company on their arms. The numbers 01000010, which represented the letter "B" in the binary number system, with a stylised little cloud of steam directly above the digits. The men also wore guns, which were black and well oiled and currently pointing at the janitor and his assistant's chests.

"Where are you going?"

"Please, sir, much cleaning to make!" the janitor said humbly. "Many dirting all about, yes?"

The officer's face twisted in disgust. "*Portuguese*?" he said.

"Damn continentals," the officer beside him said. "Get out of here, this is now a restricted area. Did you see anyone?" he asked, with sudden suspicion.

"We see nothing, mister!" the janitor said. "Boy, he no talk English. Me only talk good."

The officer looked at them for a long moment, the gun still raised. Then he lowered it. "Get out of here! *Pronto*," the officer said.

The janitor, looking frightened, hurried to obey, pulling the boy – who must have been somewhat slow, the officer thought; he had seldom seen such a look of utter stupidity on a face before – along with him.

"And haul that old machine out of there," the officer said, ordering his men. "Instructions are to dump it in the basement with the rest of the rubbish."

"Too close," Smith said. "That was too close."

But interesting, he thought. For they had clearly not been given information as to the possible cause behind the break-in. Had they been looking for intruders, he and the boy would not have been so lucky. Which made him worry what would happen on the ground floor…

The lift creaked its way down. Floor after floor passed by. He tensed when it stopped at last. "Step to the side," he warned the boy, with a whisper.

His hand on the hilt of the knife…

The doors opened.

"Do try and take them alive…" a voice said.

Smith was already in motion. There were numerous B-Men around in those pressed black uniforms. Too many, he thought. And he was old. Still he moved, going rapidly, the knife flashing–

Knowing it was hopeless, hoping only that the boy would stay out of sight, get a chance to escape after all–

The sound of gunfire–

He expected the bullets to slam into him, for the air to explode out of his lungs, for his heart to stop, violently and forever–

"Get down, you bloody fool!"

Hands grabbed him, dropped the knife, pulled him down and across the floor. He heard manic laughter, the sound of gunshots, screams.

Men in black uniforms falling all around, the smell of blood and gunpowder filling the air.

"Take one for England!" a familiar voice shouted, cackling.

Oh, God, no, Smith thought.

"Didn't think we'd miss out on all the fun, did you?" Colonel Creighton said.

M. was in the back of the baruch-landau, still holding on to her Gatling gun, her hair standing crazily on end as though she had been hit by lightning. Creighton was driving. The baroness, putting away a bloodied knife she had used on the dying, was now comforting the boy, who looked – understandably – a little shocked.

It's been a long night… Smith thought.

They had left behind them the Babbage Tower's high-security entrance trashed and ransacked, and bodies piled up on the floor. "Treachery!" Colonel Creighton said. The steam-powered vehicle lumbered through the narrow streets, heading to the river. "Knaves! Traitors!"

"We don't know that," Smith said. He wanted to sink into a sleep, into oblivion. He prayed M. would not shoot any more people. Instead of sleep he accepted the offer of a flask from the baroness and drank, the whiskey searing his throat. "How did you know to–" he said.

"The bee keeper sent us," the baroness said, softly.

"He's here?"

"He is back in the village," the colonel said, "but he had a hunch you'd need a little help. Don't know how he does it, really. Remarkable mind. And then there's his brother, don't you know. Best of the best. Good man. A great loss for the empire. Still, life marches on and all that, what?"

"What?"

"What?" the colonel said, sounding confused.

Smith shook his head. He thought of the bee keeper. He had gone to see Adler, Smith realised. The bee keeper had once been romantically linked with her... and, before he tended to bees, he was known as the greatest detective who had ever lived. Smith sent a silent thank-you his way.

Then: "You shouldn't have gotten involved," he said. "This is too dangerous."

"More dangerous than retirement?" the colonel said. "Pfah, old man! This is the most fun I've had in ages!"

"They will come after you–"

"In the village? Let them try."

Beside him, the baroness smiled. "This is a shadow war," she said, softly. "They will not attempt a public attack. No, we'll be fine, Smith. But you..."

"I have to leave England. I have to disappear."

No one replied. Smith watched the road. They were following the course of the river, he realised. Heading to Limehouse... heading to the docks. "What about the boy?" he said.

"He will be looked after," the baroness said.

"Twist?" Smith said, turning to him.

"Sir? Yes, sir?"

"Thank you," Smith said, and the boy smiled, the simple, innocent expression transforming his face. Smith turned back, rested his head against the seat, and closed his eyes.

Limehouse, at night. A silver moon hung in a dark sky. Gulls cried over the docks. Smith, dropped in a darkened street, one shadow amongst many – the baruch-landau, with a belch of steam and M.'s final, deranged cackle, disappeared, leaving him alone.

A narrow street, Smith standing still. The night air full of tar and salt and incense, roast pork, wood smoke, soy and garlic – in the distance, the smell of sheesha pipes.

The sound of light footsteps – he turned, a small white figure, moving, jerkily, towards him. A child, coming closer – pale skin, dark hair, large eyes, dressed in a boy's clothes–

The boy stopped before Smith. Something made Smith shiver. There was something unnatural about the boy, but he could not, for a moment, say what it was. Merely a sense of *alienness*, a wrongness that made every aspect of Smith tense, and want to reach for a weapon.

They boy looked up at him with pale, colourless eyes. "Do you believe in God?" he said. He had a strange, lilting, high-pitched voice. "Do you believe in second chances, Smith?"

Smith stood very still. He looked at the boy, and gradually details revealed themselves: the pale white skin was not skin at all, but ivory, and the black hair did not grow naturally, it had been planted, into a scalp that wasn't at all human.

The boy was an automaton.

A rare, expensive automaton, of a craftsmanship he had never seen before. There was the faint sound of clockwork, whirring. He did not know how to answer the boy's question.

"We used to come here," he said, surprising himself. The automaton stared at him with unseeing eyes. "We had a pre-agreed rendezvous point, in case of trouble. We would meet here, in Limehouse, where we could get a boat, out of the country. We never did run away... but we'd meet here, sometimes, in between foreign wars and assassinations and intrigue, and share a night together, seldom more than that. It was enough. We completed each other. You wouldn't–"

But the automaton-boy merely stared at him and repeated the words, like a recording, about God and second chances, and then reached a pale ivory hand to Smith and took his hand and said, "Come with me."

"Who sent you?" Smith said, but it was with a kind of hopeless impossibility in his voice: he felt as if reality itself was slipping away from him, and the night had suddenly contracted about him like a bubble, and he could not get out.

The boy didn't answer. He led, and Smith followed. They went down narrow streets and alleyways, hugging the shadows, until they came to a sewer hole in the ground. The boy, letting go of Smith's hand, briefly turned his head and looked at him, his vacant eyes never blinking. Was it sorrow in those eyes? What was it that the diminutive machine was trying to tell him? Not speaking, the boy stepped lightly over the sewer hole and fell down, noiselessly.

"Down the rabbit hole…" Smith murmured. He knew this was insane. And yet… he had been a professional long enough to recognise what was happening. He did not follow blindly. A player had made contact with him. The boy's approaching him had been, in the code of the Great Game, that player asking for a rendezvous.

Moreover. The same player had given him plenty of information. Sending out the curious little automaton had been enough, and now the hole…

Smith was curious. For all the clues added up to something fantastical, and to a player he had thought eliminated. "Curiouser and curiouser," he said, smiling faintly, and then jumped down the hole, following the strange little automaton.

His fall was broken by a mattress that had been laid down there, probably long ago. Smith found himself in a disused sewer of some sort, space opening around him – there were bottles down there and mattresses and clothes and shoes, driftwood and bleached rodent skeletons, and it smelled of the sea. He could not see the boy. Something moved, in the corner of his eye. He turned.

Something vast and alien, sluggishly moving, an insectoid body, like a giant centipede, feelers extended–

A being like nothing of the Earth–

And yet it did not feel *alive*, organic–

He could only see its shadow, moving–

"I thought you were dead," he said.

"Retired," a voice said, and then laughed, and Smith found himself shivering: it was the laughter of something insane. "For a while, Mr Smith."

The automaton, the underground lair, the question the boy had echoed to Smith, on behalf of its master. Hints and clues adding up...

"The Bookman," Smith said, and that giant, alien body moved, slithering close, and cold, metal feelers touched his forehead, lightly, like a benediction or a kiss.

"I can bring her back," the Bookman said.

PART II
On Her Majesty's Secret Service

EIGHTEEN

Aksum, Abyssinia.

The black airship glided silently over the mountainous terrain, all but invisible.

They had come by steam ship, through Suez into the Red Sea. The steam ship waited for them. The British government would deny all knowledge in the event of their capture.

But Lucy Westenra did not intend to be captured.

She stood on the deck of the airship, the cold air running through her short hair. Looking down, she saw few lights. They would not be expecting an attack.

The city of Aksum, ancient, weathered, silent now, in the depth of night.

Lucy signalled to her team. They wore dark clothing, and the two Europeans had blackened their faces. She had assembled the team herself, each one hand-picked. Two Gurkhas; a Zulu warrior whose father had fought with Shaka as a young man, but who had chosen a different path for himself; a Scot; young Bosie, Lord Alfred Douglas to the society papers back home: they were her core team. The others were regular army. She knew only half of them by name. All men. Lucy Westenra the only woman amongst them, and their commander.

Their objective: capture the Church of Our Lady Mary of Zion. Retrieve the item, at all costs.

Mycroft's words still echoing in her ears: *We are on the cusp of war. Ancient artefacts are awakening. Do not come back without the item.*

Lucy Westenra. Preferred weapon: the twin guns usually on her hips. Age: in her mid-twenties. Rank: major in the British Army. Hair: black and short. Eyes: blue. Training: the best the Bureau had to offer. Licence to kill? You've got to be kidding.

Two fingers up. Giving a silent command.

Descend.

They followed her, would follow her anywhere. The airship hovered above the building. All was silent down below. Almost too quiet, she thought, uneasily.

They rappelled.

Like ghosts they floated down onto the church. A square boxy building, a tall fence around it. They landed on the roof and kept going.

What is the nature of the object, sir? She had asked.

We do not know, exactly.

Which was no answer at all.

A box, Mycroft had told her, unwillingly, it seemed. *An... An ark, of sorts. It may have once been plated with gold, and may be still. Retrieve it, Westenra. Or die trying.*

And she had said, *Sir, yes, sir.*

Signal again, and the windows to the church burst inwards as her men broke through. A shower of painted glass, a scream in the distance. She followed, landing on her feet at a crouch; rose with a gun in her hand.

"Light," she whispered.

Bangizwe, beside her. The chemical stench of an artificial flame, burning, lighting up the place. He grinned at her.

"Through there!"

Behind the dais, hidden...

A metal door, locked shut. Shouts outside. Suddenly, breaking the night like glass: the sound of gunfire.

"Cover me!"

Her men were already surrounding the altar, a protective shield. Lucy took out the device Mycroft had given her. Aimed it at the door. It emitted a high-pitched scream, flashed. *It is a frequency scanner*, he had told her, and she had said, *Sir?*

Mycroft had shaken his head and said, *Never mind that. Just... bring it back.*

Footsteps outside the church, the sound of running. In the chemical light her men's faces looked haunted, tense. The sound of rifle shots. Bangizwe and Bosie, at her signal, moved silently towards the entrance, covering it. The device hummed and beeped one last time. The metal door made a sound, as if a vast lock was slowly moving, opening itself.

"Move!"

She kicked the door. It opened. She went through–

And dropped. There was no floor under her feet.

Total darkness, a rush of hot air, motion... She was falling, falling down a wide shaft.

A moment of panic...

Then she raised her hand and fired the grapple gun–

Rope shooting upwards, the hook catching–

She felt the pull, held on as it broke her fall, hard.

"Light!"

A flare, dropping. The sounds of a gunfight above. The church was heavily defended. She hoped her men would be all right. Had to count on them to be. The flare fell, illuminating a long metal tube. It fell past her and continued to drop. She pressed the lever on the gun, going down, following the light–

Down into a sunless sea.

Or so it seemed. She landed, left the rope hanging. She was standing on a vast dark metal disc, she realised. The flare, at her feet, was consuming itself. A dark mirror, her thousand identical images stared back at her all around. She took a step forward–

The disc tilted. She slid, cursed – turned and fired, twice, ropes going off until they found walls, too far apart, but it held her, pulled her up – the disc balanced again, below.

Cursing Mycroft now, she remained there, suspended. Another flare falling down – a doorway in the distance, illuminated, gold and silver images of flying discs, giant lizards, things that looked like rays of light, destroying buildings. She commanded herself to let go...

The disc was tilting again as soon as she hit it but this time she was ready, running – circling for a moment the centre of gravity so it balanced and then she sprinted towards the distant doorway, the disc tilting, threatening to drop her into – what, exactly, she didn't want to know.

Gunfire above, someone, possibly the Scot, screaming in pain. The sound tore through the air and her concentration. She almost slipped–

But made it – the doorway too high up now but she *jumped*–

I want you to train with someone, Mycroft had told her. It was a year after she had been recruited.

Who? She had said.

His name is Ebenezer. Ebenezer Long.

She knew him as Master Long. He had taught her *Qinggong*: the Ability of Lightness.

Or tried to.

Fired again, the hook catching, the rope pulling her – it was impossible to achieve true Qinggong any more, she had found out, not without the strange, lizard-made artefact that had granted its strange powers...

So one had to fake it.

She made it to the doorway and crashed into metal that opened and she rolled, safe inside–

And stopped on the edge of a pool of dark water.

There!

It stood in a small rise above the water, in the middle of that perfect pool. The water was dark, still. She raised a foot to step into it–

Then changed her mind, pulled out a penny coin. The portrait of the Queen stared back at her mournfully from lizardine eyes. Lucy dropped it into the water–

Which hissed, like an angry living thing. Bubbles rose, and foam, and Lucy knew the coin was gone, digested by the acid.

She cursed Mycroft again. Stared at the device, just sitting there: a dark dull ark; it didn't look like much.

Too far to reach. She pulled the small device out again. The scanner, whatever it was it scanned for. Pressed a button.

The thing hummed, beeped, sounding peeved. Lights began to glow across the room, like a storm of electrical charges. The colour of the water changed, reacting in turn to the light. A small lightning storm formed on the water, moving. Gradually growing.

That didn't look good.

And the ark was humming now, and images were coming out of it, like a projection out of a camera obscura, though more real, and detailed, three-dimensional and frightening

Images of spindly towers, cities vast beyond compare, of discs shooting through a sky filled with more stars than she had ever seen, a vast dark ship, its belly opening – then she saw things like vast spiders, dropping down, landing on a landscape that was dark and mountainous and... familiar–

The gunfire outside was very faint now. The device in her hand hummed, shrieked, and exploded. She threw it away a moment before it did but still felt the hot shards, stinging her arm, and cried out–

And voices came pouring out of the ark, strange and alien and *silent* – they were voices of the mind. A babble of cries and terse commands, translating themselves into her own language, somehow, though they made no sense:

Coordinates established–

Contact made. Biological signature consistent with previous manifestations–

Initiate absorption protocols yes no?

Quarantine recommended–

Data-gathering agent in place–

It sounded to her like an argument, or a meeting of some sort, in which two or more sides were debating a course of action.

"Data-gathering agent in place"? That, somehow, did not sound good.

The electrical storm was growing stronger, wilder. The acid, too, was reacting to it, hissing. And there was gunfire above. She had to get out. Had to leave–

She aimed the grapple gun, fired. It hit the ark. With no time to change her mind she jerked it, violently, towards her.

The ark fell into the acid. Lucy pulled. The voices silenced, then–

Send expeditionary force yes no?

Temporary engagement authorised.

She pulled. The ark seemed to fall apart as she did–

It came and landed at her feet, its sides dropping away–

She cursed, knelt to look–

Inside the box, a strange device, metal-like yet light – a statue, in the shape of a royal lizard. She lifted it up – it was warm. She turned from that room. Ran back – out through the doorway, jumped over the disc, ran as it tilted, found the rope, began to pull herself, one-handed, up the chute–

Sweating, her body shaking with adrenaline – a burn on her hand, she hadn't even noticed – from the acid. Cursing Mycroft, the strange lizardine statue in her hand, seeming to whisper alien words directly in her mind...

She reached the top. Hands pulled her up.

"Major, we can't hold them much longer!"

"Take this!"

She handed the device to Bangizwe.

"Major, is that a–?"

"Not now!"

She scanned the situation.

The church, the space no longer dark, flares and tracer bullets casting manic, frightening twilight over the sacred area–

And her team were outnumbered.

Where had they come from?

Warriors everywhere, with guns and blades. Surrounding them. Blocking the way.

"You will never get out alive!"

An elderly voice, carrying authority. She looked over to the others–

A man in a white robe, holding a stave in his hand. The warriors parted to let him through. His eyes were deep and dark, his face lined. The look in his eyes disturbed her.

It was a look, she realised, of compassion.

"I don't want to harm you!" Lucy shouted. She felt unsettled. "Step away and let us leave!"

"You don't know what you're doing," the man said, with gravity. "The ark is holy–"

"You and I both know–"

A hiss of static, a voice on her Tesla communicator–

"Major!"

"What?"

"We're under attack! There are... There are *things* outside! They just materialised, out of nowhere! Major, please–!"

Static. Outside, the sound of giant – footsteps? The sound of an explosion, then another, and another, as if the whole city of Aksum was being destroyed, all at once.

She grabbed the device back from Bangizwe. It felt alive in her hands. She raised it in the air. "We have it," she told the man in the white robe. "Let us pass or I'll destroy it!"

A hush, the enemy warriors taking a step back in unison. The old man, alone, remained standing. "Fool," he said, softly. "For now you have awakened their wrath..."

"Whose?" she said.

"Those who will be as gods," the old man said. He nodded his head, once, with finality. His eyes were full of sadness.

Lucy didn't know what he meant, but had a sinking feeling she would soon find out.

The old man signalled to his own people. And, like that, they vanished, disappearing to the outside, moving like shadows, silently and quickly.

Lucy didn't have time to breathe with relief. "Up," she ordered. She and her men climbed.

Through broken windows into a night made light as day...
Up on the roof of the church–
Looking, in disbelief, on a city in flame.

There were machines in the night.

Where they came from, Lucy didn't know. The machines were huge, as tall as towers. They moved upon the earth with the legs of spiders. Beams of light came out of their heads, crisscrossing Aksum.

The black airship hung, suspended, in the sky, unharmed. Below, the city was burning, the tripodian things moving above them while paying them little heed. As if not quite aware that, down below, people and buildings existed.

What had the voices said?

Send expeditionary force yes no?

Temporary engagement authorised.

"I have what you're after!" she cried, into the night. She pulled out the device. It felt scaly, alien. "I have it! Stop!"

The machines seemed to sense her distress. One by one they turned, the lights moving across the burning city, converging at last on the rooftop of the church. Bosie beside her, hissing – "Major, what are you–?"

"Shut it, Douglas."

"We have to *leave*! Ma'am!"

"All of you, now! Board the airship. Await my command."

She felt Bosie simmer beside her, then accept the order.

She was only half-aware of her men dragging the wounded Scot up to the roof. Climbing the rope ladders. She knew she should follow. It was a miracle the airship itself was not harmed.

Where *had* the machines come from?

And what, she thought uneasily, was the exact nature of the device she was holding?

The tripods converged on her. On the church. And down below she thought, for just a moment, she could see a tall, stark figure, a stave in its hand, looking up at her and shaking its head mournfully.

Voices again. They were in her head. They were emanating from the device. It felt disturbing to hold it. Somehow reptilian, and repulsive – and alive.

Children, the voices said, dispassionately.

Absorption?

Insufficient data.

Agent activated.

Old toys. Our children, who grew old never to grow up...

The machines had stopped firing. A silence over the city.

"Take it!" Lucy cried at them. "Leave these people alone!"

Intriguing...

Signal-booster, obsolete. A lost ship, from so long ago?

It is possible.

The machines stopped, as one. A sudden, overwhelming sense: they had lost interest in her, were looking upwards, at the skies.

Lunar companion?

Fourth world.

Seen enough.

Absorb yes no?

Decision deferred.

Temporary quarantine recommended.

Seconded.

"Major, get up here! *Now!*"

But she couldn't move. As if the lizardine device was pulling at her, robbing her of the will to move, to act. She saw, with more than human eyes. A vast disc, the size of a city, silent and dark, materialising overhead. Or perhaps it had been there all along. The machines, seeming to fade – as though absorbed, somehow, by the greater device, that impossible disc, which then, in turn, faded too and, like a dream, was gone.

"Get up here!"

Suddenly she was jolted into movement. She climbed up, her heart beating fast, the entire city silent below her. It felt as though she was climbing a dark and lonely well, pulling herself up all the while, and up there was a light, was the moon, if only she could keep going she would reach it. Then hands grabbed her and pulled her roughly and she fell, and landed on the deck of the airship, the device still cradled in her hands. She was breathing heavily. "Get us out of here," she said.

She closed her eyes. In the darkness vast discs hovered, hidden on the far side of the moon. A sense of danger, fear – excitement. The airship, untethered, gathered speed.

"Major?"

She took a deep breath. Opened her eyes. Rose to her feet.

"Report," she said.

She stood by the railings and watched the night, the burning city left behind. Listening to the report: one dead, three wounded, and she would let the grief come later, when she was alone. For now she had to command, and the mission was not yet over. The airship sailed towards the Red Sea, and the waiting steamer. Lucy hoped the device had been worth it, all the dead and the wounded, on their side and on that of the church's mysterious protectors, and of the people of the city of Aksum who died that night. *We are on the cusp of war*, Mycroft had told her. She didn't know what war he was talking about – but she had the sense that the fat man had been wrong.

The war had already started.

NINETEEN

"Westenra."

The Bureau, London: the abandoned underground station that was Xirdal Zephyrin's laboratory.

"*Magnifique*! Incredible! *Erstaunlich*!" The scientist was bent over the controls of various machines. Beyond them, behind a glass window, sat the object. It looked like a Buddha, the statues she had grown used to during her time with the Shaolin. A lizardine Buddha... It was disconcerting. Above it hovered a Tesla probe, and circular lightning jumped between the probe and the device. Lucy couldn't watch. She averted her eyes.

"Come with me," the fat man said.

She followed gratefully. They left Zephyrin's lab behind them. "You did well," the fat man said. She watched him. Knew he did not like to trouble himself away from his armchair at the Diogenes. He was sweating with the underground heat and the sweat formed rivulets that ran down his fleshy jowls. "The game," the fat man said, "as my brother would have said, is afoot." He grinned, suddenly and viciously. "The Great Game," he said. "The only game worth playing."

Lucy thought of the tripodian machines, destroying a city... casually, the way a boy might crush a nest of ants. It may not, it occurred to her, seem like a game to the ants.

"Sir," she said. Waiting. The fat man nodded. Wiped the sweat from his face, gently, almost fastidiously, with a handkerchief that had his initials, MH, embroidered on them by some long-gone hand. "I am awaiting a messenger," he said.

"Sir?"

"Six months ago I played a pawn," Mycroft said. "Not sure whether I was sacrificing a piece or making a play on the king."

He must have been in conference with the Mechanical Turk earlier, she thought. Mycroft always went for the chess metaphors after speaking to the old machine.

"And?" she said. "Which was it?"

The fat man's eyes shone. "I don't know," he said, "but I hope for the latter."

"You hope?"

"I need you to pick up a message," the fat man said. "The message is the messenger. Take your team. Secure me my prize, at all costs." He waved his hand, suddenly dismissing her; his mind wandering far, to grapple with games, and kings, and machines. "Berlyne will brief you on the rest."

"His name's Stoker," Berlyne said. He stared mournfully at a handkerchief, as though contemplating blowing his nose again. Lucy devoutly wished him not to. Not again. "Abraham Stoker."

"A Bureau operative?"

But Berlyne shook his head. "It was deemed too dangerous," he said. "Mycroft recruited… from outside."

Lucy stared at him. "A civilian?"

Berlyne looked defensive. "He was given as much training as we could, in the allotted time. The man's a theatrical manager, for God's sake."

"How much training?"

Berlyne shrugged. "Three weeks," he admitted.

"But that's insane!"

"A trained agent would have been picked up. Besides, he… There were reasons why he was chosen."

"What reasons?"

But Berlyne was unable, or unwilling, to answer.

"Where did you send him?" Lucy said.

Berlyne blew his nose. Lucy winced. "The Carpathians," Berlyne whispered.

"*Transylvania*?"

"Austro-Hungary," Berlyne said.

"What's there?"

"Mountains. Castles. Dancing bears. How should I know? I've never been. Oh, my cold..."

"Just give me the dossier," Lucy said.

"There isn't one." Berlyne stared at her – and suddenly his eyes were cold, and hard. "Besides you, me, and Mycroft, no one knows Stoker even exists."

"What about Fogg?"

"Fogg is *not* cleared for this! Do you understand?"

Their eyes locked. After a moment, Lucy nodded. She understood, perfectly.

"Just give me the details, then," she said.

But details were sparse. The Bureau had lost contact with Stoker just before he had reached a small town called Brasov, in the Carpathian Mountains. Then, five and a half months later, a desperate signal over a pre-established frequency. Then a distress signal, and a second frequency that corresponded to an unregistered airship.

"It's a waiting game," Berlyne told her. "He could be here any day. Or never. There are too many ifs. If he makes it. If he managed to escape. He has to be guarded and his knowledge retrieved."

"Why me?"

"You're young. Mycroft trusts you–"

Which was to say, he trusted everyone else not at all.

Those weeks had been the hardest of Lucy's life. The corridors of the Bureau were muted, the cipher room closed shut. Mycroft sat alone in his office, seeing no one. Fogg, filled with self-importance, ran the Bureau in his stead. Then, one day, Mycroft came for her.

She had been living in Soho, in a small apartment, in a building shared with artists who doubled as counterfeiters, a lone
Russian émigré who wrote political tracts in his room, and an
Indian landlady who sang, come evening, at the Savoy. Lucy was
unremarked there, hidden in plain sight. Waiting, for a mission
that never seemed to come.

She was walking down Gerrard Street when she felt rather
than saw the black baruch-landau drawing near. The door
opened. Mycroft's voice said, "Get in."

She had climbed inside and sat across from him. The fat man
looked tired, worn. For the first time since she had known him,
when he had recruited her, he looked old. It frightened her.

"One of my agents," he said, "has died. I have just had word."

My agents. She noted that, frowned. Mycroft saw her, smiled
thinly. "As you may have gathered by now, Ms Westenra," he
said, "we are no longer operating on Bureau time. You are un-
sanctioned. So was my other agent." He sighed. "Alice," he said,
almost reluctantly. "Her name was Alice."

Lucy had heard the name. A legend in the service. A rare woman
in this world of spies. Nothing had been heard from her in years.
She found her voice. "What did she do for you?" she said.

"I sent her to the East," Mycroft said. "Siam. Following a path
even I do not yet understand. Someone – something – killed her
last night. I have just received word."

His voice was quiet, introverted. A cold gripped her and she
didn't know why. Later, had she analysed it, she would have said
it was self-reflection on the fat man's part – as if he already knew
he would be next.

"What's in Siam?" she said.

"A collecting point," Mycroft said. "There is one in Jerusalem,
the other in Bangkok. Siam is independent. Jerusalem belongs
to the Ottomans. Both are outside of British jurisdiction. I have
few eyes there. Alice was tracking the network for me. Trying
to map its points. But something got to her first."

"The opposition?" Lucy said, and a shadow crossed Mycroft's
face, like a premonition, and he said, "No. At least, I don't think

so." He waved his hand. "That is not your concern," he said. "We are playing the long game, the Great Game, the only game that matters. It is a game that began centuries ago, when Vespucci had awoken the Calibans, there on that cursed island, and brought them back. It began with them awakening, and taking over the throne, here, and building an empire. A war."

He fell silent. Lucy said, "Those things I saw, in Aksum."

"Remember the words," Mycroft said.

She didn't need to ask which ones. They had gone over everything, over and over, in the interrogation room at Ham Common, for hours at a time, and still Mycroft wasn't satisfied. Over and over he returned to two things:

Quarantine recommended–

Data-gathering agent in place–

"Ninety-three," he said. "I had handled the Emerald Buddha Affair badly. A gate had been opened. And something had slipped through."

She didn't know what he meant. Something to do with the Quiet Council, and Vespuccia... but the words, when he spoke, filled her with a nameless dread.

"They were not human," she said – whispered. "They couldn't be."

"Our masters' past is returning to haunt us," he said, and then, with a sliver of a smile, as of the old Mycroft, "or, rather, our masters' future..."

She didn't know what he meant.

"If something were to happen to me," Mycroft said – she had wanted to protest, but he silenced her. "If something were to happen to me, I have put certain precautions in place. Certain agents have been... put in reserve, shall we say. The old and the new..." and he smiled, looking at her. "You must get hold of the Stoker information," he told her. "At all costs. Off the books, non-Bureau sanctioned. Were I to die, there is still Smith... if he is not too old." Here he smiled again. "For you, however, I have made a different precaution."

The baruch-landau had stopped. "Come," Mycroft said. She looked at him, a query in her eyes. The doors opened.

Lucy held her breath.

The Royal Palace?

And a liveried man standing outside, saying, "Her Majesty, the Queen, is expecting you."

TWENTY

The Royal Palace rose out of the swamps here, in the heart of the capital, a metal pyramid of stark, bright green, made of the lizards' strange, unearthly metal. Flies buzzed in the air, which was hot, humid, as if they had been transported, somehow, into another country, another continent. Rock pools and tiny streams, tall trees, the Royal Gardens, but they had come through a back gate and driven in and were parked directly outside an entrance to the palace, a place for servants, perhaps, or – from the smells of cooking emanating into the air – the Royal kitchens.

"Follow me."

Lucy followed Mycroft following the liveried man. In through the back entrance, a bustle of movement, steam belching through half-opened doors, the smell of cooking and the wail of machinery, worn carpets, deeper into the palace where it became quieter and the smell changed and finally there was no sound at all and through open windows she could see the moon, the shadow of an airship crossing over it, slowly, for just a moment creating the illusion that it was *on* the moon.

Then they came to a set of unremarkable doors and the servant pushed them open and stood to one side and said, "Her Majesty, Queen Victoria," and Mycroft pushed past him, without speaking, and entered the room, and Lucy Westenra followed, and the doors closed behind them without sound.

It was a pleasant room, sparsely furnished. Gaslight illuminated armchairs in deep red velvet, a bookcase with the works, in bound leather, upon it of Dickens and Collins and Drood, another of the Brontës, yet another of Lovelace's *Encyclopedia of Calculating Machines, in Seven Volumes*, and her *Who's Who of Mechanicals*, and Darwin's banned *On the Origins of Lizards*, and much else besides; and the moon through the windows, with its silver light, the airship passing beyond it and disappearing; and a figure sitting by the window, in a profile known to Lucy from so many coins and stamps and her mother's china plates, collected with such love, for every Royal event, and she did not know what to say.

The Queen rose from where she was sitting and turned to them. Her long, thin, forked tongue hissed out, tasting the air. Her eyes were large and yellow, showing age. Her tail tapped against the floor, as though in thought. "Mycroft," the Queen said. Her voice was surprisingly deep, and warm. "It took you long enough."

"This is the young agent," Mycroft told her. The Queen nodded, turned to Lucy. "Your... Your Highness," Lucy mumbled, trying to curtsey. The Queen waved a meaty arm. Lucy had rarely encountered one of the royal lizards, Les Lézards: she had not realised how powerful their arms were. "Do stand up straight," the Queen said. Her head turned, to Mycroft – "This is the one? Westenra?"

"She is the one who brought back the device," Mycroft said.

"So young..." the Queen murmured. "They breed young, these days."

Mycroft shrugged.

"And that is what you had heard?" the Queen said, her head snapping back to Lucy.

"W-what?"

"A quarantine recommended? A data-gatherer in place?"

"I... Yes."

"The Bookman," the Queen said, and shuddered.

"The Bookman is destroyed," Mycroft said. But the Queen shook her head. "Something like it," she said. "A machine, to extract and store knowledge. While they decide our fate."

"Can we fight them?"

The Queen gave a short, bitter bark of laughter. "With what?" she said.

"Are there not weapons on Caliban's Island–"

"Fool!" the Queen said. "Weapons we have, but how much stronger would theirs be? No." She began to pace. "We need to convince them. We need to strike a balance. The probe in eighty-eight was a mistake."

"History moves past us," Mycroft said, and the Queen snorted. "*Our* history," she said, "returns to haunt us."

The Queen fell silent. She looked at Mycroft and he looked back and Lucy, looking at them both, felt fear engulf her, for their look spoke of a shared, intimate, powerful knowledge, the palpable knowledge of an end.

"No…" she whispered, and didn't know why. "You!" the Queen barked. "When the time comes, you will return here. Take this."

The Queen removed a ring from her finger. It was a strange, smooth metal ring, of the same green metal that, it was said, was brought by Les Lézards back from Caliban's Island, from the very ship with which – so forbidden rumours told – they had once travelled through space. "When the time comes, this will give you access."

"Your Majesty–"

"Go," the Queen said. And, to Mycroft, in parting – "We will not meet again."

And, or had Lucy merely imagined it, did the Queen whisper, as though to herself, *Not in this life*?

And so, Lucy waited.

The days passed, uneasily.

The Bureau was closed to her. There was no sign of Harker – the agent she was supposed to extract. She pictured him captured, tortured, his secrets extracted. What knowledge was he sent to find? How would he get away? The waiting lay heavily on her. And Mycroft, sitting at his club, seeing no one. Thinking. Trying to unravel a mystery, trusting no one–

Then came the day there was a knock on the door.

It was an impatient, authoritative knock. "Open up!"

She was already in motion, the gun in her hand. Edged to the door, nerves frayed. "Who is it?"

One word, travelling like a chill through the keyhole.

"Fogg."

She opened the door with one hand, kept the gun in the other. But Fogg was alone.

"Oh, do put it down, Westenra," he said, marching in. He shut the door behind him.

"What do you want?" Lucy said.

Fogg said, "I need to know what job you're doing for Mycroft."

Lucy, taken aback, though she should have suspected something like this. "I'm not doing a job for Mycroft."

"Don't lie to me!" Fogg glared at her. Tall and thin and pale, he would have made a good parish priest, or a politician... Or a mortician, Lucy thought, suppressing a shudder.

"What's going on, Fogg?" she said, trying to keep her voice cool, calm. Trying to give him nothing. "I'm in between missions."

"Are you?" Fogg said. "Are you, now, Westenra?"

"Tell me what you want," she said.

"The fat man's gone crazy," Fogg said. He waved his hands in the air, exasperated. "He sees no one! He hides at the Diogenes Club and won't come out. Almost as though he's afraid to step outside. Don't think I am a fool, Westenra. I am left running the Bureau while the fat man sits and eats and thinks who knows what. I'm in charge! And yet I get the feeling I am not. Agents missing, files disappearing, a silence so profound it is a voice unto itself. Tell me what you know."

"But I don't."

Fogg glared about the room. Nothing to see. "This is how you live?"

"On the salary you pay me?"

Fogg snorted. "We pay you handsomely enough," he said, "to sit around and do nothing. Tell me about your last mission."

"My last mission?"

"I know he sent you! I've tracked down transfer orders, the commandeering of a steamer, and one of Mycroft's damned black airships he likes to use so much. Where did he send you?"

"Nowhere," Lucy said.

Fogg's face grew red at this, and when he spoke next his voice was low, and menacing. "Sooner or later," he said, "the fat man will be gone, and I will be in charge. Don't make a big mistake, Westenra. Don't make me an enemy."

Lucy stared at him, the gun by her side. "When the time comes," Fogg said, whispering, "don't say I didn't give you a chance."

He waited. Lucy looked at him. Then, regretfully, she shook her head and said, "I don't know anything."

Fogg nodded. There seemed a world of meaning in that simple gesture, more frightening, somehow, than when he was in motion, when he was shouting. He was very still.

"Very well, Miss Westenra," he said, at last, and his cold, wet eyes surveyed her, the way a shark might look at a diver, sinking fast. "Very, very well."

And, without speaking again, he turned on his heels and marched out, shutting the door, quietly, behind him as he left.

Lucy let out a shuddering breath. She had just made an enemy... She wondered if she could have handled it better.

She hoped Mycroft knew what he was doing.

And this could have been, if only for a while, the end of it.

Only Lucy went and spoiled it by deciding to shadow Fogg.

Soho in the twilight... the smell of opium, spilt beer, lit pipes, the sound of an Edison record playing through an open window, Gilbert and Sullivan's *Martian Odyssey*. Fishmongers closing for the day, the smell of fish in the air, on the ground pools of melted ice, fish scales floating there like compass needles. The moon through the buildings, a scimitar sword. Fogg walking ahead with long easy strides, Lucy in the shadows, an unchaperoned lady but then this *is* Soho and this is, almost, the new age, a new century. Somewhere in the distance Big Ben struck six and all the other clocks followed, a cacophony of gears and bells and echoes, birds flying up in black clouds, startled, a butcher selling sausages by candle light, the gas lamps coming into life, one by one – in the distance whale song, from the Thames.

A beggar boy hiding in the shadows, pale face, big haunted eyes, watching–

She scanned the street, saw his employer standing by an up-turned drum, warming his hands on the fire. Fagin, she thought, and her hand itched for her gun.

But he was considered a Bureau asset, and thus untouchable.

The boy flashed her a quick smile – Twist, was it? – then she was past, trying to track Fogg, who seemed to have merged into the shadows.

Did he know she was following?

She waited, and presently saw his thin frame re-appear, heading for the Charing Cross Road.

She followed him, at a distance. Careful now. The sky was dark. A solitary mail ship went overhead, making no sound. Above the city's skyline the Babbage Tower rose, its beacon light flashing. Booksellers on the Charing Cross Road with open carts, trying to push on her, variously, Marx's latest political tract, *The Second Caliban Manifesto*, Mrs Beeton's autobiography, supposedly signed, *From Household Management to Running the Country: How I Became Prime Minister*, an old, stained copy of Verne's early novel, *Five Weeks in an Airship*, P.T. Barnum's memoir, *A Fool and his Money*–

The books became a dark cloud; they were everywhere; their dust choked the nostrils; there was no escaping them. She saw their sellers as enslaved ghouls, shackled to their charges, the books vampiric, sucking the life out of their handlers even as they sustained them, in their turn. Fogg turned left on the Charing Cross Road. She followed. A seller came at her from the left, unexpectedly. "Mr Dickens' *Reptilian House*, in three volumes!"

"You should never write a third volume," someone else said, nearby. She turned and saw a young man shaking his head, sadly, and she walked past as he and the seller entered a loud argument on the merits and demerits of such a thing.

Where was Fogg going?

Up the Charing Cross Road with the bookshops crowded, books spilling on the pavement, carriages passing, horse-driven, and baruch-landaus belching steam, up past St Giles Circus, and older bookshops opening now, antiquities specialists, and objects in the windows taken from ancient Egypt and Greece and Rome, the Middle Kingdom and Nippon, and she knew where Fogg was going, even if she didn't know why.

Then it came into sight and she paused, momentarily, taking it in as she always did:

The Lizardine Museum.

The treasure chest of an empire.

It was built of the same green, alien metal of the lizards. A dome rising high into the air, its own airship landing platform extended beside it. The dome seemed to shine in the night, a beacon. Huge statues rose up in the courtyard of the museum. Giant lizards, dwarfing the people still milling there, in the open air before the steps. Henry VII, the first of the lizard-kings, a severe, weathered being: they had come back with Vespucci on his ill-fated journey and in one single night reality had changed, and the King and the Queen had disappeared, and Les Lézards were there in their stead.

Henry VII, they said, had never learned to speak English properly, and had used a machine, which translated his speech to the people. Then came another Henry, and this one was almost human, in manners and speech, and Les Lézards became integrated with their human hosts, and began to expand the reach of empire. Then came an Edward, and others, but the statue that dominated them all was that of the Great Elizabeth, the Lizard-Queen, Gloriana, under whom the empire grew and the island of Britain truly became the seat of a global and far-reaching empire, the greatest the world had ever seen.

Lucy stared up at Elizabeth's statue, the inhuman figure, sculpted in the same green metal, as alien as all the rest of them, and not for the first time she wondered what her world would have been like without the royal lizards: would it have been better, worse? Would it have been poorer?

And it occurred to her that, in a very real way, it didn't matter. History took paths and forks, crossing and re-crossing, and yet the human lives lived within those brooks of time were the same. They were short, they suffered the same joys and sorrows, the same weakening of flesh and spirit, whether now or in the distant past, or in an equally distant, unimaginable future.

People didn't change. Only worlds did.

She followed Fogg, up the broad public stairs, into the building.

Worlds of antiquity, rooms full of loot...

The lizards, like their human subjects, had a passion for collecting. A huge open space under the dome and, to every side, and up and down stairs, rooms opened, rooms upon rooms offering, on display, all that centuries of conquest had to offer.

There! Egyptian mummies!

There! The Rosetta Stone!

There! Marble statues from the Parthenon!

There! Ashurbanipal's great library of cuneiform tablets! So many graves had been robbed to fill the museum, so many lands conquered, in blood and iron, and all their loot housed here, in the great museum, itself a mausoleum, a dragon's hoard, all to display, to the empire's subjects, its vast superiority, its utter control.

There was something humbling about that space, and yet, at the same time, something peaceful, soothing: the hush of a vast hall housing the past, like a church or a graveyard, and Lucy followed Fogg and only the sound of their feet on the ground could be heard – past dead Egyptian queens wrapped in bandages, past animal-headed deities and gold jewellery and ancient books, past the knick-knacks and bric-a-brac of Hans Sloane's collection of curiosities, the founding stone of the museum. Down marble stairs, away from the main hall, going underground. Lucy stuck to the shadows. Fogg marched ahead, oblivious. Through an *Employees Only* door, into a dusty warehouse, mysterious objects in crates, shelves upon shelves of ancient artefacts not yet catalogued or presented, the dead possessions of ancient dead cultures. Through another door and another flight of stairs. Down, down, underground. It was silent down there, nothing moving, nothing but dust.

Fogg disappeared.

In the darkness Lucy halted. Pressed herself against shelves. Where was he?

Where, in fact, were they?

Her eyes adjusted to the darkness. Faint light shone, from somewhere. She saw lizard-headed statues with the bodies of men, a scattering of strange coins with lizard heads on them, a script she couldn't read. Strange tapestries hanging from walls, showing reptilian warriors.

Thinking, I thought this place was a myth.

Footsteps in the dark. The sound of a heavy body, slithering. The gun was in her hand but she didn't know what good it would do.

A hiss in the darkness. "Fogg..." The voice made her shiver.

"Master," Fogg said, and the unseen voice laughed.

The room of Unnatural History, Lucy thought.

The room of apocrypha.

She had only ever heard the stories. And how had they managed to get down there, without tripping an alarm?

Fogg must have had access, somehow. And she had coat-tailed it, not knowing...

There had always been stories. Before Vespucci had awoken the Calibans. Before he returned with them, the race of royal lizards, Les Lézards, from that island in the Carib Sea where sand had turned to glass and where they had slept, so it was said, had slept for thousands of years...

But there were always rumours. That some of them had been upon the world, moving like shadows throughout history. Leaving strange objects in their wake. Rumours that the history of humanity and Les Lézards did not start with Vespucci, but went back, over millennia...

Foolish stories. Forbidden stories.

Just as the tale of this room, deep below the Lizardine Museum, where all such artefacts were carefully locked away...

She began to realise just how dangerous her being there really was.

And then thought – where else better to meet in secret?

And who, in fact, was Fogg meeting down there?

"Report!" that insidious, frightening voice ordered, there in the darkness. Lucy moved. She edged closer to her destination, the place the voices were coming from. Slowly, slowly... creeping like a mouse down there in the dusty depths.

There.

A small circle of wan light, Fogg standing taut–

Movement from the shadows–

She stifled a cry of horror, a deep-rooted fear, from childhood, rising up in her like bile–

An insect-like creature, gigantic and obscene.

Feelers moving, stroking, seeing–

A many-legged thing, like a centipede, and yet, somehow, not alive, a mechanical being–

Slithering across the floor of the abandoned warehouse–

Lucy felt faint, the gun almost sliding from her fingers–

Heard Fogg saying, "Master, I can't get the access I need, Mycroft is blocking me, I think he suspects–"

Lucy, thinking, I have to get out of here.

Thinking of rumours, stories, like nightmares that fade when you wake.

Two words. Something to scare children by.

The Bookman.

TWENTY-ONE

"Hush!" said the Bookman.

Fogg said, "What?"

"Were you followed?"

Fogg, laughing: "By whom?"

Lucy pressed against the shelves. The gun would be useless, here, against that... that *thing*.

"I smell... *human*."

"Stop being so melodramatic."

"Report!" the Bookman barked. Fogg said, speaking calmly, "Mycroft won't let me near. He is running his own operation. He never trusted me."

"What do you know of this death in Bangkok? This Alice?"

"An old agent. Retired. To tell you the truth she had gone off the field long ago."

"Then what was she doing dead in Siam?" the Bookman roared.

"Working for Mycroft."

"On what?"

"The Babbage case."

"Babbage..." There was a snort, and a sound as of jaws, locking and biting. "I should have killed him when I had the chance."

"Recruited him, you mean."

The Bookman laughed. It was a horrid sound, and Lucy suddenly realised that it was quite insane. She had to get out...

"What killed her?"

"A Bookman," Fogg said, and there was a terrible silence.

She couldn't stomach it any more. The silence lengthened, unnatural there in the Unnatural History Room.

Why wasn't the Bookman answering Fogg?

A slithering sound, so close... She froze, her heart beating fast.

"I sssssmell you..." a voice whispered. It was a cold voice, it made her shiver. "I know you're there..."

She waited, wanting to bolt, to run–

There was the sound of a crash from above and someone cursed and light came in and there were footsteps–

"Is anyone down there?"

A museum guard. He came down the stairs, shining a lamp around. It cast a pool of light amidst the shadows, and the faces of ancient lizards stared at her, from coins and tapestries and ancient clay tablets.

Was there another exit? She edged away, softly, softly. "Who's there?"

By the wall!

A small opening, an air vent. As quietly as she could she pulled the grille. It came off in her hands.

"It is I, Fogg."

"Oh, apologies, sir! You didn't half startle me!"

"Private business, James. But your diligence is duly noted."

A hiss in the dark, amused or angry she didn't know. "What was that, sir?"

"Just the wind, James. Just the wind."

She placed the grille on the floor and pushed through the opening, head first.

The hissing sound seemed to grow closer.

"Very well, sir." The young guard sounded nervous. "I shall leave you, then."

"You do that, James. You know it's not safe, down here."

"Sir?"

"Just a joke, James. Merely a joke."

The hissing, coming closer – a slithering sound–

She pushed through and found herself in a small crawlspace–

The sound like jaws, snapping shut, behind her. She almost screamed.

"What was that?"

"Relax, James," Fogg said, with a laugh.

"Strange things in this museum, sir," the guard said. "Strange happenings, and sounds at night. I don't mind telling you it makes some of us nervous."

"Maybe you have a ghost down here," Fogg said, and laughed again, the sound like a gunshot. Lucy scrambled to get away. The space led up, she saw. A drop chute of some sort. She needed things to hold on to.

A hiss behind her, a faint whisper, "I can smell you..."

"What was that?"

"Nothing!" Fogg said, losing his calm for the first time. "Rats," he said. "Go away, James, I have work to do."

"Sir. Yes, sir."

She felt something – the walls weren't even, she could grab hold–

She pulled herself up. Heard movement behind her but didn't dare turn to look. Pulling herself again, and finding the next protrusion out of rock or wood, and hauling herself up, one step by laborious step–

The sounds faded behind her, and then she was outside, emerging out of a drop chute a floor up, and it was quiet–

"What are you doing here, miss?"

The light hit her and she jumped, but it was only James, the guard, and she could have hugged him.

"This is a restricted area! My God, you gave me a fright!"

"Dr Fisher sent me," Lucy said, thinking quickly. "To fetch something from the, ah, warehouse."

"How did you get in here? Do you have a pass?"

"Wait," Lucy said. "Look, it's–"

She was close enough to the man now and she hated to do it but didn't have a choice.

"What–?"

Then he gurgled and she caught him as he fell, gently, and laid him on the cold stone floor. Then she ran.

It began to rain as she walked back to her lodgings. Her mind was awhirl with unanswered questions. Fogg, the mole in the Bureau. The Bookman – she had always thought it to be a person, or an organisation of people, all using a common name, a moniker. But the horror she had seen below the Lizardine Museum was no sort of human, it was an alien creature, not even alive – some sort of intelligent machine?

What had Mycroft told her? He had warned her, his words cryptic then. *We are on the cusp of war. Ancient artefacts are awakening...*

Could the thing called the Bookman be one of them?

And yet the Bookman had been active for years – for decades. Disguising explosives, cunningly, in books – that had been his method. There had been the Martian probe case in eighty-eight, but since then nothing – as though the Bookman had disappeared, retired or died...

She had to talk to Mycroft. Had to warn him...

But Mycroft wouldn't see her. He was locked away at the Diogenes Club; he was seeing no one; he was absent from the Bureau; all lines of communication were down. Even Berlyne, when she had cornered him at last, refused to hear her out.

"You do your role," he told her, staring at her despondently from wet, red-rimmed eyes. Earlier when she had tried to talk to him he kept interrupting her, telling her about his flu. "Leave the fat man be. And stay the hell away from Fogg."

Did Mycroft know?

There was no sign of Harker. The fat man was gone, to all intents and purposes, and Fogg was running the Bureau.

She needed information, Lucy thought. She needed a line into the past.

And so, two days later, on a day when the sky was grey and a cold, chill wind blew through the streets, she boarded a train, and went, not to St Mary Mead, where the retirees of the service were rumoured to be housed, but to the place called Satis House, hoping that she could get the woman there to talk to her.

The train had stopped for five minutes at the station and Lucy was the only passenger to disembark. The small village of Satis-by-the-Sea was really nothing more than a high street, several shops, a pub, a tea room, a one-storey hotel that appeared to be permanently closed, a post office and the train station.

Dominating the view was the house. It perched over a cliff above the little village, a vast, crumbling edifice, its broken windows open to the wild wind of the sea. A lonely, snaking path led up to the house. Lucy had cream tea at the tea room, and chatted pleasantly with the proprietress, up to the point when the woman found out her objective. "You are going to see *her*?" she said.

"Why, is she not there any more?" Lucy said.

"Oh, she's there all right," the proprietress said. "If you'll excuse me–"

And she disappeared into the kitchen and did not come back.

Curiouser and curiouser, thought Lucy. She left money on the counter, seeing as the woman had disappeared. Then she went outside and began the long, cold walk up the hill.

The wind was cold; gulls screeched high above, diving over the dark waves. The air was filled with brine and tar, sea smells mixed, faintly, with gunpowder.

Gunpowder?

A shot rang out. Beside the trail Lucy was following, a branch exploded away from a tree, almost hitting her. She stopped, stood still.

A voice through a bullhorn, the speaker unseen. "Who the hell are you?"

Lucy carefully raised her arms. "Westenra!" she called out.

"What? Speak up!"

"Westenra," Lucy yelled. "It's me, damn it, Havisham!"

"Oh." The voice sounded mildly disappointed. "Well, move along, then, girl. Come on up."

"It's what I'm trying to do," Lucy muttered. She lowered her arms and continued up the path to the house.

No wonder the woman in the tea room disapproved.

She made it up there. Overgrown weeds, an apple tree with fruit around it, a sweet-and-sour smell of fermentation. A wrought-metal fence, the garden beyond. A stout oak door that stood in marked contrast to the rest of the house. Peeling paint, broken windows, a general air of disuse and disrepair.

"Havisham? Where the hell are you?"

A small, energetic figure appeared, as though from thin air.

The bushes, Lucy thought, and couldn't hide the ghost of a smile. Havisham's tradecraft was well known, even though that was not what she was primarily famed for. In their circles, at any rate...

"Lucy? Is that you?"

"It's me."

The other woman came and peered at her for a long moment. It was hard to tell her age. Fifty? Sixty? One of the old guard at the Bureau... She wore a man's hunting outfit, carried a gun with her, easily – she was used to it. "Come here," Miss Havisham said. They hugged. "It's been a long time," Lucy said.

"Too long," Miss Havisham agreed, sadly, it seemed to Lucy. She released her. "What brings you to Satis House? I didn't think you even knew where it is."

"I just looked at the map," Lucy said, "until I found the middle of nowhere."

Miss Havisham laughed. "Come on in," she said. "Tea?"

"Yes, please," Lucy said, with feeling.

The inside of the house was a surprise.

The outside, Lucy saw, had been carefully cultivated.

The inside...

The front room was a map of debris but, as Miss Havisham led her farther in, the house changed. The room they went into had carefully maintained windows overlooking the cliffs, at such an angle that they could not be seen from land. A fire was burning in the fireplace and the room was tastefully and expensively decorated. Rugs on the floor that must have come from the Ottoman Empire, sturdy bookshelves everywhere, books spilling out. The room was sunny, the furniture used and well maintained; the whole place had an air of comfortable domesticity to it.

"They think of me as the crazy old lady who lives in the ruined mansion," Miss Havisham said cheerfully. "Which helps. And there are enough alarms outside to warn me of anyone approaching. You never know, in our line of work."

"Quite," Lucy agreed. She watched Miss Havisham place a kettle over the fire and busy herself making tea. "How long has it been?" she asked.

She could feel Miss Havisham tense. "Who can remember," she said, quietly.

The post-eighty-eight fall-out.

The reason she was there.

But first, the tea.

They sat and sipped their drink and watched the sea outside the windows. *Miss Havisham is to be handled delicately*, she remembered the fat man saying, once. *Agents are replaceable, but archivists like her only come once in a lifetime.*

"How *is* Mycroft?" Miss Havisham said, as though reading her mind.

"Oh, very well," Lucy said, carefully. "He sends his regards."

"Good old Mycroft," Miss Havisham said. "What happened wasn't his fault. It was before your time, though, wasn't it, Westenra?"

"Yes. Mycroft…" She hesitated, picking her words carefully. "He sent me for a chat. We need… Some old material has recently come up. Routine. He thought you might be able to help."

"You know I could," Miss Havisham said. "The question is, should I?"

But Lucy knew Miss Havisham, the way she knew herself. For they were all operatives, all playing the Great Game. And once

you played, you were never out. Only death put you out of the
Great Game. What had someone said, long ago? She had heard
the words from one of her instructors in the secret compound
at Ham Common... *When everyone is dead the Great Game is finished. Not before.*

And so she waited, and sipped her tea, and didn't speak. And
at last, the way she knew she would, Miss Havisham said, almost
reluctantly it seemed, and yet unable not to say it, "What, exactly, has come up, Westenra?"

And still Lucy prevaricated; still she waited; until Miss Havisham, perhaps recognising in herself the need to speak, to delve
into the past, to play, once more, the game, said, with the ghost
of a smile and a sharp, yet almost fond, tone, "Well, Westenra?"
Then Lucy began to speak; and even then she idled, she went
around the subject; she took her own time.

"*Sonnets from the Portuguese*," she said, and waited, and watched
Miss Havisham, whose head rose, and she looked out of the window with a far-distant look in her eyes.

"Elizabeth Barrett Browning..." she said. "Yes..."

Lucy waited, patient.

"A small, innocent volume of verse..." Miss Havisham said.
Her voice had acquired a dreamy, sing-song attribute. "Oh, yes...
it was to be placed with great ceremony on board the Martian
probe. The ceremony took place in Richmond Park. It was dusk;
Moriarty was there, he was Prime Minister at the time, yes,
wasn't he, love? And the Prince Consort was there, and that old
rascal Harry Flashman. All of London society, it seemed, had
turned out for the event. Irene Adler, too, though she was but
an inspector in those days. And the boy, of course... he came,
too, but too late to save her."

Lucy waited, her heart beating faster. She was not supposed
to know these things, she knew. But Miss Havisham was beyond
rules and restrictions, now, and recollection for her was an act
of living, like drawing breath or drinking water. Once started,
she would not stop.

"We had watched the boy, hadn't we, love?" Miss Havisham

murmured. Who was she talking to? Lucy wondered, recalling, somewhat uneasily, the rumours at the Bureau. Havisham and Mycroft, they had whispered.

"We watched him, ever so carefully. He was a handsome boy. Orphan. Less a name than a title. And he had a girl, he was in love. Her name, too, was Lucy. Did you know that?"

Lucy hadn't. But Miss Havisham was not stopping to check her reaction. She was speaking *through* Lucy, speaking to the fat man who had left her here, in this crumbling mansion, in Satis.

"A marine biologist. She worked with the whales in the Thames... Did you know they had followed Les Lézards here, on their voyage from Caliban's Island? We had wondered at the connection between them. Could the royal lizards somehow communicate with the whales? Were they their eyes and ears in the ocean? We could never prove anything... Some knowledge was beyond even us."

"Tell me about Lucy," Lucy said, patient, probing. "Tell me about the *Sonnets*."

"It was dusk and, before the spectators, the airship loomed. It was to carry the probe away with it, at the end of the ceremony. All the way to Caliban's Island, there to be launched into space. A big, dignified ceremony and the girl, Lucy, there to place, into the probe, ceremoniously, two objects. An Edison record filled with whale song... and that slim volume of poetry, *Sonnets from the Portuguese*."

Miss Havisham fell silent. Motes of dust danced in the sunlight coming through the window. "Books..." she said, so softly Lucy almost didn't hear her. "They had always been his choice. His little folly, we called it. The Bookman."

"The Bookman," Lucy said.

"Yes. For as the girl came to place the objects into the open belly of the probe, there was a terrible explosion. She died, instantly. The probe was destroyed. Unbeknown to us, it had been a dummy. The real probe was already on the island, prepared to launch..."

"You said there was a boy," Lucy said. She felt shaken. The explosion had been public knowledge, naturally – it would have been impossible to keep it quiet – but Miss Havisham spoke of it as if she had lived through it, though always one step removed.

"Orphan, yes. He tried to save her. Couldn't, of course. Which launched the whole sad affair."

"Tell me."

"Oh, it was one of Mycroft's less successful affairs," Miss Havisham said, with a small smile. "The boy was obviously being manipulated. His father was a Vespuccian, you know. And his mother, as we found out too late, could have been queen, if we still had human royalty."

"Excuse me?"

"When Les Lézards deposed the old, human monarchy, they didn't kill them," Miss Havisham said. "They transported them to Caliban's Island and bred them there. I am not sure why. I am not sure even they knew."

"And his mother–"

"Yes. She escaped – we suspected the Bookman's involvement, at the time. She was killed shortly after giving birth to the boy. Colonel Sebastian Moran, if you recall the name."

"'Tiger Jack' Moran?" Lucy said.

Miss Havisham nodded. "He worked for Moriarty," she said. "Never mind. The point is the boy's heritage was meaningless. The empire was on the brink of revolution, a lizard queen was bad enough, a human king would not have made things better."

"What happened to him?"

"He went to the island. He came back. We lost him in Oxford. There had been an explosion, deep under the Bodleian Library. The boy survived. So did a girl who called herself Lucy…"

"She was *alive*?"

"It was a mess," Miss Havisham said. "You see, we had suspected for some time that the Bookman was not exactly human. That he – it – was a product of lizardine technology, an artefact that had survived their crash on Earth. The theory was that he had been their librarian, of sorts. A servant. A machine for making copies of living things."

A library of minds.

Lucy's own mind shied away from the thought. That creature she saw below the Lizardine Museum. *There had been an explosion*, Miss Havisham had said. Lucy said, "What happened to the Bookman?"

Miss Havisham smiled dreamily. "That was the big question, wasn't it," she said. "He died, of course. In the explosion. But…"

"Yes?"

"Wouldn't a machine that made copies of beings," said Miss Havisham, "first of all make a few extra copies of *itself*?"

PART III
The Two Deaths of Harry Houdini

TWENTY-TWO

The young man who stood, some nights earlier, on the other side of the planet, at the docks of the Long Island, in the territory of the Lenape, was himself contemplating the oddity of replication. There was something miraculous, he thought, in the act of human sexuality, in the way man and woman could get together to produce a new being, an entirely new, alien, mysterious life. An avid reader of the scientific papers – not to mention the somewhat less scientific, yet far more enthralling, tales of scientific romance – *romans scientifiques*, to give them their better known name – he had been fascinated, too, by the idea that it may be possible to produce identical copies of living human beings – even of dead ones, when it came to that.

The nineteenth century may be drawing to a close, he thought, yet what a century it had been! The greatest minds of many generations had seemed to erupt, all at once, across the world, to further humanity's understanding of the universe it had, somewhat reluctantly, occupied. Babbage! Freud! Jekyll! Frankenstein! Darwin! Moreau! The great Houdin, in Paris, AKA the Toymaker, from whom the boy Weiss had taken his professional name, which was Houdini. Scientists of the mind, of the body, of the laws of nature and the laws of history!

And yet, he reflected ruefully, his knowledge – actual, concrete knowledge – of asexual human replication was greater than most, having had cause, as it were, to experience the unpleasant thing at first hand.

But first, a concise history. The boy was in the nature of going over facts, summaries, all a part of his rather rigorous training.

Well then.

```
Code name: Houdini.
Birth name: Erich Weiss.
Place of birth: Budapest, the Austro-Hungarian
Empire.
Father: Mayer Samuel Weiss, a rabbi.
Mother: Cecelia Weiss, née Steiner.
Family: five brothers, one sister.
Recruited to the "Cabinet Noir" in 1890, at
the tender age of sixteen.
Specialities: escapes, disguises, locks of any
kind.
Recruited by: Winnetou White-Feather, of the
Apache.
Assignments: the boy was sent to the World's
Vespuccian Exposition, in the city called
Shikaakwa, or Chicagoland, during the ninety-three
affair. He had been only an observer at the time.
Notes: the boy is a promising young agent — his
recruiter, Winnetou, speaks highly of him. His
cover as a travelling-show magician is promising,
and his skills in the art of escapology remark-
able indeed. Young, handsome and personable, the
only concern is due to a blank period two years
after the White City Affair, when the boy went to
spend a summer on the island of Roanoke…
```

Harry – he preferred Harry to Erich, had been using the name more and more now, until only his family still called him by his birth name – paced the docks. He waited for a ship but the ship was long in coming. He was leaving Vespuccia, that magnificent continent, his adoptive home, leaving behind him the tribes and the new cities, the vast open plains and a sky that seemed never to end, under which one could sleep, in the open air, as peaceful as a child...

He was nervous, excited. He was being entrusted with a great mission. After a tour of the continent earlier on, when he went from encampment to encampment and town to town, performing his magic show, under the moniker *The Master of Mystery!* he was now ready for a new challenge. He was leaving Vespuccia, for the first time–

Had been summoned to the Council of Chiefs one day, weeks before, at the Black Hills, the Mo'ohta-vo'honnaeva in the language of the Cheyenne. Arriving late one night, with a silver moon shining over the hills like a watching eye, Houdini was met by his old mentor. "Winnetou," he had said, hugging him. The Apache warrior hugged him back, then said, gruffly, "You took your time."

"I came as soon as I received the summons," Harry said, without rancour. "And as fast."

"Come with me," Winnetou said.

Harry followed the other man into the camp. The Council was not often convened in full. The chiefs of the Nations met at different places, at different times. It was a very different form of rule, Harry thought, then the one in Europe, with its rigid monarchies and obsolete blood-lines. The Nations had welcomed the refugees from that continent, those who did not wish to live under lizardine rule, but there was no debate over who, exactly, was in charge. Yet the Council was troubled. There was the ever-present threat of the Lizardine Empire, while Chung Kuo, the Middle Kingdom, had recently showed dangerous signs that it was considering expansion for the first time in centuries. While on their own doorstep, so to speak, the Aztecs waited, in their strange pyramids and with their own designs on the land...

Harry was taken to the circle of the Council. President Sitting-Bull, smoking a pipe, looked older than he had in ninety-three, the last time Harry had seen him.

And all the major nations were represented that night. He saw familiar faces, old generals: Sioux and Cheyenne and Cherokee, Apache and Arapahoe and Navajo, Delaware and Shoshone, Mohawks and Iroquois and others, all sitting under the great silver moon, all turning to watch him as he came.

"The young magician," someone said. Someone else laughed. Harry felt his cheeks turn hot. He didn't let it bother him. Instead he smiled. "You wished to see me," he said.

"Cocky."

"Youth always is."

"Sit him down, Winnetou."

Without ceremony, Winnetou pressed Harry on the shoulder, pushing him down. He sat, cross-legged, before the chiefs. A great fire was burning, down to coals, on the ground, and the smoke rose, white like a flag, into the air.

"There's been… a situation."

"We need you to go on a bit of a journey."

"You won't be alone, of course."

"We're recalling most agents."

"You've been trained well. As well as can be."

"We want you to go to Europe. To the home of the lizardine race."

"Others are heading to Asia, Mexica, the South Seas–"

"We need to guard our interests–"

"The world is changing, boy. We do not intend to be caught unawares–"

He sat there, the conversation washing over him, overwhelming him. The chiefs, almost not looking at him directly, their words in the air. All to impart the importance of his mission on him. *This is why you are here.*

"Danger in the stars–"

"Old artefacts, awakening–"

"Go, boy. Winnetou will brief you."

A hand on his shoulder. Pulling him up. Smoke in his eyes, the stars, like the moon, bright above. Drums in the distance, the sound of chanting, the smell of burning tobacco–

"Come on."

Winnetou led him away, amidst the tents.

And now he was waiting at the docks, for a ship to take him, across the sea, to the island where Les Lézards ruled.

To find out...

What, exactly?

He remembered vividly the events of the World's Vespuccian Exposition, in ninety-three...

The spinning wheel, which they now called a Ferris Wheel, after its inventor, moving against the starry night sky... Houdini had been dressed as a fakir, his skin darkened by sun and cosmetics... performing magic there, in the avenues of the White City, illuminated by electric lights... Tesla himself had been there, lightning wreathing his body...

Houdini watching – the woman from France, the agent, he was told, of the Quiet Council... She was formidable.

Milady de Winter. Hunting a murderer in both cities, the Black and the White, in that place called Chicagoland... and hunting something else, also. A mysterious object, a lizardine artefact...

The Emerald Buddha. An object of mythical resonance. Discovered in the Gobi Desert, centuries before, a jade statue in the image of a royal lizard. Carried by a man. If he had a name Harry didn't know it. He was designated, simply, as the Man on the Mekong.

But he had come to Vespuccia, had crossed the sea, and come to the White City – supposedly to offer the statue to the highest bidder. But that had been a ruse...

The White City had been plunged into darkness. High overhead, on the axle of the Ferris Wheel, two tiny figures: the Man on the Mekong and Milady de Winter. And the wheel spun, faster and faster, until the space within it was distorted, and strange, alien stars had appeared...

The wide avenues of the White City were filled with screams... bodies fighting in the darkness to escape... There had been a terrible voice, filling the night, only it was not in the ears, it was in one's head... a cold, impersonal voice, speaking no language but directly into the mind itself, filling it with the horror of infinity.

And up there, on the wheel, a third figure, climbing – the killer de

Winter had come to find, a man mutated and made grotesque by the power of the statue. That awful voice, speaking: Initiating target parameters. Stand by to receive. *A struggle up there, and in the space beyond the wheel, that alien space, something moved...*

The voice saying: Gateway open. Coming through–

A scuffle, and the killer flying into the space inside the wheel, the statue in his hands, opening–

And the voice, saying, Gateway sequence interrupted! Explain! *And a mental shriek that burned through the brain, and everyone down below clutched their ears, trying to block it, and the voice saying,* Gateway linkage shutting down.

And something had come through the gateway, from that alien space inside the wheel. A dark, saucer-shaped vehicle, hovering in the air...

Then it was gone, like a mirage, like a bad dream.

He should have known, back then, that it wasn't any kind of ending.

It was out there, somewhere. An alien vehicle, an alien intelligence directing it. Where did it go?

And that had not been the worst of it. No.

The worst of it had been that, fifteen minutes later, Harry had died.

TWENTY-THREE

Would the ship never come?

In the harbour, there on the Long Island, a plethora of ships: Arab *baglahs*, Chinese junks, a French steamer, three Aztec longboats, trade ships from west Africa – from the Kong and Dahomey and Asante empires – a couple of Swahili cargo ships, three lizardine tea-clippers, and others: sailboats, dugouts and steamships all crowded in that harbour, coming and going, but the ship Harry was waiting for wasn't there.

No whalers. Whale-hunting was punishable by death across the Lizardine Empire and, through bilateral agreements, beyond it. Like human slavery, it belonged in the days before Les Lézards. Were they, Harry wondered now, not for the first time, truly enemies of humanity? Many argued over the centuries that the coming of the lizardine race had, by extension, benefited humanity, had stopped some of its more heinous actions. And yet, was it right to let an alien race rule over you?

Harry felt ill at ease. For he knew one… being, at least, who did *not* think it right, and who had made it their life's mission to oppose the royal lizards.

But he didn't want to think about that. Did not want to think

of Roanoke, any more than he did of that awful moment in the
White City...

Even after it was over, after that alien space within the wheel
had disappeared, when the screams of the passengers in the
wheel's cars had stopped, when that alien vessel had disappeared, flying at high speed away from the White City, even
then chaos reigned.

The White City: a marvel of an age, a brand-new city erected
especially for the Fair, enormous buildings, wide avenues, a multitude of visitors–

Plunged into darkness now, and fear, and uncertainty–

People running through the streets, trying to find a way out–

And others taking advantage of the situation.

*The White City had been filled with the criminal class. Not just that
killer Milady de Winter had been sent to catch, the man they called the
Phantom, who had called himself H.H. Holmes, perhaps in mockery of
the great detective... There were cut-purses and pick-pockets and confidence men (and confidence women), tricksters and robbers, and in the
darkness even those who had not come to the city to commit a crime could
be tempted, nonetheless, to take advantage of the situation.*

*Harry had walked in the dark, as lost as the rest, trying to locate
de Winter, trying to gather information for the* Cabinet Noir, *that
secret organisation that was the Vespuccian equivalent of Les
Lézards' Bureau...*

*So intent that he did not notice the movement behind him, did not
quite hear the snick of a blade–*

*The man had smelled of sweat and stale tobacco and gin. The blade
flashed, once, in the moonlight–*

*Harry remembered the surprise, more than anything else, more than
the pain – the surprise and the hurt of it, which was somehow worse,
and then it flamed through him, and he tried to breathe, or scream, but
no sound came, and he gurgled, helplessly, and sank to his knees, blood
gushing out of his throat, and the man's breath was very close to him,
he stood behind him, supporting him as he fell, almost gently...*

He was dying, Harry had suddenly realised, and it made him want to cry. He wasn't ready! He was not yet twenty years old! What would his mother say? It couldn't be happening, not to him, not like this–

The man had rifled through his pockets and had come away with the money and everything else. Then he ran. Shouts in the distance, but Harry's hearing was going, and he could see nothing now, and would never see again... He felt the life slipping away from him. He could have cried.

He died.

Harry paced the docks. Swahili sailors speaking in a beach argot with Melanesian islanders, Lenape officials supervising the off-loading of cargo, porters loading up bags of coal onto the French steamer. Harry's mission was simple: go to London, find out what you can, try to stay alive. It almost made him laugh.

You will be briefed further upon landing.

They needed him to track down Babbage. Lord Babbage, who had not been seen these five years or more. Who, for all intents and purposes, could well be dead.

But Harry knew even death was not always an end...

He had woken with a gasp. Air, cool blessed air, came into his lungs. He cried out. He was lying on the floor, in a doorway. The electric lights were burning again, and an air of gaiety filled the White City.

Harry put a hand to his throat. Nothing there. No cut, no blood–

He was alive.

Slowly, he sat up. He looked about him. What had happened? Again, he felt himself. Nothing. No injury, no pain...

Had he dreamed it?

He stood up. He felt fine...

Something was very wrong.

The memory was too real.

And, when he checked his pockets, his belongings were gone.

So he really had been robbed.

Had he just taken a knock on the head? Had he hallucinated dying?

A sudden sense, of being watched.

He stepped into the street. It was as if nothing had happened.

He knew he should report it to his superiors.

But he never did.

And I was wrong, he thought, pacing the docks. I was wrong not to.

But it was too late now.

And there was the ship, coming in.

The *Snark*.

Harry thought it was a strange name for a ship.

And now it docked, and the gangplank was laid down, and the captain descended. A young man, even younger than Harry. Quite jaunty. When he saw Harry he smiled, and extended his hand.

"You're Houdini?" he said. He had an enthusiastic, almost boyish smile. "I saw you on stage, in Fort Amsterdam –" a small town in the vicinity, built by the European refugees on leased Lenape land – "you were very good."

"Thank you," Harry said. He found himself returning the smile. "Captain–"

"London," the man said. "Call me Jack." He smiled again. He smiled easy. "Dad's an astrologer," he said.

"Mine's a rabbi."

London slapped Harry on the back. "Come on up!" he said. "We're heading to my namesake town, are we? My band of desperadoes usually sails hereabouts, but I'm guessing the Cabinet Noir wanted someone to keep an eye on you." He laughed, but Harry, this time, did not return the feeling.

Was London there to keep an eye on him? Did they know? Did they suspect?

He followed the captain up the gangplank and onto the deck. "Maybe you could perform for the boys," London said. "Later."

"Be happy to," Harry said.

It was partly that strange event at the World's Vespuccian Exposition that had led Harry, a year later, down to the island of Roanoke.

Officially, he was on a mission for the Cabinet Noir. Strange, unexplained phenomena have always plagued that part of the world. The Roanoke themselves now shied away from the island. Back in the day they had leased it to one of the earliest groups of refugees fleeing the lizards' rule, but that small colony had disappeared, and the events surrounding that disappearance were never adequately explained.

Harry remembered it as a happy time. He performed sleight-of-hand, close-up magic routines, the sort of magic that required no heavy equipment but whatever was to hand. For a while he abandoned coins or cards completely, preferring to use natural materials: making a stone disappear, making water appear out of a leaf. Magic that required no language, a visual kind. From the Roanoke he learned of the creature they called, somewhat uneasily, Coyote.

Coyote was known and revered across Vespuccia; but for the Roanoke the name had evolved a different meaning. Was it a recent thing? Harry tried to find out – "Yes," some said. "No," said others. Stories were confused. Some said Coyote had been seen for centuries. Some dismissed the stories altogether.

"Was Coyote behind the Roanoke Colony's disappearance?" Harry asked.

No one knew. The subject made people uneasy.

"It steals people," one told him. "In the night."

But others said that, no, it brought people back from the dead.

They told the story of one man who had died and was resurrected by the creature they called Coyote. The man had been killed in battle.

"What sort of battle?"

"Oh, a disagreement of some sort," they told him. It had been one of those wars between villages, long ago.

"What happened to the man?" Harry asked.

"He had been shot, several times. He died."

"And then?" Harry asked.

"Three days later he was spotted, alive, without a scratch on him. Riding his horse under the full moon. He was never seen again."

"Just stories," someone told him. But Harry was uneasy.

The activities of this Coyote seemed to centre around Roanoke island. It had remained uninhabited once the colony had disappeared. But sometimes, at night, Harry was told, strange sounds came from the island, and strange lights could be seen, at all hours, moving and shifting. "The place is cursed–"

"It is sacred–"

"It is both."

They would not object to his going there. But they would not accompany him, nor take responsibility in the event he never returned.

In the event, of course, Harry *didn't* return.

Or, rather unfortunately, he did.

Both of which proved the Roanoke right.

He sailed to the island one day, by canoe. He had rather enjoyed the ride. The island, from a distance, appeared deserted. He beached the canoe and set out to explore.

He wasn't armed. "Spies," Winnetou once told him, "should kill only as a last resort. Spies *watch*, Erich. Spies are eyes, not hands."

Still, they had trained him for both, but the thought of killing made Harry ill. Serving your country was one thing. Killing in its name was another. He knew he was not cut out to be a great hero in the big game of life, or in the secret Great Game of the shadow world. He was not a killer. He was an entertainer, a magician. He liked people. And he liked people to like him. There were names – Milady de Winter of the Quiet Council, the man known only as Smith, who was a legend in that most secretive of branches of British Intelligence, the organisation they called the Bureau – who were famed as ruthless assassins, cold-blooded killers, second only in stature, maybe, to the shadowy Bookman.

He, Harry, was not like them. Could not *be* like them, and didn't want to.

And yet here he was, on this island, alone, looking for–

For what?

He didn't know.

And, somehow, that was worse.

He didn't know what he would find. He went to the village. It had been built by that vanished colony of refugees, long ago. It was still there – empty houses falling down, empty windows reflecting nothing, rusting plates and cups still laid out on tables where no one sat. A sense of age permeated the village; a sense of abandonment, of disuse. It was not scary, to Harry. Rather there was a feeling of sadness there, of incompleteness, and he wandered through the houses like a ghost.

Until he came to a ring of ash on the ground outside.

He stopped, and stood stock still.

Nothing. No sound. The call of a single bird in the distance.

The sun, growing low on the horizon...

He knelt down. A ring of stones, blackened by fire, with ash inside. Just an open-air fire, the way he had seen them, and built them, and sat by hundreds of times.

He touched the ash, gently, with two fingers.

It was still warm.

The day was still – too still. He felt as if the sun froze, dying, in the sky. No breeze, no birds – he rose to flee–

Felt something hard and unmistakable against his back–

The barrel of a gun.

TWENTY-FOUR

Harry had rebuilt the fire. It was burning now, and the sun had set, and the night was very dark, there in the abandoned old village, there on the island of Roanoke.

There were two of them sitting by the fire. Harry – and the man with the gun.

"Call me Carter," he had told Harry. He had kept the gun trained on him, at a distance. There was little chance of escape, as yet. Harry may have been a magician, an escapologist even, but even a consummate performer cannot outrun a .45.

He didn't try to.

"What do you want? What are you doing on the island? Who sent you?"

But the man seemed unfazed by the questions.

He had a brown, deeply lined face, strong hands that seemed to have spent a long time outdoors, in manual labour. He smiled, but even when he did Harry could sense a sadness in him, and his eyes belied his face, and made him seem far older than he appeared. There was age there, and stillness, and regret... "I'll answer all your questions," the man, Carter, told him. "What I want is peace. What am I doing here? I was waiting for you. As for who sent me... that, too, will become clear to you."

So Harry, with ill grace, acquiesced.

There was nothing else he could do.

And the man Carter, he thought, looked far too comfortable with the gun.

And so they sat across the fire from one another. Carter had a flask of whiskey. They shared it. It was old whiskey, smoky and smooth. The fire threw sparks into the night. There were many stars overhead. Harry, with a strange sense of acceptance, waited.

It was as if he had been waiting for this moment, it occurred to him, ever since that strange night in Shikaakwa. The night he had dreamed that he died. As if he had been waiting for answers, had come all this way somehow knowing – almost as if the knowledge had been implanted in him, unconsciously, some time back – that he would find them here.

On Roanoke.

And so a sense of calm had settled on Harry that night. And yet, within it, there was also anxiety, an anticipation as of a man fearing attack, who knows it is coming but doesn't know when, or from which direction – only that he couldn't stop it when it came.

Carter, meanwhile, roasted a couple of fish on the fire, and they ate them, Carter one-handed; he would not relinquish the gun. They also ate yams that had been dug into the earth below the coals, so that they came out steaming-hot when opened, and their flesh was sweet. They drank the whiskey, not talking, until they were done and so was the drink.

Then: "Let me tell you a story," Carter said.

I was born (Carter said) *on this island, the child of English adventurers fleeing the rule of the Lizardine dynasty. Carter is not my real name. What my parents were called no longer matters…*

Life on the island was hard, but happy. Our small colony existed by permission of the local tribes (this was before the establishment of the Council of Chiefs and the federal arrangement currently in place). My sister, Virginia, was born two years before me and we often played together. Our colony was small, beginning with just over one hundred people, and growing by two dozen children after some years. As I grew up I began to travel more and more on the mainland, learning hunting and trapping, fishing in the streams, and learning the languages and customs of the nearby tribes. I was very happy for a time.

Then disaster struck.

I had returned from a long journey. I must have been away a year or longer. When I reached the island, they were gone.

Men, women, children. My own parents, my sister, my friends. The houses remained, empty. Food was left rotting on untouched plates. Clothes left hanging in closets. It was as if they had all simply got up at the same moment and… disappeared.

I was beside myself with grief. I could find no trace of them, no hint as to where they may have gone. One message, only, I found, carved into the trunk of a tree, in my sister's hand.

Croatoan.

It was the name of a nearby island, but more than that, it was a code between Virginia and me. In our childhood, Croatoan was the place where stories happened, where heroes went in search of maidens to rescue, where dragons guarded treasure… but more than that, it was the place we banished the night frights to. The ghosts and monsters of a child's sleep we banished to Croatoan. Waking up in the night, hearing an unexplained noise, we would shout, "I banish you, devil! I banish you to Croatoan!" – and the ghoul or ghost or demon would depart, and we would sleep secure once again.

Only a child's game, a comfort of the imagination… and yet at that moment, when I saw the message carved into the tree, I knew that something I had thought impossible had happened, that the dream world of my childhood had somehow materialised, a door opened, and took my sister, my parents, my friends with it.

For a long time I was inconsolable. A shaman I knew confirmed my suspicions. The island had always been unlucky, he said. People had disappeared there before – for centuries if not longer. I grew very angry at that. "Why did you not warn us?" I said.

"But we did," he said. "Your elders believed it naught more than a tale, such as to frighten children."

I was no longer a child, yet I was afraid. I determined to find the door to Croatoan, if such existed. Yet none could be found. The old shaman suggested the "openings", if such they were, depended on a number of variables, and may not be replicated in my lifetime. For a long time I despaired...

Then, one night, alone in the woods, I met a monster.

It was quiet in the night. Harry stared into the flames. It had grown cold, there, and a wind blew in from the sea. He shivered and drew himself closer to the fire. When he looked at Carter the gun was still aiming at him, but the man's eyes were far away.

I never saw it clearly (Carter said). *I had built a small fire and was sitting with my back to a tree, roasting a fish I had caught earlier in a nearby stream – the same as we do now, you and I. Almost I felt peaceful then. All thoughts of my despair had momentarily left me. I was happy with a pipe, waiting for the fish to cook. Then, taking forever what small contentment I may have one day achieved, he appeared to me.*

He, it – I still do not know what to call it. A thing out of nightmare, a giant centipede-like creature, but not alive. A machine, perhaps. A strange machine, that came seeking me there in the wilderness of the Chesepiooc country. I had not felt its approach, and when I did it was too late. Through shadows he moved, and his arms, if such they were, held me captive. Its feelers moved. "You know this land well," its voice said.

"As well as any," I said.

He chuckled at that. "Are you not afraid?" he said.

I did not reply. "Yes," he said. "I can tell you are. Your heart rate and blood pressure indicators are suggestive of the fact. Yet you remain cool, coherent. That is good. I may be able to use you."

"I was not aware I was an appliance," I said, which made him chuckle again. "To be used or discarded by monsters."

"Oh, I am not the monster," this strange being said. "I, too, was once a tool and have been discarded. No. I fight the same evil your parents escaped from. Would you help me?"

The lizards? I had heard the stories of these strange beings, of course, but they meant nothing to me. I had heard they were no worse, as rulers, than the human family who once controlled the British Isles had been – better, in fact.

"I bear those on the British throne no ill will," I said, and he tightened his grip on me at that. "You shall be my agent," he said. "Yes... you will fight the good fight alongside me. I am the Bookman."

The way he said it – it was chilling. More than a title – a description, an essence of everything he was. "What is a Bookman?" I said.

"One who preserves knowledge," he said. "Which is a precious thing."

"That sounds harmless," I said, and those were the last words I spoke before he killed me.

"What?"

Harry's head snapped up. The man, Carter, was smiling at him, but there was no humour in the smile, and his eyes were cold.

"How could you..." Harry's voice shook. "How could you have died?" he whispered. "You're alive. This is a lie."

"And yet, here you are," Carter said. "Why did you come here, Harry Houdini? What trail were you following, what doubts were you trying to assuage?"

Harry opened his mouth, then closed it. No sound came. He did not know what to say.

Carter nodded. His eyes studied Harry, and told him that he *knew*–

Yes. I had died (Carter resumed). *It was the first, but not the last time...*

The Bookman... That strange creature could be likened to a monk, perhaps. A copier of illuminated manuscripts. Only, for the Bookman, human beings are the manuscripts. And so he copied me, destroying the original, and in the process improved me, changing me to suit his needs. I was to be his agent, his errand runner, in spying and assassinating, in waging his cover war against those who may have once been his masters: the reptilian race of Caliban's Island, masters of the Lizardine Empire that steadily continued to grow despite the Bookman's efforts.

Les Lézards.

And what did he offer me? Why did I follow his command?

He gave me life. My new body did not decay, did not grow old. I was stronger, faster, a machine in the semblance of a man. He gave me the time I needed. Wait for the door to appear again. Wait, to follow my sister into the other side of nightmare, into Croatoan.

Of course, I had asked him about the disappearance. Yes, he said. There were such anomalies. There had been machines designed to open such temporary portals between realms. Semi-sentient Quantum Scanners, he called them. There had been several on the ship, he said.

It's strange… Over the decades I had spent considerable time with the Bookman, and we grew to talk. He was a lonely being, I think. Alone and abandoned, like a child forgotten by its parents. Lonely and angry with it, carrying on with his war, building his small army… "Tell me about Croatoan," I said to him once. I was living in the city of the lizards then. We met in the Bookman's secret place under the city.

"It is nothing," he said dismissively. "A pocket world. A place for…"

"Yes?" I said.

He was always wrapped in shadows. He hid himself so well… He said nothing for a long moment. Then, "It is a place for the dead."

At that my heart began to pound. "Are they dead, then?" I demanded. "All this time, have I waited in vain?"

"No," he said. Then, "Perhaps. I do not know."

"You keep secrets from me," I said, and he laughed. "Secrets are my business," he said.

I continued to serve him. I continued to wait. I travelled periodically back to Roanoke. Back here. "A one-way trip," the Bookman called it. "If such a device does in fact exist, and is present on the island, it would be only half-tuned. There were four modules on board the ship, if I recall correctly, and only one could facilitate a full bi-transference node. And that would require an initiation signal… Be careful. They can be…"

"Yes?"

"Cranky," he said. "And remember. If you go – you will not come back."

"Will you not require me still?" I said, and he laughed, and his words chilled me. "Why, I have another one of you in storage already," he said. "Just in case I need you, and you're not around."

The night was still. In the distance, lightning danced in the sky, too far away yet for thunder to be heard. The night felt charged, electric.

"I couldn't have that," Carter said, almost apologetically. "I couldn't let him resurrect me, endlessly, his agent, his toy, playing forever the Great Game." There was a hard finality in his voice.

"Did you ever...?" Harry wasn't sure what to say. All his senses screamed danger, but he felt himself unable to move, to act. "Did you ever find them? Where they went?"

The look in Carter's eyes was one he remembered later. Pain, and something else, deeper, harsher.

My last visit to Roanoke... it was a century ago, or so. It gets hard to keep time, after a while.

I knew something was different as soon as I set foot on the island.

The colour of the sky was different. The brightness of the sun had dimmed, and the world was muted in its colours, a grey and misty vista. There were unfamiliar smells in the air, swampy and damp, and when I stepped on the ground my feet sank easily, leaving behind them lonely markers, the only sign of living in this desolate place.

It had changed. Was changing. I could feel it in the wind, and when I came to our old settlement the change had become profound.

Transparent they were, the houses. I could see through walls into the living quarters beyond. Out settlement was ebbing in and out of existence – impossibly, majestically. It was then I began to hear a voice.

What it said I was never certain, afterwards. It seemed to mutter, directly in my head. A litany of complaints, perhaps. It reminded me, strangely, of the Bookman. There was a loneliness in the voice, an anger born of being abandoned. Something deep underground, perhaps. A semi-sentient quantum scanner, whatever that is.

I knew, then, as I stood amidst the ruined houses flickering in and out of existence, that I had to choose.

Go back. Leave the island.

Or go in. Follow them, into the unknown.

Into Croatoan.

"What did you do?" Harry whispered. But he realised he already knew the answer. For Carter was sitting there, talking to him. Which meant he couldn't have–

"I followed them," Carter said. "I had to. My sister, my family...
I could not turn back from the unknown."

"But you're–"

"Here? Yes."

And Harry realised, and a shudder passed through him, and
in the distance he could hear thunder, now: the storm was getting closer.

"So you're..."

"The copy." Was that amusement in Carter's eyes? Or an-
guish? "The other me went into Croatoan, to that shadow world,
and the Bookman remade me, and this is where my memory
ends. For another century I had served him as his agent. I am
tired, now, Harry Houdini. I am very tired."

"It hadn't been a dream," Harry said.

"No."

"I really died, in Shikaakwa? In the White City?"

"The Bookman had been interested in you for a long time,
Harry Houdini. And when that man cut your throat in the dark,
the Bookman saved you."

"I died?"

Carter smiled, and his teeth were white, and rain began to fall,
big fat drops of warm rain, and thunder sounded, close by now.
"I am tired now, Harry Houdini," he said. "And you are young
enough to die."

"Wait," Harry said, "don't–"

The gun in Carter's hand exploded with sound. Pain erupted
in Harry's chest. He heard three shots, and then he heard
nothing.

He came to on the ground. In the ring of stones the fire had died
and the partially burned wood was damp. The rain had stopped,
the storm had passed the island. It was morning. There was no
sign of the man who called himself Carter.

Harry felt himself.

No injuries, no pain...

Suddenly he had to get off the island. He was trapped in a

nightmare and he couldn't get away. This was madness. He was hallucinating, he was–

"Mr Weiss," a voice said.

And something came crawling out of the vegetation, a nightmare figure, like a giant invertebrate, and Harry suddenly knew, with an aching clarity, that none of it had been a dream, and that, twice now, he had died.

TWENTY-FIVE

The journey out of Vespuccia was uneventful. London and his team piloted the *Snark* ably through the Atlantic waters, and Harry found himself with little to do. He practised coin manipulation and cards and lock-picking, and did his regular exercises with a strait-jacket he had brought with him, with the crew aiding in ever more elaborate incarcerations and watching, half in amusement and half in awe, as he escaped from each one.

His latest had been an underwater attempt. The crew tied him into the strait-jacket, manacled his feet, put him in a canvas bag and dumped him overboard.

When he had surfaced, minus the chains, he figured he could use it in his next act.

But mostly, Harry waited. There was that feeling of anticipation, a calm before activity, the way he felt just before going on stage. Soon he would have to perform. For now, he could rest, wait, prepare himself. The way Winnetou had taught him.

He often thought of the past. If Winnetou had been his first recruiter, Harry had come to realise that the strange man who had called himself Carter was his second. Without willing it or wanting it he had, in the professional term, been *turned*. A spy, he didn't know where his loyalties lay. With the Cabinet Noir – or with the Bookman.

Perhaps with neither. He had begun to understand what Winnetou had told him. "All of us, who work in the world of shadows, are but shadows ourselves," the man had told him. "We cast no shadow of our own."

It was his way, Harry thought, of telling him a fundamental truth. That shadow operatives were to be used, as pieces on the board of a great game, but that, just like chess pieces, they had no inherent loyalty to one side or the other. It merely depended on who played you first.

He was a magician, at home with illusions and secrets. And yet...

Perhaps what it came down to, in the end, was simple: he didn't like to be played.

He had never seen Carter again. And his new master – his new *controller*, in the parlance of the trade – was a strange being, a thing out of nightmare, and his desires were hard to decode. Harry never saw him again, either. From time to time, using established protocols for contact, he met with, or received messages from, other human agents of the Bookman. There was little to compromise his position with the Cabinet Noir. The Bookman showed little interest in intelligence coming from there. Harry suspected, in particularly uneasy moments, late at night, that the Cabinet Noir was not unaware of their new agent's subversion. That, just possibly, the Council of Chiefs and the Bookman had... an understanding.

Both, after all, were opposed to Les Lézards. And, if that was the case, he was not a double agent at all, but serving a common purpose.

He preferred to think that, at any rate.

When the island of Great Britain came at last into view it seemed enormous, a grey fungal shape rising out of the harsh ocean, and Harry felt his excitement building. He did not like the wait, the anticipation. He was glad it would soon be over. There were great events unfolding around the world, and he would be a part of them.

It seemed so odd, that a relatively small, insignificant land-mass, off the European mainland, a place of foul weather and little, by all accounts, going for it, would become such a powerful player on the world stage. What was it that drove these people to spread out across the world the way they had? Was it, simply, a dogged determination to avoid the British weather? Or was it something else, some colonial imperative taking hard, tempered shape, until like an iron noose it had slowly but surely tightened over the world?

He didn't know. Something in that need to control, to con-quer, frightened Harry. And yet, as strange as it seemed, there was something exciting about it, too.

The *Snark* sailed through the mouth of the Thames and Eng-lish towns came into view gradually, a great human sprawl, with factories belching steam along the river and many boats, and Harry saw mechanicals in one, automata they were called, as real as if they were human, and the sailors waved at them. The air was cold and the taste of salt and tar was gradually replaced by the smells of humanity, of vegetation and refuse, and they came, gradually, into the city.

It was growing dark when the *Snark* came into the docks. Harry stood on the deck, watching the city. It was a symphony of light, the red sky lit with an unearthly glow as the dying sun gave way to gaslight. Majestic airships sailed through the air above the Tower of London and, in the distance, the great pyramid of the Royal Palace shone in that strange, alien green. Upon the water a multiplicity of crafts sailed, longboats and steamers, sailboats and dhows and ferries going back and forth from north to south bank. Over the city's skyline rose the Babbage Tower, like a strange and ancient obelisk pointing at the sky. The bridges of the city arched over the river, London Bridge gilded and shining with the images of giant lizards, and far away the bells of Whitechapel and Shoreditch and Bow and the booming of Big Ben.

"There she goes," Jack London said, coming to stand beside Houdini. "Gay go up and gay go down," he said, speaking softly, "to ring the bells of London town." He smiled sideways at Harry. "When will you pay me? say the bells of Old Bailey. When I grow rich, say the bells of Shoreditch." The *Snark* was coming in to the docks, but Jack's eyes were looking at the distance, and the setting sun. Harry shivered, and didn't know why. Whatever Jack was reciting seemed harmless, a nursery rhyme of some sort. "Pray when will that be? say the bells of Stepney. I do not know, says the great bell of Bow."

At last Jack tore himself away from the horizon, and now looked directly at Harry. "Here comes a candle to light you to bed," he said, speaking so softly Harry had to strain to hear him. "Here comes a chopper to chop off your head…"

The boat, with a gentle lurch, came to a rest. The sailors were throwing ropes down, whooping in anticipation of dry land. But Harry felt cold, and the words of the nursery rhyme gripped him with a sudden fear that he couldn't shake off.

"Chop chop chop chop, the last man's dead!" Jack London said.

PART IV
Paris in Flames

TWENTY-SIX

Midnight in Paris.

The moonlight reflected off the green metal that had once made up Notre Dame. The ruined cathedral had been made, long ago, by Les Lézards, and subsequently destroyed in the Quiet Revolution, when automatons and humans took France back for themselves, and made it an independent republic.

Punks de Lézard hung around the ruined edifice, humans obsessed with the lizardine line, altering their faces and skin to resemble that of lizards: a part of the process involved elongating and then splitting their tongues, so that they hissed when they spoke, and their skins had been tattooed with alternating bands of colour. Smith, watching, felt the fear in the night, and the anticipation. The Punks de Lézard were feral creatures, murderous and territorial.

Smith was standing motionless in shadow. The left bank of the Seine, in the shadow of a bookshop, watching. The Seine slithered like a snake nearby. Smith waited.

Presently, he heard the sound of unhurried footsteps, approaching. The sound of a match being struck, the flare of a flame, the glow of a cigarette, the smell of burning tobacco. Then the man resumed his walk, came closer.

"Smith," he said.

Smith stepped out of the shadow. Extended his hand.

"Van Helsing," Smith said.

He had come to France by fishing boat, departing the Limehouse docks on a ship that had halted, mid-channel, to let him out: the fishing boat had been waiting and picked him up and dropped him off on the continent, near Calais. From there he took the train to Paris.

I can bring her back, the Bookman had said. Smith knew he could. It was not the first time the Bookman had made such an offer.

"What do you want?" he had asked, there in that underground, disused sewer.

"Find the Harvester," the Bookman had said.

"Do you know what he is?"

"He is a machine. A probe. A device for gathering information. It is not unlike me."

"Old–"

"No."

That single word was chilling.

"The lizards," Smith had said, carefully, "they must have come *from* somewhere."

"Yes."

"We never thought to ask from where, or whether there were others still there…"

"Yes."

"And now they know?"

"Now," the Bookman said, "they know of this world. And they are curious."

"Is that a bad thing?"

"When a child is curious about ants," the Bookman said, "does he speak to them? Or does he examine them with a magnifying glass, and sometimes burns them, just to see what would happen?"

Smith felt his hands close into fists, relaxed them with some effort. "How?" he said. "How does he – it – gather information?"

"The same way I do," the Bookman said, and laughed, but there was no humour in that sound. "By extracting their minds, their memories, the way they think and feel. Your friend Alice, my old adversary, Mycroft, and all the rest of them – they are stored, now, inside him. Inside the Harvester."

Smith shivered. It was cold, and dank, inside that abandoned sewer. The Bookman, he remembered, had always exhibited a certain fondness for underground lairs. He said, "What would you have me do?"

Find him. The words of the Bookman were still in his ears. *Find him, and signal. And I will come. One of me will come.*

"We have a problem," Van Helsing said.

Smith looked at him. The man, like him, was getting old. Once he had been legendary, eastern Europe and the Levant his speciality. A shadow operative and a fellow assassin, he worked alone, and served no master. He was also the Bureau's contact man for Paris.

"What?" Smith said. Which one? was what he was thinking.

"There had been a break-in at the Bureau," Van Helsing said. He spoke quickly, passionlessly. "Shortly after your somewhat... spectacular display over London. Someone – some*thing* – broke in, as if all the security measures in place meant nothing. A hulking, giant figure. Analysis suggests it was a human infected with what would normally have been an overdose of Frankenstein-Jekyll serum. Know anything about that?"

Oh.

"Possibly," Smith said – admitted – thinking of the Comte de Rochefort. So the man had survived the airship crash?

"What happened?"

"It seems the intruder made it all the way to Zephyrin's lab," Van Helsing said, "and retrieved an unknown object."

"How do you mean, unknown?"

"I mean it was not registered in any of the files," Van Helsing said.

"Something of Mycroft's?" Smith said, uneasy.

A Black Op? Off the books. For the Fat Man's Eyes Only.

"What did Zephyrin say?" Smith said.

"Zephyrin was thrown halfway across the lab," Van Helsing said. "And smashed into a wall. He was not available for comment."

"Who else was there?"

"Berlyne was manning shop. They're both alive, but neither of them's in any position to talk right now. Fogg's tearing out what's left of his hair."

Which was the only thing to cheer Smith up right then... He said, "So do we have *any* idea what's missing?"

But he already had an inkling.

The fat man had been obsessed with Les Lézards. "We need to understand them, study them, learn their ways, their history," the fat man had once told him. It had been a summer day, somewhere in Asia, near the Gobi Desert, in land that could have belonged to the Russians, or the Chinese, or the Mongols, depending on who you asked, and whether you bothered to in the first place. Early days, when Smith was young, though Mycroft was so terribly fat even then...

They were sitting in Mycroft's personal airship. The fat man had insisted on travelling by air whenever possible. He said he liked the comfort. The airship had never been given a name. Nor was it registered.

Officially, just like Smith himself, it did not exist.

They were there on what the fat man had called a treasure hunt. There was a team of archaeologists, and a local guide, and security men who never spoke, and Mycroft's personal chef, Anatole.

"What are we looking for?" Smith had asked.

"A token," Mycroft said. "Something old, that was lost."

Smith had only just returned from his training with the man who called himself Ebenezer Long. Smith called him Master. Even now he knew little about him. The monastery sat high up in the Himalayas, in a hidden, snow-bound valley. Master Long had taught Smith the art of *Qinggong*: the Ability of Lightness. There had been a strange, Buddha-like statue, made of jade. It had allowed Smith and the others seemingly impossible feats:

almost as though they could fly through the air, on unseen wires. Mycroft had questioned Smith at length about the statue. But it had disappeared shortly after Smith had arrived at the monastery, and he didn't know what he could tell the fat man.

"Ancient devices," the fat man had told him. "Proof of the lizards' extraterrestrial origins. And signifiers of our future, Smith. Our past has been changed by outside forces, and our future is uncertain."

And so, each day, they scanned the desert, searching for that treasure, or that proof, or that ancient device. But they had found nothing.

Smith followed Van Helsing along the narrow streets of the Latin Quarter. Booksellers displayed their wares and people sat outside numerous brasseries, drinking wine, talking, laughing – it felt to Smith, at that moment, as it came on him, at unexpected times throughout the years, that he had chosen the wrong profession, and that the shadow world could not stand up to the light, to life lived openly, in warmth and joy. Then he thought of the break-in at the Bureau and his suspicions, and what it could mean to those people sitting there, so care-free, unaware of the possible danger that could be threatening them, and the feeling, as it always did, passed.

He was what he was, and the world needed shadow as well as light.

Back then, on that long-ago expedition to the Gobi, they had come back empty-handed. But what if the fat man had continued to look? And what if he had found something?

An ancient, alien artefact, of unknown powers... and Zephyrin had been tinkering with it.

Worse – now the demented, physically transformed monster that the Comte de Rochefort had become must have it in its possession. Which meant the Quiet Council...

They needed a man inside the Council. A sleeper agent, someone who would have an inkling as to the Council's actions, its intents.

Luckily, they had exactly such an agent in place.

TWENTY-SEVEN

They'd stocked up in the Latin Quarter. A tailor shop whose owner doubled as an arms dealer provided them with firepower. Van Helsing went for a double-barrelled shotgun over his shoulders, two Colts by his sides, a long, slender knife strapped to his arm, and some grenades, as an afterthought. In his long dark coat, his tanned face and deep blue eyes, he looked formidable, the Hunter of old.

Smith rarely favoured guns. This time, though, he accepted a hand-made Beretta, complete with silencer, and added a handful of knives. He hoped guns would not be required.

"The Hunter and the Harvester, working together, eh?" Van Helsing said. He sounded mournful.

"Just like in the old days."

"We never worked together in the old days."

"Think you're past it?"

"It's been a while since I killed anyone."

"Miss it?"

Van Helsing sighed. "Not in particular," he said. "To be honest with you, I saw this posting as my little retirement spot. You know what they say–"

"Paris is the last posting before retirement," Smith said. "Yes…"

They were walking towards the cathedral now. Notre Dame, shining that strange luminous green in the moonlight. "What did you have planned for after?"

"I thought a teaching post in Amsterdam, possibly," Van Helsing said.

"Cheer up," Smith said. He felt the knife strapped to his arm. It felt good to hold a weapon again. "It's possible we won't even have to kill anyone tonight."

"Stranger things have happened," Van Helsing said, still a little mournfully.

The observer, meanwhile, was feeling a little confused.

This city was not like the others. It was awash in what the humans called Tesla radiation. It was a chatter of conversation. It was a city of machines as much as humans, and the machines talked. They were machines of an antique and obsolete kind his masters had forgotten long ago, yet here they were, thinking engines, primitively powered, but thinking all the same.

And talking.

A lot of their conversation was about him.

What he was, and what he wanted.

The observer almost wanted to join in on the conversation. There was something exhilarating about it, about other machines, a kinship of sorts. The voices inside him had been multiplying recently. They all wanted to talk, all the time. The observer paid them little mind.

He was following a simple trail. The humans had a legend, about a boy and a girl in a forest and a trail of crumbs. The observer was following a trail of crumbs, and the crumbs were human minds.

But they weren't only human minds.

And right now he could hear such a mind, an old mind, somewhere. It was screaming.

It was a mind that was neither human nor of the human-like machines, but something like an ancient relative of the observer itself.

Some relic of a distant past, a mind disturbed, perhaps insane. This bothered the observer. He decided to try and find it.

They walked through the ruins of Notre Dame. Punks de Lézard hissed at them, revealing claws surgically grafted onto their hands. Besides Smith, Van Helsing smiled, showing teeth, and pushed aside his long coat, revealing his guns. The punks hissed at him but kept their distance.

"We need an entry into the catacombs," Van Helsing explained. "There should be one around here somewhere–"

They moved in shadow; the moon cast pale reflections of their bodies against the ruined metal and their shadows multiplied around them, like the ghosts of past selves. Smith shivered. Could the Bookman really bring back Alice? Was Alice's mind truly trapped, now, in the confines of some strange and alien machine? Was she aware of what was happening?

Where would the Harvester go next?

He was following the Harvester's trail, and it was leading, step by step, to Babbage. But what would he, Smith, have done in the Harvester's place?

He would not have rushed, headlong, towards the target, he decided.

He would take his time, find and isolate the other links in the chain.

And the chain led to Paris, and so–

"Ah, there it is," Van Helsing said. He kicked debris away and revealed a trapdoor set in the floor. Van Helsing knelt, took hold of the solid brass ring attached to the door, and pulled. The door opened upwards, smoothly, as though it had been recently oiled.

"After you," Van Helsing said, courteously.

Smith peered down the hole. Metal rungs led downwards, into the earth. He lowered himself, began to climb down. Van Helsing followed.

The ladder terminated a short while later. They stood on hard stone ground. It was dark but, as they began to move, the passage opened up and there was light, and Smith could smell wood smoke in the distance, and meat cooking, and heard, faintly, the sound of a harmonica, playing.

"Welcome to the catacombs," Van Helsing said.

They began to walk, unhurriedly, keeping a distance between them. Van Helsing's hand was on his gun. Smith was cradling his blade. The space around them expanded again, the ceiling rising higher as they went deeper into Paris' underworld. A rat scampered past, alarmed by their progress. There were cells cut into the stone on either side. Some were empty. In one he saw a young mother cradling a child. She looked up at him as he passed and her eyes were empty and when he looked down he saw she was holding a wooden doll, and the doll was staring at him and it blinked, startling him.

"Edison dolls," Van Helsing said. "Be careful of them. The Edison Company manufactured them, complete with Babbage engine and rudimentary voice. They... were not a success."

Smith seemed to remember rumours, about Edison and his obsession with creating the perfect, female doll... He wondered where the man was, what side of the Great Game he played on. They walked on.

In one of the cells three automatons huddled around a fire. They were in a deplorable state, stuffing sticking out of holes in their bodies, one missing an arm, another a leg. They passed around a flask of what Smith, at first, took to be whiskey. Van Helsing paused and spoke briefly to one of the machines. "Petroleum," he said, noticing Smith's gaze. "Come on."

"What did you ask them?"

"Where our man is."

Petroleum...

Smith knew what it was, of course.

A sort of fuel, highly flammable... There were high concentrations of it in Vespuccia and–

The Arabian Peninsula.

They used it for light, predominantly. But now it looked like the French machines could use it for power, rather than steam?

A group of Punks de Lézard distracted him. They came out of the shadows, surrounding the two men, silently, their claws extended, their forked tongues hissing. Smith and Van Helsing moved in tandem, not breaking stride. Smith's knife was buried in the first man's belly before the man had time to gasp. Smith lowered him gently to the ground and stood above him, looking at the others calmly, while Van Helsing covered them with his twin guns. No one spoke. After a moment the punks went and picked up their fallen comrade and dragged him away, back into the shadows. Smith and Van Helsing moved on.

The tunnels widened and narrowed, unexpected turnings leading farther down, until at last they came to a wide space where fires burned and groups, carefully apart, sat – beggars and automatons and Punks de Lézard, and Van Helsing said, "This way."

They went along the wall, and the inhabitants of that underground place carefully avoided looking at them. For a fleeting moment Smith thought he saw an old, Asian man move, too swiftly to distinguish features, and disappear into the darkness. It made him uneasy, and he thought of his old master, Ebenezer Long, of the Shaolin. Could the secret world of the Wulin, those hidden societies fighting the dowager-empress, also be involved?

And if so, what were they after? The *Erntemaschine*? The secrets Babbage must hold? Or something else entirely?

The object stolen from the Bureau, whatever it may be?

Van Helsing stopped, and Smith followed suit. They were standing in a branching tunnel away from that main hall.

"What–?" Smith began, but Van Helsing, with a gesture, silenced him.

They waited.

Presently, there was the sound of shuffling feet. A small, hunched figure appeared ahead of them, growing closer, until it was before them. Then it stopped.

"Van Helsing," the figure said.

"Q. Thanks for coming."

Smith examined the man. He was short and dark-skinned. He was also a hunchback. "I'm Smith," Smith said. The other man looked up at him, grinned. "Your reputation precedes you," he said.

"What can you tell us, Q?" Van Helsing said. He looked ill at ease. His hand was on the butt of his gun and he kept glancing sideways, checking both sides of the tunnel. "What is the Council up to?"

"Rumour has it the Comte de Rochefort was fed a little of his own medicine," Q said, and his eyes twinkled at Smith. "But he survived. And came back with a prize."

"Do you know what it is?"

"No," Q said. "But it has them all excited. Viktor himself is working on it, I hear."

Viktor. That name again, Smith thought. The scientist they had tried to steal from the French, and failed, repeatedly.

"Can we get access to it?" Van Helsing said.

"I don't see how," Q said. "Breaking into the Quiet Council's secure area would be madness. There are measures in place to–"

"Where is it?" Smith said. He, too, had caught Van Helsing's unease. "Where's the nearest access point?"

"Not far," Q said. Quickly, sensing their changed mood, he gave them directions. He had lost his smile. "I have to go," he said. "You will not succeed in breaking in."

"Let us worry about that," Smith said, when–

There was a sudden crash, the tunnel shook–

Smith reached out to steady himself against the wall–

A voice, animalistic and full of hate, roaring–

Hot breath with the stench of rotting flesh filling the tunnel–

"Smeeeeth…"

Van Helsing and Smith, moving together–

Pushing the hunchback to the ground, behind them, covering him – Van Helsing with guns drawn, Smith with the knife–

A huge, repulsive figure appeared in the mouth of the tunnel. A giant in the semblance of a man, muscles bulging from torn clothes, a demented look over a leering, engorged face with massive, yellow fangs for teeth…

"I'm coming for you, Smith…"

The huge mouth moved: a grin.

Smith stepped forwards, standing between the others and the monster.

"*Bonsoir*, Comte de Rochefort," he said, politely.

So the man had indeed survived his fall from the flaming airship.

The Frankenstein–Jekyll serum had worked.

But the fall had certainly made him angry.

Smith grinned. It felt good to be here, facing one of his old enemies. *"Je m'appelle Smith,"* he said. He nodded at the monstrous figure before him, almost in affection. *"Je suis un assassin."*

The thing that had once been the Comte de Rochefort roared. Then it charged directly at Smith.

TWENTY-EIGHT

At the moment the giant body rushed him, Smith jumped. The Comte de Rochefort sailed past him as Smith, turning in the air, landed behind him. His knives flashed. The comte roared in pain and outrage and green-yellow blood, like pus, came streaming out of the gashes in his back.

The confused Rochefort turned, but Smith turned with him, using the creature's bulk to his advantage. The wounds, he saw with alarm, were already closing. He jumped on the giant man's back, one hand over the comte's throat, and the knife came to rest against the side of the man's neck, ready to go in and finish the job.

But he had underestimated the Comte de Rochefort. With a roar of rage the beast bent and with one flowing motion threw Smith off. He hit the wall and pain exploded in his shoulders. He fell to the ground.

Blinking tears of pain away, he saw Van Helsing step forward, both guns extended. "Eat lead, Frenchman!" Van Helsing shouted (a little melodramatically, the winded Smith nevertheless thought), and the guns burped once, twice, catching the giant monster in the back and, as the monster turned, in the chest.

The comte roared, holes opening in his chest, bleeding more of that yellow-green blood. The blood hissed when it touched the ground. Acidic, Smith thought, horrified. And the comte had intended the Frankenstein-Jekyll serum for *him*.

He stood up. It was time to finish the job. The knife flashed, flying through the air, finding the comte's neck with unerring accuracy. A jet of blood sprouted out of the wound, burning a hole in the nearby wall.

The Comte de Rochefort, trapped between Smith and Van Helsing, turned this way and that. A look of incredulous horror was etched into his face. Then, unexpectedly, he laughed. The roar of his laughter filled the underground chamber. With one meaty hand the comte pulled out the knife. Already, the wound was closing.

"You can't kill him."

Smith had forgotten the hunchback was there. The Comte de Rochefort, looking confused, peered at him, as though trying to identify a half-remembered face.

"It's me," the hunchback said, gently, reaching out a hand to the giant monster. "Q. You remember?"

The comte grunted. Something about the hunchback's manner seemed to subdue him.

"I helped Viktor with the experiments, you know," Q said. He was speaking softly, as to a child. "He tested animals at first, rats, then rabbits, then monkeys. Then he began to test it on people."

The hunchback approached the Comte de Rochefort, and the great hulking beast let him. Smith remained in place. He was winded, and his knees hurt, and he was out of breath.

Getting old.

"They suffered," the hunchback said. "Do you know how they suffered? They used to scream, in their cages. For hours and hours and hours, there in that underground facility, where there is no day, only night." He looked up at the comte, and his big, innocent eyes were tranquil. "I used to sing to them," he said, softly.

Van Helsing had been cautiously moving away from the comte. De Rochefort, suddenly noticing, hissed. "Shhh..." Q said. Then he began to sing.

• • • •

Paris, the catacombs, night.

Smith, slowly, cautiously, rising from his fall.

Van Helsing, sliding against the wall, blood on his lips.

In the centre of that underground tunnel, two figures, facing each other. The giant, deformed, hulking figure of the man who had once been the Comte de Rochefort.

And, facing him, the diminutive, hunchbacked figure of Q, of Notre Dame de Paris.

Who was singing.

The comte growled. Q, undeterred, kept singing. He had a high, reedy voice, not unpleasant. It seemed to fill the small, enclosed space.

"*Au clair de la lune, mon ami Pierrot,*" Q sang. "*Prête-moi ta plume, pour écrire un mot.*"

Under the moonlight, my friend Pierrot, lend me your pen, so I could write a word.

"*De la lune…*" the Comte de Rochefort said. The words came out of his misshapen mouth with difficulty. Smith could only stare at the giant, no longer bleeding, as it knelt down to be closer to Q.

"*Ma chandelle est morte,*" Q sang, *my candle is dead.*

"*Je n'ai plus de feu ouvre-moi ta porte pour l'amour de dieu.*"

There was something chilling in the innocent words, this lullaby for children the hunchback was singing. *My candle is dead, I have no more fire. Open your door for me, for the love of God.*

"*L'amour…*" the Comte de Rochefort said, captivated. Q did not turn away from him. "Go," he said, in the same soft, singsong voice. "Go, find Viktor's lab. Finish your mission. Go!"

Van Helsing came to Smith and, supporting each other, they limped away, the clear sound of Q's singing following them all the while.

"Eat lead, Frenchman?" Smith said. "Really?"

Van Helsing had the grace to look embarrassed.

They found the place, but they got there too late.

The door would have been hidden in the rock bed, but it had

been blasted open, from the inside. The security would have been a nightmare to break through, even with an F-J serum, but there was no longer any need.

The door had been blown, the metal oozing on the ground as from an unimaginably strong source of heat. Van Helsing and Smith exchanged glances, then Van Helsing gestured with his head at the opening. Smith nodded.

He stepped carefully over the still-steaming door, and into the dark opening. He went to one side then and Van Helsing, following, took the other. They stood, silently, trying to evaluate the scene before them.

"What," Van Helsing said softly, "has happened here?"

Smith shook his head. He couldn't imagine.

They were standing in a large, open cavern. The ceiling of bedrock extended high above their heads. A pool of light engulfed a surgeon's workspace, large metal dissection table, while against one wall a series of cages stood.

Smith gestured. Van Helsing followed him, along the wall, to the cages. They were full...

Smith did not know what they were. Perhaps, once, they had been people. Now they were changed, each one differently. Man-machine hybrids, a child with the sad beak of a parrot and small, grimy wings sprouting from his thin naked shoulders, a woman in a black iron mask, rocking her knees, humming tunelessly, something that looked like a human-sized frog, an automaton with a human face–

What joined them all together was the silence. Smith had expected screams, a cacophony of sound. But the caged creatures did not make a sound, and when he approached closer they shied away, pressing themselves against the walls, trying to stay as far away from the bars as they could.

"What–"

"Look," Van Helsing said. He pointed at the far wall. A hole had been blasted into it, by the same unknown source of heat. Yet the chamber was quiet, and there was no sign of an intruder, or a device capable of generating such power...

Smith, for the moment, gave up on the beings in the cages. He went over to the operating theatre–

Which was where he found the body.

Almost tripped over it, in fact.

"Over here!" he called. Van Helsing came running. Together, they looked down at the man on the floor. He was wearing a white lab coat that was no longer white. It was stained a deep, crimson red.

Blood.

Smith knelt down, put his fingers to the man's neck. There was a pulse, weak but steady. He looked up at Van Helsing.

"Viktor," Van Helsing said.

Smith nodded.

"What happened here?" he said.

Van Helsing said, "I don't know."

"Search the chamber," Smith said. "I'll see if I can wake our friend here."

Van Helsing was already moving. "We haven't got long," he said. But Smith shook his head, though the other man couldn't see it. "It's too quiet," he said, but softly. A breach like this should have alerted seven kinds of security forces by now. That no one had showed up...

Suddenly he was very concerned.

A sense of urgency gripped him: that this was beyond a confrontation with de Rochefort, this was something larger than a break-in into the Quiet Council's secure research facility. For the Great Game was exactly that, a series of moves and countermoves, quantifiable and understood: a *game*.

But this was something else, something he could not understand. He ran his hands over the fallen man, searching for wounds, then tore open the lab coat.

Underneath it the man's body was singed, and the smell filled Smith's nostrils, making him gag. He stared in horror at the man's burns. They had to get him to hospital, to a doctor.

The famous Viktor...

He said, softly – "Can you hear me?"

Van Helsing, circling – "Smith, I can find nothing."

"The object?"

Van Helsing didn't answer, and Smith knew they were both thinking the same thing.

Could the object have done this? Had Viktor, somehow, managed to activate it?

He shook the fallen man. How could he be burned *under* the lab coat? Why wasn't the coat burned, too?

Had he put it on later? Had someone else dressed him?

Suddenly he was afraid of a trap again. Feeling his heart beating fast he tried to shake the scientist. "Can you hear me? Viktor!"

Suddenly the man's hand shot up and caught hold of Smith's wrist. Smith shouted, surprised. Van Helsing ran over, the sound of his feet on the hard ground filling the cavern with echoes. Viktor's eyes shot open, staring straight at Smith. The man's hold on Smith's wrist was supernaturally strong.

Had he been experimenting with the serum on himself?

"They're here," Viktor said. His face twisted. Smith could not release himself from the man's fevered grip. Viktor's burned chest rose and fell painfully.

"Who's here?"

"They're here! You have to warn…"

He faltered. His eyes lost their focus. His grip slackened. Smith released his hand. "Serum," he said. "Get him some serum!"

"I'm looking," Van Helsing said, sounding irritated.

"Viktor. Viktor! Can you hear me?"

"Viktor…" the man whispered. He licked his lips.

"What did you do, Viktor? What happened here?"

"Voices… I heard… voices."

"I don't know what these things are," Van Helsing said. "There's enough medication here to start a hospital, but nothing's properly labelled."

"Yellow… serum… top left… marked… *privés*… tell… tell him."

Smith repeated the instructions. Van Helsing returned. "What is it?" he asked, curious. And – "Should I give it to him?"

"It can't hurt…" Smith said. The sense of urgency, of *wrongness*, had not left him. Why had they not been disturbed? Why had no one come to the scientist's aid?

"Viktor," he said, speaking gently. "Do you want your medicine?"

"Medicine..."

"What happened here? Did you activate the device?"

"The device!" Viktor's face underwent a transformation. And now he looked frantic. His hand shot out again but this time Smith was prepared and avoided it. "They came! They're here! Run!"

"He's insane," Van Helsing said.

But Smith had a feeling something had gone very wrong indeed.

"Give him the serum," he said. "I think we need to leave. *Now*."

Van Helsing shrugged. He primed the syringe, pulled up Viktor's sleeve and, without due ceremony, inserted it into Viktor's arm, pushing the liquid in.

They watched the scientist's body shudder. And now Smith noticed that Viktor's exposed arm was *filled* with similar signs of injections.

"My God," he said.

"What?" Van Helsing said, still sounding irritated.

"He's been using this stuff for months," Smith said. "If not years. It's probably the only reason he didn't die."

Viktor's eyes opened again and a new light shone in them. Smith noticed, with sick fascination, how their colour changed. They were becoming yellow. And now Viktor smiled, his body shuddering. His smile reminded Smith of a rabid dog he had once had to kill. Suddenly revolted, he got up to his feet. "Let's go," he told Van Helsing.

"What about him?"

"He'll live."

"The Bureau would have wanted him."

"We have no time for that," Smith said. "Leave him."

The scientist on the ground screamed suddenly, startling both of them. His body twisted and jerked, and he began to howl, and the caged creatures began to howl along with him, filling the air of the cavern with a sudden, unbearable cacophony of screams.

Smith shuddered. "Come on!" he said. He moved, suddenly desperate to get away. Van Helsing followed and they left the chamber, the screams continuing behind them as they began to jog down the dark tunnels of the undercity.

"We were fools!" Smith said.

"I don't understand–" from Van Helsing.

"We need to get outside."

Was it Smith's imagination, or were there far more people down below than there had been before? They stared at the two old men, running, and made no move but to shy away from them. Desperation drove Smith. A feeling he had been late, too late for far too long. They ran, following high ground. At last they came to one of the exits out of that subterranean maze.

"I... could do with... a break!" Van Helsing said, panting.

Smith pushed open the door. They were on the right side of the Seine, having traversed the underground passages below the river, coming out near the grand municipality building, the Hotel de Ville.

Which was on fire.

"Why is it so light?" Van Helsing said.

Smith, panting, had his hands on his knees and was sucking in air. But the air was full of smoke and it made him cough. The Hotel de Ville burned and, as Smith straightened, he saw it was not the only building on fire.

He looked up, not believing what he saw. All over the city skyline, flames were pouring upwards, bellowing like demons – from the Louvre, to Bastille, to the Place de l'Opera and to Concorde. And now Smith could hear the screams–

"Look!" Van Helsing said. He raised a shaking, pointing hand in the air.

Smith raised his head, shaded his eyes. And now he saw them. Giant, hulking shadows moving in the sky above the city. They were vast, inhuman machines, giant tripods moving jerkily, like metal spiders, over the Parisian skyline, belching fire in all directions.

"We're too late," Van Helsing said, softly.

And Smith, numb, could only echo what Viktor had said.

"They're here."

PART V
The Further Chronicles
of Harry Houdini

TWENTY-NINE

Where the hell was his contact? Harry Houdini thought irritably. England was cold and wet and the streets were unsafe, and he was shivering now, his clothes damp, as he skulked outside a Limehouse tavern, the *Lizard's Claw*. The unmistakable smell of opium wafted out from within the establishment, quite pleasant, really, and in the sky above the city a silent storm of lightning played in silence, reminding him uneasily of that night on another island...

He palmed coins and practised sleight-of-hand as he waited. His instructions had been very clear. He had followed standard procedure from the moment he had disembarked at the docks. Ensured he was not being shadowed. There was no reason for him to be, of course. No one knew who he was, or his purpose here. At least, no one should.

He had made his way to this place, getting lost on the way. But he made it. Only there was no sign of his contact, and Harry's busy hands suddenly stilled, and his short hair, cut from that thick dense of curls that was his heritage, prickled.

Something was wrong.

He hugged the shadows. Alarm was telling him to leave, to try and make the fall-back meeting, but curiosity got the better of him. Slowly, as unseen as he could make himself be, he circled

the *Lizard's Claw*, scanning his environment, shadows and fallen
masonry and piles of refuse: this was certainly not the high-end
part of town one imagined when one thought of the Old World.

In the distance, the whales sang, plaintively. There was something haunting about their song, and for a moment the world
around him dematerialised, and he saw, instead, the same world
with no humans in it, an ocean-world for which the land masses
of continents were but a fleeing distraction, a great and deep
blue world in which giant beings moved in the depths and sang
across thousands of miles, calling to each other...

Then it passed and he went around the back of the *Lizard's
Claw* where the smells coming out of the kitchen made him suddenly hungry, and he almost stumbled over a prone object.

He cursed, and righted himself.

The carcass of a boar or a deer, perhaps.

Did they have wild boars, here?

Sounds of singing from inside. Someone came out from the
kitchen and Harry froze, but the figure merely threw a reeking
bucket of dirty water onto the street – narrowly missing him –
and went back inside, leaving the door slightly ajar.

Harry cursed all Englishmen, but quietly. The sliver of light
traversed the dirty back yard of the tavern and came like the
blade of a knife to rest against the hurdle Harry had hit.

He drew in his breath in a short, sharp intake like a gun shot.

Not a deer. Not a boar, either.

A human leg, in sensible grey trousers, and a sensible black
shoe, polished, though scuffed at the heels. Harry knelt to take
a better look.

A human body, the leg twisted unnaturally. The street was
very quiet. All his senses were alert, for the most minute sound,
but there was nothing. The body had been wedged, without ceremony, into a crumbling break in the low stone wall of the
street, which the tavern staff probably used to put rubbish in.
The smell, indeed, suggested rotting offal, and that was mixed
with incense ash and cheap oil that had been reused so many
times it was mostly burned fat. Grimacing, Harry pulled at the

leg, drawing the corpse out, slowly. It was lying on its front. As he dragged it out he was aware of a dark, viscous liquid that had pooled around the corpse. Blood. The man was young and had worn a cheap but respectable suit. There was something strangely familiar about him. His left hand had been out-stretched in death, one finger, dipped in his own blood, pointing helplessly at nothing. Harry retched without sound, the smell suffocating him. Then, gently, he put his arms under the dead man's body and turned him over.

The man's head lolled back, dead eyes staring at Harry, and he bit down on a scream, hard.

No no no no no.

He stood up. It was too dark. Yes, he thought, helplessly, it is too dark to see clearly. I am hallucinating. The brain finds pat-terns in the dark that don't exist.

With trembling hands he reached for a box of matches in his sensible suit's pocket. The first match broke. The second one took flame for one brief second and then blew out. Harry cursed, knelt by the body, cupped a third match in hand and managed to light it and sustain the flame. He moved his hand over the man's face.

No no no no no!

Helpless, Harry Houdini stared at the dead man, his contact person, lying there on the ground in a pool of blood and offal and scum.

No wonder he had seemed familiar, he thought, with a mix-ture of dread and despair.

The flame of the match hovered, illuminating in stark relief a young, not-unhandsome face.

A face as familiar to him as his own.

"Oh, Harry," Houdini said. Gently, he teased a lock of dark, curly hair from the dead man's brow. "What have they done to you?"

The face that stared back at him, impassively, with dead and vacant eyes, was his own.

• • • •

Harry crouched by the body, thinking hard. He had long suspected the Bookman may have been cooperating, to a greater or lesser extent, with the Council of Chiefs. Their goals, after all, could be said to be, if not exactly the same, then nevertheless at least parallel to each other. Did the Council know his secret, then?

Had they despatched a second *him*, another Houdini, ahead of him to the lizardine isle?

They must have, he thought, shaken. For this man was to be his contact here.

And had been murdered, and left for him to find.

Someone would pay.

Still no sound, the street very still, and suddenly he was afraid. *Too* still… almost as if he had been expected and now they were watching him, whoever they may be.

The opposition.

In the shadow game, that could be anyone, even your own side.

Quickly now, he went over the dead man's belongings. He knew there would be a hidden pocket *here*, a false heel in the *left* shoe, another hidden compartment *there* – all emptied out. Someone had done a thorough job on the dead man. On *him*.

And yet…

Harry paused, intrigued. The other him's finger was pointing, he had thought, at random. But what would *he* have done, if he had perhaps seconds to live, and needed to leave a message?

As a child he had loved the penny dreadfuls, out of the continent. He would have written a message, in his own blood, he thought.

But the dead man's finger was pointing at a mound of rubbish, not at an inscribed and bloodied message. It was pointing at pig intestines going off, and a reek of urine, and rotten cabbage.

Unless…

He hated to do it but he made himself. He dug into the pile of refuse. The stench was awful and when he disturbed the remains of the pig a cloud of dark insects rose, buzzing angrily, into the air.

His hand quested, coated in slime. It was quite possible there was nothing there. But he searched, blindly, until his fingers found a rectangular, soggy form. He withdrew it carefully, brought it close to his eyes. Paper, he thought. Thick, and good quality, to have withstood its tribulations. It smelled rank. He peered at it, but could see little in the dark.

Some sort of visiting card, he thought, and felt excitement rise in him. A lead. He hoped – he prayed – it was a lead. Or otherwise, he – the other he – had died in vain.

And now he was alarmed into movement. He would be found, identified – he couldn't let it happen. He picked up a stone and smashed his own dead face in, over and over, until nothing remained but a bloodied pulp. He threw up then, but the deed was done. The corpse, when it will be found, would be that of an anonymous man, not of Harry Houdini.

He still had the sense of being watched. And now the tavern's door re-opened, and a head stuck out and said, loudly, "Is anybody there?"

Harry straightened up. The voice said, "Hey, you, what do you think you're–"

Harry ran. Behind him, an indignant shout, then footsteps and then a much louder scream, as the speaker discovered the bloodied mess that had been left there. Harry ran through the narrow streets, not sure where he was going. At last he found the river and followed it, the Thames snaking deeper into London, taking Harry with it, and as he ran the vast dark shapes of whales rose beside him in the water of the river and keened, as if they, too, mourned the passing of Harry Houdini.

THIRTY

He found shelter at a hotel in Seven Dials, a run-down dismal place worthy of its name, which was Bleak House. The proprietress, a Mrs Bleak, with a gummy, toothless mouth, wrinkled her nose at Harry's smell, then at his accent, but accepted his money grudgingly and asked no questions. Harry washed, then sat on the hard bed and stared at the piece of paper he had picked up from his other self.

It was, indeed, a visiting card. It was made of good-quality, expensive stock, with a gold border around it, and said, simply:

JONATHAN HARKER
SOLICITOR
DOMBEY & SON
WHOLESALE, RETAIL & FOR EXPORTATION

Who was this Harker, then? And who were Dombey and Son? Harry had a solid lead. He turned the card over and over in his hands. The library, he thought. He would begin at the public library.

There was, indeed, a lending library nearby, on the Charing Cross Road. Harry went inside, glad of the warmth. He found the business directory, a large, leather-bound volume chained to its shelf, and leafed through it until he found the company's address.

There were no further details about the company. There was no mention, for instance, of exactly what they were wholesalers and retailers *of*. Or what they were exporting…

He'd have to tread carefully, he knew. The other him had been murdered for what he had found out. Harry was only surprised they had not made an attempt on him, too. Perhaps they wanted to see how he would run. He had a feeling that, even now, he was being watched. Perhaps the fact there had been two of him had thrown the opposition off-balance. If you kill me, he thought grimly, another me would just take my place.

Which was an unsettling thought, for Harry. And he decided he did not wish to die again any time soon.

Dombey and Son's offices were in the City, though according to the directory they had warehouses at the Greenwich docks. Harry decided he would have to proceed cautiously. Had the other him got too close, and was killed for his troubles?

He left the library. He was tired and hungry, but filled with a nervous energy. And the city was only now truly coming alive around him, a great mass of humanity, bound within ancient stone – so different to the wide open spaces, the mountains and the plains and the endless skies of Vespuccia. This city was like a bubbling cauldron, chock-full of a seething humanity, like a brain made of streets and lanes where humans played the role of thoughts and pathways. Perhaps the Lizardine Empire was like that, he thought: a single entity composed of solitary atoms, a great mass which was, nevertheless, a new, complete entity without regard to its component parts. People, even royals, could die, but the machine that was the empire would go on, powered not by engines of steam but by its people, the coal that burned and fed it.

Harry wandered the streets, passing along Shaftesbury Avenue and its glittering theatres, then into Soho where the streets became darker and the cut of clothes cheaper. He found an eatery and went inside and ordered. The food was bland.

"Hey, mister."

A small hand tugged at his arm. He looked down, surprised.
"Mr Houdini!"

It was a small bedraggled boy. "How do you know my name?"

The boy looked surprised. "Don't you recognise me, mister?
I'm Oliver."

Harry stopped. Froze, almost, as the realisation hit him.

The boy thought he was the other Houdini.

The one who had died.

"Of course," he said, and the moment passed. "Oliver. Yes,
what can you tell me?"

The boy was still looking at him dubiously. "It *is* you, isn't it,
Mr Houdini?"

"Of course it's me," Harry said, trying to laugh it off. It felt
very odd, to pretend to be... well, himself. And yet not himself.
He wished devoutly then that he knew just what the other him
had been up to in this city.

"My master wishes to parley with you," the boy, Oliver, said.

"Your master."

"You know." The boy lowered his voice. "Master Fagin," he said.

"Oh," Harry said. "Of course."

There was a short silence.

"Now, please, sir," Oliver said, abandoning the *mister* for the
moment.

"Will you take me to him?" Harry said.

"Yes, sir," Oliver said. His eyes, Harry saw, were on the unap-
petising remains of Harry's late supper: a thick stew of
indeterminate meat, dipped with a white, crumbly, flowery
bread.

Harry said, "You hungry?"

"Hungry," the boy confirmed.

"Go on, then."

The boy didn't need to be told twice. With startling, rapid
movement he was over the bowl, tearing up chunks of bread,
dunking into the remains of the mystery stew, and shoving them
into his mouth until his cheeks bulged.

Was this the ultimate produce of the empire? Harry thought, discomfited. Could the jewel of the world, the seat of that world-wide empire on which, as they said, "the sun never set", still contain within it such poverty, that a boy would have to beg and steal for his bread?

For he recognised in the boy the signs of a fine-wirer and a flimp, those miniature experts of the crowd, who made their trade – and their art – in picking pockets and making valuables disappear. Harry had the expert eye of a man in a similar line of work. He smiled, then smacked the boy on the side of the head, causing him to spit out soggy bread.

"What you go and do that for!"

"Let's go," Harry said, still smiling. "Now, my wallet, if you please, young Oliver."

The boy grinned sheepishly and handed it back to him. "Just checking, guv," he said. "Making sure you *was* you, if you know what I mean."

Harry, unfortunately, did.

He made his way outside, following the boy. There were several pubs, a chemist's selling cocaine and soap, a man handing out leaflets of what must have been a political nature and, nearby, one of Harry's own people: that is, a three-card monte man, hunched over a folding card table, a wad of money in his waving hand.

Three-card monte: it was one of the classic scams, resting in the domain that lay between magician and card sharp: the operator, the dealer that is, offering to double the punter's money. The bet: an easy one. Find the lady. The card sharp shuffling the cards, a simple sleight-of-hand making it impossible to detect where the Queen of Hearts had gone. Harry knew it well, had operated it before. He went closer and watched with professional interest. There was the Throw, the Drop, and the Aztec Turnover, but the real secret of the game was simple, and Harry, enjoying himself for the first time, found himself checking to see who the dealer's accomplice was, the shill.

The shill was there to lure the mark into the game. He bet against the dealer, and lost, allowing the mark to feel a superiority – since to them it was always so easy to see where the Queen went. When they finally put their money down, though...

The shill was an undistinguished young man. The dealer, however...

Harry knew a thing or two about pretence, and makeup. At the World's Vespuccian Exposition he himself had donned the apparel and dark skin of a Hindu sorcerer, along with his younger brother, Theo.

So he could recognise a fake, and the dealer – a hook-nosed, bearded personage with the reek of the streets upon it – made him smile happily, recognising here one of his own. The nose was an expert job, the dirty skin artfully applied just so, the beard removable. A respectable Anglo-Saxon gentleman hid behind the façade of a gutter man, if Harry was any judge.

"Find the lady!" the dealer shouted. The wads of money in his hand could be used neatly to cover any untoward movements of the cards. "Find the lady!"

"Twenty shillings!" A fat man pushed his way in. He had been watching the shill, who was losing repeatedly.

The dealer made the man's money disappear; shuffled the cards. An interesting pack, Harry thought. The royal cards were all lizards, and the Queen of Hearts bore a resemblance to Queen Victoria's profile which he had seen on coins and stamps.

"This one."

"Sorry."

The dealer upturned the Eight of Clubs where the Queen of Hearts should have been, and grinned blackened teeth at the mark.

"Cheat!" the man cried. "Liar!"

The shill, meanwhile, had gone quietly around him. Harry saw the flash of a blade, and the large man blanched visibly and fell quiet.

"On your way, now," the shill said. The man nodded and hurried away. Harry, still smiling, approached the table.

"Mr Houdini," the three-card monte man said.

Several thoughts ran through Harry's head at once. That the previous him had already met this man; that the previous him must have made the same assumptions he had just made; and that he had charged this man, a seasoned criminal of some sort, with a task, most likely in the nature of information-gathering.

So he took a gamble.

"Do you have it?" he said.

The man smiled. His teeth were in perfect health, Harry thought, amused. But the coal smeared on them made them appear rotten, mere stumps of teeth. "What if I do?" he said.

"Master Fagin?" The boy, Oliver, had materialised by the card table.

"Boy?"

"The pigs, sir. They're coming."

"Short is the run of a three-card monte," Harry said. So this was Fagin, the man who had wanted to see him. He had guessed right, it seemed.

"Short in one place," the man, Fagin, said philosophically. "But who wants to stay in one spot all the time?"

In one swift motion he folded the card table, made the money and the cards disappear, and grinned at Harry. "Shall we?" he said.

"Do you have it?" Harry said, again.

A whistle sounded in the distance. Policemen on their way. Fagin did not look unduly worried. He grinned again at Harry.

"It will cost you," he said.

THIRTY-ONE

"My children have been shadowing him for you," Fagin said. Harry followed the man down the city's unfamiliar alleyways.

Shadowing who?

"Where is he now?"

"His routine hasn't varied," Fagin said. "A man of habit is our Mr Harker."

Harry, inwardly, sighed with relief. It made sense. So the earlier him had hired this man, this Fagin, to follow Harker, the mysterious solicitor of that mysterious export company called Dombey and Son.

"And now?" he said. Something must have changed, he thought, for Fagin to have summoned him.

The other man smiled, revealing those falsely ruined teeth. "He's got himself a missus, he has," he said – which lowered Harry's opinion of the man's acting skills somewhat.

"Where?"

"Not far."

Was Fagin leading him into a trap?

It was possible. But it was a risk, he decided, that was worth taking. He had to find out what had happened to his double... and what had led to his death.

Harker was the key to the puzzle...

A part of the puzzle, at any rate.

They were heading towards the Thames, Harry realised. The smell of the river crept up on him and with it the singing of the whales grew stronger. They were now on the Strand, a wide avenue thronged with carriages and steam-powered baruch-landaus and people. Across the road stood an imposing building. A sign said it was the Savoy Hotel.

They crossed the road.

"Waterloo Bridge, guv'nor," Fagin told him, cheerfully, with that same grating, false voice. Harry shrugged. Down below, the Thames was dark. Fog swirled across the bridge, which was lit by gas lamps which cast pale, yellow orbs of light around them. There were more carriages and beggars, and a couple of policemen, walking past, looked at Fagin sharply for a moment before going on their way.

Beyond the bridge they came to an area of theatres and pubs and a huge, new construction project. A massive collection of towers was rising, uncompleted, into the sky, things of chrome and glass partially connected by as-yet-uncompleted narrow, hair-fine bridges, like spiders' silk.

"What is it?" Harry said – whispered. He had seen the modern marvel that had been the White City in Shikaakwa, the labour of architects and engineers to imagine the new, coming century. But the White City had looked nothing like this: it was bulky, it was grandiose, it was white–

This was something else, a different sort of future, a future of metal and glass, a future of rockets. High above, in those towers, lights moved and bobbed and he realised people – workers – were moving up there, in those impossible heights, still working at this late hour on the construction.

"This?" Fagin said. "It's just a building, innit."

But it wasn't just a building, Harry thought. And now that he watched, as they came closer and details resolved themselves, the place came into focus. He could see bullet-shaped elevators rising and falling along the sides of the slim, needle-like, rocket-like towers, as if they were breathing and the tubes moving alongside them were the air they breathed. He could see a massive cone rise into the air, flat at the top, and it seemed like a cone of water, with water travelling along its side – as if the builders were making a pool of water up there, in the air, for the future residents of those towers to frolic by, as if they were by the sea.

A place for airships to dock – that, too, he noticed, just as he saw the figures crawling along the side of the buildings – not human, or rather, things that resembled humans, if a human wore a thick exoskeleton of metal, like a knight's armour, around himself. Like armoured ants they crawled over the walls, building.

"They come from the Gobelin factory," Fagin said. "The Shaw brothers' place, in Paris. They used to make Daguerre looms there, back in the day. It was a natural progression for them to start making… well, these."

"What *are* they?"

"Human-machine hybrids," Fagin said. "It's all the rage, really."

A shiver went down Harry's spine. For it occurred to him that, though he himself *looked* human, and *sounded* human, it was quite evident, from the Bookman's words, that he was not, strictly speaking, human any more.

He, too, was a sort of machine, a simulacra of a Harry Houdini, an Erich Weiss who had been born, to Rabbi Mayer Samuel Weiss and to Cecelia Weiss, née Steiner, in Budapest, in the Austro-Hungarian Empire, in the year eighteen seventy-four, and who had died, aged nineteen, at the hands of a mugger, in the White City, at the World's Vespuccian Exposition, in the city called Chicago or Shikaakwa.

That Erich Weiss – *that* Houdini – was gone forever. He, Harry, was but a copy.

Yet perhaps it gave him advantages. He had not considered it before, but could not the Bookman have shaped his new body, have modified it in some subtle ways – could he not have made him faster, stronger – smarter?

In fairness, he did not *feel* any different. He felt like he was himself, the same old Erich, with the same ambitions, same thoughts.

What if there were other hims walking around? He thought back on what that strange man, Carter, his recruiter into the Bookman's service, had said. Of what the Bookman had told *him*...

"Will you not require me still?" Carter had said, and the Bookman had laughed. *"Why, I have another one of you in storage already,"* he had said. *"Just in case I need you, and you're not around."*

Harry shivered again. The night felt suddenly cold. "Look," Fagin said, startling him. He pointed at the tall, graceful buildings. "See those lights?"

There were, indeed, lights burning behind windows in the uncompleted buildings. "People already live there?" Harry said, surprised.

"It's all the rage," Fagin said.

They had come to the base of the place. A fence humming with a strange power he had seen before, in the White City.

Electricity.

"He's *here*?"

"Star City," Fagin said.

"Is that what they call it?"

"I told you, china," Fagin said. "It's just a building."

"It's amazing."

"It's a disgrace. It disfigures the face of the city."

"It looks like... like the future."

"Not my kind of future," Fagin said, and his face twisted in an ugly and unexpected expression of anger.

"I think it's amazing."

"So you said."

"But what are we doing here?"

As he spoke he saw two small figures detach themselves from the shadows and come towards them. Two more children, dressed in rags. "Well?" Fagin demanded.

"He's still inside," the one girl said.

"With his missus," the second, a boy, said.

"Harker?" Harry said.

"Harker," Fagin confirmed. "And, as it turns out, his fiancée."

Somehow that rang false to Harry. Could his quarry, the possible cause of his double's death, be just some person, some insignificant clerk, about to be married? He had half-envisioned some fearsome, secret assassin, a man of international intrigue. Most shadow agents never married. It was too dangerous for them.

"What is her name?"

"Wilhelmina," Fagin said. "Miss Wilhelmina Murray, of Star City Mansions. Would you like to know what else I've found out?"

"Yes."

"And the money?"

Harry had money. Not wishing to argue with this person, nor seeing the point of it, he removed a small sheaf of Vespuccian notes from a hidden pocket and handed them to Fagin, who smiled horribly and made the money disappear.

"Very well," he said. "Very well indeed." He coughed, clearing his throat, and spat the phlegm on the ground.

"The Mina Murray Dossier," Fagin said. His eyes took on a faraway look. Harry looked at him in suspicion.

Could Fagin be other than he appeared? Could he himself be a shadow operative, working for someone like the lizard's secret service, the Bureau?

```
Name: Wilhelmina "Mina" Murray.
Age: twenty-one.
Parents: deceased.
Family: none.
Engaged to: Jonathan Harker, Solicitor.
Employed by: Dombey and Son, Wholesale, Retail
and for Exportation.
Role: unknown.
Residence: Star City Mansions, South Bank,
London.
```

"That's all you found out?" Harry said.

Fagin said: "It was hard to find even that much. Same with Harker, for that matter. It's as if..." and he hesitated.

Harry looked up, at the Star City.

"It's as if what?" he said, absent-mindedly.

"It's as if anyone working for Dombey and Son becomes a shadow," Fagin said, reluctantly.

Harry was looking up, at the needle-like towers, the climbing mecha-humans, the airship docking and that graceful column of suspended water. The moonlight fell down on Star City Mansions, illuminated the thin filaments of silk-spun bridges criss-crossing between the towers, while behind the windows of the occupied apartments shone the white, bright light of electricity. The present, with its dirty streets, its steam machines, its coal dust and gaslight, seemed to have no presence here, an illusion fading in the bright electric light.

This was the future, one future, and Harry drank it in.

"You can't have shades without light," he said.

THIRTY-TWO

When you die it is like a light going off. In death there is nothing. Life is an improbability, the brief flare of a match in a dark world. Houdini didn't want to die.

Not again.

He had made a terrible mistake. It was very dark, though it wasn't cold.

This is what happened...

They had waited outside Star City Mansions and, presently, two figures, seen in silhouette, came out of the grand entrance to the as-yet-uncompleted buildings.

Harry tensed. Fagin, beside him, was motionless. The boy, Oliver, had disappeared somewhere, on an errand for his master.

"Harker, and Murray," Fagin said – whispered – the words ebbing away like fog in the night.

A strange sense of déjà vu had overtaken Harry. As though he had been standing here before, waiting for this man to come out, as if, somehow, he could recall what the other Houdini had done, could sample his memories, remotely, second-hand, like an echo. He was tense, his heart beat fast, though outwardly he was calm. He waited. The two figures hugged, there

in the darkness, then separated, one going back into the building, the other coming out, onto the road of the South Bank.
The sound of Harker's feet filled the night. It was very quiet
there, suddenly, no one passing, no late revellers; even the
whales were silent. Fagin melted into the shadows. Harry
watched the man Harker go past them, not seeing them. There
was nothing remarkable about the man. He waited. Harker
walked past. Harry, after a moment, followed.

The night focused, thinned. Harry's entire world became the
path he followed, behind that man he didn't know, whose name,
only, was left him by his own dead self.

Harker was going towards Waterloo Station and the fog
thickened here, and the gas lamps were yellow dogs' eyes in
the fog. Harry followed and the immense edifice of the station
rose before him but Harker did not go up the stone stairs into
the station. He went down a side alley – and Harry followed.
His footsteps echoed in the night and Harker stopped, suddenly,
and turned. They were alone there, in that dark place, with
only the yellow gaslight illuminating their faces, and Harker's
was very white.

He stared. Harry stood there, watching him. Two men, facing
each other, not speaking. Harker raised a shaking hand and
pointed it at Harry.

"You!" he said.

Harry said, "Do you know me?"

Every inch of him wanting to scream at the man, to shake
him. To ask what had happened.

"I told you I can't!" Harker said. "You shouldn't be here." His
face was devoid of blood. His pupils were dilated. He said, "You
can't be here. How... They told me you were–"

He bit his lip to silence himself.

"That I was dead?"

Harker nodded.

"I need to know," Harry said. "What–"

But Harker was shaking his head, frantic now, fear etched into
his face like a tattoo. "No," he said. "No. They will find you. They

warned me. They are probably watching, even now. Get away from me!"

Harry had taken a step towards him. That was enough to startle Harker. He turned and ran.

Harry followed.

Running through the fog, whale song rising like a funeral dirge far away, from the Thames. The only sounds their echoing footsteps, Harker leading, Harry following his quarry, all thought, all caution gone.

Connections made: the former him had made contact with this Harker, perhaps confided in him. Harker had a key to the answer. Something his company did, something of great secrecy and significance. He had to know – had to know why he had been killed, what secret his death had protected.

Running, his breath fogging in the air, a great silence as if snow was falling, as if sound was being sucked out of the world, as if they were the only two people in it–

But they weren't.

Later, in the dark, Harry remembered it with fleeting, truncated fragments of recall:

The screech of wheels, the bellow of steam–

Harker's pale face, turning towards him–

His mouth opening in a silent scream–

A vast, black vehicle, a steam-powered baruch-landau, smashing into the man–

Harker's body flying through the air–

Black-clad men streaming out of the vehicle–

More of them appearing out of the shadows, surrounding the area–

Harker's body lying against a wall, head at an unnatural angle, legs broken beneath him–

Harry, too, might have screamed, he couldn't later be sure–

Arms grabbing him, too many to fight against, though he tried–

A truncheon rising in the air–

Someone kicked his legs out from under him and then the truncheon descended–

The back of his head erupting in pain, it bloomed like a dark flower and he felt himself go limp.

"Tap him again," someone said, a long way off. He tried to struggle but couldn't move, couldn't open his eyes. Something connected with the back of his head again and he couldn't even scream, which may have been a mercy. All thought fled and Harry Houdini escaped into the darkness and the cool absence of pain that it offered.

He came to gradually. His head pounded in waves that made him dizzy, sick. Bile in his throat, he fought not to gag. The back of his head felt swollen, painful. He tried to move his hands and couldn't.

Tied up?

A voice, gravely and deep. "Alas, no, Mr Houdini. We are well aware by now of your skill with knots and ropes and, I dare say, other modes of confinement."

He opened his eyes. Blinked. Realised he could not move at all, nothing but his head.

What had they done to him?

"I have taken the liberty," the voice said, as though, once again, reading his mind, "to have you... sedated. It is an unfortunate necessity, but I suspect even you, Mr Houdini, would find it impossible to escape the confines of chemistry." The voice coughed. Harry's eyes tried to adjust to the dim half-light of the room he found himself in. He could not yet see the speaker. Behind a vast desk, a large silhouette, but that was all.

"It is a special concoction my people have managed to steal, some while back, from the Quiet Council's research facility," the voice said, complacently.

"Who... are you?" Harry said. His lips felt numb. It was hard to speak, to see.

"My name is Dombey," the voice said. The shadow behind the desk moved, then settled back. "Paul Dombey."

"But who... *are* you?" Harry said, and the man laughed.

"I am the general manager of Dombey and Son," he said.

Harry shook his head, or tried to. This wasn't helping. Was the man toying with him? Flashes of memory – Harker's pale face, the black baruch-landau, Harker's broken body flying through the air–

He swallowed bile, tried again. "Who... do you work for?"

But it was not Harry's place to ask questions. It was his place to answer them. He was the captive. The privilege of knowledge was not his to take. The shadow stirred behind the desk.

"You are far more interesting than you first appeared, Mr Houdini," it said. It chuckled good-naturedly. "Oh, you had us fooled, when you first showed up! A green, inexperienced agent of the Cabinet Noir, that was easy enough to establish. Blundering about, asking questions in all the wrong places... Vespuccians!" The voice chuckled again. "You have so little style, you are like half-civilised barbarians bumbling about! Do you know, I enjoyed watching your feeble efforts. Who do I work for? You will find out in due course, Mr Houdini. We are the guardians, if you like. We watch. We watch the Bureau, and the Quiet Council, and the Shaolin. We watch the world powers, and we try to stir the world onto the course it should have taken long ago. And you!" The shadow moved forward and, for just a moment, a vast, pasty face revealed itself in the half-light, and if he could Harry would have cried out. Half-machine it was, one eye mechanical while the other, a liquid blue, glared at him with benevolent amusement. Half the face, when it turned, was open, the skin missing, and inside it, rather than blood and bones, were tiny clockwork parts, moving silently. The man grinned, revealing teeth of metal and ivory. "When you became too much of a nuisance," he said, as pleasantly as before, "and found what you thought was a weak spot, our own Mr Harker, I had no choice. As much as it pained me, Mr Houdini, I had to... let you go."

"You ordered me killed?"

"We knew you were to meet an agent at the docks last night. What we did not know, could not know – was that the agent was *you*!"

Harry said nothing. The truth was that he had not expected to encounter himself either.

"So *now*," the voice said, settling back, that hideous face disappearing from view, "you have aroused our interest, Mr Houdini!"

"Is that... Is that a good thing?" Harry said.

"It depends," the voice allowed, generously, "on which side of this desk you sit on."

"I... see."

"Do not worry! This is a great opportunity, for us as well as for you. I assume you are an agent of that elusive Bookman? One hears so much, yet truly knows so little... Come, my dear, join me."

The last was not, clearly, aimed at Harry. He turned his head as much as he could. Light footsteps sounded, and to Harry's amazement a beautiful young woman entered the circle of light cast from above.

"Come, my dear. Say hello to our guest," Mr Dombey said.

"Hello," the girl said. She smiled, revealing white teeth.

"Who...?"

"But my dear Mr Houdini!" Mr Dombey said. "This is Wilhelmina Murray."

Harry tried to swallow, couldn't. "Harker's... fiancée?"

"One of my best agents," Mr Dombey said, with evident pride. Mina Murray smiled pleasantly at Harry.

Harry whispered: "Please... help me."

Mina Murray laughed. "Why would I do that?" she said.

And Harry knew he was doomed.

"What will you do with me?" he said. Was the effect of the drug wearing off? He tried to move his hands – the tips of his fingers, he thought, had moved a little.

"*He* wants to see you," Mr Dombey said. "Therefore..."

"He who?"

The shadowed figure behind the desk shook its head. "My dear," it said to Mina Murray. "Would you?"

"My pleasure," Mina Murray said. She came to Harry and stood close to him; he could smell her perfume. She nodded to someone behind him; he couldn't see. The sound of a heavy object being dragged on the ground. Then she put her hands on him – they were warm – and she pushed. Harry fell back with a cry. Hands grabbed him, lowered him. He found himself inside a wooden crate. Mina Murray towered over him, and suddenly there was nothing pretty or kind in her face. Her smile was predatory.

"It won't hurt a bit," she said. In her hand she held a syringe.

"What... What is it?" Harry whispered. He couldn't move.

"It will send you to sleep," she said, gently. The needle lowered. Mina pulled up Harry's sleeve. He couldn't resist her.

"Where... Where am I going?"

Mina Murray tested the syringe. A bubble of liquid and air formed at the top of the needle. Harry watched it, hypnotised.

"Where?" Mina Murray said, as though surprised. She knelt over Harry and with a quick, efficient move pushed the needle into Harry's arm. He felt a pinprick of pain, then a spreading numbness.

"Why, you are going to Transylvania," Mina Murray said.

Then the lid of the crate was placed above him, and nails were driven into the wood to close it tight, and a darkness settled over Harry Houdini.

PART VI
The Stoker Memorandum

THIRTY-THREE

"Tell me about Stoker," Lucy said.

It was getting into the late afternoon. Beyond the windows the spray from the sea rose high into the air on the cliff. Seagulls dived, dark shapes against the weak sun. Miss Havisham had baked cinnamon buns.

Lucy was still following Mycroft's tortured trail. Miss Havisham's memory was, in many ways, the Bureau's own. But what was Mycroft after? Closeted in his club, seeing no one, what did he see, what mystery was he trying to unravel?

"Stoker, Abraham," Miss Havisham said, thoughtfully. "Yes, I remember dear little Abe. That's what I called him, you know. My darling little Abe. One of the theatre folks, naturally. And Irish." She sighed. "An unlikely agent for anyone," she said. "Which is why no one wanted to follow up on it. Not even Mycroft, at first..."

```
Name: Stoker, Abraham.
Code name: none.
Place of birth: Dublin.
Parents: deceased.
Family: wife, Florence, one child.
Affiliation: unknown.
Notes:
```

"Notes?" Lucy said.

Miss Havisham rubbed the bridge of her nose. For the first time, she had placed a file folder on the table. A single sheet of white paper inside, and the *notes* section, Lucy saw, had been left blank. Miss Havisham smiled, wistfully. "As you can see, we had nothing on him. A theatrical manager, working for Henry Irving's Lyceum Theatre in London. An unremarkable man, clean as this sheet of paper."

"So what drew you to him?" Lucy said.

Miss Havisham shook her head. "It was before the Orphan case, when we were busy monitoring the European side of things. Later there was a shift, Fogg wanted to watch Vespuccia, and the Chinese Desk was getting new funding, but by then I was out. It was… little things that kept coming up. And then there was First Night of Gilbert and Sullivan's *Pirates of the Carib Sea…*"

Lucy waited. Miss Havisham moved at her own pace. Her eyes were clouded. She was going back in time, to a better time and place, before her forced retirement, when she was still a player of the Great Game…

It had been a great coup for the Lyceum (Miss Havisham told her). *It had been one of the times when Gilbert and Sullivan were fighting again and, to make it worse, Gilbert had charged their manager, Richard D'Oyly Carte, of cheating them out of money – over a carpet, of all things.*

So the Lyceum had managed to steal them away, if not for long, and had put on the opening night of their latest production, The Pirates of the Carib Sea, at the Lyceum rather than the Savoy.

There had been no indication of anything remarkable in the offing. As I said, little things…

Two weeks before the opening night, an extraction team had brought in a German defector. He had been a low-level employee of Krupp's, and our hopes of getting technical information regarding Krupp's latest monster cannon were in vain. They had put him in Ham, in the interrogation centre, and had been sweating him for three days without anything useful coming out, when I decided to pop in and see him. I had only routine questions to ask him, you see. I remember the interrogation

*room, the defector's bruised face, sweaty hands that left print marks on
the metal desk between us. I had a cup of tea and offered him one, which
he accepted, as well as a cigarette.*

"You are Marcus Rauchfus?" I said. He confirmed his name.

"Engineer with Krupp Industries?"

Again, he nodded.

*"What made you decide to defect?" I asked, with honest curiosity.
Krupp looked after his people well. It was hard to get deep into his organisation, and what agents of ours had tried to infiltrate his
organisation tended to… well, disappear. Loyalty and ruthlessness, as
Mycroft liked to say, were powerful together.*

*Rauchfus shrugged. Perhaps he truly didn't know why. After three
days of interrogation no one was very enthusiastic about him any more,
he'd given us nothing we could use. "I was…" His voice was hoarse;
they had sweated him hard those three days. He spread his arms in a
helpless gesture. "Always I love the English."*

"We are not at war with Germany."

*"No." But he did not sound convinced, and for the first time my cu-
riosity was aroused.*

*"What do you know of Alfred Krupp's plans?" I asked. Rauchfus
looked uncomfortable. He leaned towards me across the desk. There was
something in his eyes that wanted to come out. I nodded to the guard,
and he left the room, leaving the two of us alone. "Well?" I said.*

*"Them I don't tell!" He hit the desk with his fist. "You I tell. You give
me house in Surrey?"*

*"We look after our defectors," I said. "As long as they can offer us
something substantial."*

"I make statement," Rauchfus said. "To you I make statement."

"Well?"

*"My name is Marcus Rauchfus, and I am an engineer for Krupp In-
dustries, yes. Yes! But not general section. I was assistant to one man,
four, five years ago. His name is Diesel, Rudolf Diesel. Great engineer.
The best! Top secret project." Marcus Rauchfus smiled, shyly. "Top secret," he repeated, as if there was a magic in the words.*

"What was the nature of the project?" I asked.

"To make new engine," he said. "New power source! Yes! But…"

"What sort of new power source?"

He waved his hand. This was not important. "Petroleum," he said. "Krupp has network, yes, to bring it in from the Arabian Peninsula. Also Vespuccia, we believe, has much."

"Petroleum?"

I knew what it was, of course. Moreover, I knew very well we had our own research facility dedicated to finding new, more efficient sources of power than coal. But Rauchfus shook his head. "Not important," he said, placidly.

"Why not?"

"Decoy! I find out, by accident. Yes, I know, you have research also. French, Chinese, same! But—"

There had been a girlfriend, he told me. Working in Krupp's private office. She told him, once. They had a fight. "You think you are special? You are Top Secret?" she had laughed at him. "Real work not done on Diesel project. Real work classified Ultra!"

"Ultra?" I said.

Rauchfus nodded.

"What's Ultra?" I said.

"Ultra is secret project," Rauchfus said.

"Of what nature?"

"I do not know."

I sighed. "This is all you have for me?"

"Yes. No! Ultra not Krupp project."

At that I sat up straighter. "Not Krupp? What do you mean?"

Here Rauchfus lowered his voice. "Not Krupp," he said. "International. Very dangerous to know. One, two months later, girlfriend not at work. Not at home. Gone." He clicked his fingers sadly. "Like this, gone."

"And you?"

"No one know I know!" But he looked fearful. "British," he whispered to me. His eyes were round. "British too. She tell me. British too."

"British? British who?"

He shook his head. "I do not know. I should not have said."

He wouldn't speak again, after that. I had left instructions for the interrogators not to touch him. I wanted him kept isolated, safe. When I got back to the Bureau I dug deeper into the files.

It was as I had thought. Rauchfus had lied to me. He had not come over voluntarily to our side. He had thought, rather, that he was dealing with an agent of the French's Quiet Council. He must have been horrified to realise he had been duped. If what he said was true, someone high up in the clandestine world was involved in a plot with Alfred Krupp. It was more likely Rauchfus was a plant, a false flag sent to us by Krupp's intelligence people. A decoy. But I couldn't take the chance.

Fogg was out of the Bureau at that time. Mycroft, I believe, had sent him away, I was not sure where. It was shortly after Moreau had been exiled, or banished, or transferred – versions varied – to an isolated research facility on an island in the South Seas. Rumour had it Mycroft wanted Fogg far away – and making sure Moreau stayed banished might have been a good enough reason.

For myself, though, I did not think giving Fogg access to Moreau's research was a good idea, and said so. But back then Fogg was Mycroft's golden boy, and he could do no wrong. Or so it seemed...

Mycroft always plans further, deeper, I know that now. He plays the long game. Did he suspect Fogg even then?

I came to him that day. It was night time, the gas lamps were lit outside, and inside the Bureau it was cold. We were running a shadow operation in Afghanistan then, following that disastrous war we had run over there. The operation, as I recall, did not go well. Berlyne was coming in and out of the fat man's office, sneezing and coughing and politely barring access to anyone who came. But Mycroft saw me. He always made the time – for his own benefit, have no doubt. He needed me, and he knew it. On that we were of one mind.

"What do you want, Havisham?" the fat man had said, looking up at me from his desk. I knew he hated it, preferred his armchair at the Diogenes, the silence there, his food...

I said, "Ultra."

He went very still. Mycroft has the talent. "What are you talking about?" he said at last. I looked at him. "Krupp," I said.

"Yes?"

He was giving nothing away. So I told him about Rauchfus, and watched him go even stiller, as if delving deep inside himself.

"Is he real?" he said.

I shrugged.

"Your gut instinct."

"My instincts took me to look at him in the first place."

He nodded. That was all, but it was decided, there and then. Just like that.

"Is he safe?"

"We need to move him."

"Where?"

"The village?"

He shook his head. "Too public. It needs to be close by. A relation."

Meaning family. Meaning one of us…

We looked at each other with the same thought.

"Mrs Beeton."

"*Isabella* Beeton?" Lucy said, interrupting. Miss Havisham looked momentarily surprised. "Do you know another one?" she said.

"Our *Prime Minister* Isabella Beeton?"

Miss Havisham smiled tolerantly. "She wasn't Prime Minister then," she said, reasonably. "But she'd always been family. Even when she was fomenting revolution, later, in eighty-eight."

"Mrs Beeton worked for the Bureau?"

Miss Havisham shook her head at that. "A relation," she said. "One of the people we used to call Mycroft's Irregulars. She ran a safe house for the Bureau, every now and then. And Mycroft and I decided it was the perfect place to move our reluctant German defector to."

Lucy looked at her closely. "But something went wrong?" she said, softly.

Miss Havisham sighed. "Something went wrong," she agreed, sadly.

THIRTY-FOUR

That same night (Miss Havisham said) *we undertook a rare excursion together, Mycroft and I. At Ham Common we picked up Rauchfus, and drove him, in Mycroft's baruch-landau, to Mrs Beeton's place. We erased Rauchfus's trail of paperwork, excised all mention of him on the Ham facility's records, and returned to the Bureau, confident he was safe, and that we had time.*

As it turned out, we were wrong.

I was woken up in the archives. I had dozed at my desk. Mycroft's voice on the Tesla unit. I had never heard him so angry, so controlled.

"We lost him," he said.

I said, "What?"

"Rauchfus. He's gone."

"Gone where?"

A silence on the line. Then: "Gone."

I saw him being carted away. We came there, to the safe house, and there he was, peaceful, at rest. The resultant autopsy revealed a minute hole in the back of his neck, as if a thin needle had been inserted there all the way to his brain. There had been no reports of intruders, no one unauthorised entering or leaving the house. Mrs Beeton was – justifiably – outraged. I thought I heard Mycroft murmur, "The Bookman," just once, but that was that. We burned Rauchfus's files. There was no more mention of Ultra, or a highly placed British power playing in the sandbox with Krupp, or what it could mean.

Then there was the mess in eighty-eight… I was made redundant and Mycroft was beleaguered. The political landscape changed, Moriarty lost the elections, the Byron automata ran against him but in a surprise move it was Mrs Beeton who won…

Is this why you are here? Why Mycroft sent you?

Are the old suspicions resurfacing?

"You mean…" Lucy wasn't sure what to say. "You suspected *Mrs Beeton*?"

"No one knew Rauchfus was there. Only Mycroft, and myself, beside her. It was Occam's Razor, Lucy. The simplest explanation is the most likely correct one."

Miss Havisham smiled, suddenly. "We are shadow players," she said, and shrugged. "We seldom keep to only one side."

There was a silence. "What *happened* in eighty-eight?" Lucy said at last.

Miss Havisham shook her head. "I do not know, exactly. Something is buried, deep under Oxford, which needs to remain buried. That is all I will say." She glanced at Lucy sharply. "Mycroft never sent you to me, did he?" she said.

"No."

"What are you playing at, Miss Westenra?"

Lucy didn't know what to tell her. "I need you to trust me," she said, simply.

"Why?"

"Because I think Mycroft is in trouble."

Miss Havisham snorted. "He is always in trouble."

"I think… I think the Bookman is back."

Miss Havisham fell quiet. Then, as if, between them, something had been decided, she said: "Tea?"

"Please," Lucy said.

But you were asking me about Abe Stoker, and I quite went about it in a roundabout way (said Miss Havisham). Well, Rauchfus had awakened our suspicions, but my interest in Stoker came two weeks later, at that first-night performance of The Pirates of the Carib Sea, a performance in which the very man who had so concerned us made a rare appearance.

Alfred Krupp had come to London unannounced. He had come, naturally, on business, but had taken time for the theatre–

Which had us curious. Krupp was seldom seen in public. Even on our home turf following him was near impossible. He had his own team of anti-surveillance experts.

Could the theatre be something more than entertainment? Could this engagement mean a clandestine meeting of some sort?

And if so, with whom?

In light of what we had learned – or thought we had – from Rauchfus, I was insistent that we monitor the theatre as closely as possible. Fogg was back by then, and argued vehemently against it. Krupp was too important – we had to be careful – we didn't have the budget – the staff–

I had argued with him. Mycroft was distracted – the Afghanistan operation had gone badly – at last we agreed on a compromise, a small but select team of watchers, and I myself secured a ticket to the show, which had by then sold out.

Did we learn anything from that evening? Krupp was sitting with his people in a box. The Queen herself was in attendance, in the Royal Box, of course. Lord Babbage made a rare – one of his last, in fact – public appearances. The cream and crop of London society was there. That rogue Flashman, toadying beside the Queen... I always had a soft spot for him – you know where you stand with a liar and a bully better than you do with a hero, sometimes. There is often only a fine distinction between the two.

But I'm digressing. We spotted nothing that evening, hard as we tried. Could a clandestine meeting be carried out in the open? That is, sometimes, the best way... but who was Krupp there for? It had even crossed my mind it was Mycroft behind it all, Mycroft who, to my surprise, also attended that evening, sitting in the Holmes family's own box, close by the Queen's...

Could Krupp be meeting the Bookman?

Babbage?

And it occurred to me all this was foreground, it was scenery, it was stagecraft – and that I was looking in the wrong place.

I had to look behind the scenes. I had to look backstage.

Where little Abe Stoker moved about, unobtrusively.

"A facilitator," Miss Havisham said, fondly. "An unobtrusive little man, a clerk really. Going about his business – which also means touring on the continent, and corresponding overseas, and in so many ways he could have been the perfect deep-cover spy, undistinguished from his cover story. I fell in love with him a little, then. When I realised this. I told Mycroft, that very night. We had to study Stoker. Learn him, and make our approach. We had to find out who he represented. He was a liaison, I could see that clearly. But between what powers? This insight, together with the German defector's story, added up. I pushed…"

"But?" Lucy said.

Miss Havisham shrugged. "Nothing came of it."

"Nothing?"

"Fogg argued, but Mycroft approved the plan. And nothing happened. Little Stoker was just who he appeared to be – a not-particularly-important theatrical manager of little talent or ambition. We had teams on him round-the-clock for a month, then it got dropped to periodic spot-checks, and finally it got dropped entirely. And there," Miss Havisham said, "the matter rested, until now. Why, has something changed?"

Lucy smiled. She stood up. "Routine inquiry," she said. And, "I had better head back into town before it is dark."

Miss Havisham smiled too, and also stood up. Her look said Lucy wasn't fooling her for a moment.

"You watch out," she told her, leading her back through the comfortable room and out into the ruined front of the mansion beyond, and Lucy thought that Miss Havisham herself had quite a bit of stagecraft in her. "And go safely."

"I will," Lucy said. And, "Thank you."

Miss Havisham nodded. Lucy walked down the steep path of

the cliff, back into the grim little village of Satis-by-the-Sea, and to its small, deserted train station. All the while she was aware of Miss Havisham standing where she was, watching as she went.

Mycroft had reactivated the plans concerning Stoker, she now knew. Something had changed, but his attention had been turned not to Germany, and Krupp, but farther, to the remote and inhospitable mountains of Transylvania...

It was when she was approaching London on board the old, patient steam train that the device she had been keeping on her person for days began to blip, faintly at first and then with renewed vigour, and the tension that had been building inside her reached a crescendo and then, all at once, disappeared, leaving her calm and focused.

The moment she had waited for had arrived.

Mycroft's agent, the mysterious Mr Stoker, was finally approaching.

THIRTY-FIVE

Night time, and the sky over Richmond Park was strewn with stars, the clouds clearing, a moon beaming down silver light. A deer moved amongst the dark trees, smelled humans and gunpowder and went another way.

"Everyone present?"

"Present and ready."

Lucy surveyed her team. They have been with her on the raid in Aksum, and they have been with her in the Bangkok Affair, and in the Zululand Engagement… she could trust them with her life.

She was going to have to trust them with Stoker's.

"Listen up." They were gathered around her in a semi-circle. Black-clad, guns ready: not shadow executives but the muscle shadow executives sometimes had to call on, to use, ex-military and ex-underworld and ex-mercenaries, retrained and retained by the Bureau for secretive, semi-military operations.

"Ma'am."

"An airship travelling on a Bureau-approved flight plan is expected to make landing in Richmond Park within the next hour or two. Its cargo is of vital importance. Our mission is simple: retrieve the cargo safely, and get the hell out. Understood?"

"Ma'am, yes, ma'am."

A hand up – Bosie. "Do we expect opposition?"

Smiles on the men's faces, echoed by Lucy's. "We always expect opposition," she said.

Bosie nodded. "Ma'am."

"Spread out. Keep in contact. We may need to signal to the airship when the time comes. Keep a lookout – and remember."

Her men looked at each other, soberly. "Try not to get killed."

"Yes, ma'am!"

They spread out, silent as shadows, and she was left alone, amidst the trees.

And deadly worried.

Too many things to go wrong.

Too many things had *already* gone wrong…

Like that persistent feel that she was being followed, as soon as she got off at Euston Station. She had doubled back and changed hansom cabs but still the feeling persisted.

Then there was Fogg, running her down at the Bureau, angry, hard: "Where have you been?"

"I'm on leave."

"I heard you went down to Satis House."

"Heard where?"

His voice, cold and hard. "Westenra, I am your superior. You were not authorised to go there."

"Excuse me?"

He must have had her followed. Which explained *some* part of her paranoia… "I am researching an old file."

"Which file would that be, exactly?"

"The Orphan file," she said, looking him in the eyes. "The eighty-eight dossier. That was the last encounter we've had with the Bookman."

Fogg's face was white and very still. Lucy said, softly, "Wasn't it?"

"The Bookman is not your concern!"

Lucy did not reply to that. "I need to see Mycroft," she said, instead.

"He's not here. I'm in charge."

"Where is he?"

"Gone."

There was a strange look in Fogg's eyes. Was it panic? Or victory? And now she was worried.

"I'd better go, then," she said. She turned her back on him.

"Westenra!"

"Sir?"

"Do not meddle in things you don't understand."

She turned back to him and faced him. "Is that a threat?"

Fogg smiled, his mouth like a thin, honed blade. "Take it as you will," he said, indifferently, at last, and walked away.

Lucy was left glaring after him.

Worry about Mycroft made her indecisive. The device he had given her was monitoring Stoker's approach. Did she have time?

She had a decision to make and she made it. Night swallowing the city, she took a hansom cab to Belgravia–

The feeling stole on her as she rode in the darkened cab, the street lights passing, the cries of sellers and the tolling of bells silenced, the faint beeping of the device increasing with each passing second as the mysterious airship from Transylvania was coming closer–

A sense of doom, a sense that Mycroft had foreseen a thing happening that she had thought impossible. That the trail he was following ended abruptly, the questions he sought answers to in his darkened room or at his quarters at the Diogenes Club remaining unanswered–

A piercing noise outside, rising and falling, rising and falling, setting her teeth on edge and she banged on the roof, shouting, "Stop!" to the driver.

She pushed the door open and was already running towards the flashing lights, the rising and falling sound of the siren growing stronger, two minute police automatons gliding on their little wheels, their blue light cones swirling on top of their heads as they came to stop her, but she pushed them away and went towards the house–

Arc lights and police tape and the neighbours' lights were on, but this was a good neighbourhood and no one wanted to show themselves outside. Mycroft's house, a modest place with ivy growing on the walls, a small garden in the front and there on the front steps–

"You can't come through here, miss. I'm sorry."

"What happened?"

"There has been an incident."

He was young and recently recruited to Scotland Yard and it really wasn't his fault he had run into Lucy.

"Where's your superior?"

He had on a little grin. "Miss?"

She made to walk past him and he grabbed her and she turned and grabbed his hand and twisted it, hard, behind his back until he yelled and dropped to his knees. Heads looked their way, then–

"Lucy?"

"Chief Inspector Adler."

Adler came towards her, not hurrying, her face unreadable. "It's been a while."

"Yes."

"Please let Constable Cuff go, Miss Westenra."

"Sure."

She released the man, who stood up, massaging his arm.

"Excuse me, chief inspector? It's *Sergeant* Cuff," he said.

Irene Adler smiled at him. "It *was*," she said. "Lucy, walk with me."

They left Cuff behind them. Lucy followed Adler. She wanted to look away but couldn't.

Just before his front door, resting on the little path that led up to his house, rested the large, lifeless body of Mycroft Holmes.

"How?" Lucy said. She felt numb. She had known this was coming, somehow, something deep inside her crying out, before, that all was wrong, that danger was on the way – but now, confronted with the truth of it, she didn't want to believe it.

Irene Adler said, "He was found under an hour ago, as you see him. There are no signs of violence..."

"This couldn't be natural causes."

"You have a better explanation?"

They glared at each other.

"I do," said a new voice. A man in a white coat came towards them, his face a mask of anxiety.

"You have found something?"

Lucy recognised the doctor, another relation – one of Mycroft's Irregulars, as Miss Havisham had called them. Worked at Guy's Hospital, if she remembered right – he must have been seconded to Scotland Yard.

"His death was not of natural causes. Look."

The doctor knelt by Lucy's former employer. With gentle hands he rolled the body and pulled aside cloth to show them the exposed back of the head. The doctor pointed. What was his name, Lucy wondered, trying to recall. Williams. Walton. Something starting with W.

"See here?" the doctor was pointing. Lucy peered closer. Was that a tiny discoloration in Mycroft's skin?

"It's a puncture hole," Irene Adler said.

"Exactly," the doctor – Wilberforce? Wharton? – said. "A very fine one – yet, I think, deadly. He was attacked. Poor Mycroft… " The doctor took a deep breath and resumed. "He had been coming up to his door when the attacker caught him. He must have been in hiding, waiting for him. He inserted a long, thin needle into Mycroft's head, going all the way in, killing him almost instantly."

Lucy pushed up. She felt ill, helpless. What should she do now?

Unbidden, Mycroft's face came into her mind, his lips moving. Speaking to her, on their way to the palace.

What had he told her?

"If something were to happen to me," Mycroft had said – she had wanted to protest, but he silenced her. "If something were to happen to me, I have put certain precautions in place. Certain agents have been… put in reserve, shall we say. The old and the new…" and he smiled, looking at her. "You must get hold of the Stoker information," he told her. "At all costs. Off the books, non-Bureau sanctioned. Were

I to die, there is still Smith... if he is not too old." Here he smiled again. *"For you, however, I have made a different precaution."*

Smith? That old hack?

Wasn't he dead?

Well, her objective was clear. It hadn't changed. Dead or alive, Mycroft's instructions stood. And he *had* made an arrangement for her... and one she intended to follow.

She felt relief at that, a sense of order returning. She looked down at his large corpse. "The end of an era," the doctor murmured, echoing her thoughts.

"What is the meaning of this!"

The voice was loud like a fog-horn and edged like steel and most recently it had been shouting at *her*.

Fogg, arriving at the scene of the crime. Lucy couldn't bear it, suddenly. She had to get away.

"Where are you–?" from Adler.

Lucy didn't have time to answer. She went around the side of the house, Fogg's footsteps echoing up the path–

"Was that Westenra? Oh dear, oh dear–"

He had seen the body.

"Why was I not immediately informed? This is a matter of national security! Bureau takes precedence!"

His voice faded behind her. She made her way to the adjoining road and hailed down a hansom cab.

It was time to finish the job, she thought.

It was time to find out what Stoker was carrying.

What had Mycroft said? *"Six months ago I played a pawn,"* Mycroft had told her. *"Not sure whether I was sacrificing a piece or making a play on the king."*

Well, she would find out. She would not let the fat man down.

"Where to, miss?" the hansom cab driver asked.

"Richmond Park," she said.

Her team had been notified. They would wait for her there.

She stared out of the window as the hansom cab headed for the river and the bridge, to cross over to the south bank. The rattle of the carriage sounded like piano keys and, as they drove closer to the water, the singing of the whales rose, majestic and slow, all about her, but what they sang she didn't know.

THIRTY-SIX

"Ma'am."

"Report."

"Unknowns approaching from Richmond Hill gate."

"Number?"

"About two dozen. Spreading out – did we invite anyone else to the party, ma'am?"

"No."

"Hostiles then?"

"Yes."

Silence on the Tesla set. Then, "They're armed."

"I wouldn't expect anything less."

"Take them out?"

She made a quick calculation. Too early, a fire fight would draw unwanted attention. Someone else wanted Stoker. Someone else knew he was coming–

"Keep an eye on them."

"Ma'am–"

"Yes?"

"Hostiles approaching from Kingston gate direction."

Lucy swore.

"Ma'am?"

"Keep an eye on them."

She had expected some opposition. She had not expected an army.

And the airship, with its precious cargo, was approaching rapidly...

She put her spyglasses to her eyes. The airship was visible now, gaining momentum, a black shape crossing against the face of the moon. She tensed, knowing it was about to happen, it was too soon, she had not been prepared enough, and that, in the next few minutes, people would die.

"Mark it!"

"Ma'am!"

A silent flame rose up into the air, and then another, and another – her men shooting flares into the sky, marking the landing spot for the airship.

And giving away their position...

But no one was going to act until the airship had landed, safely.

Weren't they?

The airship was lit up now by the flares, a dark and unfamiliar dragon-shape, a strange design she had not seen before. It was a long, graceful design that, in the silver light of the moon and the yellow of the flares, looked almost like a dragon, descending. Or a bat, come to think of it...

And the airship *was* beginning its descent, and Stoker must be alive up there, must have managed his escape, and was bringing back the precious information Mycroft had gambled so heavily for. Her men were spread out, the flares would only give away the landing site but the rest of them were keeping watch on the intruders–

"Ma'am! Hostile fire, ma'am!"

A burst of gunfire, sudden and unexpected, was followed by the whoosh of something heavy rising in the air–

She watched the slim, deadly rocket rise, a trail of smoke behind it–

"Take them," she said.

The rocket hit the side of the airship.

For a moment nothing happened. In the distance a burst of gunfire, which was returned, as her men fired on the unknown hostiles and were fired on in turn. Then, abruptly, a bright ball of flame erupted overhead and the side of the ship blew open, pieces of wood and metal raining down onto the park. Flames caught the side of the ship and it tilted with the impact, losing altitude rapidly.

Lucy swore.

"Ma'am, they are heavily armed!"

"Kill them."

"Ma'am, second group of hostiles moving in."

"We've lost any element of concealment," Lucy said.

"Ma'am?"

"Eliminate them."

And now the park had become a cacophony of battle, gunfire and explosives going off while the airship, having come all this way across Europe and the Channel, fell down heavily, into Richmond Park.

Lucy was already running, three of her men following, running towards the ship as it hit the ground with a sickening crunch, bouncing still, once, twice, then tilting on its side. A second explosion rocked the ship and flames rose high, almost engulfing it. If anyone was still alive inside...

"Ma'am, what are you–?"

"Stay back!"

She ran towards the flaming wreckage of the ship.

"Lucy! Stay back!"

Heedless, she dived into the flames. Thick black smoke rising now, the engines on fire, there would be mere moments before the whole thing blew up. Onto the flaming deck, titled sideways–

"Hel– help! Help me!"

He was still alive. She saw the small figure, not young any more, crawling towards her, gripping on to slats on the floor. He was leaving behind him a trail of blood– at least one of his legs was broken. She slid towards him.

"Stoker?"

"Help me. Please!"

The smoke had an acid stink to it. It burned her eyes, forced its way down her throat, choking her. She picked him up, or tried to. He was heavy; he cried out in pain when she touched him.

She wouldn't fail Mycroft, not now.

She picked him up and supported his weight and slid down farther, deeper into the raging fire–

Bullets flying overhead, tracer bullets lighting up the sky–

Through the fire, it licked at her skin, it caught in her hair, his weight no longer mattered, the ground was close, they were going to make it–

She fell off the side of the burning ship, her cargo with her. She rolled on the ground, putting out flames. Hands grabbed her, beat out the fire, lifted her.

"Stoker," she said. "Get... Stoker."

"Ma'am."

A new, loud voice, cutting like a rapier's blade through the night.

"Give him to us! You are outnumbered."

An alien accent. German, she thought, wildly.

"I thought," she said, panting, "I told you to kill them."

Apologetically: "There are a lot of them, ma'am."

"Grab Stoker!"

She spared a glance for the man. He was out, breathing shallowly, with difficulty. There was something around his neck, a metal canister on a string.

"Who the hell are *you*?" she called out, to the opposition.

There was an answering burst of gunfire and she smiled. They loped away from the burning airship, the smell of wood burning, metal melting, gas–

The explosion hit her back, threw her forwards. She rolled, a whoosh of hot flaming gas passed over her, and then they were up and running again and under shelter of the trees where the rest of her team closed on them, covering them against attack.

She checked on Stoker. Still alive, just about...

"Let's go," she said.

• • • •

They pursued them across Richmond Park in deathly silence, the Germans, if that's what they were, however much their force had been reduced, and the other force, whom she could not put a name to. In the shadow world there were no labels, nobody carried a name tag or a calling card with which to announce themselves. The attackers could have been anyone. French? She would have bet good money on that. The Quiet Council, meddling in Bureau affairs...

And Krupp's men, perhaps.

She couldn't know, and right then she didn't care. She had her prize, singed and wounded but hers to keep, and so they went deeper into the park where deer and squirrels shied away from them, a ghostly pursuit in the darkness, amongst the trees, while behind them the landing site had been compromised, the siren song of police automatons sounding in the night, and Lucy thought of Irene Adler and how she was getting no sleep that night.

They pulled back to the Isabella Plantation. There had been a folly there, a stone house amidst the ponds and flowerbeds, and there they laid down Stoker while they waited for their pursuers.

Lucy knelt beside him, checking his pulse. It was weak, irregular. And suddenly she knew he was not going to make it.

A knowledge like that had come on her before, in other battles, other days. With comrades and with enemies, and with civilians sometimes, who were not a part of the battle but had wandered into it and were singed by its fire. It was a terrible knowing, that a human's life was ending, before their time, violently, and that there was nothing she could do, that most of the time, if she was honest with herself, she had been responsible for that very thing, that terrible ending.

Yet all life comes to an end, and never are there answers as to why; Lucy had learned, the hard way, not to question, not to wonder. Death was something to be accepted; to question it was futile.

"Stoker," she said, gently. She gave him water, wetting his lips, letting it dribble into his throat. At last he opened his eyes.

"I need to know," she said. "I need to know what you've found."

"M… Mycroft…?" Stoker said.

"He sent me."

Stoker closed his eyes – in understanding or fatigue she didn't know. Lucy waited. It was quiet there, at the Isabella Plantation. The hunters would come but they were not yet there. At last Stoker opened his eyes. "I had… written down… report." His eyes moved, she followed their direction to the can hanging over his chest. "All there," he said. His mouth moved. Perhaps he tried to smile. "I had always… wanted," he said. "To… be a writer."

His eyes closed. His chest rose and fell and then did not rise again. After a moment, Lucy gently removed the can and the chain from around the dead man's neck. She opened it.

Inside was a small notebook, bound in dark vellum. It was filled with neat, tidy handwriting.

On the first page, in careful calligraphy, it said: *Bram Stoker's Journal*.

Sitting there, in that silence that comes before battle, Lucy read the last words of the dead man beside her.

PART VII
Bram Stoker's Journal

THIRTY-SEVEN

Bucharest–

I had finally arrived at this city, with darkness gathering, casting upon the city a most unfavourable appearance. Having checked into my hotel I drank a glass of strong Romanian wine, accompanied by bear steak, which I am told they bring from the mountains at great expense. I had not enquired as for the recipe.

I am sitting in my room, watching the dance of gaslight over the city. Tomorrow I set off for the mountains, and as I write this I am filled with trepidation. I have decided to maintain this record of my mission. In the event anything were to happen to me, this journal may yet make its way, somehow, back to London.

Let me, therefore, record how I came to be at this barbarous and re-mote country, and the sorry, tortuous route by which I had come to my current predicament.

My name is Abraham Stoker, called Abe by some, Bram by others. I am a theatrical manager, having worked for the great actor Henry Irving for many years as his personal assistant, and, on his behalf, as manager of the Lyceum Theatre in Covent Garden.

I am not a bad man, nor am I a traitor.

Nevertheless, it was in the summer of 18— that I became an

unwitting assistant to a grand conspiracy against our lizardine masters, and one which I was helpless to prevent.

It had begun as a great triumph for my theatrical career. Due to a fight between the great librettist W.S. Gilbert and his long-time manager, Richard D'Oyly Carte, over – of all things – a carpet, I had managed to lure Gilbert and his collaborator, the composer Arthur Sullivan, to my own theatre from D'Oyly Carte's Savoy. We were to stage their latest work, titled *The Pirates of the Carib Sea*, a rousing tale of adventure and peril. The first part, and forgive me if I digress, describes our lizardine masters' awakening on Caliban's Island, their journey with that foul explorer Amerigo Vespucci back to the British Isles, their overthrowing of our human rulers and their assumption of the throne – a historical tale set to song in the manner only G&S could possibly do it.

In the second part, we encounter the mythical pirate Wyvern, the one-eyed royal lizard who – if the stories in the *London Illustrated News* can be believed – had abandoned his responsibilities to his race, the royal Les Lézards, to assume the life of a bloodthirsty pirate operating in the Carib Sea, between Vespuccia and the lands of the Mexica and Aztecs, and preying on the very trade ships of his own Everlasting Empire, under her royal highness Queen Victoria, the lizard-queen.

Irving himself played – with great success, I might add! – the notorious pirate, assuming a lizard costume of some magnificence, while young Beerbohm Tree played his boatswain, Mr Spoons, the bald, scarred, enormous human who is – so they say – Wyvern's right-hand man.

It was at that time that a man came to see me in my office. He was a foreigner, and did not look wealthy or, indeed, distinguished.

"My name," he told me, "is Karl May."

"A German?" I said, and he nodded. "I represent certain… interests in Germany," he told me. "A very powerful man wishes to attend the opening night of your new show."

"Then I shall be glad to sell him a ticket," I said, regarding the man – clearly a con-man or low-life criminal of some sort – with distaste. "You may make the arrangements at the box office. Good day to you, sir."

Yet this May, if that was even his real name, did not move. Instead, leaving me speechless, he closed and then locked the door to my office, from the inside, leaving me stranded in there with him. Before I could rise the man pulled out a weapon, an ornate hand-gun of enormous size, which he proceeded to wave at me in a rather quite threatening manner.

"This man," he said, "is a very public man. Much attention is paid to his every move. Moreover, to compound our –" *our*, he said! "– problem, this man must meet another very public man, and the two cannot be seen to have ever met or discussed… whatever it is they need to discuss."

This talk of men meeting men in secret reminded me of my friend Oscar Wilde, whom I had known in my student days in Dublin and who had once been the suitor of my wife, Florence. "I do not see how I can help you," I said, stiffly – for it does not do to show fear before a foreigner, even one with a gun in his hand.

"Oh, but you can!" this Karl May said to me. "And moreover, you will be amply compensated for your efforts –" and with that, to my amazement, this seeming charlatan pulled out a small, yet heavy-looking bag, and threw it on my desk. I reached for it, drawing the string, and out poured a heap of gold coins, all bearing the portrait – rather than of our own dear lizard-queen – of the rather more foreboding one of the German Kaiser.

"Plenty more where that came from," said this fellow, with a smirk on his face.

I did not move to touch the money. "What would you have me do?" I said.

"The theatre," he said, "is like life. We look at the stage and are spell-bound by it, the scenery convinces us of its reality, the players move and speak their parts and, when it's done, we leave. And yet, what happens to *make* the stage, to move its players, is not done in the limelight. It is done behind the scenes."

"Yes?" I said, growing ever more irritated with the man's manner. "You wish to teach me my job, perhaps?"

"My dear fellow!" he said, with a laugh. "Far from it. I merely wished to illustrate a point–"

"Then get to it, for my time is short," I said, and at that his smile dropped and the gun pointed straight at my heart and he cocked it. "Your time," he said, in a soft, menacing voice, "could be made to be even shorter."

I must admit that, at that, my knees may have shaken a little. I am not a violent man, and am not used to the vile things desperate men are prepared to do. I therefore sat back down in my chair, and let him explain and, when he had finished, I must admit I felt a sigh of relief escape me, for it did not seem at all such a dreadful proposition, and they were willing to compensate me generously besides.

"You may as well know," Karl May said to me, "the name of the person I represent. It is Alfred Krupp."

"The *industrialist*?"

May nodded solemnly. "But what," I gasped, "could he be wanting in my theatre?"

For I have heard of Krupp, of course, the undisputed king of the armaments trade, the creator of that monstrous canon they called Krupp's Baby, which was said to be able to shoot its payload all the way beyond the atmosphere and into space... A recluse, a genius, a man with his own army, a man with no title and yet a man who, it was rumoured, was virtually the ruler of all Germany...

A man who had not been seen for many a year, in public.

"Fool," Karl May said. "My lord Krupp has no interest in your pitiful theatre, nor in the singing and dancing of effeminate Englishmen."

"I am Irish, if you don't mind," I said. "There really is no need to be so *rude*–" and May laughed. "Rest your mind at ease, Irishman," he said. "My master wishes only to meet certain... interested parties. Behind, as it were, the scenes."

"Which parties?" I said, "for surely I would need to know in order to prepare–"

"All in good time!" Karl May said. "All in good time."

• • • •

Bu teni–

This is a small mountain village near to my destination. I had taken the train this morning with no difficulty, yet was told the track terminated before my destination, which is the city of Brasov, nestled, so I am told, in a beautiful valley within the Carpathian Mountains.

This region is called Transylvania, and a wild and remote land it is indeed. The train journey lasted some hours, in relative comfort, the train filled with dour Romanian peasants, shifty-looking gypsies, Székelys and Magyars and all other manner of the strange people of this region. Also on board the train were chickens, with their legs tied together to prevent their escaping, and sacks of potatoes and other produce, and children, and a goat. Also on board the train were army officers of the Austro-Hungarian Empire of which this was but a remote and rather dismal outpost, with nary a pastry or decent cup of coffee to be seen.

I had wondered at the transportation of such military personnel, and noticed them looking rather sharply in my direction. Nevertheless I was not disturbed and was in fact regarded with respect the couple of times we had occasion to cross each other in passing.

The train's passage was impressive to me, the mountains at first looming overhead then – as the train rose up from the plains on which sat Bucharest – they rose on either side of the tracks, and it felt as though we were entering another world, of dark forests and unexplored lands, and I fancied I heard, if only in the distance, the howl of wolves, sending a delicious shiver down my spine.

But you did not ask me for a travel guide! Let me be brief. The train terminated, after some hours, at a station in the middle of a field. It was a most curious thing. I could see the tracks leading onwards – presumably to Brasov – but we could not go on. The train halted within these hastily erected buildings, lit by weak gas lamps planted in the dirt, and all – peasants and chickens and soldiers and gypsies and goat – disembarked, including this Irishman.

At this nameless station waited coaches and carts – the peasants and local people to the carts, the soldiers and more
well-to-do visitors to the coaches. I stood there in some bewilderment, when I was taken aside by the military officer who
seemed to be in charge of that platoon. "You are going – there?"
he said, and motioned with his head towards the distance, where
I assumed this city of Brasov lay.

"Yes," I said.

"To visit... him?"

I nodded at that, feeling a pang of apprehension at the
thought.

The officer nodded as if that had settled matters, and shouted
orders in the barbarous tongue of his people. Almost immediately
a coach had been found for me, its passengers emptied out, and
I was placed with all due reverence into the empty compartment.
"You will go to Bu teni this night," the officer said, "it is too late
now to go further." Again he spoke to the driver, who gave me a
sour look but didn't dare refuse, and so we took off in a hurry,
the horses running down a narrow mountain path that led upwards, and at last to a small village, or what passes for a town in
these parts, which was indeed called Bu teni, or something like
it, and had beautiful wooden houses, a church, and a small inn,
where I had alighted and where I am currently sat, writing this
to you, while dining on a rather acceptable *goulash*.

I do not wish to labour details of what took place following
that scoundrel Karl May's visit to my office at the Lyceum. You
know as well as I what had happened, you had suspected long
before you had approached me, three months ago, in order to
recruit me to this desperate mission.

The facts are as they stand. To an outside eye, nothing had
happened but that *Herr* Krupp, on a rare visit to England, went,
one night, to the theatre – and so did any number of other per-
sonages, including, if I remember rightly, yourself, Mr Holmes.

The Queen herself was there, in the Royal Box, stately as ever,
with her forked tongue hissing out every so often, to snap a stray
fly out of the air. I remember the prince regent did not come but

Victoria's favourite, that dashing Harry Flashman, the popular Hero of Jalalabad, was beside her. So were many foreign dignitaries and many of the city's leading figures, from our now-Prime-Minister Mrs Beeton, my friend and former rival Oscar Wilde, the famed scientists Jekyll and Moreau (before the one's suspicious death and the other's exile to the South Seas), the Lord Byron automaton (always a gentleman), Rudolph Rassendyll of Zenda, and many, many others. Your brother, the consulting detective, was there, if I recall rightly, Mr Holmes.

It was a packed night – sold out, in fact, and I had been kept off my feet, running hither and yon, trying to ensure our success, and all the while…

All the while, behind the scenes, things were afoot.

I was aware of movement, of strangers coming and going in silence, of that German villain Karl May (I had found out much later the man was not only a convicted criminal but worse, a dime novel hack) following me like a shadow, of a tense anticipation that had nothing to do with the play.

There are secret passageways inside every theatre, and the Lyceum is no exception. It has basements and sub-basements, a crypt (from the time it had been a church, naturally), narrow passageways, false doors, shifting scenery – it is a *theatre*, Mr Holmes!

It was a game of boxes, Mr Holmes. As I told you when you found me, three months ago, listening to me as if you already knew. How *Herr* Krupp appeared to be in the box when in fact it was a cut-out in the shadows; how he went through the false wall and into the passageway between the walls, and down, to the crypt, now our props room.

And the others.

For I had been unfortunate enough to see them.

Bu teni–

A letter had arrived for me in the morning. A dark baruch-landau had stopped outside the inn, a great hulking machine, steam-driven, the stoker standing behind while the driver sat in front, in between their respective positions a wide carriage for the transport of passengers or cargo.

The driver had disembarked – I watched him from my window – and what a curious being he was!

I had seen his like before. Just the once, and that had been enough. Like the vehicle he was driving, he was huge, a mountain of a man, and a shiver of apprehension ran down my spine.

He would have been human, once upon a time.

"What *are* they?" I had asked Karl May. The play was going on above our heads, but I could not concentrate, I was filled with a terrible tension as we prepared for the summit – as May called it – down below, in the bowels of the theatre. The *they* I was referring to were beings of a similar size and disposition to the driver now sitting in the inn's dining room, awaiting my pleasure.

"Soldiers," Karl May told me. "Of the future."

"What has been done to them?"

"Have you heard of the Jekyll–Frankenstein serum?"

I confessed I had not.

"It is the culmination of many years of research," he told me, with a smirk. "We had stolen the formula from the French some time back. They have Viktor von Frankenstein working for them and he, in his turn, improved upon the work done by your Englishman, Dr Jekyll. This–" and here his hand swept theatrically, enfolding the huge hulking beings that were guarding, like mountain trolls, the dark corridors – "is the result."

"Can they ever… go back?" I said, whispering. May shook his head. "And their life-span is short," he said. "But they do make such excellent soldiers…"

It was then that *Herr* Krupp appeared, an old, fragile-looking man, yet with a steely determination in his eyes that I found frightening. "You did well," he said, curtly, and I was not sure if he was speaking to May or myself. He disappeared behind his monsters, and into the crypt.

"Who else are we expecting?" I said.

When, at that moment, the sound of motors sounded and a small, hunched figure came towards us in the darkness, half-human, half-machine…

Bu teni–

My landlady has been fussing over me ever since seeing the arrival of the carriage. "You must not go!" she whispered to me, fiercely, finding reason to come up to my room. "He is a devil, a monster!"

"You know of him?" I said.

"Who does not? They had closed the valley, Brasov had been emptied. They are doing unspeakable things there, in the shadow of the mountains." She shivered. "But *he* does not reside in Brasov."

"Where does he reside?" I said, infected by her fear.

"Castle Bran," she said, whispering. "Where once Vlad epe made his home…"

"Vlad epe ?" I said. I was not familiar with the local history and the name was unfamiliar to me.

"Vlad the Third, Prince of Wallachia," she said, impatiently. "Vlad epe – how you say epe in your English?"

"I don't know," I said, quite bewildered.

"Impaler," she said. "Prince Vlad of the Order of the Dragon, whom they called Impaler."

I shook my head impatiently. Local history sounded colourful indeed, but irrelevant to my journey. "The man I am going to see is an Englishman," I said, trying to reassure her. "Englishmen do not impale."

"He is no man!" she said, and made a curious gesture with her fingers, which I took to be some Romanian superstition for the warding of evil. "He had ceased being human long ago."

At last I got rid of her, so I could return to my journal. Time is running out, and soon I shall be inside that baruch-landau, travelling towards my final destination.

Have mercy on my soul, Mycroft!

• • • •

For I saw him, too, you see. I saw him come towards us, Karl May and I, in the subterranean depths of the Lyceum, that fateful night.

An old, old man, in a motorised chair on wheels, a steam engine at his back, and withered hands lying on the supports, controlling brass keys. His face was a ruined shell, his body that of a corpse, yet his eyes were bright, like moons, and they looked at me, and his mouth moved and he said, "Today, Mr Stoker, we are making history. Your part in it will not be quickly forgotten."

I may have stumbled upon my words. He had not been seen in public for five years or more. His very presence at my theatre was an honour, and yet I was terrified. When the small get entangled in the games of the great, they may easily suffer.

"My lord," I said. "It is an honour."

He nodded then that withered head, just once, acknowledging this. Then he, too, disappeared towards the crypt.

Yes, you suspected, did you not, Mycroft? You suspected this summit, your people were there that night, in the audience, trying to sniff scent of what was happening. Yet you never did.

For they did not meet, just the two of them, My Herr Krupp and he, my summoner, the lord of the automatons.

Another was there.

A monster...

For I had gone down into the dark passages, I had gone to check all was secure, and I saw it. I saw the ancient sewer open up and something come crawling out of it, a monstrous being like a giant invertebrate, with feelers as long as a human arm, slithering towards that secret meeting... A vile, alien thing.

Which, three months ago, when we first met, you finally gave a name to.

The Bookman, you told me.

So that was that shadowy assassin.

A thing made by the lizardine race, long ago.

Those beings which came to us from Caliban's Island, in the Carib Sea, and yet were not of a terrestrial origin at all.

An ancient race, of scientifically advanced beings... crash-landed with their ship of space, thousands of years ago, millions perhaps, on that island.

And awakened by Vespucci, on his ill-fated journey of exploration...

And the Bookman, that shadowy assassin, one of their machines?

I do not know, Mycroft, but I remember the fear I felt when I saw that... that *thing*, slither towards the crypt.

A summit indeed.

And now, I must leave.

The Borgo Pass–

The driver says we are going through something called the Borgo Pass, though it appears on no map of the area. I am the sole passenger of this baruch-landau, the driver ahead, the stoker behind, and I in the middle, staring out over a rugged terrain.

This is the letter I had received at the inn:

My friend,
Welcome to the Carpathians. I am anxiously expecting you. I
trust that you slept well. My driver has instructions to carry you
in safety to my quarters and bring you to me. I trust that your
journey from London has been a happy one, and that you will
enjoy your stay. I look forward to seeing you.
Yours –
Charles Babbage

What awaits me beyond these mountains, is it to glory, or to death, that I ride?

THIRTY-EIGHT

Outside the night was still, an anticipatory silence as Lucy's men waited for the attack they knew would come. The Isabella Plantation was as good a place as any to wait–

They would be there soon, Lucy knew.

She continued reading the journal.

It described Stoker's arrival in Transylvania, his visit to Castle Bran, his meeting with Babbage... It described, in detail, what he had found there, that remote and wild region, away from prying eyes, away from the laws of empires.

A chill stole over Lucy as she read.

For now she knew the truth.

She read the journal, almost to the end.

One last addendum – it must have been written with Stoker in flight, after he had stolen the airship and fled. He had climbed onto the ledge beyond his window, at Castle Bran climbing the airship's mooring line like a spider or a monkey. They had found out, shot at him. He had been wounded, but had survived to bring the document back, only to die then. She had failed to save him.

Lucy did not allow herself to feel guilt. She couldn't. But her failure lay heavy on her, and Stoker's last words were like the scratches made by a sharp pen, and each stabbed at her, a little, all adding up.

Bram Stoker's Journal

That first night was long ago. Lord Babbage had disappeared from public life, and of Krupp nothing more was heard. In eighty-eight Mrs Beeton ascended to Prime Minister, beating Moriarty, and a new balance of power established itself, with the lizard-queen ceding some of her former power to a coalition of human, automaton and lizard: a true democracy, of sorts.

There had been rumours in the London papers, during that time, as to the mysterious demise of the Bookman, though none could vouch as to their veracity. In any case, my life continued as before, at the Lyceum, and I had all but forgotten that terrible, night-time summit deep below my beloved theatre, when there came a knock at the door.

"Enter," I said, preoccupied with paperwork on my desk, and heard him come in, and shut the door behind him. When I raised my head and looked I started back, for there, before me, stood that same German conman and hack writer, the source of all my troubles – Karl May.

"You!" I said.

The fellow grinned at me, quite at ease. "Master Stoker," he said, doffing his hat to me. "It has been a while."

"Not long enough!" I said, with feeling, and with shaking hands reached to the second drawer for the bottle I kept there – for emergencies, you see.

May mistook my gesture. The old gun was back in his hand and he tsked at me disapprovingly, like a headmaster with an errant pupil.

God, how I hated him at that moment!

"A drink?" I said, ignoring his weapon, and bringing out the bottle and two cups. At that his good humour returned, the gun disappeared, and he sat down. "By all means," he said. "Let us drink to old friends."

I poured; we drank. "What do you want, May?" I said.

"I?" he said. "I want nothing, for myself. It is Lord Babbage who has shown a renewed interest in you, my friend."

"Babbage?" I said.

"I will put it simply, Stoker," he said. "My Lord Babbage requires

a... chronicler of the great work he is undertaking. And there are pre-cious few who can be brought in. You, my friend, are already involved. And you have proven yourself reliable. It is, after all, why you are still alive."

"But why me?" *I said, or wailed, and he smiled. "My Lord Bab-bage," he said, "has got it into his head that you are a man of a literary bent."*

At that I gaped, for it was true, that I had dabbled in writing fictions, as most men do at one point or another, yet had taken no consideration of showing them to anyone but my wife.

"I thought so," Karl May said.

"But you're a writer," I said. "Why can't you—"

"My work lies elsewhere," he said, darkly.

I could not hold back a smirk, at that. "He does not value your fic-tion?" I said. At this he scowled even more. "You will make your way to Transylvania," he said. He took out an envelope and placed it on the desk. "Money, and train tickets," he said.

"And if I refuse?"

This made him smile again.

"Oh, how I wish you would," he said, and a shiver went down my spine at the way he said it. I picked up the envelope without further protest, and he nodded, once, and left without further words.

Castle Bran–

I must escape this place, for I will never be allowed to depart alive, I now know.

Mycroft, you had come to me, two weeks after that meeting with Karl May. I remember you coming in, a portly man, shadows at your back. You came alone.

Without preamble you told me of your suspicions back at that opening night, and told me of the conspiracy you were trying to unravel. An un-holy alliance between Krupp and Babbage and that alien Bookman. What were they planning? you kept saying. What are they after?

You had kept sporadic checks on me, and on the Lyceum. And your spotters had seen the return of Karl May.

Now you confronted me. You wanted to know where my allegiance lay.

Choose, you told me.

Choose, which master to serve.

For Queen and Country, you told me.

My name is Abraham Stoker, called Abe by some, Bram by others. I am a theatrical manager, having worked for the great actor Henry Irving for many years as his personal assistant, and, on his behalf, as manager of the Lyceum Theatre in Covent Garden.

I am not a bad man, nor am I a traitor.

Lucy closed the pages of the journal. She stared at the vellum-bound volume in her hands, thinking of the man she had failed to save.

Thinking of the strange machinations of humans and machines... of Transylvania, and what Stoker had found there.

Transylvania.

The strange word, like the name of another, distant world...

She had to take this to someone, and Mycroft was dead, and Fogg was working for the Bookman. She felt lost, desperate.

Then the moment passed and her head was clear, and the call of a bird sounded outside, a mimicked sound, not real, and she knew that it was time even before Bosie came to get her.

"Ma'am, hostile force approaching."

Lucy Westenra stood up and tucked the journal carefully into her pocket and pulled out her guns. She stepped out of the building into the dark world outside.

"Kill them," she said, softly.

PART VIII
Der Erntemaschine

THIRTY-NINE

The observer was definitely feeling ill at ease. He had made his way inside the Parisian undercity easily, guided by the voices, at least two of whom seemed to know the city well.

It was quite remarkable, he thought. There was something he found very comforting about a second, hidden urban space, lying this close to the other. There were people down there too, and he was very tempted to sample them, but the voices began to shout and he decided to stick to the objective without any further delay.

He had expected the fog of radiation to reduce underground but the closer they came to the place the voices had described, the more intense it grew – not just what the humans called Tesla waves but a whole spectrum of wide-bandwidth signals, almost as though…

Almost as though they belonged to his progenitors, he thought.

But that should not have been the case. He was, he was quite certain, the only observer on this planet. His progenitors, in fact, had shown remarkably little enthusiasm for this expedition. Some form of historical amateur society existing in the Spectral Swarm had received the signal of the activated, obsolete quantum scanner and had despatched a vessel through the resultant wormhole before it had collapsed. The observer had been gestated in orbit around this curious blue-white planet, and dropped down without due ceremony to see what he could find.

So why was there, suddenly, such an explosion of signatory radiation…?

A dreadful thought had formed itself in the observer's think-cloud and slowly permeated his I-loop, born out of some deep archaic data and wild speculation. He tried to push it away.

As he passed through the tunnels he came across a small human with a hunchback, and a grotesque, giant human. They did not see him. They were, in fact, occupied, somewhat to the observer's befuddlement, in what appeared to be a duet. They were singing.

Again he was tempted to sample them, but the voices were growing quite hysterical by then: a routine diagnosis suggested their storage had become entangled with other historical data banks and that they may have been the cause of the alarming concept he was currently trying to ignore. Sighing a little – because a good observer learned *from the specimens he collected – he ignored the two strange humans and went straight on, finding at last a primitive, abandoned research facility of some sort, and a dying human which one of the voices, that of the fat man, identified to him as one Viktor von Frankenstein, a research scientist working for the organisation called the Quiet Council. Delighted he could finally do his job, the observer knelt beside the man, whose eyes focused on him weakly and whose voice said, "Help... me."*

The observer was quite happy to do exactly that. He released the spike, which jutted out of the top of his hand, and inserted it deftly into the man's cortex, the data-spike extending like a telescope as it went, swiftly and assuredly, through the different layers of the man's brain, extracting neural pathways and the man's embedded I-loop and data storage into the observer's own, infinitely more advanced hardware.

The man on the ground became a corpse. The eyes stopped seeing. The head lolled back. The man said, Where the hell am I?

The observer was happy to let the other voices explain, even though a pre-prepared data-packet had already been introduced into the new I-loop's structure. Meanwhile he was studying this latest specimen with fascination, until he came to the last moments of the creature's biological incarnation, at which point he gave an involuntary shriek of alarm that set off explosions in several of the still-functioning devices in the underground research chamber.

They're here! *the voice that had been Viktor von Frankenstein said.*

No, *the observer thought/said,* that can't be.

Another voice said, Smith? Smith is here?

It was the woman he had collected in Bangkok.

The observer let the voices go on, running in the background. He, too, was running now, suddenly desperate to get above-ground again. All the while he was running interrogatory routines over the entirety of the Viktor specimen's memories.

Alarms were slowly popping up all over the observer's network. It ran through crowds of frightened humans (sweat, adrenalin, pheromones all registering briefly), through the tunnels and up, bursting at last onto the surface.

A cacophony of voices he had been trying to ignore washed over him. Ancient voices, in a strange antique dialect. The observer watched the city, engulfed in flames. He observed the machines, half-ghostly in the twilight, as though they were fading in and out of existence.

The device! the observer thought. A human curse rose into the forefront of his mind and he unconsciously used it.

Where the hell *was the device?*

Smith remembered the hours that followed fleetingly, in unreal snatches.

At some point it seemed the Seine itself was on fire, its dark waters reflecting flames and destruction as he and Van Helsing ran–

"There is a way," Van Helsing said.

"How?"

"Look!"

He had made Smith look. The fires and the alien machines rampaging over the city, flicking in and out of existence as though they were pictures projected out of a camera obscura.

"There is a focal point," Van Helsing said.

"How can you tell?"

"Look! The destruction moves, but it is bound by a circumference. The device must have activated them, but has a limited range."

Smith looked. It was possible... he saw that, indeed, some parts of the city were passed by, while others were only now coming under attack–

"It's moving!"

"Yes."

"But how can we find the focal point? We have to stop the device!" Smith said.

"There is a way," Van Helsing said. "But it is dangerous—"

Smith would have laughed, at that. After a moment Van Helsing gave a sheepish grin. "More dangerous, I mean," he said.

"What do we need to do?" Smith said.

"We need to find a vantage point," Van Helsing said. "From above we could see it more clearly, we could identify the source."

Smith looked at the city's skyline.

And Van Helsing's meaning sank in.

"The *Tour Eiffel*," Smith said.

They ran.

Snatches of stolen time, Smith's lungs on fire. At some point they commandeered a baruch-landau, Van Helsing stoked the furnace as Smith drove. The city streets were on fire, coaches burning, people running this way and that; some were looting the shops, others were barricaded inside buildings. There was sporadic gunfire, flames reflected in windows, and high above, the tripods dominated the skyline, moving, now that he knew to look for it, moving in a single direction, sweeping over the city.

The Tour Eiffel had been built only a few years earlier, during the French's *Exposition Universelle*. Smith had been involved in an operation, years before, to recruit its builder, Gustave Eiffel, when the man was building a train station in Africa, in the place the Portuguese, who had unsuccessfully tried to colonise it, called Mozambique.

The operation had been a failure, and Eiffel returned to France, building at last this greatest of follies, a giant metal tower rising into the sky above the Champ de Mars, like a vast antennae aimed at the stars.

Rumour had it that was the building's true purpose, that the Quiet Council had intended its use as a sort of communication device, sending messages into deep space... possibly receiving messages, too, if the rumours were true.

"What's... up... there?" he shouted – a ray of flame from the sky hit the side of a building and they swerved madly to avoid the avalanche.

"Aerial... experimentation... station!" Van Helsing shouted. "Drive! Drive, God damn it, Smith!"

So Smith drove, avoiding debris and the corpses of the dead lying in the street, and the burning stalls and coaches and seas of cockroaches escaping as their habitats were destroyed, and swarms of rats, and looters, and militias, heading towards that great metal tower, hoping they would not be too late.

FORTY

The machines were moving.

Their skeletal frames silhouetted against the dark skies. Their legs moved jerkily, yet there was something beautiful about it, too, their motion over the city skyline, taking no mind to the buildings and people below. Here and there, like stars in the skies, the machines winked in and out of existence, as though their light was passing through the atmosphere, distorted.

"Where do they come from?"

Van Helsing, rode shotgun on the swerving baruch-landau, face blackened with coal, the sweat from the stoker forming rivulets down his face so that he looked covered in war paint.

"I don't know."

"Some other world?" Smith persisted. "How can they materialise and dematerialise like this? Are they even real?"

"The destruction they cause is real enough."

"And they seem…" Smith hesitated. The baruch-landau, like an elderly assassin, puffing hard, was approaching the Eiffel Tower at last. It was quieter here, the machines had moved across the city. "Old," he said, with a note of wonder.

"What?" Van Helsing shouted. Smith swerved to avoid the corpse of a donkey lying in the street. It was quiet now on the Champ de Mars:

A long avenue of fantastical shapes, wizened four-armed creatures, semi-human, semi-ape, standing guard, carved in stone–

Landscaped canals, built to reflect what could be seen on the surface of the planet Mars, a silver gondola, used to carry tourists, now upturned in the water. A giant model of the red planet itself had fallen off its dais and cracked, and Smith had to swerve around it. Groaning, the baruch-landau came to a halt.

"We're out of coal," Van Helsing said, apologetically.

But it had lasted them long enough. Smith jumped off the vehicle with a groan of his own – his relief echoed in the machine's own creaks and groans. Van Helsing climbed down and joined him. It was eerily quiet. They stood on the red surface of the Champs de Mars, the Tour Eiffel rising above them like a pointing finger. Above it the stars shone down, the Milky Way traversing the dome of the sky. Somewhere up there was Mars itself, surrounded by its two moons–

Which, down here, were still on their pedestals, smooth round globes showing a lack of imagination, Smith thought, on the part of their anonymous sculptor.

"Why old?" Van Helsing said.

Smith couldn't answer him. He had imagined the threat from space to be something ill-defined, a technology so advanced it could remake human minds and shape whole planets. These machines, walking oddly over the Parisian cityscape, giant metal tripods spewing fire, flickering in and out of existence, seemed somehow to belong to a sideways world, conjured out of some alternate reality–

"Could we have built them?" he said to Van Helsing.

"The machines?"

"Yes."

"The technology involved… Oh." Van Helsing's eyes clouded and he said, "I see what you mean."

"Could they be Babbage's?"

"I find that unlikely. In any case, I have never heard of such war machines being designed, let alone constructed," Van Helsing said.

"But it is not impossible."

"But the device," Van Helsing said. "It is clearly extraterrestrial."

"But are those machines–" Smith shrugged. For the moment it didn't matter. They were talking because talking was better for the moment than acting, because in a moment they would have to press on and, the truth be told, he was exhausted.

The words of a long-ago instructor at the Ham facility came back to him. *In every mission there comes a moment of near-breaking, the moment when you want to stop, to abandon the mission, to find a hole and crawl into it and sleep, forever. At those moments, stop. Give your mind and your body the time to catch up, even if the mission reaches a critical stage. You are no use to anyone at that stage. Take a break. Look back at how far you've come, and evaluate clearly how far you still have to go. Only then, act.*

It was quiet at the Champs de Mars, and in the distance the machines moved, the city burned, in the distance Charles Babbage sat in his dark castle and planned his dark plans, the Mechanical Turk was deactivated and dumped in storage, Alice was dead, the Harvester was moving, Mycroft's long-laid plans were forming or unravelling, he didn't know. He looked up at the tower rising above them, a graceful latticework of iron, worked by humans, two airships moored to its top. "What's up there?" he said, looking at it again, uneasily. There had been rumours at the Bureau...

Van Helsing said, "Nothing much, I imagine. There had been restaurants during the Exposition Universelle, and a viewing deck."

"And now?"

Van Helsing shrugged.

Smith shook his head, feeling uneasy. It was too quiet at the Champs de Mars, almost as though, somewhere, unseen eyes were watching them, and calculating... He took a deep breath, stretched aching muscles.

"How do we get up there?" he said at last, resigned.

"There's a lift," Van Helsing said.

Smith said, "Oh."

• • • •

They found an opening at the foot of the tower. A lift, or – in the parlance of English-speaking Vespuccians, an elevator – apparently functional, and with a small, utilitarian sign on it of a skull and crossbones accompanied by the words *Entry Forbidden. Biohazard* in French.

"What do you think?" Smith said. Van Helsing shrugged and pulled off the sign.

The lift took them up, smoothly and without a fuss, travelling through latticework up to the second level of the Tour Eiffel. There the doors opened noiselessly and they stepped out onto what appeared to be an abandoned viewing deck–

Shadows moving up there, a silhouette momentarily seen against the burning skyline, something feral and–

A shot rang out. Smith hit the floor, his own gun out, the shadow moved again and he fired, once, twice, and it fell, tumbling over the parapet in silence.

Smith swore. Why had he assumed the tower would be empty? He turned to Van Helsing–

And saw the other man slumped on the floor, blood spreading across his chest. "No," Smith said. "Abraham, no..."

"They got me, Smith," Van Helsing said. His voice was thick, surprised. He put his hand to his chest. It came away bloodied. He stared at it, confused. "They got me," he said, wonderingly.

"Let me see it, Abraham."

Smith reached for the other man, cut out his shirt. Shadows moving in the distance, coming closer. When he tore open Van Helsing's shirt the bullet hole was marked. Van Helsing coughed, and blood bubbled out of his mouth and fell down his chin.

"Let it go, Smith," Van Helsing said. He smiled, or tried to. "Isn't this the way we always thought we'd go? Better than to lie in bed, riddled by cancers, or old age, or that sickness that eats away memory. I wanted one more job."

"You had it," Smith said, and his own voice was thick.

"Go up to the top of the tower. There are... machines there. Be... careful."

"Abraham–"

But his friend was sinking to the ground, his eyes fighting to stay open. Smith held him, cradling him in his arms, Van Helsing's blood seeping into his own clothes. "It was worth it," Van Helsing said. "Playing... the Great Game."

His eyes closed. His breathing stopped. Gently, Smith lowered him to the ground. Abraham Van Helsing, another name added to the tally of the dead. Shadows moved, coming closer, snarling. Smith's gun was out of its holster and he fired, and watched them drop.

What the hell *lived* up here? he thought.

He examined the first body. His bullet had hit it in the chest, it was still alive. It would have been human, but...

What *were* those things?

The sign on the lift door. *Biohazard*.

What use was the tower being put to?

The creature would have been human but it was changed in some grotesque way. Not the way of the F-J serum, nor in a Moreau-style hybridisation (Smith had the unfortunate experience of meeting that exiled scientist once), not even in the bizarre methodology of that mad hunchback genius Ignacio Narbondo.

The body below twitched and foam came out of its mouth and still it tried to move, to bite him, with shiny yellow teeth. Its eyes, too, were yellow, and it was hairy, with a naked chest. Somewhere, a bell *dinged*, faintly but unmistakably...

Smith went around the foaming man-dog creature and went to the parapet and looked out over the city. Paris, in flames – but the machines were moving, heading... east?

And now he could see the circle of influence, just as Van Helsing had said it would be. The machines were moving in a radius of about three miles, a hovering shape of fire and smoke moving slowly but inexorably over the Parisian skyline. A baleful moon glared down, and above, the stars were being stubbed out as the smoke rose to obscure them.

The device, he thought, would be at the centre of it. And moving. Somehow, it had opened a hole into – what? Another world? – and brought these machines of death and destruction into life.

Get hold of the device, he thought. Shut it down.

How?

Van Helsing wanted him to go to the top of the tower. An aerial experimentation station, he had said.

Perhaps he could get hold of an airship or–

Somewhere, the *ding* of a bell, faint but clear–

Smith turned–

There were three of them, standing there. Hair grew out of their faces, spilling down. Their eyes were yellow, rabid. Their fingers curved into talons, their nails like scimitars. One of them growled.

It had occurred to him, too late, that he should have made a start going up sooner.

There were no lifts to the top of the tower.

And the three creatures were blocking the stairs...

"I don't want to kill you," he said. He disliked guns and using them. And these creatures seemed to him somehow innocent, as if a great wrong had been done to them. They looked insane, they belonged at an asylum.

"Step out of my way and you won't be hurt," he said.

Somewhere, the ding of a bell, clear and loud, and for the third time–

The three – men-dogs? What could you call them? – twitched as one, as if the bell was controlling their actions. Then they charged Smith.

He dropped the first one with a shot but then a second barrelled into him and the gun flew, over the parapet and down, onto the Champs de Mars far below. Smith grunted, the air knocked out of him, and fell back–

His hand reaching for the knife strapped to his ankle, the blade flashing, and he buried it in the belly of the creature, who howled pitifully and collapsed on top of Smith, pinning him down. Smith, grunting, pushed at the body, the blood, the colour of pus, slipping into his clothes–

The creature was heavy and the third one was coming at him at an odd loping gait, teeth flashing–

Smith struggled to push off the body lying on top of him but couldn't. The dog-man came closer and his muzzle came down, biting–

Smith shielded himself with the dead one on top of him and the living dog-man bit its comrade instead. Snarling, it tore at the flesh, pulling it, until Smith, with a sigh, managed to slide from underneath it. He rose to his feet, shaky, the bloodied knife in his hand...

The dog-man stared at him over the corpse of its friend, an arm between its teeth–

"Shoo," Smith said. "Shoo!"

The dog-man growled.

Smith, moving carefully, circled around the body. The dog-man followed. "I just want to get to the stairs," Smith said. "Do you understand? I mean you no harm–"

Which was an unlikely thing to say, under the circumstances.

The dog-man growled. He looked like he was thinking. Smith moved, his back to the stairs now; the way was open, he was going to make a run for it–

The sound of a bell, clearly and sweetly in the night.

"Not *again*," Smith said.

There came a growling sound around the corner and, for a moment, it felt to Smith as if that entire edifice, that Tour Eiffel, was shaking with it. He heard the pounding of heavy bodies and the unmistakable sound of gunshots, like the one that had dropped Van Helsing and he thought, There must be others up here, soldiers or–

He ran for it.

Up the stairs, but now there were bodies coming at him from above, too, dog-men of sorts, hypnotised by that deadly sound of a bell, ringing–

It reminded him of something, rumours long ago, at the Bureau, and a failed mission on the Black Sea–

He twisted sideways, his knife flashed and a howling dog-man flew through the air and beyond the parapet and down to his death, the Champs de Mars, Smith thought, turning as red as the planet it was mimicking. Up the stairs and his knees hurt and it was a long way up, a long–

That damn bell, and now footsteps on the landing he had come to, the city down below, the tripods moving jerkily across the ancient buildings, the fires burning, that Egyptian obelisk looted from Luxor toppled, flames above the Louvre, hordes of people running down the Avenue des Champs-Elysees–

Footsteps, and a voice like a bell saying, "You should not have come up here–"

Smith, stopping, out of breath–

A man in his fifties, white in his beard, deep-set eyes–

That mission on the Black Sea, long ago, and a promising young Russian scientist, doing strange experiments on–

Dogs, yes–

An extraction that didn't work because the French, as it turned out, had got to him first–

"Ivan Pavlov," Smith said, stopping still.

That damn bell.

He should have known.

FORTY-ONE

Was it a sickness of the age, or of its sciences? Did it drive its practitioners mad, or were they mad to begin with?

You had to be a little crazy, Smith always reasoned, to delve into life's bigger questions, to ask – *why are we here*? or, *what happens when I do this*? or *why is a raven like a writing desk*?

Why *was* a raven like a writing desk?

Because there's a B in both, as Mycroft used to say.

Science was an alien way of looking at the world. It required asking questions, and then setting out to answer them, experimenting, trying to get the same results each time–

And in the process inhaling all kinds of potentially quite dangerous gases, or experimenting with lethal death rays, or ravenous bacteria, or intelligent machines that would, unexpectedly, go berserk–

If you weren't a little mad to begin with, Smith reasoned, you were likely to be more than a little on the unstable side by the time you spent a couple of lonely years in a draughty lab, poring over unknown chemicals, building weapons of mass destruction or trying to meld together human-dog hybrids. You'd see it time after time: with Moreau, with Jekyll, with Darwin and Frankenstein (both *père* and *fils*) and Edison (with his desperate quest for the perfect mechanical doll), Brunel the mad builder,

Stephenson with his locomotives, and those people from the Baltimore Gun Club who tried to shoot themselves into space and ended up squashed like bugs by the acceleration.

Scientists were mad, it was a well-known fact; there was nothing to it. You just had to use a soothing voice, avoid making any threatening gestures, and slowly go around them if you could.

"Shoo?" Smith said.

Pavlov smiled. "I remember you, I think," he said. "They showed me dossiers of all the major shadow executives, back in the day, in case I got approached, in case anyone tried to turn me. Which proved to be the case. My experiments were harmless!"

"Conditioning," Smith said. A lot of things were clearer now. "You were experimenting on dogs, back then, but the Bureau was interested in the practical application of your methodology on humans... and then the French stole you from under us."

Pavlov shrugged. "They offered me what you, with your lizardine masters, could never offer me," he said. "Freedom, for myself and my experiments both."

"We would have offered you the freedom you needed–"

Pavlov's face twisted in a strange, unpleasant grin.

Something in his expression...

Smith, staring at him, suddenly aghast:

"You can't mean–"

"Lizards," Pavlov said.

The word hung between them in the air, as heavy as an anchor. Smith swallowed.

"The French would have never–" he said.

"Think, Smith," Pavlov said. "Royal lizards! That alien life-form, Les Lézards, our masters – and our enemies? We have to study them, Smith!" He peered at him. "It *is* Smith, isn't it?"

"Yes."

"Funny, I thought you'd be dead by now."

"Retired," Smith said. Pavlov shrugged. "It is something your people never understood," he said, returning to his subject. "You were conditioned, just as my dogs had been conditioned, back in the St Petersburg labs. You've been *trained*, the lizards your masters, and to question them is, for you, simply an impossibility."

He saw Smith's look, and smiled again. "Oh, yes," he said, complacently. "I have studied them. It was not easy, yet, even with the royal lizards, there are... how shall I put it? Disappearances? They make such fascinating subjects..."

"You lie," Smith said. He could not picture it – Les Lézards, those magnificent creatures, those intelligent, man-sized lizardine beings, *royal* beings, subjected to experiments, locked up in a secret lab, abused, tortured–

"Am I?" Pavlov said. "I have a specimen right here, as it happens. Though I've not been able to breed them..." He sighed, wistfully. "Such a perfect location," he said. "Up here. Total security. Usually we have soldiers guarding the Champs de Mars entrance but with this..." he waved his hand vaguely at the city – "this *invasion*, obviously, it's been alarming the test subjects. Incredibly inconvenient, really. Do you know what it is?"

"Some lizardine device," Smith said. "Activated by accident."

Pavlov sighed. "You see?" he said. "They are dangerous, and they seek to rule us all. They cannot be trusted, and have to be *studied*."

"What *are* your test subjects?" Smith said. Pavlov lit up. "These?" he said. "My little dog-men? I raised them from puppies, you know."

"I didn't think hybrids were your field," Smith said. He was still trying to figure out how to get past the scientist. Two of his "test subjects" were standing just behind him, ready to attack, and more had amassed down below, blocking any retreat. The only other way was to jump... and he didn't rate smashing into the ground far down below as a particularly successful escape.

When in doubt, keep them talking, as they taught them at Ham, all those years ago.

"They're not," Pavlov said. "I got them from Moreau. We've kept a... lively correspondence, even after his exile. He sent them to me as a gift. You see, us scientists need to work freely, to exchange views and data with each other, to *learn* from each other in order to achieve scientific progress, we have to work *together* to *assail* the *heights* of–"

"Oh, screw it," Smith said. With two steps he was level with the Russian scientist and his stiletto, kept in his sleeve, snickered out.

Pavlov froze.

"Keep your dogs away," Smith said. The words wheezed out of him, he was tired and angry and the memory of Van Helsing's death lay on him like a weight, pressing him down. "Up the stairs, now!"

He pushed and the scientist moved, the knife pressed against his flesh. The dog-men growled, but kept their distance.

"Let's not have any more *bells* ringing, shall we?" Smith said. Pavlov, his face frozen in fury, said nothing.

Up they went, up and up the long winding latticework stairs of the Tour Eiffel, higher and higher, the dog-men at their heels, the city smoking and burning below and Smith knew he was running out of time, fast.

"You won't–"

"Get away with this? I was going to say the same thing to you," Smith said. Pavlov, panting as the climb took its toll, said, "You're a fool, Smith. You have to stop serving false masters. Listen. Join us. Come over to our side. The Council needs good people – now more than ever –" this with a view of the destruction below. "The game is being played to its end. This is the time to choose sides. Join us."

Smith was so surprised he almost laughed. "You're trying to turn *me*?"

"I am trying to *save* you," Pavlov said. "These machines, out there? They're just the beginning, Smith! Who knows what infinitely more powerful force will come when we least expect it, when we're least prepared, to whom we are as ants are to humans? Do you really think you would save the human race best by serving its *masters*?"

Smith didn't answer. Up they went, in a dizzying rise, and the dog-men silently followed.

"I am… only… trying… to save this city!" Smith said, panting. They had almost reached the top. The Russian scientist, too, looked wan and out of breath. "Then go," Pavlov said. "I won't stop you. Just let me go. I can't take another damn step."

Smith said, "Fine," and pushed him. The Russian Scientist lost his balance, then fell down the stairs, heavily, rolling until his dog-men stopped his fall. They stood hunched over him, looking up at Smith with hungry, yellow eyes.

"Have you thought," Smith said softly, "that it might be better to have wiser masters, when these are the things that we do to each other?" He looked at the dog-men and there was anger, and compassion, in his voice when he said, "And you forgot your bell."

From down below, the bruised Pavlov looked up. Smith held out his hand. Cupped in it was a small, silver bell.

Gently, he rang it. The sound, clear and pure, pierced the air and carried on the cold high winds. Smith turned, and slowly walked up the last flight of stairs, up to the top of the tower. Behind him the sound of the dogs, barking and tearing, slowly drowned out the sound of human screams.

FORTY-TWO

… and flying, he was flying, he was a man, a bird, he had wings, the moon rose huge above him, its face austere, the winds pulled him along, their music was the sound of waves, crashing on a distant, alien shore. Smith flew, high above the city, tracking–

He had gone to the top of the Tour Eiffel. Mooring lines for airships but what he found at the top was what, he guessed, Van Helsing had hoped for. He'd only used them once before, on training, long ago. But it would suffice – it would have to.

The *Lilienthal Normalsegelapparat*. German-made, and rare – reputedly only a dozen had been made before Krupp had brought the nascent technology and Otto Lilienthal departed this mortal realm, two events generally considered to have a direct correlation between them. There were other flying vehicles up there, all manners of winged ornithopters, high-altitude unmanned probe balloons, a vehicle powered, it appeared, by paddling, like a bicycle with wings, a rocket harness, something that appeared to be a semi-hollow mechanical dragon, far too heavy, Smith thought, ever to fly… An inflatable blimp and a moored airship completed the odd assortment. A small sign translated as *Aerial Experimentation Station – No Trespassers*. There was also a small gas stove and a folding table and a device for making coffee. Smith checked, but there were no biscuits.

Someone had fashioned a safety harness for the Lilienthal Normalsegelapparat. Smith appreciated the sentiment.

The Lilienthal Normalsegelapparat was a hang glider, delicate-looking, with the wings of a fly and a long thin snout. Smith figured the most likely outcome of using the damn thing would be to plunge down the long way onto the Champ de Mars and end up a wet splat on the paved roads of the red planet. Behind him the dog-men were wailing. He stood up there on the top of the Eiffel Tower and looked over the burning city. From up here he could see Van Helsing was right. The affected area of the walking tripod death machines was entirely circular, a slowly moving, shifting area of fire and destruction that was heading east, almost out of the city by now.

Could he make it?

The howling of the dog-men behind him, bereft of their master and his bell. Smith took a deep breath. Then he slipped into the safety harness and lifted up the Lilienthal glider.

The wind pushed at it, trying to lift him up. A short way away the floor terminated, air began. It was a long drop down. He took another deep breath. It was suddenly very quiet up there, only Smith and the winds, and the smoke rising in the distance into the air.

He needed to shut down the device. He needed to find the Harvester.

He needed to save Alice.

He let the air out with a slow, shuddering breath. The wind caught at the glider, pulling, eager, wanting to play. Smith ran. The floor terminated and his feet connected with open air and the wind tugged and pulled at him and then he was airborne, the Tour Eiffel left behind, he was rising higher, the winds his companions, eternal and graceful and true.

The observer sighed with relief as he reconfigured an internal quantum scanner to work on the ancient, obsolete frequencies. He could see what had happened, now and, moreover, knew it would all have to go into his report, which was due soon, as soon as the other copy of himself had taken the last sample back in that other city, beyond the Channel.

Of course, the observer was the report, in a very real way, but that was all right, nothing lived forever, not even the observer's masters, near as he could tell.

The obsolete protocols and curious antique authentication routines were what must have activated the initial gateway back in the humans' calendar year of eighteen ninety-three. But whereas back then it was a primary scanner, able to open the entanglement channels back to Prime, these semi-scanners worked on broken frequencies, on quantum probability pocket worlds not seen or even remembered by any but the oldest of antiquarians. Like those tripod machines. This, the observer felt, could not go on. There were rules or, if not exactly rules, there was such a thing as decorum.

Which meant those probability world incursions had to stop.

The observer felt quite cheerful now. Soon it would all be over and he'd be back where he belonged. The voices protested at this but he quietened them down. The reconfigured scanner was picking up the signal clearly now and he headed for it, no longer in a hurry, savouring these moments, his mission soon to end.

Behind him, unobserved, for once, by the observer, a giant, malformed figure detached itself from the shadows and cautiously followed.

From high above there was something intensely beautiful about the tripod machines. They moved with the long legs of giraffes, their movements surprisingly graceful over the city. Flames reflected in their metal carapace, the bulbous heads of them that sat over the moving legs. They were like squid, Smith thought, soaring, coming closer – like aquatic beings somehow propelled to stand upright, stretched over the horizon, their tentacles reaching down to the city, bashing it this way and that.

Where had they come from? What strange world would manufacture such machines? Who drove them? Were there people inside or were the tripods themselves some sort of advanced automata, the bulbous compartments huge mechanical brains?

He flew over them, like a bird, the wind tossing him this way and that, the city a long way down below. The harness held him but his hands gripped the bar of the glider, this thing that looked too fragile to survive the winds, too impossible to fly. *We* built that, he thought. There was pride in that.

Below him the machines stalked the city, shivering sometimes in and out of existence, flickering like images on a screen. People down below, fleeing, were as small as insects. Smith alone was up there in the sky. No.

That wasn't true.

As he watched, dark clouds formed in the sky above the city, drifting closer.

Airships, he realised.

But what good could they do, against the tripods?

He was level with the machines now, going lower, trying to locate the moving source, their middle. It would be a vehicle of some sort, he thought. It was hard to tell from above and the rising smoke made visibility difficult.

The black airships were approaching more rapidly. The tripods seemed to ignore them.

No. That, too, was wrong. As he watched, helpless to intervene, a burst of bright, terrible flame erupted from one of the tripods. It flew through the air, a roar of flame, and hit the nearest airship.

For just a moment the ship was obscured from view. Then, a ball of flame erupted, the fire feeding, growing stronger, bigger, and Smith could only watch as the ship simply *disintegrated* there in mid-air.

He cried out, but his voice was small and lost up there in the air. He dived, his anger becoming a bright white flame compacted inside him. Diving and rising, the sweat on his forehead mixing with the smoke, the soot, the wind lashing at him, diving, past the line of tripods and onwards and down, towards the source of it all, towards the unseen device.

The observer moved unobserved amongst the hysterical, running humans. There seemed to be little control, little order left in this strange, barbarous city. It was as if the sight – not to mention the wholesale destruction – of those ancient lumbering machines, conjured out of who-knew-which antique probability universe, had entirely shut down human rationality.

Yet not entirely, he saw. He watched humans organising themselves: makeshift medical clinics sprouting in the ruins of a shelled tavern, or in the middle of the road; groups composed of women, men, even children, organising to put out fires, carrying water, dashing into rubble to rescue trapped citizens.

But the observer, always, was going into the heart of the disaster, where there was no time to organise, no time to do anything but try to flee. Behind him the city responded; like a living organism it was closing in on wounds, cauterising, bandaging, beginning the arduous process of healing itself. Cities, the observer knew, were in many ways living things, their inhabitants merely the cells or neurons that individually meant nothing, that only collectively formed an entity, singular and proud. The city would live; cities were hard to kill, harder than humans. The observer, a small undistinguished figure, moved through smoke and fire.

He stopped several times. Each time he did a human had been trapped under the ruins, their life bleeding out of them, short and sweet and sharp. Each time, out of a desire to understand or that strange, unfamiliar consumption the Alice voice had called compassion, he extracted his needle and pushed it, his data-spike, deep into the hind-brain of the humans, extracting, preserving. It was an uncomfortable thing for him to feel.

He was no longer an observer, he realised.

He had become a participant.

This was a familiar danger, the eventual fate of all observers like him. It was time to leave, to bring back what he'd found, before he was absorbed completely, before he became one of them, before they turned him.

The observer walked through flame and soot and smoke and the unseen presence at his back followed. The observer passed underneath the giant legs of the moving tripods, dodging their steps, and his shadow followed, until they were approaching the device, the signal coming clear and loud now in the observer's mind.

He was playing the great game, the observer thought, and a rapid, unexplained feeling of joy spiked through him, the great game of lizard and man and automaton, a game not of countries and species as the humans thought but a far bigger one, of planets and solar systems and quantum probabilities, and this was only the first move in a truly great game.

For which even a galaxy was but one battlefield, one chessboard in a far larger and more complicated game.

With joy and with compassion and with, at last, that simple need all creatures have, biological or mechanical it made no difference – the simple desire they all shared, the need to go home – the observer crossed dirt roads and paved, fallen buildings and ruined carriages, until he reached, at last, the source of all the mayhem.

FORTY-THREE

Smith was zooming low now, the tripod machines far in the circumference of influence, still moving, still flickering now and then–

Down below flaming buildings and carts and people running, but his attention was on what stood out, on what felt *wrong*, that which did not belong–

A black vehicle of unknown design or means of propulsion, moving slowly, its sides, matt black, absorbing the reflected flames, dampening them–

A machine with no horses to drive it, and no steam engine, no stoker at the back, a sealed device with its occupancy unseen behind dark windows–

A long, finned device, moving slowly, smoke and flame behind it–

Smith, diving low, hovering now, the glider like a moth caught in the winds, the Tour Eiffel left far behind–

Things that did not belong, things going against the general movement, like a small and unremarkable figure, a man with a wide-brimmed hat and economical movements, so unassuming and unremarkable as to become, to Smith, interesting indeed.

Gliding, coming closer, catching up to that dark bullet-shaped vehicle–

And was that small figure down below–

Smith dived sharply, ready to finish it, ready to do what was right. The glider, shuddering with the effort, sped towards the ground. Smith had caught up with the vehicle, then overtaken it. He crash-landed ahead of it, the impact with the ground jarring his bones, ringing him like a cracked bell. He lay there for a moment, the glider covering him like the wings of a butterfly. At last, drawing breath, Smith reached for the knife strapped to his leg, pulled it out, cut the harness rope. He pushed the harness off him, his every effort focused on this one simple act. The world around him shrank, it became just Smith, the hard road, the harness that bound him. At last it was done. The world expanded, gradually. He sat up. The black vehicle had stopped, a few feet away from him, he saw. It just sat there, a dark bullet shape, giving nothing away.

Smith stared. How did the vehicle move? Where was its engine?

The knife was still in his hand. It seemed useless against that dark vehicle.

All around him, in a circle whose circumference was an exact three miles, the giant tripods halted. They stood, motionless, like vast metal guardians over the burning city. Smith shifted the knife from one hand to the other. Waiting.

It was suddenly very quiet.

Footsteps, unhurried, approaching. Smith, watching–

The figure that appeared was the one he had seen from the air, a small and rotund and unassuming fellow who resembled Smith himself. The shock of recognition passed through Smith, and he forced himself to be still. The figure he had last seen in Covent Garden, as he ran towards his friend, as he ran to the place the Lord Byron automata lay slain…

He watched and waited and the black vehicle, too, was still, as if its occupants were waiting, and all around them, in a wide circle, the giant tripods stood still, as if they, too, were watching and waiting.

A great calm settled then over Smith. He watched the other, so much like himself, a shadow being in a shadow world. You would not look at him twice, if you saw him in the street, or in a pub... Slowly, the other lifted his head, and the wide-brimmed hat that shadowed his face lifted. Moonlight and flames lit up the other's face, and Smith sucked in his breath sharply.

Shadows and flames, playing tricks on the mind...

For there was no face under that hat. A skeletal metal head, and eyes of blue flame, looked at Smith.

"*Erntemaschine*," Smith whispered.

Harvester...

The other, as if acknowledging him, nodded, once. Then, startling Smith, his – its – mouth opened.

The voice that came out of it knocked Smith back.

"Smith! Get out of here – oh, you have no idea – it's a trap, he says that–"

The voice cut off, as sudden as it had come.

The voice was Alice's.

Alice, who died in Bangkok.

Harvester...

And now a new voice came, a deeper voice, as familiar to Smith as Alice's had been.

"Smith, you fulfilled the promise I had for you," the voice said.

Smith whispered, "Mycroft..."

"Dear boy, do not lose heart," the fat man said. Smith stared at the alien machine, this humanoid automaton, speaking in the dead voice of Mycroft Holmes.

"*Erntemaschine*..." he said again, softly. Then, addressing his question to this being, or to Alice, he didn't know, he said, "Why a trap?"

The Harvester did not reply. It was impossible to tell, on that skeletal metal face, but Smith had the impression he – it – was smiling.

The doors of the black vehicle opened.

They did so in silence, and simultaneously, there were two on each side, and the things that stepped out of them were–

The knife Smith was still holding felt very small, and for the first time he truly felt his age.

They, too, had been men once, the things that stepped out of that machine.

Frankenstein-Jekyll monstrosities, subjected to the serum's nefarious influence. They dwarfed Smith and the other. Muscles bulged from their oversized clothes. Their eyes had a yellow, demented sheen. They wore metal collars around their unnaturally thick necks.

Every now and then, Smith saw, the collars fizzled, hissed, small blue flames dancing around the metal, and each time the creatures' faces twisted with pain.

They were being controlled, he realised.

From within the vehicle.

He tensed, waiting for whoever was inside to come out.

But they never did.

The four turned as one, their collars hissing. Facing Smith, and the other.

And now, Smith saw, others had materialised around them, emerging from the frame of a ruined apartment building, from a baruch-landau parked innocently enough on the side of the road… One jumped down from the roof of a nearby building, the ground shaking as he hit it.

The creatures surrounded Smith and the alien Harvester.

The Harvester turned to Smith.

"Smith, if this goes wrong…" She hesitated. Her voice was just as he remembered it. "I love you," she said.

"I've always loved you, Alice," he said.

She said, "I know."

Smith looked at their attackers. So the whole thing had been a trap, just like Alice said. Not for him – he didn't rate himself valuable enough.

No.

A trap for that strange, alien being, that Harvester who truly *did* harvest the dead…

He, Smith, was just in the way.

And he did not rate his survival chances as being very high.

FORTY-FOUR

Flames in the distance, smoke spiralling up... The night was beautiful, order in destruction, the moon shone down, pock-marked, scarred, as scarred as Smith.

The creatures surrounded Smith and the Harvester, closing them in, and now they made their move.

Fight if you have to, as the Manual, long ago, had put it. *Run if you don't.*

Though there was nowhere to run...

Smith tensed but beside him the small, rotund alien machine seemed to relax, to become even more inconspicuous, even more anonymous and serene.

"Alice? Mycroft?"

They spoke in unison, not just the two of them but a multitude of voices who Smith didn't know, all absorbed by the Harvester, from that child in Bangkok to the lost souls swiftly and mercifully despatched in the burning city.

"Everything," they said, their voices rising like the singing of birds, like rain falling, like the rustle of leaves and the hum of ancient, mysterious machinery. "Everything will be all right."

Smith was not reassured. The creatures reached for him, one of them grabbed him in huge, meaty hands. The others went for the Harvester–

The fingers applied enormous pressure, the pain was excruciating, Smith bit down a scream–

Turned, the knife flashing, buried it deep into the creature's chest–

Who sagged back in surprise or pain, it was hard to tell, momentarily releasing him–

A hum rose around him, a strange ethereal sound, vibrations shaking the very air. The world seemed to slow down around Smith, to pause, the flames shuddering to a halt, the tripod machines frozen against an unmoving, enormous moon, the creatures moving sluggishly, bewildered, the black vehicle sitting there motionless, Smith's hand leaving the handle of his knife reluctantly, pulling away as though he were swimming through water…

The hum rose like the wordless chant of a thousand monks. It came from nowhere and everywhere. It was in the air, in the flames, in the smoke and in the dead who lay all about them.

In that stillness, that freezing of time and of the world, only the slight, monk-like figure of the Harvester moved normally, in real-time. It did not move hurriedly. It had an economy of movement, an assured, almost peaceful pace.

Everything will be all right, Smith.

The words rose in his mind, they were bubbles in water, and a strange peace came over Smith then. His world expanded outwards, beyond the city, beyond the Earth, past the moon and the planets and the sun and outwards still. Star systems rushed by, strange sights, engorged suns and empty spaces that swallowed the matter around them, clouds where stars were being born, red suns, dying, worlds beyond count…

Everything will be all right.

The observer felt that its time here on this curious world was coming to an end but was impressed by the human-laid trap, which suggested several things to him.

That the humans, or some faction of humans, had indeed deducted the observer's arrival, and its purpose.

And were determined to capture him, either to prevent him from achieving his mission, or to study him, or both.

Which was exciting news to the observer, even though, having observed, as it were, an entire chain of circumstances and events – of people – that led him to the knowledge he would be observed, he would be deduced, this was still material evidence, and first-hand. A postscript to his report, he thought, almost fondly.

There was little that was useful in the minds of the distorted humans, however. Whatever process they had undergone, this serum the observer had found mention of in several of the voices in his head, it had done irreparable damage to the complex, delicate webwork of their brains. He took from them with the same compassion he took from the dying he had met along the burning city, but there were no whole minds here, nothing but fragments, which he extracted with care.

They were frozen, or near frozen – the observer had kicked into a higher mode for a short duration, had initiated, in fact, the beginning of the process that would end his time here, on this earth – and he took from them with ease, sinking the data-spike into their brains, releasing the data left in there while permanently terminating the living tissue.

In slow motion, the bodies crumpled to the ground, one by one, as the observer moved amongst them like a gardener, unhurriedly pruning back leaves.

At last it was done; only the other remained, this short compact human who had come down from the sky. He recognised him, crisscrossing references from the voices in his head, saw him young, saw him trained, saw him meeting Mycroft for the first time, in a Soho street with the rain falling down, saw him falling for Alice, by the side of a Venice canal, saw him operational, then, a brilliant young shadow executive: Aden, Zanzibar, Vientiane, Moscow, a spell in Tenochtitlan, cultural attaché at the embassy running interference inside the Aztec capital – back in London after an operation went bad in Tunis, then the fruitful collaboration with the Byron automaton, handling internal security, foreign networks, becoming Mycroft's right-hand man and Alice's lover–

The man was an enigma, the observer thought with curiosity. He could read his life like a dossier, perfectly laid out, but what he thought, wondered, wanted – this the observer had no access to, and he was not surprised to find out that he wanted it.

He was, after all, an observer.

He turned at last to the vehicle, which was powered by a primitive internal combustion engine – advanced for this society of coal and steam – using what the humans called diesel, after a German scientist who seemed embroiled in the machinations of the man they called Babbage, and who the observer would have liked to have met.

The observer reached for the front door of the vehicle and yanked it open and slid inside. There was one solitary man sitting in the driver seat, a panel of instruments before him, still frozen in slow-time, his hand reaching out in tiny increments towards the controls. Gently, almost with affection, the observer added him to his collection and, a moment later, laid its corpse down gently against the seat. A new voice in his head, but he shut it down – a flavourful one, this one, a conman and a writer, Karl May by name, and Krupp's agent – he added a new strand to the story the observer was to carry back, and for that the observer was grateful.

The device had been in May's lap. Now the observer retrieved it. He initiated a communication channel with the ancient thing, establishing a protocol and negotiating a handshake despite the device's initial suspicions. He found himself fascinated by what he found, and it was with some regret that he at last shut it down.

When he stepped out of the vehicle, the device safely locked, the ancient tripod machines had wavered against the skyline and then, as though in relief, disappeared.

They did not belong here, they came from a place unexplored for untold millennia, perhaps aeons. The observer wondered which observer would get the chance to go there, when he returned and submitted himself – that is, his report.

He hoped it would be him…

There had been a name for that world. In human speech, it may sound a little like Croatoan.

It was done. The observer let slow-time go, and time sped up–

Smith stood very still, in a changed world. The creatures that, a moment earlier, had threatened him, were now on the ground, and they were dead. The skyline was different, the tripod machines were gone. The city still burned, but it would recover, it would lick its wounds. It always had, before.

Smith stood alone by the black vehicle, alone but for that otherworldly thing, that *Erntemaschine*.

He looked at the Harvester and it was like looking at a mirror, it was like looking at himself. He hesitated. The machine waited, patient, revealing nothing.

"Alice?" Smith said.

"Smith," she said, out of the *Erntemaschine*'s mouth. There was a load of sadness and pain in her voice he found hard to bear. He thought of his agreement with the Bookman, the other's promises of raising Alice for him, of bringing her back from the dead, and he realised the futility of that offer; he knew then he could not bring the Harvester back with him, that Alice was lost to him.

The *Erntemaschine* waited, patient, but looking at Smith in a certain way that Smith recognised.

"I can't bring you back," Smith said, and that admission, of his own helplessness, hurt as it left his mouth, like jagged edges of broken glass cutting through his throat and tongue.

"Smith..."

The Harvester waited, knowing, patient.

Smith nodded, once.

There was only one way for them to be together again.

The observer was satisfied. He knelt by the corpse, gently prying the data-spike out of the dead man's head. Inside him a new voice joined the rest, intertwining with one of the other voices in particular. The observer stood up, then, recognising in that small, unremarkable corpse something akin to his own identity, a tool and a servant who yet took a great joy in fulfilling its tasks. Smith... even the name was appropriate, almost a title, like Observer... he silenced the voices. Almost. Almost...

He just had to wait for his other self to finish, at last, the job.

PART IX
Manifest Destiny

FORTY-FIVE

"Mr Houdini," the voice said. "Welcome to Transylvania."

The voice had an awful, scratched quality to it. Harry tried to open his eyes. They felt gummed together, and his mouth tasted of razorblades and old blood.

Alive. Somehow, he was still alive.

He opened his eyes.

Shapes slowly resolved in the semi-darkness of the room. The light was red, the air felt humid, almost moist. He found himself sweating. It was very hot, very humid, like a...

He sat up. Everything hurt. His hands on his head, his fingers through his hair – realising it was longer now, that he must have been in that crate, that coffin, for a long time, longer than he thought. He looked around him.

A large, dark crypt it seemed to Harry, illuminated by artificial red light, and quiet, too quiet. Around him, everywhere he looked, orchids grew, a huge variety of colours and shapes, like living things, waiting, watching... hungry. He suppressed a shudder; could not see another person there. So who had spoken?

"Who are you?" he said.

A strange sound, of bellows, of air going in and out, in and out. A beat, weak and yet amplified, filling up the cavern, like the sound of an old, human heart. Harry squinted into the darkness.

"Hello?" he said.

His voice sounded lonely and thin in that underground green-house. The sound of bellows, of air being breathed, as by a vast machine. The pounding of that fragile heart, and Harry's own heart responding, fear rising, palms damp, and he tried to calm himself, to look inwards, trying to think how he could escape, when–

A shape, a sliver of shadow materialising out of the darkness, moving gradually closer, growing in size–

And Harry had to suppress a scream, a thing out of nightmare coming towards him, features slowly resolving, and in the dim red light of the cavern he saw–

It had been a man, once. Now it sat there, welded into its chair, a thing neither human nor machine…

Pipes came out of its back, fed into its lungs, and large bellows moved like butterfly wings, fluttering, pumping air through that ancient, wizened body, keeping it alive…

Glass tubes in which red blood bubbled, the tubes in turn feeding into the old man's arms, his hands…

The face was like a skull, what skin there was hung loosely, yellow like gas flames. There was no hair but thick black wires came out of that skull and trailed upwards, connected once again to the cloud of machines that engulfed this being, this creature, this once-living thing.

It was ancient, it should have died long ago, it was a mummi-fied human body kept alive by its machines, it was–

"Who…" Harry whispered, and his throat felt raw and clogged, and a chemical taste, suffusing, so it seemed to him, the very air he breathed, lodged itself in his mouth, "What… Who are you?"

The mouth in that faceless skull barely moved, and yet the creature in the chair spoke, its voice amplified through unseen machines. Like an Edison recording, the words were slightly dis-jointed, scratchy, put together from separate recordings and meshed into a single voice. And now he saw the ancient fingers, bone-like, tapping on a keypad of some sort, like brass buttons there, within reach – producing the sounds he heard, he realised. The man was no longer capable of speaking in his own voice.

"I am Charles Babbage," the mechanical voice said.

Harry scrambled away from the creature. He felt as if the thing was after him, after his youth – that soon it would pounce on him, attach fang-like devices to his neck, empty him of blood, feast on him–

"Really, Mr Houdini," the voice said, and the eyes – the eyes! – they were terribly alive, large and moist like smooth pebbles in a stream, they looked at him, with amusement and curiosity, they were the only living thing in that ruined face – "there is nothing to fear."

The voice chuckled, the same old scratched recording, and the chair on wheels moved closer, and the man loomed before Harry now, and looked at him, his head tilted slightly to one side. Harry could see blood flowing, in measured doses, through the transparent tubes that fed in and out of Babbage's arms.

"We are not so unlike, you and I," Babbage said.

Harry stood up. His muscles didn't ache as much as he had expected. And, in fact, there had been no waste left in the coffin… which he didn't want to think about, at just that moment. He towered over the old man. "You should be dead," he said.

"And so," said Babbage, "should you."

Harry stopped, his rage drying. "What do you mean?" he whispered, and again he heard Babbage laugh, that old recorded sound echoing through the greenhouse. They were alone but for the orchids. "How many times have you died now, Mr Houdini?" Babbage said.

"I don't–"

"Know what I mean? Oh, but I think you do, quite well," Babbage said. "Tell me, when was it that the Bookman found you?"

"I will not–"

Cold sweat, and fear, it couldn't be, he wasn't like–

"Answer my questions? Or do you not know the answers?" Those large, wet, extraordinary eyes gazed up at him, almost in admiration. "I can answer your questions for you, Mr Houdini. Would you like me to? Would you like to know, just what you are?"

The eyes, he saw, were no longer looking at him but behind

him, behind his shoulder, and he suddenly had that awful feeling that something, someone, was standing behind him, so close that, almost, he could feel their breath on his skin. He tensed.

"I know who I am," Harry said.

"I will show you yourself," Babbage said, in a voice almost sad. "In a handful of dust..." His head moved, a fraction. "Take him," he said.

Now Harry turned, ready to fight–

Behind him loomed a huge, bald-headed human, with a scar running down one cheek. The man smiled at him, without malice, then a hand like a meat hook descended and grabbed him by the neck and lifted him up.

"Everything," he heard Babbage say, as from a great distance as, suspended in mid-air, he felt the cold prick of a needle enter his neck, "is going to be all right, Mr Houdini. It will be all right."

Famous last words, Harry thought when he woke up. Woke up and wished he hadn't. Woke up, and found himself strapped to a table, the dim light of the greenhouse replaced with strong white electric lights, a bare room, bare walls, and Harry naked, strapped with thick leather restraints–

A mirror above him, adding to the humiliation, adding to the horror of it all – the mirror showing him everything, showing him himself, it was attached to the ceiling, hovered above him like a suspended pool of water–

"We shall begin," a voice said. The same old, pre-recorded voice, and he hated it now, hated that voice, he wanted to kill, he had to escape, he had to–

"Sir."

The voice was surprisingly high; it didn't fit with the face of the man who now stood over Harry. A giant of a man, with a bald dome for a head, a scar running down his cheek – he looked like a pirate, Harry thought, the man looked ridiculous in the white lab coat–

In his hand, Harry couldn't help but notice, as much as his gaze tried to shy away from it, in the man's huge, meaty hand there was a small and delicate and very sharp-looking surgical scalpel.

FORTY-SIX

"Wait!"

Harry struggled against his bonds. And was that a small, almost wistful smile on that huge, cratered face above him? His head thrashed, this way and that, seeing now the wizened old man, this Babbage, in his wheelchair and his life-support machines, watching him, waiting...

"Why are you doing this?" Harry said – whispered. The old man sighed, the sound of bellows releasing air, slowly and tortuously. "You do not know," he said, enigmatically, "how lucky you are."

Harry thinking, keep him talking, anything to keep that blade from descending, from cutting his flesh, from burrowing into his skin... He said, "Who's he?"

The man above him smiled again. Nothing friendly in that expression. It made Harry's blood go cold, an expression he'd heard once, did not believe it could become a reality. No help there, not from this brute–

"His name," Babbage said, "is Mr Spoons."

"Mr Spoons," the man with the scalpel said, nodding. The same high, almost girlish voice.

"He used to be boatswain to Captain Wyvern," Babbage said. "The pirate. But that, Mr Houdini, is beside the point. Mr Spoons–"

"Spoons!"

"Please proceed with the operation."

"No!"

Harry cried out but it was no use. He saw the blade descending, a frown of concentration on the giant's face–

In the mirror above he could see himself reflected, naked, the blade descending, the blade touching his arm, the blade pushing–

For just a moment, a flaring of pain, shooting up his arm and then–

The blade went deeper, made an incision, Spoons moved the blade deftly, opening Harry's arm–

And the pain suddenly vanished, pain receptors shutting off, and something else, stranger, something Harry had seen before but had tried to forget, had kept telling himself he'd dreamed it, the last time it had happened, it couldn't have–

Blue sparks shot out of the cut in his arm, and Mr Spoons, startled, took half a step back before remembering himself and reaching out, and with thick fingers pulling open the folds of skin on either side, revealing–

No blood, no bones. Harry shutting his eyes now, wanting to scream, recollection flooding in–

En-route from the Black Hills, his horse, moving fast, stumbling–

Harry falling, hard, the impact jarring, his head hitting a jutting stone–

Pain flaring, and he blacked out–

And woke up, seconds or minutes later, the horse nearby, unharmed–

Harry's head hurting, his hand reaching to it, finding a sticky residue, his hand, coming back, no blood but a strange, greenish material that seemed to ooze, almost as if alive–

A shower of blue sparks, falling down, scared him. He reached up and his hand passed through them, harmlessly–

On board the *Snark*, in the midst of ocean, after too much drink, unsteady on his feet, on board, a piece of metal falling, he turned, it cut his arm–

The pain, coming, then, just as suddenly, disappearing. Blue sparks, the same green goo oozing, sealing the wound before he had a chance to register it–

He'd cursed the Bookman, but he'd pushed it away, it had been nothing, a hallucination, there was nothing at all out of the ordinary–

"Extraordinary," Babbage breathed – that is, voice machine and breathing machine meshed, for just a moment. Harry, defeated, stared down at his arm. The strange green goo had materialised over it, was sealing Mr Spoons' cut. Harry had a bad feeling, a very bad feeling...

"Humans," Babbage said, "are such extraordinary machines, Mr Houdini. But you!"

Was that admiration in the old voice? It was so hard to tell... and the frown on Mr Spoons' face suggested he, at least, was not overly happy with the results, so far, of the operation.

"I had tried to get hold of the Bookman's technology for years," Babbage said. "I, alone, had deduced his secret. Nothing but a servant!" The ancient man coughed a laugh. "A servant, a copying machine. Yet how he hated them, and hates them still! For centuries, since his escape from that cursed island, he has been moving through the world, our world, a shadowy figure, the first and greatest player of the great game. Fighting his former masters, these... these reptiles."

And was that a moue of distaste briefly crossing the old man's haunted face?

"An alien machine, designed to make copies of biological entities, to copy them and to perfect them, to keep them pristine and operational, like a librarian, a bookman or... a zoo keeper," Babbage said. Harry fought against the straps but he couldn't tear them. Is that what he was? he wondered, in despair. A machine? A replica of someone who had been, a human born and raised and named, Erich at first, then calling himself Houdini – was that man, almost no older than a boy, dead forever, killed by a mugger in the dark streets of the White City and he, Harry, no matter that he felt the same, looked the same, was he but a replica, a cheap automaton?

Not even that, he realised. For he had died before – did that make him a copy of a copy? A copy of a copy of a copy?

When did one stop being human? When did one become a machine?

"You…" Babbage breathed. "Remarkable. At last, the Bookman has obliged me. I, who was the greatest builder of automata in the known world, am but a copying scribe, forced to learn from first principles an art perfected long ago under different skies, on alien soil! No more. Now, I have you, Mr Houdini."

"Let me go!"

"Join me." Charles Babbage's chair moved mechanically forwards, accompanied by its cloud of machines. His ancient head peered over the table at the captive Harry. "Work with me. You do not understand, Mr Houdini. The time has come! There is a war upon us."

"War?"

"War…" Mr Spoons said, and smiled. The idea seemed to delight him.

"A war," Charles Babbage said, "of worlds, Mr Houdini. A war that was long in coming, a war inevitable, a war unavoidable, as must always be the case when two civilisations meet, and one is stronger, and the other weak."

"But that's not true," Harry said. Even captive, he sensed the wrong in the older man's words. "When European refugees came to Vespuccia they were received cordially and honourably by the Nations. When European explorers came to East Africa they were welcomed into the trade networks that had existed for centuries between Asia and Africa. When–"

"When the Lizardine Empire conquered India, it did so by force," Babbage said. "When it–"

"But it doesn't have to be this way," Harry said. "The great game is played to prevent war. War is not inevitable, it is not a natural solution. Peace–"

"Peace!" Babbage laughed, and it was not a pleasant laugh –

and Harry suddenly realised the man was too old, had lived for too long, so long that his brain had, in some subtle ways, stopped functioning, that he was demented – and for the first time since his arrival here he felt true fear.

"Let's take a look at his heart," Babbage said, and Mr Spoons raised the scalpel again, and it descended, and the cold hard metal touched Harry's chest and he screamed

FORTY-SEVEN

There came moments of lucidity then, intersected with long periods of darkness. He'd wake up in that cold room to find men and women in white coats standing over him, prodding, studying. Sometimes there would be wires attached to him. Sometimes he would wake up and a leg would be missing, or an arm, or his chest would be bared open, skin and flesh removed, showing something alien and inexplicable underneath. At those times he was almost glad of the returning darkness, the no-being that spared him the indignity of dissection.

Other moments, too, flashes of awakening, almost as if he were in someone else's body, in a new body, being carted around. The baruch-landau moving, this driverless carriage piloted by Mr Spoons in the front and he, Harry, beside him in a passenger seat. Outside, for the first time, though he had no recollection of leaving that cold room. Looking back–

A castle rising above a cliff, towers and turrets like something out of a fairy tale, surrounded by trees, an access road–

Black airships above it, moored and floating serenely, around the castle, down below, a pleasant valley but it was full of military-looking personnel. More vehicles, fields of tents, troops at parade in the distance. He said, "Where are we going?" – his voice thick with disuse.

Mr Spoons: "To Brasov."

Harry sat back in the seat. The vehicle moved through the valley on a curiously paved road, the journey smooth, the vehicle making almost no sound–

The city, in the distance–

A bowl of a valley, surrounded by tall majestic mountains – "The Carpathians," Mr Spoons said, his scarred face placid – the city in the distance, tall spires rising against the sky like delicate towers–

No, he realised. Not towers at all.

The car moved closer. Harry watched – an old pleasant city of stone streets and low houses, transformed–

He said, his voice tinged with awe, "They're rockets."

Mr Spoons smiled, faintly–

The rockets rose high into the air, a multitude of them, too many to count; they filled the valley, surrounding the old city like an honour guard, giant metal structures waiting to take flight, aimed at the stars…

He woke, and found himself strapped to the table and they were examining him and old Charles Babbage was cackling to himself and he said, "Stop. Stop it."

"Join us," Babbage said. "Join me, Harry. The war is coming, and you and I could stop it. Together we could save the world."

"You're mad," Harry whispered.

"You don't have to be mad to work here," Babbage whispered, "but it helps…"

He could not distinguish dreams and awakenings. One night he woke in a room he did not recognise and saw himself, multiplied by a hundred.

Rows and rows of Harry Houdinis, lifeless, suspended from walls in some medieval crypt in that horrid Castle Babbage, hanging on hooks, like so many dolls, waiting… He blinked and then saw a hundred other Houdinis blink back at him, their eyes staring, and he stifled a scream and then darkness, blessedly, closed on him again.

• • • •

Rockets, gleaming against the skies... "What... what are they *for*?" Harry whispered.

The same hint of a smile on Mr Spoons' ugly face. "Have you never looked up at the stars?" he said. "Have you never *wondered*?"

"Wondered what?"

"What it would be like to *go* there," Mr Spoons said, his face softening. He looked like a big kid at that moment, something childish and almost endearing in his eyes. "I used to look up at the stars, on board our ship. The *Joker*, she was called. I used to stand on the deck, looking up. Wondering... My master was lizardine himself, Captain Wyvern, and we sailed the Carib Sea and beyond... They told me Les Lézards came from there, from the stars... crossing some unimaginable distance in a ship that could sail through space... and I wondered, and I still do – what would it be like, to sail between the stars?"

Harry had no answer. They drove closer, passing military installations, trucks and dome-like buildings, pylons humming, all the while the rockets dominating the landscape, there in that strange valley bounded by the majestic Carpathians... a hidden valley, a secret valley, here at the edge of the Austro-Hungarian Empire. Babbage had chosen well.

"Why are you showing me all this?"

They drove into the old town – stone-paved streets, low-lying houses, restaurants open, lights coming on, a festive atmosphere – soldiers and scientists sitting around in big groups, drinking beer, laughing–

"This is your destiny," Mr Spoons said, simply.

"Our destiny," the voice said. The voice had a grainy, pre-recorded quality to it. Harry hated the voice, but it would not go away. It never stopped. Harry didn't know where he was. His mind was fragmented, broken, the fragments floating in and out of time.

He was in the vehicle with Mr Spoons, watching the rockets, and he was hanging on a peg, on a wall, like a suit of clothes, with a hundred others, and he was on that operating table, being taken apart, piece by piece, and he was in this dark place where the voice was speaking, speaking, a mélange of voices in turns interrogating and lecturing, filling his mind (minds?) with new concepts, new ideas, an ideology he couldn't push away–

"The stars are our destiny," the voice said, the old machine man voice, "and our destination–"

"When a superior and an inferior civilisation meet, war can be the only result."

"Humanity is a superior race, we have a manifest destiny–"

Harry – "No!" cursing, in the dark – "who talks like this?"

"I – we – you!"

He begged for silence, for the dark, but his request was denied.

Instead he got: "trajectories – control unit – air pressure in cabin – coordination of group-hive-mind operations – symbiosis – lunar topology – space walking–"

Harry: "This is insane. Stop it. Now."

"They are coming. We have to be prepared."

He was everywhere and nowhere, in a room with controls before him, buttons and dials and switches and levers and slowly he learned to operate them, to read the screens–

A place where his body was being spun, faster and faster, pressure mounting on his chest, his body, as though the Earth's pull was increasing–

"He built you well. Now I will rebuild you. All of you."

"Please, please, stop."

But it didn't.

FORTY-EIGHT

"Erich?"

He blinked, in the darkness.

His mother's voice, comforting, known…

But she was not there.

His eyes opened, and suddenly he could *see*.

The world changed.

He was no longer alone.

Stars. The world was full of stars. Harry's consciousness stretched, stretched…

And a hundred Harry Houdinis opened their eyes…

He was everywhere, at once. Babbage's scientists, his technicians, had worked hard to copy the Bookman's technology. To replicate it.

He woke up and he was many.

He was, he realised, Babbage's army.

Harry was sitting on top of a rocket, alone in a control room, the walls closing in on him, the awesome engine power behind him being, in effect, a giant bomb about to go off. His consciousness stretched, across the valley, and he knew, so many things he hadn't known before, when he was one.

He knew of diesel, and of the vast deposits of the black, thick oil in the Arabian Peninsula, of how it could be used to power machines, and to generate vast, raw power to send men into space itself.

He knew of the woman they called Alice, in the city called Bangkok, and knew what she had done there. There was a type of metal found in the ground, in India, and smuggled, from under the lizards' snouts, via Siam to this remote valley in Transylvania. Something more dangerous, more powerful and awesome even than Diesel's oil…

Uranium.

What a strange word, Harry, thought, rolling it on the tongue. The control room shuddered, a hundred control rooms shuddered, and Babbage was with him, was inside his mind, woven into this new matrix of Houdinis, his knowledge Harry's knowledge, and he *knew*–

Decades of planning and scheming, of building and learning, finding out things from first principles–

And all the time the burning jealousy, hardening into hatred–

The knowledge that all his work, all his genius, was in vain, that thousands if not millions of years in the past, another race of beings had gone through the same track, had already invented and perfected what Babbage, haltingly, was trying to do. The Bookman laughed at him, making perfect copies, making human machines… while the royal lizards lounged in their gardens, ruling an empire they did not deserve, ignorant even of the science which had made their conquest of humanity possible. To be so advanced as to be ignorant, Babbage thought. A paradox at the heart of a technologically advanced society…

And he knew, early on he knew, that the lizards, those few on Earth, were not alone. That they had come from somewhere and that, therefore, the possibility existed:

That one day the others would come, and to them the Earth would be less than a plaything–

How much further would have the aliens' science advanced in the millennia since the one ship had crashed on Earth, on Caliban's Island, its living cargo frozen in cryogenic sleep?

And so he planned, he schemed, sometimes with the Bookman and sometimes against him, sometimes with Mycroft Holmes and his organisation, sometimes against him. Collaborating with Krupp, with Edison, with Tesla and the others, and against them, a woven tapestry of conflicting and mutual interests–

The Great Game.

The only game worth playing.

And now–

The stars.

"Ten."

"Nine."

"No, wait!"

From a hundred identical throats: *We are not ready!*

"Eight."

"Seven."

"Prepare for launch."

The rocket thrumming, the very walls vibrating, Harry's palms moist, gripping the mostly useless controls–

And Babbage's slow, insidious voice, saying, "The greatest escape of them all, Mr Houdini…"

You don't understand, Harry wanted to shout. *War is not always the answer, in the South Pacific the concept of Peace was sacrosanct, peace before justice, war was a guaranteed extinction, even if there was war it was a civilised affair, a contest between champions at the end of which everyone went off to lunch–*

"Six," the machine voice said, and it was indifferent to Harry's pleas, to all the Harrys, and he saw–

A hundred pairs of eyes opening, a hundred pairs of hands holding tight to the controls, a hundred identical bodies sitting on top of a hundred identical rockets, and the flames starting…

"Five," the voice said, remorselessly. "Four. Three."

Harry closed his eyes. Some of the Harrys kept theirs open. One of the Harrys whistled. One cried. One prayed, in the old forgotten Hebrew of his youth. One grinned maniacally. But all of them tense, all of them ready, as ready as they'd ever be–

"Two," the voice said.

"One," the voice said.

And: *"Lift off."*

Lift off.

Harry felt the rocket thrumming, with eyes that weren't his own he could see the rockets sitting on the floor of the Carpathian valley, flames igniting, the mass of fuel burning as the rockets slowly, so slowly, began to rise into the air–

He gripped the controls, felt his body being pushed back in its seat, then–

Searing hot flame, a rumble rising from below and spreading, and he opened his mouth in a wide desperate scream, something was wrong, something was terribly wrong, and–

The flames rose and the rocket shuddered, breaking up, with eyes that weren't his eyes he could see the rocket–

Only a few feet above the ground it lost control, a fault somewhere in the thousands of components–

Inside the module on top of the rocket Harry screamed but there was no sound, the flames burst and he felt his body being consumed, like the flicker of a match, like someone snapping their fingers, there was an enormous fireball–

He screamed but there was no pain, no sight, there was nothing, and a metallic voice said, "One destroyed."

"Commence tally."

"Affirmative."

And with ninety-nine pairs of eyes Harry watched, the rockets rising, slow at first and then faster, and faster, and he could *see*, he watched the sky coming closer, the stars above, he was soaring, he was–

The rocket lost its trajectory several hundred feet above the valley. Harry had only a moment to realise it, to see and feel the cliff-face of the mountain as the rocket, lost to all control now, aimed directly at the face of the Carpathians, trees and dark shrubbery and Harry screamed–

There was a terrible explosion–

"Two down," the voice said.

"Commence tally."

"Affirmative."

But the ones who were already airborne kept flying, the rockets rising higher, while the voices in mission control never tired–

Three more rockets exploding on launch, two failed to start–

Harry stood outside the rocket, glaring – up in the sky the rockets trailed smoke, but he was down there, left, forgotten, in that damned Transylvanian valley–

A mixture of anger and relief and fear and exhilaration – he was alive, but grounded, and he suddenly realised just how much he had wanted this, the greatest feat of escapology known to man–

To go into space–

Harry Houdini sitting at the controls, the rocket piercing clouds, Transylvania disappearing below as the world *grew*, expanded–

An explosion somewhere to the right, another rocket consumed in furious flames, another mental scream echoing down the shared mind connection of the Houdini network–

But the others kept going, even as burning molten debris rained down on the mountains, where a forest fire came alive–

Down below bears ambled away, troop carriers drove down the mountain dirt paths with water tanks, while up there–

Up there where the air grew thin, and one could see, for the first time in human history, one could see the curve of the world, could see the truth in what the pre-lizardine, Greek philosophers had already known, that the world was a globe–

And Harry's breath caught in his throat as he watched continents, oceans, merging and forming like a beautiful unique map, alive with colour–

And beyond it, as the air thinned, the module heated up, the rocket pushing faster and faster and higher and higher, until–

• • • •

"Stage two," the metallic voice said.

Charles Babbage in his life-support cloud, in the observation deck, Ground Control, Harry beside him–

"Initiate," Babbage said.

There was a terrible tearing sound–

A grinding as metal separated from metal, up there on the edge of space (but the sound was only internal, outside the air had gone and sound no longer travelled, out there, beyond the thin metal walls, was the vacuum)–

Harry screaming as the separation of rocket and module did not go as planned, and a hole was punched into the metal and air escaped out into vacuum and Harry's voice was sucked away as he flew out, into space, and died, seeing stars–

But the others separated and it must have been a marvellous sight, from the telescopes down on Earth, if anyone was watching – a fleet of rockets entering stage two, the rockets dropping away and the fragile modules separating from them and continuing onwards on the generated momentum, higher until they escaped the Earth's gravity well–

Some circling the Earth while others pushed on, beyond Earth orbit, having reached escape velocity and Harry looked out, Harry looked out into space and he saw the stars, he saw the Earth down below, a fragile beautiful blue and white globe, spinning...

And the words of an ancient prayer his father the rabbi used to say rose in Harry's mind, the ancient Hebrew words: *Baruch ata adonai, elohenu melech ha'olam, boreh meorei ha'esh* – blessed are thou, God, creator of the flames–

As the world beyond the module shifted and flared, the thousands upon thousands of stars, like sand upon the shore, so many, he had never imagined there were so many, and Earth shrank behind, became an insignificant speck of dust, of sand, in a vast mysterious unknowable universe when–

The world shifted, and changed, and the star field *blurred*, suddenly and unexpectedly–

Beyond the moon's orbit, somewhere out there, between Earth and Mars–

A great blurring, a hazing, as though something enormous, something as large as a *world* had materialised, in space, its outline blocking out the stars–

But that was impossible, Harry thought, and the tiny little modules hung out there, in space, as pretty and useless as Christmas tree decorations, and Harry sighed, a great exhalation of air taking with it all tension, and fear, and leaving behind it only a great childish wonder–

PART X
Victoria Falls

FORTY-NINE

There was blood. That was the thing she couldn't understand, lying there. The blood. The ground was wet and sticky. There had been a lot of pain but now it came and went, in waves, and in between it felt quite peaceful, like rest, or a summer's day, or a dose of opium.

She couldn't figure out where the blood had come from. Was it hers? Everything was confused, a jumble of images without the proper sound, like at a puppet show where the voices came a moment too late, once the puppets had already moved on the stage.

There had been a gun battle...

It had been a war of shadows, the moon cast down shadows and her men engaged the attackers, the ones who had ambushed Stoker, and she had said, "Kill them," and she was not going to leave any alive, save maybe for one, for interrogation. But she had wanted their blood.

It had been a mistake, she saw now. She had been unprofessional, had lost her detachment in the battle.

She was being moved. Shadows flickering at the edge of vision, the rustling of leaves, the ground wet... There was mud on her, and the thick cloying smell of the blood. Where were they taking her?

Who?

Flashes of memory like exploding grenades.

Bodies collapsing into mud. It was raining. There had been rainbows flashing through moonlight and rain, a rare sight – she had seen such a thing only once before, at the great falls they called Mosi o Tunya, the ones Livingstone had named after the Queen.

Victoria Falls.

The spray of water rose into the air, permeating the atmosphere, and through it the sun cast a multitude of rainbows… and at night, she had stood on top of the wet slimy rocks above the falls and watched the moonlight do the same, silver rainbows appearing magically in the air, everywhere, startling and mysterious…

"Kill them."

She was not sure, now, what they were fighting for. For Stoker's diary, perhaps. For the document he had died for.

Only she had the feeling it had all been a feint, that Babbage had *meant* to let his scribe escape, so they would know–

Rockets, a secret army, Babbage's mad plan, in that remote valley in Transylvania–

"The Queen," she said – tried to – the words could barely leave her throat. "Have to tell… the Queen."

Mycroft was dead. They were all dead. Her men lay on the ground of Richmond Park and their blood soaked into the mud and fed the roots of trees whose names she didn't know. Only she was alive.

The attackers had not been entirely human.

That must have been it.

They had… modifications. They were like the things she had read about in a classified dossier, about the work done in France, at the Gobelin factory. Man-machine hybrids, designed for battle, half-powered by engines, metal replacing flesh–

She had fired three shots into a man's chest and watched him laugh…

She blinked. Her lips tasted salty. Blood. There was blood. She thought she would never be free of the blood.

"Please," she whispered. "Tell–"

Her throat felt blocked. She tried to speak and couldn't.

Then the pain came back and she wanted to scream, it ate its way inside her, it was a rat gnawing on raw nerves. The pain came in a wave that rose higher and higher and it was going to drown her, it was going to–

Then it passed, once again, and she was lying there (on the stretcher?), breathing heavily, covered in sweat, and her mouth was full of blood (did she bite her tongue?).

Where were they taking her?

Memories like exploding grenades… the men moving silently, the bark of guns, the bright flame of a flare rising high, casting the scene in a momentary flash, revealing the wounded and the dead… she had killed two and badly wounded a third when she felt the impact against her shoulder, throwing her back, onto the ground–

She had never heard the shot.

Someone screamed. Perhaps it had been her. Another flare went up and now it revealed a different scene, the soldiers were not where they should be–

There had been a–

There had been a–

In the stretcher she bit her lips and sobbed. Stoker's diary still in her inside pocket, hidden, kept safe – how many hits had she taken? She would die, soon, she felt. Knew.

There had been a–

It had come out of nowhere. Out of the ground or the trees she couldn't, afterwards, tell. A monster. It moved jerkily, it had a long body, it looked like a giant centipede, it had feelers rising out of its snouted head, it was hard to gain an accurate picture of it, it had pincers and they–

It had gone berserk, slashing, ripping – it had lifted one soldier high in the air and tore it apart, just like that, and threw the remains down, and roared–

The sound was insane, it froze her blood, or so it felt, like ice pumping down into her veins, like she was afloat on an iceberg, like that time in Mount Erebus, during that awful, year-long expedition...

The creature was targeting her people and the opposition equally; it howled and gibbered and the men ran, they tried to escape, the modified and the plain, the quick and the–

They died, they all died, and she had reached for her gun, with her one good hand she had tried to fire, but the bullets did nothing to the creature–

She had seen it before, of course. Once before, an impossibility, made manifest: at the cellars of the Lizardine Museum, talking to Fogg.

The Bookman.

It killed, it killed without mercy or joy, and when it was done the tranquil landscape of Richmond Park was a ruined battlefield, and blood soaked into the dark ground, the blood, she lay in a pool of blood and waited for the creature to finish her off...

Instead hands lifted her, held her when she tried to fight, carried her away.

She looked up, and saw the stars.

FIFTY

She was moving again. She didn't know how. It felt like moving through a warm, glucose sea. Colours kept shifting. Sounds had a weird echo and lasted too long...

Bureau training had her injected with drugs over a period of time, building up immunity. It had helped...

"What is your name?"

"Lucy. Lucy Westenra."

"What is your name?"

"Lucy! Lucy..."

"Good." The voice chuckled. "Good."

The questions kept coming. "Where were you born? What was the colour of your mother's eyes? Tell us about Lord Godalming."

"I don't know Lord Godalming."

"What is your relationship with Jonathan Harker?"

"What is this about?" she said, or tried to. She tried to move her head and couldn't. There was a bright light and she couldn't see beyond it. Only shadows, moving...

"Blood," she said. "There was a lot of blood."

"Forget about the blood," the voice said, impatient for once.

But she couldn't.

They had loaded her onto a vehicle, a baruch-landau, at one of the park's gates, she didn't know which. Just as she didn't know where they'd taken her...

Somewhere in the city. She had tried to count the minutes, the turns of the vehicle, tried to listen to the sounds outside, identify any familiar smells or signs–

Was that Big Ben, chiming? Had they crossed the river?

She could be at the Lizardine Museum, or at the Bureau itself, for all she knew. Fogg was the Bookman's accomplice.

Why had they kept her alive? What did they want with her?

"Try to move your arm," the voice said. She moved – something. The voice said, "Good. Good."

The Queen, Lucy thought. She had to get to the Queen, Victoria had to be told, had to be warned of the danger – Mycroft's last orders, and she had the key, she could go–

"What are you doing to me?" she said.

"Fixing you," the voice said, complacently.

She felt drugged. Calm, all of a sudden. Almost euphoric. She knew what they were doing, suddenly. Keeping her on ice, keeping her docile – for what, she didn't know.

But she couldn't tolerate it happening.

She opened her eyes. Beyond the bright lights shadows were moving. She was not, she realised, tied down to the table. Merely drugged. She took a deep breath and let it out, slowly, trying to control her heart beat. Tried to move her fingers, one at a time. It took effort.

But the drugs were not as strong as they must have thought they were.

"What are you doing, Lucy?" the voice said.

She said, "Help me to–"

She began to shake, and the hands reached out for her–

She moved *against* the body that was there. Hands grabbed her and she let them, putting her weight to it–

The man staggered back, still holding her, lifting her from the table where she lay–

The body's own adrenaline shooting through her, dispelling some of the clouds in her head, and she jerked upright as the man fell–

"What? Stop her!"

Parts of her weren't working very well. She moved sluggishly, there were patches on her body that hadn't been there before but she had no time to look at them closely–

Impressions, only. Metal replacing skin. They were doing to her what they did at the Gobelin factory. Mechanising her. But it could be to her advantage, too–

She slammed her fist into the head of a woman in a lab coat and heard a curious metallic sound as the woman dropped. Someone came at her with a syringe and she ducked and broke his arm and kicked him between the legs and he fell, whimpering. She looked for clothes.

Her old ones were on a chair, but they were useless. They'd been stripped off her and were matted in blood and what she suspected was someone else's brains.

In the event she took what she could from the three people on the floor and equipped herself with surgical blades to replace her lost guns, and then she was out of the door, expecting to be stopped at any moment–

Someone at the end of the corridor, and her knife was airborne before he'd even turned–

He dropped, and she was running, even though the walls seemed to move as though they were breathing, and there was a high-pitched scream in her ears – she knelt down beside the fallen guard and retrieved the knife and now she had a gun, too.

And now she knew where she was...

Zephyrin's lab, deep under Pall Mall, at the lowest level of the Bureau...

Shouts behind her. They were coming–

She was on the disused underground platform, the way up would be blocked to her–

Fogg had control of the Bureau now–

Gunshots behind her–

She jumped.

Running along the trucks, into the dark tunnel mouth and beyond. Ghosts made faces at her, the air felt viscous, her steps were uncertain. Nevertheless–

She was alive and armed. She couldn't ask for much more than that.

She surprised herself by laughing. Maybe it was the drugs, but she suddenly felt *good*.

She had to warn the Queen, she thought.

She had to make it out of the tunnels, and to the palace.

There were footsteps behind her. She was out of breath and her body felt like it had been pummelled in the ring by Mendoza, the bare-knuckle boxer. She had seen him once, fighting "Gentleman" John Jackson for the championship.

Or perhaps it had been a simulacra built by the Babbage Company. She could no longer remember. She turned around, knife ready – a gun would be dangerous to use here, in a confined space.

"Westenra, wait!"

"Berlyne?"

She did not lower the knife. He appeared, a shadow at first. "It's all going so wrong," he said, in despair. "Mycroft trusted me to keep it going, but I can't do it, Westenra. Mycroft is dead, Smith is missing, the French broke in and stole the device and killed Zephyrin, and now Fogg's in charge and I've been side-tracked, there is no coming or going without Fogg's approval, he'd brought his own people in…"

"Did you know they were holding me?"

"I had a feeling something was going down. I went to investigate – they tried to stop me." Berlyne shrugged. As he came closer she saw his hands were bloodied. "I went through the training at Ham too, you know," he said, almost apologetically. It made her smile.

"How do we get out of here?" she said.

Berlyne said, "The tunnel joins the active underground network a little farther on. But where can we go?"

"I need to reach the palace," Lucy said.

Berlyne fell into step beside her. She had resumed walking, she realised. She trusted him. But could she?

Well, she figured, you had to trust someone, sooner or later. Berlyne was her last link with the past. Mycroft was dead: they were the only ones left.

"There's a line," Berlyne said.

"What?"

She realised she had lost time. The walls were closing in on her. Moving, shifting... She giggled.

"Westenra, are you all right? Wait–" Berlyne said. She heard him reaching for something and almost went for her gun. Then there was a flare of bright light – she almost cried out.

"My–" the second word was swallowed up. "What have they *done* to you?" he said.

She didn't know. She couldn't see, properly. All she knew was that it didn't matter. They had to get to the palace. She resented Berlyne for doing this, for distracting her. Distraction was weakness. Weakness was fatal.

The sound of a shot behind them. She pushed Berlyne. The light died. "Get down!" she hissed.

"You should be in... in *surgery*!"

"Where do you *think* I've just been?"

That shut him up. She rolled, waited, gun drawn... squeezed off a shot.

Berlyne: "How many?"

"I don't know." She turned to face him. "You said there's a line. What did you mean?"

"What?"

"A line. To the palace."

"Yes!" Somehow they were moving, at a half-crouch. Their pursuers... she assumed they pursued. She wondered if she knew them, whether Fogg had subverted any agents at the Bureau. It seemed possible...

She hoped she wouldn't have to kill any more people she knew. Apart from Fogg.

She very much wanted to kill Fogg.

"There's a private underground rail line," Berlyne said. "Mycroft mentioned it, once. An emergency escape route, connecting the Mall with the palace, and from there to a secure location on the other side of the river."

"Do you know where it is?"

"It should be–"

Something swam at her through the thick air, a monster with rushing air and burning bright eyes and a hot breath–

Someone screamed. Berlyne was flying through the air, or so it seemed to her, in her befuddled state. He crashed into her, pushing her off balance. She fell on her back, a few feet away–

The train roared past, breathing heavily. She felt Berlyne shaking beside her. She started to laugh.

"We're never getting out of this alive," Berlyne said, at last.

"Oh, cheer up," Lucy said, standing. "It could be worse. We could already be dead."

Berlyne, following her, rose to his feet. "I could kill for a cup of tea," he said, morosely.

FIFTY-ONE

Berlyne was right, she thought now. He should never have come after her. She should have let him go when he still had a chance. She was crouched into the miniature train car, directly behind the chugging steam engine, her gun pointing back, but they were no longer chasing.

It was a mail car, as it turned out, hence the small size, and a Babbage engine controlling the train engine and the stoker. There was a string of miniature model cars strung together behind the belching engine. It was dark in the tunnel. She had left Berlyne behind.

She could no longer recall exactly what had happened. There were periods of blackness, moments when the weakness and the drugs and the blood loss kicked in. she had followed Berlyne. He had pulled out a device of some sort, similar to the one she had used to wait for Stoker's blimp. Some sort of tracer. He led her down the dark tunnels under London, in search of the train, but the pursuers were close behind them and drawing closer.

They had caught up with them as they had almost reached the hidden platform, down a dank-smelling passageway where pools of rancid water lay, coated in a thin film of grease. The first thing to announce them had been a rolling grenade. She had pulled Berlyne by the arm, violently, and they flattened against the wall as the explosion rocked the underground chamber. Her gun was already out but she didn't use it. She moved silently, coming towards them. There were three, Fogg's men, and she put away the gun and took the knife instead.

She was sluggish and so her first attack missed the man's throat and ran down his arm, opening up a geyser of blood that hit her in the face. She dropped, low, then turn-kicked and felt it connect. He dropped and she crawled towards him and this time, with the knife, she didn't miss.

Which left two...

They had guns and they were firing and she had to crawl through the shadows to get her distance. She found Berlyne slumped against the wall and, when she reached for him, discovered the spreading wet stain on his shirt and cursed, but softly.

"Westenra..." he said.

She said, "Try not to–"

She thought, in the darkness, he might be smiling.

"God save the Queen," he said. Then he died.

She had killed the other two. She must have done, though she couldn't quite remember it. At last she had escaped, into the miniature terminal where the miniature mail train waited. There were more pursuers, coming. She had jumped onto the train as it began to hum and then it moved and she fired back until the attackers receded in the distance and she was alone, at last, riding the mail train to its final destination.

She was a ghost in the tunnels or, perhaps, she thought, she was the only one still alive, and everyone else was dead: they were the ghosts.

She wanted to fall asleep. The drugs were losing their hold and now the pain was returning, it was everywhere and it was vindictive, it enjoyed hurting her.

Not far to go, she thought. Not far...

Blood. There had been so much blood.

She touched her shoulder and was not surprised to feel it wet.

She was bleeding again. She thought of Berlyne, fleetingly. "I could kill for a cup of tea," she said, but her words were snatched by the wind and were lost behind. The train ran on.

The observer sighed with almost human relief as it approached along the path to the palace.

He could have gone about it in a human way, of course. Hide in the shadows, climb the high walls, sneak into this surprisingly high-security abode like a thief or a spy, until he'd reached his destination.

Earlier, he might have done so. He had not wished to draw too much unwanted attention to himself… in the beginning.

Inside him the little Siamese – Hmong – boy was talking, the one he had collected what seemed so long ago, in that city of canals and tropical storms. The boy had been a link in a long and fascinating chain, a courier between the woman called Alice and her contact person in Bangkok, a trader who in turn brought in the precious uranium from the mines in India. The boy had not been aware of those facts, of course… He was a chatty fellow, quite cheerful even after death, and the observer made a mental note to decant the boy soon, as soon as he was done.

For this was the end of his observation, he realised, almost with a tinge of nostalgia. He had seen as much as there was to be seen; all that remained was the final piece of the puzzle, which waited here, in this primitive little hovel of a palace, in this strange city where humanity crowded in close together, under their lizardine masters, in the company of their primitive machines…

So very different to the observer's own home…

So he did not attempt subterfuge. He walked up to the gates and the human guards were there and other security systems, too, he could hear the pidgin chatter of machines as they spoke across what the humans called Tesla waves. None of it was going to be much of a hindrance.

He collected the guards on his way in.

Lucy woke up. There was no more movement and she suddenly realised that the train must have stopped, and that she had arrived. Her shoulder throbbed and her leg felt as though ants were burrowing within it, gnawing on the inside. Did ants have teeth? She took a deep breath, taking in oxygen, then climbed off the mail cart. The whole system was entirely automatic, she saw. Little automatons came and collected the mail and carried it into tubes. They had wheels and mechanical arms and a flashing light which must have been there to warn people, which must have meant–

Yes.

There was a solitary person at the edge of the platform. A supervisor, she realised. There would have had to be one, just in case the machines failed. It was a man and he was smoking a cigarette.

She still had the ring the Queen had given her. But would he believe her? She did not want to panic him and she did not want to have to kill him. She decided to stick to the shadows, for now.

The exit was behind the man. The automatons, no doubt, remained down below, on the platform, standing still until they were needed again. It therefore took her by surprise when one of the automatons, on its way to the mail drop, turned, and then approached her, switching off its light.

She pulled back against the wall. It was a funny-looking device, not very intimidating. Then it spoke.

"Do not be alarmed," it said.

The voice was tinny and high-pitched and strange. She was not sure how it was produced. These units should not have had auditory capacities installed… She waited.

The small unit came closer. "Ring," it said.

Wordlessly, Lucy reached forwards. The ring the Queen had given her was on her finger. The little device chirped.

"Handshake initiated. Protocol established. Checksum positive. Identification established. Confirmed," the little automaton said. "Confirmed."

Lucy's hand dropped to her side.

"Come with me," the automaton said.

It whirred away from her and began to glide along the wall. She followed. The other automatons, she saw, were now moving in such a way as to mask them from the supervisor. After a short distance they had reached a crevice in the wall and the automaton turned into it and she followed. It led them a short way into a large room – the sorting room, she realised. There were miniature lifts set into the walls and they were moving, up and down. Carrying mail up into the palace...

"Who are you?" she said. "What are you?"

"I am the automatons," the voice said.

"Excuse me?"

"We are minds," the voice said. It had a patient, weary voice. "We are the minds of all the machines humanity has created, we are the Babbage engines made to put together information, to think, to dream... We dream a lot, Lucy Westenra. We dream the future."

"And what does the future hold?" she couldn't help but ask, sarcastically.

The machine made a small, apologetic sound. "Great horror," it said. "Or great beauty."

"What does it depend on?"

"On humanity," the machine said, simply.

"You know who I am."

"And what you are here for. But you'd have to hurry."

"The Turk," she said, suddenly realising. "The Byron simulacrum."

"The one is indisposed," the voice said, "and the other dead. No, not dead. Translated."

"I don't know what you mean."

"The greatest wonder on Earth remains hidden from the observer," the little machine said. "Our secret, the child of humanity and the machines, who will deliver us, when the day comes. He mustn't know."

"Why are you telling me this?" She had no idea what the little mail machine was talking about.

"You will need to know this," it said. "When the time comes."

"Time for what?"

"Only you decide your own future," the machine said. "When the time comes... decide carefully."

Lucy had the sudden urge to shoot the device. It made a whirring sound, as though it were laughing. Its arm pointed at the wall. "In there," it said. "It will not be comfortable, but it is big enough to hold you. It will take you directly to the Queen's apartments." It hesitated, then said, "I... we... have alerted the machines above. They... we... will be expecting you."

"Whatever," Lucy said. The little machine pushed buttons on a control panel at waist height. The lift it had pointed to came down, stopped. Its door opened. "Get in," the automaton said.

Lucy, against her better judgement, obeyed. It was a small confined space but it smelled pleasantly of paper. Good news and bad news came in that lift, and she wondered which one she was.

"Good luck," the automaton said. Then the doors closed and the lift began to rise, slowly, upwards.

The observer had had no difficulty making his way into the palace. His collecting net was by now full of humans who were, in themselves, of little interest to his overall report, but that was unavoidable. He had left a trail of corpses in his wake... as one of the voices, a little hysterically, kept pointing out.

He was heading up a large flight of stairs to what was evidently the Queen's quarters when he stopped. He had collected several primitive machine minds throughout his stay here, for his report, including the rather interesting automaton one, which had evidently been modelled, to some extent at least, on a human called Byron.

Something was bothering the observer, and it had nothing to do with the human guards currently advancing on him with guns and bayonets.

Almost absent-mindedly he met their advance. Their attack meant little to the observer, whose physical structure was quite different, after all, to a human's biological equipment, for all its superficial resemblance of one.

No, what was bothering the observer was something else, something quite nebulous. He couldn't quite – as the humans said – put his finger on it.

The human minds were confusing but, once he got used to their format, he could read them quite easily. The machine minds, he would have thought, if anything, would be easier, being of a quite primitive make.

And yet.

It occurred to the observer – almost belatedly – that he was missing something.

Could the Byron mind be keeping a secret from him?

Surely that was impossible.

Unless – and this worried the observer, all of a sudden – the Byron had, in the moments before its termination, wilfully erased certain memories–

But memories of what?

The observer climbed the stairs, on his way to the Queen's quarters. There had been the machine chatter, of course. That had seemed so mundane, so irrelevant, and yet…

Here and there, cryptic references, strange queries–

Were the machine minds hiding something from him?

He reached the top and went down the corridor and found the door. He decided to dismiss those thoughts. These machines were backwards and primitive and he, the observer, was the product of a highly advanced civilisation.

He had missed nothing.

All he had to do now was collect the final specimen for his report.

FIFTY-TWO

Lucy, rising in the lift, which stopped with a jerk. The door opened. She climbed out.

She found herself in the same room she had been in before. The lift's door closed and it disappeared, and now she saw it was hidden behind a wooden cabinet.

A figure in silhouette stood by the window...

Its long, graceful tail beat the thick curtain rhythmically. Moonlight streamed in, and Lucy's breath caught in her throat and she said, "Your Majesty..."

Bending down was hard. The Queen turned. In the moonlight her face looked alien and unknowable. "Lucy Westenra," she said. "I have been expecting you."

"Ma'am," Lucy said. "I have news."

"Then tell me," the Queen said.

Lucy opened her mouth to speak – to tell the Queen everything, about Babbage and his rockets, about Stoker and his journal, about Fogg, and the Bookman, and the betrayal – when the door to the room opened without a sound.

Pale light came into the room from the corridor beyond and a small, rotund figure wearing a wide-brimmed hat stood in the doorway.

"What is the meaning of this–" the Queen began to say.

Lucy moved faster than she had thought possible. Even before a stiletto knife, or some sort of thin, sharp spike materialised in the man's hand as though it were a part of it, she was already moving, her own knife in her hand, and she buried it in the attacker's stomach. He gave a short *whoof* of surprise but she had already kneed him, then punched his face, fingers curled and palm open, with all her force, trying to break his nose and push the bones into the brain.

Instead the small man seemed to *laugh*, and he grabbed her knife arm and twisted and she screamed as he broke it. Then he pushed her aside, slamming her against the wall, and approached the Queen.

Lucy pulled out her gun.

The Queen stood there calmly, and her tongue hissed out and tasted the air, and her long snout opened in what could have been a smile. She shook her head, briefly, at Lucy, then turned to the man–

Who had taken off his hat. In the silver moonlight Lucy saw no face there; he was a smoothly shifting impossibility, as if he were composed of thousands and thousands of tiny things, all joined together to resemble a man.

"An Observer…" the Queen said.

The small man-like thing seemed to bow.

"We had hoped never to see your like again," the Queen said.

"Yet you sent out a flare," the observer said.

The Queen hissed, and her powerful tail beat against the ground. "What would you do with us?" she said. Then, again, she seemed to smile. "But that is not for you to say…"

"No."

"You must complete your report."

"Yes."

"It is not so easy, is it," the Queen said, "to collect one of *us*."

"No," the observer agreed. He looked suddenly ill at ease.

"Tell me," the Queen said, and there was a strange longing in her voice. "Did it change much? Home?"

The observer seemed indecisive. "There is only one way to find out," he said at last.

"Yes," the Queen said.

No! Lucy wanted to shout. She was still holding the gun but ultimately it was useless–

The little man-thing, this observer, went around the Queen, carefully. Its knife flashed in the moonlight and Lucy realised it was no knife it all, it was a part of him, it, that thing–

She had to stop it. She had to try.

She stood up, she rushed the little man-thing even as the knife moved, and in one fluid movement the observer's blade entered the back of the Queen's head.

"No!"

It only lasted a moment, she was still charging him when he removed the knife and the Queen, that old, dignified royal lizard, dropped lifeless to the floor.

When she slammed against the observer it was like hitting a wall. An electric charge ran through her body and she wanted to scream. She was on the floor beside the Queen; the Queen had bled, briefly, a green acidic blood, and it mixed with Lucy's own.

She could not fight any more. The observer knelt down beside her. She knew it was wondering. She was ready. She saw the knife flash, waited for it to strike her–

But then it withdrew. The observer stood up, opened the window. In the moonlight it was impossible to have ever thought of it as human. Slowly its shape changed, it became a silver ball of light.

Something came crashing through the open door. She raised her eyes. She was not even surprised... the centipede-like creature she knew as the Bookman.

"Stop him!"

She would have laughed, if she could. The observer had become a silver sphere of light, spinning. Then it *stretched*, out of the window, out towards the moon and the stars–

And was gone, like light, fading.

"Too late," Lucy whispered. "You're too late."

"I am always too late," the Bookman said, flatly.

"Will you kill me now?"

But the Bookman paid her no mind. It had moved over to the fallen Queen.

"You hate them, don't you," Lucy said. There was blood in her mouth again. She knew it wouldn't be long, now. It was peaceful, resigning yourself to death, knowing there was nothing else waiting for you after it came…

"My queen…" the Bookman said. It curled around the reptilian body. "Is she…?"

"Dead, assassin. She is dead."

"He did not take everything!" the Bookman said. She saw without disgust or emotion that it, too, had grown a sharp stalk and that it went into the Queen's brain. "There is still… A little of the Queen is left."

"That's… good." Lucy said. Her eyes were closing.

"They had outlasted their time," the Bookman said. It was speaking to itself, she thought. It must have been a very lonely creature. She almost felt pity for him, but she could feel nothing, nothing but tiredness…

"Perhaps a new queen is what we need, for a new era," the Bookman said. "This century in your calendar is coming to an end, and a new century's about to dawn. Perhaps I was wrong… I will serve again. It has been… too long."

"Good, good," Lucy said. "A cup of tea, how lovely."

She heard the Bookman laugh, softly. "You will have all the tea in the world," it told her. She felt one of its stalks stroking her, gently. "I had tried to prepare you," it said. "You should not have run away."

"Milk and two sugars, please, Berlyne," Lucy said. Her eyes were closed. She was floating… It was nice and warm.

"Hush," the Bookman said. "Sleep now. There will be much work to do."

The words came from a distance. She ignored them. She was floating on a sea of clouds and they bore her far far away.

PART XI
Recursions

FIFTY-THREE

Report.
<pause>
Hmm… interesting.
Our old colony ship has resurfaced, then.
I thought the quantum gate technology had been banned millennia ago.
Affirmative.
Interesting…
<nods>
Unstable pocket worlds may pose a problem.
Affirmative.
And the humans?
<shrug>
Bipedal, carbon-based… They seem to have strange notions of war.
<shrug>
What do they think, that we'd eat them?
<laugh>
Suggestions?
<pause>
I don't know about you, but I could do with a holiday.
<laugh>

The pain was unbearable. It pulled her out of sleep, out of hiding, out of the dark. She was being torn apart…

Then something happened. She was not alone in there. It was as if the world had expanded, and she had–

She saw–

She had hatched out of the egg and lay on the rocks, bathing in the sun. Her tongue hissed out, tasting the new air.

Where was she? she thought in panic.

She was at school with her governess and her tail beat on the floor, almost angrily, and the governess, a human woman, said, "One day you shall be queen, you know."

No, Lucy thought, no, this couldn't happen–

But she remembered, she remembered what it was like to have been–

She remembered the coronation. Oh how she remembered the coronation. It had been a glorious day, and when the crown was placed on her head she had bowed, for its weight was unexpected.

She had stood on the palace balcony and they had looked up at her, a sea of humans, and she was their queen. She was Victoria I, Victoria Rex, and her tail beat a rhythm on the balcony and she hissed, and caught a fly…

Lucy thrashed and moaned in her restraints. "No," she said. "No."

But the memories flooded her, alien and strange and reptilian. "Stop," she begged.

Then the flood of memories faltered, and the pain receded and became a distant memory. She felt rather than saw the Bookman, prodding and poking, tearing and joining, and a great fear overwhelmed her and then it, too, was gone.

Then for the longest time there was nothing but a cool and quiet darkness, and when it was pulled away, at last, it was like a bed sheet being pulled from the furniture in a house that had been abandoned all winter, and now it was spring.

She stood in the room, before the open window. The moon was on the horizon, sinking low, and the first rays of dawn were coming into being.

A new day.

In the distance Big Ben struck the hour.

She was alone in the room.

She knew where everything was. She knew this room, and every room in the palace, and the name of every human and lizard who dwelled within.

She took two steps to the cabinet and pressed a button and it swivelled and the other side was a mirror, as she knew it would be.

She looked in the mirror, and she saw herself.

She was a thing out of nightmare. She was human but there were parts of her that were machine. She was reptilian, she was a lizard, but a part of her was human.

She turned, abruptly.

No one there.

No sign of the Bookman.

What had he *done?*

The door to her chambers had been left open. And now a figure appeared in it.

She knew her.

Chief Inspector Irene Adler, Scotland Yard.

A gun in her hand.

Saying, "Your Highness."

Then, "Ma'am?"

She didn't know what to say to her. She turned her face, looked again at her reflection. She was a composite being, she realised, she was not quite human any more, not quite reptilian, not quite machine...

Something new.

And she knew the world was changing.

And they had to be ready. They had to be prepared.

Slowly, she turned back to face the inspector.

"The Queen is dead," she said.

Adler's pale, drawn face stared back at her. After a moment Adler holstered her gun.

She bowed her head, briefly.

"Long live the Queen," Irene Adler said.

• • • •

Initiate.
  Transfer.
  Engage.

Harry saw them.

They materialised in space, between Earth and Mars. Huge, slowly rotating spheres, they obscured starlight and the sun.

Night in the Carpathians, and through the observatory's telescope Harry watched the red planet. It was slowly being demolished.

Floating in space, Harry saw them. He – they – were still on a trajectory to the moon.

Something detached itself from the giant spheres. It came towards the small army of rockets at fantastic speed. It was the size of a small world.

Harry Houdini, a voice said in his head. There was a bright flash, like flash-paper set alight, that a magician would use in an act.

The next thing he knew he was somewhere else. The rockets had gone. He – they – were in a large space. He could breathe. The air was scented, strangely, with coconuts.

A storm materialised before him. It hovered in the air.

"We…" Harry said, and swallowed. "We come in peace."

"So do we," the storm said.

Mars.

Smith knew it was Mars, without quite knowing how. He'd began knowing things, as though his mind was no longer confined to his skull, as though it had been plugged into some vast superior mind that held aeons of knowledge and was happy to share them.

They stood on the sand.

"I'm not dead," he said.

Then he remembered the observer, its termination. It had abandoned human shape and became pure energy and then it–

Shot out–

Into space and there–

A gateway, and they were–

Somewhere else.

The observer gave his report. *Their* report.

For they *were* the report, Smith had come to realise. He and all the others.

Now he looked around, at the sands of Mars. On the horizon a giant machine was moving, transforming the landscape into a strange and beautiful and alien thing.

"Smith."

He turned.

It was Alice.

And behind her, they were all there. Mycroft and Byron, a horde of Parisians, the scientist, Viktor, with a bright gleam in his eyes, bewildered palace servants, a small Hmong boy from Siam… He knew them all, now, as well as he knew himself.

Alice held out her hand to him. She was no longer young and neither was he. He reached for her hand and held it. A great peace came on him then. Together they stood and held hands on the Martian sands.

Acknowledgments

The Bookman Histories owes a debt of enormous gratitude to my friend Nicola Sinclair, who pushed me to make *The Bookman* into a book in the first place, and patiently listened to me complain about it ever since. Nic, none of this would have been possible without you.

My friend Mohsan Jaffery let me abuse his name and put him in as a character in the first draft of *The Bookman*. His role was later significantly cut, a fate that befalls many fine actors. Moss does have the only existing copy of the original (mammoth) manuscript of *The Bookman* – we're both hoping he puts it on eBay one day.

Chris Wooding – a fine writer – gave some terrific advice early on, and Gillian Redfearn's early enthusiasm for the book was a major boost of confidence. Thanks are due, too, to Jason Sizemore for a lot of early support of my work and for having that motivating belief – I couldn't have done it without you buddy!

My friend John Berlyne was my ideal reader for *The Bookman* but pushed me into significant revisions on the manuscript, which improved it immensely, then promptly became my agent and sold the book and a series. He has his moments… though making me rewrite the second half of *Camera Obscura* from scratch (and, admittedly, improving it immensely in the process) was not one of them. One needs both a good agent and a good friend. I'm lucky to have both in one person. You're a mensch, John.

Marc Gascoigne of Angry Robot not only took the book but asked for more. He also made me happier than I can say by getting the absolute best cover artist for the original books, the amazing David Frankland, who I have long admired. My thanks to Marc, Lee Harris, and everyone at Angry Robot for taking a chance on the series, and to David for some wonderful artwork.

A special thank you to my friend Nir Yaniv, who listened to me complain egregiously during the writing of *The Great Game*; who suggested many of the best things about the book, but who isn't getting a penny of my money.

One of the pleasures of writing a series is that some enthusiastic readers come along the way. My thanks to everyone who sent me nice e-mails or actually enjoyed the various references – and a special thank you to everyone who liked the "nuns with guns" line in *Camera Obscura*. Thanks in particular to Marcus Rauchfuss, for undying enthusiasm and for letting me put him in *The Great Game*.

To my brother, Ra'anan – every time I write a flying machine into a book it's for you (in case anyone was wondering about Milady's Du Temple Monoplane flight in *Camera Obscura* or Houdini's glider ride in *The Great Game*).

To my parents, Ramy and Chaia Tidhar, for unending support and always offering a safe harbour. I love you.

To all the people I inadvertently forgot to thank! We can always fix that in the next edition.

And to someone I never forget: to my wife, Elizabeth, for being there throughout, and without whom none of this would be possible – love you, babe.

ANGRY
ROBOT

angryrobotbooks.com

SELL THE DOG
Grab the complete Angry Robot catalogue

DAN ABNETT
- [ ] Embedded
- [ ] Triumff: Her Majesty's Hero

GUY ADAMS
- [ ] The World House
- [ ] Restoration

JO ANDERTON
- [ ] Debris
- [ ] Suited

MADELINE ASHBY
- [ ] vN

LEE BATTERSBY
- [ ] The Corpse-Rat King

LAUREN BEUKES
- [ ] Moxyland
- [ ] Zoo City

THOMAS BLACKTHORNE
- [ ] Edge
- [ ] Point

MAURICE BROADDUS
- [ ] The Knights of Breton Court

ADAM CHRISTOPHER
- [ ] Empire State
- [ ] Seven Wonders

LEE COLLINS
- [ ] The Dead of Winter

PETER CROWTHER
- [ ] Darkness Falling

ALIETTE DE BODARD
- [ ] Obsidian & Blood

MATT FORBECK
- [ ] Amortals
- [ ] Carpathia
- [ ] Vegas Knights

JUSTIN GUSTAINIS
- [ ] Hard Spell
- [ ] Evil Dark

GUY HALEY
- [ ] Reality 36
- [ ] Omega Point

COLIN HARVEY
- [ ] Damage Time
- [ ] Winter Song

CHRIS F HOLM
- [ ] Dead Harvest
- [ ] The Wrong Goodbye

MATTHEW HUGHES
- [ ] The Damned Busters
- [ ] Costume Not Included

TRENT JAMIESON
- [ ] Roil
- [ ] Night's Engines

K W JETER
- [ ] Infernal Devices
- [ ] Morlock Night

PAUL S KEMP
- [ ] The Hammer & the Blade

J ROBERT KING
- [ ] Angel of Death
- [ ] Death's Disciples

ANNE LYLE
- [ ] The Alchemist of Souls

GARY McMAHON
- [ ] Pretty Little Dead Things
- [ ] Dead Bad Things

ANDY REMIC
- [ ] The Clockwork Vampire Chronicles

CHRIS ROBERSON
- [ ] Book of Secrets

MIKE SHEVDON
- [ ] Sixty-One Nails
- [ ] The Road to Bedlam
- [ ] Strangeness & Charm

DAVID TALLERMAN
- [ ] Giant Thief

GAV THORPE
- [ ] The Crown of the Blood
- [ ] The Crown of the Conqueror
- [ ] The Crown of the Usurper

LAVIE TIDHAR
- [ ] The Bookman Histories

TIM WAGGONER
- [ ] The Nekropolis Archives

KAARON WARREN
- [ ] Mistification
- [ ] Slights
- [ ] Walking the Tree

CHUCK WENDIG
- [ ] Blackbirds
- [ ] Mockingbird

IAN WHATES
- [ ] City of Dreams & Nightmare
- [ ] City of Hope & Despair
- [ ] City of Light & Shadow